JOSEPH CONRAD

was born Teodor Jozef Konrad Korzeniowski in 1857 in what was then Russian Poland. Orphaned at the age of eleven, he lived with an uncle in Cracow, and in 1874 boarded the Vienna Express ''as a man might get into a dream'' and went to France to seek his fortune. After four years of adventure in Marseilles—years devoted to such diverse enterprises as the *légitimiste* cause, apprenticeship on French ships, and a mysterious smuggling episode, he took a berth on a British freighter and thus began his fateful seventeen-year odyssey at sea. The paradox of a Pole and a seaman writing novels in English long prevented readers from recognizing the enormous importance of Conrad's writing. Ignorant of the English language at twenty, Conrad completed more than sixteen novels and seven volumes of short stories—works that were to mark him as one of the greatest English prose stylists. He died in Kent, England in 1924.

Also available from Carroll & Graf:
  Sea Stories by Joseph Conrad
  The Inheritors by Joseph Conrad and Ford Madox Ford
  Romance by Joseph Conrad and Ford Madox Ford

JOSEPH CONRAD

EASTERN SKIES WESTERN SEAS

Carroll & Graf Publishers, Inc.
New York

First Carroll & Graf edition 1990
All rights reserved

Carroll & Graf Publishers, Inc
260 Fifth Avenue
New York, NY 10001

ISBN: 0-88184-595-7

Manufactured in the United States of America

Contents

JOSEPH CONRAD
EASTERN SKIES
WESTERN SEAS

Almayer's Folly

CHAPTER ONE

K ASPAR! Makan!"
The well-known shrill voice startled Almayer from his dream of splendid future into the unpleasant realities of the present hour. An unpleasant voice too. He had heard it for many years, and with every year he liked it less. No matter; there would be an end to all this soon.

He shuffled uneasily, but took no further notice of the call. Leaning with both his elbows on the balustrade of the verandah, he went on looking fixedly at the great river that flowed—indifferent and hurried—before his eyes. He liked to look at it about the time of sunset; perhaps because at that time the sinking sun would spread a glowing gold tinge on the waters of the Pantai, and Almayer's thoughts were often busy with gold; gold he had failed to secure; gold the others had secured—dishonestly, of course—or gold he meant to secure yet, through his own honest exertions, for himself and Nina. He absorbed himself in his dream of wealth and power away from this coast where he had dwelt for so many years, forgetting the bitterness of toil and strife in the vision of a great and splendid reward. They would live in Europe, he and his daughter. They would be rich and respected. Nobody would think of her mixed blood in the presence of her great beauty and of his immense wealth. Witnessing her triumphs he would grow young again, he would forget the twenty-five years of heart-breaking struggle on this coast where he felt like a prisoner. All this was nearly within his reach. Let only Dain return! And return soon he must—in his own interest, for his own share. He was now more than a week late! Perhaps he would return to-night.

Such were Almayer's thoughts as, standing on the verandah of his new but already decaying house—that last failure of his life—he looked on the broad river. There was no tinge of gold on it this evening, for it had been swollen by the rains, and rolled an angry and muddy flood under his inattentive eyes, carrying small drift-wood and big dead logs, and whole uprooted trees with branches and foliage, amongst which the water swirled and roared angrily.

One of those drifting trees grounded on the shelving shore, just by the house, and Almayer, neglecting his dream, watched it with languid interest. The tree swung slowly round, amid the hiss and foam of the water, and soon getting free of the obstruction began to move down stream again, rolling slowly over, raising upwards a long, denuded branch, like a hand lifted in mute appeal to heaven against the river's brutal and unnecessary violence. Almayer's interest in the fate of that tree increased rapidly. He leaned over to see if it would clear the low point below. It did; then he drew back, thinking that now its course was free down to the sea, and he envied the lot of that inanimate thing now growing small and indistinct in the deepening darkness. As he lost sight of it altogether he began to wonder how far out to sea it would drift. Would the current carry it north or south? South, probably, till it drifted in sight of Celebes, as far as Macassar, perhaps!

Macassar! Almayer's quickened fancy distanced the tree on its imaginary voyage, but his memory lagging behind some twenty years or more in point of time saw a young and slim Almayer, clad all in white and modest-looking, landing from the Dutch mail-boat on the dusty jetty of Macassar, coming to woo fortune in the godowns of old Hudig. It was an important epoch in his life, the beginning of a new existence for him. His father, a subordinate official employed in the Botanical Gardens of Buitenzorg, was no doubt delighted to place his son in such a firm. The young man himself too was nothing loth to leave the poisonous shores of Java, and the meagre comforts of the parental bungalow, where the father grumbled all day at the stupidity of native gardeners, and the mother from the depths of her long easy-chair bewailed the lost glories of Amsterdam, where she had been brought up, and of her position as the daughter of a cigar dealer there.

Almayer had left his home with a light heart and a lighter pocket, speaking English well, and strong in arithmetic; ready to conquer the world, never doubting that he would.

After those twenty years, standing in the close and stifling heat of a Bornean evening, he recalled with pleasurable regret the image of Hudig's lofty and cool warehouses with their long and straight avenues of gin cases and bales of Manchester goods; the big door swinging noiselessly; the dim light of the place, so delightful after the glare of the streets; the little railed-off spaces amongst piles of merchandise where the Chinese clerks, neat, cool, and sad-eyed, wrote rapidly and in silence amidst the din of the working gangs rolling casks or shifting cases to a muttered song, ending with a desperate yell. At the upper end, facing the great door, there was a larger space railed off, well lighted; there the noise was subdued by distance, and above it rose the soft and continuous clink of silver guilders which other discreet Chinamen were counting and piling up under the supervision of Mr. Vinck, the cashier, the genius presiding in the place—the right hand of the Master.

In that clear space Almayer worked at his table not far from a little green painted door, by which always stood a Malay in a red sash and turban, and whose hand, holding a small string dangling from above, moved up and down with the regularity of a machine. The string worked a punkah on the other side of the green door, where the so-called private office was, and where old Hudig—the Master—sat enthroned, holding noisy receptions. Sometimes the little door would fly open disclosing to the outer world, through the bluish haze of tobacco smoke, a long table loaded with bottles of various shapes and tall water pitchers, rattan easy-chairs occupied by noisy men in sprawling attitudes, while the Master would put his head through and, holding by the handle, would grunt confidentially to Vinck; perhaps send an order thundering down the warehouse, or spy a hesitating stranger and greet him with a friendly roar, "Welcome, Gapitan! ver' you gome vrom? Bali, eh? Got bonies? I vant bonies! Vant all you got; ha! ha! ha! Gome in!" Then the stranger was dragged in, in a tempest of yells, the door was shut, and the usual noises refilled the place; the song of the workmen, the rumble of barrels, the scratch of rapid pens; while above all rose the musical chink of broad silver pieces streaming ceaselessly through the yellow fingers of the attentive Chinamen.

At that time Macassar was teeming with life and commerce. It was the point in the islands where tended all those bold spirits who, fitting out schooners on the Australian coast, invaded the Malay Archipelago in search of money and adventure. Bold, reckless, keen in business, not disinclined for a brush with the pirates that were to be found on many a coast as yet, making money fast, they used to have a general "rendezvous" in the bay for purposes of trade and dissipation. The Dutch merchants called those men English pedlars; some of them were undoubtedly gentlemen for whom that kind of life had a charm; most were seamen; the acknowledged king of them all was Tom Lingard, he whom the Malays, honest or dishonest, quiet fishermen or desperate cut-throats, recognized as "the Rajah-Laut"—the King of the Sea.

Almayer had heard of him before he had been three days in Macassar, had heard the stories of his smart business transactions, his loves, and also of his desperate fights with the Sulu pirates, together with the romantic tale of some child—a girl—found in a piratical prau by the victorious Lingard, when, after a long contest, he boarded the craft, driving the crew overboard. This girl, it was generally known, Lingard had adopted, was having her educated in some convent in Java, and spoke of her as "my daughter." He had sworn a mighty oath to marry her to a white man before he went home and to leave her all his money. "And Captain Lingard has lots of money," would say Mr. Vinck solemnly, with his head on one side, "lots of money; more than Hudig!" And after a pause—just to let his hearers recover from their astonishment at such an incredible assertion—he would add in an explanatory whisper, "You know, he has discovered a river."

That was it! He had discovered a river! That was the fact placing old Lingard so much above the common crowd of sea-going adventurers who traded with Hudig in the daytime and drank champagne, gambled, sang noisy songs, and made love to half-caste girls under the broad verandah of the Sunda Hotel at night. Into that river, whose entrances himself only knew, Lingard used to take his assorted cargo of Manchester goods, brass gongs, rifles and gunpowder. His brig *Flash*, which he commanded himself, would on those occasions disappear quietly during the night from the roadstead while his companions were sleeping off the effects of the midnight carouse, Lingard seeing them drunk under the table before going on board, himself unaffected by any amount of liquor. Many tried to follow him and find that land of plenty for gutta-percha and rattans, pearl shells and birds' nests, wax and gum-dammar, but the little *Flash* could outsail every craft in those seas. A few of them came to grief on hidden sandbanks and coral reefs, losing their all and barely escaping with life from the cruel grip of this sunny and smiling sea; others got discouraged; and for many years the green and peaceful-looking islands guarding the entrances to the promised land kept their secret with all the merciless serenity of tropical nature. And so Lingard came and went on his secret or open expeditions, becoming a hero in Almayer's eyes by the boldness and enormous profits of his ventures, seeming to Almayer a very great man indeed as he saw him marching up to the warehouse, grunting a "how are you?" to Vinck, or greeting Hudig, the Master, with a boisterous "Hallo, old pirate! Alive yet?" as a preliminary to transacting business behind the little green door. Often of an evening, in the silence of the then deserted warehouse, Almayer putting away his papers before driving home with Mr. Vinck, in whose household he lived, would pause listening to the noise of a hot discussion in the private office, would hear the deep and monotonous growl of the Master, and the roared-out interruptions of Lingard—two mastiffs fighting over a marrowy bone. But to Almayer's ears it sounded like a quarrel of Titans—a battle of the gods.

After a year or so Lingard, having been brought often in contact with Almayer in the course of business, took a sudden and, to the onlookers, a rather inexplicable fancy to the young man. He sang his praises, late at night, over a convivial glass to his cronies in the Sunda Hotel, and one fine morning electrified Vinck by declaring that he must have "that young fellow for a supercargo. Kind of captain's clerk. Do all my quill-driving for me." Hudig consented. Almayer, with youth's natural craving for change, was nothing loth, and packing his few belongings, started in the *Flash* on one of those long cruises when the old seaman was wont to visit almost every island in the archipelago. Months slipped by, and Lingard's friendship seemed to increase. Often pacing the deck with Almayer, when the faint night breeze, heavy with aromatic exhalations of the islands, shoved the brig gently along under the peaceful and sparkling sky, did the old seaman open his heart to his entranced listener. He spoke of his past life, of escaped dangers, of big profits in his trade, of new combinations that were in the future to bring profits bigger still. Often he had mentioned his daughter, the girl found in the pirate prau, speaking of her with a strange assumption of fatherly tenderness. "She must be a big girl now," he used to say. "It's nigh unto four years since I have seen her! Damme, Almayer, if I don't think we will run into Sourabaya this trip." And after such a declaration he always dived into his cabin muttering to himself, "Something must be done—must be done." More than once he would astonish Almayer by walking up to him rapidly, clearing his throat with a powerful "Hem!" as if he intended to say something, and then turning abruptly away to lean over the bulwarks in silence, and watch, motionless, for hours, the gleam and sparkle of the phosphorescent sea along the ship's side. It was the night before arriving in Sourabaya when one of those attempts at confidential communication succeeded. After clearing his throat he spoke. He spoke to some purpose. He wanted Almayer to marry his adopted daughter. "And don't you kick because you're white!" he shouted, suddenly, not giving the surprised young man the time to say a word. "None of that with me! Nobody will see the colour of your wife's skin. The dollars are too thick for that, I tell you! And mind you, they will be thicker yet before I die. There will be millions, Kaspar! Millions I say! And all for her—and for you, if you do what you are told."

Startled by the unexpected proposal, Almayer hesitated, and remained silent for a minute. He was gifted with a strong and active imagination, and in that short space of time he saw, as in a flash of dazzling light, great piles of shining guilders, and realized all the possibilities of an opulent existence. The consideration, the indolent ease of life—for which he felt himself so well fitted—his ships, his warehouses, his merchandise (old Lingard would not live for ever), and, crowning all, in the far future gleamed like a fairy palace the big mansion in Amsterdam, that earthly paradise of his dreams, where made king amongst men by old Lingard's money, he would pass the

evening of his days in inexpressible splendour. As to the other side of
the picture—the companionship for life of a Malay girl, that legacy
of a boatful of pirates—there was only within him a confused consciousness of shame that he a white man—— Still, a convent education
of four years—and then she may mercifully die. He was always lucky,
and money is powerful! Go through it. Why not? He had a vague idea
of shutting her up somewhere, anywhere, out of his gorgeous future.
Easy enough to dispose of a Malay woman, a slave, after all, to his
Eastern mind, convent or no convent, ceremony or no ceremony.

He lifted his head and confronted the anxious yet irate seaman.

"I—of course—anything you wish, Captain Lingard."

"Call me father, my boy. She does," said the mollified old adven-
turer. "Damme, though, if I didn't think you were going to refuse.
Mind you, Kaspar, I always get my way, so it would have been no use.
But you are no fool."

He remembered well that time—the look, the accent, the words, the
effect they produced on him, his very surroundings. He remembered
the narrow slanting deck of the brig, the silent sleeping coast, the
smooth black surface of the sea with a great bar of gold laid on it by
the rising moon. He remembered it all, and he remembered his feelings of mad exultation at the thought of that fortune thrown into
his hands. He was no fool then, and he was no fool now. Circumstances had been against him; the fortune was gone, but hope
remained.

He shivered in the night air, and suddenly became aware of the
intense darkness which, on the sun's departure, had closed in upon the
river, blotting out the outlines of the opposite shore. Only the fire of
dry branches lit outside the stockade of the Rajah's compound called
fitfully into view the ragged trunks of the surrounding trees, putting
a stain of glowing red halfway across the river where the drifting logs
were hurrying toward the sea through the impenetrable gloom. He had
a hazy recollection of having been called some time during the evening by his wife. To his dinner probably. But a man busy contemplating the wreckage of his past in the dawn of new hopes cannot be
hungry whenever his rice is ready. Time he went home, though; it
was getting late.

He stepped cautiously on the loose planks towards the ladder. A
lizard, disturbed by the noise, emitted a plaintive note and scurried
through the long grass growing on the bank. Almayer descended the
ladder carefully, now thoroughly recalled to the realities of life by the
care necessary to prevent a fall on the uneven ground where the stones,
decaying planks, and half-sawn beams were piled up in inextricable
confusion. As he turned towards the house where he lived—"my old
house" he called it—his ear detected the splash of paddles away in the

darkness of the river. He stood still in the path, attentive and surprised at anybody being on the river at this late hour during such a heavy freshet. Now he could hear the paddles distinctly, and even a rapidly exchanged word in low tones, the heavy breathing of men fighting with the current, and hugging the bank on which he stood. Quite close, too, but it was too dark to distinguish anything under the overhanging bushes.

"Arabs, no doubt," muttered Almayer to himself, peering into the solid blackness. "What are they up to now? Some of Abdulla's business; curse him!"

The boat was very close now.

"Oh, ya! Man!" hailed Almayer.

The sound of voices ceased, but the paddles worked as furiously as before. Then the bush in front of Almayer shook, and the sharp sound of the paddles falling into the canoe rang in the quiet night. They were holding on to the bush now; but Almayer could hardly make out an indistinct dark shape of a man's head and shoulders above the bank.

"You Abdulla?" said Almayer, doubtfully.

A grave voice answered—

"Tuan Almayer is speaking to a friend. There is no Arab here."

Almayer's heart gave a great leap.

"Dain!" he exclaimed. "At last! at last! I have been waiting for you every day and every night. I had nearly given you up."

"Nothing could have stopped me from coming back here," said the other, almost violently. "Not even death," he whispered to himself.

"This is a friend's talk, and is very good," said Almayer, heartily. "Drop down to the jetty and let your men cook their rice in my campong while we talk in the house."

There was no answer to that invitation.

"What is it?" asked Almayer, uneasily. "There is nothing wrong with the brig, I hope?"

"The brig is where no Orang Blanda can lay his hands on her," said Dain, with a gloomy tone in his voice, which Almayer, in his elation, failed to notice.

"Right," he said. "But where are all your men? There are only two with you."

"Listen, Tuan Almayer," said Dain. "To-morrow's sun shall see me in your house, and then we will talk. Now I must go to the Rajah."

"To the Rajah! Why? What do you want with Lakamba?"

"Tuan, to-morrow we talk like friends. I must see Lakamba to-night."

"Dain, you are not going to abandon me now, when all is ready?" asked Almayer, in a pleading voice.

"Have I not returned? But I must see Lakamba first for your good and mine."

The shadowy head disappeared abruptly. The bush, released from the grasp of the bowman, sprung back with a swish, scattering a shower of muddy water over Almayer, as he bent forward, trying to see.

In a little while the canoe shot into the streak of light that streamed on the river from the big fire on the opposite shore, disclosing the outline of two men bending to their work, and a third figure in the stern flourishing the steering paddle, his head covered with an enormous round hat, like a fantastically exaggerated mushroom.

Almayer watched the canoe till it passed out of the line of light. Shortly after the murmur of many voices reached him across the water. He could see the torches being snatched out of the burning pile, and rendering visible for a moment the gate in the stockade round which they crowded. Then they went in; the torches disappeared, and the scattered fire sent out only a dim and fitful glare.

Almayer stepped homewards with long strides and mind uneasy. Surely Dain was not thinking of playing him false. It was absurd. Dain and Lakamba were both too much interested in the success of his scheme. Trusting to Malays was poor work; but then even Malays have some sense and understand their own interest. All would be well—must be well. At this point in his meditation he found himself at the foot of the steps leading to the verandah of his home. From the low point of land where he stood he could see both branches of the river. The main stream of the Pantai was lost in complete darkness, for the fire at the Rajah's had gone out altogether; but up the Sambir reach his eye could follow the long line of Malay houses crowding the bank, with here and there a dim light twinkling through bamboo walls, or a smoky torch burning on the platforms built out over the river. Further away, where the island ended in a low cliff, rose a dark mass of buildings towering above the Malay structures. Founded solidly on a firm ground with plenty of space, starred by many lights burning strong and white, with a suggestion of paraffin and lamp-glasses, stood the house and the godowns of Abdulla bin Selim, the great trader of Sambir. To Almayer the sight was very distasteful, and he shook his fist towards the buildings that in their evident prosperity looked to him cold and insolent, and contemptuous of his own fallen fortunes.

He mounted the steps of his house slowly.

In the middle of the verandah there was a round table. On it a paraffin lamp without a globe shed a hard glare on the three inner sides. The fourth side was open, and faced the river. Between the rough supports of the high-pitched roof hung torn rattan screens. There was no ceiling, and the harsh brilliance of the lamp was toned above into a soft half-light that lost itself in the obscurity amongst the rafters. The front wall was cut in two by the doorway of a central passage closed by a red curtain. The women's room opened into that passage, which led to the back courtyard and to the cooking shed. In one of the side walls there was a doorway. Half obliterated words—"Office: Lingard and Co."—were still legible on the dusty door, which looked as if it had not been opened for a very long time. Close to the other side wall stood a bent-wood rocking chair, and by the table and about the verandah four wooden armchairs straggled forlornly, as if ashamed of their shabby surroundings. A heap of common mats lay in one corner, with an old hammock slung diagonally above. In the other corner, his head wrapped in a piece of red calico, huddled into a shapeless heap, slept a Malay, one of Almayer's domestic slaves—"my own people," he used to call them. A numerous and representative assembly of moths were holding high revels round the lamp to the spirited music of swarming mosquitoes. Under the palm-leaf thatch lizards raced on the beams calling softly. A monkey, chained to one of the verandah supports—retired for the night under the eaves— peered and grinned at Almayer, as it swung to one of the bamboo roof sticks and caused a shower of dust and bits of dried leaves to settle on the shabby table. The floor was uneven, with many withered plants and dried earth scattered about. A general air of squalid neglect pervaded the place. The light breeze from the river swayed gently the tattered blinds, sending from the woods opposite a faint and sickly perfume as of decaying flowers.

Under Almayer's heavy tread the boards of the verandah creaked loudly. The sleeper in the corner moved uneasily, muttering indistinct words. There was a slight rustle behind the curtained doorway, and a soft voice asked in Malay, "Is it you, father?"

"Yes, Nina. I am hungry. Is everybody asleep in this house?"

Almayer spoke jovially and dropped with a contented sigh into the armchair nearest to the table. Nina Almayer came through the curtained doorway followed by an old Malay woman, who busied herself in setting upon the table a plateful of rice and fish, a jar of water and a bottle half full of genever. After carefully placing before her master a cracked glass tumbler and a tin spoon she went away noiselessly. Nina stood by the table, one hand lightly resting on its edge, the other hanging listlessly by her side. Her face turned towards the outer darkness, through which her dreamy eyes seemed to see some entrancing picture, wore a look of impatient expectancy. She was tall for a half-caste, with the correct profile of the father, modified and strengthened by the squareness of the lower part of the face inherited from her maternal ancestors—the Sulu pirates. Her firm mouth, with the lips slightly parted and disclosing a gleam of white teeth, put a vague suggestion of ferocity into the impatient expression of her features. And yet her dark and perfect eyes had all the tender softness common to Malay women, but with a gleam of superior intelligence; they looked out gravely, wide open and steady, as if facing something invisible to all other eyes. She stood there all in white, straight, flexible, graceful, unconscious of herself, her low but broad forehead crowned with a shining mass of long black hair that fell in heavy tresses over her shoulders, and made her pale olive complexion look paler still by the contrast of its coal-black hue.

Almayer attacked his rice greedily, but after a few mouthfuls he paused, spoon in hand, and looked at his daughter curiously.

"Did you hear a boat pass about half an hour ago, Nina?" he asked.

The girl gave him a quick glance, and moving away from the light stood with her back to the table.

"I heard nothing," she said, slowly.

"There was a boat. At last! Dain himself; and he went on to Lakamba. I know it, for he told me so. I spoke to him, but he would not come here to-night. Promised to come to-morrow."

He swallowed another spoonful, then said—

"I am almost happy to-night, Nina. I can see the end of a long road, and it leads us away from this miserable swamp. We shall soon get away from here, I and you, my dear little girl, and then——"

He rose from the table and stood looking fixedly before him as if contemplating some enchanting vision.

"And then," he went on, "we shall be happy, you and I. Live rich and respected far from here, and forget this life, and all this struggle, and all this misery."

He approached his daughter and passed his hand caressingly over her hair.

"It is bad to have to trust a Malay," he said, "but I must own that this Dain is a perfect gentleman—a perfect gentleman," he repeated.

"Did you ask him to come here, father?" inquired Nina, not looking at him.

"Well, of course. We shall start on the day after to-morrow," said Almayer, joyously. "We must not lose any time. Are you glad, little girl?"

She was as tall as himself, but he liked to recall the time when she was little and they were all in all to each other.

"I am glad," she said, very low.

"Of course," said Almayer, vivaciously, "you cannot imagine what is before you. I myself have not been to Europe, but I have heard my mother talk so often that I seem to know all about it. We shall live a—a glorious life. You shall see."

Again he stood silent by his daughter's side looking at that enchanting vision. After a while he shook his fist towards the sleeping settlement.

"Ah! my friend Abdulla," he cried, "we shall see who will have the best of it after all these years!"

He looked up the river and remarked calmly:

"Another thunderstorm. Well! No thunder will keep me awake to-night, I know! Good-night, little girl," he whispered tenderly, kissing her cheek. "You do not seem to be very happy to-night, but to-morrow you will show a brighter face. Eh?"

Nina had listened to her father, unmoved, with her half-closed eyes still gazing into the night now made more intense by a heavy thunder-cloud that had crept down from the hills blotting out the stars, merging sky, forest, and river into one mass of almost palpable blackness. The faint breeze had died out, but the distant rumble of thunder and pale flashes of lightning gave warning of the approaching storm. With a sigh the girl turned towards the table.

Almayer was in his hammock now, already half asleep.

"Take the lamp, Nina," he muttered, drowsily. "This place is full of mosquitoes. Go to sleep, daughter."

But Nina put the lamp out and turned back again towards the balustrade of the verandah. She stood with her arm round the wooden support looking eagerly towards the Pantai reach. And motionless there in the oppressive calm of the tropical night she could see at each flash of lightning the forest lining both banks up the river, bending before the furious blast of wind the upper reach of the river whipped into white foam, and the black clouds torn into fantastic shapes trailing low over the swaying trees. Round her all was as yet stillness and peace, but she could hear afar off the driving roar, and hiss of heavy rain, the wash of the waves on the tormented river. It came nearer and nearer, with loud thunder-claps and long flashes of vivid lightning, followed by short periods of appalling blackness. When the storm reached the low point dividing the river, the whole house shook while the rain pattered loudly on the palm-leaf roof. The thunder spoke in one prolonged roll, and the incessant lightning disclosed a turmoil of leaping waters, driving logs, and the big trees bending before a brutal and merciless force.

Undisturbed by the nightly event of the rainy monsoon, the father slept quietly, oblivious alike of his hopes, his misfortunes, his friends, and his enemies; and the daughter stood motionless, at each flash of lightning eagerly scanning the broad river with a steady and anxious gaze.

When, in compliance with Lingard's abrupt demand, Almayer consented to wed the Malay girl, no one knew that on the day when the interesting young convert had lost all her natural relations and found a white father, she had been fighting desperately like the rest of them on board the prau, and was only prevented from leaping overboard, like the few other survivors, by a severe wound in the leg. There, on the fore-deck of the prau, old Lingard found her under a heap of dead and dying pirates, and had her carried on the poop of the *Flash* before the Malay craft was set on fire and sent adrift. She was conscious, and in the great peace and stillness of the tropical evening succeeding the turmoil of the battle, she watched all she held dear on earth after her own savage manner, drift away into the gloom in a great roar of flame and smoke. She lay there unheeding the careful hands attending to her wound, silent and absorbed in gazing at the funeral pile of those brave men she had so much admired and so well helped in their contest with the redoubtable "Rajah-Laut."

The light night breeze fanned the brig gently to the southwards, and the great blaze of light got smaller and smaller till it twinkled only on the horizon like a setting star. It set: the heavy canopy of smoke reflected the glare of hidden flames for a short time and then disappeared also.

She realized that with this vanishing gleam her old life departed too. Thenceforth there was slavery in the far countries, amongst strangers, in unknown and perhaps terrible surroundings. There was in her the dread of the unknown; but otherwise she accepted her position calmly, for was she not a daughter of warriors, conquered in battle, and did she not belong rightfully to the victorious Rajah? Even the evident kindness of the terrible old man must spring, she thought, from admiration for his captive, and the flattered vanity eased for her the pangs of sorrow after such an awful calamity. Perhaps had she known of the high walls, the quiet gardens, and the silent nuns of the Samarang convent, where her destiny was leading her, she would have sought death in her dread and hate of such a restraint. But in imagination she pictured to herself the usual life of a Malay girl—the usual succession of heavy work and fierce love, of intrigues, gold ornaments, of domestic drudgery, and of that great but occult influence which is one of the few rights of half-savage womankind. But her destiny in the rough hands of the old sea-dog, acting under unreasoning impulses of the heart, took a strange and to her a terrible shape. She bore it all—the restraint and the teaching and the new faith—with calm submission, concealing her hate and contempt for all that new life. She learned the language very easily, yet understood but little of the new faith the good sisters taught her, assimilating quickly only the superstitious elements of the religion. She called Lingard father, gently and caressingly, at each of his short and noisy visits, under the clear impression that he was a great and dangerous power it was good to propitiate. Was he not now her master? And during those long four years she nourished a hope of finding favour in his eyes and ultimately becoming his wife, counsellor, and guide.

Those dreams of the future were dispelled by the Rajah Laut's "fiat," which made Almayer's fortune, as that young man fondly hoped. And dressed in the hateful finery of Europe, the young convert stood before the altar with an unknown and sulky-looking white man. For Almayer was uneasy, a little disgusted, and greatly inclined to run away. A judicious fear of the adopted father-in-law and a just regard for his own material welfare prevented him from making a scandal; yet, while swearing fidelity, he was concocting plans for getting rid of the pretty Malay girl in a more or less distant future. She, however, had retained enough of conventual teaching to understand well that according to white men's law she was going to be Almayer's companion and not his slave, and promised to herself to act accordingly.

So when the *Flash* freighted with materials for building a new house left the harbour of Batavia, taking away the young couple into the unknown Borneo, she did not carry on her deck so much love and happiness as old Lingard was wont to boast of before his casual friends in the verandahs of various hotels. The old seaman himself was perfectly happy. Now he had done his duty by the girl. "You know I made her an orphan," he often concluded solemnly, when talking about his own affairs to a scratch audience of shore loafers—as it was his habit to do. And the approbative shouts of his half-intoxicated auditors filled his simple soul with delight and pride. "I carry everything right through," was another of his sayings, and in pursuance of that principle he pushed the building of house and godowns on the Pantai River with feverish haste. The house for the young couple; the godowns for the big trade Almayer was going to develop while he (Lingard) would be able to give himself up to some mysterious work which was only spoken of in hints, but was understood to relate to gold and diamonds in the interior of the island. Almayer was impatient too. Had he known what was before him he might not have been so eager and full of hope as he stood watching the last canoe of the Lingard expedition disappear in the bend up the river. When, turning round, he beheld the pretty little house, the godowns built neatly by an army of Chinese carpenters, the new jetty round which were clustered the trading canoes, he felt a sudden elation in the thought that the world was his.

But the world had to be conquered first, and its conquest was not so easy as he thought. He was very soon made to understand that he was not wanted in that corner of it where old Lingard and his own weak will placed him, in the midst of unscrupulous intrigues and of a fierce trade competition. The Arabs had found out the river, had established a trading post in Sambir, and where they traded they would be masters and suffer no rival. Lingard returned unsuccessful from his first expedition, and departed again spending all the profits of the legitimate trade on his mysterious journeys. Almayer struggled with the difficulties of his position, friendless and unaided, save for the protection given to him for Lingard's sake by the old Rajah, the predecessor of Lakamba. Lakamba himself, then living as a private individual on a rice clearing, seven miles down the river, exercised all his inflence towards the help of the white man's enemies, plotting against the old Rajah and Almayer with a certainty of combination, pointing clearly to a profound knowledge of their most secret affairs. Outwardly friendly, his portly form was often to be seen on Almayer's verandah; his green turban and gold-embroidered jacket shone in the front rank of the decorous throng of Malays coming to greet Lingard on his returns from the interior; his salaams were of the lowest, and his handshakings of the heartiest, when welcoming the old trader. But his small eyes took in the signs of the times, and he departed from those interviews with a satisfied and furtive smile to hold long consultations with his friend and ally, Syed Abdulla, the chief of the Arab trading post, a man of great wealth and of great influence in the islands.

It was currently believed at that time in the settlement that Lakamba's visits to Almayer's house were not limited to those official interviews. Often on moonlight nights the belated fishermen of Sambir saw a small canoe shooting out from the narrow creek at the back of the white man's house, and the solitary occupant paddle cautiously down the river in the deep shadows of the bank; and those events, duly reported, were discussed round the evening fires far into the night with the cynicism of expression common to Malays. Almayer went on struggling desperately, but with a feebleness of purpose depriving him of all chance of success against men so unscrupulous and resolute as his rivals the Arabs. The trade fell away from the large godowns, and the godowns themselves rotted piecemeal. The old man's banker, Hudig of Macassar, failed, and with this went the whole available capital. The profits of past years had been swallowed up in Lingard's exploring craze. Lingard was in the interior—perhaps dead—at all events giving no sign of life. Almayer stood alone in the midst of those adverse circumstances, deriving only a little comfort from the companionship of his little daughter, born two years after the marriage, and at the time some six years old. His wife had soon commenced to treat him with a savage contempt expressed by sulky silence, only occasionally varied by outbursts of savage invective. He felt she hated him, and saw her jealous eyes watching himself and the child with almost an expression of hate. She was jealous of the little girl's evident preference for the father, and Almayer felt he was not safe with that woman in the house. While she was burning the furniture, and tearing down the pretty curtains in her unreasoning hate of those signs of civilization, Almayer, cowed by these outbursts of savage nature, meditated in silence on the best way of getting rid of her. He thought of everything; even planned murder in an undecided and feeble sort of way, but dared do nothing—expecting every day the return of Lingard with news of some immense good fortune. Lingard returned indeed, but aged, ill, a ghost of his former self, with the fire of fever burning in his sunken eyes, almost the only survivor of the numerous expedition. But he was successful at last! Untold riches were in his grasp; he wanted more money—only a little more to realize a dream of fabulous fortune. And Hudig had failed! Almayer scraped all he could together, but the old man wanted more. If Almayer could not get it he would go to Singapore—to Europe even, but before all to Singapore; and he would take the little Nina with him. The child must be brought up decently. He had good friends in Singapore who would take care of her and have her taught properly. All would be well, and that girl, upon whom the old seaman seemed to have transferred all his former affection for the mother, would be the richest woman in the East—in the world even. So old Lingard shouted, pacing the verandah with his heavy quarter-deck step, gesticulating with a smouldering cheroot; ragged, dishevelled, enthusiastic; and Almayer, sitting huddled up on a pile of mats, thought with dread of the separation from the only human being he loved—with greater dread still, perhaps, of the scene with his wife, the savage tigress deprived of her young. She will poison me, thought the poor wretch, well aware of that easy and final manner of solving the social, political, or family problems in Malay life.

To his great surprise she took the news very quietly, giving only him and Lingard a furtive glance, and saying not a word. This, however, did not prevent her the next day from jumping into the river and swimming after the boat in which Lingard was carrying away the nurse with the screaming child. Almayer had to give chase with his whale-boat and drag her in by the hair in the midst of cries and curses enough to make heaven fall. Yet after two days spent in wailing, she returned to her former mode of life, chewing betel-nut, and sitting all day amongst her women in stupefied idleness. She aged very rapidly after that, and only roused herself from her apathy to acknowledge by a scathing remark or an insulting exclamation the accidental presence of her husband. He had built for her a riverside hut in the compound where she dwelt in perfect seclusion. Lakamba's visits had ceased when, by a convenient decree of Providence the old ruler of Sambir departed this life. Lakamba reigned in his stead now, having been well served by his Arab friends with the Dutch authorities. Syed Abdulla was the great man and trader of the Pantai. Almayer lay ruined and helpless under the close-meshed net of their intrigues, owing his life only to his supposed knowledge of Lingard's valuable secret. Lingard had disappeared. He wrote once from Singapore saying the child was well, and under the care of a Mrs. Vinck, and that he himself was going to Europe to raise money for the great enterprise. He was coming back soon. There would be no difficulties, he wrote. People would rush in with their money. Evidently they did not, for there was only one letter more from him saying he was ill, had found no relation living, but little else besides. Then came a complete silence. Europe had swallowed up the Rajah Laut apparently, and Almayer looked vainly westward for a ray of light out of the gloom of his shattered hopes. Years passed, and the rare letters from Mrs. Vinck, later from the girl herself, were the only thing to be looked to to make life bearable amongst the triumphant savagery of the river. Almayer lived now alone, having even ceased to visit his debtors who would not pay, sure of Lakamba's protection. The faithful Sumatrese Ali cooked his rice and made his coffee, for he dared not trust any one else, and least of all his wife. He killed time wandering sadly in the overgrown paths round the house, visiting the ruined godowns where a few brass guns covered with verdigris and only a few broken cases of mouldering Manchester goods reminded him of the good early times when all this was full of life and merchandise, and he overlooked a busy scene on the river bank, his little daughter by his side. Now the upcountry canoes glided past the little rotten wharf of Lingard and Co., to paddle up the Pantai branch, and cluster round the new jetty belonging to Abdulla. Not that they loved Abdulla, but they dared not trade with the man whose star had set. Had they done so they knew there was no mercy to be expected from Arab or Rajah; no rice to be got on credit in times of scarcity from either; and Almayer could not help them, having at times hardly enough for himself. Almayer, in his isolation and despair, often envied his near neighbour the Chinaman, Jim-Eng, whom he could see stretched on a pile of cool mats, a wooden pillow under his head, an opium pipe in his nerveless fingers. He did not seek, however, consolation in opium—perhaps it was too expensive —perhaps his white man's pride saved him from that degradation; but most likely it was the thought of his little daughter in the far-off

Straits Settlements. He heard from her oftener since Abdulla bought a steamer, which ran now between Singapore and the Pantai settlement every three months or so. Almayer felt himself nearer his daughter. He longed to see her, and planned a voyage to Singapore, but put off his departure from year to year, always expecting some favourable turn of fortune. He did not want to meet her with empty hands and with no words of hope on his lips. He could not take her back into that savage life to which he was condemned himself. He was also a little afraid of her. What would she think of him? He reckoned the years. A grown woman. A civilized woman, young and hopeful; while he felt old and hopeless, and very much like those savages round him. He asked himself what was going to be her future. He could not answer that question yet, and he dared not face her. And yet he longed after her. He hesitated for years.

His hesitation was put an end to by Nina's unexpected appearance in Sambir. She arrived in the steamer under the captain's care. Almayer beheld her with surprise not unmixed with wonder. During those ten years the child had changed into a woman, black-haired, olive-skinned, tall, and beautiful, with great sad eyes, where the startled expression common to Malay womankind was modified by a thoughtful tinge inherited from her European ancestry. Almayer thought with dismay of the meeting of his wife and daughter, of what this grave girl in European clothes would think of her betel-nut chewing mother, squatting in a dark hut, disorderly, half naked, and sulky. He also feared an outbreak of temper on the part of that pest of a woman he had hitherto managed to keep tolerably quiet, thereby saving the remnants of his dilapidated furniture. And he stood there before the closed door of the hut in the blazing sunshine listening to the murmur of voices, wondering what went on inside, wherefrom all the servant-maids had been expelled at the beginning of the interview, and now stood clustered by the palings with half-covered faces in a chatter of curious speculation. He forgot himself there trying to catch a stray word through the bamboo walls, till the captain of the steamer (who had walked up with the girl) fearing a sunstroke, took him under the arm and led him into the shade of his own verandah where Nina's trunk stood already, having been landed by the steamer's men. As soon as Captain Ford had his glass before him and his cheroot lighted, Almayer asked for the explanation of his daughter's unexpected arrival. Ford said little beyond generalizing in vague but violent terms upon the foolishness of women in general, and of Mrs. Vinck in particular.

"You know, Kaspar," said he, in conclusion, to the excited Almayer, "it is deucedly awkward to have a half-caste girl in the house. There's such a lot of fools about. There was that young fellow from the bank who used to ride to the Vinck bungalow early and late. That old woman thought it was for that Emma of hers. When she found out what he wanted exactly, there was a row, I can tell you. She would not have Nina—not an hour longer—in the house. Fact is, I heard of this affair and took the girl to my wife. My wife is a pretty good woman—as women go—and upon my word we would have kept the girl for you, only she would not stay. Now, then! Don't flare up, Kaspar. Sit still. What can you do? It is better so. Let her stay with you. She was never happy over there. Those two Vinck girls are no better than dressed-up monkeys. They slighted her. You can't make her white. It's no use you swearing at me. You can't. She is a good girl for all that, but she would not tell my wife anything. If you want to know, ask her yourself; but if I was you I would leave her alone. You are welcome to her passage money, old fellow, if you are short now." And the skipper, throwing away his cigar, walked off to "wake them up on board," as he expressed it.

Almayer vainly expected to hear of the cause of his daughter's return from his daughter's lips. Not that day, not on any other day did she ever allude to her Singapore life. He did not care to ask, awed by the calm impassiveness of her face, by those solemn eyes looking past him on the great, still forests sleeping in majestic repose to the murmur of the broad river. He accepted the situation, happy in the gentle and protecting affection the girl showed him, fitfully enough, for she had (as he called it) her bad days when she used to visit her mother and remain long hours in the riverside hut, coming out as inscrutable as ever, but with a contemptuous look and a short word ready to answer any of his speeches. He got used even to that, and on those days kept quiet, although greatly alarmed by his wife's influence upon the girl. Otherwise Nina adapted herself wonderfully to the circumstances of a half-savage and miserable life. She accepted without question or apparent disgust the neglect, the decay, the poverty of the household, the absence of furniture, and the preponderance of rice diet on the family table. She lived with Almayer in the little house (now sadly decaying) built originally by Lingard for the young couple. The Malays discussed eagerly her arrival. There were at the beginning crowded levées of Malay women with their children, seeking eagerly after "Ubat" for all the ills of the flesh from the young Mem Putih. In the cool of the evening grave Arabs in long white shirts and yellow sleeveless jackets walked slowly on the dusty path by the riverside towards Almayer's gate, and made solemn calls upon that Unbeliever under shallow pretences of business, only to get a glimpse of the young girl in a highly decorous manner. Even Lakamba came out of his stockade in a great pomp of war canoes and red umbrellas, and landed on the rotten little jetty of Lingard and Co. He came, he said, to buy a couple of brass guns as a present to his friend the chief of Sambir

Dyaks; and while Almayer, suspicious but polite, busied himself in unearthing the old popguns in the godowns, the Rajah sat in an arm-chair on the verandah, surrounded by his respectful retinue waiting in vain for Nina's appearance. She was in one of her bad days, and remained in her mother's hut watching with her the ceremonious proceedings on the verandah. The Rajah departed, baffled but cour-teous, and soon Almayer began to reap the benefit of improved re-lations with the ruler in the shape of the recovery of some debts, paid to him with many apologies and many a low salaam by debtors till then considered hopelessly insolvent. Under these improving circum-stances Almayer brightened up a little. All was not lost perhaps. Those Arabs and Malays saw at last that he was a man of some ability, he thought. And he began, after his manner, to plan great things, to dream of great fortunes for himself and Nina. Especially for Nina! Under these vivifying impulses he asked Captain Ford to write to his friends in England making inquiries after Lingard. Was he alive or dead? If dead, had he left any papers, documents; any indications or hints as to his great enterprise? Meantime he had found amongst the rubbish in one of the empty rooms a notebook belonging to the old adventurer. He studied the crabbed handwriting of its pages and often grew meditative over it. Other things also woke him up from his apathy. The stir made in the whole of the island by the establishment of the British Borneo Company affected even the sluggish flow of the Pantai life. Great changes were expected; annexation was talked of; the Arabs grew civil. Almayer began building his new house for the use of the future engineers, agents, or settlers of the new Company. He spent every available guilder on it with a confiding heart. One thing only disturbed his happiness; his wife came out of her seclusion, importing her green jacket, scant sarongs, shrill voice, and witch-like appearance, into his quiet life in the small bungalow. And his daughter seemed to accept that savage intrusion into their daily existence with wonderful equanimity. He did not like it, but dared say nothing.

CHAPTER THREE

The deliberations conducted in London have a far-reaching im-portance, and so the decision issued from the fog-veiled offices of the Borneo Company darkened for Almayer the brilliant sunshine of the Tropics, and added another drop of bitterness to the cup of his dis-enchantments. The claim to that part of the East Coast was aban-doned, leaving the Pantai river under the nominal power of Holland. In Sambir there was joy and excitement. The slaves were hurried out of sight into the forest and jungle, and the flags were run up to tall poles in the Rajah's compound in expectation of a visit from Dutch man-of-war boats.

The frigate remained anchored outside the mouth of the river, and the boats came up in tow of the steam launch, threading their way cautiously amongst a crowd of canoes filled with gaily dressed Malays. The officer in command listened gravely to the loyal speeches of Lakamba, returned the salaams of Abdulla, and assured those gentlemen in choice Malay of the great Rajah's—down in Batavia—friendship and good-will towards the ruler and inhabitants of this model state of Sambir.

Almayer from his verandah watched across the river the festive proceedings, heard the report of brass guns saluting the new flag presented to Lakamba, and the deep murmur of the crowd of spectators surging round the stockade. The smoke of the firing rose in white clouds on the green background of the forests, and he could not help comparing his own fleeting hopes to the rapidly disappearing vapour. He was by no means patriotically elated by the event, yet he had to force himself into a gracious behaviour when, the official reception being over, the naval officers of the Commission crossed the river to pay a visit to the solitary white man of whom they had heard, no doubt wishing also to catch a glimpse of his daughter. In that they were disappointed, Nina refusing to show herself; but they seemed easily consoled by the gin and cheroots set before them by the hospitable Almayer; and sprawling comfortably on the lame armchairs under the shade of the verandah, while the blazing sunshine outside seemed to set the great river simmering in the heat, they filled the little bungalow with the unusual sounds of European languages, with noise and laughter produced by naval witticisms at the expense of the fat Lakamba whom they had been complimenting so much that very morning. The younger men in an access of good fellowship made their host talk, and Almayer, excited by the sight of European faces, by the sound of European voices, opened his heart before the sympathizing strangers, unaware of the amusement the recital of his many misfortunes caused to those future admirals. They drank his health, wished him many big diamonds and a mountain of gold, expressed even an envy of the high destinies awaiting him yet. Encouraged by so much friendliness, the grey-headed and foolish dreamer invited his guests to visit his new house. They went there through the long grass in a straggling procession while their boats were got ready for the return down the river in the cool of the evening. And in the great empty rooms where the tepid wind entering through the sashless windows whirled gently the dried leaves and the dust of many days of neglect, Almayer in his white jacket and flowered sarong, surrounded by a circle of glittering uniforms, stamped his foot to show the solidity of the neatly-fitting floors and expatiated upon the beauties and convenience of the building. They listened and assented, amazed by the wonderful simplicity and the foolish hopefulness of the man, till Almayer, carried away by his excitement, disclosed his regret at the non-arrival of the English, "who knew how to develop a rich country," as he expressed it. There was a general laugh amongst the Dutch officers at that unsophisticated statement, and a move was made towards the boats; but when Almayer, stepping cautiously on the rotten boards of the Lingard jetty, tried to approach the chief of the Commission with some timid hints anent the protection required by the Dutch subject against the wily Arabs, that salt water diplomat told him significantly that the Arabs were better subjects than Hollanders who dealt illegally in gunpowder with the Malays. The innocent Almayer recognized there at once the oily tongue of Abdulla and the solemn persuasiveness of Lakamba, but ere he had time to frame an indignant protest the steam launch and the string of boats moved rapidly down the river leaving him on the jetty, standing open-mouthed in his surprise and anger. There are thirty miles of river from Sambir to the gem-like islands of the estuary where the frigate was awaiting the return of the boats. The moon rose long before the boats had traversed half that distance, and the black forest sleeping peacefully under her cold rays woke up that night to the ringing laughter in the small flotilla provoked by some reminiscence of Almayer's lamentable narrative. Salt-water jests at the poor man's expense were passed from boat to boat, the non-appearance of his daughter was commented upon with severe displeasure, and the half-finished house built for the reception of Englishmen received on that joyous night the name of "Almayer's Folly" by the unanimous vote of the lighthearted seamen.

For many weeks after this visit life in Sambir resumed its even and uneventful flow. Each day's sun shooting its morning rays above the tree-tops lit up the usual scene of daily activity. Nina walking on the path that formed the only street in the settlement saw the accustomed sight of men lolling on the shady side of the houses, on the high platforms; of women busily engaged in husking the daily rice; of naked brown children racing along the shady and narrow paths leading to the clearings. Jim-Eng, strolling before his house, greeted her with a friendly nod before climbing up indoors to seek his beloved opium pipe. The elder children clustered round her, daring from long acquaintance, pulling the skirts of her white robe with their dark fingers, and showing their brilliant teeth in expectation of a shower of glass beads. She greeted them with a quiet smile, but always had a few friendly words for a Siamese girl, a slave owned by Bulangi, whose numerous wives were said to be of a violent temper. Well-founded rumour said also that the domestic squabbles of that industrious cultivator ended generally in a combined assault of all his wives upon the Siamese slave. The girl herself never complained—perhaps from dictates of prudence, but more likely through the strange, resigned apathy of half-savage womankind. From early morning she was to be seen on the paths amongst the houses—by the riverside or on the jetties, the tray of pastry, it was her mission to sell, skilfully balanced on her head. During the great heat of the day she usually sought refuge in Almayer's campong, often finding shelter in a shady corner of the verandah, where she squatted with her tray before her, when invited by Nina. For "Mem Putih" she had always a smile, but the presence of Mrs. Almayer, the very sound of her shrill voice, was the signal for a hurried departure.

To this girl Nina often spoke; the other inhabitants of Sambir seldom or never heard the sound of her voice. They got used to the silent figure moving in their midst calm and white-robed, a being from another world and incomprehensible to them. Yet Nina's life for all her outward composure, for all the seeming detachment from the things and people surrounding her, was far from quiet, in consequence of Mrs. Almayer being much too active for the happiness and even safety of the household. She had resumed some intercourse with Lakamba, not personally, it is true (for the dignity of that potentate kept him inside his stockade), but through the agency of that potentate's prime minister, harbour master, financial adviser, and general factotum. That gentleman—of Sulu origin—was certainly endowed with statesmanlike qualities, although he was totally devoid of personal charms. In truth he was perfectly repulsive, possessing only one eye and a pock-marked face, with nose and lips horribly disfigured by the smallpox. This unengaging individual often strolled into Almayer's garden in unofficial costume, composed of a piece of pink calico round his waist. There at the back of the house, squatting on his heels on scattered embers, in close proximity to the great iron boiler, where the family daily rice was being cooked by the women under Mrs. Almayer's superintendence, did that astute negotiator carry on long conversations in Sulu language with Almayer's wife. What the subject of their discourses was might have been guessed from the subsequent domestic scenes by Almayer's hearthstone.

Of late Almayer had taken to excursions up the river. In a small canoe with two paddlers and the faithful Ali for a steersman he would disappear for a few days at a time. All his movements were no doubt closely watched by Lakamba and Abdulla, for the man once in the confidence of Rajah Laut was supposed to be in possession of valuable secrets. The coast population of Borneo believes implicitly in diamonds of fabulous value, in gold mines of enormous richness in the interior. And all those imaginings are heightened by the difficulty of penetrating far inland, especially on the northeast coast, where the Malays and the river tribes of Dyaks or Head-hunters are eternally quarrelling. It is true enough that some gold reaches the coast in the hands of those Dyaks when, during short periods of truce in the desultory warfare, they visit the coast settlements of Malays. And so the wildest exaggerations are built up and added to on the slight basis of that fact.

Almayer in his quality of white man—as Lingard before him—had somewhat better relations with the upriver tribes. Yet even his excursions were not without danger, and his returns were eagerly looked for by the impatient Lakamba. But every time the Rajah was disappointed. Vain were the conferences by the rice-pot of his factotum Babalatchi with the white man's wife. The white man himself was impenetrable—impenetrable to persuasion, coaxing, abuse; to soft words and shrill revilings; to desperate beseechings or murderous threats; for Mrs. Almayer, in her extreme desire to persuade her husband into an alliance with Lakamba, played upon the whole gamut of passion. With her soiled robe wound tightly under the armpits across her lean bosom, her scant greyish hair tumbled in disorder over her projecting cheek-bones, in suppliant attitude, she depicted with shrill volubility the advantages of close union with a man so good and so fair dealing.

"Why don't you go to the Rajah?" she screamed. "Why do you go back to those Dyaks in the great forest? They should be killed. You cannot kill them, you cannot; but our Rajah's men are brave! You tell the Rajah where the old white man's treasure is. Our Rajah is good! He is our very grandfather. He will kill those wretched Dyaks, and you shall have half the treasure. Oh, Kaspar, tell where the treasure is! Tell me! Tell me out of the old man's surat where you read so often at night."

On those occasions Almayer sat with rounded shoulders bending to the blast of this domestic tempest, accentuating only each pause in the torrent of his wife's eloquence by an angry growl, "There is no treasure! Go away, woman!" Exasperated by the sight of his patiently bent back, she would at last walk round so as to face him across the table, and clasping her robe with one hand she stretched the other lean arm and clawlike hand to emphasize, in a passion of anger and contempt, the rapid rush of scathing remarks and bitter cursings heaped on the head of the man unworthy to associate with brave Malay chiefs. It ended generally by Almayer rising slowly, his long pipe in hand, his face set into a look of inward pain, and walking away in silence. He descended the steps and plunged into the long grass on his way to the solitude of his new house, dragging his feet in a state of physical collapse from disgust and fear before that fury. She followed to the head of the steps, and sent the shafts of indiscriminate abuse after the retreating form. And each of those scenes was concluded by a piercing shriek, reaching him far away. "You know, Kaspar, I am your wife! your own Christian wife after your own Blanda law!" For she knew that this was the bitterest thing of all; the greatest regret of that man's life.

All these scenes Nina witnessed unmoved. She might have been deaf, dumb, without any feeling as far as any expression of opinion went. Yet oft when her father had sought the refuge of the great dusty rooms of "Almayer's Folly," and her mother, exhausted by rhetorical efforts, squatted wearily on her heels with her back against the leg of the table, Nina would approach her curiously, guarding her skirts from betel juice besprinkling the floor, and gaze down upon her as one might look into the quiescent crater of a volcano after a destructive eruption. Mrs. Almayer's thoughts after these scenes were usually turned into a channel of childhood reminiscences, and she gave them utterance in a kind of monotonous recitative—slightly disconnected, but generally describing the glories of the Sultan of Sulu, his great splendour, his power, his great prowess, the fear which benumbed the hearts of white men at the sight of his swift piratical praus. And these muttered statements of her grandfather's might were mixed up with bits of later recollections, where the great fight with the "White Devil's" brig and the convent life in Samarang occupied the principal place. At that point she usually dropped the thread of her narrative, and pulling out the little brass cross, always suspended round her neck, she contemplated it with superstitious awe. That superstitious feeling connected with some vague talismanic properties of the little bit of metal and the still more hazy but terrible notion of some bad Djinns and horrible torments invented, as she thought, for her especial punishment by the good Mother Superior in case of the loss of the above charm, were Mrs. Almayer's only theological outfit for the stormy road of life. Mrs. Almayer had at least something tangible to cling to, but Nina, brought up under the Protestant wing of the proper Mrs. Vinck, had not even a little piece of brass to remind her of past teaching. And listening to the recital of those savage glories, those barbarous fights and savage feasting, to the story of deeds valorous, albeit somewhat bloodthirsty, where men of her mother's race shone far above the Orang Blanda, she felt herself irresistibly fascinated, and saw with vague surprise the narrow mantle of civilized morality, in which good-meaning people had wrapped her young soul, fall away and leave her shivering and helpless as if on the edge of some deep and unknown abyss. Strangest of all, this abyss did not frighten her when she was under the influence of the witch-like being she called her mother. She seemed to have forgotten in civilized surroundings her life before the time when Lingard had, so to speak, kidnapped her from Brow. Since then she had had Christian teaching, social education, and a good glimpse of civilized life. Unfortunately her teachers did not understand her nature, and the education ended in a scene of humiliation, in an outburst of contempt from white people for her mixed blood. And now she had lived on the river for three years with a savage mother and a father walking about amongst pitfalls, with his head in the clouds, weak, irresolute, and unhappy. She had lived a life devoid of all the decencies of civilization, in miserable domestic conditions; she had breathed the atmosphere of sordid plottings for gain, of the no less disgusting intrigues and crimes for lust or money; and those things, together with the domestic quarrels, were the only events of her three years' existence. She did not die from despair and disgust the first month, as she expected and almost hoped for. On the contrary, at the end of half a year it had seemed to her that she had known no other life. Her young mind having been unskilfully permitted to glance at better things, and then thrown back again into the hopeless quagmire of barbarism, full of strong and uncontrolled passions, had lost the power to discriminate. It seemed to Nina that there was no change and no difference. Whether they traded in brick godowns or on the muddy river bank; whether they reached after much or little; whether they made love under the shadows of the great trees or in the shadow of the cathedral on the Singapore promenade; whether they plotted for their own ends under the protection of laws and according to the rules of Christian conduct, or whether they sought the gratification of their desires with the savage cunning and the unrestrained fierceness of natures as innocent of culture as their own immense and gloomy forests, Nina saw only the same manifestations of love and hate and of sordid greed chasing the uncertain dollar in all its multifarious and vanishing shapes. To her resolute nature, however, after all these years, the savage and uncompromising sincerity of purpose shown by her Malay kinsmen seemed at last preferable to the sleek hypocrisy, to the polite disguises, to the virtuous pretences of such white people as she had had the misfortune to come in contact with. After all it was her life; it was going to be her life, and so thinking she fell more and more under the influence of her mother. Seeking, in her ignorance, a better side to that life, she listened with avidity to the old woman's tales of the departed glories of the Rajahs, from whose race she had sprung, and she became gradually more indifferent, more contemptuous of the white side of her descent represented by a feeble and traditionless father.

Almayer's difficulties were by no means diminished by the girl's presence in Sambir. The stir caused by her arrival had died out, it is true, and Lakamba had not renewed his visits; but about a year after the departure of the man-of-war boats the nephew of Abdulla, Syed

Reshid, returned from his pilgrimage to Mecca, rejoicing in a green jacket and the proud title of Hadji. There was a great letting off of rockets on board the steamer which brought him in, and a great beating of drums all night in Abdulla's compound, while the feast of welcome was prolonged far into the small hours of the morning. Reshid was the favourite nephew and heir of Abdulla, and that loving uncle, meeting Almayer one day by the riverside, stopped politely to exchange civilities and to ask solemnly for an interview. Almayer suspected some attempt at a swindle, or at any rate something unpleasant, but of course consented with a great show of rejoicing. Accordingly the next evening, after sunset, Abdulla came, accompanied by several other grey-beards and by his nephew. That young man—of a very rakish and dissipated appearance—affected the greatest indifference as to the whole of the proceedings. When the torch-bearers had grouped themselves below the steps, the visitors had seated themselves on various lame chairs, Reshid stood apart in the shadow, examining his aristocratically small hands with great attention. Almayer, surprised by the great solemnity of his visitors, perched himself on the corner of the table with a characteristic want of dignity quickly noted by the Arabs with grave disapproval. But Abdulla spoke now, looking straight past Almayer at the red curtain hanging in the doorway, where a slight tremor disclosed the presence of women on the other side. He began by neatly complimenting Almayer upon the long years they had dwelt together in cordial neighbourhood, and called upon Allah to give him many more years to gladden the eyes of his friends by his welcome presence. He made a polite allusion to the great consideration shown him (Almayer) by the Dutch "Commissie," and drew thence the flattering inference of Almayer's great importance amongst his own people. He—Abdulla—was also important amongst all the Arabs, and his nephew Reshid would be heir of that social position and of great riches. Now Reshid was a Hadji. He was possessor of several Malay women, went on Abdulla, but it was time he had a favourite wife, the first of the four allowed by the Prophet. And, speaking with well-bred politeness, he explained further to the dumbfounded Almayer that, if he would consent to the alliance of his offspring with that true believer and virtuous man Reshid, she would be mistress of all the splendours of Reshid's house, the first wife of the first Arab in the Islands, when he—Abdulla—had been called to the joys of Paradise by Allah the All-merciful. "You know, Tuan," he said, in conclusion, "the other women would be her slaves, and Reshid's house is great. From Bombay he has brought great divans, and costly carpets, and European furniture. There is also a great looking-glass in a frame shining like gold. What could a girl want more?" And while Almayer looked upon him in silent dismay Abdulla spoke in a more confidential tone, waving his attendants away, and finished his speech by pointing out the material advantages of such an alliance, and offering to settle upon Almayer three thousand dollars as a sign of his sincere friendship and the price of the girl.

Poor Almayer was nearly having a fit. Burning with the desire of taking Abdulla by the throat, he had but to think of his helpless position in the midst of lawless men to comprehend the necessity of diplomatic conciliation. He mastered his impulses, and spoke politely and coldly, saying the girl was young and was the apple of his eye. Tuan Reshid, a Faithful and a Hadji, would not want an infidel woman in his harem; and, seeing Abdulla smile sceptically at that last objection, he remained silent, not trusting himself to speak more, not daring to refuse point-blank, nor yet to say anything compromising. Abdulla understood the meaning of that silence, and rose to take leave with a grave salaam. He wished his friend Almayer "a thousand years," and moved down the steps, helped dutifully by Reshid. The torch-bearers shook their torches, scattering a shower of sparks into the river, and the cortège moved off, leaving Almayer agitated but greatly relieved by their departure. He dropped into a chair and watched the glimmer of the lights amongst the tree trunks till they disappeared and complete silence succeeded the tramp of feet and the murmur of voices. He did not move till the curtain rustled and Nina came out on the verandah and sat in the rocking-chair, where she used to spend many hours every day. She gave a slight rocking motion to her seat, leaning back with half-closed eyes, her long hair shading her face from the smoky light of the lamp on the table. Almayer looked at her furtively, but the face was as impassible as ever. She turned her head slightly towards her father, and, speaking, to his great surprise, in English, asked—

"Was that Abdulla here?"

"Yes," said Almayer—"just gone."

"And what did he want, father?"

"He wanted to buy you for Reshid," answered Almayer, brutally, his anger getting the better of him, and looking at the girl as if in expectation of some outbreak of feeling. But Nina remained apparently unmoved, gazing dreamily into the black night outside.

"Be careful, Nina," said Almayer, after a short silence and rising from his chair, "when you go paddling alone into the creeks in your canoe. That Reshid is a violent scoundrel, and there is no saying what he may do. Do you hear me?"

She was standing now, ready to go in, one hand grasping the curtain in the doorway. She turned round, throwing her heavy tresses back by a sudden gesture.

"Do you think he would dare?" she asked, quickly, and then turned again to go in, adding in a lower tone, "He would not dare. Arabs are all cowards."

Almayer looked after her, astonished. He did not seek the repose of his hammock. He walked the floor absently, sometimes stopping by the balustrade to think. The lamp went out. The first streak of dawn broke over the forest; Almayer shivered in the damp air. "I give it up," he muttered to himself, lying down wearily. "Damn those women! Well! If the girl did not look as if she wanted to be kidnapped!"

And he felt a nameless fear creep into his heart, making him shiver again.

CHAPTER FOUR

That year, towards the breaking up of the southwest monsoon, disquieting rumours reached Sambir. Captain Ford, coming up to Almayer's house for an evening's chat, brought late numbers of the *Straits Times* giving the news of Acheen war and of the unsuccessful Dutch expedition. The Nakhodas of the rare trading praus ascending the river paid visits to Lakamba, discussing with that potentate the unsettled state of affairs, and wagged their heads gravely over the recital of Orang Blanda exaction, severity, and general tyranny, as exemplified in the total stoppage of gunpowder trade and the rigorous visiting of all suspicious craft trading in the straits of Macassar. Even the loyal soul of Lakamba was stirred into a state of inward discontent by the withdrawal of his licence for powder and by the abrupt confiscation of one hundred and fifty barrels of that commodity by the gunboat *Princess Amelia*, when, after a hazardous voyage, it had almost reached the mouth of the river. The unpleasant news was given him by Reshid, who, after the unsuccessful issue of his matrimonial projects, had made a long voyage amongst the islands for trading purposes; had bought the powder for his friend, and was overhauled and deprived of it on his return when actually congratulating himself on his acuteness in avoiding detection. Reshid's wrath was principally directed against Almayer, whom he suspected of having notified the Dutch authorities of the desultory warfare carried on by the Arabs and the Rajah with the upriver Dyak tribes.

To Reshid's great surprise the Rajah received his complaints very coldly, and showed no signs of vengeful disposition towards the white man. In truth, Lakamba knew very well that Almayer was perfectly innocent of any meddling in state affairs; and besides, his attitude towards that much persecuted individual was wholly changed in consequence of a reconciliation effected between him and his old enemy by Almayer's newly-found friend, Dain Maroola.

Almayer had now a friend. Shortly after Reshid's departure on his commercial journey, Nina, drifting slowly with the tide in the canoe on her return home after one of her solitary excursions, heard in one of the small creeks a splashing of heavy ropes dropping in the water and the prolonged song of Malay seamen when some heavy pulling is to be done. Through the thick fringe of bushes hiding the mouth of the creek she saw the tall spars of some European-rigged sailing vessel overtopping the summits of the Nipa palms. A brig was being hauled out of the small creek into the main stream. The sun had set, and during the short moments of twilight Nina saw the brig, aided by the evening breeze and the flowing tide, head towards Sambir under her set foresail. The girl turned her canoe out of the main river into one of the many narrow channels amongst the wooded islets, and paddled vigorously over the black and sleepy backwaters towards Sambir. Her canoe brushed the water-palms, skirted the short spaces of muddy bank where sedate alligators looked at her with lazy unconcern, and, just as darkness was setting in, shot out into the broad junction of the two main branches of the river, where the brig was already at anchor with sails furled, yards squared, and decks seemingly untenanted by any human being. Nina had to cross the river and pass pretty close to the brig in order to reach home on the low promontory between the two branches of the Pantai. Up both branches, in the houses built on the banks and over the water, the lights twinkled already, reflected in the still waters below. The hum of voices, the occasional cry of a child, the rapid and abruptly interrupted roll of a wooden drum, together with some distant hailing in the darkness by the returning fishermen, reached her over the broad expanse of the river. She hesitated a little before crossing, the sight of such an unusual object as an European-rigged vessel causing her some uneasiness, but the river in its wide expansion was dark enough to render a small canoe invisible. She urged her small craft with swift strokes of her paddle, kneeling in the bottom and bending forward to catch any suspicious sound while she steered towards the little jetty of Lingard and Co., to which the strong light of the paraffin lamp shining on the whitewashed verandah of Almayer's bungalow served as a convenient guide. The jetty itself, under the shadow of the bank overgrown by drooping bushes, was hidden in darkness. Before even she could see it she heard the hollow bumping of a large boat against its rotten posts, and heard also the murmur of whispered conversation in that boat whose white paint and great dimensions, faintly visible on nearer approach, made her rightly guess that it belonged to the brig just anchored. Stopping her course by a rapid motion of her paddle, with another swift stroke she sent it whirling away from the wharf and steered for a little rivulet which gave access to the back courtyard of the house. She landed at the muddy head of the creek and made her way towards the house over the trodden grass of the courtyard. To the left, from the cooking shed, shone a red glare through the banana plantation she skirted, and the noise of feminine laughter reached her from there in the silent evening. She rightly judged her mother was not near, laughter and Mrs. Almayer not being close neighbours. She must be in the house, thought Nina, as she ran lightly up the inclined plane of shaky planks leading to the back door of the narrow passage dividing the house in two. Outside the doorway, in the black shadow, stood the faithful Ali.

"Who is there?" asked Nina.

"A great Malay man has come," answered Ali, in a tone of suppressed excitement. "He is a rich man. There are six men with lances. Real Soldat, you understand. And his dress is very brave. I have seen his dress. It shines! What jewels! Don't go there, Mem Nina. Tuan said not; but the old Mem is gone. Tuan will be angry. Merciful Allah! what jewels that man has got!"

Nina slipped past the outstretched hand of the slave into the dark passage where, in the crimson glow of the hanging curtain, close by its other end, she could see a small dark form crouching near the wall. Her mother was feasting her eyes and ears with what was taking place on the front verandah, and Nina approached to take her share in the rare pleasure of some novelty. She was met by her mother's extended arm and by a low murmured warning not to make a noise.

"Have you seen them, mother?" asked Nina, in a breathless whisper.

Mrs. Almayer turned her face towards the girl, and her sunken eyes shone strangely in the red half-light of the passage.

"I saw him," she said, in an almost inaudible tone, pressing her daughter's hand with her bony fingers. "A great Rajah has come to Sambir—a Son of Heaven," muttered the old woman to herself. "Go away, girl!"

The two women stood close to the curtain, Nina wishing to approach the rent in the stuff, and her mother defending the position with angry obstinacy. On the other side there was a lull in the conversation, but the occasional light tinkling of some ornaments, the clink of metal scabbards, or of brass siri-vessels passed from hand to hand, was audible during the short pause. The women struggled silently, when there was a shuffling noise and the shadow of Almayer's burly form fell on the curtain.

The women ceased struggling and remained motionless. Almayer had stood up to answer his guest, turning his back to the doorway, unaware of what was going on on the other side. He spoke in a tone of regretful irritation.

"You have come to the wrong house, Tuan Maroola, if you want to trade as you say. I was a trader once, not now, whatever you may have heard about me in Macassar. And if you want anything, you will not find it here; I have nothing to give, and want nothing myself. You should go to the Rajah here; you can see in the daytime his houses across the river, there, where those fires are burning on the shore. He will help you and trade with you. Or, better still, go to the Arabs over there," he went on bitterly, pointing with his hand towards the houses of Sambir. "Abdulla is the man you want. There is nothing he would not buy, and there is nothing he would not sell; believe me, I know him well."

He waited for an answer a short time, then added—

"All that I have said is true, and there is nothing more."

Nina, held back by her mother, heard a soft voice reply with a calm evenness of intonation peculiar to the better class Malays—

"Who would doubt a white Tuan's words? A man seeks his friends where his heart tells him. Is this not true also? I have come, although so late, for I have something to say which you may be glad to hear. To-morrow I shall go to the Sultan; a trader wants the friendship of great men. Then I shall return here to speak serious words, if Tuan permits. I shall not go to the Arabs; their lies are very great! What are they? Chelakka!"

Almayer's voice sounded a little more pleasantly in reply.

"Well, as you like. I can hear you to-morrow at any time if you have anything to say. Bah! After you have seen the Sultan Lakamba you will not want to return here, Inchi Dain. You will see. Only mind, I will have nothing to do with Lakamba. You may tell him so. What is your business with me, after all?"

"To-morrow we talk, Tuan, now I know you," answered the Malay. "I speak English a little, so we can talk and nobody will understand, and then——"

He interrupted himself suddenly, asking surprised, "What's that noise, Tuan?"

Almayer had also heard the increasing noise of the scuffle recommenced on the women's side of the curtain. Evidently Nina's strong curiosity was on the point of overcoming Mrs. Almayer's exalted sense of social proprieties. Hard breathing was distinctly audible, and the curtain shook during the contest, which was mainly physical, although Mrs. Almayer's voice was heard in angry remonstrance with its usual want of strictly logical reasoning, but with the well-known richness of invective.

"You shameless woman! Are you a slave?" shouted shrilly the irate matron. "Veil your face, abandoned wretch! You white snake, I will not let you!"

Almayer's face expressed annoyance and also doubt as to the advisability of interfering between mother and daughter. He glanced at his Malay visitor, who was waiting silently for the end of the uproar in an attitude of amused expectation, and waving his hand contemptuously he murmured—

"It is nothing. Some women."

The Malay nodded his head gravely, and his face assumed an expression of serene indifference, as etiquette demanded after such an explanation. The contest was ended behind the curtain, and evidently the younger will had its way, for the rapid shuffle and click of Mrs. Almayer's high-heeled sandals died away in the distance. The tranquillized master of the house was going to resume the conversation when, struck by an unexpected change in the expression of his guest's countenance, he turned his head and saw Nina standing in the doorway.

After Mrs. Almayer's retreat from the field of battle, Nina, with a contemptuous exclamation, "It's only a trader," had lifted the conquered curtain and now stood in full light, framed in the dark background of the passage, her lips slightly parted, her hair in disorder after the exertion, the angry gleam not yet faded out of her glorious and sparkling eyes. She took in at a glance the group of white-clad lancemen standing motionless in the shadow of the far-off end of the verandah, and her gaze rested curiously on the chief of that imposing cortège. He stood, almost facing her, a little on one side, and struck by the beauty of the unexpected apparition had bent low, elevating his joint hands above his head in a sign of respect accorded by Malays only to the great of this earth. The crude light of the lamp shone on the gold embroidery of his black silk jacket, broke in a thousand sparkling rays on the jeweled hilt of his kriss protruding from under the many folds of the red sarong gathered into a sash round his waist, and played on the precious stones of the many rings on his dark fingers. He straightened himself up quickly after the low bow, putting his hand with a graceful ease on the hilt of his heavy short sword ornamented with brilliantly dyed fringes of horsehair. Nina, hesitating on the threshold, saw an erect lithe figure of medium height with a breadth of shoulder suggesting great power. Under the folds of a blue turban, whose fringed ends hung gracefully over the left shoulder, was a face full of determination and expressing a reckless good-humour, not devoid, however, of some dignity. The squareness of lower jaw, the full red lips, the mobile nostrils, and the proud carriage of the head gave the impression of a being half-savage, untamed, perhaps cruel, and corrected the liquid softness of the almost feminine eye, that general characteristic of the race. Now, the first surprise over, Nina saw those eyes fixed upon her with such an uncontrolled expression of admiration and desire that she felt a hitherto unknown feeling of shyness, mixed with alarm and some delight, enter and penetrate her whole being. Confused by those unusual sensations she stopped in the doorway and instinctively drew the lower part of the curtain across her face, leaving only half a rounded cheek, a stray tress, and one eye exposed, wherewith to contemplate the gorgeous and bold being so unlike in appearance to the rare specimens of traders she had seen before on that same verandah.

Dain Maroola, dazzled by the unexpected vision, forgot the confused Almayer, forgot his brig, his escort staring in open-mouthed admiration, the object of his visit and all things else, in his overpowering desire to prolong the contemplation of so much loveliness met so suddenly in such an unlikely place—as he thought.

"It is my daughter," said Almayer, in an embarrassed manner. "It is of no consequence. White women have their customs, as you know, Tuan, having travelled much, as you say. However, it is late; we will finish our talk to-morrow."

Dain bent low trying to convey in a last glance towards the girl the bold expression of his overwhelming admiration. The next minute he was shaking Almayer's hand with grave courtesy, his face wearing a look of stolid unconcern as to any feminine presence. His men filed off, and he followed them quickly, closely attended by a thick-set, savage-looking Sumatrese he had introduced before as the commander of his brig. Nina walked to the balustrade of the verandah and saw the sheen of moonlight on the steel spear-heads and heard the rhythmic jingle of brass anklets as the men moved in single file towards the jetty. The boat shoved off after a little while, looming large in the full light of the moon, a black shapeless mass in the slight haze hanging over the water. Nina fancied she could distinguish the graceful figure of the trader standing erect in the stern sheets, but in a little while all the outlines got blurred, confused, and soon disappeared in the folds of white vapour shrouding the middle of the river.

Almayer had approached his daughter, and leaning with both arms over the rail, was looking moodily down on the heap of rubbish at the foot of the verandah.

"What was all that noise just now?" he growled peevishly, without looking up. "Confound you and your mother! What did she want? What did you come out for?"

"She did not want to let me come out," said Nina. "She is angry. She says the man just gone is some Rajah. I think she is right now."

"I believe all you women are crazy," snarled Almayer. "What's that to you, to her, to anybody? The man wants to collect trepang and birds' nests on the islands. He told me so, that Rajah of yours. He will come to-morrow. I want you both to keep away from the house, and let me attend to my business in peace."

Dain Maroola came the next day and had a long conversation with

Almayer. This was the beginning of a close and friendly intercourse which, at first, was much remarked in Sambir, till the population got used to the frequent sight of many fires burning in Almayer's campong, where Maroola's men were warming themselves during the cold nights of the northeast monsoon, while their master had long conferences with the Tuan Putih—as they styled Almayer amongst themselves. Great was the curiosity in Sambir on the subject of the new trader. Had he seen the Sultan? What did the Sultan say? Had he given any presents? What would he sell? What would he buy? Those were the questions broached eagerly by the inhabitants of bamboo houses built over the river. Even in more substantial buildings, in Abdulla's house, in the residences of principal traders, Arab, Chinese, and Bugis, the excitement ran high, and lasted many days. With inborn suspicion they would not believe the simple account of himself the young trader was always ready to give. Yet it had all the appearance of truth. He said he was a trader, and sold rice. He did not want to buy gutta-percha or beeswax, because he intended to employ his numerous crew in collecting trepang on the coral reefs outside the river, and also in seeking for birds' nests on the mainland. Those two articles he professed himself ready to buy if there were any to be obtained in that way. He said he was from Bali, and a Brahmin, which last statement he made good by refusing all food during his often repeated visits to Lakamba's and Almayer's houses. To Lakamba he went generally at night and had long audiences. Babalatchi, who was always a third party at those meetings of potentate and trader, knew how to resist all attempts on the part of the curious to ascertain the subject of so many long talks. When questioned with languid courtesy by the grave Abdulla he sought refuge in a vacant stare of his one eye, and in the affectation of extreme simplicity.

"I am only my master's slave," murmured Babalatchi, in a hesitating manner. Then as if making up his mind suddenly for a reckless confidence he would inform Abdulla of some transaction in rice, repeating the words, "A hundred big bags the Sultan bought; a hundred, Tuan!" in a tone of mysterious solemnity. Abdulla, firmly persuaded of the existence of some more important dealings, received, however, the information with all the signs of respectful astonishment. And the two would separate, the Arab cursing inwardly the wily dog, while Babalatchi went on his way walking on the dusty path, his body swaying, his chin with its few grey hairs pushed forward, resembling an inquisitive goat bent on some unlawful expedition. Attentive eyes watched his movements. Jim-Eng, descrying Babalatchi far away, would shake off the stupor of an habitual opium smoker and, tottering on to the middle of the road, would await the approach of that important person ready with hospitable invitation. But Babalatchi's discretion was proof even against the combined assaults of good fellowship and of strong gin generously administered by the openhearted Chinaman. Jim-Eng, owning himself beaten, was left uninformed with the empty bottle, and gazed sadly after the departing form of the statesman of Sambir pursuing his devious and unsteady way, which, as usual, led him to Almayer's compound. Ever since a reconciliation had been effected by Dain Maroola between his white friend and the Rajah, the one-eyed diplomatist had again become a frequent guest in the Dutchman's house. To Almayer's great disgust he was to be seen there at all times, strolling about in an abstracted kind of way on the verandah, skulking in the passages, or else popping round unexpected corners, always willing to engage Mrs. Almayer in confidential conversation. He was very shy of the master himself, as if suspicious that the pent-up feelings of the white man towards his person might find vent in a sudden kick. But the cooking shed was his favourite place, and he became an habitual guest there, squatting for hours amongst the busy women, with his chin resting on his knees, his lean arms clasped round his legs, and his one eye roving uneasily—the very picture of watchful ugliness. Almayer wanted more than once to complain to Lakamba of his Prime Minister's intrusion, but Dain dissuaded him. "We cannot say a word here that he does not hear," growled Almayer.

"Then come and talk on board the brig," retorted Dain, with a quiet smile. "It is good to let the man come here. Lakamba thinks he knows much. Perhaps the Sultan thinks I want to run away. Better let the one-eyed crocodile sun himself in your campong, Tuan."

And Almayer assented unwillingly muttering vague threats of personal violence, while he eyed malevolently the aged statesman sitting with quiet obstinacy by his domestic rice-pot.

CHAPTER FIVE

At last the excitement had died out in Sambir. The inhabitants got used to the sight of comings and goings between Almayer's house and the vessel, now moored to the opposite bank, and speculation as to the feverish activity displayed by Almayer's boatmen in repairing old canoes ceased to interfere with the due discharge of domestic duties by the women of the Settlement. Even the baffled Jim-Eng left off troubling his muddled brain with secrets of trade, and relapsed by the aid of his opium pipe into a state of stupefied bliss, letting Babalatchi pursue his way past his house uninvited and seemingly unnoticed.

So on that warm afternoon, when the deserted river sparkled under the vertical sun, the statesman of Sambir could, without any hindrance from friendly inquirers, shove off his little canoe from under the bushes, where it was usually hidden during his visits to Almayer's compound. Slowly and languidly Babalatchi paddled, crouching low in the boat, making himself small under his enormous sun hat to escape the scorching heat reflected from the water. He was not in a hurry; his master, Lakamba, was surely reposing at this time of the day. He would have ample time to cross over and greet him on his waking with important news. Will he be displeased? Will he strike his ebony wood staff angrily on the floor, frightening him by the incoherent violence of his exclamations; or will he squat down with a good-humoured smile, and, rubbing his hands gently over his stomach with a familiar gesture, expectorate copiously into the brass siri-vessel, giving vent to a low, approbative murmur? Such were Babalatchi's thoughts as he skilfully handled his paddle, crossing the river on his way to the Rajah's campong, whose stockades showed from behind the dense foliage of the bank just opposite to Almayer's bungalow.

Indeed, he had a report to make. Something certain at last to confirm the daily tale of suspicions, the daily hints of familiarity, of stolen glances he had seen, of short and burning words he had overheard exchanged between Dain Maroola and Almayer's daughter. Lakamba had, till then, listened to it all, calmly and with evident distrust; now he was going to be convinced, for Babalatchi had the proof; had it this very morning, when fishing at break of day in the creek over which stood Bulangi's house. There from his skiff he saw Nina's long canoe drift past, the girl sitting in the stern bending over Dain, who was stretched in the bottom with his head resting on the girl's knees. He saw it. He followed them, but in a short time they took to the paddles and got away from under his observant eye. A few minutes afterwards he saw Bulangi's slave-girl paddling in a small dug-out to the town with her cakes for sale. She also had seen them in the grey dawn. And Babalatchi grinned confidentially to himself at the recollection of the slave-girl's discomposed face, of the hard look in her eyes, of the tremble in her voice, when answering his questions. That little Taminah evidently admired Dain Maroola. That was good! And Babalatchi laughed aloud at the notion; then becoming suddenly serious, he began by some strange association of ideas to speculate upon the price for which Bulangi would, possibly, sell the girl. He shook his head sadly at the thought that Bulangi was a hard man, and had refused one hundred dollars for that same Taminah only a few weeks ago; then he became suddenly aware that the canoe had drifted too far down during his meditation. He shook off the despondency caused by the certitude of Bulangi's mercenary disposition, and, taking up his paddle, in a few strokes sheered alongside the water-gate of the Rajah's house.

That afternoon Almayer, as was his wont lately, moved about on the water-side, overlooking the repairs to his boats. He had decided at

last. Guided by the scraps of information contained in old Lingard's
pocket-book, he was going to seek for the rich gold-mine, for that place
where he had only to stoop to gather up an immense fortune and
realize the dream of his young days. To obtain the necessary help he
had shared his knowledge with Dain Maroola, he had consented to
be reconciled with Lakamba, who gave his support to the enterprise
on condition of sharing the profits; he had sacrificed his pride, his
honour, and his loyalty in the face of the enormous risk of his undertaking, dazzled by the greatness of the results to be achieved by this
alliance so distasteful yet so necessary. The dangers were great, but
Maroola was brave; his men seemed as reckless as their chief, and
with Lakamba's aid success seemed assured.

For the last fortnight Almayer was absorbed in the preparations,
walking amongst his workmen and slaves in a kind of waking trance,
where practical details as to the fitting out of the boats were mixed
up with vivid dreams of untold wealth, where the present misery of
burning sun, of the muddy and malodorous river bank disappeared in
a gorgeous vision of a splendid future existence for himself and Nina.
He hardly saw Nina during these last days, although the beloved daughter was ever present in his thoughts. He hardly took notice of Dain,
whose constant presence in his house had become a matter of course
to him now they were connected by a community of interests. When
meeting the young chief he gave him an absent greeting and passed
on, seemingly wishing to avoid him, bent upon forgetting the hated
reality of the present by absorbing himself in his work, or else by
letting his imagination soar far above the tree-tops into the great white
clouds away to the westward, where the paradise of Europe was awaiting the future Eastern millionaire. And Maroola, now the bargain was
struck and there was no more business to be talked over, evidently
did not care for the white man's company. Yet Dain was always about
the house, but he seldom stayed long by the riverside. On his daily
visits to the white man the Malay chief preferred to make his way
quietly through the central passage of the house, and would come out
into the garden at the back, where the fire was burning in the cooking
shed, with the rice kettle swinging over it, under the watchful supervision of Mrs. Almayer. Avoiding that shed, with its black smoke and
the warbling of soft, feminine voices, Dain would turn to the left.
There, on the edge of a banana plantation, a clump of palms and
mango trees formed a shady spot, a few scattered bushes giving it a
certain seclusion into which only the serving women's chatter or an
occasional burst of laughter could penetrate. Once in, he was invisible;
and hidden there, leaning against the smooth trunk of a tall palm, he
waited with gleaming eyes and an assured smile to hear the faint rustle
of dried grass under the light footsteps of Nina.

From the very first moment when his eyes beheld this—to him—perfection of loveliness he felt in his inmost heart the conviction that she would be his; he felt the subtle breath of mutual understanding passing between their two savage natures, and he did not want Mrs. Almayer's encouraging smiles to take every opportunity of approaching the girl; and every time he spoke to her, every time he looked into her eyes, Nina, although averting her face, felt as if this bold-looking being who spoke burning words into her willing ear was the embodiment of her fate, the creature of her dreams—reckless, ferocious, ready with flashing kriss for his enemies, and with passionate embrace for his beloved—the ideal Malay chief of her mother's tradition.

She recognized with a thrill of delicious fear the mysterious consciousness of her identity with that being. Listening to his words, it seemed to her she was born only then to a knowledge of a new existence, that her life was complete only when near him, and she abandoned herself to a feeling of dreamy happiness, while with half-veiled face and in silence—as became a Malay girl—she listened to Dain's words giving up to her the whole treasure of love and passion his nature was capable of with all the unrestrained enthusiasm of a man totally untrammelled by any influence of civilized self-discipline.

And they used to pass many a delicious and fast fleeting hour under the mango trees behind the friendly curtain of bushes till Mrs. Almayer's shrill voice gave the signal of unwilling separation. Mrs. Almayer had undertaken the easy task of watching her husband lest he should interrupt the smooth course of her daughter's love affair, in which she took a great and benignant interest. She was happy and proud to see Dain's infatuation, believing him to be a great and powerful chief, and she found also a gratification of her mercenary instincts in Dain's open-handed generosity.

On the eve of the day when Babalatchi's suspicions were confirmed by ocular demonstration, Dain and Nina had remained longer than usual in their shady retreat. Only Almayer's heavy step on the verandah and his querulous clamour for food decided Mrs. Almayer to lift a warning cry. Maroola leaped lightly over the low bamboo fence, and made his way through the banana plantation down to the muddy shore of the back creek, while Nina walked slowly towards the house to minister to her father's wants, as was her wont every evening. Almayer felt happy enough that evening; the preparations were nearly completed; to-morrow he would launch his boats. In his mind's eye he saw the rich prize in his grasp; and, with tin spoon in his hand, he was forgetting the plateful of rice before him in the fanciful arrangement of some splendid banquet to take place on his arrival in Amsterdam. Nina, reclining in the long chair, listened absently to the few disconnected words escaping from her father's lips. Expedition! Gold! What did she care for all that? But at the name of Maroola mentioned by her father she was all attention. Dain was going down the river with his brig to-morrow to remain away for a few days, said Almayer. It was very annoying, this delay. As soon as Dain returned they would have to start without loss of time, for the river was rising. He would not be surprised if a great flood was coming. And he pushed away his plate with an impatient gesture on rising from the table. But now Nina heard him not. Dain going away! That's why he had ordered her, with that quiet masterfulness it was her delight to obey, to meet him at break of day in Bulangi's creek. Was there a paddle in her canoe? she thought. Was it ready? She would have to start early—at four in the morning, in a very few hours.

She rose from her chair, thinking she would require rest before the long pull in the early morning. The lamp was burning dimly, and her father, tired with the day's labour, was already in his hammock. Nina put the lamp out and passed into a large room she shared with her mother on the left of the central passage. Entering, she saw that Mrs. Almayer had deserted the pile of mats serving her as bed in one corner of the room, and was now bending over the opened lid of her large wooden chest. Half a shell of cocoanut filled with oil, where a cotton rag floated for a wick, stood on the floor, surrounding her with a ruddy halo of light shining through the black and odorous smoke. Mrs. Almayer's back was bent, and her head and shoulders hidden in the deep box. Her hands rummaged in the interior, where a soft clink as of silver money could be heard. She did not notice at first her daughter's approach, and Nina, standing silently by her, looked down on many little canvas bags ranged in the bottom of the chest, wherefrom her mother extracted handfuls of shining guilders and Mexican dollars, letting them stream slowly back again through her claw-like fingers. The music of tinkling silver seemed to delight her, and her eyes sparkled with the reflected gleam of freshly-minted coins. She was muttering to herself: "And this, and this, and yet this! Soon he will give more—as much more as I ask. He is a great Rajah—a Son of Heaven! And she will be a Ranee—he gave all this for her! Who ever gave anything for me? I am a slave! Am I? I am the mother of a great Ranee!" She became aware suddenly of her daughter's presence, and ceased her droning, shutting the lid down violently; then, without rising from her crouching position, she looked up at the girl standing by with a vague smile on her dreamy face.

"You have seen. Have you?" she shouted, shrilly. "That is all mine, and for you. It is not enough! He will have to give more before he takes you away to the southern island where his father is king. You hear me? You are worth more, granddaughter of Rajahs! More! More!"

The sleepy voice of Almayer was heard on the verandah recommending silence. Mrs. Almayer extinguished the light and crept into her corner of the room. Nina laid down on her back on a pile of soft mats, her hands entwined under her head, gazing through the shutterless hole, serving as a window at the stars twinkling on the black sky; she was awaiting the time of start for her appointed meeting-place. With quiet happiness she thought of that meeting in the great forest, far from all human eyes and sounds. Her soul, lapsing again into the savage mood, which the genius of civilization working by the hand of Mrs. Vinck could never destroy, experienced a feeling of pride and of some slight trouble at the high value her worldly-wise mother had put upon her person; but she remembered the expressive glances and words of Dain, and, tranquillized, she closed her eyes in a shiver of pleasant anticipation.

There are some situations where the barbarian and the, so-called, civilized man meet upon the same ground. It may be supposed that Dain Maroola was not exceptionally delighted with his prospective mother-in-law, nor that he actually approved of that worthy woman's appetite for shining dollars. Yet on that foggy morning when Babalatchi, laying aside the cares of state, went to visit his fish-baskets in the Bulangi creek, Maroola had no misgivings, experienced no feelings but those of impatience and longing, when paddling to the east side of the island forming the backwater in question. He hid his canoe in the bushes and strode rapidly across the islet, pushing with impatience through the twigs of heavy undergrowth intercrossed over his path. From motives of prudence he would not take his canoe to the meeting-place, as Nina had done. He had left it in the main stream till his return from the other side of the island. The heavy warm fog was closing rapidly round him, but he managed to catch a fleeting glimpse of a light away to the left, proceeding from Bulangi's house. Then he could see nothing in the thickening vapour, and kept to the path only by a sort of instinct, which also led him to the very point on the opposite shore he wished to reach. A great log had stranded there, at right angles to the bank, forming a kind of jetty against which the swiftly flowing stream broke with a loud ripple. He stepped on it with a quick but steady motion, and in two strides found himself at the outer end, with the rush and swirl of the foaming water at his feet.

Standing there alone, as if separated from the world; the heavens, earth; the very water roaring under him swallowed up in the thick veil of the morning fog, he breathed out the name of Nina before him into the apparently limitless space, sure of being heard, instinctively sure of the nearness of the delightful creature; certain of her being aware of his near presence as he was aware of hers.

The bow of Nina's canoe loomed up close to the log, canted high out of the water by the weight of the sitter in the stern. Maroola laid his hand on the stem and leaped lightly in, giving it a vigorous shove off. The light craft, obeying the new impulse, cleared the log by a hair's breadth, and the river, with obedient complicity, swung it broadside to the current, and bore it off silently and rapidly between the invisible banks. And once more Dain, at the feet of Nina, forgot the world, felt himself carried away helpless by a great wave of supreme emotion, by a rush of joy, pride, and desire; understood once more with overpowering certitude that there was no life possible without that being he held clasped in his arms with passionate strength in a prolonged embrace.

Nina disengaged herself gently with a low laugh.

"You will overturn the boat, Dain," she whispered.

He looked into her eyes eagerly for a minute and let her go with a sigh, then lying down in the canoe he put his head on her knees, gazing upwards and stretching his arms backwards till his hands met round the girl's waist. She bent over him, and, shaking her head, framed both their faces in the falling locks of her long black hair.

And so they drifted on, he speaking with all the rude eloquence of a savage nature giving itself up without restraint to an overmastering passion, she bending low to catch the murmur of words sweeter to her than life itself. To those two nothing existed then outside the gunwales of the narrow and fragile craft. It was their world, filled with their intense and all-absorbing love. They took no heed of thickening mist, or of the breeze dying away before sunrise; they forgot the existence of the great forests surrounding them, of all the tropical nature awaiting the advent of the sun in a solemn and impressive silence.

Over the low river-mist hiding the boat with its freight of young passionate life and all-forgetful happiness, the stars paled, and a silvery-grey tint crept over the sky from the eastward. There was not a breath of wind, not a rustle of stirring leaf, not a splash of leaping fish to disturb the serene repose of all living things on the banks of the great river. Earth, river, and sky were wrapped up in a deep sleep from which it seemed there would be no waking. All the seething life and movement of tropical nature seemed concentrated in the ardent eyes, in the tumultuously beating hearts of the two beings drifting in the canoe, under the white canopy of mist, over the smooth surface of the river.

Suddenly a great sheaf of yellow rays shot upwards from behind the black curtain of trees lining the banks of the Pantai. The stars went out; the little black clouds at the zenith glowed for a moment with crimson tints, and the thick mist, stirred by the gentle breeze, the sigh of waking nature, whirled round and broke into fantastically torn pieces, disclosing the wrinkled surface of the river sparkling in the broad light of day. Great flocks of white birds wheeled screaming above the swaying tree-tops. The sun had risen on the east coast.

Dain was the first to return to the cares of everyday life. He rose and glanced rapidly up and down the river. His eye detected Baba-latchi's boat astern, and another small black speck on the glittering water, which was Taminah's canoe. He moved cautiously forward, and, kneeling, took up a paddle; Nina at the stern took hers. They bent their bodies to the work, throwing up the water at every stroke, and the small craft went swiftly ahead, leaving a narrow wake fringed with a lacelike border of white and gleaming foam. Without turning his head, Dain spoke.

"Somebody behind us, Nina. We must not let him gain. I think he is too far to recognize us."

"Somebody before us also," panted out Nina, without ceasing to paddle.

"I think I know," rejoined Dain. "The sun shines over there, but I fancy it is the girl Taminah. She comes down every morning to my brig to sell cakes—stays often all day. It does not matter; steer more into the bank; we must get under the bushes. My canoe is hidden not far from here."

As he spoke his eyes watched the broad-leaved nipas which they were brushing in their swift and silent course.

"Look out, Nina," he said at last; "there, where the water palms end and the twigs hang down under the leaning tree. Steer for the big green branch."

He stood up attentive, and the boat drifted slowly in shore, Nina guiding it by a gentle and skilful movement of her paddle. When near enough Dain laid hold of the big branch, and leaning back shot the canoe under a low green archway of thickly matted creepers giving access to a miniature bay formed by the caving in of the bank during the last great flood. His own boat was there anchored by a stone, and he stepped into it, keeping his hand on the gunwale of Nina's canoe. In a moment the two little nutshells with their occupants floated quietly side by side, reflected by the black water in the dim light strug-gling through a high canopy of dense foliage; while above, away up in the broad day, flamed immense red blossoms sending down on their heads a shower of great dew-sparkling petals that descended rotating slowly in a continuous and perfumed stream; and over them, under them, in the sleeping water; all around them in a ring of luxuriant vegetation bathed in the warm air charged with strong and harsh per-fumes, the intense work of tropical nature went on: plants shooting upward, entwined, interlaced in inextricable confusion, climbing madly and brutally over each other in the terrible silence of a desperate struggle towards the life-giving sunshine above—as if struck with sudden horror at the seething mass of corruption below, at the death and decay from which they sprang.

"We must part now," said Dain, after a long silence. "You must return at once, Nina. I will wait till the brig drifts down here, and shall get on board then."

"And will you be long away, Dain?" asked Nina, in a low voice.

"Long!" exclaimed Dain. "Would a man willingly remain long in a dark place? When I am not near you, Nina, I am like a man that is blind. What is life to me without light?"

Nina leaned over, and with a proud and happy smile took Dain's face between her hands, looking into his eyes with a fond yet questioning gaze. Apparently she found there the confirmation of the words just said, for a feeling of grateful security lightened for her the weight of sorrow at the hour of parting. She believed that he, the descendant of many great Rajahs, the son of a great chief, the master of life and death, knew the sunshine of life only in her presence. An immense wave of gratitude and love welled forth out of her heart towards him. How could she make an outward and visible sign of all she felt for the man who had filled her heart with so much joy and so much pride? And in the great tumult of passion, like a flash of lightning came to her the reminiscence of that despised and almost forgotten civilization she had only glanced at in her days of restraint, of sorrow, and of anger. In the cold ashes of that hateful and miserable past she would find the sign of love, the fitting expression of the boundless felicity of the present, the pledge of a bright and splendid future. She threw her arms around Dain's neck and pressed her lips to his in a long and burning kiss. He closed his eyes, surprised and frightened at the storm raised in his breast by the strange and to him hitherto unknown contact, and long after Nina had pushed her canoe into the river he remained motionless, without daring to open his eyes, afraid to lose the sensation of intoxicating delight he had tasted for the first time.

Now he wanted but immortality, he thought, to be the equal of gods, and the creature that could open so the gates of paradise must be his—soon would be his for ever!

He opened his eyes in time to see through the archway of creepers the bows of his brig come slowly into view, as the vessel drifted past on its way down the river. He must go on board now, he thought; yet he was loth to leave the place where he had learned to know what happiness meant. "Time yet. Let them go," he muttered to himself; and he closed his eyes again under the red shower of scented petals, trying to recall the scene with all its delight and all its fear.

He must have been able to join his brig in time, after all, and found much occupation outside, for it was in vain that Almayer looked for his friend's speedy return. The lower reach of the river where he so often and so impatiently directed his eyes remained deserted, save for the rapid flitting of some fishing canoe; but down the upper reaches came black clouds and heavy showers heralding the final setting in of the rainy season with its thunderstorms and great floods making the river almost impossible of ascent for native canoes.

Almayer, strolling along the muddy beach between his houses, watched uneasily the river rising inch by inch, creeping slowly nearer to the boats, now ready and hauled up in a row under the cover of dripping Kajang-mats. Fortune seemed to elude his grasp, and in his weary tramp backwards and forwards under the steady rain falling from the lowering sky, a sort of despairing indifference took possession of him. What did it matter? It was just his luck! Those two infernal savages, Lakamba and Dain, induced him, with their promises of help, to spend his last dollar in the fitting out of boats, and now one of them was gone somewhere, and the other shut up in his stockade would give no sign of life. No, not even the scoundrelly Babalatchi, thought Almayer, would show his face near him, now they had sold him all the rice, brass gongs, and cloth necessary for his expedition. They had his very last coin, and did not care whether he went or stayed. And with a gesture of abandoned discouragement Almayer would climb up slowly to the verandah of his new house to get out of the rain, and leaning on the front rail with his head sunk between his shoulders he would abandon himself to the current of bitter thoughts, oblivious of the flight of time and the pangs of hunger, deaf to the shrill cries of his wife calling him to the evening meal. When, roused from his sad meditations by the first roll of the evening thunderstorm, he stumbled slowly towards the glimmering light of his old house, his half-dead hope made his ears preternaturally acute to any sound on the river. Several nights in succession he had heard the splash of paddles and had seen the indistinct form of a boat, but when hailing the shadowy apparition, his heart bounding with sudden hope of hearing Dain's voice, he was disappointed each time by the sulky answer conveying to him the intelligence that the Arabs were on the river, bound on a visit to the home-staying Lakamba. This caused him many sleepless nights, spent in speculating upon the kind of villainy those estimable personages were hatching now. At last, when all hope seemed dead, he was overjoyed on hearing Dain's voice; but Dain also appeared very anxious to see Lakamba, and Almayer felt uneasy owing to a deep and ineradicable distrust as to that ruler's disposition towards himself. Still, Dain had returned at last. Evidently he meant to keep to his bargain. Hope revived, and that night Almayer slept soundly, while Nina watched the angry river under the lash of the thunderstorm sweeping onward towards the sea.

Dain was not long in crossing the river after leaving Almayer. He landed at the water-gate of the stockade enclosing the group of houses which composed the residence of the Rajah of Sambir. Evidently some-body was expected there, for the gate was open, and men with torches were ready to precede the visitor up the inclined plane of planks leading to the largest house where Lakamba actually resided, and where all the business of state was invariably transacted. The other buildings within the enclosure served only to accommodate the nu-merous household and the wives of the ruler.

Lakamba's own house was a strong structure of solid planks, raised on high piles, with a verandah of split bamboos surrounding it on all sides; the whole was covered in by an immensely high-pitched roof of palmleaves, resting on beams blackened by the smoke of many torches.

The building stood parallel to the river, one of its long sides facing the water-gate of the stockade. There was a door in the short side looking up the river, and the inclined plank-way led straight from the gate to that door. By the uncertain light of smoky torches, Dain no-ticed the vague outlines of a group of armed men in the dark shadows to his right. From that group Babalatchi stepped forward to open the door, and Dain entered the audience chamber of the Rajah's residence. About one-third of the house was curtained off, by heavy stuff of European manufacture, for that purpose; close to the curtain there was a big armchair of some black wood, much carved, and before it a rough deal table. Otherwise the room was only furnished with mats in great profusion. To the left of the entrance stood a rude arm-rack, with three rifles with fixed bayonets in it. By the wall, in the shadow, the body-guard of Lakamba—all friends or relations—slept in a confused heap of brown arms, legs, and multi-coloured garments, from whence issued an occasional snore or a subdued groan of some uneasy sleeper. An European lamp with a green shade standing on the table made all this indistinctly visible to Dain.

"You are welcome to your rest here," said Babalatchi, looking at Dain interrogatively.

"I must speak to the Rajah at once," answered Dain.

Babalatchi made a gesture of assent, and, turning to the brass gong suspended under the arm-rack, struck two sharp blows.

The ear-splitting din woke up the guard. The snores ceased; out-stretched legs were drawn in; the whole heap moved, and slowly re-solved itself into individual forms with much yawning and rubbing of sleepy eyes; behind the curtains there was a burst of feminine chatter; then the bass voice of Lakamba was heard.

"Is that the Arab trader?"

"No, Tuan," answered Babalatchi; "Dain has returned at last. He is here for an important talk, bitcharra—if you mercifully consent."

Evidently Lakamba's mercy went so far—for in a short while he came out from behind the curtain—but it did not go to the length of inducing him to make an extensive toilet. A short red sarong tightened hastily round his hips was his only garment. The merciful ruler of Sambir looked sleepy and rather sulky. He sat in the arm-chair, his knees well apart, his elbows on the arm-rests, his chin on his breast, breathing heavily and waiting malevolently for Dain to open the important talk.

But Dain did not seem anxious to begin. He directed his gaze towards Babalatchi, squatting comfortably at the feet of his master, and remained silent with a slightly bent head as if in attentive expectation of coming words of wisdom.

Babalatchi coughed discreetly, and, leaning forward, pushed over a few mats for Dain to sit upon, then lifting up his squeaky voice he assured him with eager volubility of everybody's delight at this long-looked-for return. His heart had hungered for the sight of Dain's face, and his ears were withering for the want of the refreshing sound of his voice. Everybody's hearts and ears were in the same sad predicament, according to Babalatchi, as he indicated with a sweeping gesture the other bank of the river where the settlement slumbered peacefully, unconscious of the great joy awaiting it on the morrow when Dain's presence amongst them would be disclosed. "For"—went on Babalatchi—"what is the joy of a poor man if not the open hand of a generous trader or of a great——"

Here he checked himself abruptly with a calculated embarrassment of manner, and his roving eye sought the floor, while an apologetic smile dwelt for a moment on his misshapen lips. Once or twice during this opening speech an amused expression flitted across Dain's face, soon to give way, however, to an appearance of grave concern. On Lakamba's brow a heavy frown had settled, and his lips moved angrily as he listened to his Prime Minister's oratory. In the silence that fell upon the room when Babalatchi ceased speaking arose a chorus of varied snores from the corner where the body-guard had resumed their interrupted slumbers, but the distant rumble of thunder filling then Nina's heart with apprehension for the safety of her lover passed unheeded by those three men intent each on their own purposes, for life or death.

After a short silence, Babalatchi, discarding now the flowers of polite eloquence, spoke again, but in short and hurried sentences and in a low voice. They had been very uneasy. Why did Dain remain so long absent? The men dwelling on the lower reaches of

the river heard the reports of big guns and saw a fire-ship of the
Dutch amongst the islands of the estuary. So they were anxious.
Rumours of a disaster had reached Abdulla a few days ago, and since
then they had been waiting for Dain's return under the apprehension
of some misfortune. For days they had closed their eyes in fear, and
woke up alarmed, and walked abroad trembling, like men before an
enemy. And all on account of Dain. Would he not allay their fears
for his safety, not for themselves? They were quiet and faithful, and
devoted to the great Rajah in Batavia—may his fate lead him ever
to victory for the joy and profit of his servants! "And here," went
on Babalatchi, "Lakamba my master was getting thin in his anxiety
for the trader he had taken under his protection; and so was Abdulla,
for what would wicked men not say if perchance——"

"Be silent, fool!" growled Lakamba, angrily.

Babalatchi subsided into silence with a satisfied smile, while Dain,
who had been watching him as if fascinated, turned with a sigh of
relief towards the ruler of Sambir. Lakamba did not move, and, without
raising his head, looked at Dain from under his eyebrows, breathing
audibly, with pouted lips, in an air of general discontent.

"Speak! O Dain!" he said at last. "We have heard many rumours.
Many nights in succession has my friend Reshid come here with bad
tidings. News travels fast along the coast. But they may be untrue;
there are more lies in men's mouths in these days than when I was
young, but I am not easier to deceive now."

"All my words are true," said Dain, carelessly. "If you want to know
what befell my brig, then learn that it is in the hands of the Dutch.
Believe me, Rajah," he went on, with sudden energy, "the Orang
Blanda have good friends in Sambir, or else how did they know I
was coming thence?"

Lakamba gave Dain a short and hostile glance. Babalatchi rose
quietly, and, going to the arm-rack, struck the gong violently.

Outside the door there was a shuffle of bare feet; inside, the guard
woke up and sat staring in sleepy surprise.

"Yes, you faithful friend of the white Rajah," went on Dain, scornfully, turning to Babalatchi, who had returned to his place, "I have
escaped, and I am here to gladden your heart. When I saw the Dutch
ship I ran the brig inside the reefs and put her ashore. They did
not dare to follow with the ship, so they sent the boats. We took
to ours and tried to get away, but the ship dropped fireballs at us,
and killed many of my men. But I am left, O Babalatchi! The Dutch
are coming here. They are seeking for me. They're coming to ask
their faithful friend Lakamba and his slave Babalatchi. Rejoice!"

But neither of his hearers appeared to be in a joyful mood. Lakamba
had put one leg over his knee, and went on gently scratching it with

a meditative air, while Babalatchi, sitting cross-legged, seemed suddenly to become smaller and very limp, staring straight before him
vacantly. The guard evinced some interest in the proceedings, stretching themselves full length on the mats to be nearer the speaker. One
of them got up and now stood leaning against the arm-rack, playing
absently with the fringes of his sword-hilt.

Dain waited till the crash of thunder had died away in distant
mutterings before he spoke again.

"Are you dumb, O ruler of Sambir, or is the son of a great Rajah
unworthy of your notice? I am come here to seek refuge and to warn
you, and want to know what you intend doing."

"You came here because of the white man's daughter," retorted
Lakamba, quickly. "Your refuge was with your father, the Rajah of
Bali, the Son of Heaven, the 'Anak Agong' himself. What am I to
protect great princes? Only yesterday I planted rice in a burnt clearing;
to-day you say I hold your life in my hand."

Babalatchi glanced at his master. "No man can escape his fate,"
he murmured piously. "When love enters a man's heart he is like a
child—without any understanding. Be merciful, Lakamba," he added,
twitching the corner of the Rajah's sarong warningly.

Lakamba snatched away the skirt of the sarong angrily. Under the
dawning comprehension of intolerable embarrassments caused by
Dain's return to Sambir he began to lose such composure as he had
been, till then, able to maintain; and now he raised his voice loudly
above the whistling of the wind and the patter of rain on the roof
in the hard squall passing over the house.

"You came here first as a trader with sweet words and great promises,
asking me to look the other way while you worked your will on the
white man there. And I did. What do you want now? When I was
young I fought. Now I am old, and want peace. It is easier for me
to have you killed than to fight the Dutch. It is better for me."

The squall had now passed, and, in the short stillness of the lull
in the storm, Lakamba repeated softly, as if to himself, "Much easier.
Much better."

Dain did not seem greatly discomposed by the Rajah's threatening
words. While Lakamba was speaking he had glanced once rapidly
over his shoulder, just to make sure that there was nobody behind
him, and, tranquillized in that respect, he had extracted a siri-box
out of the folds of his waist-cloth, and was wrapping carefully the
little bit of betel-nut and a small pinch of lime in the green leaf
tendered him politely by the watchful Babalatchi. He accepted this
as a peace-offering from the silent statesman—a kind of mute protest
against his master's undiplomatic violence, and as an omen of a
possible understanding to be arrived at yet. Otherwise Dain was not

uneasy. Although recognizing the justice of Lakamba's surmise that
he had come back to Sambir only for the sake of the white man's
daughter, yet he was not conscious of any childish lack of understanding, as suggested by Babalatchi. In fact, Dain knew very well
that Lakamba was too deeply implicated in the gunpowder smuggling
to care for an investigation by the Dutch authorities into that matter.
When sent off by his father, the independent Rajah of Bali, at the
time when the hostilities between Dutch and Malays threatened to
spread from Sumatra over the whole archipelago, Dain had found
all the big traders deaf to his guarded proposals, and above the
temptation of the great prices he was ready to give for gunpowder.
He went to Sambir as a last and almost hopeless resort, having heard
in Macassar of the white man there, and of the regular steamer trading
from Singapore—allured also by the fact that there was no Dutch
resident on the river, which would make things easier, no doubt. His
hopes got nearly wrecked against the stubborn loyalty of Lakamba
arising from well-understood self-interest; but at last the young man's
generosity, his persuasive enthusiasm, the prestige of his father's great
name, overpowered the prudent hesitation of the ruler of Sambir.
Lakamba would have nothing to do himself with any illegal traffic.
He also objected to the Arabs being made use of in that matter; but
he suggested Almayer, saying that he was a weak man easily persuaded,
and that his friend, the English captain of the steamer, could be made
very useful—very likely even would join in the business, smuggling
the powder in the steamer without Abdulla's knowledge. There again
Dain met in Almayer an unexpected resistance; Lakamba had to send
Babalatchi over with the solemn promise that his eyes would be shut
in friendship for the white man, Dain paying for the promise and
the friendship in good silver guilders of the hated Orang Blanda.
Almayer, at last consenting, said the powder would be obtained, but
Dain must trust him with dollars to send to Singapore in payment for
it. He would induce Ford to buy and smuggle it in the steamer on
board the brig. He did not want any money for himself out of the
transaction, but Dain must help him in his great enterprise after
sending off the brig. Almayer had explained to Dain that he could
not trust Lakamba alone in that matter; he would be afraid of losing
his treasure and his life through the cupidity of the Rajah; yet the
Rajah had to be told, and insisted on taking a share in that operation,
or else his eyes would remain shut no longer. To this Almayer had
to submit. Had Dain not seen Nina he would have probably refused
to engage himself and his men in the projected expedition to Gunong
Mas—the mountain of gold. As it was he intended to return with
half of his men as soon as the brig was clear of the reefs, but the
persistent chase given him by the Dutch frigate had forced him to

run south and ultimately to wreck and destroy his vessel in order to preserve his liberty, or perhaps even his life. Yes, he had come back to Sambir for Nina, although aware that the Dutch would look for him there, but he had also calculated his chances of safety in Lakamba's hands. For all his ferocious talk, the merciful ruler would not kill him, for he had long ago been impressed with the notion that Dain possessed the secret of the white man's treasure; neither would he give him up to the Dutch, for fear of some fatal disclosure of complicity in the treasonable trade. So Dain felt tolerably secure as he sat meditating quietly his answer to the Rajah's bloodthirsty speech. Yes, he would point out to him the aspect of his position should he—Dain—fall into the hands of the Dutch and should he speak the truth. He would have nothing more to lose then, and he would speak the truth. And if he did return to Sambir, disturbing thereby Lakamba's peace of mind, what then? He came to look after his property. Did he not pour a stream of silver into Mrs. Almayer's greedy lap? He had paid, for the girl, a price worthy of a great prince, although unworthy of that delightfully maddening creature for whom his untamed soul longed in an intensity of desire far more tormenting than the sharpest pain. He wanted his happiness. He had the right to be in Sambir.

He rose, and, approaching the table, leaned both his elbows on it; Lakamba responsively edged his seat a little closer, while Babalatchi scrambled to his feet and thrust his inquisitive head between his master's and Dain's. They interchanged their ideas rapidly, speaking in whispers into each other's faces, very close now, Dain suggesting, Lakamba contradicting, Babalatchi conciliating and anxious in his vivid apprehension of coming difficulties. He spoke most, whispering earnestly, turning his head slowly from side to side so as to bring his solitary eye to bear upon each of his interlocutors in turn. Why should there be strife? said he. Let Tuan Dain, whom he loved only less than his master, go trustfully into hiding. There were many places for that. Bulangi's house away in the clearing was best. Bulangi was a safe man. In the network of crooked channels no white man could find his way. White men were strong, but very foolish. It was undesirable to fight them, but deception was easy. They were like silly women—they did not know the use of reason, and he was a match for any of them—went on Babalatchi, with all the confidence of deficient experience. Probably the Dutch would seek Almayer. Maybe they would take away their countryman if they were suspicious of him. That would be good. After the Dutch went away Lakamba and Dain would get the treasure without any trouble, and there would be one person less to share it. Did he not speak wisdom? Will Tuan Dain go to Bulangi's house till the danger is over, go at once?

Dain accepted this suggestion of going into hiding with a certain sense of conferring a favour upon Lakamba and the anxious statesman, but he met the proposal of going at once with a decided no, looking Babalatchi meaningly in the eye. The statesman sighed as a man accepting the inevitable would do, and pointed silently towards the other bank of the river. Dain bent his head slowly.

"Yes, I am going there," he said.

"Before the day comes?" asked Babalatchi.

"I am going there now," answered Dain, decisively. "The Orang Blanda will not be here before to-morrow night, perhaps, and I must tell Almayer of our arrangements."

"No, Tuan. No; say nothing," protested Babalatchi. "I will go over myself at sunrise and let him know."

"I will see," said Dain, preparing to go.

The thunderstorm was recommencing outside, the heavy clouds hanging low overhead now. There was a constant rumble of distant thunder punctuated by the nearer sharp crashes, and in the continuous play of blue lightning the woods and the river showed fitfully, with all the elusive distinctness of detail characteristic of such a scene. Outside the door of the Rajah's house Dain and Babalatchi stood on the shaking verandah as if dazed and stunned by the violence of the storm. They stood there amongst the cowering forms of the Rajah's slaves and retainers seeking shelter from the rain, and Dain called aloud to his boatmen, who responded with an unanimous "Ada! Tuan!" while they looked uneasily at the river.

"This is a great flood!" shouted Babalatchi into Dain's ear. "The river is very angry. Look! Look at the drifting logs! Can you go?"

Dain glanced doubtfully on the livid expanse of seething water bounded far away on the other side by the narrow black line of the forests. Suddenly, in a vivid white flash, the low point of land with the bending trees on it and Almayer's house, leaped into view, flickered and disappeared. Dain pushed Babalatchi aside and ran down to the water-gate followed by his shivering boatmen.

Babalatchi backed slowly in and closed the door, then turned round and looked silently upon Lakamba. The Rajah sat still, glaring stonily upon the table, and Babalatchi gazed curiously at the perplexed mood of the man he had served so many years through good and evil fortune. No doubt the one-eyed statesman felt within his savage and much sophisticated breast the unwonted feelings of sympathy with, and perhaps even pity for, the man he called his master. From the safe position of a confidential adviser, he could, in the dim vista of past years, see himself—a casual cut-throat—finding shelter under that man's roof in the modest rice-clearing of early beginnings. Then came a long period of unbroken success, of wise counsels, and deep plottings resolutely carried out by the fearless Lakamba, till the whole east coast from Poulo Laut to Tanjong Batu listened to Babalatchi's wisdom speaking through the mouth of the ruler of Sambir. In those long years how many dangers escaped, how many enemies bravely faced, how many white men successfully circumvented! And now he looked upon the result of so many years of patient toil: the fearless Lakamba cowed by the shadow of an impending trouble. The ruler was growing old, and Babalatchi, aware of an uneasy feeling at the pit of his stomach, put both his hands there with a suddenly vivid and sad perception of the fact that he himself was growing old too; that the time of reckless daring was past for both of them, and that they had to seek refuge in prudent cunning. They wanted peace; they were disposed to reform; they were ready even to retrench so as to have the wherewithal to bribe the evil days away, if bribed away they could be. Babalatchi sighed for the second time that night as he squatted again at his master's feet and tendered him his betel-nut box in mute sympathy. And they sat there in close yet silent communion of betel-nut chewers, moving their jaws slowly, expectorating decorously into the wide-mouthed brass vessel they passed to one another, and listening to the awful din of the battling elements outside.

"There is a very great flood," remarked Babalatchi, sadly.

"Yes," said Lakamba. "Did Dain go?"

"He went, Tuan. He ran down to the river like a man possessed of the Sheitan himself."

There was another long pause.

"He may get drowned," suggested Lakamba at last, with some show of interest.

"The floating logs are many," answered Babalatchi, "but he is a good swimmer," he added languidly.

"He ought to live," said Lakamba; "he knows where the treasure is."

Babalatchi assented with an ill-humoured grunt. His want of success in penetrating the white man's secret as to the locality where the gold was to be found was a sore point with the statesman of Sambir, as the only conspicuous failure in an otherwise brilliant career.

A great peace had now succeeded the turmoil of the storm. Only the little belated clouds, which hurried past overhead to catch up with the main body flashing silently in the distance, sent down short showers that pattered softly with a soothing hiss over the palm-leaf roof.

Lakamba roused himself from his apathy with an appearance of having grasped the situation at last.

"Babalatchi," he called briskly, giving him a slight kick.

"Ada Tuan! I am listening."

"If the Orang Blanda come here, Babalatchi, and take Almayer to Batavia to punish him for smuggling gunpowder, what will he do, you think?"

"I do not know, Tuan."

"You are a fool," commented Lakamba, exultingly. "He will tell them where the treasure is, so as to find mercy. He will."

Babalatchi looked up at his master and nodded his head with by no means a joyful surprise. He had not thought of this; there was a new complication.

"Almayer must die," said Lakamba, decisively, "to make our secret safe. He must die quietly, Babalatchi. You must do it."

Babalatchi assented, and rose wearily to his feet. "To-morrow?" he asked.

"Yes; before the Dutch come. He drinks much coffee," answered Lakamba, with seeming irrelevancy.

Babalatchi stretched himself yawning, but Lakamba, in the flattering consciousness of a knotty problem solved by his own unaided intellectual efforts, grew suddenly very wakeful.

"Babalatchi," he said to the exhausted statesman, "fetch the box of music the white captain gave me. I cannot sleep."

At this order a deep shade of melancholy settled upon Babalatchi's features. He went reluctantly behind the curtain and soon reappeared carrying in his arms a small hand-organ, which he put down on the table with an air of deep dejection. Lakamba settled himself comfortably in his armchair.

"Turn, Babalatchi, turn," he murmured, with closed eyes.

Babalatchi's hand grasped the handle with the energy of despair, and as he turned, the deep gloom on his countenance changed into an expression of hopeless resignation. Through the open shutter the notes of Verdi's music floated out on the great silence over the river and forest. Lakamba listened with closed eyes and a delighted smile; Babalatchi turned, at times dozing off and swaying over, then catching himself up in a great fright with a few quick turns of the handle. Nature slept in an exhausted repose after the fierce turmoil, while under the unsteady hand of the statesman of Sambir the Trovatore fitfully wept, wailed, and bade good-bye to his Leonore again and again in a mournful round of tearful and endless iteration.

The bright sunshine of the clear mistless morning, after the stormy night, flooded the main path of the settlement leading from the low shore of the Pantai branch of the river to the gate of Abdulla's compound. The path was deserted this morning; it stretched its dark yellow surface, hard beaten by the tramp of many bare feet, between the clusters of palm trees, whose tall trunks barred it with strong black lines at irregular intervals, while the newly risen sun threw the shadows of their leafy heads far away over the roofs of the buildings lining the river, even over the river itself as it flowed swiftly and silently past the deserted houses. For the houses were deserted too. On the narrow strip of trodden grass intervening between their open doors and the road, the morning fires smouldered untended, sending thin fluted columns of smoke into the cool air, and spreading the thinnest veil of mysterious blue haze over the sunlit solitude of the settlement. Almayer, just out of his hammock, gazed sleepily at the unwonted appearance of Sambir, wondering vaguely at the absence of life. His own house was very quiet; he could not hear his wife's voice, nor the sound of Nina's footsteps in the big room, opening on the verandah, which he called his sitting-room, whenever, in the company of white men, he wished to assert his claims to the commonplace decencies of civilization. Nobody ever sat there; there was nothing there to sit upon, for Mrs. Almayer in her savage moods, when excited by the reminiscences of the piratical period of her life, had torn off the curtains to make sarongs for the slave-girls, and had burnt the showy furniture piecemeal to cook the family rice. But Almayer was not thinking of his furniture now. He was thinking of Dain's return, of Dain's nocturnal interview with Lakamba, of its possible influence on his long-matured plans, now nearing the period of their execution. He was also uneasy at the non-appearance of Dain who had promised him an early visit. "The fellow had plenty of time to cross the river," he mused, "and there was so much to be done to-day. The settling of details for the early start on the morrow; the launching of the boats; the thousand and one finishing touches. For the expedition must start complete, nothing should be forgotten, nothing should——"

The sense of the unwonted solitude grew upon him suddenly, and in the unusual silence he caught himself longing even for the usually unwelcome sound of his wife's voice to break the oppressive stillness which seemed, to his frightened fancy, to portend the advent of some new misfortune. "What has happened?" he muttered half aloud, as he shuffled in his imperfectly adjusted slippers towards the balustrade of the verandah. "Is everybody asleep or dead?"

The settlement was alive and very much awake. It was awake ever since the early break of day, when Mahmat Banjer, in a fit of unheard-of energy, arose and, taking up his hatchet, stepped over the sleeping forms of his two wives and walked shivering to the water's edge to make sure that the new house he was building had not floated away during the night.

The house was being built by the enterprising Mahmat on a large raft, and he had securely moored it just inside the muddy point of land at the junction of the two branches of the Pantai so as to be out of the way of drifting logs that would no doubt strand on the point during the freshet. Mahmat walked through the wet grass saying bourrouh, and cursing softly to himself the hard necessities of active life that drove him from his warm couch into the cold of the morning. A glance showed him that his house was still there, and he congratulated himself on his foresight in hauling it out of harm's way, for the increasing light showed him a confused wrack of drift-logs, half-stranded on the muddy flat, interlocked into a shapeless raft by their branches, tossing to and fro and grinding together in the eddy caused by the meeting currents of the two branches of the river. Mahmat walked down to the water's edge to examine the rattan moorings of his house just as the sun cleared the trees of the forest on the opposite shore. As he bent over the fastenings he glanced again carelessly at the unquiet jumble of logs and saw there something that caused him to drop his hatchet and stand up, shading his eyes with his hand from the rays of the rising sun. It was something red, and the logs rolled over it, at times closing round it, sometimes hiding it. It looked to him at first like a strip of red cloth. The next moment Mahmat had made it out and raised a great shout.

"Ah ya! There!" yelled Mahmat. "There's a man amongst the logs." He put the palms of his hand to his lips and shouted, enunciating distinctly, his face turned towards the settlement: "There's a body of a man in the river! Come and see! A dead—stranger!"

The women of the nearest house were already outside kindling the fires and husking the morning rice. They took up the cry shrilly, and it travelled so from house to house, dying away in the distance. The men rushed out excited but silent, and ran towards the muddy point where the unconscious logs tossed and ground and bumped and rolled over the dead stranger with the stupid persistency of inanimate things. The women followed, neglecting their domestic duties and disregarding the possibilities of domestic discontent, while groups of children brought up the rear, warbling joyously, in the delight of unexpected excitement.

Almayer called aloud for his wife and daughter, but receiving no response, stood listening intently. The murmur of the crowd reached him faintly, bringing with it the assurance of some unusual event. He glanced at the river just as he was going to leave the verandah and checked himself at the sight of a small canoe crossing over from the Rajah's landing-place. The solitary occupant (in whom Almayer soon recognized Babalatchi) effected the crossing a little below the house and paddled up to the Lingard jetty in the dead water under the bank. Babalatchi clambered out slowly and went on fastening his canoe with fastidious care, as if not in a hurry to meet Almayer, whom he saw looking at him from the verandah. This delay gave Almayer time to notice and greatly wonder at Babalatchi's official get-up. The statesman of Sambir was clad in a costume befitting his high rank. A loudly checkered sarong encircled his waist and from its many folds peeped out the silver hilt of the kriss that saw the light only on great festivals or during official receptions. Over the left shoulder and across the otherwise unclad breast of the aged diplomatist glistened a patent leather belt bearing a brass plate with the arms of Netherlands under the inscription, "Sultan of Sambir." Babalatchi's head was covered by a red turban, whose fringed ends falling over the left cheek and shoulder gave to his aged face a ludicrous expression of joyous recklessness. When the canoe was at last fastened to his satisfaction he straightened himself up, shaking down the folds of his sarong, and moved with long strides towards Almayer's house, swinging regularly his long ebony staff, whose gold head ornamented with precious stones flashed in the morning sun. Almayer waved his hand to the right towards the point of land, to him invisible, but in full view from the jetty.

"Oh, Babalatchi! oh!" he called out; "what is the matter there? can you see?"

Babalatchi stopped and gazed intently at the crowd on the river bank, and after a little while the astonished Almayer saw him leave the path, gather up his sarong in one hand, and break into a trot through the grass towards the muddy point. Almayer, now greatly interested, ran down the steps of the verandah. The murmur of men's voices and the shrill cries of women reached him quite distinctly now, and as soon as he turned the corner of his house he could see the crowd on the low promontory swaying and pushing round some object of interest. He could indistinctly hear Babalatchi's voice, then the crowd opened before the aged statesman and closed after him with an excited hum, ending in a loud shout.

As Almayer approached the throng a man ran out and rushed past him towards the settlement, unheeding his call to stop and explain the cause of this excitement. On the very outskirts of the crowd

Almayer found himself arrested by an unyielding mass of humanity, regardless of his entreaties for a passage, insensible to his gentle pushes as he tried to work his way through it towards the riverside.

In the midst of his gentle and slow progress he fancied suddenly he had heard his wife's voice in the thickest of the throng. He could not mistake very well Mrs. Almayer's high-pitched tones, yet the words were too indistinct for him to understand their purport. He paused in his endeavours to make a passage for himself, intending to get some intelligence from those around him, when a long and piercing shriek rent the air, silencing the murmurs of the crowd and the voices of his informants. For a moment Almayer remained as if turned into stone with astonishment and horror, for he was certain now that he had heard his wife wailing for the dead. He remembered Nina's unusual absence, and maddened by his apprehensions as to her safety, he pushed blindly and violently forward, the crowd falling back with cries of surprise and pain before his frantic advance.

On the point of land in a little clear space lay the body of the stranger just hauled out from amongst the logs. On one side stood Babalatchi, his chin resting on the head of his staff and his one eye gazing steadily at the shapeless mass of broken limbs, torn flesh, and bloodstained rags. As Almayer burst through the ring of horrified spectators, Mrs. Almayer threw her own head-veil over the upturned face of the drowned man, and, squatting by it, with another mournful howl, sent a shiver through the now silent crowd. Mahmat, dripping wet, turned to Almayer, eager to tell his tale.

In the first moment of reaction from the anguish of his fear the sunshine seemed to waver before Almayer's eyes, and he listened to words spoken around him without comprehending their meaning. When, by a strong effort of will, he regained the possession of his senses, Mahmat was saying—

"That is the way, Tuan. His sarong was caught in the broken branch, and he hung with his head under water. When I saw what it was I did not want it here. I wanted it to get clear and drift away. Why should we bury a stranger in the midst of our houses for his ghost to frighten our women and children? Have we not enough ghosts about this place?"

A murmur of approval interrupted him here. Mahmat looked reproachfully at Babalatchi.

"But the Tuan Babalatchi ordered me to drag the body ashore"— he went on looking round at his audience, but addressing himself only to Almayer—"and I dragged him by the feet; in through the mud I have dragged him, although my heart longed to see him float down the river to strand perchance on Bulangi's clearing—may his father's grave be defiled!"

There was subdued laughter at this, for the enmity of Mahmat and Bulangi was a matter of common notoriety and of undying interest to the inhabitants of Sambir. In the midst of that mirth Mrs. Almayer wailed suddenly again.

"Allah! What ails the woman!" exclaimed Mahmat, angrily. "Here, I have touched this carcass which came from nobody knows where, and have most likely defiled myself before eating rice. By orders of Tuan Babalatchi I did this thing to please the white man. Are you pleased, O Tuan Almayer? And what will be my recompense? Tuan Babalatchi said a recompense there will be, and from you. Now consider. I have been defiled and if not defiled I may be under the spell. Look at his ankles! Who ever heard of a corpse appearing during the night amongst the logs with gold anklets on its legs? There is witchcraft there. However," added Mahmat, after a reflective pause, "I will have the anklet if there is permission, for I have a charm against the ghosts and am not afraid. God is great!"

A fresh outburst of noisy grief from Mrs. Almayer checked the flow of Mahmat's eloquence. Almayer, bewildered, looked in turn at his wife, at Mahmat, at Babalatchi, and at last arrested his fascinated gaze on the body lying on the mud with covered face in a grotesquely unnatural contortion of mangled and broken limbs, one twisted and lacerated arm, with white bones protruding in many places through the torn flesh, stretched out; the hand with outspread fingers nearly touching his foot.

"Do you know who this is?" he asked of Babalatchi, in a low voice.

Babalatchi, staring straight before him, hardly moved his lips, while Mrs. Almayer's persistent lamentations drowned the whisper of his murmured reply intended only for Almayer's ear.

"It was fate. Look at your feet, white man. I can see a ring on those torn fingers which I know well."

Saying this, Babalatchi stepped carelessly forward, putting his foot as if accidentally on the hand of the corpse and pressing it into the soft mud. He swung his staff menacingly towards the crowd, which fell back a little.

"Go away," he said sternly, "and send your women to their cooking fires, which they ought not to have left to run after a dead stranger. This is men's work here. I take him now in the name of the Rajah. Let no man remain here but Tuan Almayer's slaves. Now go!"

The crowd reluctantly began to disperse. The women went first, dragging away the children that hung back with all their weight on the maternal hand. The men strolled slowly after them in ever forming and changing groups that gradually dissolved as they neared the settlement and every man regained his own house with steps quickened by the hungry anticipation of the morning rice. Only on the slight elevation where the land sloped down towards the muddy point a few men, either friends or enemies of Mahmat, remained gazing curiously for some time longer at the small group standing around the body on the river bank.

"I do not understand what you mean, Babalatchi," said Almayer. "What is the ring you are talking about? Whoever he is, you have trodden the poor fellow's hand right into the mud. Uncover his face," he went on, addressing Mrs. Almayer, who, squatting by the head of the corpse, rocked herself to and fro, shaking from time to time her dishevelled grey locks, and muttering mournfully.

"Hai!" exclaimed Mahmat, who had lingered close by. "Look, Tuan; the logs came together so," and here he pressed the palms of his hands together, "and his head must have been between them, and now there is no face for you to look at. There are his flesh and his bones, the nose, and the lips, and maybe his eyes, but nobody could tell the one from the other. It was written the day he was born that no man could look at him in death and be able to say, 'This is my friend's face.'"

"Silence, Mahmat; enough!" said Babalatchi, "and take thy eyes off his anklet, thou eater of pig's flesh. Tuan Almayer," he went on, lowering his voice, "have you seen Dain this morning?"

Almayer opened his eyes wide and looked alarmed. "No," he said quickly; "haven't you seen him? Is he not with the Rajah? I am waiting; why does he not come?"

Babalatchi nodded his head sadly.

"He is come, Tuan. He left last night when the storm was great and the river spoke angrily. The night was very black, but he had within him a light that showed the way to your house as smooth as a narrow backwater, and the many logs no bigger than wisps of dried grass. Therefore he went; and now he lies here." And Babalatchi nodded his head towards the body.

"How can you tell?" said Almayer, excitedly, pushing his wife aside. He snatched the cover off and looked at the formless mass of flesh, hair, and drying mud, where the face of the drowned man should have been. "Nobody can tell," he added, turning away with a shudder.

Babalatchi was on his knees wiping the mud from the stiffened fingers of the outstretched hand. He rose to his feet and flashed before Almayer's eyes a gold ring set with a large green stone.

"You know this well," he said. "This never left Dain's hand. I had to tear the flesh now to get it off. Do you believe now?"

Almayer raised his hands to his head and let them fall listlessly by his side in the utter abandonment of despair. Babalatchi, looking at him curiously, was astonished to see him smile. A strange fancy had taken possession of Almayer's brain, distracted by this new misfortune. It seemed to him that for many years he had been falling into a deep precipice. Day after day, month after month, year after year, he had been falling, falling, falling; it was a smooth, round, black thing, and the black walls had been rushing upwards with wearisome rapidity. A great rush, the noise of which he fancied he could hear yet; and now, with an awful shock, he had reached the bottom, and behold! he was alive and whole, and Dain was dead with all his bones broken. It struck him as funny. A dead Malay; he had seen many dead Malays without any emotion; and now he felt inclined to weep, but it was over the fate of a white man he knew; a man that fell over a deep precipice and did not die. He seemed somehow to himself to be standing on one side, a little way off, looking at a certain Almayer who was in great trouble. Poor, poor fellow! Why doesn't he cut his throat? He wished to encourage him; he was very anxious to see him lying dead over that other corpse. Why does he not die and end this suffering? He groaned aloud unconsciously and started with affright at the sound of his own voice. Was he going mad? Terrified by the thought he turned away and ran towards his house repeating to himself, "I am not going mad; of course not, no, no, no!" He tried to keep a firm hold of the idea. Not mad, not mad. He stumbled as he ran blindly up the steps repeating fast and ever faster those words wherein seemed to lie his salvation. He saw Nina standing there, and wished to say something to her, but could not remember what, in his extreme anxiety not to forget that he was not going mad, which he still kept repeating mentally as he ran round the table, till he stumbled against one of the armchairs and dropped into it exhausted. He sat staring wildly at Nina, still assuring himself mentally of his own sanity and wondering why the girl shrank from him in open-eyed alarm. What was the matter with her? This was foolish. He struck the table violently with his clenched fist and shouted hoarsely, "Give me some gin! Run!" Then, while Nina ran off, he remained in the chair, very still and quiet, astonished at the noise he had made.

Nina returned with a tumbler half filled with gin, and found her father staring absently before him. Almayer felt very tired now, as if he had come from a long journey. He felt as if he had walked miles and miles that morning and now wanted to rest very much. He took the tumbler with a shaking hand, and as he drank his teeth chattered against the glass which he drained and set down heavily on the table. He turned his eyes slowly towards Nina standing beside him, and said steadily—

"Now all is over, Nina. He is dead, and I may as well burn all my boats."

He felt very proud of being able to speak so calmly. Decidedly he was not going mad. This certitude was very comforting, and he went on talking about the finding of the body, listening to his own voice complacently. Nina stood quietly, her hand resting lightly on her father's shoulder, her face unmoved, but every line of her features, the attitude of her whole body expressing the most keen and anxious attention.

"And so Dain is dead," she said coldly, when her father ceased speaking.

Almayer's elaborately calm demeanour gave way in a moment to an outburst of violent indignation.

"You stand there as if you were only half alive, and talk to me," he exclaimed angrily, "as if it was a matter of no importance. Yes, he is dead! Do you understand? Dead! What do you care? You never cared; you saw me struggle, and work, and strive, unmoved; and my suffering you could never see. No, never. You have no heart, and you have no mind, or you would have understood that it was for you, for your happiness I was working. I wanted to be rich; I wanted to get away from here. I wanted to see white men bowing low before the power of your beauty and your wealth. Old as I am I wished to seek a strange land, a civilization to which I am a stranger, so as to find a new life in the contemplation of your high fortunes, of your triumphs, of your happiness. For that I bore patiently the burden of work, of disappointment, of humiliation amongst these savages here, and I had it all nearly in my grasp."

He looked at his daughter's attentive face and jumped to his feet upsetting the chair.

"Do you hear? I had it all there; so; within reach of my hand."

He paused, trying to keep down his rising anger, and failed.

"Have you no feeling?" he went on. "Have you lived without hope?" Nina's silence exasperated him; his voice rose, although he tried to master his feelings.

"Are you content to live in this misery and die in this wretched hole? Say something, Nina; have you no sympathy? Have you no word of comfort for me? I that loved you so."

He waited for a while for an answer, and receiving none shook his fist in his daughter's face.

"I believe you are an idiot!" he yelled.

He looked round for the chair, picked it up and sat down stiffly. His anger was dead within him, and he felt ashamed of his outburst, yet relieved to think that now he had laid clear before his daughter the inner meaning of his life. He thought so in perfect good faith, deceived by the emotional estimate of his motives, unable to see the crookedness of his ways, the unreality of his aims, the futility of his regrets. And now his heart was filled only with a great tenderness and love for his daughter. He wanted to see her miserable, and to share with her his despair; but he wanted it only as all weak natures long for a companionship in misfortune with beings innocent of its cause. If she suffered herself she would understand and pity him; but now she would not, or could not, find one word of comfort or love for him in his dire extremity. The sense of his absolute loneliness came home to his heart with a force that made him shudder. He swayed and fell forward with his face on the table, his arms stretched straight out, extended and rigid. Nina made a quick movement towards her father and stood looking at the grey head, on the broad shoulders shaken convulsively by the violence of feelings that found relief at last in sobs and tears.

Nina sighed deeply and moved away from the table. Her features lost the appearance of stony indifference that had exasperated her father into his outburst of anger and sorrow. The expression of her face, now unseen by her father, underwent a rapid change. She had listened to Almayer's appeal for sympathy, for one word of comfort, apparently indifferent, yet with her breast torn by conflicting impulses raised unexpectedly by events she had not foreseen, or at least did not expect to happen so soon. With her heart deeply moved by the sight of Almayer's misery, knowing it in her power to end it with a word, longing to bring peace to that troubled heart, she heard with terror the voice of her overpowering love commanding her to be silent. And she submitted after a short and fierce struggle of her old self against the new principle of her life. She wrapped herself up in absolute silence, the only safeguard against some fatal admission. She could not trust herself to make a sign, to murmur a word for fear of saying too much; and the very violence of the feelings that stirred the innermost recesses of her soul seemed to turn her person into a stone. The dilated nostrils and the flashing eyes were the only signs of the storm raging within, and those signs of his daughter's emotion Almayer did not see, for his sight was dimmed by self-pity, by anger, and by despair.

Had Almayer looked at his daughter as she leant over the front rail of the verandah he could have seen the expression of indifference give way to a look of pain and that again pass away, leaving the glorious beauty of her face marred by deep-drawn lines of watchful anxiety. The long grass in the neglected courtyard stood very straight before her eyes in the noonday heat. From the river-bank there were voices and a shuffle of bare feet approaching the house; Babalatchi could be heard giving directions to Almayer's men, and Mrs. Almayer's subdued wailing became audible as the small procession bearing the body of the drowned man and headed by that sorrowful matron turned the corner of the house. Babalatchi had taken the broken anklet off the man's leg, and now held it in his hand as he moved by the side of the bearers, while Mahmat lingered behind timidly, in the hopes of the promised reward.

"Lay him there," said Babalatchi to Almayer's men, pointing to a pile of drying planks in front of the verandah. "Lay him there. He was a Kaffir and the son of a dog, and he was the white man's friend. He drank the white man's strong water," he added, with affected horror. "That I have seen myself."

The men stretched out the broken limbs on two planks they had laid level, while Mrs. Almayer covered the body with a piece of white cotton cloth, and after whispering for some time with Babalatchi departed to her domestic duties. Almayer's men, after laying down their burden, dispersed themselves in quest of shady spots wherein to idle the day away. Babalatchi was left alone by the corpse that lay rigid under the white cloth in the bright sunshine.

Nina came down the steps and joined Babalatchi, who put his hand to his forehead, and squatted down with great deference.

"You have a bangle there," said Nina, looking down on Babalatchi's upturned face and into his solitary eye.

"I have, Mem Putih," returned the polite statesman. Then turning towards Mahmat he beckoned him closer, calling out, "Come here!"

Mahmat approached with some hesitation. He avoided looking at Nina, but fixed his eyes on Babalatchi.

"Now, listen," said Babalatchi, sharply. "The ring and the anklet you have seen, and you know they belonged to Dain the trader, and to no other. Dain returned last night in a canoe. He spoke with the Rajah, and in the middle of the night left to cross over to the white man's house. There was a great flood, and this morning you found him in the river."

"By his feet I dragged him out," muttered Mahmat under his breath. "Tuan Babalatchi, there will be a recompense!" he exclaimed aloud.

Babalatchi held up the gold bangle before Mahmat's eyes. "What I have told you, Mahmat, is for all ears. What I give you now is for your eyes only. Take."

Mahmat took the bangle eagerly and hid it in the folds of his waist-cloth. "Am I a fool to show this thing in a house with three women in it?" he growled. "But I shall tell them about Dain the trader, and there will be talk enough."

He turned and went away, increasing his pace as soon as he was outside Almayer's compound.

Babalatchi looked after him till he disappeared behind the bushes. "Have I done well, Mem Putih?" he asked, humbly addressing Nina.

"You have," answered Nina. "The ring you may keep yourself."

Babalatchi touched his lips and forehead, and scrambled to his feet. He looked at Nina, as if expecting her to say something more, but Nina turned towards the house and went up the steps, motioning him away with her hand.

Babalatchi picked up his staff and prepared to go. It was very warm, and he did not care for the long pull to the Rajah's house. Yet he must go and tell the Rajah—tell of the event; of the change in his plans; of all his suspicions. He walked to the jetty and began casting off the rattan painter of his canoe.

The broad expanse of the lower reach, with its shimmering surface dotted by the black specks of the fishing canoes, lay before his eyes. The fishermen seemed to be racing. Babalatchi paused in his work, and looked on with sudden interest. The man in the foremost canoe, now within hail of the first houses of Sambir, laid in his paddle and stood up shouting—

"The boats! the boats! The man-of-war's boats are coming! They are here!"

In a moment the settlement was again alive with people rushing to the riverside. The men began to unfasten their boats, the women stood in groups looking towards the bend down the river. Above the trees lining the reach a slight puff of smoke appeared like a black stain on the brilliant blue of the cloudless sky.

Babalatchi stood perplexed, the painter in his hand. He looked down the reach, then up towards Almayer's house, and back again at the river as if undecided what to do. At last he made the canoe fast again hastily, and ran towards the house and up the steps of the verandah.

"Tuan! Tuan!" he called, eagerly. "The boats are coming. The man-of-war's boats. You had better get ready. The officers will come here, I know."

Almayer lifted his head slowly from the table, and looked at him stupidly.

"Mem Putih!" exclaimed Babalatchi to Nina, "look at him. He does not hear. You must take care," he added meaningly.

Nina nodded to him with an uncertain smile, and was going to speak, when a sharp report from the gun mounted in the bow of the steam launch that was just then coming into view arrested the words on her parted lips. The smile died out, and was replaced by the old look of anxious attention. From the hills far away the echo came back like a long-drawn and mournful sigh, as if the land had sent it in answer to the voice of its masters.

The news as to the identity of the body lying now in Almayer's compound spread rapidly over the settlement. During the forenoon most of the inhabitants remained in the long street discussing the mysterious return and the unexpected death of the man who had become known to them as the trader. His arrival during the northeast monsoon, his long sojourn in their midst, his sudden departure with his brig, and, above all, the mysterious appearance of the body, said to be his, amongst the logs, were subjects to wonder at and to talk over and over again with undiminished interest. Mahmat moved from house to house and from group to group, always ready to repeat his tale: how he saw the body caught by the sarong in a forked log; how Mrs. Almayer coming, one of the first, at his cries, recognized it, even before he had it hauled on shore; how Babalatchi ordered him to bring it out of the water. "By the feet I dragged him in, and there was no head," exclaimed Mahmat, "and how could the white man's wife know who it was? She was a witch, it was well known. And did you see how the white man himself ran away at the sight of the body? Like a deer he ran!" And here Mahmat imitated Almayer's long strides, to the great joy of the beholders. And for all his trouble he had nothing. The ring with the green stone Tuan Babalatchi kept. "Nothing! Nothing!" He spat down at his feet in sign of disgust, and left that group to seek further on a fresh audience.

The news spreading to the furthermost parts of the settlement found out Abdulla in the cool recess of his godown, where he sat overlooking his Arab clerks and the men loading and unloading the up-country canoes. Reshid, who was busy on the jetty, was summoned into his uncle's presence and found him, as usual, very calm and even cheerful, but very much surprised. The rumour of the capture or destruction of Dain's brig had reached the Arab's ears three days before from the sea-fishermen and through the dwellers on the lower reaches of the river. It had been passed upstream from neighbour to neighbour till Bulangi, whose clearing was nearest to the settlement, had brought that news himself to Abdulla whose favour he courted. But rumour also spoke of a fight and of Dain's death on board his own vessel. And now all the settlement talked of Dain's visit to the Rajah and of his death when crossing the river in the dark to see Almayer. They could not understand this. Reshid thought that it was very strange. He felt uneasy and doubtful. But Abdulla, after the first shock of surprise, with the old age's dislike for solving riddles, showed a becoming resignation. He remarked that the man was dead now at all events, and consequently no more dangerous. Where was the use to wonder at the decrees of Fate, especially if they were propitious to the True Believers? And with a pious ejaculation to Allah the Merciful, the Compassionate, Abdulla seemed to regard the incident as closed for the present.

Not so Reshid. He lingered by his uncle, pulling thoughtfully his neatly trimmed beard.

"There are many lies," he murmured. "He has been dead once before, and came to life to die again now. The Dutch will be here before many days and clamour for the man. Shall I not believe my eyes sooner than the tongues of women and idle men?"

"They say that the body is being taken to Almayer's compound," said Abdulla. "If you want to go there you must go before the Dutch arrive here. Go late. It should not be said that we have been seen inside that man's enclosure lately."

Reshid assented to the truth of this last remark and left his uncle's side. He leaned against the lintel of the big doorway and looked idly across the courtyard through the open gate on to the main road of the settlement. It lay empty, straight, and yellow under the flood of light. In the hot noontide the smooth trunks of palm trees, the outlines of the houses, and away there at the other end of the road the roof of Almayer's house visible over the bushes on the dark background of forest, seemed to quiver in the heat radiating from the steaming earth. Swarms of yellow butterflies rose, and settled to rise again in short flights before Reshid's half-closed eyes. From under his feet arose the dull hum of insects in the long grass of the courtyard. He looked on sleepily.

From one of the side paths amongst the houses a woman stepped out on the road, a slight girlish figure walking under the shade of a large tray balanced on its head. The consciousness of something moving stirred Reshid's half-sleeping senses into a comparative wakefulness. He recognized Taminah, Bulangi's slave-girl, with her tray of cakes for sale—an apparition of daily recurrence and of no importance whatever. She was going towards Almayer's house. She could be made useful. He roused himself up and ran towards the gate calling out, "Taminah O!" The girl stopped, hesitated, and came back slowly. Reshid waited, signing to her impatiently to come nearer.

When near Reshid Taminah stood with downcast eyes. Reshid looked at her a while before he asked—

"Are you going to Almayer's house? They say in the settlement that Dain the trader, he that was found drowned this morning, is lying in the white man's campong."

"I have heard this talk," whispered Taminah; "and this morning by the riverside I saw the body. Where it is now I do not know."

"So you have seen it?" asked Reshid, eagerly. "Is it Dain? You have seen him many times. You would know him."

The girl's lips quivered and she remained silent for a while breathing quickly.

"I have seen him, not a long time ago," she said at last. "The talk is true; he is dead. What do you want from me, Tuan? I must go."

Just then the report of the gun fired on board the steam launch was heard, interrupting Reshid's reply. Leaving the girl he ran to the house, and met in the courtyard Abdulla coming towards the gate.

"The Orang Blanda are come," said Reshid, "and now we shall have our reward."

Abdulla shook his head doubtfully. "The white men's rewards are long in coming," he said. "White men are quick in anger and slow in gratitude. We shall see."

He stood at the gate stroking his grey beard and listening to the distant cries of greeting at the other end of the settlement. As Taminah was turning to go he called her back.

"Listen, girl," he said: "there will be many white men in Almayer's house. You shall be there selling your cakes to the men of the sea. What you see and what you hear you may tell me. Come here before the sun sets and I will give you a blue handkerchief with red spots. Now go, and forget not to return."

He gave her a push with the end of his long staff as she was going away and made her stumble.

"This slave is very slow," he remarked to his nephew, looking after the girl with great disfavour.

Taminah walked on, her tray on the head, her eyes fixed on the ground. From the open doors of the houses were heard, as she passed, friendly calls inviting her within for business purposes, but she never heeded them, neglecting her sales in the preoccupation of intense thinking. Since the very early morning she had heard much, she had also seen much that filled her heart with a joy mingled with great suffering and fear. Before the dawn, before she left Bulangi's house to paddle up to Sambir she had heard voices outside the house when all in it but herself were asleep. And now, with her knowledge of the words spoken in the darkness, she held in her hand a life and carried in her breast a great sorrow. Yet from her springy step, erect figure, and face veiled over by the every-day look of apathetic indifference, nobody could have guessed of the double load she carried under the visible burden of the tray piled up high with cakes manufactured by the thrifty hands of Bulangi's wives. In that supple figure straight as an arrow, so graceful and free in its walk, behind those soft eyes that spoke of nothing but of unconscious resignation, there slept all feelings and all passions, all hopes and all fears, the curse of life and the consolation of death. And she knew nothing of it all. She lived like the tall palms amongst whom she was passing now, seeking the light, desiring the sunshine, fearing the storm, unconscious of either. The slave had no hope, and knew of no change. She knew of no other sky, no other water, no other forest, no other world, no other life. She had no wish, no hope, no love, no fear, except of a blow, and no vivid feeling but that of occasional hunger, which was seldom, for Bulangi was rich and rice was plentiful in the solitary house in his clearing. The absence of pain and hunger was her happiness, and when she felt unhappy she was simply tired, more than usual, after the day's labour. Then in the hot nights of the southwest monsoon she slept dreamlessly under the bright stars on the platform built outside the house and over the river. Inside they slept too: Bulangi by the door; his wives further in; the children with their mothers. She could hear their breathing; Bulangi's sleepy voice; the sharp cry of a child soon hushed with tender words. And she closed her eyes to the murmur of the water below her, to the whisper of the warm wind above, ignorant of the never-ceasing life of that tropical nature that spoke to her in vain with the thousand faint voices of the near forest, with the breath of tepid wind; in the heavy scents that lingered around her head; in the white wraiths of morning mist that hung over her in the solemn hush of all creation before the dawn.

Such had been her existence before the coming of the brig with the strangers. She remembered well that time; the uproar in the settlement, the never-ending wonder, the days and nights of talk and excitement. She remembered her own timidity with the strange men, till the brig moored to the bank became in a manner part of the settlement, and the fear wore off in the familiarity of constant intercourse. The call on board then became part of her daily round. She walked hesitatingly up the slanting planks of the gangway amidst the encouraging shouts and more or less decent jokes of the men idling over the bulwarks. There she sold her wares to those men that spoke so loud and carried themselves so free. There was a throng, a constant coming and going; calls interchanged, orders given and executed with shouts; the rattle of blocks, the flinging about of coils of rope. She sat out of the way under the shade of the awning, with her tray before her, the veil drawn well over her face, feeling shy amongst so many men. She smiled at all buyers, but spoke to none, letting their jests pass with stolid unconcern. She heard many tales told around her of far-off countries, of strange customs, of events stranger still. Those men were brave; but the most fearless of them spoke of their chief with fear. Often the man they called their master passed before her, walking erect and indifferent, in the pride of youth, in the flash of rich dress, with a tinkle of gold ornaments, while everybody stood aside watching anxiously for a movement of his lips, ready to do his bidding. Then all her life seemed to rush into her eyes, and from under her veil she gazed at him, charmed yet fearful to attract attention. One day he noticed her and asked, "Who is that girl?" "A slave, Tuan! A girl that sells cakes," a dozen voices replied together. She rose in terror to run on shore, when he called her back; and as she stood trembling with head hung down before him, he spoke kind words, lifting her chin with his hand and looking into her eyes with a smile. "Do not be afraid," he said. He never spoke to her any more. Somebody called out from the river-bank; he turned away and forgot her existence. Taminah saw Almayer standing on the shore with Nina on his arm. She heard Nina's voice calling out gaily, and saw Dain's face brighten with joy as he leaped on shore. She hated the sound of that voice ever since.

After that day she left off visiting Almayer's compound, and passed the noon hours under the shade of the brig awning. She watched for his coming with heart beating quicker and quicker, as he approached, into a wild tumult of newly-aroused feelings of joy and hope and fear that died away with Dain's retreating figure, leaving her tired out, as if after a struggle, sitting still for a long time in dreamy languor. Then she paddled home slowly in the afternoon, often letting her canoe float with the lazy stream in the quiet backwater of the river. The paddle hung idle in the water as she sat in the stern, one hand supporting her chin, her eyes wide open, listening intently to the whispering of her heart that seemed to swell at last into a song of extreme sweetness. Listening to that song she husked the rice at home; it dulled her ears to the shrill bickerings of Bulangi's wives, to the sound of angry reproaches addressed to herself. And when the sun was near its setting she walked to the bathing-place and heard it as she stood on the tender grass of the low bank, her robe at her feet, and looked at the reflection of her figure on the glass-like surface of the creek. Listening to it she walked slowly back, her wet hair hanging over her shoulders; laying down to rest under the bright stars, she closed her eyes to the murmur of the water below, of the warm wind above; to the voice of nature speaking through the faint noises of the great forest, and to the song of her own heart.

She heard, but did not understand, and drank in the dreamy joy of her new existence without troubling about its meaning or its end, till the full consciousness of life came to her through pain and anger. And she suffered horribly the first time she saw Nina's long canoe drift silently past the sleeping house of Bulangi, bearing the two lovers into the white mist of the great river. Her jealousy and rage culminated into a paroxysm of physical pain that left her lying panting on the river-bank, in the dumb agony of a wounded animal. But she went on moving patiently in the enchanted circle of slavery, going through her task day after day with all the pathos of the grief she could not express, even to herself, locked within her breast. She shrank from Nina as she would have shrunk from the sharp blade of a knife cutting into her flesh, but she kept on visiting the brig to feed her dumb, ignorant soul on her own despair. She saw Dain many times. He never spoke, he never looked. Could his eyes see only one woman's image? Could his ears hear only one woman's voice? He never noticed her; not once.

And then he went away. She saw him and Nina for the last time on that morning when Babalatchi, while visiting his fish baskets, had his suspicions of the white man's daughter's love affair with Dain confirmed beyond the shadow of doubt. Dain disappeared, and Taminah's heart, where lay useless and barren the seeds of all love and of all hate, the possibilities of all passions and of all sacrifices, forgot its joys and its sufferings when deprived of the help of the senses. Her half-formed, savage mind, the slave of her body—as her body was the slave of another's will—forgot the faint and vague image of the ideal that had found its beginning in the physical promptings of her savage nature. She dropped back into the torpor of her former life and found consolation—even a certain kind of happiness—in the thought that now Nina and Dain were separated, probably for ever. He would forget. This thought soothed the last pangs of dying jealousy that had nothing now to feed upon, and Taminah found peace. It was like the dreary tranquillity of a desert, where there is peace only because there is no life.

And now he had returned. She had recognized his voice calling aloud in the night for Bulangi. She had crept out after her master to listen closer to the intoxicating sound. Dain was there, in a boat, talking to Bulangi. Taminah, listening with arrested breath, heard another voice. The maddening joy, that only a second before she thought herself incapable of containing within her fast-beating heart, died out, and left her shivering in the old anguish of physical pain that she had suffered once before at the sight of Dain and Nina. Nina spoke now, ordering and entreating in turns, and Bulangi was refusing, expostulating, at last consenting. He went in to take a paddle from the heap lying behind the door. Outside the murmur of two voices went on, and she caught a word here and there. She understood that he was fleeing from white men, that he was seeking a hiding-place, that he was in some danger. But she heard also words which woke the rage of jealousy that had been asleep for so many days in her bosom. Crouching low on the mud in the black darkness amongst the piles, she heard the whisper in the boat that made light of toil, of privation, of danger, of life itself, if in exchange there could be but a short moment of close embrace, a look from the eyes, the feel of light breath, the touch of soft lips. So spoke Dain as he sat in the canoe holding Nina's hands while waiting for Bulangi's return; and Taminah, supporting herself by the slimy pile, felt as if a heavy weight was crushing her down, down into the black oily water at her feet. She wanted to cry out; to rush at them and tear their vague shadows apart; to throw Nina into the smooth water, cling to her close, hold her to the bottom where that man could not find her. She could not cry, she could not move. Then footsteps were heard on the bamboo platform above her head; she saw Bulangi get into his smallest canoe and take the lead, the other boat following, paddled by Dain and Nina. With a slight splash of the paddles dipped stealthily into the water, their indistinct forms passed before her aching eyes and vanished in the darkness of the creek.

She remained there in the cold and wet, powerless to move, breathing painfully under the crushing weight that the mysterious hand of Fate had laid so suddenly upon her slender shoulders, and shivering, she felt within a burning fire, that seemed to feed upon her very life. When the breaking day had spread a pale golden ribbon over the black outline of the forests, she took up her tray and departed towards the settlement, going about her task purely from the force of habit. As she approached Sambir she could see the excitement and she heard with momentary surprise of the finding of Dain's body. It was not true, of course. She knew it well. She regretted that he was not dead. She should have liked Dain to be dead, so as to be parted from that woman—from all women. She felt a strong desire to see Nina, but without any clear object. She hated her, and feared her, and she felt an irresistible impulse pushing her towards Almayer's house to see the white woman's face, to look close at those eyes, to hear again that voice, for the sound of which Dain was ready to risk his liberty, his life even. She had seen her many times; she had heard her voice daily for many months past. What was there in her? What was there in that being to make a man speak as Dain had spoken, to make him blind to all other faces, deaf to all other voices?

She left the crowd by the riverside, and wandered aimlessly among the empty houses, resisting the impulse that pushed her towards Almayer's campong to seek there in Nina's eyes the secret of her own misery. The sun mounting higher, shortened the shadows and poured down upon her a flood of light and of stifling heat as she passed on from shadow to light, from light to shadow amongst the houses, the bushes, the tall trees, in her unconscious flight from the pain in her own heart. In the extremity of her distress she could find no words to pray for relief, she knew of no heaven to send her prayer to, and she wandered on with tired feet in the dumb surprise and terror at the injustice of the suffering inflicted upon her without cause and without redress.

The short talk with Reshid, the proposal of Abdulla steadied her a little and turned her thoughts into another channel. Dain was in some danger. He was hiding from white men. So much she had overheard last night. They all thought him dead. She knew he was alive, and she knew of his hiding-place. What did the Arabs want to know about the white men? The white men want with Dain? Did they wish to kill him? She could tell them all—no, she would say nothing, and in the night she would go to him and sell him his life for a word, for a smile, for a gesture even, and be a slave in far-off countries, away from Nina. But there were dangers. The one-eyed Babalatchi who knew everything; the white man's wife!—she was a witch. Perhaps they would tell. And then there was Nina. She must hurry on and see.

In her impatience she left the path and ran towards Almayer's dwelling through the undergrowth between the palm trees. She came out at the back of the house, where a narrow ditch, full of stagnant water that overflowed from the river, separated Almayer's campong from the rest of the settlement. The thick bushes growing on the bank were hiding from her sight the large courtyard with its cooking shed. Above them rose several thin columns of smoke, and from behind the sound of strange voices informed Taminah that the Men of the Sea belonging to the warship had already landed and were camped between the ditch and the house. To the left one of Almayer's slave-girls came down to the ditch and bent over the shiny water, washing a kettle. To the right the tops of the banana plantation, visible above the bushes, swayed and shook under the touch of invisible hands gathering the fruit. On the calm water several canoes moored to a heavy stake were crowded together, nearly bridging the ditch just at the place where Taminah stood. The voices in the courtyard rose at times into an outburst of calls, replies, and laughter, and then died away into a silence that soon was broken again by a fresh clamour. Now and again the thin blue smoke rushed out thicker and blacker, and drove in odorous masses over the creek, wrapping her for a moment in a suffocating veil; then, as the fresh wood caught well alight, the smoke vanished in the bright sunlight, and only the scent of aromatic wood drifted afar, to leeward of the crackling fires.

Taminah rested her tray on a stump of a tree, and remained standing with her eyes turned towards Almayer's house, whose roof and part of a whitewashed wall were visible over the bushes. The slave-girl finished her work, and after looking for a while curiously at Taminah, pushed her way through the dense thicket back to the courtyard. Round Taminah there was now a complete solitude. She threw herself down on the ground, and hid her face in her hands. Now when so close she had no courage to see Nina. At every burst of louder voices from the courtyard she shivered in the fear of hearing Nina's voice. She came to the resolution of waiting where she was till dark, and then going straight to Dain's hiding-place. From where she was she could watch the movements of white men, of Nina, of all Dain's friends, and of all his enemies. Both were hateful alike to her, for both would take him away beyond her reach. She hid herself in the long grass to wait anxiously for the sunset that seemed so slow to come.

On the other side of the ditch, behind the bush, by the clear fires, the seamen of the frigate had encamped on the hospitable invitation of Almayer. Almayer, roused out of his apathy by the prayers and importunity of Nina, had managed to get down in time to the jetty so as to receive the officers at their landing. The lieutenant in command accepted his invitation to his house with the remark that in any case their business was with Almayer—and perhaps not very pleasant, he added. Almayer hardly heard him. He shook hands with them absently and led the way towards the house. He was scarcely conscious of the polite words of welcome he greeted the strangers with, and afterwards repeated several times over again in his efforts to appear at ease. The agitation of their host did not escape the officer's eyes, and the chief confided to his subordinate, in a low voice, his doubts as to Almayer's sobriety. The young sub-lieutenant laughed and expressed in a whisper the hope that the white man was not intoxicated enough to neglect the offer of some refreshments. "He does not seem very dangerous," he added, as they followed Almayer up the steps of the verandah.

"No, he seems more of a fool than a knave; I have heard of him," returned the senior.

They sat around the table. Almayer with shaking hands made gin cocktails, offered them all round, and drank himself, with every gulp feeling stronger, steadier, and better able to face all the difficulties of his position. Ignorant of the fate of the brig he did not suspect the real object of the officer's visit. He had a general notion that something must have leaked out about the gunpowder trade, but apprehended nothing beyond some temporary inconvenience. After emptying his glass he began to chat easily, lying back in his chair with one of his legs thrown negligently over the arm. The lieutenant astride on his chair, a glowing cheroot in the corner of his mouth, listened with a sly smile from behind the thick volumes of smoke that escaped from his compressed lips. The young sub-lieutenant, leaning with both elbows on the table, his head between his hands, looked on sleepily in the torpor induced by fatigue and the gin. Almayer talked on—

"It is a great pleasure to see white faces here. I have lived here many years in great solitude. The Malays, you understand, are not company for a white man; moreover they are not friendly; they do not understand our ways. Great rascals they are. I believe I am the only white man on the east coast that is a settled resident. We get visitors from Macassar or Singapore sometimes—traders, agents, or explorers, but they are rare. There was a scientific explorer here a year or more ago. He lived in my house: drank from morning to night. He lived joyously for a few months, and when the liquor he brought with him was gone he returned to Batavia with a report on the mineral wealth of the interior. Ha, ha, ha! Good, is it not?"

He ceased abruptly and looked at his guests with a meaningless stare. While they laughed he was reciting to himself the old story: "Dain dead, all my plans destroyed. This is the end of all hope and of all things." His heart sank within him. He felt a kind of deadly sickness.

"Very good. Capital!" exclaimed both officers.

Almayer came out of his despondency with another burst of talk.

"Eh! what about the dinner? You have got a cook with you. That's all right. There is a cooking shed in the other courtyard. I can give you a goose. Look at my geese—the only geese on the east coast—perhaps on the whole island. Is that your cook? Very good. Here, Ali, show this Chinaman the cooking place and tell Mem Almayer to let him have room there. My wife, gentlemen, does not come out; my daughter may. Meantime have some more drink. It is a hot day."

The lieutenant took the cigar out of his mouth, looked at the ash critically, shook it off and turned towards Almayer.

"We have a rather unpleasant business with you," he said.

"I am sorry," returned Almayer. "It can be nothing very serious, surely."

"If you think an attempt to blow up forty men at least, not a serious matter you will not find many people of your opinion," retorted the officer sharply.

"Blow up! What? I know nothing about it," exclaimed Almayer. "Who did that, or tried to do it?"

"A man with whom you had some dealings," answered the lieutenant. "He passed here under the name of Dain Maroola. You sold him the gunpowder he had in that brig we captured."

"How did you hear about the brig?" asked Almayer. "I know nothing about the powder he may have had."

"An Arab trader of this place has sent the information about your goings on here to Batavia, a couple of months ago," said the officer. "We were waiting for the brig outside, but he slipped past us at the mouth of the river, and we had to chase the fellow to the southward. When he sighted us he ran inside the reefs and put the brig ashore. The crew escaped in boats before we could take possession. As our boats neared the craft it blew up with a tremendous explosion; one of the boats being too near got swamped. Two men drowned—that is the result of your speculation, Mr. Almayer. Now we want this Dain. We have good grounds to suppose he is hiding in Sambir. Do you know where he is? You had better put yourself right with the authorities as much as possible by being perfectly frank with me. Where is this Dain?"

Almayer got up and walked towards the balustrade of the verandah. He seemed not to be thinking of the officer's question. He looked at the body lying straight and rigid under its white cover on which the sun, declining amongst the clouds to the westward, threw a pale tinge of red. The lieutenant waited for the answer, taking quick pulls at his half-extinguished cigar. Behind them Ali moved noiselessly laying the table, ranging solemnly the ill-assorted and shabby crockery, the tin spoons, the forks with broken prongs, and the knives with saw-like blades and loose handles. He had almost forgotten how to prepare the table for white men. He felt aggrieved; Mem Nina would not help him. He stepped back to look at his work admiringly, feeling very proud. This must be right; and if the master afterwards is angry and swears, then so much the worse for Mem Nina. Why did she not help? He left the verandah to fetch the dinner.

"Well, Mr. Almayer, will you answer my question as frankly as it is put to you?" asked the lieutenant, after a long silence.

Almayer turned round and looked at his interlocutor steadily. "If you catch this Dain what will you do with him?" he asked.

The officer's face flushed. "This is not an answer," he said, annoyed.

"And what will you do with me?" went on Almayer, not heeding the interruption.

"Are you inclined to bargain?" growled the other. "It would be bad policy, I assure you. At present I have no orders about your person, but we expected your assistance in catching this Malay."

"Ah!" interrupted Almayer, "just so: you can do nothing without me, and I, knowing the man well, am to help you in finding him."

"This is exactly what we expect," assented the officer. "You have broken the law, Mr. Almayer, and you ought to make amends."

"And save myself?"

"Well, in a sense yes. Your head is not in any danger," said the lieutenant, with a short laugh.

"Very well," said Almayer, with decision, "I shall deliver the man up to you."

Both officers rose to their feet quickly, and looked for their side-arms which they had unbuckled. Almayer laughed harshly.

"Steady, gentlemen!" he exclaimed. "In my own time and in my own way. After dinner, gentlemen, you shall have him."

"This is preposterous," urged the lieutenant. "Mr. Almayer, this is no joking matter. The man is a criminal. He deserves to hang. While we dine he may escape; the rumour of our arrival——"

Almayer walked towards the table. "I give you my word of honour, gentlemen, that he shall not escape; I have him safe enough."

"The arrest should be effected before dark," remarked the young sub.

"I shall hold you responsible for any failure. We are ready, but can do nothing just now without you," added the senior, with evident annoyance.

Almayer made a gesture of assent. "On my word of honour," he repeated vaguely. "And now let us dine," he added briskly.

Nina came through the doorway and stood for a moment holding the curtain aside for Ali and the old Malay woman bearing the dishes; then she moved towards the three men by the table.

"Allow me," said Almayer pompously. "This is my daughter. Nina, these gentlemen, officers of the frigate outside, have done me the honour to accept my hospitality."

Nina answered the low bows of the two officers by a slow inclination of the head and took her place at the table opposite her father. All sat down. The coxswain of the steam launch came up carrying some bottles of wine.

"You will allow me to have this put upon the table?" said the lieutenant to Almayer.

"What! Wine! You are very kind. Certainly. I have none myself. Times are very hard."

The last words of his reply were spoken by Almayer in a faltering voice. The thought that Dain was dead recurred to him vividly again, and he felt as if an invisible hand was gripping his throat. He reached for the gin bottle while they were uncorking the wine and swallowed a big gulp. The lieutenant, who was speaking to Nina, gave him a quick glance. The young sub began to recover from the astonishment and confusion caused by Nina's unexpected appearance and great beauty. "She was very beautiful and imposing," he reflected, "but after all a half-caste girl." This thought caused him to pluck up heart and look at Nina sideways. Nina, with composed face, was answering in a low, even voice the elder officer's polite questions as to the country and her mode of life. Almayer pushed his plate away and drank his guest's wine in gloomy silence.

CHAPTER NINE

"Can I believe what you tell me? It is like a tale for men that listen only half awake by the camp fire, and it seems to have run off a woman's tongue."

"Who is there here for me to deceive, O Rajah?" answered Babalatchi. "Without you I am nothing. All I have told you I believe to be true. I have been safe for many years in the hollow of your hand. This is no time to harbour suspicions. The danger is very great. We should advise and act at once, before the sun sets."

"Right. Right," muttered Lakamba, pensively.

They had been sitting for the last hour together in the audience chamber of the Rajah's house, for Babalatchi, as soon as he had witnessed the landing of the Dutch officers, had crossed the river to report to his master the events of the morning, and to confer with him upon the line of conduct to pursue in the face of altered circumstances. They were both puzzled and frightened by the unexpected turn the events had taken. The Rajah, sitting crosslegged on his chair, looked fixedly at the floor; Babalatchi was squatting close by in an attitude of deep dejection.

"And where did you say he is hiding now?" asked Lakamba, breaking at last the silence full of gloomy forebodings in which they both had been lost for a long while.

"In Bulangi's clearing—the furthest one, away from the house. They went there that very night. The white man's daughter took him there. She told me so herself, speaking to me openly, for she is half white and has no decency. She said she was waiting for him while he was here; then, after a long time, he came out of the darkness and fell at her feet exhausted. He lay like one dead, but she brought him back to life in her arms, and made him breathe again with her own breath. That is what she said, speaking to my face, as I am speaking now to you, Rajah. She is like a white woman and knows no shame."

He paused, deeply shocked. Lakamba nodded his head. "Well, and then?" he asked.

"They called the old woman," went on Babalatchi, "and he told them all—about the brig, and how he tried to kill many men. He knew the Orang Blanda were very near, although he had said nothing to us about that; he knew his great danger. He thought he had killed many, but there were only two dead, as I have heard from the men of the sea that came in the warship's boats."

"And the other man, he that was found in the river?" interrupted Lakamba.

"That was one of his boatmen. When his canoe was overturned by the logs those two swam together, but the other man must have been hurt. Dain swam, holding him up. He left him in the bushes when he went up to the house. When they all came down his heart had ceased to beat; then the old woman spoke; Dain thought it was good. He took off his anklet and broke it, twisting it round the man's foot. His ring he put on that slave's hand. He took off his sarong and clothed that thing that wanted no clothes, the two women holding it up meanwhile, their intent being to deceive all eyes and to mislead the minds in the settlement, so that they could swear to the thing that was not, and that there could be no treachery when the white men came. Then Dain and the white woman departed to call up Bulangi and find a hiding-place. The old woman remained by the body."

"Hai!" exclaimed Lakamba. "She has wisdom."

"Yes, she has a Devil of her own to whisper counsel in her ear," assented Babalatchi. "She dragged the body with great toil to the point where many logs were stranded. All these things were done in the darkness after the storm had passed away. Then she waited. At the first sign of daylight she battered the face of the dead with a heavy stone, and she pushed him amongst the logs. She remained near, watching. At sunrise Mahmat Banjer came and found him. They all believed; I myself was deceived, but not for long. The white man believed, and, grieving, fled to his house. When we were alone, I, having doubts, spoke to the woman, and she, fearing my anger and your might, told me all, asking for help in saving Dain."

"He must not fall into the hands of the Orang Blanda," said Lakamba; "but let him die, if the thing can be done quietly."

"It cannot, Tuan! Remember there is that woman who, being half white, is ungovernable, and would raise a great outcry. Also the officers are here. They are angry enough already. Dain must escape; he must go. We must help him now for our own safety."

"Are the officers very angry?" inquired Lakamba, with interest.

"They are. The principal chief used strong words when speaking to me—to me when I salaamed in your name. I do not think," added Babalatchi, after a short pause and looking very worried—"I do not think I saw a white chief so angry before. He said we were careless or even worse. He told me he would speak to the Rajah, and that I was of no account."

"Speak to the Rajah!" repeated Lakamba, thoughtfully. "Listen, Babalatchi: I am sick, and shall withdraw; you cross over and tell the white men."

"Yes," said Babalatchi, "I am going over at once; and as to Dain?"

"You get him away as you can best. This is a great trouble in my heart," sighed Lakamba.

Babalatchi got up, and, going close to his master, spoke earnestly.

"There is one of our praus at the southern mouth of the river. The Dutch warship is to the northward watching the main entrance. I shall send Dain off to-night in a canoe, by the hidden channels, on board the prau. His father is a great prince, and shall hear of our generosity. Let the prau take him to Ampanam. Your glory shall be great, and your reward in powerful friendship. Almayer will no doubt deliver the dead body as Dain's to the officers, and the foolish white men shall say, "This is very good; let there be peace." And the trouble shall be removed from your heart, Rajah."

"True! true!" said Lakamba.

"And, this being accomplished by me who am your slave, you shall reward with a generous hand. That I know! The white man is grieving for the lost treasure, in the manner of white men who thirst after dollars. Now, when all other things are in order, we shall perhaps obtain the treasure from the white man. Dain must escape, and Almayer must live."

"Now go, Babalatchi, go!" said Lakamba, getting off his chair. "I am very sick, and want medicine. Tell the white chief so."

But Babalatchi was not to be got rid of in this summary manner. He knew that his master, after the manner of the great, liked to shift the burden of toil and danger on to his servants' shoulders, but in the difficult straits in which they were now the Rajah must play his part. He may be very sick for the white men, for all the world if he liked, as long as he would take upon himself the execution of part at least of Babalatchi's carefully thought-of plan. Babalatchi wanted a big canoe manned by twelve men to be sent out after dark towards Bulangi's clearing. Dain may have to be overpowered. A man in love cannot be expected to see clearly the path of safety if it leads him away from the object of his affections, argued Babalatchi, and in that case they would have to use force in order to make him go. Would the Rajah see that trusty men manned the canoe? The thing must be done secretly. Perhaps the Rajah would come himself, so as to bring all the weight of his authority to bear upon Dain if he should prove obstinate and refuse to leave his hiding-place. The Rajah would not commit himself to a definite promise, and anxiously pressed Babalatchi to go, being afraid of the white men paying him an unexpected visit. The aged statesman reluctantly took his leave and went into the courtyard.

Before going down to his boat Babalatchi stopped for a while in the big open space where the thick-leaved trees put black patches of shadow which seemed to float on a flood of smooth, intense light that rolled up to the houses and down to the stockade and over the river, where it broke and sparkled in thousands of glittering wavelets, like a band woven of azure and gold edged with the brilliant green of the forests guarding both banks of the Pantai. In the perfect calm before the coming of the afternoon breeze the irregularly jagged line of tree-tops stood unchanging, as if traced by an unsteady hand on the clear blue of the hot sky. In the space sheltered by the high palisades there lingered the smell of decaying blossoms from the surrounding forest, a taint of drying fish; with now and then a whiff of acrid smoke from the cooking fires when it eddied down from under the leafy boughs and clung lazily about the burnt-up grass.

As Babalatchi looked up at the flagstaff overtopping a group of low trees in the middle of the courtyard the tricolour flag of the Netherlands stirred slightly for the first time since it had been hoisted that morning on the arrival of the man-of-war boats. With a faint rustle of trees the breeze came down in light puffs, playing capriciously for a time with this emblem of Lakamba's power, that was also the mark of his servitude; then the breeze freshened in a sharp gust of wind, and the flag flew out straight and steady above the trees. A dark shadow ran along the river, rolling over and covering up the sparkle of declining sunlight. A big white cloud sailed slowly across the darkening sky, and hung to the westward as if waiting for the sun to join it there. Men and things shook off the torpor of the hot afternoon and stirred into life under the first breath of the sea breeze.

Babalatchi hurried down to the water-gate; yet before he passed through it he paused to look round the courtyard, with its light and shade, with its cheery fires, with the groups of Lakamba's soldiers and retainers scattered about. His own house stood amongst the other buildings in that enclosure, and the statesman of Sambir asked himself with a sinking heart when and how would it be given him to return to that house. He had to deal with a man more dangerous than any wild beast of his experience: a proud man, a man wilful after the manner of princes, a man in love. And he was going forth to speak to that man words of cold and worldly wisdom. Could anything be more appalling? What if that man should take umbrage at some fancied slight to his honour or disregard of his affections and suddenly "amok"? The wise adviser would be the first victim, no doubt, and death would be his reward. And underlying the horror of this situation there was the danger of those meddlesome fools, the white men. A vision of comfortless exile in far-off Madura rose up before Babalatchi. Wouldn't that be worse than death itself? And there was that half-white woman with threatening eyes. How could he tell what an incomprehensible creature of that sort would or would not do? She knew so much that she made the killing of Dain an impossibility. That much was certain. And yet the sharp, rough-edged kriss is a good and discreet friend, thought Babalatchi, as he examined his own lovingly, and put it back in the sheath, with a sigh of regret, before unfastening his canoe. As he cast off the painter, pushed out into the stream, and took up his paddle, he realized vividly how unsatisfactory it was to have women mixed up in state affairs. Young women, of course. For Mrs. Almayer's mature wisdom, and for the easy aptitude in intrigue that comes with years to the feminine mind, he felt the most sincere respect.

He paddled leisurely, letting the canoe drift down as he crossed towards the point. The sun was high yet, and nothing pressed. His work would commence only with the coming of darkness. Avoiding the Lingard jetty, he rounded the point, and paddled up the creek at the back of Almayer's house. There were many canoes lying there, their noses all drawn together, fastened all to the same stake. Babalatchi pushed his little craft in amongst them and stepped on shore. On the other side of the ditch something moved in the grass.

"Who's that hiding?" hailed Babalatchi. "Come out and speak to me."

Nobody answered. Babalatchi crossed over, passing from boat to boat, and poked his staff viciously in the suspicious place. Taminah jumped up with a cry.

"What are you doing here?" he asked, surprised. "I have nearly stepped on your tray. Am I a Dyak that you should hide at my sight?"

"I was weary, and—I slept," whispered Taminah, confusedly.

"You slept! You have not sold anything to-day, and you will be beaten when you return home," said Babalatchi.

Taminah stood before him abashed and silent. Babalatchi looked her over carefully with great satisfaction. Decidedly he would offer fifty dollars more to that thief Bulangi. The girl pleased him.

"Now you go home. It is late," he said sharply. "Tell Bulangi that I shall be near his house before the night is half over, and that I want him to make all things ready for a long journey. You understand? A long journey to the southward. Tell him that before sunset, and do not forget my words."

Taminah made a gesture of assent, and watched Babalatchi recross the ditch and disappear through the bushes bordering Almayer's compound. She moved a little further off the creek and sank in the grass again, lying down on her face, shivering in dry-eyed misery.

Babalatchi walked straight towards the cooking shed looking for Mrs. Almayer. The courtyard was in a great uproar. A strange Chinaman had possession of the kitchen fire and was noisily demanding another saucepan. He hurled objurgations, in the Canton dialect and bad Malay, against the group of slave-girls standing a little way off, half frightened, half amused, at his violence. From the camping fires round which the seamen of the frigate were sitting came words of encouragement, mingled with laughter and jeering. In the midst of this noise and confusion Babalatchi met Ali, an empty dish in his hand.

"Where are the white men?" asked Babalatchi.

"They are eating on the front verandah," answered Ali. "Do not stop me, Tuan. I am giving the white men their food and am busy."

"Where's Mem Almayer?"

"Inside the passage. She is listening to the talk."

Ali grinned and passed on; Babalatchi ascended the plankway to the rear verandah, and beckoning out Mrs. Almayer, engaged her in earnest conversation. Through the long passage, closed at the further end by the red curtain, they could hear from time to time Almayer's voice mingling in conversation with an abrupt loudness that made Mrs. Almayer look significantly at Babalatchi.

"Listen," she said. "He has drunk much."

"He has," whispered Babalatchi. "He will sleep heavily to-night."

Mrs. Almayer looked doubtful.

"Sometimes the devil of strong gin makes him keep awake, and he walks up and down the verandah all night, cursing; then we stand afar off," explained Mrs. Almayer, with the fuller knowledge born of twenty odd years of married life.

"But then he does not hear, nor understand, and his hand, of course, has no strength. We do not want him to hear to-night."

"No," assented Mrs. Almayer, energetically, but in a cautiously subdued voice. "If he hears he will kill."

Babalatchi looked incredulous.

"Hai Tuan, you may believe me. Have I not lived many years with that man? Have I not seen death in that man's eyes more than once when I was younger and he guessed at many things? Had he been a man of my own people I would not have seen such a look twice; but he——"

With a contemptuous gesture she seemed to fling unutterable scorn on Almayer's weak-minded aversion to sudden bloodshed.

"If he has the wish but not the strength, then what do we fear?" asked Babalatchi, after a short silence during which they both listened to Almayer's loud talk till it subsided into the murmur of general conversation. "What do we fear?" repeated Babalatchi again.

"To keep the daughter whom he loves he would strike into your heart and mine without hesitation," said Mrs. Almayer. "When the girl is gone he will be like the devil unchained. Then you and I had better beware."

"I am an old man and fear not death," answered Babalatchi, with a mendacious assumption of indifference. "But what will you do?"

"I am an old woman, and wish to live," retorted Mrs. Almayer. "She is my daughter also. I shall seek safety at the feet of our Rajah, speaking in the name of the past when we both were young, and he——"

Babalatchi raised his hand.

"Enough. You shall be protected," he said soothingly.

Again the sound of Almayer's voice was heard, and again interrupting their talk, they listened to the confused but loud utterance coming in bursts of unequal strength, with unexpected pauses and noisy repetitions that made some words and sentences fall clear and distinct on their ears out of the meaningless jumble of excited shoutings emphasized by the thumping of Almayer's fist upon the table. On the short intervals of silence, the high complaining note of tumblers, standing close together and vibrating to the shock, lingered, growing fainter, till it leapt up again into tumultuous ringing, when a new idea started a new rush of words and brought down the heavy hand again. At last the quarrelsome shouting ceased, and the thin plaint of disturbed glass died away into reluctant quietude.

Babalatchi and Mrs. Almayer had listened curiously, their bodies bent and their ears turned towards the passage. At every louder shout they nodded at each other with a ridiculous affectation of scandalized propriety, and they remained in the same attitude for some time after the noise had ceased.

"This is the devil of gin," whispered Mrs. Almayer. "Yes; he talks like that sometimes when there is nobody to hear him."

"What does he say?" inquired Babalatchi, eagerly. "You ought to understand."

"I have forgotten their talk. A little I understood. He spoke without any respect of the white ruler in Batavia, and of protection, and said he had been wronged; he said that several times. More I did not understand. Listen! Again he speaks!"

"Tse! tse! tse!" clicked Babalatchi, trying to appear shocked, but with a joyous twinkle of his solitary eye. "There will be great trouble between those white men. I will go round now and see. You tell your daughter that there is a sudden and a long journey before her, with much glory and splendour at the end. And tell her that Dain must go, or he must die, and that he will not go alone."

"No, he will not go alone," slowly repeated Mrs. Almayer, with a thoughtful air, as she crept into the passage after seeing Babalatchi disappear round the corner of the house.

The statesman of Sambir, under the impulse of vivid curiosity, made his way quickly to the front of the house, but once there he moved slowly and cautiously as he crept step by step up the stairs of the verandah. On the highest step he sat down quietly, his feet on the steps below, ready for flight should his presence prove unwelcome. He felt pretty safe so. The table stood nearly endways to him, and he saw Almayer's back; at Nina he looked full face, and had a side view of both officers; but of the four persons sitting at the table only Nina and the younger officer noticed his noiseless arrival. The momentary dropping of Nina's eyelids acknowledged Babalatchi's presence; she then spoke at once to the young sub, who turned towards her with attentive alacrity, but her gaze was fastened steadily on her father's face while Almayer was speaking uproariously.

". . . disloyalty and unscrupulousness! What have you ever done to make me loyal? You have no grip on this country. I had to take care of myself, and when I asked for protection I was met with threats and contempt, and had Arab slander thrown in my face. I! a white man!"

"Don't be violent, Almayer," remonstrated the lieutenant; "I have heard all this already."

"Then why do you talk to me about scruples? I wanted money, and I gave powder in exchange. How could I know that some of your wretched men were going to be blown up? Scruples! Pah!"

He groped unsteadily amongst the bottles, trying one after another, grumbling to himself the while. "No more wine," he muttered discontentedly.

"You have had enough, Almayer," said the lieutenant, as he lighted a cigar. "Is it not time to deliver to us your prisoner? I take it you have that Dain Maroola stowed away safely somewhere. Still we had better get that business over, and then we shall have more drink. Come! don't look at me like this."

Almayer was staring with stony eyes, his trembling fingers fumbling about his throat.

"Gold," he said with difficulty. "Hem! A hand on the windpipe, you know. Sure you will excuse. I wanted to say—a little gold for a little powder. What's that?"

"I know, I know," said the lieutenant soothingly.

"No! You don't know. Not one of you knows!" shouted Almayer. "The government is a fool, I tell you. Heaps of gold. I am the man that knows; I and another one. But he won't speak. He is——"

He checked himself with a feeble smile, and, making an unsuccessful attempt to pat the officer on the shoulder, knocked over a couple of empty bottles.

"Personally you are a fine fellow," he said very distinctly, in a patronizing manner. His head nodded drowsily as he sat muttering to himself.

The two officers looked at each other helplessly.

"This won't do," said the lieutenant, addressing his junior. "Have the men mustered in the compound here. I must get some sense out of him. Hi! Almayer! Wake up, man. Redeem your word. You gave your word. You gave your word of honour, you know."

Almayer shook off the officer's hand with impatience, but his ill-humour vanished at once, and he looked up, putting his forefinger to the side of his nose.

"You are very young; there is time for all things," he said, with an air of great sagacity.

The lieutenant turned towards Nina, who, leaning back in her chair, watched her father steadily.

"Really I am very much distressed by all this for your sake," he exclaimed. "I do not know," he went on, speaking with some embarrassment, "whether I have any right to ask you anything, unless, perhaps, to withdraw from this painful scene, but I feel that I must—for your father's good—suggest that you should—I mean if you have any influence over him you ought to exert it now to make him keep the promise he gave me before he—before he got into this state."

He observed with discouragement that she seemed not to take any notice of what he said, sitting still with half-closed eyes.

"I trust——" he began again.

"What is the promise you speak of?" abruptly asked Nina, leaving her seat and moving towards her father.

"Nothing that is not just and proper. He promised to deliver to us a man who in time of profound peace took the lives of innocent men to escape the punishment he deserved for breaking the law. He planned his mischief on a large scale. It is not his fault if it failed, partially. Of course you have heard of Dain Maroola. Your father secured him, I understand. We know he escaped up this river. Perhaps you——"

"And he killed white men!" interrupted Nina.

"I regret to say they were white. Yes, two white men lost their lives through that scoundrel's freak."

"Two only!" exclaimed Nina.

The officer looked at her in amazement.

"Why! why! You——" he stammered, confused.

"There might have been more," interrupted Nina. "And when you get this—this scoundrel, will you go?"

The lieutenant, still speechless, bowed his assent.

"Then I would get him for you if I had to seek him in a burning fire," she burst out with intense energy. "I hate the sight of your white faces. I hate the sound of your gentle voices. That is the way you speak to women, dropping sweet words before any pretty face. I have heard your voices before. I hoped to live here without seeing any other white face but this," she added in a gentler tone, touching lightly her father's cheek.

Almayer ceased his mumbling and opened his eyes. He caught hold of his daughter's hand and pressed it to his face, while Nina with the other hand smoothed his rumpled grey hair, looking defiantly over her father's head at the officer, who had now regained his composure and returned her look with a cool, steady stare. Below, in front of the verandah, they could hear the tramp of seamen mustering there ac-

cording to orders. The sub-lieutenant came up the steps, while Babalatchi stood up uneasily and, with finger on lip, tried to catch Nina's
eye.

"You are a good girl," whispered Almayer, absently, dropping his
daughter's hand.

"Father! father!" she cried, bending over him with passionate entreaty. "See those two men looking at us. Send them away. I cannot
bear it any more. Send them away. Do what they want and let them
go."

She caught sight of Babalatchi and ceased speaking suddenly, but
her foot tapped the floor with rapid beats in a paroxysm of nervous
restlessness. The two officers stood close together looking on curiously.

"What has happened? What is the matter?" whispered the younger
man.

"Don't know," answered the other, under his breath. "One is furious, and the other is drunk. Not so drunk, either. Queer this. Look!"

Almayer had risen, holding on to his daughter's arm. He hesitated
a moment, then he let go his hold and lurched half-way across the verandah. There he pulled himself together, and stood very straight,
breathing hard and glaring round angrily.

"Are the men ready?" asked the lieutenant.

"All ready, sir."

"Now, Mr. Almayer, lead the way," said the lieutenant.

Almayer rested his eyes on him as if he saw him for the first time.

"Two men," he said thickly. The effort of speaking seemed to interfere with his equilibrium. He took a quick step to save himself from
a fall, and remained swaying backwards and forwards. "Two men," he
began again, speaking with difficulty. "Two white men—men in uniform—honourable men. I want to say—men of honour. Are you?"

"Come! None of that," said the officer impatiently. "Let us have
that friend of yours."

"What do you think I am?" asked Almayer, fiercely.

"You are drunk, but not so drunk as not to know what you are doing. Enough of this tomfoolery," said the officer sternly, "or I will have
you put under arrest in your own house."

"Arrest!" laughed Almayer, discordantly. "Ha! ha! ha! Arrest! Why,
I have been trying to get out of this infernal place for twenty years,
and I can't. You hear, man! I can't, and never shall! Never!"

He ended his words with a sob, and walked unsteadily down the
stairs. When in the courtyard the lieutenant approached him, and took
him by the arm. The sub-lieutenant and Babalatchi followed close.

"That's better, Almayer," said the officer encouragingly. "Where are
you going to? There are only planks there. Here," he went on, shaking
him slightly, "do we want the boats?"

"No," answered Almayer, viciously. "You want a grave."

"What? Wild again! Try to talk sense."

"Grave!" roared Almayer, struggling to get himself free. "A hole in the ground. Don't you understand? You must be drunk. Let me go! Let go, I tell you!"

He tore away from the officer's grasp, and reeled towards the planks where the body lay under its white cover; then he turned round quickly, and faced the semicircle of interested faces. The sun was sinking rapidly, throwing long shadows of house and trees over the courtyard, but the light lingered yet on the river, where the logs went drifting past in midstream, looking very distinct and black in the pale red glow. The trunks of the trees in the forest on the east bank were lost in gloom while their highest branches swayed gently in the departing sunlight. The air felt heavy and cold in the breeze, expiring in slight puffs that came over the water.

Almayer shivered as he made an effort to speak, and again with an uncertain gesture he seemed to free his throat from the grip of an invisible hand. His bloodshot eyes wandered aimlessly from face to face.

"There!" he said at last. "Are you all there? He is a dangerous man."

He dragged at the cover with hasty violence, and the body rolled stiffly off the planks and fell at his feet in rigid helplessness.

"Cold, perfectly cold," said Almayer, looking round with a mirthless smile. "Sorry can do no better. And you can't hang him, either. As you observe, gentlemen," he added gravely, "there is no head, and hardly any neck."

The last ray of light was snatched away from the tree-tops, the river grew suddenly dark, and in the great stillness the murmur of the flowing water seemed to fill the vast expanse of grey shadow that descended upon the land.

"This is Dain," went on Almayer to the silent group that surrounded him. "And I have kept my word. First one hope, then another, and this is my last. Nothing is left now. You think there is one dead man here? Mistake, I 'sure you. I am much more dead. Why don't you hang me?" he suggested suddenly, in a friendly tone, addressing the lieutenant. "I assure, assure you it would be a mat—matter of form altog—altogether."

These last words he muttered to himself, and walked zigzagging towards his house. "Get out!" he thundered at Ali, who was approaching timidly with offers of assistance. From afar, scared groups of men and women watched his devious progress. He dragged himself up the stairs by the banister, and managed to reach a chair into which he fell heavily. He sat for awhile panting with exertion and anger, and looking round vaguely for Nina; then making a threatening gesture towards the compound, where he had heard Babalatchi's voice, he overturned the table with his foot in a great crash of smashed crockery. He muttered yet menacingly to himself, then his head fell on his breast, his eyes closed, and with a deep sigh he fell asleep.

That night—for the first time in its history—the peaceful and flourishing settlement of Sambir saw the lights shining about "Almayer's Folly." These were the lanterns of the boats hung up by the seamen under the verandah where the two officers were holding a court of inquiry into the truth of the story related to them by Babalatchi. Babalatchi had regained all his importance. He was eloquent and persuasive, calling Heaven and Earth to witness the truth of his statements. There were also other witnesses. Mahmat Banjer and a good many others underwent a close examination that dragged its weary length far into the evening. A messenger was sent for Abdulla, who excused himself from coming on the score of his venerable age, but sent Reshid. Mahmat had to produce the bangle, and saw with rage and mortification the lieutenant put it in his pocket as one of the proofs of Dain's death, to be sent in with the official report of the mission. Babalatchi's ring was also impounded for the same purpose, but the experienced statesman was resigned to that loss from the very beginning. He did not mind as long as he was sure that the white men believed. He put that question to himself earnestly as he left, one of the last, when the proceedings came to a close. He was not certain. Still, if they believed only for a night, he would put Dain beyond their reach and feel safe himself. He walked away fast, looking from time to time over his shoulder in the fear of being followed, but he saw and heard nothing.

"Ten o'clock," said the lieutenant, looking at his watch and yawning. "I shall hear some of the captain's complimentary remarks when we get back. Miserable business, this."

"Do you think all this is true?" asked the younger man.

"True! It is just possible. But if it isn't true what can we do? If we had a dozen boats we could patrol the creeks; and that wouldn't be much good. That drunken madman was right; we haven't enough hold on this coast. They do what they like. Are our hammocks slung?"

"Yes, I told the coxswain. Strange couple over there," said the sub, with a wave of his hand towards Almayer's house.

"Hem! Queer, certainly. What have you been telling her? I was attending to the father most of the time."

"I assure you I have been perfectly civil," protested the other warmly.

"All right. Don't get excited. She objects to civility, then, from what I understand. I thought you might have been tender. You know we are on service."

"Well, of course. Never forget that. Coldly civil. That's all."

They both laughed a little, and not feeling sleepy began to pace the verandah side by side. The moon rose stealthily above the trees, and suddenly changed the river into a stream of scintillating silver. The forest came out of the black void and stood sombre and pensive over the sparkling water. The breeze died away into a breathless calm.

Seamanlike, the two officers tramped measuredly up and down without exchanging a word. The loose planks rattled rhythmically under their steps with obtrusive dry sound in the perfect silence of the night. As they were wheeling round again the younger man stood attentive.

"Did you hear that?" he asked.

"No!" said the other. "Hear what?"

"I thought I heard a cry. Ever so faint. Seemed a woman's voice. In that other house. Ah! Again! Hear it?"

"No," said the lieutenant, after listening awhile. "You young fellows always hear women's voices. If you are going to dream you had better get into your hammock. Good-night."

The moon mounted higher, and the warm shadows grew smaller and crept away as if hiding before the cold and cruel light.

CHAPTER TEN

"It has set at last," said Nina to her mother pointing towards the hills behind which the sun had sunk. "Listen, mother, I am going now to Bulangi's creek, and if I should never return——"

She interrupted herself, and something like doubt dimmed for a moment the fire of suppressed exaltation that had glowed in her eyes and had illuminated the serene impassiveness of her features with a ray of eager life during all that long day of excitement—the day of joy and anxiety, of hope and terror, of vague grief and indistinct delight. While the sun shone with that dazzling light in which her love was born and grew till it possessed her whole being, she was kept firm in her unwavering resolve by the mysterious whisperings of desire which filled her heart with impatient longing for the darkness that would mean the end of danger and strife, the beginning of happiness, the fulfilling of love, the completeness of life. It had set at last! The short tropical twilight went out before she could draw the long breath of relief; and now the sudden darkness seemed to be full of menacing voices calling upon her to rush headlong into the unknown; to be true to her own impulses to give herself up to the passion she had evoked and shared. He was waiting! In the solitude of the secluded clearing, in the vast silence of the forest he was waiting alone, a fugitive in fear of his life. Indifferent to his danger he was waiting for her. It was for her only that he had come; and now as the time approached when he should have his reward, she asked herself with dismay what meant that chilling doubt of her own will and of her own desire? With an effort she shook off the fear of the passing weakness. He should have his reward. Her woman's love and her woman's honour overcame the faltering distrust of that unknown future waiting for her in the darkness of the river.

"No, you will not return," muttered Mrs. Almayer, prophetically. "Without you he will not go, and if he remains here——" She waved her hand towards the lights of "Almayer's Folly," and the unfinished sentence died out in a threatening murmur.

The two women had met behind the house, and now were walking slowly together towards the creek where all the canoes were moored. Arrived at the fringe of bushes they stopped by a common impulse, and Mrs. Almayer, laying her hand on her daughter's arm, tried in vain to look close into the girl's averted face. When she attempted to speak her first words were lost in a stifled sob that sounded strangely coming from that woman who, of all human passions, seemed to know only those of anger and hate.

"You are going away to be a great Ranee," she said at last, in a voice that was steady enough now, "and if you be wise you shall have much power that will endure many days, and even last into your old age. What have I been? A slave all my life, and I have cooked rice for a man who had no courage and no wisdom. Hai! I! even I, was given in gift by a chief and a warrior to a man that was neither. Hai! Hai!"

She wailed to herself softly, lamenting the lost possibilites of murder and mischief that could have fallen to her lot had she been mated with a congenial spirit. Nina bent down over Mrs. Almayer's slight form and scanned attentively, under the stars that had rushed out on the black sky and now hung breathless over that strange parting, her mother's shrivelled features, and looked close into the sunken eyes that could see into her own dark future by the light of a long and a painful experience. Again she felt herself fascinated, as of old, by her mother's exalted mood and by the oracular certainty of expression which, together with her fits of violence, had contributed not a little to the reputation for witchcraft she enjoyed in the settlement.

"I was a slave, and you shall be a queen," went on Mrs. Almayer, looking straight before her; "but remember men's strength and their weakness. Tremble before his anger, so that he may see your fear in the light of day; but in your heart you may laugh, for after sunset he is your slave."

"A slave! He! The master of life! You do not know him, mother."

Mrs. Almayer condescended to laugh contemptuously.

"You speak like a fool of a white woman," she exclaimed. "What do you know of men's anger and of men's love? Have you watched the sleep of men weary of dealing death? Have you felt about you the strong arm that could drive a kriss deep into a beating heart? Yah! you are a white woman, and ought to pray to a woman god!"

"Why do you say this? I have listened to your words so long that I have forgotten my old life. If I was white would I stand here, ready to go? Mother, I shall return to the house and look once more at my father's face."

"No!" said Mrs. Almayer, violently. "No, he sleeps now the sleep of gin; and if you went back he might awake and see you. No, he shall never see you. When the terrible old man took you away from me when you were little, you remember——"

"It was such a long time ago," murmured Nina.

"I remember," went on Mrs. Almayer, fiercely. "I wanted to look at your face again. He said no! I heard you cry and jumped into the river. You were his daughter then; you are my daughter now. Never shall you go back to that house; you shall never cross this courtyard again. No! no!"

Her voice rose almost to a shout. On the other side of the creek there was a rustle in the long grass. The two women heard it, and listened for a while in startled silence.

"I shall go," said Nina, in a cautious but intense whisper. "What is your hate or your revenge to me?"

She moved towards the house, Mrs. Almayer clinging to her and trying to pull her back.

"Stop, you shall not go!" she gasped.

Nina pushed away her mother impatiently and gathered up her skirts for a quick run, but Mrs. Almayer ran forward and turned round, facing her daughter with outstretched arms.

"If you move another step," she exclaimed, breathing quickly, "I shall cry out. Do you see those lights in the big house? There sit two white men, angry because they cannot have the blood of the man you love. And in those dark houses," she continued, more calmly as she pointed towards the settlement, "my voice could wake up men that would lead the Orang Blanda soldiers to him who is waiting—for you."

She could not see her daughter's face, but the white figure before her stood silent and irresolute in the darkness. Mrs. Almayer pursued her advantage.

"Give up your old life! Forget!" she said in entreating tones. "Forget that you ever looked at a white face; forget their words; forget their thoughts. They speak lies. And they think lies because they despise us that are better than they are, but not so strong. Forget their friendship and their contempt; forget their many gods. Girl, why do you want to remember the past when there is a warrior and a chief ready to give many lives—his own life—for one of your smiles?"

While she spoke she pushed gently her daughter towards the canoes, hiding her own fear, anxiety, and doubt under the flood of passionate words that left Nina no time to think and no opportunity to protest, even if she had wished it. But she did not wish it now. At the bottom of that passing desire to look again at her father's face there was no strong affection. She felt no scruples and no remorse at leaving suddenly that man whose sentiment towards herself she could not understand, she could not even see. There was only an instinctive clinging to old life, to old habits, to old faces; that fear of finality which lurks in every human breast and prevents so many heroisms and so many crimes. For years she had stood between her mother and her father, the one so strong in her weakness, the other so weak where he could have been strong. Between those two beings so dissimilar, so antagonistic, she stood with mute heart wondering and angry at the fact of her own existence. It seemed so unreasonable, so humiliating to be flung there in that settlement and to see the days rush by into the past, without a hope, a desire, or an aim that would justify the life she had to endure in ever-growing weariness. She had little belief and no sympathy for her father's dreams; but the savage ravings of her mother chanced to strike a responsive chord, deep down somewhere in her despairing heart; and she dreamed dreams of her own with the persistent absorption of a captive thinking of liberty within the walls of his prison cell. With the coming of Dain she found the road to freedom by obeying the voice of the new-born impulses, and with surprised joy she thought she could read in his eyes the answer to all the questionings of her heart. She understood now the reason and the aim of life; and in the triumphant unveiling of that mystery she threw away disdainfully her past with its sad thoughts, its bitter feelings and its faint affections, now withered and dead in contact with her fierce passion.

Mrs. Almayer unmoored Nina's own canoe and, straightening herself painfully, stood, painter in hand, looking at her daughter.

"Quick," she said; "get away before the moon rises, while the river is dark. I am afraid of Abdulla's slaves. The wretches prowl in the night often, and might see and follow you. There are two paddles in the canoe."

Nina approached her mother and touched lightly with her lips the wrinkled forehead. Mrs. Almayer snorted contemptuously in protest against that tenderness which she, nevertheless, feared could be contagious.

"Shall I ever see you again, mother?" murmured Nina.

"No," said Mrs. Almayer, after a short silence. "Why should you return here where it is my fate to die? You will live far away in splendour and might. When I hear of white men driven from the islands, then I shall know that you are alive, and that you remember my words."

"I shall always remember," returned Nina, earnestly; "but where is my power, and what can I do?"

"Do not let him look too long in your eyes, nor lay his head on your knees without reminding him that men should fight before they rest. And if he lingers, give him his kriss yourself and bid him go, as the wife of a mighty prince should do when the enemies are near. Let him slay the white men that come to us to trade, with prayers on their lips and loaded guns in their hands. Ah"—she ended with a sigh—"they are on every sea, and on every shore; and they are very many!"

She swung the bow of the canoe towards the river, but did not let go the gunwale, keeping her hand on it in irresolute thoughtfulness. Nina put the point of the paddle against the bank, ready to shove off into the stream.

"What is it, mother?" she asked, in a low voice. "Do you hear anything?"

"No," said Mrs. Almayer, absently. "Listen, Nina," she continued, abruptly, after a slight pause, "in after years there will be other women——"

A stifled cry in the boat interrupted her, and the paddle rattled in the canoe as it slipped from Nina's hands, which she put out in a protesting gesture. Mrs. Almayer fell on her knees on the bank and leaned over the gunwale so as to bring her own face close to her daughter's.

"There will be other women," she repeated firmly; "I tell you that, because you are half white, and may forget that he is a great chief, and that such things must be. Hide your anger, and do not let him see on your face the pain that will eat your heart. Meet him with joy in your eyes and wisdom on your lips, for to you he will turn in sadness or in doubt. As long as he looks upon many women your power will last, but should there be one, one only with whom he seems to forget you, then——"

"I could not live," exclaimed Nina, covering her face with both her hands. "Do not speak so, mother; it could not be."

"Then," went on Mrs. Almayer, steadily, "to that woman, Nina, show no mercy."

She moved the canoe down towards the stream by the gunwale, and gripped it with both her hands, the bow pointing into the river.

"Are you crying?" she asked sternly of her daughter, who sat still with covered face. "Arise, and take your paddle, for he has waited long enough. And remember, Nina, no mercy; and if you must strike, strike with a steady hand."

She put out all her strength, and swinging her body over the water, shot the light craft far into the stream. When she recovered herself from the effort she tried vainly to catch a glimpse of the canoe that seemed to have dissolved suddenly into the white mist trailing over the heated waters of the Pantai. After listening for a while intently on her knees, Mrs. Almayer rose with a deep sigh, while two tears wandered slowly down her withered cheeks. She wiped them off quickly with a wisp of her grey hair as if ashamed of herself, but could not stifle another loud sigh, for her heart was heavy and she suffered much, being unused to tender emotions. This time she fancied she had heard a faint noise, like the echo of her own sigh, and she stopped, straining her ears to catch the slightest sound, and peering apprehensively towards the bushes near her.

"Who is there?" she asked, in an unsteady voice, while her imagination peopled the solitude of the riverside with ghost-like forms. "Who is there?" she repeated faintly.

There was no answer: only the voice of the river murmuring in sad monotone behind the white veil seemed to swell louder for a moment, to die away again in a soft whisper of eddies washing against the bank.

Mrs. Almayer shook her head as if in answer to her own thoughts, and walked quickly away from the bushes, looking to the right and left watchfully. She went straight towards the cooking shed, observing that the embers of the fire there glowed more brightly than usual, as if somebody had been adding fresh fuel to the fires during the evening. As she approached, Babalatchi, who had been squatting in the warm glow, rose and met her in the shadow outside.

"Is she gone?" asked the anxious statesman, hastily.

"Yes," answered Mrs. Almayer. "What are the white men doing? When did you leave them?"

"They are sleeping now, I think. May they never wake!" exclaimed Babalatchi, fervently. "Oh! but they are devils, and made much talk and trouble over that carcass. The chief threatened me twice with his hand, and said he would have me tied up to a tree. Tie me up to a tree! Me!" he repeated, striking his breast violently.

Mrs. Almayer laughed tauntingly.

"And you salaamed and asked for mercy. Men with arms by their side acted otherwise when I was young."

"And where are they, the men of your youth? You mad woman!" retorted Babalatchi, angrily. "Killed by the Dutch. Aha! But I shall live to deceive them. A man knows when to fight and when to tell peaceful lies. You would know that if you were not a woman."

But Mrs. Almayer did not seem to hear him. With bent body and outstretched arm she appeared to be listening to some noise behind the shed.

"There are strange sounds," she whispered, with evident alarm. "I have heard in the air the sounds of grief, as of a sigh and weeping. That was by the riverside. And now again I heard——"

"Where?" asked Babalatchi, in an altered voice. "What did you hear?"

"Close here. It was like a breath long drawn. I wish I had burnt the paper over the body before it was buried."

"Yes," assented Babalatchi. "But the white men had him thrown into a hole at once. You know he found his death on the river," he added cheerfully, "and his ghost may hail the canoes, but would leave the land alone."

Mrs. Almayer, who had been craning her neck to look round the corner of the shed, drew back her head.

"There is nobody there," she said, reassured. "Is it not time for the Rajah war-canoe to go to the clearing?"

"I have been waiting for it here, for I myself must go," explained Babalatchi. "I think I will go over and see what makes them late. When will you come? The Rajah gives you refuge."

"I shall paddle over before the break of day. I cannot leave my dollars behind," muttered Mrs. Almayer.

They separated. Babalatchi crossed the courtyard towards the creek to get his canoe, and Mrs. Almayer walked slowly to the house, ascended the plankway, and passing through the back verandah entered the passage leading to the front of the house; but before going in she turned in the doorway and looked back at the empty and silent courtyard, now lit up by the rays of the rising moon. No sooner she had disappeared, however, than a vague shape flitted out from amongst the stalks of the banana plantation, darted over the moonlit space, and fell in the darkness at the foot of the verandah. It might have been the shadow of a driving cloud, so noiseless and rapid was its passage, but for the trail of disturbed grass, whose feathery heads trembled and swayed for a long time in the moonlight before they rested motionless and gleaming, like a design of silver sprays embroidered on a sombre background.

Mrs. Almayer lighted the cocoanut lamp, and lifting cautiously the red curtain, gazed upon her husband, shading the light with her hand. Almayer, huddled up in the chair, one of his arms hanging down, the other thrown across the lower part of his face as if to ward off an invisible enemy, his legs stretched straight out, slept heavily, unconscious of the unfriendly eyes that looked upon him in disparaging criticism. At his feet lay the overturned table, amongst a wreck of crockery and broken bottles. The appearance as of traces left by a desperate struggle was accentuated by the chairs, which seemed to have been scattered violently all over the place, and now lay about the

verandah with a lamentable aspect of inebriety in their helpless attitudes. Only Nina's big rocking-chair, standing black and motionless on
its high runners, towered above the chaos of demoralized furniture,
unflinchingly dignified and patient, waiting for its burden.

With a last scornful look towards the sleeper, Mrs. Almayer passed
behind the curtain into her own room. A couple of bats, encouraged
by the darkness and the peaceful state of affairs, resumed their silent
and oblique gambols above Almayer's head, and for a long time the
profound quiet of the house was unbroken, save for the deep breathing
of the sleeping man and the faint tinkle of silver in the hands of the
woman preparing for flight. In the increasing light of the moon that
had risen now above the night mist, the objects on the verandah came
out strongly outlined in black splashes of shadow with all the uncompromising ugliness of their disorder, and a caricature of the sleeping
Almayer appeared on the dirty whitewash of the wall behind him in a
grotesquely exaggerated detail of attitude and feature enlarged to a
heroic size. The discontented bats departed in quest of darker places,
and a lizard came out in short, nervous rushes, and, pleased with the
white table-cloth, stopped on it in breathless immobility that would
have suggested sudden death had it not been for the melodious call he
exchanged with a less adventurous friend hiding amongst the lumber
in the courtyard. Then the boards in the passage creaked, the lizard
vanished, and Almayer stirred uneasily with a sigh: slowly, out of the
senseless annihilation of drunken sleep, he was returning, through the
land of dreams, to waking consciousness. Almayer's head rolled from
shoulder to shoulder in the oppression of his dream; the heavens had
descended upon him like a heavy mantle, and trailed in starred folds
far under him. Stars above, stars all round him; and from the stars
under his feet rose a whisper full of entreaties and tears, and sorrowful
faces flitted amongst the clusters of light filling the infinite space below.
How escape from the importunity of lamentable cries and from the
look of staring, sad eyes in the faces which pressed round him till he
gasped for breath under the crushing weight of worlds that hung over
his aching shoulders? Get away! But how? If he attempted to move he
would step off into nothing, and perish in the crashing fall of that
universe of which he was the only support. And what were the voices
saying? Urging him to move! Why? Move to destruction! Not likely!
The absurdity of the thing filled him with indignation. He got a firmer
foothold and stiffened his muscles in heroic resolve to carry his burden
to all eternity. And ages passed in the superhuman labour, amidst the
rush of circling worlds; in the plaintive murmur of sorrowful voices
urging him to desist before it was too late—till the mysterious power
that had laid upon him the giant task seemed at last to seek his destruction. With terror he felt an irresistible hand shaking him by the

shoulder, while the chorus of voices swelled louder into an agonized prayer to go, go before it is too late. He felt himself slipping, losing his balance, as something dragged at his legs, and he fell. With a faint cry he glided out of the anguish of perishing creation into an imperfect waking that seemed to be still under the spell of his dream.

"What? What?" he murmured sleepily, without moving or opening his eyes. His head still felt heavy, and he had not the courage to raise his eyelids. In his ears there still lingered the sound of entreating whisper.—"Am I awake?—Why do I hear the voices?" he argued to himself, hazily.—"I cannot get rid of the horrible nightmare yet.—I have been very drunk.—What is that shaking me? I am dreaming yet.—I must open my eyes and be done with it. I am only half awake, it is evident."

He made an effort to shake off his stupor and saw a face close to his, glaring at him with staring eyeballs. He closed his eyes again in amazed horror and sat up straight in the chair, trembling in every limb. What was this apparition?—His own fancy, no doubt.—His nerves had been much tried the day before—and then the drink! He would not see it again if he had the courage to look.—He would look directly.—Get a little steadier first.—So.—Now.

He looked. The figure of a woman standing in the steely light, her hands stretched forth in a suppliant gesture, confronted him from the far-off end of the verandah; and in the space between him and the obstinate phantom floated the murmur of words that fell on his ears in a jumble of torturing sentences, the meaning of which escaped the utmost efforts of his brain. Who spoke the Malay words? Who ran away? Why too late—and too late for what? What meant those words of hate and love mixed so strangely together, the ever-recurring names falling on his ears again and again—Nina, Dain; Dain, Nina? Dain was dead, and Nina was sleeping, unaware of the terrible experience through which he was now passing. Was he going to be tormented for ever, sleeping or waking, and have no peace either night or day? What was the meaning of this?

He shouted the last words aloud. The shadowy woman seemed to shrink and recede a little from him towards the doorway, and there was a shriek. Exasperated by the incomprehensible nature of his torment, Almayer made a rush upon the apparition, which eluded his grasp, and he brought up heavily against the wall. Quick as lightning he turned round and pursued fiercely the mysterious figure fleeing from him with piercing shrieks that were like fuel to the flames of his anger. Over the furniture, round the overturned table, and now he had it cornered behind Nina's chair. To the left, to the right they dodged, the chair rocking madly between them, she sending out shriek after shriek at every feint, and he growling meaningless curses through his hard-set teeth. Oh! the fiendish noise that split his head and seemed to choke his breath.—It would kill him.—It must be stopped! An insane desire to crush that yelling thing induced him to cast himself recklessly over the chair with a desperate grab, and they came down together in a cloud of dust amongst the splintered wood. The last shriek died out under him in a faint gurgle, and he had secured the relief of absolute silence.

He looked at the woman's face under him. A real woman. He knew her. By all that is wonderful! Taminah! He jumped up ashamed of his fury and stood perplexed, wiping his forehead. The girl struggled to a kneeling posture and embraced his legs in a frenzied prayer for mercy.

"Don't be afraid," he said, raising her. "I shall not hurt you. Why do you come to my house in the night? And if you had to come, why not go behind the curtain where the women sleep?"

"The place behind the curtain is empty," gasped Taminah, catching her breath between the words. "There are no women in your house any more, Tuan. I saw the old Mem go away before I tried to wake you. I did not want your women, I wanted you."

"Old Mem!" repeated Almayer. "Do you mean my wife?"

She nodded her head.

"But of my daughter you are not afraid?" said Almayer.

"Have you not heard me?" she exclaimed. "Have I not spoken for a long time when you lay there with eyes half open? She is gone too."

"I was asleep. Can you not tell when a man is sleeping and when awake?"

"Sometimes," answered Taminah in a low voice; "sometimes the spirit lingers close to a sleeping body and may hear. I spoke a long time before I touched you, and I spoke softly for fear it would depart at a sudden noise and leave you sleeping for ever. I took you by the shoulder only when you began to mutter words I could not understand. Have you not heard, then, and do you know nothing?"

"Nothing of what you said. What is it? Tell again if you want me to know."

He took her by the shoulder and led her unresisting to the front of the verandah into a stronger light. She wrung her hands with such an appearance of grief that he began to be alarmed.

"Speak," he said. "You made noise enough to wake even dead men. And yet nobody living came," he added to himself in an uneasy whisper. "Are you mute? Speak!" he repeated.

In a rush of words which broke out after a short struggle from her trembling lips she told him the tale of Nina's love and her own jealousy. Several times he looked angrily into her face and told her to be silent; but he could not stop the sounds that seemed to him to run out in a hot stream, swirl about his feet, and rise in scalding waves about him, higher, higher, drowning his heart, touching his lips with a feel of molten lead, blotting out his sight in scorching vapour, closing over his head, merciless and deadly. When she spoke of the deception as to Dain's death of which he had been the victim only that day, he glanced again at her with terrible eyes, and made her falter for a second, but he turned away directly, and his face suddenly lost all expression in a stony stare far away over the river. Ah! the river! His old friend and his old enemy, speaking always with the same voice as he runs from year to year bringing fortune or disappointment, happiness or pain, upon the same varying but unchanged surface of glancing currents and swirling eddies. For many years he had listened to the passionless and soothing murmur that sometimes was the song of hope, at times the song of triumph, of encouragement; more often the whisper of consolation that spoke of better days to come. For so many years! So many years! And now to the accompaniment of that murmur he listened to the slow and painful beating of his heart. He listened attentively, wondering at the regularity of its beats. He began to count mechanically. One, two. Why count? At the next beat it must stop. No heart could suffer so and beat so steadily for long. Those regular strokes as of a muffled hammer that rang in his ears must stop soon. Still beating unceasing and cruel. No man can bear this: and is this the last, or will the next one be the last?—How much longer? O God! how much longer? His hand weighed heavier unconsciously on the girl's shoulder, and she spoke the last words of her story crouching at his feet with tears of pain and shame and anger. Was her revenge to fail her? This white man was like a senseless stone. Too late! Too late!

"And you saw her go?" Almayer's voice sounded harshly above her head.

"Did I not tell you?" she sobbed, trying to wriggle gently out from under his grip. "Did I not tell you that I saw the witchwoman push the canoe? I lay hidden in the grass and heard all the words. She that we used to call the white Mem wanted to return to look at your face, but the witchwoman forbade her, and——"

She sank lower yet on her elbow, turning half round under the downward push of the heavy hand, her face lifted up to him with spiteful eyes.

"And she obeyed," she shouted out in a half-laugh, half-cry of pain. "Let me go, Tuan. Why are you angry with me? Hasten, or you will be too late to show your anger to the deceitful woman."

Almayer dragged her up to her feet and looked close into her face while she struggled, turning her head away from his wild stare.

"Who sent you here to torment me?" he asked, violently. "I do not believe you. You lie."

He straightened his arm suddenly and flung her across the verandah towards the doorway, where she lay immobile and silent, as if she had left her life in his grasp, a dark heap, without a sound or a stir.

"Oh! Nina!" whispered Almayer, in a voice in which reproach and love spoke together in pained tenderness. "Oh! Nina! I do not believe."

A light draught from the river ran over the courtyard in a wave of bowing grass and, entering the verandah, touched Almayer's forehead with its cool breath, in a caress of infinite pity. The curtain in the women's doorway blew out and instantly collapsed with startling helplessness. He stared at the fluttering stuff.

"Nina!" cried Almayer. "Where are you, Nina?"

The wind passed out of the empty house in a tremulous sigh, and all was still.

Almayer hid his face in his hands as if to shut out a loathsome sight. When, hearing a slight rustle, he uncovered his eyes, the dark heap by the door was gone.

CHAPTER ELEVEN

In the middle of a shadowless square of moonlight, shining on a smooth and level expanse of young rice-shoots, a little shelter-hut perched on high posts, the pile of brushwood near by and the glowing embers of a fire with a man stretched before it, seemed very small and as if lost in the pale green iridescence reflected from the ground. On three sides of the clearing, appearing very far away in the deceptive light, the big trees of the forest, lashed together with manifold bonds by a mass of tangled creepers, looked down at the growing young life at their feet with the sombre resignation of giants that had lost faith in their strength. And in the midst of them the merciless creepers clung to the big trunks in cable-like coils, leaped from tree to tree, hung in thorny festoons from the lower boughs, and, sending slender tendrils on high to seek out the smallest branches, carried death to their victims in an exulting riot of silent destruction.

On the fourth side, following the curve of the bank of that branch of the Pantai that formed the only access to the clearing, ran a black line of young trees, bushes, and thick second growth, unbroken save for a small gap chopped out in one place. At that gap began the narrow footpath leading from the water's edge to the grass-built shelter used by the night watchers when the ripening crop had to be protected from the wild pigs. The pathway ended at the foot of the piles on which the hut was built, in a circular space covered with ashes and bits of burnt wood. In the middle of that space, by the dim fire, lay Dain.

He turned over on his side with an impatient sigh, and, pillowing his head on his bent arm, lay quietly with his face to the dying fire. The glowing embers shone redly in a small circle, throwing a gleam into his wide-open eyes. His body was weary with the exertion of the past few days, his mind more weary still with the strain of solitary waiting for his fate. Never before had he felt so helpless. He had heard the report of the gun fired on board the launch, and he knew that his life was in untrustworthy hands, and that his enemies were very near.

During the slow hours of the afternoon he had roamed about on the edge of the forest, or, hiding in the bushes, watched the creek with unquiet eyes for some sign of danger. He feared not death, yet he desired ardently to live, for life to him was Nina. She had promised to come, to follow him, to share his danger and his splendour. But with her by his side he cared not for danger, and without her there could be no splendour and no joy in existence. Crouching in his shady hiding-place, he closed his eyes, trying to evoke the gracious and charming image of the white figure that for him was the beginning and the end of life. With eyes shut tight, his teeth hard set, he tried in a great effort of passionate will to keep his hold on that vision of supreme delight. In vain! His heart grew heavy as the figure of Nina faded away to be replaced by another vision this time—a vision of armed men, of angry faces, of glittering arms—and he seemed to hear the hum of excited and triumphant voices as they discovered him in his hiding-place. Startled by the vividness of his fancy, he would open his eyes, and, leaping out into the sunlight, resume his aimless wanderings around the clearing. As he skirted in his weary march the edge of the forest he glanced now and then into its dark shade, so enticing in its deceptive appearance of coolness, so repellent with its unrelieved gloom, where lay, entombed and rotting, countless generations of trees, and where their successors stood as if mourning, in dark green foliage, immense and helpless, awaiting their turn. Only the parasites seemed to live there in a sinuous rush upwards into the air and sunshine, feeding on the dead and the dying alike, and crowning their victims with pink and blue flowers that gleamed amongst the boughs, incongruous and cruel, like a strident and mocking note in the solemn harmony of the doomed trees.

A man could hide there, thought Dain, as he approached a place where the creepers had been torn and hacked into an archway that might have been the beginning of a path. As he bent down to look through he heard angry grunting, and a sounder of wild pig crashed away in the undergrowth. An acrid smell of damp earth and of decaying leaves took him by the throat, and he drew back with a scared face, as if he had been touched by the breath of Death itself. The very air seemed dead in there—heavy and stagnating, poisoned with the corruption of countless ages. He went on, staggering on his way, urged by the nervous restlessness that made him feel tired yet caused him to loathe the very idea of immobility and repose. Was he a wild man to hide in the woods and perhaps be killed there—in the darkness —where there was no room to breathe? He would wait for his enemies in the sunlight, where he could see the sky and feel the breeze. He knew how a Malay chief should die. The sombre and desperate fury, that peculiar inheritance of his race, took possession of him, and he glared savagely across the clearing towards the gap in the bushes by the riverside. They would come from there. In imagination he saw them now. He saw the bearded faces and the white jackets of the officers, the light on the levelled barrels of the rifles. What is the bravery of the greatest warrior before the firearms in the hand of a slave? He would walk towards them with a smiling face, with his hands held out in a sign of submission till he was very near them. He would speak friendly words—come nearer yet—yet nearer—so near that they could touch him with their hands and stretch them out to make him a captive. That would be the time; with a shout and a leap he would be in the midst of them, kriss in hand, killing, killing, killing, and would die with the shouts of his enemies in his ears, their warm blood spurting before his eyes.

Carried away by his excitement, he snatched the kriss hidden in his sarong, and, drawing a long breath, rushed forward, struck at the empty air, and fell on his face. He lay as if stunned in the sudden reaction from his exaltation, thinking that, even if he died thus gloriously, it would have to be before he saw Nina. Better so. If he saw her again he felt that death would be too terrible. With horror he, the descendant of Rajahs and of conquerors, had to face the doubt of his own bravery. His desire of life tormented him in a paroxysm of agonizing remorse. He had not the courage to stir a limb. He had lost faith in himself, and there was nothing else in him of what makes a man. The suffering remained, for it is ordered that it should abide in the human body even to the last breath, and fear remained. Dimly he could look into the depths of his passionate love, see its strength and its weakness, and felt afraid.

The sun went down slowly. The shadow of the western forest marched over the clearing, covered the man's scorched shoulders with its cool mantle, and went on hurriedly to mingle with the shadows of other forests on the eastern side. The sun lingered for a while amongst the light tracery of the higher branches, as if in friendly reluctance to abandon the body stretched in the green paddy-field. Then Dain, revived by the cool of the evening breeze, sat up and stared round him. As he did so the sun dipped sharply, as if ashamed of being detected in a sympathizing attitude, and the clearing, which during the day was all light, became suddenly all darkness, where the fire gleamed like an eye. Dain walked slowly towards the creek, and, divesting himself of his torn sarong, his only garment, entered the water cautiously. He had had nothing to eat that day, and had not dared show himself in daylight by the water-side to drink. Now, as he swam silently, he swallowed a few mouthfuls of water that lapped about his lips. This did him good, and he walked with greater confidence in himself and others as he returned towards the fire. Had he been betrayed by Lakamba all would have been over by this. He made up a big blaze, and while it lasted dried himself, and then lay down by the embers. He could not sleep, but he felt a great numbness in all his limbs. His restlessness was gone, and he was content to lie still, measuring the time by watching the stars that rose in endless succession above the forest, while the slight puffs of wind under the cloudless sky seemed to fan their twinkle into a greater brightness. Dreamily he assured himself over and over again that she would come, till the certitude crept into his heart and filled him with a great peace. Yes, when the next day broke, they would be together on the great blue sea that was like life—away from the forests that were like death. He murmured the name of Nina into the silent space with a tender smile: this seemed to break the spell of stillness, and far away by the creek a frog croaked loudly as if in answer. A chorus of loud roars and plaintive calls rose from the mud along the line of bushes. He laughed heartily; doubtless it was their love-song. He felt affectionate towards the frogs and listened, pleased with the noisy life near him.

When the moon peeped above the trees he felt the old impatience and the old restlessness steal over him. Why was she so late? True, it was a long way to come with a single paddle. With what skill and what endurance could those small hands manage a heavy paddle! It was very wonderful—such small hands, such soft little palms that knew how to touch his cheek with a feel lighter than the fanning of a butterfly's wing. Wonderful! He lost himself lovingly in the contemplation of this tremendous mystery, and when he looked at the moon again it had risen a hand's breadth above the trees. Would she come? He forced himself to lie still, overcoming the impulse to rise and rush round the clearing again. He turned this way and that; at last, quivering with the effort, he lay on his back, and saw her face among the stars looking down on him.

The croaking of frogs suddenly ceased. With the watchfulness of a hunted man Dain sat up, listening anxiously, and heard several splashes in the water as the frogs took rapid headers into the creek. He knew that they had been alarmed by something, and stood up suspicious and attentive. A slight grating noise, then the dry sound as of two pieces of wood struck against each other. Somebody was about to land! He took up an armful of brushwood, and, without taking his eyes from the path, held it over the embers of his fire. He waited, undecided, and saw something gleam amongst the bushes; then a white figure came out of the shadows and seemed to float towards him in the pale light. His heart gave a great leap and stood still, then went on shaking his frame in furious beats. He dropped the brushwood upon the glowing coals, and had an impression of shouting her name—of rushing to meet her; yet he emitted no sound, he stirred not an inch, but he stood silent and motionless like chiselled bronze under the moonlight that streamed over his naked shoulders. As he stood still, fighting with his breath, as if bereft of his senses by the intensity of his delight, she walked up to him with quick, resolute steps, and, with the appearamce of one about to leap from a dangerous height, threw both her arms round his neck with a sudden gesture. A small blue gleam crept amongst the dry branches, and the crackling of reviving fire was the only sound as they faced each other in the speechless emotion of that meeting; then the dry fuel caught at once, and a bright hot flame shot upwards in a blaze as high as their heads, and in its light they saw each other's eyes.

Neither of them spoke. He was regaining his senses in a slight tremor that ran upwards along his rigid body and hung about his trembling lips. She drew back her head and fastened her eyes on his in one of those long looks that are a woman's most terrible weapon; a look that is more stirring than the closest touch, and more dangerous than the thrust of a dagger, because it also whips the soul out of the body, but leaves the body alive and helpless, to be swayed here and there by the capricious tempests of passion and desire; a look that enwraps the whole body, and that penetrates into the innermost recesses of the being, bringing terrible defeat in the delirious uplifting of accomplished conquest. It has the same meaning for the man of the forests and the sea as for the man threading the paths of the more dangerous wilderness of houses and streets. Men that have felt in their breasts the awful exultation such a look awakens become mere things of to-day—which is paradise; forget yesterday—which was suffering; care not for to-morrow—which may be perdition. They wish to live under that look for ever. It is the look of woman's surrender.

He understood, and, as if suddenly released from his invisible bonds, fell at her feet with a shout of joy, and, embracing her knees, hid his head in the folds of her dress, murmuring disjointed words of gratitude and love. Never before had he felt so proud as now, when at the feet of that woman that half belonged to his enemies. Her fingers played with his hair in an absent-minded caress as she stood absorbed in thought. The thing was done. Her mother was right. The man was her slave. As she glanced down at his kneeling form she felt a great pitying tenderness for that man she used to call—even in her thoughts—the master of life. She lifted her eyes and looked sadly at the southern heavens under which lay the path of their lives—her own, and that man's at her feet. Did he not say himself that she was the light of his life? She would be his light and his wisdom; she would be his greatness and his strength; yet hidden from the eyes of all men she would be, above all, his only and lasting weakness. A very woman! In the sublime vanity of her kind she was thinking already of moulding a god from the clay at her feet. A god for others to worship. She was content to see him as he was now, and to feel him quiver at the slightest touch of her light fingers. And while her eyes looked sadly at the southern stars a faint smile seemed to be playing about her firm lips. Who can tell in the fitful light of a camp fire? It might have been a smile of triumph, or of conscious power, or of tender pity, or perhaps, of love.

She spoke softly to him, and he rose to his feet, putting his arm round her in quiet consciousness of his ownership; she laid her head on his shoulder with a sense of defiance to all the world in the encircling protection of that arm. He was hers with all his qualities and his faults. His strength and his courage, his recklessness and his daring, his simple wisdom and his savage cunning—all were hers. As they passed together out of the red light of the fire into the silver shower of rays that fell upon the clearing he bent his head over her face, and she saw in his eyes the dreamy intoxication of boundless felicity from the close touch of her slight figure clasped to his side. With a rhythmical swing of their bodies they walked through the light towards the outlying shadows of the forests that seemed to guard their happiness in solemn immobility. Their forms melted in the play of light and shadow at the foot of the big trees, but the murmur of tender words lingered over the empty clearing, grew faint, and died out. A sigh as of immense sorrow passed over the land in the last effort of the dying breeze, and in the deep silence which succeeded, the earth and the heavens were suddenly hushed up in the mournful contemplation of human love and human blindness.

They walked slowly back to the fire. He made for her a seat out of the dry branches, and, throwing himself down at her feet, lay his head in her lap and gave himself up to the dreamy delight of the passing hour. Their voices rose and fell, tender or animated as they spoke of their love and of their future. She, with a few skilful words spoken from time to time, guided his thoughts, and he let his happiness flow in a stream of talk passionate and tender, grave or menacing, according to the mood which she evoked. He spoke to her of his own island, where the gloomy forests and the muddy rivers were unknown. He spoke of its terraced fields, of the murmuring clear rills of sparkling water that flowed down the sides of great mountains, bringing life to the land and joy to its tillers. And he spoke also of the mountain peak that rising lonely above the belt of trees knew the secrets of the passing clouds, and was the dwelling-place of the mysterious spirit of his race, of the guardian genius of his house. He spoke of vast horizons swept by fierce winds that whistled high above the summits of burning mountains. He spoke of his forefathers that conquered ages ago the island of which he was to be the future ruler. And then as, in her interest, she brought her face nearer to his, he, touching lightly the thick tresses of her long hair, felt a sudden impulse to speak to her of the sea he loved so well; and he told her of its never-ceasing voice, to which he had listened as a child, wondering at its hidden meaning that no living man has penetrated yet; of its enchanting glitter; of its senseless and capricious fury; how its surface was for ever changing, and yet always enticing, while its depths were for ever the same, cold and cruel, and full of the wisdom of destroyed life. He told her how it held men slaves of its charm for a lifetime, and then, regardless of their devotion, swallowed them up, angry at their fear of its mystery, which it would never disclose, not even to those that loved it most. While he talked, Nina's head had been gradually sinking lower, and her face almost touched his now. Her hair was over his eyes, her breath was on his forehead, her arms were about his body. No two beings could be closer to each other, yet she guessed rather than understood the meaning of his last words that came out after a slight hesitation in a faint murmur, dying out imperceptibly into a profound and significant silence: "The sea, O Nina, is like a woman's heart."

She closed his lips with a sudden kiss, and answered in a steady voice—

"But to the men that have no fear, O master of my life, the sea is ever true."

Over their heads a film of dark, thread-like clouds, looking like immense cobwebs drifting under the stars, darkened the sky with the presage of the coming thunderstorm. From the invisible hills the first distant rumble of thunder came in a prolonged roll which, after tossing about from hill to hill, lost itself in the forests of the Pantai. Dain and Nina stood up, and the former looked at the sky uneasily.

"It is time for Babalatchi to be here," he said. "The night is more than half gone. Our road is long, and a bullet travels quicker than the best canoe."

"He will be here before the moon is hidden behind the clouds," said Nina. "I heard a splash in the water," she added. "Did you hear it too?"

"Alligator," answered Dain shortly, with a careless glance towards the creek. "The darker the night," he continued, "the shorter will be our road, for then we could keep in the current of the main stream, but if it is light—even no more than now—we must follow the small channels of sleeping water, with nothing to help our paddles."

"Dain," interposed Nina, earnestly, "it was no alligator. I heard the bushes rustling near the landing-place."

"Yes," said Dain, after listening awhile. "It cannot be Babalatchi, who would come in a big war canoe, and openly. Those that are coming, whoever they are, do not wish to make much noise. But you have heard, and now I can see," he went on quickly. "It is but one man. Stand behind me, Nina. If he is a friend he is welcome; if he is an enemy you shall see him die."

He laid his hand on his kriss, and waited the approach of his unexpected visitor. The fire was burning very low, and small clouds—precursors of the storm—crossed the face of the moon in rapid succession, and their flying shadows darkened the clearing. He could not make out who the man might be, but he felt uneasy at the steady advance of the tall figure walking on the path with a heavy tread, and hailed it with a command to stop. The man stopped at some little distance, and Dain expected him to speak, but all he could hear was his deep breathing. Through a break in the flying clouds a sudden and fleeting brightness descended upon the clearing. Before the darkness closed in again Dain saw a hand holding some glittering object extended towards him, heard Nina's cry of "Father!" and in an instant the girl was between him and Almayer's revolver. Nina's loud cry woke up the echoes of the sleeping woods, and the three stood still as if waiting for the return of silence before they would give expression to their various feelings. At the appearance of Nina, Almayer's arm fell by his side, and he made a step forward. Dain pushed the girl gently aside.

"Am I a wild beast that you should try to kill me suddenly and in the dark, Tuan Almayer?" said Dain, breaking the strained silence. "Throw some brushwood on the fire," he went on, speaking to Nina, "while I watch my white friend, lest harm should come to you or to me, O delight of my heart!"

Almayer ground his teeth and raised his arm again. With a quick bound Dain was at his side: there was a short scuffle, during which one chamber of the revolver went off harmlessly, then the weapon, wrenched out of Almayer's hand, whirled through the air and fell in the bushes. The two men stood close together, breathing hard. The replenished fire threw out an unsteady circle of light and shone on the terrified face of Nina, who looked at them with outstretched hands.

"Dain!" she cried out warningly, "Dain!"

He waved his hand towards her in a reassuring gesture, and, turning to Almayer, said with great courtesy—

"Now we may talk, Tuan. It is easy to send out death, but can your wisdom recall the life? She might have been harmed," he continued, indicating Nina. "Your hand shook much; for myself I was not afraid."

"Nina!" exclaimed Almayer, "come to me at once. What is this sudden madness? What bewitched you? Come to your father, and together we shall try to forget this horrible nightmare!"

He opened his arms with the certitude of clasping her to his breast in another second. She did not move. As it dawned upon him that she did not mean to obey he felt a deadly cold creep into his heart, and pressing the palms of his hands to his temples, he looked down on the ground in mute despair. Dain took Nina by the arm and led her towards her father.

"Speak to him in the language of his people," he said. "He is grieving—as who would not grieve at losing thee, my pearl! Speak to him the last words he shall hear spoken by that voice, which must be very sweet to him, but is all my life to me."

He released her, and, stepping back a few paces out of the circle of light, stood in the darkness looking at them with calm interest. The reflection of a distant flash of lightning lit up the clouds over their heads, and was followed after a short interval by the faint rumble of thunder, which mingled with Almayer's voice as he began to speak.

"Do you know what you are doing? Do you know what is waiting for you if you follow that man? Have you no pity for yourself? Do you know that you shall be at first his plaything and then a scorned slave, a drudge, and a servant of some new fancy of that man?"

She raised her hand to stop him, and turning her head slightly, asked—

"You hear this Dain! Is it true?"

"By all the gods!" came the impassioned answer from the darkness—"by heaven and earth, by my head and thine I swear: this is a white man's lie. I have delivered my soul into your hands for ever; I breathe with your breath, I see with your eyes, I think with your mind, and I take you into my heart for ever."

"You thief!" shouted the exasperated Almayer.

A deep silence succeeded this outburst, then the voice of Dain was heard again.

"Nay, Tuan," he said in a gentle tone, "that is not true also. The girl came of her own will. I have done no more but to show her my love like a man; she heard the cry of my heart, and she came, and the dowry I have given to the woman you call your wife."

Almayer groaned in his extremity of rage and shame. Nina laid her hand lightly on his shoulder, and the contact, light as the touch of a falling leaf, seemed to calm him. He spoke quickly, and in English this time.

"Tell me," he said—"tell me, what have they done to you, your mother and that man? What made you give yourself up to that savage? For he is a savage. Between him and you there is a barrier that nothing can remove. I can see in your eyes the look of those who commit suicide when they are mad. You are mad. Don't smile. It breaks my heart. If I were to see you drowning before my eyes, and I without the power to help you, I could not suffer a greater torment. Have you forgotten the teaching of so many years?"

"No," she interrupted, "I remember it well. I remember how it ended also. Scorn for scorn, contempt for contempt, hate for hate. I am not of your race. Between your people and me there is also a barrier that nothing can remove. You ask why I want to go, and I ask you why I should stay."

He staggered as if struck in the face, but with a quick, unhesitating grasp she caught him by the arm and steadied him.

"Why you should stay!" he repeated slowly, in a dazed manner, and stopped short, astounded at the completeness of his misfortune.

"You told me yesterday," she went on again, "that I could not understand or see your love for me: it is so. How can I? No two human beings understand each other. They can understand but their own voices. You wanted me to dream your dreams, to see your own visions —the visions of life amongst the white faces of those who cast me out from their midst in angry contempt. But while you spoke I listened to the voice of my own self; then this man came, and all was still; there was only the murmur of his love. You call him a savage! What do you call my mother, your wife?"

"Nina!" cried Almayer, "take your eyes off my face."

She looked down directly, but continued speaking only a little above a whisper.

"In time," she went on, "both our voices, that man's and mine, spoke together in a sweetness that was intelligible to our ears only. You were speaking of gold then, but our ears were filled with the song of our love, and we did not hear you. Then I found that we could see through each other's eyes: that he saw things that nobody but myself and he could see. We entered a land where no one could follow us, and least of all you. Then I began to live."

She paused. Almayer sighed deeply. With her eyes still fixed on the ground she began speaking again.

"And I mean to live. I mean to follow him. I have been rejected with scorn by the white people, and now I am a Malay! He took me in his arms, he laid his life at my feet. He is brave; he will be powerful, and I hold his bravery and his strength in my hand, and I shall make him great. His name shall be remembered long after both our bodies are laid in the dust. I love you no less than I did before, but I shall never leave him, for without him I cannot live."

"If he understood what you have said," answered Almayer, scornfully, "he must be highly flattered. You want him as a tool for some incomprehensible ambition of yours. Enough, Nina. If you do not go down at once to the creek, where Ali is waiting with my canoe, I shall tell him to return to the settlement and bring the Dutch officers here. You cannot escape from this clearing, for I have cast adrift your canoe. If the Dutch catch this hero of yours they will hang him as sure as I stand here. Now go."

He made a step towards his daughter and laid hold of her by the shoulder, his other hand pointing down the path to the landing-place.

"Beware!" exclaimed Dain; "this woman belongs to me!"

Nina wrenched herself free and looked straight at Almayer's angry face.

"No, I will not go," she said with desperate energy. "If he dies I shall die too!"

"You die?" said Almayer, contemptuously. "Oh, no! You shall live a life of lies and deception till some other vagabond comes along to sing; how did you say that? The song of love to you! Make up your mind quickly."

He waited for a while, and then added meaningly—

"Shall I call out to Ali?"

"Call out," she answered in Malay, "you that cannot be true to your own countrymen. Only a few days ago you were selling the powder of their destruction; now you want to give up to them the man that yesterday you called your friend. Oh, Dain," she said, turning towards the motionless but attentive figure in the darkness, "instead of bringing you life I bring you death, for he will betray unless I leave you for ever!"

Dain came into the circle of light, and, throwing his arm around Nina's neck, whispered in her ear—

"I can kill him where he stands, before a sound can pass his lips. For you it is to say yes or no. Babalatchi cannot be far now."

He straightened himself up, taking his arm off her shoulder, and confronted Almayer, who looked at them both with an expression of concentrated fury.

"No!" she cried, clinging to Dain in wild alarm. "No! Kill me! Then perhaps he will let you go. You do not know the mind of a white man. He would rather see me dead than standing where I am. Forgive me, your slave, but you must not." She fell at his feet sobbing violently and repeating, "Kill me! Kill me!"

"I want you alive," said Almayer, speaking also in Malay, with sombre calmness. "You go, or he hangs. Will you obey?"

Dain shook Nina off, and, making a sudden lunge, struck Almayer full in the chest with the handle of his kriss, keeping the point towards himself.

"Hai, look! It was easy for me to turn the point the other way," he said in his even voice. "Go, Tuan Putih," he added with dignity. "I give you your life, my life, and her life. I am the slave of this woman's desire, and she wills it so."

There was not a glimmer of light in the sky now, and the tops of the trees were as invisible as their trunks, being lost in the mass of clouds that hung low over the woods, the clearing, and the river. Every outline had disappeared in the intense blackness that seemed to have destroyed everything but space. Only the fire glimmered like a star forgotten in this annihilation of all visible things, and nothing was heard after Dain ceased speaking but the sobs of Nina, whom he held in his arms, kneeling beside the fire. Almayer stood looking down at them in gloomy thoughtfulness. As he was opening his lips to speak they were startled by a cry of warning by the riverside, followed by the splash of many paddles and the sound of voices.

"Babalatchi!" shouted Dain, lifting up Nina as he got upon his feet quickly.

"Ada! Ada!" came the answer from the panting statesman who ran up the path and stood amongst them. "Run to my canoe," he said to Dain excitedly, without taking any notice of Almayer. "Run! we must go. That woman has told them all!"

"What woman?" asked Dain, looking at Nina. Just then there was only one woman in the whole world for him.

"The she-dog with white teeth; the seven times accursed slave of Bulangi. She yelled at Abdulla's gate till she woke up all Sambir. Now the white officers are coming guided by her and Reshid. If you want to live, do not look at me, but go!"

"How do you know this?" asked Almayer.

"Oh, Tuan! what matters how I know! I have only one eye, but I saw lights in Abdulla's house and in his campong as we were paddling past. I have ears, and while we lay under the bank I have heard the messengers sent out to the white men's house."

"Will you depart without that woman who is my daughter?" said Almayer, addressing Dain, while Babalatchi stamped with impatience, muttering, "Run! Run at once!"

"No," answered Dain, steadily, "I will not go; to no man will I abandon this woman."

"Then kill me and escape yourself," sobbed out Nina.

He clasped her close, looking at her tenderly, and whispered, "We will never part, O Nina!"

"I shall not stay here any longer," broke in Babalatchi, angrily. "This is great foolishness. No woman is worth a man's life. I am an old man, and I know."

He picked up his staff, and, turning to go, looked at Dain as if offering him his last chance of escape. But Dain's face was hidden amongst Nina's black tresses, and he did not see this last appealing glance.

Babalatchi vanished in the darkness. Shortly after his disappearance they heard the war canoe leave the landing-place in the swish of the numerous paddles dipped in the water together. Almost at the same time Ali came up from the riverside, two paddles on his shoulder.

"Our canoe is hidden up the creek, Tuan Almayer," he said, "in the dense bush where the forest comes down to the water. I took it there because I heard from Babalatchi's paddlers that the white men are coming here."

"Wait for me there," said Almayer, "but keep the canoe hidden."

He remained silent, listening to Ali's footsteps, then turned to Nina.

"Nina," he said sadly "will you have no pity for me?"

There was no answer. She did not even turn her head, which was pressed close to Dain's breast.

He made a movement as if to leave them and stopped. By the dim glow of the burning-out fire he saw their two motionless figures. The woman's back turned to him with the long black hair streaming down over the white dress, and Dain's calm face looking at him above her head.

"I cannot," he muttered to himself. After a long pause he spoke again a little lower, but in an unsteady voice, "It would be too great a disgrace. I am a white man." He broke down completely there, and went on tearfully, "I am a white man, and of good family. Very good family," he repeated, weeping bitterly. "It would be a disgrace . . . all over the island, . . . the only white man on the east coast. No, it cannot be . . . white men finding my daughter with this Malay. My daughter!" he cried aloud, with a ring of despair in his voice.

He recovered his composure after a while and said distinctly—

"I will never forgive you, Nina—never! If you were to come back to me now, the memory of this night would poison all my life. I shall try to forget. I have no daughter. There used to be a half-caste woman in my house, but she is going even now. You, Dain, or whatever your name may be, I shall take you and that woman to the island at the mouth of the river myself. Come with me."

He led the way, following the bank as far as the forest. Ali answered to his call, and, pushing their way through the dense bush, they stepped into the canoe hidden under the overhanging branches. Dain laid Nina in the bottom, and sat holding her head on his knees. Almayer and Ali each took up a paddle. As they were going to push out Ali hissed warningly. All listened.

In the great stillness before the bursting out of the thunderstorm they could hear the sound of oars working regularly in their row-locks. The sound approached steadily, and Dain, looking through the branches, could see the faint shape of a big white boat. A woman's voice said in a cautious tone—

"There is the place where you may land white men; a little higher —there!"

The boat was passing them so close in the narrow creek that the blades of the long oars nearly touched the canoe.

"Way enough! Stand by to jump on shore! He is alone and unarmed," was the quiet order in a man's voice, and in Dutch.

Somebody else whispered: "I think I can see a glimmer of a fire through the bush." And then the boat floated past them, disappearing instantly in the darkness.

"Now," whispered Ali, eagerly, "let us push out and paddle away."

The little canoe swung into the stream, and as it sprung forward in response to the vigorous dig of the paddles they could hear an angry shout.

"He is not by the fire. Spread out, men, and search for him!"

Blue lights blazed out in different parts of the clearing, and the shrill voice of a woman cried in accents of rage and pain—

"Too late! O senseless white men! He has escaped!"

CHAPTER TWELVE

"That is the place," said Dain, indicating with the blade of his paddle a small islet about a mile ahead of the canoe—"that is the place where Babalatchi promised that a boat from the prau would come for me when the sun is overhead. We will wait for that boat there."

Almayer, who was steering, nodded without speaking, and by a slight sweep of his paddle laid the head of the canoe in the required direction.

They were just leaving the southern outlet of the Pantai, which lay behind them in a straight and long vista of water shining between

two walls of thick verdure that ran downwards and towards each other,
till at last they joined and sank together in the far-away distance. The
sun, rising above the calm waters of the Straits, marked its own path
by a streak of light that glided upon the sea and darted up the wide
reach of the river, a hurried messenger of light and life to the gloomy
forests of the coast; and in this radiance of the sun's pathway floated
the black canoe heading for the islet which lay bathed in sunshine,
the yellow sands of its encircling beach shining like an inlaid golden
disc on the polished steel of the unwrinkled sea. To the north and
south of it rose other islets, joyous in their brilliant colouring of green
and yellow, and on the main coast the sombre line of mangrove bushes
ended to the southward in the reddish cliffs of Tanjong Mirrah, advancing into the sea, steep and shadowless under the clear light of the
early morning.

The bottom of the canoe grated upon the sand as the little craft
ran upon the beach. Ali leaped on shore and held on while Dain
stepped out carrying Nina in his arms, exhausted by the events and
the long travelling during the night. Almayer was the last to leave the
boat, and together with Ali ran it higher up on the beach. Then Ali,
tired out by the long paddling, laid down in the shade of the canoe,
and incontinently fell asleep. Almayer sat sideways on the gunwale,
and with his arms crossed on his breast, looked to the southward
upon the sea.

After carefully laying Nina down in the shade of the bushes growing in the middle of the islet, Dain threw himself beside her and
watched in silent concern the tears that ran down from under her
closed eyelids, and lost themselves in that fine sand upon which they
both were lying face to face. These tears and this sorrow were for
him a profound and disquieting mystery. Now, when the danger was
past, why should she grieve? He doubted her love no more than he
would have doubted the fact of his own existence, but as he lay looking ardently in her face, watching her tears, her parted lips, her very
breath, he was uneasily conscious of something in her he could not
understand. Doubtless she had the wisdom of perfect beings. He
sighed. He felt something invisible that stood between them, something that would let him approach her so far, but no farther. No
desire, no longing, no effort of will or length of life could destroy
this vague feeling of their difference. With awe but also with great
pride he concluded that it was her own incomparable perfection. She
was his, and yet she was like a woman from another world. His! His!
He exulted in the glorious thought; nevertheless her tears pained him.

With a wisp of her own hair which he took in his hand with timid
reverence he tried in an access of clumsy tenderness to dry the tears
that trembled on her eyelashes. He had his reward in a fleeting smile

that brightened her face for the short fraction of a second, but soon the tears fell faster than ever, and he could bear it no more. He rose and walked towards Almayer, who still sat absorbed in his contemplation of the sea. It was a very, very long time since he had seen the sea—that sea that leads everywhere, brings everything, and takes away so much. He had almost forgotten why he was there, and dreamily he could see all his past life on the smooth and boundless surface that glittered before his eyes.

Dain's hand laid on Almayer's shoulder recalled him with a start from some country very far away indeed. He turned round, but his eyes seemed to look rather at the place where Dain stood than at the man himself. Dain felt uneasy under the unconscious gaze.

"What do you want?" asked Almayer.

"She is crying," murmured Dain, softly.

"She is crying! Why?" asked Almayer, indifferently.

"I came to ask you. My Ranee smiles when looking at the man she loves. It is the white woman that is crying now. You would know."

Almayer shrugged his shoulders and turned away again towards the sea.

"Go, Tuan Putih," urged Dain. "Go to her; her tears are more terrible to me than the anger of gods."

"Are they? You will see them more than once. She told me she could not live without you," answered Almayer, speaking without the faintest spark of expression in his face, "so it behoves you to go to her quick, for fear you may find her dead."

He burst into a loud and unpleasant laugh which made Dain stare at him with some apprehension, but got off the gunwale of the boat and moved slowly towards Nina, glancing up at the sun as he walked.

"And you go when the sun is overhead?" he said.

"Yes, Tuan. Then we go," answered Dain.

"I have not long to wait," muttered Almayer. "It is most important for me to see you go. Both of you. Most important," he repeated, stopping short and looking at Dain fixedly.

He went on again towards Nina, and Dain remained behind. Almayer approached his daughter and stood for a time looking down on her. She did not open her eyes, but hearing footsteps near her, murmured in a low sob, "Dain."

Almayer hesitated for a minute and then sank on the sand by her side. She, not hearing a responsive word, not feeling a touch, opened her eyes—saw her father, and sat up suddenly with a movement of terror.

"Oh, father!" she murmured faintly, and in that word there was expressed regret and fear and dawning hope.

"I shall never forgive you, Nina," said Almayer, in a dispassionate voice. "You have torn my heart from me while I dreamt of your happiness. You have deceived me. Your eyes that for me were like truth itself lied to me in every glance—for how long? You know that best. When you were caressing my cheek you were counting the minutes to the sunset that was the signal for your meeting with that man —there!"

He ceased, and they both sat silent side by side, not looking at each other, but gazing at the vast expanse of the sea. Almayer's words had dried Nina's tears, and her look grew hard as she stared before her into the limitless sheet of blue that shone limpid, unwaving, and steady like heaven itself. He looked at it also, but his features had lost all expression, and life in his eyes seemed to have gone out. The face was a blank, without a sign of emotion, feeling, reason, or even knowledge of itself. All passion, regret, grief, hope, or anger—all were gone, erased by the hand of fate, as if after this last stroke everything was over and there was no need for any record. Those few who saw Almayer during the short period of his remaining days were always impressed by the sight of that face that seemed to know nothing of what went on within: like the blank wall of a prison enclosing sin, regrets, and pain, and wasted life, in the cold indifference of mortar and stones.

"What is there to forgive?" asked Nina, not addressing Almayer directly, but more as if arguing with herself. "Can I not live my own life as you have lived yours? The path you would have wished me to follow has been closed to me by no fault of mine."

"You never told me," muttered Almayer.

"You never asked me," she answered, "and I thought you were like the others and did not care. I bore the memory of my humiliation alone, and why should I tell you that it came to me because I am your daughter? I knew you could not avenge me."

"And yet I was thinking of that only," interrupted Almayer, "and I wanted to give you years of happiness for the short day of your suffering. I only knew of one way."

"Ah! but it was not my way!" she replied. "Could you give me happiness without life? Life!" she repeated with sudden energy that sent the word ringing over the sea. "Life that means power and love," she added in a low voice.

"That!" said Almayer, pointing his finger at Dain standing close by and looking at them in curious wonder.

"Yes, that!" she replied, looking her father full in the face and noticing for the first time with a slight gasp of fear the unnatural rigidity of his features.

"I would have rather strangled you with my own hands," said Almayer, in an expressionless voice which was such a contrast to the desperate bitterness of his feelings that it surprised even himself. He asked himself who spoke, and, after looking slowly round as if expecting to see somebody, turned again his eyes towards the sea.

"You say that because you do not understand the meaning of my words," she said sadly. "Between you and my mother there never was any love. When I returned to Sambir I found the place which I thought would be a peaceful refuge for my heart, filled with weariness and hatred—and mutual contempt. I have listened to your voice and to her voice. Then I saw that you could not understand me; for was I not part of that woman? Of her who was the regret and shame of your life? I had to choose—I hesitated. Why were you so blind? Did you not see me struggling before your eyes? But, when he came, all doubt disappeared, and I saw only the light of the blue and cloudless heaven——"

"I will tell you the rest," interrupted Almayer: "when that man came I also saw the blue and the sunshine of the sky. A thunderbolt has fallen from that sky, and suddenly all is still and dark around me for ever. I will never forgive you, Nina; and to-morrow I shall forget you! I shall never forgive you," he repeated with mechanical obstinacy while she sat, her head bowed down as if afraid to look at her father.

To him it seemed of the utmost importance that he should assure her of his intention of never forgiving. He was convinced that his faith in her had been the foundation of his hopes, the motive of his courage, of his determination to live and struggle, and to be victorious for her sake. And now his faith was gone, destroyed by her own hands; destroyed cruelly, treacherously, in the dark; in the very moment of success. In the utter wreck of his affections and of all his feelings, in the chaotic disorder of his thoughts, above the confused sensation of physical pain that wrapped him up in a sting as of a whiplash curling round him from his shoulders down to his feet, only one idea remained clear and definite—not to forgive her; only one vivid desire—to forget her. And this must be made clear to her—and to himself—by frequent repetition. That was his idea of his duty to himself—to his race—to his respectable connections; to the whole universe unsettled and shaken by this frightful catastrophe of his life. He saw it clearly and believed he was a strong man. He had always prided himself upon his unflinching firmness. And yet he was afraid. She had been all in all to him. What if he should let the memory of his love for her weaken the sense of his dignity? She was a remarkable woman; he could see that; all the latent greatness of his nature—in which he honestly believed—had been transfused into that slight, girlish figure. Great things could be done! What if he should suddenly take her to his heart, forget his shame, and pain, and anger, and—follow her! What if he changed his heart if not his skin and made her life easier between the two loves that would guard her from any mischance! His heart yearned for her. What if he should say that his love for her was greater than . . .

"I will never forgive you, Nina!" he shouted, leaping up madly in the sudden fear of his dream.

This was the last time in his life that he was heard to raise his voice. Henceforth he spoke always in a monotonous whisper like an instrument of which all the strings but one are broken in a last ringing clamour under a heavy blow.

She rose to her feet and looked at him. The very violence of his cry soothed her in an intuitive conviction of his love, and she hugged to her breast the lamentable remnants of that affection with the unscrupulous greediness of women who cling desperately to the very scraps and rags of love, any kind of love, as a thing that of right belongs to them and is the very breath of their life. She put both her hands on Almayer's shoulders, and looking at him half tenderly, half playfully, she said—

"You speak so because you love me."

Almayer shook his head.

"Yes, you do," she insisted softly; then after a short pause she added, "and you will never forget me."

Almayer shivered slightly. She could not have said a more cruel thing.

"Here is the boat coming now," said Dain, his arm outstretched towards a black speck on the water between the coast and the islet.

They all looked at it and remained standing in silence till the little canoe came gently on the beach and a man landed and walked towards them. He stopped some distance off and hesitated.

"What news?" asked Dain.

"We have had orders secretly and in the night to take off from this islet a man and a woman. I see the woman. Which of you is the man?"

"Come, delight of my eyes," said Dain to Nina. "Now we go, and your voice shall be for my ears only. You have spoken your last words to the Tuan Putih, your father. Come."

She hesitated for a while, looking at Almayer, who kept his eyes steadily on the sea, then she touched his forehead in a lingering kiss, and a tear—one of her tears—fell on his cheek and ran down his immovable face.

"Good-bye," she whispered, and remained irresolute till he pushed her suddenly into Dain's arms.

"If you have any pity for me," murmured Almayer, as if repeating some sentence learned by heart, "take that woman away."

He stood very straight, his shoulders thrown back, his head held high, and looked at them as they went down the beach to the canoe, walking enlaced in each other's arms. He looked at the line of their footsteps marked in the sand. He followed their figures moving in the crude blaze of the vertical sun, in that light violent and vibrating, like a triumphal flourish of brazen trumpets. He looked at the man's brown shoulders, at the red sarong round his waist; at the tall, slender, dazzling white figure he supported. He looked at the white dress, at the falling masses of the long black hair. He looked at them embarking, and at the canoe growing smaller in the distance, with rage, despair, and regret in his heart, and on his face a peace as that of a carved image of oblivion. Inwardly he felt himself torn to pieces, but Ali who—now aroused—stood close to his master, saw on his features the blank expression of those who live in that hopeless calm which sightless eyes only can give.

The canoe disappeared, and Almayer stood motionless with his eyes fixed on its wake. Ali from under the shade of his hand examined the coast curiously. As the sun declined, the sea-breeze sprang up from the northward and shivered with its breath the glassy surface of the water.

"Dapat!" exclaimed Ali, joyously. "Got him, master! Got prau! Not there! Look more Tanah Mirrah side. Aha! That way! Master, see? Now plain. See?"

Almayer followed Ali's forefinger with his eyes for a long time in vain. At last he sighted a triangular patch of yellow light on the red background of the cliffs of Tanjong Mirrah. It was the sail of the prau that had caught the sunlight and stood out, distinct with its gay tint, on the dark red of the cape. The yellow triangle crept slowly from cliff to cliff, till it cleared the last point of land and shone brilliantly for a fleeting minute on the blue of the open sea. Then the prau bore up to the southward: the light went out of the sail, and all at once the vessel itself disappeared, vanishing in the shadow of the steep headland that looked on, patient and lonely, watching over the empty sea.

Almayer never moved. Round the little islet the air was full of the talk of the rippling water. The crested wavelets ran up the beach audaciously, joyously, with the lightness of young life, and died quickly, unresistingly, and graciously, in the wide curves of transparent foam on the yellow sand. Above the white clouds sailed rapidly southwards as if intent upon overtaking something. Ali seemed anxious.

"Master," he said timidly, "time to get house now. Long way off to pull. All ready, sir."

"Wait," whispered Almayer.

Now she was gone his business was to forget, and he had a strange notion that it should be done systematically and in order. To Ali's great dismay he fell on his hands and knees, and, creeping along the sand, erased carefully with his hand all traces of Nina's footsteps. He piled up small heaps of sand, leaving behind him a line of miniature graves right down to the water. After burying the last slight imprint of Nina's slipper he stood up, and, turning his face towards the headland where he had last seen the prau, he made an effort to shout out loud again his firm resolve to never forgive. Ali watching him uneasily saw only his lips move, but heard no sound. He brought his foot down with a stamp. He was a firm man—firm as a rock. Let her go. He never had a daughter. He would forget. He was forgetting already.

Ali approached him again, insisting on immediate departure, and this time he consented, and they went together towards their canoe, Almayer leading. For all his firmness he looked very dejected and feeble as he dragged his feet slowly through the sand on the beach; and by his side—invisible to Ali—stalked that particular fiend whose mission it is to jog the memories of men, lest they should forget the meaning of life. He whispered into Almayer's ear a childish prattle of many years ago. Almayer, his head bent on one side, seemed to listen to his invisible companion, but his face was like the face of a man that has died struck from behind—a face from which all feelings and all expression are suddenly wiped off by the hand of unexpected death.

They slept on the river that night, mooring their canoe under the bushes and lying down in the bottom side by side, in the absolute exhaustion that kills hunger, thirst, all feeling and all thought in the overpowering desire for that deep sleep which is like the temporary annihilation of the tired body. Next day they started again and fought doggedly with the current all the morning, till about midday they reached the settlement and made fast their little craft to the jetty of Lingard and Co. Almayer walked straight to the house, and Ali followed, paddles on shoulder, thinking that he would like to eat something. As they crossed the front courtyard they noticed the abandoned look of the place. Ali looked in at the different servants' houses: all were empty. In the back courtyard there was the same absence of sound and life. In the cooking shed the fire was out and the black embers were cold. A tall, lean man came stealthily out of the banana plantation, and went away rapidly across the open space looking at them with big, frightened eyes over his shoulder. Some vagabond without a master; there were many such in the settlement, and they looked upon Almayer as their patron. They prowled about his premises and picked their living there, sure that nothing worse could befall them than a shower of curses when they got in the way of the white man, whom they trusted and liked, and called a fool amongst themselves. In the house, which Almayer entered through the back verandah, the only living thing that met his eyes was his small monkey, which hungry and unnoticed for the last two days, began to cry and complain in monkey language as soon as it caught sight of the familiar face. Almayer soothed it with a few words and ordered Ali to bring in some bananas, then while Ali was gone to get them he stood in the doorway of the front verandah looking at the chaos of overturned furniture. Finally he picked up the table and sat on it while the monkey let itself down from the roof-stick by its chain and perched on his shoulder. When the bananas came they had their breakfast together; both hungry, both eating greedily and showering the skins round them recklessly, in the trusting silence of perfect friendship. Ali went away, grumbling, to cook some rice himself, for all the women about the house had disappeared; he did not know where. Almayer did not seem to care, and, after he finished eating, he sat on the table swinging his legs and staring at the river as if lost in thought.

After some time he got up and went to the door of a room on the right of the verandah. That was the office. The office of Lingard and Co. He very seldom went in there. There was no business now, and he did not want an office. The door was locked, and he stood biting his lower lip, trying to think of the place where the key could be. Suddenly he remembered: in the women's room hung upon a nail. He went over to the doorway where the red curtain hung down in motionless folds, and hesitated for a moment before pushing it aside with his shoulder as if breaking down some solid obstacle. A great square of sunshine entering through the window lay on the floor. On the left he saw Mrs. Almayer's big wooden chest, the lid thrown back, empty; near it the brass nails of Nina's European trunk shone in the large initials N. A. on the cover. A few of Nina's dresses hung on wooden pegs, stiffened in a look of offended dignity at their abandonment. He remembered making the pegs himself and noticed that they were very good pegs. Where was the key? He looked round and saw it near the door where he stood. It was red with rust. He felt very much annoyed at that, and directly afterwards wondered at his own feeling. What did it matter? There soon would be no key—no door—nothing! He paused, key in hand, and asked himself whether he knew well what he was about. He went out again on the verandah and stood by the table thinking. The monkey jumped down, and, snatching a banana skin, absorbed itself in picking it to shreds industriously.

"Forget!" muttered Almayer, and that word started before him a sequence of events, a detailed programme of things to do. He knew perfectly well what was to be done now. First this, then that, and then forgetfulness would come easy. Very easy. He had a fixed idea that if he should not forget before he died he would have to remember to all eternity. Certain things had to be taken out of his life, stamped out of sight, destroyed, forgotten. For a long time he stood in deep thought, lost in the alarming possibilities of unconquerable memory, with the fear of death and eternity before him. "Eternity!" he said aloud, and the sound of that word recalled him out of his reverie. The monkey started, dropped the skin, and grinned up at him amicably.

He went towards the office door and with some difficulty managed to open it. He entered in a cloud of dust that rose under his feet. Books open with torn pages bestrewed the floor; other books lay about grimy and black, looking as if they had never been opened. Account books. In those books he had intended to keep day by day a record of his rising fortunes. Long time ago. A very long time. For many years there had been no record to keep on the blue and red ruled pages! In the middle of the room the big office desk, with one of its legs broken, careened over like the hull of a stranded ship; most of the drawers had fallen out, disclosing heaps of paper yellow with age and dirt. The revolving office chair stood in its place, but he found the pivot set fast when he tried to turn it. No matter. He desisted, and his eyes wandered slowly from object to object. All those things had cost a lot of money at the time. The desk, the paper, the torn books, and the broken shelves, all under a thick coat of dust. The very dust and bones of a dead and gone business. He looked at all these things, all that was left after so many years of work, of strife, of weariness, of discouragement, conquered so many times. And all for what? He stood thinking mournfully of his past life till he heard distinctly the clear voice of a child speaking amongst all this wreck, ruin, and waste. He started with a great fear in his heart, and feverishly began to rake in the papers scattered on the floor, broke the chair into bits, splintered the drawers by banging them against the desk, and made a big heap of all that rubbish in one corner of the room.

He came out quickly, slammed the door after him, turned the key, and, taking it out, ran to the front rail of the verandah, and, with a great swing of his arm, sent the key whizzing into the river. This done he went back slowly to the table, called the monkey down, unhooked its chain, and induced it to remain quiet in the breast of his jacket. Then he sat again on the table and looked fixedly at the door of the room he had just left. He listened also intently. He heard a dry sound of rustling sharp cracks as of dry wood snapping; a whirr like that of a bird's wings when it rises suddenly, and then he saw a thin stream of smoke come through the keyhole. The monkey struggled under his coat. Ali appeared with his eyes starting out of his head.

"Master! House burn!" he shouted.

Almayer stood up holding by the table. He could hear the yells of alarm and surprise in the settlement. Ali wrung his hands, lamenting aloud.

"Stop this noise, fool!" said Almayer, quietly. "Pick up my hammock and blankets and take them to the other house. Quick, now!"

The smoke burst through the crevices of the door, and Ali, with the hammock in his arms, cleared in one bound the steps of the verandah.

"It has caught well," muttered Almayer to himself. "Be quiet, Jack," he added, as the monkey made a frantic effort to escape from its confinement.

The door split from top to bottom, and a rush of flame and smoke drove Almayer away from the table to the front rail of the verandah. He held on there till a great roar overhead assured him that the roof was ablaze. Then he ran down the steps of the verandah, coughing, half choked with the smoke that pursued him in bluish wreaths curling about his head.

On the other side of the ditch, separating Almayer's courtyard from the settlement, a crowd of the inhabitants of Sambir looked at the burning house of the white man. In the calm air the flames rushed up on high, coloured pale brick-red, with violet gleams in the strong sunshine. The thin column of smoke ascended straight and unwavering till it lost itself in the clear blue of the sky, and in the great empty space between the two houses the interested spectators could see the tall figure of the Tuan Putih, with bowed head and dragging feet, walking slowly away from the fire towards the shelter of "Almayer's Folly."

In that manner did Almayer move into his new house. He took possession of the new ruin, and in the undying folly of his heart set himself to wait in anxiety and pain for that forgetfulness which was so slow to come. He had done all he could. Every vestige of Nina's existence had been destroyed; and now with every sunrise he asked himself whether the longed-for oblivion would come before sunset, whether it would come before he died? He wanted to live only long enough to be able to forget, and the tenacity of his memory filled him with dread and horror of death; for should it come before he could accomplish the purpose of his life he would have to remember for ever! He also longed for loneliness. He wanted to be alone. But he was not. In the dim light of the rooms with their closed shutters, in the bright sunshine of the verandah, wherever he went, whichever way he turned, he saw the small figure of a little maiden with pretty olive face, with long black hair, her little pink robe slipping off her shoulders, her big eyes looking up at him in the tender trustfulness of a petted child. Ali did not see anything, but he also was aware of the presence of a child in the house. In his long talks by the evening fires of the settlement he used to tell his intimate friends of Almayer's strange doings. His master had turned sorcerer in his old age. Ali said that often when Tuan Putih had retired for the night he could hear him talking to something in his room. Ali thought that it was a spirit in the shape of a child. He knew his master spoke to a child from certain expressions and words his master used. His master spoke in Malay a little, but mostly in English, which he, Ali, could understand. Master spoke to the child at times tenderly, then he would weep over it, laugh at it, scold it, beg of it to go away; curse it. It was a bad and stubborn spirit. Ali thought his master had imprudently called it up, and now could not get rid of it. His master was very brave; he was not afraid to curse this spirit in the very Presence; and once he fought with it. Ali had heard a great noise as of running about inside the room and groans. His master groaned. Spirits do not groan. His master was brave, but foolish. You cannot hurt a spirit. Ali expected to find his master dead next morning, but he came out very early, looking much older than the day before, and had no food all day.

So far Ali to the settlement. To Captain Ford he was much more communicative, for the good reason that Captain Ford had the purse and gave orders. On each of Ford's monthly visits to Sambir Ali had to go on board with a report about the inhabitant of "Almayer's Folly." On his first visit to Sambir, after Nina's departure, Ford had taken charge of Almayer's affairs. They were not cumbersome. The shed for the storage of goods was empty, the boats had disappeared, appropriated—generally in night-time—by various citizens of Sambir in need of means of transport. During a great flood the jetty of Lingard and Co. left the bank and floated down the river, probably in search of more cheerful surroundings; even the flock of geese—"the only geese on the east coast"—departed somewhere, preferring the unknown dangers of the bush to the desolation of their old home. As time went on the grass grew over the black patch of ground where the old house used to stand, and nothing remained to mark the place of the dwelling that had sheltered Almayer's young hopes, his foolish dream of splendid future, his awakening, and his despair.

Ford did not often visit Almayer, for visiting Almayer was not a pleasant task. At first he used to respond listlessly to the old seaman's boisterous inquiries about his health; he even made efforts to talk, asking for news in a voice that made it perfectly clear that no news from this world had any interest for him. Then gradually he became more silent—not sulkily—but as if he was forgetting how to speak. He used also to hide in the darkest rooms of the house where Ford had to seek him out guided by the patter of the monkey galloping before him. The monkey was always there to receive and introduce Ford. The little animal seemed to have taken complete charge of its master, and whenever it wished for his presence on the verandah it would tug perseveringly at his jacket, till Almayer obediently came out into the sunshine, which he seemed to dislike so much.

One morning Ford found him sitting on the floor of the verandah, his back against the wall, his legs stretched stiffly out, his arms hanging by his side. His expressionless face, his eyes open wide with immobile pupils, and the rigidity of his pose, made him look like an immense man-doll broken and flung there out of the way. As Ford came up the steps he turned his head slowly.

"Ford," he murmured from the floor, "I cannot forget."

"Can't you?" said Ford, innocently, with an attempt at joviality: "I wish I was like you. I am losing my memory—age, I suppose; only the other day my mate——"

He stopped, for Almayer had got up, stumbled, and steadied himself on his friend's arm.

"Hallo! You are better to-day. Soon be all right," said Ford, cheerfully, but feeling rather scared.

Almayer let go his arm and stood very straight with his head up and shoulders thrown back, looking stonily at the multitude of suns shining in ripples of the river. His jacket and his loose trousers flapped in the breeze on his thin limbs.

"Let her go!" he whispered in a grating voice. "Let her go. To-morrow I shall forget. I am a firm man, . . . firm as a . . . rock, . . . firm. . . ."

Ford looked at his face—and fled. The skipper was a tolerably firm man himself—as those who had sailed with him could testify—but Almayer's firmness was altogether too much for his fortitude.

Next time the steamer called in Sambir Ali came on board early with a grievance. He complained to Ford that Jim-Eng the Chinaman had invaded Almayer's house, and actually had lived there for the last month.

"And they both smoke," added Ali.

"Phew! Opium, you mean?"

Ali nodded, and Ford remained thoughtful; then he muttered to himself, "Poor devil! The sooner the better now." In the afternoon he walked up to the house.

"What are you doing here?" he asked of Jim-Eng, whom he found strolling about on the verandah.

Jim-Eng explained in bad Malay, and speaking in that monotonous, uninterested voice of an opium smoker pretty far gone, that his house was old, the roof leaked, and the floor was rotten. So, being an old friend for many, many years, he took his money, his opium, and two pipes, and came to live in this big house.

"There is plenty of room. He smokes, and I live here. He will not smoke long," he concluded.

"Where is he now?" asked Ford.

"Inside. He sleeps," answered Jim-Eng, wearily.

Ford glanced in through the doorway. In the dim light of the room he could see Almayer lying on his back on the floor, his head on a wooden pillow, the long white beard scattered over his breast, the yellow skin of the face, the half-closed eyelids showing the whites of the eye only. . . .

He shuddered and turned away. As he was leaving he noticed a long strip of faded red silk, with some Chinese letters on it, which Jim-Eng had just fastened to one of the pillars.

"What's that?" he asked.

"That," said Jim-Eng, in his colourless voice, "that is the name of the house. All the same like my house. Very good name."

Ford looked at him for awhile and went away. He did not know what the crazy-looking maze of the Chinese inscription on the red silk meant. Had he asked Jim-Eng, that patient Chinaman would have informed him with proper pride that its meaning was: "House of heavenly delight."

In the evening of the same day Babalatchi called on Captain Ford. The captain's cabin opened on deck, and Babalatchi sat astride on the high step, while Ford smoked his pipe on the settee inside. The steamer was leaving next morning, and the old statesman came as usual for a last chat.

"We had news from Bali last moon," remarked Babalatchi. "A grandson is born to the old Rajah, and there is great rejoicing."

Ford sat up interested.

"Yes," went on Babalatchi, in answer to Ford's look. "I told him. That was before he began to smoke."

"Well, and what?" asked Ford.

"I escaped with my life," said Babalatchi, with perfect gravity, "because the white man is very weak and fell as he rushed upon me." Then, after a pause, he added, "She is mad with joy."

"Mrs. Almayer, you mean?"

"Yes, she lives in our Rajah's house. She will not die soon. Such women live a long time," said Babalatchi, with a slight tinge of regret in his voice. "She has dollars, and she has buried them, but we know where. We had much trouble with those people. We had to pay a fine and listen to threats from the white men, and now we have to be careful." He sighed and remained silent for a long while. Then with energy:

"There will be fighting. There is a breath of war on the islands. Shall I live long enough to see? . . . Ah, Tuan!" he went on, more quietly, "the old times were best. Even I have sailed with Lanun men, and boarded in the night silent ships with white sails. That was before an English Rajah ruled in Kuching. Then we fought amongst ourselves and were happy. Now when we fight with you we can only die!"

He rose to go. "Tuan," he said, "you remember the girl that man Bulangi had? Her that caused all the trouble?"

"Yes," said Ford. "What of her?"

"She grew thin and could not work. Then Bulangi, who is a thief and a pig-eater, gave her to me for fifty dollars. I sent her amongst my women to grow fat. I wanted to hear the sound of her laughter, but she must have been bewitched, and . . . she died two days ago. Nay, Tuan. Why do you speak bad words? I am old—that is true—but why should I not like the sight of a young face and the sound of a young voice in my house?" He paused, and then added with a little mournful laugh, "I am like a white man talking too much of what is not men's talk when they speak to one another."

And he went off looking very sad.

The crowd massed in a semicircle before the steps of "Almayer's Folly," swayed silently backwards and forwards, and opened out before the group of white-robed and turbaned men advancing through the grass towards the house. Abdulla walked first, supported by Reshid and followed by all the Arabs in Sambir. As they entered the lane made by the respectful throng there was a subdued murmur of voices, where the word "Mati" was the only one distinctly audible. Abdulla stopped and looked round slowly.

"Is he dead?" he asked.

"May you live!" answered the crowd in one shout, and then there succeeded a breathless silence.

Abdulla made a few paces forward and found himself for the last time face to face with his old enemy. Whatever he might have been once he was not dangerous now, lying stiff and lifeless in the tender light of the early day. The only white man on the east coast was dead, and his soul, delivered from the trammels of his earthly folly, stood now in the presence of Infinite Wisdom. On the upturned face there was that serene look which follows the sudden relief from anguish and pain, and it testified silently before the cloudless heaven that the man lying there under the gaze of indifferent eyes had been permitted to forget before he died.

Abdulla looked down sadly at this Infidel he had fought so long and had bested so many times. Such was the reward of the Faithful! Yet in the Arab's old heart there was a feeling of regret for that thing gone out of his life. He was leaving fast behind him friendships, and enmities, successes, and disappointments—all that makes up a life; and before him was only the end. Prayer would fill up the remainder of the days allotted to the True Believer! He took in his hand the beads that hung at his waist.

"I found him here, like this, in the morning," said Ali, in a low and awed voice.

Abdulla glanced coldly once more at the serene face.

"Let us go," he said, addressing Reshid.

And as they passed through the crowd that fell back before them, the beads in Abdulla's hand clicked, while in a solemn whisper he breathed out piously the name of Allah! The Merciful! The Compassionate!

Karain: A Memory

W E KNEW him in those unprotected days when we were content to hold in our hands our lives and our property. None of us, I believe, has any property now, and I hear that many, negligently, have lost their lives; but I am sure that the few who survive are not yet so dim-eyed as to miss in the befogged respectability of their newspapers the intelligence of various native risings in the Eastern Archipelago. Sunshine gleams between the lines of those short paragraphs—sunshine and the glitter of the sea. A strange name wakes up memories; the printed words scent the smoky atmosphere of to-day faintly, with the subtle and penetrating perfume as of land breezes breathing through the starlight of bygone nights; a signal fire gleams like a jewel on the high brow of a sombre cliff; great trees, the advanced sentries of immense forests, stand watchful and still over sleeping stretches of open water; a line of white surf thunders on an empty beach, the shallow water foams on the reefs; and green islets scattered through the calm of noonday lie upon the level of a polished sea, like a handful of emeralds on a buckler of steel.

There are faces too—faces dark, truculent, and smiling; the frank audacious faces of men barefooted, well armed and noiseless. They thronged the narrow length of our schooner's decks with their ornamented and barbarous crowd, with the variegated colours of checkered sarongs, red turbans, white jackets, embroideries; with the gleam of scabbards, gold rings, charms, armlets, lance blades, and jewelled handles of their weapons. They had an independent bearing, resolute eyes, a restrained manner; and we seem yet to hear their soft voices speaking of battles, travels, and escapes; boasting with composure, joking quietly; sometimes in well-bred murmurs extolling their own valour, our generosity; or celebrating with loyal enthusiasm the virtues of their ruler. We remember the faces, the eyes, the voices, we see again the gleam of silk and metal; the murmuring stir of that crowd, brilliant, festive, and martial; and we seem to feel the touch of friendly brown hands that, after one short grasp, return to rest on a chased hilt. They were Karain's people—a devoted following. Their movements hung on his lips; they read their thoughts in his eyes; he murmured to them nonchalantly of life and death, and they accepted his words humbly, like gifts of fate. They were all free men, and when speaking to him said, "Your slave." On his passage voices died out as though he had walked guarded by silence; awed whispers followed him. They called him their war-chief. He was the ruler of three villages on a narrow plain; the master of an insignificant foothold on the earth— of a conquered foothold that, shaped like a young moon, lay ignored between the hills and the sea.

From the deck of our schooner, anchored in the middle of the bay, he indicated by a theatrical sweep of his arm along the jagged outline of the hills the whole of his domain; and the ample movement seemed to drive back its limits, augmenting it suddenly into something so immense and vague that for a moment it appeared to be bounded only by the sky. And really, looking at that place, landlocked from the sea and shut off from the land by the precipitous slopes of mountains, it was difficult to believe in the existence of any neighbourhood. It was still, complete, unknown, and full of a life that went on stealthily with a troubling effect of solitude; of a life that seemed unaccountably empty of anything that would stir the thought, touch the heart, give a hint of the ominous sequence of days. It appeared to us a land without memories, regrets, and hopes; a land where nothing could survive the coming of the night, and where each sunrise, like a dazzling act of special creation, was disconnected from the eve and the morrow.

Karain swept his hand over it. "All mine!" He struck the deck with his long staff; the gold head flashed like a falling star; very close behind him a silent old fellow in a richly embroidered black jacket alone of all the Malays around did not follow the masterful gesture with a look. He did not even lift his eyelids. He bowed his head behind his master, and without stirring held hilt up over his right shoulder a long blade in a silver scabbard. He was there on duty, but without curiosity, and seemed weary, not with age, but with the possession of a burdensome secret of existence. Karain, heavy and proud, had a lofty pose and breathed calmly. It was our first visit, and we looked about curiously.

The bay was like a bottomless pit of intense light. The circular sheet of water reflected a luminous sky, and the shores enclosing it made an opaque ring of earth floating in an emptiness of transparent blue. The hills, purple and arid, stood out heavily on the sky: their summits seemed to fade into a coloured tremble as of ascending vapour; their steep sides were streaked with the green of narrow ravines; at their foot lay rice-fields, plantain-patches, yellow sands. A torrent wound about like a dropped thread. Clumps of fruit-trees marked the villages; slim palms put their nodding heads together above the low houses; dried palm-leaf roofs shone afar, like roofs of gold, behind the dark colonnades of tree-trunks; figures passed vivid and vanishing; the smoke of fires stood upright above the masses of flowering bushes; bamboo fences glittered, running away in broken lines between the fields. A sudden cry on the shore sounded plaintive in the distance, and ceased abruptly, as if stifled in the downpour of sunshine. A puff of breeze made a flash of darkness on the smooth water, touched our faces, and became forgotten. Nothing moved. The sun blazed down into a shadowless hollow of colours and stillness.

It was the stage where, dressed splendidly for his part, he strutted, incomparably dignified, made important by the power he had to awaken an absurd expectation of something heroic going to take place —a burst of action or song—upon the vibrating tone of a wonderful sunshine. He was ornate and disturbing, for one could not imagine what depth of horrible void such an elaborate front could be worthy to hide. He was not masked—there was too much life in him, and a mask is only a lifeless thing; but he presented himself essentially as an actor, as a human being aggressively disguised. His smallest acts were prepared and unexpected, his speeches grave, his sentences ominous like hints and complicated like arabesques. He was treated with a solemn respect accorded in the irreverent West only to the monarchs of the stage, and he accepted the profound homage with a sustained dignity seen nowhere else but behind the footlights and in the condensed falseness of some grossly tragic situation. It was almost impossible to remember who he was—only a petty chief of a conveniently isolated corner of Mindanao, where we could in comparative safety break the law against the traffic in firearms and ammunition with the natives. What would happen should one of the moribund Spanish gun-boats be suddenly galvanized into a flicker of active life did not trouble us, once we were inside the bay—so completely did it appear out of the reach of a meddling world; and besides, in those days we were imaginative enough to look with a kind of joyous equanimity on any chance there was of being quietly hanged somewhere out of the way of diplomatic remonstrance. As to Karain, nothing could happen to him unless what happens to all—failure and death; but his quality was to appear clothed in the illusion of unavoidable success. He seemed too effective, too necessary there, too much of an essential condition for the existence of his land and his people, to be destroyed by anything short of an earthquake. He summed up his race, his country, the elemental force of ardent life, of tropical nature. He had its luxuriant strength, its fascination; and, like it, he carried the seed of peril within.

In many successive visits we came to know his stage well—the purple semicircle of hills, the slim trees leaning over houses, the yellow sands, the streaming green of ravines. All that had the crude and blended colouring, the appropriateness almost excessive, the suspicious immobility of a painted scene; and it enclosed so perfectly the accomplished acting of his amazing pretences that the rest of the world seemed shut out forever from the gorgeous spectacle. There could be nothing outside. It was as if the earth had gone on spinning, and had left that crumb of its surface alone in space. He appeared utterly cut off from everything but the sunshine, and that even seemed to be made for him alone. Once when asked what was on the other side of the hills, he said, with a meaning smile, "Friends and enemies—many enemies; else why should I buy your rifles and powder?" He was always like this—word-perfect in his part, playing up faithfully to the mysteries and certitudes of his surroundings. "Friends and enemies"—nothing else. It was impalpable and vast. The earth had indeed rolled away from under his land, and he, with his handful of people, stood surrounded by a silent tumult as of contending shades. Certainly no sound came from outside. "Friends and enemies!" He might have added, "and memories," at least as far as he himself was concerned; but he neglected to make that point then. It made itself later on, though; but it was after the daily performance—in the wings, so to speak, and with the lights out. Meantime he filled the stage with barbarous dignity. Some ten years ago he had led his people—a scratch lot of wandering Bugis—to the conquest of the bay, and now in his august care they had forgotten all the past, and had lost all concern for the future. He gave them wisdom, advice, reward, punishment, life or death, with the same serenity of attitude and voice. He understood irrigation and the art of war—the qualities of weapons and the craft of boatbuilding. He could conceal his heart; had more endurance; he could swim longer, and steer a canoe better than any of his people; he could shoot straighter, and negotiate more tortuously than any man of his race I knew. He was an adventurer of the sea, an outcast, a ruler—and my very good friend. I wish him a quick death in a stand-up fight, a death in sunshine; for he had known remorse and power, and no man can demand more from life. Day after day he appeared before us, incomparably faithful to the illusions of the stage, and at sunset the night descended upon him quickly, like a falling curtain. The seamed hills became black shadows towering high upon a clear sky; above them the glittering confusion of stars resembled a mad turmoil stilled by a gesture; sounds ceased, men slept, forms vanished—and the reality of the universe alone remained—a marvellous thing of darkness and glimmers.

But it was at night that he talked openly, forgetting the exactions of his stage. In the daytime there were affairs to be discussed in state. There were at first between him and me his own splendour, my shabby suspicions, and the scenic landscape that intruded upon the reality of our lives by its motionless fantasy of outline and colour. His followers thronged round him; above his head the broad blades of their spears made a spiked halo of iron points, and they hedged him from humanity by the shimmer of silks, the gleam of weapons, the excited and respectful hum of eager voices. Before sunset he would take leave with ceremony, and go off sitting under a red umbrella, and escorted by a score of boats. All the paddles flashed and struck together with a mighty splash that reverberated loudly in the monumental amphitheatre of hills. A broad stream of dazzling foam trailed behind the flotilla. The canoes appeared very black on the white hiss of water; turbaned heads swayed back and forth; a multitude of arms in crimson and yellow rose and fell with one movement; the spearmen upright in the bows of canoes had variegated sarongs and gleaming shoulders like bronze statues; the muttered strophes of the paddlers' song ended periodically in a plaintive shout. They diminished in the distance; the song ceased; they swarmed on the beach in the long shadows of the western hills. The sunlight lingered on the purple crests, and we could see him leading the way to his stockade, a burly bareheaded figure walking far in advance of a straggling *cortège*, and swinging regularly an ebony staff taller than himself. The darkness deepened fast; torches gleamed fitfully, passing behind bushes; a long hail or two trailed in the silence of the evening; and at last the night stretched its smooth veil over the shore, the lights, and the voices.

Then, just as we were thinking of repose, the watchmen of the schooner would hail a splash of paddles away in the starlit gloom of the bay; a voice would respond in cautious tones, and our serang, putting his head down the open skylight, would inform us without surprise, "That Rajah, he coming. He here now." Karain appeared noiselessly in the doorway of the little cabin. He was simplicity itself then; all in white; muffled about his head; for arms only a kriss with a plain buffalo-horn handle, which he would politely conceal within a fold of his sarong before stepping over the threshold. The old sword-bearer's face, the worn-out and mournful face so covered with wrinkles that it seemed to look out through the meshes of a fine dark net, could be seen close above his shoulders. Karain never moved without that attendant, who stood or squatted close at his back. He had a dislike of an open space behind him. It was more than a dislike—it resembled fear, a nervous preoccupation of what went on where he could not see. This, in view of the evident and fierce loyalty that surrounded him, was inexplicable. He was there alone in the midst of devoted men; he was safe from neighbourly ambushes, from fraternal ambitions; and yet more than one of our visitors had assured us that their ruler could not bear to be alone. They said, "Even when he eats and sleeps there is always one on the watch near him who has strength and weapons." There was indeed always one near him, though our informants had no conception of that watcher's strength and weapons, which were both shadowy and terrible. We knew, but only later on, when we had heard the story. Meantime we noticed that, even during the most important interviews, Karain would often give a start, and interrupting his discourse, would sweep his arm back with a sudden movement, to feel whether the old fellow was there. The old fellow, impenetrable and weary, was always there. He shared his food, his repose, and his thoughts; he knew his plans, guarded his secrets; and, impassive behind his master's agitation, without stirring the least bit, murmured above his head in a soothing tone some words difficult to catch.

It was only on board the schooner, when surrounded by white faces, by unfamiliar sights and sounds, that Karain seemed to forget the strange obsession that wound like a black thread through the gorgeous pomp of his public life. At night we treated him in a free and easy manner, which just stopped short of slapping him on the back, for there are liberties one must not take with a Malay. He said himself that on such occasions he was only a private gentleman coming to see other gentlemen whom he supposed as well born as himself. I fancy that to the last he believed us to be emissaries of Government, darkly official persons furthering by our illegal traffic some dark scheme of high statecraft. Our denials and protestations were unavailing. He only smiled with discreet politeness and inquired about the Queen. Every visit began with that inquiry; he was insatiable of details; he was fascinated by the holder of a sceptre the shadow of which, stretching from the westward over the earth and over the seas, passed far beyond his own hand's-breadth of conquered land. He multiplied questions; he could never know enough of the Monarch of whom he spoke with wonder and chivalrous respect—with a kind of affectionate awe! Afterwards, when we had learned that he was the son of a woman who had many years ago ruled a small Bugis state, we came to suspect that the memory of his mother (of whom he spoke with enthusiasm) mingled somehow in his mind with the image he tried to form for himself of the far-off Queen whom he called Great, Invincible, Pious, and Fortunate. We had to invent details at last to satisfy his craving curiosity; and our loyalty must be pardoned, for we tried to make them fit for his august and resplendent ideal. We talked. The night slipped over us, over the still schooner, over the sleeping land, and over the sleepless sea that thundered amongst the reefs outside the bay. His paddlers, two trustworthy men, slept in the canoe at the foot of our side-ladder. The old confidant, relieved from duty, dozed on his heels, with his back against the companion-doorway; and Karain sat squarely in the ship's wooden armchair, under the slight sway of the cabin lamp, a cheroot between his dark fingers, and a glass of lemonade before him. He was amused by the fizz of the thing, but after a sip or two would let it get flat, and with a courteous wave of his hand ask for a fresh bottle. He decimated our slender stock; but we did not begrudge it to him, for, when he began, he talked well. He must have been a great Bugis dandy in his time, for even then (and when we knew him he was no longer young) his splendour was spotlessly neat, and he dyed his hair a light shade of brown. The quiet dignity of his bearing transformed the dim-lit cuddy of the schooner into an audience-hall. He talked of inter-island politics with an ironic and melancholy shrewdness. He had travelled much, suffered not a little, intrigued, fought. He knew native Courts, European Settlements, the forests, the sea, and, as he said himself, had spoken in his time to many great men. He liked to talk with me because I had known some of these men: he seemed to think that I could understand him, and, with a fine confidence, assumed that I, at least, could appreciate how much greater he was himself. But he preferred to talk of his native country—a small Bugis state on the island of Celebes. I had visited it some time before, and he asked eagerly for news. As men's names came up in conversation he would say, "We swam against one another when we were boys"; or, "We hunted the deer together—he could use the noose and the spear as well as I." Now and then his big dreamy eyes would roll restlessly; he frowned or smiled, or he would become pensive, and, staring in silence, would nod slightly for a time at some regretted vision of the past.

His mother had been the ruler of a small semi-independent state on the sea-coast at the head of the Gulf of Boni. He spoke of her with pride. She had been a woman resolute in affairs of state and of her own heart. After the death of her first husband, undismayed by the turbulent opposition of the chiefs, she married a rich trader, a Korinchi man of no family. Karain was her son by that second marriage, but his unfortunate descent had apparently nothing to do with his exile. He said nothing as to its cause, though once he let slip with a sigh, "Ha! my land will not feel any more the weight of my body." But he related willingly the story of his wanderings, and told us all about the conquest of the bay. Alluding to the people beyond the hills, he would murmur gently, with a careless wave of the hand, "They came over the hills once to fight us, but those who got away never came again." He thought for a while, smiling to himself. "Very few got away," he added, with proud serenity. He cherished the recollections of his successes; he had an exulting eagerness for endeavour; when he talked, his aspect was warlike, chivalrous, and uplifting. No wonder his people admired him. We saw him once walking in daylight amongst the houses of the settlement. At the doors of huts groups of women turned to look after him, warbling softly, and with gleaming eyes; armed men stood out of the way, submissive and erect; others approached from the side, bending their backs to address him humbly; an old woman stretched out a draped lean arm—"Blessings on thy head!" she cried from a dark doorway; a fiery-eyed man showed above the low fence of a plantain-patch a streaming face, a bare breast scarred in two places, and bellowed out pantingly after him, "God give victory to our master!" Karain walked fast, and with firm long strides; he answered greetings right and left by quick piercing glances. Children ran forward between the houses, peeped fearfully round corners; young boys kept up with him, gliding between bushes: their eyes gleamed through the dark leaves. The old sword-bearer, shouldering the silver scabbard, shuffled hastily at his heels with bowed head, and his eyes on the ground. And in the midst of a great stir they passed swift and absorbed, like two men hurrying through a great solitude.

In his council hall he was surrounded by the gravity of armed chiefs, while two long rows of old headmen dressed in cotton stuffs squatted on their heels, with idle arms hanging over their knees. Under the thatch roof supported by smooth columns, of which each one had cost the life of a straight-stemmed young palm, the scent of flowering hedges drifted in warm waves. The sun was sinking. In the open courtyard suppliants walked through the gate, raising, when yet far off, their joined hands above bowed heads, and bending low in the bright stream of sunlight. Young girls, with flowers in their laps, sat under the wide-spreading boughs of a big tree. The blue smoke of wood fires spread in a thin mist above the high-pitched roofs of houses that had glistening walls of woven reeds, and all round them rough wooden pillars under the sloping eaves. He dispensed justice in the shade; from a high seat he gave orders, advice, reproof. Now and then the hum of approbation rose louder, and idle spearmen that lounged listlessly against the posts, looking at the girls, would turn their heads slowly. To no man had been given the shelter of so much respect, confidence, and awe. Yet at times he would lean forward and appear to listen as for a far-off note of discord, as if expecting to hear some faint voice, the sound of light footsteps; or he would start half up in his seat, as though he had been familiarly touched on the shoulder. He glanced back with apprehension; his aged follower whispered inaudibly at his ear; the chiefs turned their eyes away in silence, for the old wizard, the man who could command ghosts and send evil spirits against enemies, was speaking low to their ruler. Around the short stillness of the open place the trees rustled faintly, the soft laughter of girls playing with the flowers rose in clear bursts of joyous sound. At the end of upright spear-shafts the long tufts of dyed horse-hair waved crimson and filmy in the gust of wind; and beyond the blaze of hedges the brook of limpid quick water ran invisible and loud under the drooping grass of the bank, with a great murmur, passionate and gentle.

After sunset, far across the fields and over the bay, clusters of torches could be seen burning under the high roofs of the council shed. Smoky red flames swayed on high poles, and the fiery blaze flickered over faces, clung to the smooth trunks of palm-trees, kindled bright sparks on the rims of metal dishes standing on fine floor-mats. That obscure adventurer feasted like a king. Small groups of men crouched in tight circles round the wooden platters; brown hands hovered over snowy heaps of rice. Sitting upon a rough couch apart from the others, he leaned on his elbow with inclined head; and near him a youth improvised in a high tone a song that celebrated his valour and wisdom. The singer rocked himself to and fro, rolling frenzied eyes; old women hobbled about with dishes, and men, squatting low, lifted their heads to listen gravely without ceasing to eat. The song of triumph vibrated in the night, and the stanzas rolled out mournful and fiery like the thoughts of a hermit. He silenced it with a sign, "Enough!" An owl hooted far away, exulting in the delight of deep gloom in dense foliage; overhead lizards ran in the attap thatch, calling softly; the dry leaves of the roof rustled; the rumour of mingled voices grew louder suddenly. After a circular and startled glance, as of a man waking up abruptly to the sense of danger, he would throw himself back, and under the downward gaze of the old sorcerer take up, wide-eyed, the slender thread of his dream. They watched his moods; the swelling rumour of animated talk subsided like a wave on a sloping beach. The chief is pensive. And above the spreading whisper of lowered voices only a light rattle of weapons would be heard, a single louder word distinct and alone, or the grave ring of a big brass tray.

CHAPTER THREE

For two years at short intervals we visited him. We came to like him, to trust him, almost to admire him. He was plotting and preparing a war with patience, with foresight—with a fidelity to his purpose and with a steadfastness of which I would have thought him racially incapable. He seemed fearless of the future, and in his plans displayed a sagacity that was only limited by his profound ignorance of the rest of the world. We tried to enlighten him, but our attempts to make clear the irresistible nature of the forces which he desired to arrest failed to discourage his eagerness to strike a blow for his own primitive ideas. He did not understand us, and replied by arguments that almost drove one to desperation by their childish shrewdness. He was absurd and unanswerable. Sometimes we caught glimpses of a sombre, glowing fury within him—a brooding and vague sense of wrong, and a concentrated lust of violence which is dangerous in a native. He raved like one inspired. On one occasion, after we had been talking to him late in his campong, he jumpd up. A great, clear fire blazed in the grove; lights and shadows danced together between the trees; in the still night bats flitted in and out of the boughs like fluttering flakes of denser darkness. He snatched the sword from the old man, whizzed it out of the scabbard, and thrust the point into the earth. Upon the thin, upright blade the silver hilt, released, swayed before him like something alive. He stepped back a pace, and in a deadened tone spoke fiercely to the vibrating steel: "If there is virtue in the fire, in the iron, in the hand that forged thee, in the words spoken over thee, in the desire of my heart, and in the wisdom of thy makers,—then we shall be victorious together!" He drew it out, looked along the edge. "Take," he said over his shoulder to the old sword-bearer. The other, unmoved on his hams, wiped the point with a corner of his sarong, and returning the weapon to its scabbard, sat nursing it on his knees without a single look upwards. Karain, suddenly very calm, reseated himself with dignity. We gave up remonstrating after this, and let him go his way to an honourable disaster. All we could do for him was to see to it that the powder was good for the money and the rifles serviceable, if old.

But the game was becoming at last too dangerous; and if we, who had faced it pretty often, thought little of the danger, it was decided for us by some very respectable people sitting safely in counting-houses that the risks were too great, and that only one more trip could be made. After giving in the usual way many misleading hints as to our destination, we slipped away quietly, and after a very quick passage entered the bay. It was early morning, and even before the anchor went to the bottom the schooner was surrounded by boats.

The first thing we heard was that Karain's mysterious sword-bearer had died a few days ago. We did not attach much importance to the news. It was certainly difficult to imagine Karain without his inseparable follower; but the fellow was old, he had never spoken to one of us, we hardly ever had heard the sound of his voice; and we had come to look upon him as upon something inanimate, as a part of our friend's trappings of state—like that sword he had carried, or the fringed red umbrella displayed during an official progress. Karain did not visit us in the afternoon as usual. A message of greeting and a present of fruit and vegetables came off for us before sunset. Our friend paid us like a banker, but treated us like a prince. We sat up for him till midnight. Under the stern awning bearded Jackson jingled an old guitar and sang, with an execrable accent, Spanish love-songs; while young Hollis and I, sprawling on the deck, had a game of chess by the light of a cargo lantern. Karain did not appear. Next day we were busy unloading, and heard that the Rajah was unwell. The expected invitation to visit him ashore did not come. We sent friendly messages, but, fearing to intrude upon some secret council, remained on board. Early on the third day we had landed all the powder and rifles, and also a six-pounder brass gun with its carriage which we had subscribed together for a present for our friend. The afternoon was sultry. Ragged edges of black clouds peeped over the hills, and invisible thunderstorms circled outside, growling like wild beasts. We got the schooner ready for sea, intending to leave next morning at daylight. All day a merciless sun blazed down into the bay, fierce and pale, as if at white heat. Nothing moved on the land. The beach was empty, the villages seemed deserted; the trees far off stood in unstirring clumps, as if painted; the white smoke of some invisible bush-fire spread itself low over the shores of the bay like a settling fog. Late in the day three of Karain's chief men, dressed in their best and armed to the teeth, came off in a canoe, bringing a case of dollars. They were gloomy and languid, and told us they had not seen their Rajah for five days. No one had seen him! We settled all accounts, and after shaking hands in turn and in profound silence, they descended one after another into their boat, and were paddled to the shore, sitting close together, clad in vivid colours, with hanging heads: the gold embroideries of their jackets flashed dazzlingly as they went away gliding on the smooth water, and not one of them looked back once. Before sunset the growling clouds carried with a rush the ridge of hills, and came tumbling down the inner slopes. Everything disappeared; black whirling vapours filled the bay, and in the midst of them the schooner swung here and there in the shifting gusts of wind. A single clap of thunder detonated in the hollow with a violence that seemed capable of bursting into small pieces the ring of high land, and a warm deluge descended. The wind died out. We panted in the close cabin; our faces streamed; the bay outside hissed as if boiling; the water fell in perpendicular shafts as heavy as lead; it swished about the deck, poured off the spars, gurgled, sobbed, splashed, murmured in the blind night. Our lamp burned low. Hollis, stripped to the waist, lay stretched out on the lockers, with closed eyes and motionless like a despoiled corpse; at his head Jackson twanged the guitar, and gasped out in sighs a mournful dirge about hopeless love and eyes like stars. Then we heard startled voices on deck crying in the rain, hurried footsteps overhead, and suddenly Karain appeared in the doorway of the cabin. His bare breast and his face glistened in the light; his sarong, soaked, clung about his legs; he had his sheathed kriss in his left hand; and wisps of wet hair, escaping from under his red kerchief, stuck over his eyes and down his cheeks. He stepped in with a headlong stride and looking over his shoulder like a man pursued. Hollis turned on his side quickly and opened his eyes. Jackson clapped his big hand over the strings and the jingling vibration died suddenly. I stood up.

"We did not hear your boat's hail!" I exclaimed.

"Boat! The man's swum off," drawled out Hollis from the locker. "Look at him!"

He breathed heavily, wild-eyed, while we looked at him in silence. Water dripped from him, made a dark pool, and ran crookedly across the cabin floor. We could hear Jackson, who had gone out to drive away our Malay seamen from the doorway of the companion; he swore menacingly in the patter of a heavy shower, and there was a great commotion on deck. The watchmen, scared out of their wits by the glimpse of a shadowy figure leaping over the rail, straight out of the night as it were, had alarmed all hands.

Then Jackson, with glittering drops of water on his hair and beard, came back looking angry, and Hollis, who, being the youngest of us, assumed an indolent superiority, said without stirring, "Give him a dry sarong—give him mine; it's hanging up in the bathroom." Karain laid the kriss on the table, hilt inwards, and murmured a few words in a strangled voice.

"What's that?" asked Hollis, who had not heard.

"He apologizes for coming in with a weapon in his hand," I said, dazedly.

"Ceremonious beggar. Tell him we forgive a friend . . . on such a night," drawled out Hollis. "What's wrong?"

Karain slipped the dry sarong over his head, dropped the wet one at his feet, and stepped out of it. I pointed to the wooden armchair—his armchair. He sat down very straight, said "Ha!" in a strong voice; a short shiver shook his broad frame. He looked over his shoulder uneasily, turned as if to speak to us, but only stared in a curious blind manner, and again looked back. Jackson bellowed out, "Watch well on deck there!" heard a faint answer from above, and reaching out with his foot slammed-to the cabin door.

"All right now," he said.

Karain's lips moved slightly. A vivid flash of lightning made the two round sternports facing him glimmer like a pair of cruel and phosphorescent eyes. The flame of the lamp seemed to wither into brown dust for an instant, and the looking-glass over the little sideboard leaped out behind his back in a smooth sheet of livid light. The roll of thunder came near, crashed over us; the schooner trembled, and the great voice went on, threatening terribly, into the distance. For less than a minute a furious shower rattled on the decks. Karain looked slowly from face to face, and then the silence became so profound that we all could hear distinctly the two chronometers in my cabin ticking along with unflagging speed against one another.

And we three, strangely moved, could not take our eyes from him. He had become enigmatical and touching, in virtue of that mysterious cause that had driven him through the night, and through the thunderstorm to the shelter of the schooner's cuddy. Not one of us doubted that we were looking at a fugitive, incredible as it appeared to us. He was haggard, as though he had not slept for weeks; he had become lean, as though he had not eaten for days. His cheeks were hollow, his eyes sunk, the muscles of his chest and arms twitched slightly as if after an exhausting contest. Of course it had been a long swim off to the schooner; but his face showed another kind of fatigue, the tormented weariness, the anger and the fear of a struggle against a thought, an idea—against something that cannot be grappled, that never rests—a shadow, a nothing, unconquerable and immortal, that preys upon life. We knew it as though he had shouted it at us. His chest expanded time after time, as if it could not contain the beating of his heart. For a moment he had the power of the possessed—the power to awaken in the beholders wonder, pain, pity, and a fearful near sense of things invisible, of things dark and mute, that surround the loneliness of mankind. His eyes roamed about aimlessly for a moment, then became still. He said with effort—

"I came here . . . I leaped out of my stockade as after a defeat. I ran in the night. The water was black. I left him calling on the edge of black water. . . . I left him standing alone on the beach. I swam . . . he called out after me . . . I swam . . ."

He trembled from head to foot, sitting very upright and gazing straight before him. Left whom? Who called? We did not know. We could not understand. I said at all hazards—

"Be firm."

The sound of my voice seemed to steady him into a sudden rigidity, but otherwise he took no notice. He seemed to listen, to expect something for a moment, then went on—

"He cannot come here—therefore I sought you. You men with white faces who despise the invisible voices. He cannot abide your unbelief and your strength."

He was silent for a while, then exclaimed softly—

"Oh! the strength of unbelievers!"

"There's no one here but you—and we three," said Hollis, quietly. He reclined with his head supported on elbow and did not budge.

"I know," said Karain. "He has never followed me here. Was not the wise man ever by my side? But since the old wise man, who knew of my trouble, has died, I have heard the voice every night. I shut myself up—for many days—in the dark. I can hear the sorrowful murmurs of women, the whisper of the wind, of the running waters; the clash of weapons in the hands of faithful men, their footsteps—and his voice! . . . Near . . . So! In my ear! I felt him near . . . His breath passed over my neck. I leaped out without a cry. All about me men slept quietly. I ran to the sea. He ran by my side without footsteps, whispering, whispering old words—whispering into my ear in his old voice. I ran into the sea; I swam off to you, with my kriss between my teeth. I, armed, I fled before a breath—to you. Take me away to your land. The wise old man has died, and with him is gone the power of his words and charms. And I can tell no one. No one. There is no one here faithful enough and wise enough to know. It is only near you, unbelievers, that my trouble fades like a mist under the eye of day."

He turned to me.

"With you I go!" he cried in a contained voice. "With you, who know so many of us. I want to leave this land—my people . . . and him—there!"

He pointed a shaking finger at random over his shoulder. It was hard for us to bear the intensity of that undisclosed distress. Hollis stared at him hard. I asked gently—

"Where is the danger?"

"Everywhere outside this place," he answered, mournfully. "In every place where I am. He waits for me on the paths, under the trees, in the place where I sleep—everywhere but here."

He looked round the little cabin, at the painted beams, at the tarnished varnish of bulkheads; he looked round as if appealing to all its shabby strangeness, to the disorderly jumble of unfamiliar things that belong to an inconceivable life of stress, of power, of endeavour, of unbelief—to the strong life of white men, which rolls on irresistible and hard on the edge of outer darkness. He stretched out his arms as if to embrace it and us. We waited. The wind and rain had ceased, and the stillness of the night round the schooner was as dumb and complete as if a dead world had been laid to rest in a grave of clouds. We expected him to speak. The necessity within him tore at his lips. There are those who say that a native will not speak to a white man. Error. No man will speak to his master; but to a wanderer and a friend, to him who does not come to teach or to rule, to him who asks for nothing and accepts all things, words are spoken by the camp-fires, in the shared solitude of the sea, in riverside villages, in resting-places surrounded by forests—words are spoken that take no account of race or colour. One heart speaks—another one listens; and the earth, the sea, the sky, the passing wind and the stirring leaf, hear also the futile tale of the burden of life.

He spoke at last. It is impossible to convey the effect of his story. It is undying, it is but a memory, and its vividness cannot be made clear to another mind, any more than the vivid emotions of a dream. One must have seen his innate splendour, one must have known him before—looked at him then. The wavering gloom of the little cabin; the breathless stillness outside, through which only the lapping of water against the schooner's sides could be heard; Hollis's pale face, with steady dark eyes; the energetic head of Jackson held up between two big palms, and with the long yellow hair of his beard flowing over the strings of the guitar lying on the table; Karain's upright and motionless pose, his tone—all this made an impression that cannot be forgotten. He faced us across the table. His dark head and bronze torso appeared above the tarnished slab of wood, gleaming and still as if cast in metal. Only his lips moved, and his eyes glowed, went out, blazed again, or stared mournfully. His expressions came straight from his tormented heart. His words sounded low, in a sad murmur as of running water; at times they rang loud like the clash of a war-gong—or trailed slowly like weary travellers—or rushed forward with the speed of fear.

CHAPTER FOUR

This is, imperfectly, what he said—

"It was after the great trouble that broke the alliance of the four states of Wajo. We fought amongst ourselves, and the Dutch watched from afar till we were weary. Then the smoke of their fire-ships was seen at the mouth of our rivers, and their great men came in boats full of soldiers to talk to us of protection and peace. We answered with caution and wisdom, for our villages were burnt, our stockades weak, the people weary, and the weapons blunt. They came and went; there had been much talk, but after they went away everything seemed to be as before, only their ships remained in sight from our coast, and very soon their traders came amongst us under a promise of safety. My brother was a Ruler, and one of those who had given the promise. I was young then, and had fought in the war, and Pata Matara had fought by my side. We had shared hunger, danger, fatigue, and victory. His eyes saw my danger quickly, and twice my arm had preserved his life. It was his destiny. He was my friend. And he was great amongst us—one of those who were near my brother, the Ruler. He spoke in council, his courage was great, he was the chief of many villages round the great lake that is in the middle of our country as the heart is in the middle of a man's body. When his sword was carried into a campong in advance of his coming, the maidens whispered wonderingly under the fruit-trees, the rich men consulted together in the shade, and a feast was made ready with rejoicing and songs. He had the favour of the Ruler and the affecton of the poor. He loved war, deer hunts, and the charms of women. He was the possessor of jewels, of lucky weapons, and of men's devotion. He was a fierce man; and I had no other friend.

"I was the chief of a stockade at the mouth of the river, and collected tolls for my brother from the passing boats. One day I saw a Dutch trader go up the river. He went up with three boats, and no toll was demanded from him, because the smoke of Dutch war-ships stood out from the open sea, and we were too weak to forget treaties. He went up under the promise of safety, and my brother gave him protection. He said he came to trade. He listened to our voices, for we are men who speak openly and without fear; he counted the number of our spears, he examined the trees, the running waters, the grasses of the bank, the slopes of our hills. He went up to Matara's country and obtained permission to build a house. He traded and planted. He despised our joys, our thoughts, and our sorrows. His face was red, his hair like flame, and his eyes pale, like a river mist; he moved heavily, and spoke with a deep voice; he laughed aloud like a fool, and knew no courtesy in his speech. He was a big, scornful man, who looked into women's faces and put his hand on the shoulders of free men as though he had been a noble-born chief. We bore with him. Time passed.

"Then Pata Matara's sister fled from the campong and went to live in the Dutchman's house. She was a great and wilful lady: I had seen her once carried high on slaves' shoulders amongst the people, with uncovered face, and I had heard all men say that her beauty was extreme, silencing the reason and ravishing the heart of the beholders. The people were dismayed; Matara's face was blackened with that disgrace, for she knew she had been promised to another man. Matara went to the Dutchman's house, and said, 'Give her up to die—she is the daughter of chiefs.' The white man refused and shut himself up, while his servants kept guard night and day with loaded guns. Matara raged. My brother called a council. But the Dutch ships were near, and watched our coast greedily. My brother said, 'If he dies now our land will pay for his blood. Leave him alone till we grow stronger and the ships are gone.' Matara was wise; he waited and watched. But the white man feared for her life and went away.

"He left his house, his plantations, and his goods! He departed, armed and menacing, and left all—for her! She had ravished his heart!

From my stockade I saw him put out to sea in a big boat. Matara and I watched him from the fighting platform behind the pointed stakes. He sat cross-legged, with his gun in his hands, on the roof at the stern of his prau. The barrel of his rifle glinted aslant before his big red face. The broad river was stretched under him—level, smooth, shining, like a plain of silver; and his prau, looking very short and black from the shore, glided along the silver plain and over into the blue of the sea.

"Thrice Matara, standing by my side, called aloud her name with grief and imprecations. He stirred my heart. It leaped three times; and three times with the eye of my mind I saw in the gloom within the enclosed space of the prau a woman with streaming hair going away from her land and her people. I was angry—and sorry. Why? And then I also cried out insults and threats. Matara said, 'Now they have left our land their lives are mine. I shall follow and strike—and, alone, pay the price of blood.' A great wind was sweeping toward the setting sun over the empty river. I cried, 'By your side I will go!' He lowered his head in sign of assent. It was his destiny. The sun had set, and the trees swayed their boughs with a great noise above our heads.

"On the third night we two left our land together in a trading prau.

"The sea met us—the sea, wide, pathless, and without voice. A sailing prau leaves no track. We went south. The moon was full; and, looking up, we said to one another, 'When the next moon shines as this one, we shall return and they will be dead.' It was fifteen years ago. Many moons have grown full and withered and I have not seen my land since. We sailed south; we overtook many praus; we examined the creeks and the bays; we saw the end of our coast, of our island—a steep cape over a disturbed strait, where drift the shadows of shipwrecked praus and drowned men clamour in the night. The wide sea was all round us now. We saw a great mountain burning in the midst of water; we saw thousands of islets scattered like bits of iron fired from a big gun; we saw a long coast of mountain and lowlands stretching away in sunshine from west to east. It was Java. We said, 'They are there; their time is near, and we shall return or die cleansed from dishonour.'

"We landed. Is there anything good in that country? The paths run straight and hard and dusty. Stone campongs, full of white faces, are surrounded by fertile fields, but every man you meet is a slave. The rulers live under the edge of a foreign sword. We ascended mountains, we traversed valleys; at sunset we entered villages. We asked everyone, 'Have you seen such a white man?' Some stared; others laughed; women gave us food, sometimes, with fear and respect, as though we had been distracted by the visitation of God; but some did not understand our language, and some cursed us, or, yawning, asked with contempt the reason of our quest. Once, as we were going away, an old man called after us, 'Desist!'

"We went on. Concealing our weapons, we stood humbly aside before the horsemen on the road; we bowed low in the courtyards of chiefs who were no better than slaves. We lost ourselves in the fields, in the jungle; and one night, in a tangled forest, we came upon a place where crumbling old walls had fallen amongst the trees, and where strange stone idols—carved images of devils with many arms and legs, with snakes twined round their bodies, with twenty heads and holding a hundred swords—seemed to live and threaten in the light of our camp-fire. Nothing dismayed us. And on the road, by every fire, in resting-places, we always talked of her and of him. Their time was near. We spoke of nothing else. No! not of hunger, thirst, weariness, and faltering hearts. No! we spoke of him and her! Of her! And we thought of them—of her! Matara brooded by the fire. I sat and thought and thought, till suddenly I could see again the image of a woman, beautiful, and young, and great and proud, and tender, going away from her land and her people. Matara said, 'When we find them we shall kill her first to cleanse the dishonour—then the man must die.' I would say, 'It shall be so; it is your vengeance.' He stared long at me with his big sunken eyes.

"We came back to the coast. Our feet were bleeding, our bodies thin. We slept in rags under the shadow of stone enclosures; we prowled, soiled and lean, about the gateways of white men's courtyards. Their hairy dogs barked at us, and their servants shouted from afar, 'Begone!' Low-born wretches, that keep watch over the streets of stone campongs, asked us who we were. We lied, we cringed, we smiled with hate in our hearts, and we kept looking here, looking there for them— for the white man with hair like flame, and for her, for the woman who had broken faith, and therefore must die. We looked. At last in every woman's face I thought I could see hers. We ran swiftly. No! Sometimes Matara would whisper, 'Here is the man,' and we waited, crouching. He came near. It was not the man—those Dutchmen are all alike. We suffered the anguish of deception. In my sleep I saw her face, and was both joyful and sorry. . . . Why? . . . I seemed to hear a whisper near me. I turned swiftly. She was not there! And as we trudged wearily from stone city to stone city I seemed to hear a light footstep near me. A time came when I heard it always, and I was glad. I thought, walking dizzy and weary in sunshine on the hard paths of white men—I thought, She is there—with us! . . . Matara was sombre. We were often hungry.

"We sold the carved sheaths of our krisses—the ivory sheaths with golden ferules. We sold the jewelled hilts. But we kept the blades— for them. The blades that never touch but kill—we kept the blades for her. . . . Why? She was always by our side. . . . We starved. We begged. We left Java at last.

"We went West, we went East. We saw many lands, crowds of strange faces, men that live in trees and men who eat their old people. We cut rattans in the forest for a handful of rice, and for a living swept the decks of big ships and heard curses heaped upon our heads. We toiled in villages; we wandered upon the seas with the Bajow people, who have no country. We fought for pay; we hired ourselves to work for Goram men, and were cheated; and under the orders of rough white faces we dived for pearls in barren bays, dotted with black rocks, upon a coast of sand and desolation. And everywhere we watched, we listened, we asked. We asked traders, robbers, white men. We heard jeers, mockery, threats—words of wonder and words of contempt. We never knew rest; we never thought of home, for our work was not done. A year passed, then another. I ceased to count the number of nights, of moons, of years. I watched over Matara. He had my last handful of rice; if there was water enough for one he drank it; I covered him up when he shivered with cold; and when the hot sickness came upon him I sat sleepless through many nights and fanned his face. He was a fierce man, and my friend. He spoke of her with fury in the daytime, with sorrow in the dark; he remembered her in health, in sickness. I said nothing; but I saw her every day— always! At first I saw only her head, as of a woman walking in the low mist on a river bank. Then she sat by the fire. I saw her! I looked at her! She had tender eyes and a ravishing face. I murmured to her in the night. Matara said sleepily sometimes, 'To whom are you talking? Who is there?' I answered quickly, 'No one' . . . It was a lie! She never left me. She shared the warmth of our fire, she sat on my couch of leaves, she swam on the sea to follow me. . . . I saw her! . . . I tell you I saw her long black hair spread behind her upon the moonlit water as she struck out with bare arms by the side of a swift prau. She was beautiful, she was faithful, and in the silence of foreign countries she spoke to me very low in the language of my people. No one saw her; no one heard her; she was mine only! In daylight she moved with a swaying walk before me upon the weary paths; her figure was straight and flexible like the stem of a slender tree; the heels of her feet were round and polished like shells of eggs; with her round arm she made signs. At night she looked into my face. And she was sad! Her eyes were tender and frightened; her voice soft and pleading. Once I murmured to her, 'You shall not die,' and she smiled . . . ever after she smiled! . . . She gave me courage to bear weariness and hardships. Those were times of pain, and she soothed me. We wandered patient in our search. We knew deception, false hopes; we knew captivity, sickness, thirst, misery, despair . . . Enough! We found them! . . ."

He cried out the last words and paused. His face was impassive, and he kept still like a man in a trance. Hollis sat up quickly, and spread his elbows on the table. Jackson made a brusque movement, and accidentally touched the guitar. A plaintive resonance filled the cabin with confused vibrations and died out slowly. Then Karain began to speak again. The restrained fierceness of his tone seemed to rise like a voice from outside, like a thing unspoken but heard; it filled the cabin and enveloped in its intense and deadened murmur the motionless figure in the chair.

"We were on our way to Atjeh, where there was war; but the vessel ran on a sandbank, and we had to land in Delli. We had earned a little money, and had bought a gun from some Selangore traders; only one gun, which was fired by the spark of a stone: Matara carried it. We landed. Many white men lived there, planting tobacco on conquered plains, and Matara . . . But no matter. He saw him! . . . The Dutchman! . . . At last! . . . We crept and watched. Two nights and a day we watched. He had a house—a big house in a clearing in the midst of his fields; flowers and bushes grew around; there were narrow paths of yellow earth between the cut grass, and thick hedges to keep people out. The third night we came armed, and lay behind a hedge.

"A heavy dew seemed to soak through our flesh and made our very entrails cold. The grass, the twigs, the leaves, covered with drops of water, were gray in the moonlight. Matara, curled up in the grass, shivered in his sleep. My teeth rattled in my head so loud that I was afraid the noise would wake up all the land. Afar, the watchmen of white men's houses struck wooden clappers and hooted in the darkness. And, as every night, I saw her by my side. She smiled no more! . . . The fire of anguish burned in my breast, and she whispered to me with compassion, with pity, softly—as women will; she soothed the pain of my mind; she bent her face over me—the face of a woman who ravishes the hearts and silences the reason of men. She was all mine, and no one could see her—no one of living mankind! Stars shone through her bosom, through her floating hair. I was overcome with regret, with tenderness, with sorrow. Matara slept . . . Had I slept? Matara was shaking me by the shoulder, and the fire of the sun was drying the grass, the bushes, the leaves. It was day. Shreds of white mist hung between the branches of trees.

"Was it night or day? I saw nothing again till I heard Matara breathe quickly where he lay, and then outside the house I saw her. I saw them both. They had come out. She sat on a bench under the wall, and twigs laden with flowers crept high above her head, hung over her hair. She had a box on her lap, and gazed into it, counting the increase of her pearls. The Dutchman stood by looking on; he smiled down at her; his white teeth flashed; the hair on his lip was like two twisted flames. He was big and fat, and joyous, and without fear. Matara tipped fresh priming from the hollow of his palm, scraped the flint with his thumb-nail, and gave the gun to me. To me! I took it . . . O fate!

"He whispered into my ear, lying on his stomach, 'I shall creep close and then amok . . . let her die by my hand. You take aim at the fat swine there. Let him see me strike my shame off the face of the earth—and then . . . you are my friend—kill with a sure shot.' I said nothing; there was no air in my chest—there was no air in the world. Matara had gone suddenly from my side. The grass nodded. Then a bush rustled. She lifted her head.

"I saw her! The consoler of sleepless nights, of weary days; the companion of troubled years! I saw her! She looked straight at the place where I crouched. She was there as I had seen her for years—a faithful wanderer by my side. She looked with sad eyes and had smiling lips; she looked at me . . . Smiling lips! Had I not promised that she should not die!

"She was far off and I felt her near. Her touch caressed me, and her voice murmured, whispered above me, around me, 'Who shall be thy companion, who shall console thee if I die?' I saw a flowering thicket to the left of her stir a little . . . Matara was ready . . . I cried aloud—'Return!'

"She leaped up; the box fell; the pearls streamed at her feet. The big Dutchman by her side rolled menacing eyes through the still sunshine. The gun went up to my shoulder. I was kneeling and I was firm—firmer than the trees, the rocks, the mountains. But in front of the steady long barrel the fields, the house, the earth, the sky swayed to and fro like shadows in a forest on a windy day. Matara burst out of the thicket; before him the petals of torn flowers whirled high as if driven by a tempest. I heard her cry; I saw her spring with open arms in front of the white man. She was a woman of my country and of noble blood. They are so! I heard her shriek of anguish and fear— and all stood still! The fields, the house, the earth, the sky stood still —while Matara leaped at her with uplifted arm. I pulled the trigger, saw a spark, heard nothing; the smoke drove back into my face, and then I could see Matara roll over head first and lie with stretched arms at her feet. Ha! A sure shot! The sunshine fell on my back colder than the running water. A sure shot! I flung the gun after the shot. Those two stood over the dead man as though they had been bewitched by a charm. I shouted at her, 'Live and remember!' Then for a time I stumbled about in a cold darkness.

"Behind me there were great shouts, the running of many feet;

strange men surrounded me, cried meaningless words into my face, pushed me, dragged me, supported me . . . I stood before the big Dutchman: he stared as if bereft of his reason. He wanted to know, he talked fast, he spoke of gratitude, he offered me food, shelter, gold —he asked many questions. I laughed in his face. I said, 'I am a Korinchi traveller from Perak over there, and know nothing of that dead man. I was passing along the path when I heard a shot, and your senseless people rushed out and dragged me here.' He lifted his arms, he wondered, he could not believe, he could not understand, he clamoured in his own tongue! She had her arms clasped round his neck, and over her shoulder stared back at me with wide eyes. I smiled and looked at her; I smiled and waited to hear the sound of her voice. The white man asked her suddenly, 'Do you know him?' I listened—my life was in my ears! She looked at me long, she looked at me with unflinching eyes, and said aloud, 'No! I never saw him before.' . . . What! Never before? Had she forgotten already? Was it possible? Forgotten already—after so many years—so many years of wandering, of companionship, of trouble, of tender words! Forgotten already! . . . I tore myself out from the hands that held me and went away without a word . . . They let me go.

"I was weary. Did I sleep? I do not know. I remember walking upon a broad path under a clear starlight; and that strange country seemed so big, the rice-fields so vast, that, as I looked around, my head swam with the fear of space. Then I saw a forest. The joyous starlight was heavy upon me. I turned off the path and entered the forest, which was very sombre and very sad."

CHAPTER FIVE

Karain's tone had been getting lower and lower, as though he had been going away from us, till the last words sounded faint but clear, as if shouted on a calm day from a very great distance. He moved not. He stared fixedly past the motionless head of Hollis, who faced him, as still as himself. Jackson had turned sideways, and with elbow on the table shaded his eyes with the palm of his hand. And I looked on, surprised and moved; I looked at that man, loyal to a vision, betrayed by his dream, spurned by his illusion, and coming to us un- believers for help—against a thought. The silence was profound; but it seemed full of noiseless phantoms, of things sorrowful, shadowy, and mute, in whose invisible presence the firm, pulsating beat of the two ship's chronometers ticking off steadily the seconds of Greenwich Time seemed to me a protection and a relief. Karain stared stonily; and looking at his rigid figure, I thought of his wanderings, of that obscure

Odyssey of revenge, of all the men that wander amongst illusions; of the illusions as restless as men; of the illusions faithful, faithless; of the illusions that give joy, that give sorrow, that give pain, that give peace; of the invincible illusions that can make life and death appear serene, inspiring, tormented, or ignoble.

A murmur was heard; that voice from outside seemed to flow out of a dreaming world into the lamplight of the cabin. Karain was speaking.

"I lived in the forest.

"She came no more. Never! Never once! I lived alone. She had forgotten. It was well. I did not want her; I wanted no one. I found an abandoned house in an old clearing. Nobody came near. Sometimes I heard in the distance the voices of people going along a path. I slept; I rested; there was wild rice, water from a running stream—and peace! Every night I sat alone by my small fire before the hut. Many nights passed over my head.

"Then, one evening, as I sat by my fire after having eaten, I looked down on the ground and began to remember my wanderings. I lifted my head. I had heard no sound, no rustle, no footsteps—but I lifted my head. A man was coming towards me across the small clearing. I waited. He came up without a greeting and squatted down into the firelight. Then he turned his face to me. It was Matara. He stared at me fiercely with his big sunken eyes. The night was cold; the heat died suddenly out of the fire, and he stared at me. I rose and went away from there, leaving him by the fire that had no heat.

"I walked all that night, all next day, and in the evening made up a big blaze and sat down—to wait for him. He had not come into the light. I heard him in the bushes here and there, whispering, whispering. I understood at last—I had heard the words before, 'You are my friend—kill with a sure shot.'

"I bore it as long as I could—then leaped away, as on this very night I leaped from my stockade and swam to you. I ran—I ran crying like a child left alone and far from the houses. He ran by my side, without footsteps, whispering, whispering—invisible and heard. I sought people—I wanted men around me! Men who had not died! And again we two wandered. I sought danger, violence, and death. I fought in the Atjeh war, and a brave people wondered at the valiance of a stranger. But we were two; he warded off the blows . . . Why? I wanted peace, not life. And no one could see him; no one knew—I dared tell no one. At times he would leave me, but not for long; then he would return and whisper or stare. My heart was torn with a strange fear, but could not die. Then I met an old man.

"You all knew him. People here called him my sorcerer, my servant and sword-bearer; but to me he was father, mother, protection, refuge and peace. When I met him he was returning from a pilgrimage, and I heard him intoning the prayer of sunset. He had gone to the holy place with his son, his son's wife, and a little child; and on their return, by the favour of the Most High, they all died: the strong man, the young mother, the little child—they died; and the old man reached his country alone. He was a pilgrim serene and pious, very wise and very lonely. I told him all. For a time we lived together. He said over me words of compassion, of wisdom, of prayer. He warded from me the shade of the dead. I begged him for a charm that would make me safe. For a long time he refused; but at last, with a sigh and a smile, he gave me one. Doubtless he could command a spirit stronger than the unrest of my dead friend, and again I had peace; but I had become restless, and a lover of turmoil and danger. The old man never left me. We travelled together. We were welcomed by the great; his wisdom and my courage are remembered where your strength, O white men, is forgotten! We served the Sultan of Sula. We fought the Spaniards. There were victories, hopes, defeats, sorrow, blood, women's tears . . . What for? . . . We fled. We collected wanderers of a warlike race and came here to fight again. The rest you know. I am the ruler of a conquered land, a lover of war and danger, a fighter and a plotter. But the old man has died, and I am again the slave of the dead. He is not here now to drive away the reproachful shade—to silence the lifeless voice! The power of his charm has died with him. And I know fear; and I hear the whisper, 'Kill! kill! kill!' . . . Have I not killed enough? . . ."

For the first time that night a sudden convulsion of madness and rage passed over his face. His wavering glances darted here and there like scared birds in a thunderstorm. He jumped up, shouting—

"By the spirits that drink blood: by the spirits that cry in the night: by all the spirits of fury, misfortune, and death, I swear—some day I will strike into every heart I meet—I . . ."

He looked so dangerous that we all three leaped to our feet, and Hollis, with the back of his hand, sent the kriss flying off the table. I believe we shouted together. It was a short scare, and the next moment he was again composed in his chair, with three white men standing over him in rather foolish attitudes. We felt a little ashamed of ourselves. Jackson picked up the kriss, and, after an inquiring glance at me, gave it to him. He received it with a stately inclination of the head and stuck it in the twist of his sarong, with punctilious care to give his weapon a pacific position. Then he looked up at us with an austere smile. We were abashed and reproved. Hollis sat sideways on the table and, holding his chin in his hand, scrutinized him in pensive silence. I said—

"You must abide with your people. They need you. And there is forgetfulness in life. Even the dead cease to speak in time."

"Am I a woman, to forget long years before an eyelid has had the time to beat twice?" he exclaimed, with bitter resentment. He startled me. It was amazing. To him his life—that cruel mirage of love and peace—seemed as real, as undeniable, as theirs would be to any saint, philosopher, or fool of us all. Hollis muttered—

"You won't soothe him with your platitudes."

Karain spoke to me.

"You know us. You have lived with us. Why?—we cannot know; but you understand our sorrows and our thoughts. You have lived with my people, and you understand our desires and our fears. With you I will go. To your land—to your people. To your people, who live in unbelief; to whom day is day, and night is night—nothing more, because you understand all things seen, and despise all else! To your land of unbelief, where the dead do not speak, where every man is wise, and alone—and at peace!"

"Capital description," murmured Hollis, with the flicker of a smile.

Karain hung his head.

"I can toil, and fight—and be faithful," he whispered, in a weary tone, "but I cannot go back to him who waits for me on the shore. No! Take me with you . . . Or else give me some of your strength— of your unbelief . . . A charm! . . ."

He seemed utterly exhausted.

"Yes, take him home," said Hollis, very low, as if debating with himself. "That would be one way. The ghosts there are in society, and talk affably to ladies and gentlemen, but would scorn a naked human being—like our princely friend. . . . Naked . . . Flayed! I should say. I am sorry for him. Impossible—of course. The end of all this shall be," he went on, looking up at us—"the end of this shall be, that some day he will run amuck amongst his faithful subjects and send *ad patres* ever so many of them before they make up their minds to the disloyalty of knocking him on the head."

I nodded. I thought it more than probable that such would be the end of Karain. It was evident that he had been hunted by his thought along the very limit of human endurance, and very little more pressing was needed to make him swerve over into the form of madness peculiar to his race. The respite he had during the old man's life made the return of the torment unbearable. That much was clear.

He lifted his head suddenly; we had imagined for a moment that he had been dozing.

"Give me your protection—or your strength!" he cried. "A charm . . . a weapon!"

Again his chin fell on his breast. We looked at him, then looked at

one another with suspicious awe in our eyes, like men who come unexpectedly upon the scene of some mysterious disaster. He had given
himself up to us; he had thrust into our hands his errors and his torment, his life and his peace; and we did not know what to do with that
problem from the outer darkness. We three white men, looking at the
Malay, could not find one word to the purpose amongst us—if indeed there existed a word that could solve that problem. We pondered,
and our hearts sank. We felt as though we three had been called to
the very gate of Infernal Regions to judge, to decide the fate of a
wanderer coming suddenly from a world of sunshine and illusions.

"By Jove, he seems to have a great idea of our power," whispered
Hollis, hopelessly. And then again there was a silence, the feeble plash
of water, the steady tick of chronometers. Jackson, with bare arms
crossed, leaned his shoulders against the bulkhead of the cabin. He was
bending his head under the deck beam; his fair beard spread out magnificently over his chest; he looked colossal, ineffectual, and mild.
There was something lugubrious in the aspect of the cabin; the air in
it seemed to become slowly charged with the cruel chill of helplessness,
with the pitiless anger of egoism against the incomprehensible form of
an intruding pain. We had no idea what to do; we began to resent
bitterly the hard necessity to get rid of him.

Hollis mused, muttered suddenly with a short laugh, "Strength . . .
Protection . . . Charm." He slipped off the table and left the cuddy
without a look at us. It seemed a base desertion. Jackson and I exchanged indignant glances. We could hear him rummaging in his
pigeon-hole of a cabin. Was the fellow actually going to bed? Karain
sighed. It was intolerable!

Then Hollis reappeared, holding in both hands a small leather box.
He put it down gently on the table and looked at us with a queer
gasp, we thought, as though he had from some cause become speechless for a moment, or were ethically uncertain about producing that
box. But in an instant the insolent and unerring wisdom of his youth
gave him the needed courage. He said, as he unlocked the box with
a very small key, "Look as solemn as you can, you fellows."

Probably we looked only surprised and stupid, for he glanced over
his shoulder, and said angrily—

"This is no play; I am going to do something for him. Look serious.
Confound it! . . . Can't you lie a little . . . for a friend!"

Karain seemed to take no notice of us, but when Hollis threw open
the lid of the box his eyes flew to it—and so did ours. The quilted
crimson satin of the inside put a violent patch of colour into the
sombre atmosphere; it was something positive to look at—it was
fascinating.

CHAPTER SIX

Hollis looked smiling into the box. He had lately made a dash home through the Canal. He had been away six months, and only joined us again just in time for this last trip. We had never seen the box before. His hands hovered above it; and he talked to us ironically, but his face became as grave as though he were pronouncing a powerful incantation over the things inside.

"Every one of us," he said, with pauses that somehow were more offensive than his words—"every one of us, you'll admit, has been haunted by some woman . . . And . . . as to friends . . . dropped by the way . . . Well! . . . ask yourselves . . ."

He paused. Karain stared. A deep rumble was heard high up under the deck. Jackson spoke seriously—

"Don't be so beastly cynical."

"Ah! You are without guile," said Hollis, sadly. "You will learn . . . Meantime this Malay has been our friend . . ."

He repeated several times thoughtfully, "Friend . . . Malay. Friend, Malay," as though weighing the words against one another, then went on more briskly—

"A good fellow—a gentleman in his way. We can't, so to speak, turn our backs on his confidence and belief in us. Those Malays are easily impressed—all nerves, you know—therefore . . ."

He turned to me sharply.

"You know him best," he said, in a practical tone. "Do you think he is fanatical—I mean very strict in his faith?"

I stammered in profound amazement that "I did not think so."

"It's on account of its being a likeness—an engraved image," muttered Hollis, enigmatically, turning to the box. He plunged his fingers into it. Karain's lips were parted and his eyes shone. We looked into the box.

There were there a couple of reels of cotton, a packet of needles, a bit of silk ribbon, dark blue; a cabinet photograph, at which Hollis stole a glance before laying it on the table face downwards. A girl's portrait, I could see. There were, amongst a lot of various small objects, a bunch of flowers, a narrow white glove with many buttons, a slim packet of letters carefully tied up. Amulets of white men! Charms and talismans! Charms that keep them straight, that drive them crooked, that have the power to make a young man sigh, an old man smile. Potent things that procure dreams of joy, thoughts of regret; that soften hard hearts, and can temper a soft one to the hardness of steel. Gifts of heaven—things of earth . . .

Hollis rummaged in the box.

And it seemed to me, during that moment of waiting, that the cabin of the schooner was becoming filled with a stir invisible and living as of subtle breaths. All the ghosts driven out of the unbelieving West by men who pretend to be wise and alone and at peace—all the homeless ghosts of an unbelieving world—appeared suddenly round the figure of Hollis bending over the box; all the exiled and charming shades of loved women; all the beautiful and tender ghosts of ideals, remembered, forgotten, cherished, execrated; all the cast-out and reproachful ghosts of friends admired, trusted, traduced, betrayed, left dead by the way—they all seemed to come from the inhospitable regions of the earth to crowd into the gloomy cabin, as though it had been a refuge and, in all the unbelieving world, the only place of avenging belief. . . . It lasted a second—all disappeared. Hollis was facing us alone with something small that glittered between his fingers. It looked like a coin.

"Ah! here it is," he said.

He held it up. It was a sixpence—a Jubilee sixpence. It was gilt; it had a hole punched near the rim. Hollis looked towards Karain.

"A charm for our friend," he said to us. "The thing itself is of great power—money, you know—and his imagination is struck. A loyal vagabond; if only his puritanism doesn't shy at a likeness . . ."

We said nothing. We did not know whether to be scandalized, amused, or relieved. Hollis advanced towards Karain, who stood up as if startled, and then, holding the coin up, spoke in Malay.

"This is the image of the Great Queen, and the most powerful thing the white men know," he said, solemnly.

Karain covered the handle of his kriss in sign of respect, and stared at the crowned head.

"The Invincible, the Pious," he muttered.

"She is more powerful than Suleiman the Wise, who commanded the genii, as you know," said Hollis, gravely. "I shall give this to you."

He held the sixpence in the palm of his hand, and looking at it thoughtfully, spoke to us in English.

"She commands a spirit, too—the spirit of her nation; a masterful, conscientious, unscrupulous, unconquerable devil . . . that does a lot of good—incidentally . . . a lot of good . . . at times—and wouldn't stand any fuss from the best ghost out for such a little thing as our friend's shot. Don't look thunderstruck, you fellows. Help me to make him believe—everything's in that."

"His people will be shocked," I murmured.

Hollis looked fixedly at Karain, who was the incarnation of the very essence of still excitement. He stood rigid, with head thrown back; his eyes rolled wildly, flashing; the dilated nostrils quivered.

"Hang it all!" said Hollis at last, "he is a good fellow. I'll give him something that I shall really miss."

He took the ribbon out of the box, smiled at it scornfully, then with a pair of scissors cut out a piece from the palm of the glove.

"I shall make him a thing like those Italian peasants wear, you know."

He sewed the coin in the delicate leather, sewed the leather to the ribbon, tied the ends together. He worked with haste. Karain watched his fingers all the time.

"Now then," he said—then stepped up to Karain. They looked close into one another's eyes. Those of Karain stared in a lost glance, but Hollis's seemed to grow darker and looked out masterful and compelling. They were in violent contrast together—one motionless and the colour of bronze, the other dazzling white and lifting his arms, where the powerful muscles rolled slightly under a skin that gleamed like satin. Jackson moved near with the air of a man closing up to a chum in a tight place. I said impressively, pointing to Hollis——

"He is young, but he is wise. Believe him!"

Karain bent his head: Hollis threw lightly over it the dark-blue ribbon and stepped back.

"Forget, and be at peace!" I cried.

Karain seemed to wake up from a dream. He said, "Ha!" shook himself as if throwing off a burden. He looked round with assurance. Someone on deck dragged off the skylight cover, and a flood of light fell into the cabin. It was morning already.

"Time to go on deck," said Jackson.

Hollis put on a coat, and we went up, Karain leading.

The sun had risen beyond the hills, and their long shadows stretched far over the bay in the pearly light. The air was clear, stainless, and cool. I pointed at the curved line of yellow sands.

"He is not there," I said, emphatically, to Karain. "He waits no more. He has departed forever."

A shaft of bright hot rays darted into the bay between the summits of two hills, and the water all round broke out as if by magic into a dazzling sparkle.

"No! He is not there waiting," said Karain, after a long look over the beach. "I do not hear him," he went on, slowly. "No!"

He turned to us.

"He has departed again—forever!" he cried.

We assented vigorously, repeatedly, and without compunction. The great thing was to impress him powerfully; to suggest absolute safety—the end of all trouble. We did our best; and I hope we affirmed our faith in the power of Hollis's charm efficiently enough to put the matter beyond the shadow of a doubt. Our voices rang around him joyously in the still air, and above his head the sky, pellucid, pure, stainless, arched its tender blue from shore to shore and over the bay, as if to envelop the water, the earth, and the man in the caress of its light.

The anchor was up, the sails hung still, and a half-a-dozen big boats were seen sweeping over the bay to give us a tow out. The paddlers in the first one that came alongside lifted their heads and saw their ruler standing amongst us. A low murmur of surprise arose—then a shout of greeting.

He left us, and seemed straightway to step into the glorious splendour of his stage, to wrap himself in the illusion of unavoidable success. For a moment he stood erect, one foot over the gangway, one hand on the hilt of his kriss, in a martial pose; and, relieved from the fear of outer darkness, he held his head high, he swept a serene look over his conquered foothold on the earth. The boats far off took up the cry of greeting; a great clamour rolled on the water; the hills echoed it, and seemed to toss back at him the words invoking long life and victories.

He descended into a canoe, and as soon as he was clear of the side we gave him three cheers. They sounded faint and orderly after the wild tumult of his loyal subjects, but it was the best we could do. He stood up in the boat, lifted up both his arms, then pointed to the infallible charm. We cheered again; and the Malays in the boats stared—very much puzzled and impressed. I wondered what they thought; what he thought; . . . what the reader thinks?

We towed out slowly. We saw him land and watch us from the beach. A figure approached him humbly but openly—not at all like a ghost with a grievance. We could see other men running towards him. Perhaps he had been missed? At any rate there was a great stir. A group formed itself rapidly near him, and he walked along the sands, followed by a growing *cortège* and kept nearly abreast of the schooner. With our glasses we could see the blue ribbon on his neck and a patch of white on his brown chest. The bay was waking up. The smokes of morning fires stood in faint spirals higher than the heads of palms; people moved between the houses; a herd of buffaloes galloped clumsily across a green slope; the slender figures of boys brandishing sticks appeared black and leaping in the long grass; a coloured line of women, with water bamboos on their heads, moved swaying through a thin grove of fruit-trees. Karain stopped in the midst of his men and waved his hand; then, detaching himself from the splendid group, walked alone to the water's edge and waved his hand again. The schooner passed out to sea between the steep headlands that shut in the bay, and at the same instant Karain passed out of our life forever.

But the memory remains. Some years afterwards I met Jackson, in the Strand. He was magnificent as ever. His head was high above the crowd. His beard was gold, his face red, his eyes blue; he had a wide-brimmed gray hat and no collar or waistcoat; he was inspiring; he had just come home—had landed that very day! Our meeting caused an eddy in the current of humanity. Hurried people would run against us, then walk round us, and turn back to look at that giant. We tried to compress seven years of life into seven exclamations; then, suddenly appeased, walked sedately along, giving one another the news of yesterday. Jackson gazed about him, like a man who looks for landmarks, then stopped before Bland's window. He always had a passion for firearms; so he stopped short and contemplated the row of weapons, perfect and severe, drawn up in a line behind the black-framed panes. I stood by his side. Suddenly he said—

"Do you remember Karain?"

I nodded.

"The sight of all this made me think of him," he went on, with his face near the glass . . . and I could see another man, powerful and bearded, peering at him intently from amongst the dark and polished tubes that can cure so many illusions. "Yes; it made me think of him," he continued, slowly. "I saw a paper this morning; they are fighting over there again. He's sure to be in it. He will make it hot for the caballeros. Well, good luck to him, poor devil! He was perfectly stunning."

We walked on.

"I wonder whether the charm worked—you remember Hollis's charm, of course. If it did . . . never was a sixpence wasted to better advantage! Poor devil! I wonder whether he got rid of that friend of his. Hope so. . . . Do you know, I sometimes think that——"

I stood still and looked at him.

"Yes . . . I mean, whether the thing was so, you know . . . whether it really happened to him. . . . What do you think?"

"My dear chap," I cried, "you have been too long away from home. What a question to ask! Only look at all this."

A watery gleam of sunshine flashed from the west and went out between two long lines of walls; and then the broken confusion of roofs, the chimney-stacks, the gold letters sprawling over the fronts of houses, the sombre polish of windows, stood resigned and sullen under the falling gloom. The whole length of the street, deep as a well and narrow like a corridor, was full of a sombre and ceaseless stir. Our ears were filled by a headlong shuffle and beat of rapid footsteps and an underlying rumour—a rumour vast, faint, pulsating, as of panting breaths, of beating hearts, of gasping voices. Innumerable eyes stared straight in front, feet moved hurriedly, blank faces flowed, arms swung.

Over all, a narrow ragged strip of smoky sky wound about between the high roofs, extended and motionless, like a soiled streamer flying above the rout of a mob.

"Ye-e-e-s," said Jackson, meditatively.

The big wheels of hansoms turned slowly along the edge of sidewalks; a pale-faced youth strolled, overcome by weariness, by the side of his stick and with the tails of his overcoat flapping gently near his heels; horses stepped gingerly on the greasy pavement, tossing their heads; two young girls passed by, talking vivaciously and with shining eyes; a fine old fellow strutted, red-faced, stroking a white moustache; and a line of yellow boards with blue letters on them approached us slowly, tossing on high behind one another like some queer wreckage adrift upon a river of hats.

"Ye-e-es," repeated Jackson. His clear blue eyes looked about, contemptuous, amused and hard, like the eyes of a boy. A clumsy string of red, yellow, and green omnibuses rolled swaying, monstrous and gaudy; two shabby children ran across the road; a knot of dirty men with red neckerchiefs round their bare throats lurched along, discussing filthily; a ragged old man with a face of despair yelled horribly in the mud the name of a paper; while far off, amongst the tossing heads of horses, the dull flash of harnesses, the jumble of lustrous panels and roofs of carriages, we could see a policeman, helmeted and dark, stretching out a rigid arm at the crossing of the streets.

"Yes; I see it," said Jackson, slowly. "It is there; it pants, it runs, it rolls; it is strong and alive; it would smash you if you didn't look out; but I'll be hanged if it is yet as real to me as . . . as the other thing . . . say, Karain's story."

I think that, decidedly, he had been too long away from home.

The Planter of Malata

CHAPTER ONE

IN THE private editorial office of the principal newspaper in a great colonial city two men were talking. They were both young. The stouter of the two, fair, and with more of an urban look about him, was the editor and part-owner of the important newspaper.

The other's name was Renouard. That he was exercised in his mind about something was evident on his fine bronzed face. He was a lean, lounging, active man. The journalist continued the conversation.

"And so you were dining yesterday at old Dunster's."

He used the word old not in the endearing sense in which it is sometimes applied to intimates, but as a matter of sober fact. The Dunster in question was old. He had been an eminent colonial states-man, but had now retired from active politics after a tour in Europe and a lengthy stay in England, during which he had had a very good press indeed. The colony was proud of him.

"Yes. I dined there," said Renouard. "Young Dunster asked me just as I was going out of his office. It seemed to be like a sudden thought. And yet I can't help suspecting some purpose behind it. He was very pressing. He swore that his uncle would be very pleased to see me. Said his uncle had mentioned lately that the granting to me of the Malata concession was the last act of his official life."

"Very touching. The old boy sentimentalises over the past now and then."

"I really don't know why I accepted," continued the other. "Senti-ment does not move me very easily. Old Dunster was civil to me of course, but he did not even inquire how I was getting on with my silk plants. Forgot there was such a thing probably. I must say there were more people there than I expected to meet. Quite a big party."

"I was asked," remarked the newspaper man. "Only I couldn't go. But when did you arrive from Malata?"

"I arrived yesterday at daylight. I am anchored out there in the bay —off Garden Point. I was in Dunster's office before he had finished reading his letters. Have you ever seen young Dunster reading his letters? I had a glimpse of him through the open door. He holds the paper in both hands, hunches his shoulders up to his ugly ears, and brings his long nose and thick lips on to it like a sucking apparatus. A commercial monster."

"Here we don't consider him a monster," said the newspaper man looking at his visitor thoughtfully.

"Probably not. You are used to seeing his face and the faces of others. I don't know how it is that, when I come to town, the appearance of the people in the street strikes me with such force. They seem so awfully expressive."

"And not charming."

"Well—no. Not as a rule. The effect is forcible without being clear. . . . I know that you think it's because of my solitary manner of life away there."

"Yes. I do think so. It is demoralising. You don't see any one for months at a stretch. You're leading an unhealthy life."

The other hardly smiled and murmured the admission that true enough it was a good eleven months since he had been in town last.

"You see," insisted the other. "Solitude works like a sort of poison. And then you perceive suggestions in faces—mysterious and forcible, that no sound man would be bothered with. Of course you do."

Geoffrey Renouard did not tell his journalist friend that the suggestions of his own face, the face of a friend, bothered him as much as the others. He detected a degrading quality in the touches of age which every day adds to a human countenance. They moved and disturbed him, like the signs of a horrible inward travail which was frightfully apparent to the fresh eye he had brought from his isolation in Malata, where he had settled after five strenuous years of adventure and exploration.

"It's a fact," he said, "that when I am at home in Malata I see no one consciously. I take the plantation boys for granted."

"Well, and we here take the people in the streets for granted. And that's sanity."

The visitor said nothing to this for fear of engaging a discussion. What he had come to seek in the editorial office was not controversy, but information. Yet somehow he hesitated to approach the subject. Solitary life makes a man reticent in respect of anything in the nature of gossip, which those to whom chatting about their kind is an everyday exercise regard as the commonest use of speech.

"You very busy?" he asked.

The Editor making red marks on a long slip of printed paper threw the pencil down.

"No. I am done. Social paragraphs. This office is the place where everything is known about everybody—including even a great deal of nobodies. Queer fellows drift in and out of this room. Waifs and strays from home, from up-country, from the Pacific. And, by the way, last time you were here you picked up one of that sort for your assistant—didn't you?"

"I engaged an assistant only to stop your preaching about the evils of solitude," said Renouard hastily; and the pressman laughed at the half-resentful tone. His laugh was not very loud, but his plump person shook all over. He was aware that his younger friend's deference to his advice was based only on an imperfect belief in his wisdom—or his sagacity. But it was he who had first helped Renouard in his plans of exploration: the five-years' programme of scientific adventure, of work, of danger and endurance, carried out with such distinction and rewarded modestly with the lease of Malata island by the frugal colonial government. And this reward, too, had been due to the journalist's advocacy with word and pen—for he was an influential man in the community. Doubting very much if Renouard really liked him, he was himself without great sympathy for a certain side of that man which he could not quite make out. He only felt it obscurely to be his real personality—the true—and, perhaps, the absurd. As, for instance, in that case of the assistant. Renouard had given way to the arguments of his friend and backer—the argument against the unwholesome effect of solitude, the argument for the safety of companionship even if quarrelsome. Very well. In this docility he was sensible and even likeable. But what did he do next? Instead of taking counsel as to the choice with his old backer and friend, and a man, besides, knowing everybody employed and unemployed on the pavements of the town, this extraordinary Renouard suddenly and almost surreptitiously picked up a fellow—God knows who—and sailed away with him back to Malata in a hurry; a proceeding obviously rash and at the same time not quite straight. That was the sort of thing. The secretly unforgiving journalist laughed a little longer and then ceased to shake all over.

"Oh, yes. About that assistant of yours. . . ."

"What about him?" said Renouard, after waiting a while, with a shadow of uneasiness on his face.

"Have you nothing to tell me of him?"

"Nothing except. . . ." Incipient grimness vanished out of Renouard's aspect and his voice, while he hesitated as if reflecting seriously before he changed his mind. "No. Nothing whatever."

"You haven't brought him along with you by chance—for a change."

The Planter of Malata stared, then shook his head, and finally murmured carelessly: "I think he's very well where he is. But I wish you could tell me why young Dunster insisted so much on my dining with his uncle last night. Everybody knows I am not a society man."

The Editor exclaimed at so much modesty. Didn't his friend know that he was their one and only explorer—that he was the man experimenting with the silk plant. . . .

"Still, that doesn't tell me why I was invited yesterday. For young Dunster never thought of this civility before. . . ."

"Our Willie," said the popular journalist, "never does anything without a purpose, that's a fact."

"And to his uncle's house too!"

"He lives there."

"Yes. But he might have given me a feed somewhere else. The extraordinary part is that the old man did not seem to have anything special to say. He smiled kindly on me once or twice, and that was all. It was quite a party, sixteen people."

The Editor then, after expressing his regret that he had not been able to come, wanted to know if the party had been entertaining.

Renouard regretted that his friend had not been there. Being a man whose business or at least whose profession was to know everything that went on in this part of the globe, he could probably have told him something of some people lately arrived from home, who were amongst the guests. Young Dunster (Willie), with his large shirt front and streaks of white skin shining unpleasantly through the thin black hair plastered over the top of his head, bore down on him and introduced him to that party, as if he had been a trained dog or a child phenomenon. Decidedly, he said, he disliked Willie—one of these large oppressive men. . . .

A silence fell, and it was as if Renouard were not going to say anything more when, suddenly, he came out with the real object of his visit to the editorial room.

"They looked to me like people under a spell."

The Editor gazed at him appreciatively, thinking that, whether the effect of solitude or not, this was a proof of a sensitive perception of the expression of faces.

"You omitted to tell me their name, but I can make a guess. You mean Professor Moorsom, his daughter and sister—don't you?"

Renouard assented. Yes, a white-haired lady. But from his silence, with his eyes fixed, yet avoiding his friend, it was easy to guess that it was not in the white-haired lady that he was interested.

"Upon my word," he said, recovering his usual bearing. "It looks to me as if I had been asked there only for the daughter to talk to me."

He did not conceal that he had been greatly struck by her appearance. Nobody could have helped being impressed. She was different from everybody else in that house, and it was not only the effect of her London clothes. He did not take her down to dinner. Willie did that. It was afterwards, on the terrace. . . .

The evening was delightfully calm. He was sitting apart and alone, and wishing himself somewhere else—on board the schooner for choice, with the dinner-harness off. He hadn't exchanged forty words altogether during the evening with the other guests. He saw her suddenly all by herself coming towards him along the dimly lighted terrace, quite from a distance.

She was tall and supple, carrying nobly on her straight body a head of a character which to him appeared peculiar, something—well—pagan, crowned with a great wealth of hair. He had been about to rise, but her decided approach caused him to remain on the seat. He had not looked much at her that evening. He had not that freedom of gaze acquired by the habit of society and the frequent meetings with strangers. It was not shyness, but the reserve of a man not used to the world and to the practice of covert staring, with careless curiosity. All he had captured by his first, keen, instantly lowered glance was the impression that her hair was magnificently red and her eyes very black. It was a troubling effect, but it had been evanescent; he had forgotten it almost till very unexpectedly he saw her coming down the terrace slow and eager, as if she were restraining herself, and with a rhythmic upward undulation of her whole figure. The light from an open window fell across her path, and suddenly all that mass of arranged hair appeared incandescent, chiselled and fluid, with the daring suggestion of a helmet of burnished copper and the flowing lines of molten metal. It kindled in him an astonished admiration. But he said nothing of it to his friend the Editor. Neither did he tell him that her approach woke up in his brain the image of love's infinite grace and the sense of the inexhaustible joy that lives in beauty. No! What he imparted to the Editor were no emotions, but mere facts conveyed in a deliberate voice and in uninspired words.

"That young lady came and sat down by me. She said: 'Are you French, Mr. Renouard?'"

He had breathed a whiff of perfume of which he said nothing either—of some perfume he did not know. Her voice was low and distinct. Her shoulders and her bare arms gleamed with an extraordinary splendour, and when she advanced her head into the light he saw the admirable contour of the face, the straight fine nose with delicate nostrils, the exquisite crimson brush-stroke of the lips on this oval without colour. The expression of the eyes was lost in a shadowy mysterious play of jet and silver, stirring under the red coppery gold of the hair as though she had been a being made of ivory and precious metals changed into living tissue.

". . . I told her my people were living in Canada, but that I was brought up in England before coming out here. I can't imagine what interest she could have in my history."

"And you complain of her interest?"

The accent of the all-knowing journalist seemed to jar on the Planter of Malata.

"No!" he said in a deadened voice that was almost sullen. But after a short silence he went on. "Very extraordinary. I told her I came out to wander at large in the world when I was nineteen, almost directly after I left school. It seems that her late brother was in the same school a couple of years before me. She wanted me to tell her what I did at first when I came out here; what other men found to do when they came out—where they went, what was likely to happen to them—as if I could guess and foretell from my experience the fates of men who come out here with a hundred different projects, for hundreds of different reasons—for no reason but restlessness—who come, and go, and disappear! Preposterous. She seemed to want to hear their histories. I told her that most of them were not worth telling."

The distinguished journalist leaning on his elbow, his head resting against the knuckles of his left hand, listened with great attention, but gave no sign of that surprise which Renouard, pausing, seemed to expect.

"You know something," the latter said brusquely. The all-knowing man moved his head slightly and said, "Yes. But go on."

"It's just this. There is no more to it. I found myself talking to her of my adventures, of my early days. It couldn't possibly have interested her. Really," he cried, "this is most extraordinary. Those people have something on their minds. We sat in the light of the window, and her father prowled about the terrace, with his hands behind his back and his head drooping. The white-haired lady came to the dining-room window twice—to look at us I am certain. The other guests began to go away—and still we sat there. Apparently these people are staying with the Dunsters. It was old Mrs. Dunster who put an end to the thing. The father and the aunt circled about as if they were afraid of interfering with the girl. Then she got up all at once, gave me her hand, and said she hoped she would see me again."

While he was speaking Renouard saw again the sway of her figure in a movement of grace and strength—felt the pressure of her hand— heard the last accents of the deep murmur that came from her throat so white in the light of the window, and remembered the black rays of her steady eyes passing off his face when she turned away. He remembered all this visually, and it was not exactly pleasurable. It was rather startling like the discovery of a new faculty in himself. There are faculties one would rather do without—such, for instance, as seeing

through a stone wall or remembering a person with this uncanny vividness. And what about those two people belonging to her with their air
of expectant solicitude! Really, those figures from home got in front
of one. In fact, their persistence in getting between him and the solid
forms of the everyday material world had driven Renouard to call on
his friend at the office. He hoped that a little common, gossipy information would lay the ghost of that unexpected dinner-party. Of
course the proper person to go to would have been young Dunster,
but he couldn't stand Willie Dunster—not at any price.

In the pause the Editor had changed his attitude, faced his desk,
and smiled a faint knowing smile.

"Striking girl—eh?" he said.

The incongruity of the word was enough to make one jump out
of the chair. Striking! That girl striking! Stri . . . ! But Renouard
restrained his feelings. His friend was not a person to give oneself away
to. And, after all, this sort of speech was what he had come there to
hear. As, however, he had made a movement he resettled himself comfortably and said, with very creditable indifference, that yes—she was,
rather. Especially amongst a lot of over-dressed frumps. There wasn't
one woman under forty there.

"Is that the way to speak of the cream of our society; the 'top of the
basket,' as the French say?" the Editor remonstrated with mock indignation. "You aren't moderate in your expressions—you know."

"I express myself very little," interjected Renouard seriously.

"I will tell you what you are. You are a fellow that doesn't count
the cost. Of course you are safe with me, but will you never learn. . . ."

"What struck me most," interrupted the other, "is that she should
pick me out for such a long conversation."

"That's perhaps because you were the most remarkable of the men
there."

Renouard shook his head.

"This shot doesn't seem to me to hit the mark," he said calmly.
"Try again."

"Don't you believe me? Oh, you modest creature. Well, let me assure
you that under ordinary circumstances it would have been a good shot.
You are sufficiently remarkable. But you seem a pretty acute customer
too. The circumstances are extraordinary. By Jove, they are!"

He mused. After a time the Planter of Malata dropped a negligent—

"And you know them."

"And I know them," assented the all-knowing Editor, soberly, as
though the occasion were too special for a display of professional
vanity; a vanity so well known to Renouard that its absence augmented
his wonder and almost made him uneasy as if portending bad news
of some sort.

"You have met those people?" he asked.

"No. I was to have met them last night, but I had to send an apology to Willie in the morning. It was then that he had the bright idea to invite you to fill the place, from a muddled notion that you could be of use. Willie is stupid sometimes. For it is clear that you are the last man able to help."

"How on earth do I come to be mixed up in this—whatever it is?" Renouard's voice was slightly altered by nervous irritation. "I only arrived here yesterday morning."

CHAPTER TWO

His friend the Editor turned to him squarely. "Willie took me into consultation, and since he seems to have let you in I may just as well tell you what is up. I shall try to be as short as I can. But in confidence —mind!"

He waited. Renouard, his uneasiness growing on him unreasonably, assented by a nod, and the other lost no time in beginning. Professor Moorsom—physicist and philosopher—fine head of white hair, to judge from the photographs—plenty of brains in the head too—all these famous books—surely even Renouard would know. . . .

Renouard muttered moodily that it wasn't his sort of reading, and his friend hastened to assure him earnestly that neither was it his sort —except as a matter of business and duty, for the literary page of that newspaper which was his property (and the pride of his life). The only literary newspaper in the Antipodes could not ignore the fashionable philosopher of the age. Not that anybody read Moorsom at the Antipodes, but everybody had heard of him—women, children, dock labourers, cabmen. The only person (besides himself) who had read Moorsom, as far as he knew, was old Dunster, who used to call himself a Moorsomian (or was it Moorsomite) years and years ago, long before Moorsom had worked himself up into the great swell he was now, in every way. . . . Socially too. Quite the fashion in the highest world.

Renouard listened with profoundly concealed attention. "A charlatan," he muttered languidly.

"Well—no. I should say not. I shouldn't wonder though if most of his writing had been done with his tongue in his cheek. Of course. That's to be expected. I tell you what: the only really honest writing is to be found in newspapers and nowhere else—and don't you forget it."

The Editor paused with a basilisk stare till Renouard had conceded a casual: "I dare say," and only then went on to explain that old

Dunster, during his European tour, had been made rather a lion of in London, where he stayed with the Moorsoms—he meant the father and the girl. The professor had been a widower for a long time.

"She doesn't look just a girl," muttered Renouard. The other agreed. Very likely not. Had been playing the London hostess to tip-top people ever since she put her hair up, probably.

"I don't expect to see any girlish bloom on her when I do have the privilege," he continued. "Those people are staying with the Dunsters *incog.*, in a manner, you understand—something like royalties. They don't deceive anybody, but they want to be left to themselves. We have even kept them out of the paper—to oblige old Dunster. But we shall put your arrival in—our local celebrity."

"Heavens!"

"Yes. Mr. G. Renouard, the explorer, whose indomitable energy, etc., and who is now working for the prosperity of our country in another way on his Malata plantation . . . And, by the by, how's the silk plant—flourishing?"

"Yes."

"Did you bring any fibre?"

"Schooner-full."

"I see. To be transhipped to Liverpool for experimental manufacture, eh? Eminent capitalists at home very much interested, aren't they?"

"They are."

A silence fell. Then the Editor uttered slowly: "You will be a rich man some day."

Renouard's face did not betray his opinion of that confident prophecy. He didn't say anything till his friend suggested in the same meditative voice—

"You ought to interest Moorsom in the affair too—since Willie has let you in."

"A philosopher!"

"I suppose he isn't above making a bit of money. And he may be clever at it for all you know. I have a notion that he's a fairly practical old cove. . . . Anyhow," and here the tone of the speaker took on a tinge of respect, "he has made philosophy pay."

Renouard raised his eyes, repressed an impulse to jump up, and got out of the arm-chair slowly. "It isn't perhaps a bad idea," he said. "I'll have to call there in any case."

He wondered whether he had managed to keep his voice steady, its tone unconcerned enough; for his emotion was strong though it had nothing to do with the business aspect of this suggestion. He moved in the room in vague preparation for departure, when he heard a soft laugh. He spun about quickly with a frown, but the Editor was not laughing at him. He was chuckling across the big desk at the wall: a preliminary of some speech for which Renouard, recalled to himself, waited silent and mistrustful.

"No! You would never guess! No one would ever guess what these people are after. Willie's eyes bulged out when he came to me with the tale."

"They always do," remarked Renouard with disgust. "He's stupid."

"He was startled. And so was I after he told me. It's a search party. They are out looking for a man. Willie's soft heart's enlisted in the cause."

Renouard repeated: "Looking for a man." He sat down suddenly as if on purpose to stare. "Did Willie come to you to borrow the lantern," he asked sarcastically, and got up again for no apparent reason.

"What lantern?" snapped the puzzled Editor, and his face darkened with suspicion. "You, Renouard, are always alluding to things that aren't clear to me. If you were in politics, I, as a party journalist, wouldn't trust you further than I could see you. Not an inch further. You are such a sophisticated beggar. Listen: the man is the man Miss Moorsom was engaged to for a year. He couldn't have been a nobody, anyhow. But he doesn't seem to have been very wise. Hard luck for the young lady."

He spoke with feeling. It was clear that what he had to tell appealed to his sentiment. Yet, as an experienced man of the world, he marked his amused wonder. Young man of good family and connections, going everywhere, yet not merely a man about town, but with a foot in the two big F's.

Renouard lounging aimlessly in the room turned round: "And what the devil's that?" he asked faintly.

"Why Fashion and Finance," explained the Editor. "That's how I call it. There are the three R's at the bottom of the social edifice and the two F's on the top. See?"

"Ha! Ha! Excellent! Ha! Ha!" Renouard laughed with stony eyes.

"And you proceed from one set to the other in this democratic age," the Editor went on with unperturbed complacency. "That is if you are clever enough. The only danger is in being too clever. And I think something of the sort happened here. That swell I am speaking of got himself into a mess. Apparently a very ugly mess of a financial character. You will understand that Willie did not go into details with me. They were not imparted to him with very great abundance either. But a bad mess—something of the criminal order. Of course he was innocent. But he had to quit all the same."

"Ha! Ha!" Renouard laughed again abruptly, staring as before. "So there's one more big F in the tale."

"What do you mean?" inquired the Editor quickly, with an air as if his patent were being infringed.

"I mean—Fool."

"No. I wouldn't say that. I wouldn't say that."

"Well—let him be a scoundrel then. What the devil do I care."

"But hold on! You haven't heard the end of the story."

Renouard, his hat on his head already, sat down with the disdainful smile of a man who had discounted the moral of the story. Still he sat down and the Editor swung his revolving chair right round. He was full of unction.

"Imprudent, I should say. In many ways money is as dangerous to handle as gunpowder. You can't be too careful either as to who you are working with. Anyhow there was a mighty flashy burst up, a sensation, and—his familiar haunts knew him no more. But before he vanished he went to see Miss Moorsom. That very fact argues for his innocence—don't it? What was said between them no man knows—unless the professor had the confidence from his daughter. There couldn't have been much to say. There was nothing for it but to let him go—was there?—for the affair had got into the papers. And perhaps the kindest thing would have been to forget him. Anyway the easiest. Forgiveness would have been more difficult, I fancy, for a young lady of spirit and position drawn into an ugly affair like that. Any ordinary young lady, I mean. Well, the fellow asked nothing better than to be forgotten, only he didn't find it easy to do so himself, because he would write home now and then. Not to any of his friends though. He had no near relations. The professor had been his guardian. No, the poor devil wrote now and then to an old retired butler of his late father, somewhere in the country, forbidding him at the same time to let any one know of his whereabouts. So that worthy old ass would go up and dodge about the Moorsom's town house, perhaps waylay Miss Moorsom's maid, and then would write to 'Master Arthur' that the young lady looked well and happy, or some such cheerful intelligence. I dare say he wanted to be forgotten, but I shouldn't think he was much cheered by the news. What would you say?"

Renouard, his legs stretched out and his chin on his breast, said nothing. A sensation which was not curiosity, but rather a vague nervous anxiety, distinctly unpleasant, like a mysterious symptom of some malady, prevented him from getting up and going away.

"Mixed feelings," the Editor opined. "Many fellows out here receive news from home with mixed feelings. But what will his feelings be when he hears what I am going to tell you now? For we know he has not heard yet. Six months ago a city clerk, just a common drudge of finance, gets himself convicted of a common embezzlement or something of that kind. Then seeing he's in for a long sentence he thinks of making his conscience comfortable, and makes a clean breast of an old story of tampered with, or else suppressed, documents, a story which clears altogether the honesty of our ruined gentleman. That embezzling fellow was in a position to know, having been employed by the firm before the smash. There was no doubt about the character being cleared—but where the cleared man was nobody could tell. Another sensation in society. And then Miss Moorsom says: 'He will come back to claim me, and I'll marry him.' But he didn't come back. Between you and me I don't think he was much wanted—except by Miss Moorsom. I imagine she's used to having her own way. She grew impatient, and declared that if she knew where the man was she would go to him. But all that could be got out of the old butler was that the last envelope bore the postmark of our beautiful city; and that this was the only address of 'Master Arthur' that he ever had. That and no more. In fact the fellow was at his last gasp—with a bad heart. Miss Moorsom wasn't allowed to see him. She had gone herself into the country to learn what she could, but she had to stay downstairs while the old chap's wife went up to the invalid. She brought down the scrap of intelligence I've told you of. He was already too far gone to be cross-examined on it, and that very night he died. He didn't leave behind him much to go by, did he? Our Willie hinted to me that there had been pretty stormy days in the professor's house, but—here they are. I have a notion she isn't the kind of everyday young lady who may be permitted to gallop about the world all by herself—eh? Well, I think it rather fine of her, but I quite understand that the professor needed all his philosophy under the circumstances. She is his only child now—and brilliant—what? Willie positively spluttered trying to describe her to me; and I could see directly you came in that you had an uncommon experience."

Renouard, with an irritated gesture, tilted his hat more forward on his eyes, as though he were bored. The Editor went on with the remark that to be sure neither he (Renouard) nor yet Willie were much used to meeting girls of that remarkable superiority. Willie when learning business with a firm in London, years before, had seen none but boardinghouse society, he guessed. As to himself in the good old days, when he trod the glorious flags of Fleet Street, he neither had access to, nor yet would have cared for the swells. Nothing interested him then but parliamentary politics and the oratory of the House of Commons.

He paid to this not very distant past the tribute of a tender, reminiscent smile, and returned to his first idea that for a society girl her action was rather fine. All the same the professor could not be very pleased. The fellow if he was as pure as a lily now was just about as devoid of the goods of the earth. And there were misfortunes, however undeserved, which damaged a man's standing permanently. On the other hand, it was difficult to oppose cynically a noble impulse—not to speak of the great love at the root of it. Ah! Love! And then the lady was quite capable of going off by herself. She was of age, she had money of her own, plenty of pluck too. Moorsom must have concluded that it was more truly paternal, more prudent too, and generally safer all round to let himself be dragged into this chase. The aunt came along for the same reasons. It was given out at home as a trip round the world of the usual kind.

Renouard had risen and remained standing with his heart beating, and strangely affected by this tale, robbed as it was of all glamour by the prosaic personality of the narrator. The Editor added: "I've been asked to help in the search—you know."

Renouard muttered something about an appointment and went out into the street. His inborn sanity could not defend him from a misty creeping jealousy. He thought that obviously no man of that sort could be worthy of such a woman's devoted fidelity. Renouard, however, had lived long enough to reflect that a man's activities, his views, and even his ideas may be very inferior to his character; and moved by a delicate consideration for that splendid girl he tried to think out for the man a character of inward excellence and outward gifts—some extraordinary seduction. But in vain. Fresh from months of solitude and from days at sea, her splendour presented itself to him absolutely unconquerable in its perfection, unless by her own folly. It was easier to suspect her of this than to imagine in the man qualities which would be worthy of her. Easier and less degrading. Because folly may be generous—could be nothing else but generosity in her; whereas to imagine her subjugated by something common was intolerable.

Because of the force of the physical impression he had received from her personality (and such impressions are the real origins of the deepest movements of our soul) this conception of her was even inconceivable. But no Prince Charming has ever lived out of a fairy tale. He doesn't walk the worlds of Fashion and Finance—and with a stumbling gait at that. Generosity. Yes. It was her generosity. But this generosity was altogether regal in its splendour, almost absurd in its lavishness—or, perhaps, divine.

In the evening, on board his schooner, sitting on the rail, his arms folded on his breast and his eyes fixed on the deck, he let the darkness catch him unawares in the midst of a meditation on the mechanism of sentiment and the springs of passion. And all the time he had an abiding consciousness of her bodily presence. The effect on his senses had been so penetrating that in the middle of the night, rousing up suddenly, wide-eyed in the darkness of his cabin, he did not create a faint mental vision of her person for himself, but, more intimately affected, he scented distinctly the faint perfume she used, and could almost have sworn that he had been awakened by the soft rustle of her dress. He even sat up listening in the dark for a time, then sighed and lay down again, not agitated but, on the contrary, oppressed by the sensation of something that had happened to him and could not be undone.

CHAPTER THREE

In the afternoon he lounged into the editorial office, carrying with affected nonchalance that weight of the irremediable he had felt laid on him suddenly in the small hours of the night—that consciousness of something that could no longer be helped. His patronising friend informed him at once that he had made the acquaintance of the Moorsom party last night. At the Dunster's, of course. Dinner.

"Very quiet. Nobody there. It was much better for the business. I say . . ."

Renouard, his hand grasping the back of a chair, stared down at him dumbly.

"Phew! That's a stunning girl. . . . Why do you want to sit on that chair? It's uncomfortable!"

"I wasn't going to sit on it." Renouard walked slowly to the window, glad to find in himself enough self-control to let go the chair instead of raising it on high and bringing it down on the Editor's head.

"Willie kept on gazing at her with tears in his boiled eyes. You should have seen him bending sentimentally over her at dinner."

"Don't," said Renouard in such an anguished tone that the Editor turned right round to look at his back.

"You push your dislike of young Dunster too far. It's positively morbid," he disapproved mildly. "We can't be all beautiful after thirty. . . . I talked a little, about you mostly, to the professor. He appeared to be interested in the silk plant—if only as a change from the great subject. Miss Moorsom didn't seem to mind when I confessed to her that I had taken you into the confidence of the thing. Our Willie approved too. Old Dunster with his white beard seemed to give me his blessing. All those people have a great opinion of you, simply because I told them that you've led every sort of life one can think of before you got struck on exploration. They want you to make suggestions. What do you think 'Master Arthur' is likely to have taken to?"

"Something easy," muttered Renouard without unclenching his teeth.

"Hunting man. Athlete. Don't be hard on the chap. He may be riding boundaries, or droving cattle, or humping his swag about the back-blocks away to the devil—somewhere. He may be even prospecting at the back of beyond—this very moment."

"Or lying dead drunk in a roadside pub. It's late enough in the day for that."

The Editor looked up instinctively. The clock was pointing at a quarter to five. "Yes, it is," he admitted. "But it needn't be. And he may have lit out into the Western Pacific all of a sudden—say in a trading schooner. Though I really don't see in what capacity. Still . . ."

"Or he may be passing at this very moment under this very window."

"Not he . . . and I wish you would get away from it to where one can see your face. I hate talking to a man's back. You stand there like a hermit on a sea-shore growling to yourself. I tell you what it is, Geoffrey, you don't like mankind."

"I don't make my living by talking about mankind's affairs," Renouard defended himself. But he came away obediently and sat down in the arm-chair. "How can you be so certain that your man isn't down there in the street?" he asked. "It's neither more nor less probable than every single one of your other suppositions."

Placated by Renouard's docility the Editor gazed at him for a while. "Aha! I'll tell you how. Learn then that we have begun the campaign. We have telegraphed his description to the police of every township up and down the land. And what's more we've ascertained definitely that he hasn't been in this town for the last three months at least. How much longer he's been away we can't tell."

"That's very curious."

"It's very simple. Miss Moorsom wrote to him, to the post office here, directly she returned to London after her excursion into the country to see the old butler. Well—her letter is still lying there. It has not been called for. Ergo, this town is not his usual abode. Personally, I never thought it was. But he cannot fail to turn up some time or other. Our main hope lies just in the certitude that he must come to town sooner or later. Remember he doesn't know that the butler is dead, and he will want to inquire for a letter. Well, he'll find a note from Miss Moorsom."

Renouard, silent, thought that it was likely enough. His profound distaste for this conversation was betrayed by an air of weariness darkening his energetic sun-tanned features, and by the augmented dreaminess of his eyes. The Editor noted it as a further proof of that immoral detachment from mankind, of that callousness of sentiment fostered by the unhealthy conditions of solitude—according to his own favourite theory. Aloud he observed that as long as a man had not given up correspondence he could not be looked upon as lost. Fugitive criminals had been tracked in that way by justice, he reminded his friend; then suddenly changed the bearing of the subject somewhat by asking if Renouard had heard from his people lately, and if every member of his large tribe was well and happy.

"Yes, thanks."

The tone was curt, as if repelling a liberty. Renouard did not like being asked about his people, for whom he had a profound and remorseful affection. He had not seen a single human being to whom he was related, for many years, and he was extremely different from them all.

On the very morning of his arrival from his island he had gone to a set of pigeon-holes in Willie Dunster's outer office and had taken out from a compartment labelled "Malata" a very small accumulation of envelopes, a few addressed to himself, and one addressed to his assistant, all to the care of the firm, W. Dunster and Co. As opportunity offered, the firm used to send them on to Malata either by a man-of-war schooner going on a cruise, or by some trading craft proceeding that way. But for the last four months there had been no opportunity.

"You going to stay here some time?" asked the Editor, after a longish silence.

Renouard, perfunctorily, did see no reason why he should make a long stay.

"For health, for your mental health, my boy," rejoined the newspaper man. "To get used to human faces so that they don't hit you in the eye so hard when you walk about the streets. To get friendly with your kind. I suppose that assistant of yours can be trusted to look after things?"

"There's the half-caste too. The Portuguese. He knows what's to be done."

"Aha!" The Editor looked sharply at his friend. "What's his name?"

"Who's name?"

"The assistant's you picked up on the sly behind my back."

Renouard made a slight movement of impatience.

"I met him unexpectedly one evening. I thought he would do as well as another. He had come from up country and didn't seem happy in a town. He told me his name was Walter. I did not ask him for proofs, you know."

"I don't think you get on very well with him."

"Why? What makes you think so."

"I don't know. Something reluctant in your manner when he's in question."

"Really. My manner! I don't think he's a great subject for conversation, perhaps. Why not drop him?"

"Of course! You wouldn't confess to a mistake. Not you. Nevertheless I have my suspicions about it."

Renouard got up to go, but hesitated, looking down at the seated Editor.

"How funny," he said at last with the utmost seriousness, and was making for the door, when the voice of his friend stopped him.

"You know what has been said of you? That you couldn't get on with anybody you couldn't kick. Now, confess—is there any truth in the soft impeachment?"

"No," said Renouard. "Did you print that in your paper?"

"No. I didn't quite believe it. But I will tell you what I believe. I believe that when your heart is set on some object you are a man that doesn't count the cost to yourself or others. And this shall get printed some day."

"Obituary notice?" Renouard dropped negligently.

"Certain—some day."

"Do you then regard yourself as immortal?"

"No, my boy. I am not immortal. But the voice of the press goes on for ever. . . . And it will say that this was the secret of your great success in a task where better men than you—meaning no offence—did fail repeatedly."

"Success," muttered Renouard, pulling-to the office door after him with considerable energy. And the letters of the word PRIVATE like a row of white eyes seemed to stare after his back sinking down the staircase of that temple of publicity.

Renouard had no doubt that all the means of publicity would be put at the service of love and used for the discovery of the loved man. He did not wish him dead. He did not wish him any harm. We are all equipped with a fund of humanity which is not exhausted without many and repeated provocations—and this man had done him no evil. But before Renouard had left old Dunster's house, at the conclusion of the call he made there that very afternoon, he had discovered in himself the desire that the search might last long. He never really flattered himself that it might fail. It seemed to him that there was no other course in this world for himself, for all mankind, but resignation. And he could not help thinking that Professor Moorsom had arrived at the same conclusion too.

Professor Moorsom, slight frame of middle height, a thoughtful keen head under the thick wavy hair, veiled dark eyes under straight eyebrows, and with an inward gaze which when disengaged and arriving at one seemed to issue from an obscure dream of books, from the limbo of meditation, showed himself extremely gracious to him. Renouard guessed in him a man whom an incurable habit of investigation and analysis had made gentle and indulgent; inapt for action, and more sensitive to the thoughts than to the events of existence. Withal not crushed, sub-ironic without a trace of acidity, and with a simple manner which put people at ease quickly. They had a long conversation on the terrace commanding an extended view of the town and the harbour.

The splendid immobility of the bay resting under his gaze, with its grey spurs and shining indentations, helped Renouard to regain his self-possession, which he had felt shaken, in coming out on the terrace, into the setting of the most powerful emotion of his life, when he had sat within a foot of Miss Moorsom with fire in his breast, a humming in his ears, and in a complete disorder of his mind. There was the very garden seat on which he had been enveloped in the radiant spell. And presently he was sitting on it again with the professor talking of her. Near by the patriarchal Dunster leaned forward in a wicker arm-chair, benign and a little deaf, his big hand to his ear with the innocent eagerness of his advanced age remembering the fires of life.

It was with a sort of apprehension that Renouard looked forward to seeing Miss Moorsom. And strangely enough it resembled the state of mind of a man who fears disenchantment more than sortilege. But he need not have been afraid. Directly he saw her in a distance at the other end of the terrace he shuddered to the roots of his hair. With her approach the power of speech left him for a time. Mrs. Dunster and her aunt were accompanying her. All these people sat down; it was an intimate circle into which Renouard felt himself cordially admitted; and the talk was of the great search which occupied all their minds. Discretion was expected by these people, but of reticence as to the object of the journey there could be no question. Nothing but ways and means and arrangements could be talked about.

By fixing his eyes obstinately on the ground, which gave him an air of reflective sadness, Renouard managed to recover his self-possession. He used it to keep his voice in a low key and to measure his words on the great subject. And he took care with a great inward effort to make them reasonable without giving them a discouraging complexion. For he did not want the quest to be given up, since it would mean her going away with her two attendant grey-heads to the other side of the world.

He was asked to come again, to come often and take part in the counsels of all these people captivated by the sentimental enterprise of a declared love. On taking Miss Moorsom's hand he looked up, would have liked to say something, but found himself voiceless, with his lips suddenly sealed. She returned the pressure of his fingers, and he left her with her eyes vaguely staring beyond him, an air of listening for an expected sound, and the faintest possible smile on her lips—a smile not for him, evidently, but the reflection of some deep and inscrutable thought.

CHAPTER FOUR

He went on board his schooner. She lay white, and as if suspended, in the crepuscular atmosphere of sunset mingling with the ashy gleam of the vast anchorage. He tried to keep his thoughts as sober, as reasonable, as measured as his words had been, lest they should get away from him and cause some sort of moral disaster. What he was afraid of in the coming night was sleeplessness and the endless strain of that wearisome task. It had to be faced however. He lay on his back, sighing profoundly in the dark, and suddenly beheld his very own self, carrying a small bizarre lamp, reflected in a long mirror inside a room in an empty and unfurnished palace. In this startling image of himself he recognised somebody he had to follow—the frightened guide of his dream. He traversed endless galleries, no end of lofty halls, innumerable doors. He lost himself utterly—he found his way again. Room succeeded room. At last the lamp went out, and he stumbled against some object which, when he stooped for it, he found to be very cold and heavy to lift. The sickly white light of dawn showed him the head of a statue. Its marble hair was done in the bold lines of a helmet, on its lips the chisel had left a faint smile, and it resembled Miss Moorsom. While he was staring at it fixedly, the head began to grow light in his fingers, to diminish and crumble to pieces, and at last turned into a handful of dust, which was blown away by a puff of wind so chilly that he woke up with a desperate shiver and leaped headlong out of his bed-place. The day had really come. He sat down by the cabin table, and taking his head between his hands, did not stir for a very long time.

Very quiet, he set himself to review this dream. The lamp, of course, he connected with the search for a man. But on closer examination he perceived that the reflection of himself in the mirror was not really the true Renouard, but somebody else whose face he could not remember. In the deserted palace he recognised a sinister adaptation by his brain of the long corridors with many doors, in the great building in which his friend's newspaper was lodged on the first floor. The marble head with Miss Moorsom's face! Well! What other face could he have dreamed of? And her complexion was fairer than Parian marble, than the heads of angels. The wind at the end was the morning breeze entering through the open porthole and touching his face before the schooner could swing to the chilly gust.

Yes! And all this rational explanation of the fantastic made it only more mysterious and weird. There was something daemonic in that dream. It was one of those experiences which throw a man out of conformity with the established order of his kind and make him a creature of obscure suggestions.

Henceforth, without ever trying to resist, he went every afternoon to the house where she lived. He went there as passively as if in a dream. He could never make out how he had attained the footing of intimacy in the Dunster mansion above the bay—whether on the ground of personal merit or as the pioneer of the vegetable silk industry. It must have been the last, because he remembered distinctly, as distinctly as in a dream, hearing old Dunster once telling him that his next public task would be a careful survey of the Northern Districts to discover tracts suitable for the cultivation of the silk plant. The old man wagged his beard at him sagely. It was indeed as absurd as a dream.

Willie of course would be there in the evening. But he was more of a figure out of a nightmare, hovering about the circle of chairs in his dress-clothes like a gigantic, repulsive, and sentimental bat. "Do away with the beastly cocoons all over the world," he buzzed in his blurred, waterlogged voice. He affected a great horror of insects of all kinds. One evening he appeared with a red flower in his button-hole. Nothing could have been more disgustingly fantastic. And he would also say to Renouard: "You may yet change the history of our country. For economic conditions do shape the history of nations. Eh? What?" And he would turn to Miss Moorsom for approval, lowering protectingly his spatulous nose and looking up with feeling from under his absurd eyebrows, which grew thin, in the manner of canebrakes, out of his spongy skin. For this large, bilious creature was an economist and a sentimentalist, facile to tears, and a member of the Cobden Club.

In order to see as little of him as possible Renouard began coming earlier so as to get away before his arrival, without curtailing too much the hours of secret contemplation for which he lived. He had given up trying to deceive himself. His resignation was without bounds. He accepted the immense misfortune of being in love with a woman who was in search of another man only to throw herself into his arms. With such desperate precision he defined in his thoughts the situation, the consciousness of which traversed like a sharp arrow the sudden silences of general conversation. The only thought before which he quailed was the thought that this could not last; that it must come to an end. He feared it instinctively as a sick man may fear death. For it seemed to him that it must be the death of him followed by a lightless, bottomless pit. But his resignation was not spared the torments of jealousy: the cruel, insensate, poignant, and imbecile jealousy, when it seems that a woman betrays us simply by this that she exists, that she breathes—and when the deep movements of her nerves or her soul become a matter of distracting suspicion, of killing doubt, of mortal anxiety.

In the peculiar condition of their sojourn Miss Moorsom went out very little. She accepted this seclusion at the Dunster's mansion as in a hermitage, and lived there, watched over by a group of old people, with lofty endurance of a condescending and strong-headed goddess. It was impossible to say if she suffered from anything in the world, and whether this was the insensibility of a great passion concentrated on itself, or a perfect restraint of manner, or the indifference of superiority so complete as to be sufficient to itself. But it was visible to Renouard that she took some pleasure in talking to him at times. Was it because he was the only person near her age? Was this, then, the secret of his admission to the circle?

He admired her voice as well poised as her movements, as her attitudes. He himself had always been a man of tranquil tones. But the power of fascination had torn him out of his very nature so completely that to preserve his habitual calmness from going to pieces had become a terrible effort. He used to go from her on board the schooner exhausted, broken, shaken up, as though he had been put to the most exquisite torture. When he saw her approaching he always had a moment of hallucination. She was a misty and fair creature, fitted for invisible music, for the shadows of love, for the murmurs of waters. After a time (he could not be always staring at the ground) he would summon up all his resolution and look at her. There was a sparkle in the clear obscurity of her eyes; and when she turned them on him they seemed to give a new meaning to life. He would say to himself that another man would have found long before the happy release of madness, his wits burnt to cinders in that radiance. But no such luck for him. His wits had come unscathed through the furnaces of hot suns, of blazing deserts, of flaming angers against the weaknesses of men and the obstinate cruelties of hostile nature.

Being sane he had to be constantly on his guard against falling into adoring silences or breaking out into wild speeches. He had to keep watch on his eyes, his limbs, on the muscles of his face. Their conversations were such as they could be between these two people: she a young lady fresh from the thick twilight of four million people and the artificiality of several London seasons; he the man of definite conquering tasks, the familiar of wide horizons, and in his very repose holding aloof from these agglomerations of units in which one loses one's importance even to oneself. They had no common conversational small change. They had to use the great pieces of general ideas, but they exchanged them trivially. It was no serious commerce. Perhaps she had not much of that coin. Nothing significant came from her. It could not be said that she had received from the contacts of the external world impressions of a personal kind, different from other women. What was ravishing in her was her quietness and, in her grave attitudes, the unfailing brilliance of her femininity. He did not know what there was under that ivory forehead so splendidly shaped, so gloriously crowned. He could not tell what were her thoughts, her feelings. Her replies were reflective, always preceded by a short silence, while he hung on her lips anxiously. He felt himself in the presence of a mysterious being in whom spoke an unknown voice, like the voice of oracles, bringing everlasting unrest to the heart.

He was thankful enough to sit in silence with secretly clenched teeth, devoured by jealousy—and nobody could have guessed that his quiet deferential bearing to all these grey-heads was the supreme effort of stoicism, that the man was engaged in keeping a sinister watch on his tortures lest his strength should fail him. As before, when grappling with other forces of nature, he could find in himself all sorts of courage except the courage to run away.

It was perhaps from the lack of subjects they could have in common that Miss Moorsom made him so often speak of his own life. He did not shrink from talking about himself, for he was free from that exacerbated, timid vanity which seals so many vain-glorious lips. He talked to her in his restrained voice, gazing at the tip of her shoe, and thinking that the time was bound to come soon when her very inattention would get weary of him. And indeed on stealing a glance he would see her dazzling and perfect, her eyes vague, staring in mournful immobility, with a drooping head that made him think of a tragic Venus arising before him, not from the foam of the sea, but from a distant, still more formless, mysterious, and potent immensity of mankind.

CHAPTER FIVE

One afternoon Renouard stepping out on the terrace found nobody there. It was for him, at the same time, a melancholy disappointment and a poignant relief.

The heat was great, the air was still, all the long windows of the house stood wide open. At the further end, grouped round a lady's worktable, several chairs disposed sociably suggested invisible occupants, a company of conversing shades. Renouard looked toward them with a sort of dread. A most elusive, faint sound of ghostly talk issuing from one of the rooms added to the illusion and stopped his already hesitating footsteps. He leaned over the balustrade of stone near a squat vase holding a tropical plant of a bizarre shape. Professor Moorsom coming up from the garden with a book under his arm and a white parasol held over his bare head, found him there and, closing the parasol, leaned over by his side with a remark on the increasing heat of the season. Renouard assented and changed his position a little; the other, after a short silence, administered unexpectedly a question which, like the blow of a club on the head, deprived Renouard of the power of speech and even thought, but, more cruel, left him quivering with apprehension, not of death but of everlasting torment. Yet the words were extremely simple.

"Something will have to be done soon. We can't remain in a state of suspended expectation for ever. Tell me what do you think of our chances?"

Renouard, speechless, produced a faint smile. The professor confessed in a jocular tone his impatience to complete the circuit of the globe and be done with it. It was impossible to remain quartered on the dear excellent Dunsters for an indefinite time. And then there were the lectures he had arranged to deliver in Paris. A serious matter.

That lectures by Professor Moorsom were a European event and that brilliant audiences would gather to hear them Renouard did not know. All he was aware of was the shock of this hint of departure. The menace of separation fell on his head like a thunderbolt. And he saw the absurdity of his emotion, for hadn't he lived all these days under the very cloud? The professor, his elbows spread out, looked down into the garden and went on unburdening his mind. Yes. The department of sentiment was directed by his daughter, and she had plenty of volunteered moral support; but he had to look after the practical side of life without assistance.

"I have the less hesitation in speaking to you about my anxiety, because I feel you are friendly to us and at the same time you are detached from all these sublimities—confound them."

"What do you mean?" murmured Renouard.

"I mean that you are capable of calm judgment. Here the atmosphere is simply detestable. Everybody has knuckled under to sentiment. Perhaps your deliberate opinion could influence . . ."

"You want Miss Moorsom to give it up?"

The professor turned to the young man dismally.

"Heaven only knows what I want."

Renouard leaning his back against the balustrade folded his arms on his breast, appeared to meditate profoundly. His face, shaded softly by the broad brim of a planter's panama hat, with the straight line of the nose level with the forehead, the eyes lost in the depth of the setting, and the chin well forward, had such a profile as may be seen amongst the bronzes of classical museums, pure under a crested helmet—recalled vaguely a Minerva's head.

"This is the most troublesome time I ever had in my life," exclaimed the professor testily.

"Surely the man must be worth it," muttered Renouard with a pang of jealousy traversing his breast like a self-inflicted stab.

Whether enervated by the heat or giving way to pent-up irritation the professor surrendered himself to the mood of sincerity.

"He began by being a pleasantly dull boy. He developed into a pointlessly clever young man, without, I suspect, ever trying to understand anything. My daughter knew him from childhood. I am a busy man, and I confess that their engagement was a complete surprise to me. I wish their reasons for that step had been more naïve. But simplicity was out of fashion in their set. From a worldly point of view he seems to have been a mere baby. Of course, now, I am assured that he is the victim of his noble confidence in the rectitude of his kind. But that's mere idealising of a sad reality. For my part I will tell you that from the very beginning I had the gravest doubts of his dishonesty. Unfortunately my clever daughter hadn't. And now we behold the reaction. No. To be earnestly dishonest one must be really poor. This was only a manifestation of his extremely refined cleverness. The complicated simpleton. He had an awful awakening though."

In such words did Professor Moorsom give his "young friend" to understand the state of his feelings toward the lost man. It was evident that the father of Miss Moorsom wished him to remain lost. Perhaps the unprecedented heat of the season made him long for the cool spaces of the Pacific, the sweep of the ocean's free wind along the promenade decks, cumbered with long chairs, of a ship steaming toward the Californian coast. To Renouard the philosopher appeared simply the most treacherous of fathers. He was amazed. But he was not at the end of his discoveries.

"He may be dead," the professor murmured.

"Why? People don't die here sooner than in Europe. If he had gone to hide in Italy, for instance, you wouldn't think of saying that."

"Well! And suppose he has become morally disintegrated. You know he was not a strong personality," the professor suggested moodily. "My daughter's future is in question here."

Renouard thought that the love of such a woman was enough to pull any broken man together—to drag a man out of his grave. And he thought this with inward despair, which kept him silent as much almost as his astonishment. At last he managed to stammer out a generous—

"Oh! Don't let us even suppose . . ."

The professor struck in with a sadder accent than before—

"It's good to be young. And then you have been a man of action, and necessarily a believer in success. But I have been looking too long at life not to distrust its surprises. Age! Age! Here I stand before you a man full of doubts and hesitation—*spe lentus, timidus futuri.*"

He made a sign to Renouard not to interrupt, and in a lowered voice, as if afraid of being overheard, even there, in the solitude of the terrace—

"And the worst is that I am not even sure how far this sentimental pilgrimage is genuine. Yes. I doubt my own child. It's true that she's a woman . . ."

Renouard detected with horror a tone of resentment, as if the professor had never forgiven his daughter for not dying instead of his son. The latter noticed the young man's stony stare.

"Ah! you don't understand. Yes, she's clever, open-minded, popular, and—well, charming. But you don't know what it is to have moved, breathed, existed, and even triumphed in the mere smother and froth of life—the brilliant froth. There thoughts, sentiments, opinions, feelings, actions too, are nothing but agitation in empty space—to amuse life—a sort of superior debauchery, exciting and fatiguing, meaning nothing, leading nowhere. She is the creature of that circle. And I ask myself if she is obeying the uneasiness of an instinct seeking its satisfaction, or is it a revulsion of feeling, or is she merely deceiving her own heart by this dangerous trifling with romantic images. And everything is possible—except sincerity, such as only stark, struggling humanity can know. No woman can stand that mode of life in which women rule, and remain a perfectly genuine, simple human being. . . . Ah! There's some people coming out."

He moved off a pace, then turning his head: "Upon my word! I would be infinitely obliged to you if you could throw a little cold water . . ." and at a vaguely dismayed gesture of Renouard, he added: "Don't be afraid. You wouldn't be putting out a sacred fire."

Renouard could hardly find words for a protest: "I assure you that I never talk with Miss Moorsom—on—on—that. And if you, her father . . ."

"I envy you your innocence," sighed the professor. "A father is only an everyday person. Flat. Stale. Moreover, my child would naturally mistrust me. We belong to the same set. Whereas you carry with you the prestige of the unknown. You have proved yourself to be a force."

Thereupon the professor, followed by Renouard, joined the circle of all the inmates of the house assembled at the other end of the terrace about a tea-table: three white heads and that resplendent vision of woman's glory, the sight of which had the power to flutter his heart like a reminder of the mortality of his frame.

He avoided the seat by the side of Miss Moorsom. The others were talking together languidly. Unnoticed he looked at that woman so marvellous that centuries seemed to lie between them. He was oppressed and overcome at the thought of what she could give to some man who really would be a force! What a glorious struggle with this amazon. What noble burden for the victorious strength.

Dear old Mrs. Dunster was dispensing tea, looking from time to time with interest toward Miss Moorsom. The aged statesman having eaten a raw tomato and drunk a glass of milk (a habit of his early farming days, long before politics, when, pioneer of wheat growing, he demonstrated the possibility of raising crops on ground looking barren enough to discourage a magician), smoothed his white beard, and struck lightly Renouard's knee with his big wrinkled hand.

"You had better come back to-night and dine with us quietly."

He liked this young man, a pioneer, too, in more than one direction. Mrs. Dunster added: "Do. It will be very quiet. I don't even know if Willie will be home for dinner." Renouard murmured his thanks, and left the terrace to go on board the schooner. While lingering in the drawing-room doorway he heard the resonant voice of old Dunster uttering oracularly—

" . . . the leading man here some day. . . . Like me."

Renouard let the thin summer portière of the doorway fall behind him. The voice of Professor Moorsom said—

"I am told that he has made an enemy of almost every man who had to work with him."

"That's nothing. He did his work. . . . Like me."

"He never counted the cost they say. Not even of lives."

Renouard understood that they were talking of him. Before he could move away, Mrs. Dunster struck in placidly—

"Don't let yourself be shocked by the tales you may hear of him, my dear. Most of it is envy."

Then he heard Miss Moorsom's voice replying to the old lady—

"Oh! I am not easily deceived. I think I may say I have an instinct for truth."

He hastened away from that house with his heart full of dread.

CHAPTER SIX

On board the schooner, lying on the settee on his back with the knuckles of his hands pressed over his eyes, he made up his mind that he would not return to that house for dinner—that he would never go back there any more. He made up his mind some twenty times. The knowledge that he had only to go up on the quarter deck, utter quietly the words: "Man the windlass," and that the schooner springing into life would run a hundred miles out to sea before sunrise, deceived his struggling will. Nothing easier! Yet, in the end, this young man, almost ill-famed for his ruthless daring, the inflexible leader of two tragically successful expeditions, shrank from that act of savage energy, and began, instead, to hunt for excuses.

No! It was not for him to run away like an incurable who cuts his throat. He finished dressing and looked at his own impassive face in the saloon mirror scornfully. While being pulled on shore in the gig, he remembered suddenly the wild beauty of a waterfall seen when hardly more than a boy, years ago, in Menado. There was a legend of a governor-general of the Dutch East Indies, on official tour, committing suicide on that spot by leaping into the chasm. It was supposed that a painful disease had made him weary of life. But was there ever a visitation like his own, at the same time binding one to life and so cruelly mortal!

The dinner was indeed quiet. Willie, given half an hour's grace, failed to turn up, and his chair remained vacant by the side of Miss Moorsom. Renouard had the professor's sister on his left, dressed in an expensive gown becoming her age. That maiden lady in her wonderful preservation reminded Renouard somehow of a wax flower under glass. There were no traces of the dust of life's battles on her anywhere. She did not like him very much in the afternoons, in his white drill suit and planter's hat, which seemed to her an unduly Bohemian costume for calling in a house where there were ladies. But in the evening, lithe and elegant in his dress clothes and with his pleasant, slightly veiled voice, he always made her conquest afresh. He might have been anybody distinguished—the son of a duke. Falling under that charm probably (and also because her brother had given her a hint), she attempted to open her heart to Renouard, who was watching with all the power of his soul her niece across the table. She spoke to him as frankly as though that miserable mortal envelope, emptied of everything but hopeless passion, were indeed the son of a duke.

Inattentive, he heard her only in snatches, till the final confidential burst: ". . . glad if you would express an opinion. Look at her, so charming, such a great favourite, so generally admired! It would be too sad. We all hoped she would make a brilliant marriage with somebody very rich and of high position, have a house in London and in the country, and entertain us all splendidly. She's so eminently fitted for it. She has such hosts of distinguished friends! And then—this instead! . . . My heart really aches."

Her well-bred if anxious whisper was covered by the voice of Professor Moorsom discoursing subtly down the short length of the dinner table on the Impermanency of the Measurable to his venerable disciple. It might have been a chapter in a new and popular book of Moorsomian philosophy. Patriarchal and delighted, old Dunster leaned forward a little, his eyes shining youthfully, two spots of colour at the roots of his white beard; and Renouard, glancing at the senile excitement, recalled the words heard on those subtle lips, adopted their scorn for his own, saw their truth before this man ready to be amused by the side of the grave. Yes! Intellectual debauchery in the froth of existence! Froth and fraud!

On the same side of the table Miss Moorsom never once looked toward her father, all her grace as if frozen, her red lips compressed, the faintest rosiness under her dazzling complexion, her black eyes burning motionless, and the very coppery gleams of light lying still on the waves and undulation of her hair. Renouard fancied himself over-turning the table, smashing crystal and china, treading fruit and flowers under foot, seizing her in his arms, carrying her off in a tumult of shrieks from all these people, a silent frightened mortal, into some profound retreat as in the age of Cavern men. Suddenly everybody got up, and he hastened to rise too, finding himself out of breath and quite unsteady on his feet.

On the terrace the philosopher, after lighting a cigar, slipped his hand condescendingly under his "dear young friend's" arm. Renouard regarded him now with the profoundest mistrust. But the great man seemed really to have a liking for his young friend—one of those mysterious sympathies, disregarding the differences of age and position, which in this case might have been explained by the failure of philosophy to meet a very real worry of a practical kind.

After a turn or two and some casual talk the professor said suddenly: "My late son was in your school—do you know? I can imagine that had he lived and you had ever met you would have understood each other. He too was inclined to action."

He sighed, then shaking off the mournful thought and with a nod at the dusky part of the terrace where the dress of his daughter made a luminous stain: "I really wish you would drop in that quarter a few sensible, discouraging words."

Renouard disengaged himself from that most perfidious of men under the pretence of astonishment, and stepping back a pace—

"Surely you are making fun of me, Professor Moorsom," he said with a low laugh, which was really a sound of rage.

"My dear young friend! It's no subject for jokes, to me. . . . You don't seem to have any notion of your prestige," he added, walking away toward the chairs.

"Humbug!" thought Renouard, standing still and looking after him. "And yet! And yet! What if it were true?"

He advanced then toward Miss Moorsom. Posed on the seat on which they had first spoken to each other, it was her turn to watch him coming on. But many of the windows were not lighted that evening. It was dark over there. She appeared to him luminous in her clear dress, a figure without shape, a face without features, awaiting his approach, till he got quite near to her, sat down, and they had exchanged a few insignificant words. Gradually she came out like a magic painting of charm, fascination, and desire, glowing mysteriously on the dark background. Something imperceptible in the lines of her attitude, in the modulations of her voice, seemed to soften that suggestion of calm unconscious pride which enveloped her always like a mantle. He, sensitive like a bond slave to the moods of the master, was moved by the subtle relenting of her grace to an infinite tenderness. He fought down the impulse to seize her by the hand, lead her down into the garden away under the big trees, and throw himself at her feet uttering words of love. His emotion was so strong that he had to cough slightly, and not knowing what to talk to her about he began to tell her of his mother and sisters. All the family were coming to London to live there, for some little time at least.

"I hope you will go and tell them something of me. Something seen," he said pressingly.

By this miserable subterfuge, like a man about to part with his life, he hoped to make her remember him a little longer.

"Certainly," she said. "I'll be glad to call when I get back. But that 'when' may be a long time."

He heard a light sigh. A cruel jealous curiosity made him ask—

"Are you growing weary, Miss Moorsom?"

A silence fell on his low-spoken question.

"Do you mean heart weary?" sounded Miss Moorsom's voice. "You don't know me, I see."

"Ah! Never despair," he muttered.

"This, Mr. Renouard, is a work of reparation. I stand for truth here. I can't think of myself."

He could have taken her by the throat for every word seemed an insult to his passion; but he only said—

"I never doubted the—the—nobility of your purpose."

"And to hear the word weariness pronounced in this connection surprises me. And from a man too who, I understand, has never counted the cost."

"You are pleased to tease me," he said directly he had recovered his voice and had mastered his anger. It was as if Professor Moorsom had dropped poison in his ear which was spreading now and tainting his passion, his very jealousy. He mistrusted every word that came from those lips on which his life hung. "How can you know anything of men who do not count the cost?" he asked in his gentlest tones.

"From hearsay—a little."

"Well, I assure you they are like the others, subject to suffering, victims of spells. . . ."

"One of them, at least, speaks very strangely."

She dismissed the subject after a short silence. "Mr. Renouard, I had a disappointment this morning. This mail brought me a letter from the widow of the old butler—you know. I expected to learn that she had heard from—from here. But no. No letter arrived home since we left."

Her voice was calm. His jealousy couldn't stand much more of this sort of talk; but he was glad that nothing had turned up to help the search; glad blindly, unreasonably—only because it would keep her longer in his sight—since she wouldn't give up.

"I am too near her," he thought, moving a little farther on the seat. He was afraid in the revulsion of feeling of flinging himself on her hands, which were lying on her lap, and covering them with kisses. He was afraid. Nothing, nothing could shake that spell—not if she were ever so false, stupid, or degraded. She was fate itself. The extent of his misfortune plunged him in such a stupor that he failed at first to hear the sound of voices and footsteps inside the drawing-room. Willie had come home—and the Editor was with him.

They burst out on the terrace babbling noisily, and then pulling themselves together stood still, surprising—and as if themselves surprised.

CHAPTER SEVEN

They had been feasting a poet from the bush, the latest discovery of the Editor. Such discoveries were the business, the vocation, the pride and delight of the only apostle of letters in the hemisphere, the solitary patron of culture, the Slave of the Lamp—as he subscribed himself at the bottom of the weekly literary page of his paper. He had had no difficulty in persuading the virtuous Willie (who had festive instincts) to help in the good work, and now they had left the poet lying asleep on the hearthrug of the editorial room and had rushed to the Dunster mansion wildly. The Editor had another discovery to announce. Swaying a little where he stood he opened his mouth very wide to shout the one word "Found!" Behind him Willie flung both his hands above his head and let them fall dramatically. Renouard saw the four white-headed people at the end of the terrace rise all together from their chairs with an effect of sudden panic.

"I tell you—he—is—found," the patron of letters shouted emphatically.

"What is this!" exclaimed Renouard in a choked voice. Miss Moorsom seized his wrist suddenly, and at that contact fire ran through all his veins, a hot stillness descended upon him in which he heard the blood—or the fire—beating in his ears. He made a movement as if to rise, but was restrained by the convulsive pressure on his wrist.

"No, no." Miss Moorsom's eyes stared black as night, searching the

space before her. Far away the Editor strutted forward, Willie following with his ostentatious manner of carrying his bulky and oppressive
carcass which, however, did not remain exactly perpendicular for two
seconds together.

"The innocent Arthur . . . Yes. We've got him." The Editor became very business-like. "Yes, this letter has done it."

He plunged into an inside pocket for it, slapped the scrap of paper
with his open palm. "From that old woman. William had it in his
pocket since this morning when Miss Moorsom gave it to him to show
me. Forgot all about it till an hour ago. Thought it was of no importance. Well, no! Not till it was properly read."

Renouard and Miss Moorsom emerged from the shadows side by
side, a well-matched couple, animated yet statuesque in their calmness
and in their pallor. She had let go his wrist. On catching sight of
Renouard the Editor exclaimed: "What—you here!" in a quite shrill
voice.

There came a dead pause. All the faces had in them something
dismayed and cruel.

"He's the very man we want," continued the Editor. "Excuse my
excitement. You are the very man, Renouard. Didn't you tell me that
your assistant called himself Walter? Yes? Thought so. But here's that
old woman—the butler's wife—listen to this. She writes: All I can tell
you, Miss, is that my poor husband directed his letters to the name of
H. Walter."

Renouard's violent but repressed exclamation was lost in a general
murmur and shuffle of feet. The Editor made a step forward, bowed
with creditable steadiness.

"Miss Moorsom, allow me to congratulate you from the bottom of
my heart on the happy—er—issue . . ."

"Wait," muttered Renouard irresolutely.

The Editor jumped on him in the manner of their old friendship.
"Ah, you! You are a fine fellow too. With your solitary ways of life
you will end by having no more discrimination than a savage. Fancy
living with a gentleman for months and never guessing. A man, I am
certain, accomplished, remarkable, out of the common, since he had
been distinguished" (he bowed again) "by Miss Moorsom, whom we
all admire."

She turned her back on him.

"I hope to goodness you haven't been leading him a dog's life,
Geoffrey," the Editor addressed his friend in a whispered aside.

Renouard seized a chair violently, sat down, and propping his
elbow on his knee leaned his head on his hand. Behind him the sister
of the professor looked up to heaven and wrung her hands stealthily.
Mrs. Dunster's hands were clasped forcibly under her chin, but she,

dear soul, was looking sorrowfully at Willie. The model nephew! In this strange state! So very much flushed! The careful disposition of the thin hairs across Willie's bald spot was deplorably disarranged, and the spot itself was red and, as it were, steaming.

"What's the matter, Geoffrey?" The Editor seemed disconcerted by the silent attitudes round him, as though he had expected all these people to shout and dance. "You have him on the island—haven't you?"

"Oh, yes: I have him there," said Renouard, without looking up.

"Well, then!" The Editor looked helplessly around as if begging for response of some sort. But the only response that came was very unexpected. Annoyed at being left in the background, and also because very little drink made him nasty, the emotional Willie turned malignant all at once, and in a bibulous tone surprising in a man able to keep his balance so well—

"Aha! But you haven't got him here—not yet!" he sneered. "No! You haven't got him yet."

This outrageous exhibition was to the Editor like the lash to a jaded horse. He positively jumped.

"What of that? What do you mean? We—haven't—got—him—here. Of course he isn't here! But Geoffrey's schooner is here. She can be sent at once to fetch him here. No! Stay! There's a better plan. Why shouldn't you all sail over to Malata, professor? Save time! I am sure Miss Moorsom would prefer . . ."

With a gallant flourish of his arm he looked for Miss Moorsom. She had disappeared. He was taken aback somewhat.

"Ah! H'm. Yes. . . . Why not. A pleasure cruise, delightful ship, delightful season, delightful errand, del . . . No! There are no objections. Geoffrey, I understand, has indulged in a bungalow three sizes too large for him. He can put you all up. It will be a pleasure for him. It will be the greatest privilege. Any man would be proud of being an agent of this happy reunion. I am proud of the little part I've played. He will consider it the greatest honour. Geoff, my boy, you had better be stirring to-morrow bright and early about the preparations for the trip. It would be criminal to lose a single day."

He was as flushed as Willie, the excitement keeping up the effect of the festive dinner. For a time Renouard, silent, as if he had not heard a word of all that babble, did not stir. But when he got up it was to advance toward the Editor and give him such a hearty slap on the back that the plump little man reeled in his tracks and looked quite frightened for a moment.

"You are a heaven-born discoverer and a first-rate manager. . . . He's right. It's the only way. You can't resist the claim of sentiment, and you must even risk the voyage to Malata. . . ." Renouard's voice sank.

"A lonely spot," he added, and fell into thought under all these eyes converging on him in the sudden silence. His slow glance passed over all the faces in succession, remaining arrested on Professor Moorsom, stony eyed, a smouldering cigar in his fingers, and with his sister standing by his side.

"I shall be infinitely gratified if you consent to come. But, of course, you will. We shall sail to-morrow evening then. And now let me leave you to your happiness."

He bowed, very grave, pointed suddenly his finger at Willie who was swaying about with a sleepy frown. . . . "Look at him. He's overcome with happiness. You had better put him to bed . . ." and disappeared while every head on the terrace was turned to Willie with varied expressions.

Renouard ran through the house. Avoiding the carriage road he fled down the steep short cut to the shore, where his gig was waiting. At his loud shout the sleeping Kanakas jumped up. He leaped in. "Shove off. Give way!" and the gig darted through the water. "Give way! Give way!" She flew past the wool-clippers sleeping at their anchors each with the open unwinking eye of the lamp in the rigging; she flew past the flagship of the Pacific squadron, a great mass all dark and silent, heavy with the slumbers of five hundred men, and where the invisible sentries heard his urgent "Give way! Give way!" in the night. The Kanakas, panting, rose off the thwarts at every stroke. Nothing could be fast enough for him! And he ran up the side of his schooner shaking the ladder noisily with his rush.

On deck he stumbled and stood still.

Wherefore this haste? To what end, since he knew well before he started that he had a pursuer from whom there was no escape?

As his foot touched the deck his will, his purpose he had been hurrying to save, died out within him. It had been nothing less than getting the schooner under-way, letting her vanish silently in the night from amongst these sleeping ships. And now he was certain he could not do it. It was impossible! And he reflected that whether he lived or died such an act would lay him under a dark suspicion from which he shrank. No, there was nothing to be done.

He went down into the cabin and, before even unbuttoning his overcoat, took out of the drawer the letter addressed to his assistant; that letter which he had found in the pigeon-hole labelled "Malata" in young Dunster's outer office, where it had been waiting for three months some occasion for being forwarded. From the moment of dropping it in the drawer he had utterly forgotten its existence—till now, when the man's name had come out so clamorously. He glanced at the common envelope, noted the shaky and laborious handwriting: H. Walter, Esqre. Undoubtedly the very last letter the old butler had posted before his illness, and in answer clearly to one from "Master Arthur" instructing him to address in the future: "Care of Messrs. W. Dunster and Co." Renouard made as if to open the envelope, but paused, and, instead, tore the letter deliberately in two, in four, in eight. With his hand full of pieces of paper he returned on deck and scattered them overboard on the dark water, in which they vanished instantly.

He did it slowly, without hesitation or remorse. H. Walter, Esqre, in Malata. The innocent Arthur—— What was his name? The man sought for by that woman who as she went by seemed to draw all the passion of the earth to her without effort, not deigning to notice, naturally, as other women breathed the air. But Renouard was no longer jealous of her very existence. Whatever its meaning it was not for that man he had picked up casually on obscure impulse, to get rid of the tiresome expostulations of a so-called friend; a man of whom he really knew nothing—and now a dead man. In Malata. Oh, yes! He was there secure enough, untroubled in his grave. In Malata. To bury him was the last service Renouard had rendered to his assistant before leaving the island on this trip to town.

Like many men ready enough for arduous enterprises Renouard was inclined to evade the small complications of existence. This trait of his character was composed of a little indolence, some disdain, and a shrinking from contests with certain forms of vulgarity—like a man who would face a lion and go out of his way to avoid a toad. His intercourse with the meddlesome journalist was that merely outward intimacy without sympathy some young men get drawn into easily. It had amused him rather to keep that "friend" in the dark about the fate of his assistant. Renouard had never needed other company than his own, for there was in him something of the sensitiveness of a dreamer who is easily jarred. He had said to himself that the all-knowing one would only preach again about the evils of solitude and worry his head off in favour of some forlornly useless protégé of his. Also the inquisitiveness of the Editor had irritated him and had closed his lips in sheer disgust.

And now he contemplated the noose of consequences drawing tight around him.

It was the memory of that diplomatic reticence which on the terrace had stifled his first cry which would have told them all that the man sought for was not to be met on earth any more. He shrank from the absurdity of hearing the all-knowing one, and not very sober at that, turning on him with righteous reproaches—

"You never told me. You gave me to understand that your assistant was alive, and now you say he's dead. Which is it? Were you lying then or are you lying now?" No! the thought of such a scene was not to be borne. He had sat down appalled, thinking: "What shall I do now?"

His courage had oozed out of him. Speaking the truth meant the Moorsoms going away at once—while it seemed to him that he would give the last shred of his rectitude to secure a day more of her company. He sat on—silent. Slowly, from confused sensations, from his talk with the professor, the manner of the girl herself, the intoxicating familiarity of her sudden hand-clasp, there had come to him a half glimmer of hope. The other man was dead. Then! . . . Madness, of course—but he could not give it up. He had listened to that confounded busybody arranging everything—while all these people stood around assenting, under the spell of that dead romance. He had listened scornful and silent. The glimmers of hope, of opportunity, passed before his eyes. He had only to sit still and say nothing. That and no more. And what was truth to him in the face of that great passion which had flung him prostrate in spirit at her adored feet!

And now it was done! Fatality had willed it! With the eyes of a mortal struck by the maddening thunderbolt of the gods, Renouard looked up to the sky, an immense black pall dusted over with gold, on which great shudders seemed to pass from the breath of life affirming its sway.

CHAPTER EIGHT

At last, one morning, in a clear spot of a glassy horizon charged with heraldic masses of black vapours, the island grew out from the sea, showing here and there its naked members of basaltic rock through the rents of heavy foliage. Later, in the great spilling of all the riches of sunset, Malata stood out green and rosy before turning into a violet shadow in the autumnal light of the expiring day. Then came the night. In the faint airs the schooner crept on past a sturdy squat headland, and it was pitch dark when her head-sails ran down, she turned short on her heel, and her anchor bit into the sandy bottom of the edge of the outer reef; for it was too dangerous then to attempt entering the little bay full of shoals. After the last solemn flutter of the mainsail the murmuring voices of the Moorsom party lingered, very frail, in the black stillness.

They were sitting aft, on chairs, and nobody made a move. Early in the day, when it had become evident that the wind was failing, Renouard, basing his advice on the shortcomings of his bachelor establishment, had urged on the ladies the advisability of not going ashore in the middle of the night. Now he approached them in a constrained manner (it was astonishing the constraint that had reigned between him and his guests all through the passage) and renewed his arguments. No one ashore would dream of his bringing any visitors with him. Nobody would even think of coming off. There was only one old canoe on the plantation. And landing in the schooner's boats would be awkward in the dark. There was the risk of getting aground on some shallow patches. It would be best to spend the rest of the night on board.

There was really no opposition. The professor smoking a pipe, and very comfortable in an ulster buttoned over his tropical clothes, was the first to speak from his long chair.

"Most excellent advice."

Next to him Miss Moorsom assented by a long silence. Then in a voice as of one coming out of a dream—

"And so this is Malata," she said. "I have often wondered . . ."

A shiver passed through Renouard. She had wondered! What about? Malata was himself. He and Malata were one. And she wondered! She had . . .

The professor's sister leaned over toward Renouard. Through all these days at sea the man's—the found man's—existence had not been alluded to on board the schooner. That reticence was part of the general constraint lying upon them all. She, herself, certainly had not been exactly elated by this finding—poor Arthur, without money, without prospects. But she felt moved by the sentiment and romance of the situation.

"Isn't it wonderful," she whispered out of her white wrap, "to think of poor Arthur sleeping there, so near to our dear lovely Felicia, and not knowing the immense joy in store for him to-morrow."

There was such artificiality in the wax-flower lady that nothing in this speech touched Renouard. It was but the simple anxiety of his heart that he was voicing when he muttered gloomily—

"No one in the world knows what to-morrow may hold in store."

The mature lady had a recoil as though he had said something impolite. What a harsh thing to say—instead of finding something nice and appropriate. On board, where she never saw him in evening clothes, Renouard's resemblance to a duke's son was not so apparent to her. Nothing but his—ah—bohemianism remained. She rose with a sort of ostentation.

"It's late—and since we are going to sleep on board to-night . . ." she said. "But it does seem so cruel."

The professor started up eagerly, knocking the ashes out of his pipe. "Infinitely more sensible, my dear Emma."

Renouard waited behind Miss Moorsom's chair.

She got up slowly, moved one step forward, and paused looking at the shore. The blackness of the island blotted out the stars with its vague mass like a low thundercloud brooding over the waters and ready to burst into flame and crashes.

"And so—this is Malata," she repeated dreamily, moving toward the cabin door. The clear cloak hanging from her shoulders, the ivory face—for the night had put out nothing of her but the gleams of her hair—made her resemble a shining dream woman uttering words of wistful inquiry. She disappeared without a sign, leaving Renouard penetrated to the very marrow by the sounds that came from her body like a mysterious resonance of an exquisite instrument.

He stood stock still. What was this accidental touch which had evoked the strange accent of her voice? He dared not answer that question. But he had to answer the question of what was to be done now. Had the moment of confession come? The thought was enough to make one's blood run cold.

It was as if those people had a premonition of something. In the taciturn days of the passage he had noticed their reserve even amongst themselves. The professor smoked his pipe moodily in retired spots. Renouard had caught Miss Moorsom's eyes resting on himself more than once with a peculiar and grave expression. He fancied that she avoided all opportunities of conversation. The maiden lady seemed to nurse a grievance. And now what had he to do?

The lights on the deck had gone out one after the other. The schooner slept.

About an hour after Miss Moorsom had gone below without a sign or a word for him, Renouard got out of his hammock slung in the waist under the midship awning—for he had given up all the accommodation below to his guests. He got out with a sudden swift movement, flung off his sleeping jacket, rolled his pyjamas up his thighs, and stole forward, unseen by the one Kanaka of the anchor-watch. His white torso, naked like a stripped athlete's, glimmered ghostly in the deep shadows of the deck. Unnoticed he got out of the ship over the knight-heads, ran along the back rope, and seizing the dolphin-striker firmly with both hands, lowered himself into the sea without a splash.

He swam away, noiseless like a fish, and then struck boldly for the land, sustained, embraced by the tepid water. The gentle, voluptuous heave of its breast swung him up and down slightly; sometimes a wavelet murmured in his ears; from time to time, lowering his feet, he felt for the bottom on a shallow patch to rest and correct his direction. He landed at the lower end of the bungalow garden, into the dead stillness of the island. There were no lights. The plantation seemed to sleep as profoundly as the schooner. On the path a small shell cracked under his naked heel.

The faithful half-caste foreman going his rounds cocked his ears at the sharp sound. He gave one enormous start of fear at the sight of the swift white figure flying at him out of the night. He crouched in terror, and then sprang up and clicked his tongue in amazed recognition.

"Tse! Tse! The master!"

"Be quiet, Luiz, and listen to what I say."

Yes, it was the master, the strong master who was never known to raise his voice, the man blindly obeyed and never questioned. He talked low and rapidly in the quiet night, as if every minute were precious. On learning that three guests were coming to stay Luiz clicked his tongue rapidly. These clicks were the uniform, stenographic symbols of his emotions, and he could give them an infinite variety of meaning. He listened to the rest in a deep silence hardly affected by the low, "Yes, master," whenever Renouard paused.

"You understand?" the latter insisted. "No preparations are to be made till we land in the morning. And you are to say that Mr. Walter has gone off in a trading schooner on a round of the islands."

"Yes, master."

"No mistakes—mind!"

"No, master."

Renouard walked back toward the sea. Luiz following him, proposed to call out half a dozen boys and man the canoe.

"Imbecile!"

"Tse! Tse! Tse!"

"Don't you understand that you haven't seen me?"

"Yes, master. But what a long swim. Suppose you drown."

"Then you can say of me and of Mr. Walter what you like. The dead don't mind."

Renouard entered the sea and heard a faint Tse! Tse! Tse! of concern from the half-caste, who had already lost sight of the master's dark head on the overshadowed water.

Renouard set his direction by a big star that, dipping on the horizon, seemed to look curiously into his face. On this swim back he felt the mournful fatigue of all that length of the traversed road, which brought him no nearer to his desire. It was as if his love had sapped the invisible supports of his strength. There came a moment when it seemed to him that he must have swum beyond the confines of life. He had a sensation of eternity close at hand, demanding no effort— offering its peace. It was easy to swim like this beyond the confines of life looking at a star. But the thought: "They will think I dared not face them and committed suicide," caused a revolt of his mind which carried him on. He returned on board, as he had left, unheard and unseen. He lay in his hammock utterly exhausted and with a confused feeling that he had been beyond the confines of life, somewhere near a star, and that it was very quiet there.

CHAPTER NINE

Sheltered by the squat headland from the first morning sparkle of the sea the little bay breathed a delicious freshness. The party from the schooner landed at the bottom of the garden. They exchanged insignificant words in studiously casual tones. The professor's sister put up a long-handled eyeglass as if to scan the novel surroundings, but in reality searching for poor Arthur anxiously. Having never seen him otherwise than in his town clothes she had no idea what he would look like. It had been left to the professor to help his ladies out of the boat because Renouard, as if intent on giving directions, had stepped forward at once to meet the half-caste Luiz hurrying down the path. In the distance, in front of the dazzlingly sunlit bungalow, a row of dark-faced house boys, unequal in stature and varied in complexion, preserved the immobility of a guard of honour.

Luiz had taken off his soft felt hat before coming within earshot. Renouard bent his head to his rapid talk of domestic arrangements he meant to make for the visitors; another bed in the master's room for the ladies and a cot for the gentleman to be hung in the room opposite where—where Mr. Walter—here he gave a scared look all round—Mr. Walter—had died.

"Very good," assented Renouard in an even undertone. "And remember what you have to say of him."

"Yes, master. Only"—he wriggled slightly and put one bare foot on the other for a moment in apologetic embarrassment—"only I—I—don't like to say it."

Renouard looked at him without anger, without any sort of expression. "Frightened of the dead? Eh? Well—all right. I will say it myself—I suppose once for all. . . ." Immediately he raised his voice very much.

"Send the boys down to bring up the luggage."

"Yes, master."

Renouard turned to his distinguished guests who, like a personally conducted party of tourists, had stopped and were looking about them. "I am sorry," he began with an impassive face. "My man has just told me that Mr. Walter . . ." he managed to smile, but didn't correct himself . . . "has gone in a trading schooner on a short tour of the islands, to the westward."

This communication was received in profound silence.

Renouard forgot himself in the thought: "It's done!" But the sight of the string of boys marching up to the house with suitcases and dressing-bags rescued him from that appalling abstraction.

"All I can do is to beg you to make yourselves at home . . . with what patience you may."

This was so obviously the only thing to do that everybody moved on at once. The professor walked alongside Renouard, behind the two ladies.

"Rather unexpected—this absence."

"Not exactly," muttered Renouard. "A trip has to be made every year to engage labour."

"I see . . . And he . . . How vexingly elusive the poor fellow has become! I'll begin to think that some wicked fairy is favouring this love tale with unpleasant attentions."

Renouard noticed that the party did not seem weighed down by this new disappointment. On the contrary they moved with a freer step. The professor's sister dropped her eyeglass to the end of its chain. Miss Moorsom took the lead. The professor, his lips unsealed, lingered in the open: but Renouard did not listen to that man's talk. He looked after that man's daughter—if indeed that creature of irresistible seductions were a daughter of mortals. The very intensity of his desire, as if his soul were streaming after her through his eyes, defeated his object of keeping hold of her as long as possible with, at least, one of his senses. Her moving outlines dissolved into a misty coloured shimmer of a woman made of flame and shadows crossing the threshold of his house.

The days which followed were not exactly such as Renouard had feared—yet they were not better than his fears. They were accursed in all the moods they brought him. But the general aspect of things was quiet. The professor smoked innumerable pipes with the air of a worker on his holiday, always in movement and looking at things with that mysteriously sagacious aspect of men who are admittedly wiser than the rest of the world. His white head of hair—whiter than anything within the horizon except the broken water on the reefs—was glimpsed in every part of the plantation always on the move under the white parasol. And once he climbed the headland and appeared suddenly to those below, a white speck elevated in the blue, with a diminutive but statuesque effect.

Felicia Moorsom remained near the house. Sometimes she could be seen with a despairing expression scribbling rapidly in her lock-up diary. But only for a moment. At the sound of Renouard's footsteps she would turn toward him her beautiful face, adorable in that calm which was like a wilful, like a cruel ignoring of her tremendous power.

THE PLANTER OF MALATA 201

Whenever she sat on the veranda, on a chair more specially reserved
for her use, Renouard would stroll up and sit on the steps near her,
mostly silent, and often not trusting himself to turn his glance on
her. She, very still, with her eyes half closed, looked down on his head
—so that to a beholder (such as Professor Moorsom, for instance) she
would appear to be turning over in her mind profound thoughts about
that man sitting at her feet, his shoulders bowed a little, his hands
listless—as if vanquished. And, indeed, the moral poison of falsehood
has such a decomposing power that Renouard felt his old personality
turn to dead dust. Often, in the evening, when they sat outside conversing languidly in the dark, he felt that he must rest his forehead
on her feet and burst into tears.

The professor's sister suffered from some little strain caused by the
unstability of her own feelings toward Renouard. She could not tell
whether she really did dislike him or not. At times he appeared to
her most fascinating; and, though he generally ended by saying something shockingly crude, she could not resist her inclination to talk with
him—at least not always. One day when her neice had left them alone
on the veranda she leaned forward in her chair—speckless, resplendent,
and, in her way, almost as striking a personality as her niece, who
did not resemble her in the least. "Dear Felicia has inherited her hair
and the greatest part of her appearance from her mother," the maiden
lady used to tell people.

She leaned forward then, confidentially.

"Oh! Mr. Renouard! Haven't you something comforting to say?"

He looked up, as surprised as if a voice from heaven had spoken
with this perfect society intonation, and by the puzzled profundity of
his blue eyes fluttered the wax flower of refined womanhood. She
continued. "For—I can speak to you openly on this tiresome subject
—only think what a terrible strain this hope deferred must be for
Felicia's heart—for her nerves."

"Why speak to me about it," he muttered, feeling half choked
suddenly.

"Why! As a friend—a well-wisher—the kindest of hosts. I am afraid
we are really eating you out of house and home." She laughed a little.
"Ah! When, when will this suspense be relieved! That poor lost Arthur!
I confess that I am almost afraid of the great moment. It will be
like seeing a ghost."

"Have you ever seen a ghost?" asked Renouard in a dull voice.

She shifted her hands a little. Her pose was perfect in its ease and
middle-aged grace.

"Not actually. Only in a photograph. But we have many friends who
had the experience of apparitions."

"Ah! They see ghosts in London," mumbled Renouard, not looking at her.

"Frequently—in a certain very interesting set. But all sorts of people do. We have a friend, a very famous author—his ghost is a girl. One of my brother's intimates is a very great man of science. He is friendly with a ghost . . . Of a girl too," she added in a voice as if struck for the first time by the coincidence. "It is the photograph of that apparition which I have seen. Very sweet. Most interesting. A little cloudy naturally. . . . Mr. Renouard! I hope you are not a sceptic. It's so consoling to think . . ."

"Those plantation boys of mine see ghosts too," said Renouard grimly.

The sister of the philosopher sat up stiffly. What crudeness! It was always so with this strange young man.

"Mr. Renouard! How can you compare the superstitious fancies of your horrible savages with the manifestations . . ."

Words failed her. She broke off with a very faint primly angry smile. She was perhaps the more offended with him because of that flutter at the beginning of the conversation. And in a moment, with perfect tact and dignity, she got up from her chair and left him alone.

Renouard didn't even look up. It was not the displeasure of the lady which deprived him of his sleep that night. He was beginning to forget what simple, honest sleep was like. His hammock from the ship had been hung for him on a side veranda, and he spent his nights in it on his back, his hands folded on his chest, in a sort of half-conscious, oppressed stupor. In the morning he watched with unseeing eyes the headland come out a shapeless inkblot against the thin light of the false dawn, pass through all the stages of daybreak to the deep purple of its outlined mass nimbed gloriously with the gold of the rising sun. He listened to the vague sounds of waking within the house: and suddenly he became aware of Luiz standing by the hammock—obviously troubled.

"What's the matter?"

"Tse! Tse! Tse!"

"Well, what now? trouble with the boys?"

"No, master. The gentleman when I take him his bath water he speak to me. He ask me—he ask—when, when I think Mr. Walter, he come back."

The half-breed's teeth chattered slightly. Renouard got out of the hammock.

"And he is here all the time—eh?"

Luiz nodded a scared affirmative, but at once protested, "I no see him. I never. Not I! The ignorant wild boys say they see . . . Something! Ough!"

He clapped his teeth on another short rattle, and stood there, shrunk, blighted like a man in a freezing blast.

"And what did you say to the gentleman?"

"I say I don't know—and I clear out. I—I don't like to speak of him."

"All right. We shall try to lay that poor ghost," said Renouard gloomily, going off to a small hut near by to dress. He was saying to himself: "This fellow will end by giving me away. The last thing that I . . . No! That mustn't be." And feeling his hand being forced he discovered the whole extent of his cowardice.

CHAPTER TEN

That morning wandering about his plantation, more like a frightened soul than its creator and master, he dodged the white parasol bobbing up here and there like a buoy adrift on a sea of dark-green plants. The crop promised to be magnificent, and the fashionable philosopher of the age took other than a merely scientific interest in the experiment. His investments were judicious, but he had always some little money lying by for experiments.

After lunch, being left alone with Renouard, he talked a little of cultivation and such matters. Then suddenly:

"By the way, is it true what my sister tells me, that your plantation boys have been disturbed by a ghost?"

Renouard, who since the ladies had left the table was not keeping such a strict watch on himself, came out of his abstraction with a start and a stiff smile.

"My foreman had some trouble with them during my absence. They funk working in a certain field on the slope of the hill."

"A ghost here!" exclaimed the amused professor. "Then our whole conception of the psychology of ghosts must be revised. This island has been uninhabited probably since the dawn of ages. How did a ghost come here. By air or water? And why did it leave its native haunts. Was it from misanthropy? Was he expelled from some community of spirits?"

Renouard essayed to respond in the same tone. The words died on his lips. Was it a man or a woman ghost, the professor inquired.

"I don't know." Renouard made an effort to appear at ease. He had, he said, a couple of Tahitians amongst his boys—a ghost-ridden race. They had started the scare. They had probably brought their ghost with them.

"Let us investigate the matter, Renouard," proposed the professor half in earnest. "We may make some interesting discoveries as to the state of primitive minds, at any rate."

This was too much. Renouard jumped up and leaving the room went out and walked about in front of the house. He would allow no one to force his hand. Presently the professor joined him outside. He carried his parasol, but had neither his book nor his pipe with him. Amiably serious he laid his hand on his "dear young friend's" arm.

"We are all of us a little strung up," he said. "For my part I have been like sister Anne in the story. But I cannot see anything coming. Anything that would be the least good for anybody—I mean."

Renouard had recovered sufficiently to murmur coldly his regret of this waste of time. For that was what, he supposed, the professor had in his mind.

"Time," mused Professor Moorsom. "I don't know that time can be wasted. But I will tell you, my dear friend, what this is: it is an awful waste of life. I mean for all of us. Even for my sister, who has got a headache and is gone to lie down."

He shook gently Renouard's arm. "Yes, for all of us! One may meditate on life endlessly, one may even have a poor opinion of it—but the fact remains that we have only one life to live. And it is short. Think of that, my young friend."

He released Renouard's arm and stepped out of the shade opening his parasol. It was clear that there was something more in his mind than mere anxiety about the date of his lectures for fashionable audiences. What did the man mean by his confounded platitudes? To Renouard, scared by Luiz in the morning (for he felt that nothing could be more fatal than to have his deception unveiled otherwise than by personal confession) this talk sounded like encouragement or a warning from that man who seemed to him to be very brazen and very subtle. It was like being bullied by the dead and cajoled by the living into a throw of dice for a supreme stake.

Renouard went away to some distance from the house and threw himself down in the shade of a tree. He lay there perfectly still with his forehead resting on his folded arms, light headed and thinking. It seemed to him that he must be on fire, then that he had fallen into a cool whirlpool, a smooth funnel of water swirling about with nauseating rapidity. And then (it must have been a reminiscence of his boyhood) he was walking on the dangerous thin ice of a river, unable to turn back. . . . Suddenly it parted from shore to shore with a loud crack like the report of a gun.

With one leap he found himself on his feet. All was peace, stillness, sunshine. He walked away from there slowly. Had he been a gambler he would have perhaps been supported in a measure by the mere excitement. But he was not a gambler. He had always disdained that artificial manner of challenging the fates. The bungalow came into view, bright and pretty, and all about everything was peace, stillness, sunshine. . . .

While he was plodding toward it he had a disagreeable sense of the dead man's company at his elbow. The ghost! He seemed to be everywhere but in his grave. Could one ever shake him off? he wondered. At that moment Miss Moorsom came out on the veranda; and at once, as if by a mystery of radiating waves, she roused a great tumult in his heart, shook earth and sky together—but he plodded on. Then like a grave song-note in the storm her voice came to him ominously.

"Ah! Renouard. . . ." He came up and smiled calmly, but she was very serious. "I can't keep still any longer. Is there time to walk up this headland and back before dark?"

The shadows were lying lengthened on the ground; all was stillness and peace. "No," said Renouard, feeling suddenly as steady as a rock. "But I can show you a view from the central hill which your father has not seen—a view of reefs and of broken water without end, and of great wheeling clouds of sea-birds."

She came down the veranda steps at once and they moved off. "You go first," he proposed, "and I'll direct you. To the left."

She was wearing a short nankin skirt, a muslin blouse; he could see through the thin stuff the skin of her shoulders, of her arms. The noble delicacy of her neck caused him a sort of transport. "The path begins where these three palms are. The only palms on the island."

"I see."

She never turned her head. After a while she observed: "This path looks as if it had been made recently."

"Quite recently," he assented very low.

They went on climbing steadily without exchanging another word; and when they stood on the top she gazed a long time before her. The low evening mist veiled the further limit of the reefs. Above the enormous and melancholy confusion, as of a fleet of wrecked islands, the restless myriads of sea-birds rolled and unrolled dark ribbons on the sky, gathered in clouds, soared and stooped like a play of shadows, for they were too far for them to hear their cries.

Renouard broke the silence in low tones.

"They'll be settling for the night presently." She made no sound. Round them all was peace and declining sunshine. Near by the topmost pinnacle of Malata, resembling the top of a buried tower, rose a rock, weather-worn, grey, weary of watching the monotonous centuries of the Pacific. Renouard leaned his shoulders against it. Felicia Moorsom faced him suddenly, her splendid black eyes full on his face as though she had made up her mind at last to destroy his wits once and for all. Dazzled, he lowered his eyelids slowly.

"Mr. Renouard! There is something strange in all this. Tell me where he is?"

He answered deliberately.

"On the other side of this rock. I buried him there myself."

She pressed her hands to her breast, struggled for her breath for a moment, then: "Ohhh! . . . You buried him! . . . What sort of man are you? . . . You dared not tell! . . . He is another of your victims? . . . You dared not confess that evening. . . . You must have killed him. What could he have done to you? . . . You fastened on him some atrocious quarrel and . . ."

Her vengeful aspect, her poignant cries left him as unmoved as the weary rock against which he leaned. He only raised his eyelids to look at her and lowered them slowly. Nothing more. It silenced her. And as if ashamed she made a gesture with her hand, putting away from her that thought. He spoke, quietly ironic at first.

"Ha! the legendary Renouard of sensitive idiots—the ruthless adventurer—the ogre with a future. That was a parrot cry, Miss Moorsom. I don't think that the greatest fool of them all ever dared hint such a stupid thing of me that I killed men for nothing. No, I had noticed this man in a hotel. He had come from up country I was told, and was doing nothing. I saw him sitting there lonely in a corner like a sick crow, and I went over one evening to talk to him. Just on impulse. He wasn't impressive. He was pitiful. My worst enemy could have told you he wasn't good enough to be one of Renouard's victims. It didn't take me long to judge that he was drugging himself. Not drinking. Drugs."

"Ah! It's now that you are trying to murder him," she cried.

"Really. Always the Renouard of shop-keepers' legend. Listen! I would never have been jealous of him. And yet I am jealous of the air you breathe, of the soil you tread on, of the world that sees you —moving free—not mine. But never mind. I rather liked him. For a certain reason I proposed he should come to be my assistant here. He said he believed this would save him. It did not save him from death. It came to him as it were from nothing—just a fall. A mere slip and tumble of ten feet into a ravine. But it seems he had been hurt before up country—by a horse. He ailed and ailed. No, he was not a steel-tipped man. And his poor soul seemed to have been damaged too. It gave way very soon."

"This is tragic!" Felicia Moorsom whispered with feeling. Renouard's lips twitched, but his level voice continued mercilessly.

"That's the story. He rallied a little one night and said he wanted to tell me something. I, being a gentleman, he said, he could confide in me. I told him that he was mistaken. That there was a good deal of a plebeian in me, that he couldn't know. He seemed disappointed.

He muttered something about his innocence and something that sounded like a curse on some woman, then turned to the wall and—just grew cold."

"On a woman," cried Miss Moorsom indignantly. "What woman?"

"I wonder!" said Renouard, raising his eyes and noting the crimson of her ear-lobes against the live whiteness of her complexion, the sombre, as if secret, night splendour of her eyes under the writhing flames of her hair. "Some woman who wouldn't believe in that poor innocence of his. . . . Yes. You probably. And now you will not believe in me—not even in me who must in truth be what I am—even to death. No! You won't. And yet, Felicia, a woman like you and a man like me do not often come together on this earth."

The flame of her glorious head scorched his face. He flung his hat far away, and his suddenly lowered eyelids brought out startlingly his resemblance to antique bronze, the profile of Pallas, still, austere, bowed a little in the shadow of the rock. "Oh! If you could only understand the truth that is in me!" he added.

She waited, as if too astounded to speak, till he looked up again, and then with unnatural force as if defending herself from some unspoken aspersion: "It's I who stand for truth here! Believe in you! In you, who by a heartless falsehood—and nothing else, nothing else, do you hear?—have brought me here, deceived, cheated, as in some abominable farce!" She sat down on a boulder, rested her chin in her hands, in the pose of simple grief—mourning for herself.

"It only wanted this. Why! Oh! Why is it that ugliness, ridicule, and baseness must fall across my path."

On that height, alone with the sky, they spoke to each other as if the earth had fallen away from under their feet.

"Are you grieving for your dignity? He was a mediocre soul and could have given you but an unworthy existence."

She did not even smile at those words, but, superb, as if lifting a corner of the veil, she turned on him slowly.

"And do you imagine I would have devoted myself to him for such a purpose! Don't you know that reparation was due to him from me? A sacred debt—a fine duty. To redeem him would not have been in my power—I know it. But he was blameless, and it was for me to come forward. Don't you see that in the eyes of the world nothing could have rehabilitated him so completely as his marriage with me? No word of evil could be whispered of him after I had given him my hand. As to giving myself up to anything less than the shaping of a man's destiny—if I thought I could do it I would abhor myself. . . ." She spoke with authority in her deep, fascinating, unemotional voice. Renouard meditated, gloomy, as if over some sinister riddle of a beautiful sphinx met on the wild road of his life.

"Yes. Your father was right. You are one of these aristocrats . . ."

She drew herself up haughtily.

"What do you say? My father! . . . I an aristocrat."

"Oh! I don't mean that you are like the men and women of the time of armours, castles, and great deeds. Oh, no! They stood on the naked soil, had traditions to be faithful to, had their feet on this earth of passions and death which is not a hothouse. They would have been too plebeian for you since they had to lead, to suffer with, to understand the commonest humanity. No, you are merely of the topmost layer, disdainful and superior, the mere pure froth and bubble on the inscrutable depths which some day will toss you out of existence. But you are you! You are you! You are the eternal love itself—only, O Divinity, it isn't your body, it is your soul that is made of foam."

She listened as if in a dream. He had succeeded so well in his effort to drive back the flood of his passion that his life itself seemed to run with it out of his body. At that moment he felt as one dead speaking. But the headlong wave returning with tenfold force flung him on her suddenly, with open arms and blazing eyes. She found herself like a feather in his grasp, helpless, unable to struggle, with her feet off the ground. But this contact with her, maddening like too much felicity, destroyed its own end. Fire ran through his veins, turned his passion to ashes, burnt him out and left him empty, without force—almost without desire. He let her go before she could cry out. And she was so used to the forms of repression enveloping, softening the crude impulses of old humanity that she no longer believed in their existence as if it were an exploded legend. She did not recognise what had happened to her. She came safe out of his arms without a struggle, not even having felt afraid.

"What's the meaning of this?" she said, outraged but calm in a scornful way.

He got down on his knees in silence, bent low to her very feet, while she looked down at him, a little surprised, without animosity, as if merely curious to see what he would do. Then, while he remained bowed to the ground pressing the hem of her skirt to his lips, she made a slight movement. He got up.

"No," he said. "Were you ever so much mine what could I do with you without your consent? No. You don't conquer a wraith, cold mist, stuff of dreams, illusion. It must come to you and cling to your breast. And then! Oh! And then!"

All ecstasy, all expression went out of his face.

"Mr. Renouard," she said, "though you can have no claim on my consideration after having decoyed me here for the vile purpose, apparently, of gloating over me as your possible prey, I will tell you that I am not perhaps the extraordinary being you think I am. You may believe me. Here I stand for truth itself."

"What's that to me what you are?" he answered. "At a sign from you I would climb up to the seventh heaven to bring you down to earth for my own—and if I saw you steeped to the lips in vice, in crime, in mud, I would go after you, take you to my arms—wear you for an incomparable jewel on my breast. And that's love—true love —the gift and the curse of the gods. There is no other."

The truth vibrating in his voice made her recoil slightly, for she was not fit to hear it—not even a little—not even one single time in her life. It was revolting to her; and in her trouble, perhaps prompted by the suggestion of his name or to soften the harshness of expression, for she was obscurely moved, she spoke to him in French.

"*Assez! J'ai horreur de tout cela*," she said.

He was white to his very lips, but he was trembling no more. The dice had been cast, and not even violence could alter the throw. She passed by him unbendingly, and he followed her down the path. After a time she heard him saying:

"And your dream is to influence a human destiny?"

"Yes!" she answered curtly, unabashed, with a woman's complete assurance.

"Then you may rest content. You have done it."

She shrugged her shoulders slightly. But just before reaching the end of the path she relented, stopped, and went back to him.

"I don't suppose you are very anxious for people to know how near you came to absolute turpitude. You may rest easy on that point. I shall speak to my father, of course, and we will agree to say that he has died—nothing more."

"Yes," said Renouard in a lifeless voice. "He is dead. His very ghost shall be done with presently."

She went on, but he remained standing stock still in the dusk. She had already reached the three palms when she heard behind her a loud peal of laughter, cynical and joyless, such as is heard in smoking-rooms at the end of a scandalous story. It made her feel positively faint for a moment.

CHAPTER ELEVEN

Slowly a complete darkness enveloped Geoffrey Renouard. His resolution had failed him. Instead of following Felicia into the house, he had stopped under the three palms, and leaning against a smooth trunk had abandoned himself to a sense of an immense deception and the feeling of extreme fatigue. This walk up the hill and down again was like the supreme effort of an explorer trying to penetrate the interior of an unknown country, the secret of which is too well defended by its cruel and barren nature. Decoyed by a mirage, he had gone too far—so far that there was no going back. His strength was at an end. For the first time in his life he had to give up, and with a sort of despairing self-possession he tried to understand the cause of the defeat. He did not ascribe it to that absurd dead man.

The hesitating shadow of Luiz approached him unnoticed till it spoke timidly. Renouard started.

"Eh? What? Dinner waiting? You must say I beg to be excused. I can't come. But I shall see them to-morrow morning, at the landing place. Take your orders from the professor as to the sailing of the schooner. Go now."

Luiz, dumbfounded, retreated into the darkness. Renouard did not move, but hours afterward, like the bitter fruit of his immobility, the words: "I had nothing to offer to her vanity," came from his lips in the silence of the island. And it was then only that he stirred, only to wear the night out in restless tramping up and down the various paths of the plantation. Luiz, whose sleep was made light by the consciousness of some impending change, heard footsteps passing by his hut, the firm tread of the master; and turning on his mats emitted a faint Tse! Tse! Tse! of deep concern.

Lights had been burning in the bungalow almost all through the night; and with the first sign of day began the bustle of departure. House-boys walked processionally carrying suitcases and dressing-bags down to the schooner's boat, which came to the landing place at the bottom of the garden. Just as the rising sun threw its golden nimbus around the purple shape of the headland, the Planter of Malata was perceived pacing bareheaded the curve of the little bay. He exchanged a few words with the sailing master of the schooner, then remained by the boat, standing very upright, his eyes on the ground, waiting.

He had not long to wait. Into the cool, overshadowed garden the professor descended first, and came jauntily down the path in a lively cracking of small shells. With his closed parasol hooked on his forearm, and a book in his hand, he resembled a banal tourist more than was permissible to a man of his unique distinction. He waved the disengaged arm from a distance, but at close quarters, arrested before Renouard's immobility, he made no offer to shake hands. He seemed to appraise the aspect of the man with a sharp glance, and made up his mind.

"We are going back by Suez," he began almost boisterously. "I have been looking up the sailing lists. If the zephyrs of your Pacific are only moderately propitious I think we are sure to catch the mail boat due in Marseilles on the 18th of March. This will suit me excellently. . . ." He lowered his tone. "My dear young friend, I'm deeply grateful to you."

Renouard's set lips moved.

"Why are you grateful to me?"

"Ah? Why? In the first place you might have made us miss the next boat, mightn't you? . . . I don't thank you for your hospitality. You can't be angry with me for saying that I am truly thankful to escape from it. But I am grateful to you for what you have done, and—for being what you are."

It was difficult to define the flavour of that speech, but Renouard received it with an austerely equivocal smile. The professor stepping into the boat opened his parasol and sat down in the stern-sheets waiting for the ladies. No sound of human voice broke the fresh silence of the morning while they walked the broad path, Miss Moorsom a little in advance of her aunt.

When she came abreast of him Renouard raised his head.

"Good-bye, Mr. Renouard," she said in a low voice, meaning to pass on; but there was such a look of entreaty in the blue gleam of his sunken eyes that after an imperceptible hesitation she laid her hand, which was ungloved, in his extended palm.

"Will you condescend to remember me?" he asked, while an emotion with which she was angry made her pale cheeks flush and her black eyes sparkle.

"This is a strange request for you to make," she said, exaggerating the coldness of her tone.

"Is it? Impudent, perhaps. Yet I am not so guilty as you think; and bear in mind that to me you can never make reparation."

"Reparation? To you! It is you who can offer me no reparation for the offence against my feelings—and my person; for what reparation can be adequate for your odious and ridiculous plot so scornful in its implication, so humiliating to my pride. No! I don't want to remember you."

Unexpectedly, with a tightening grip, he pulled her nearer to him, and looking into her eyes with fearless despair—

"You'll have to. . . . I shall haunt you," he said firmly.

Her hand was wrenched out of his grasp before he had time to release it. Felicia Moorsom stepped into the boat, sat down by the side of her father, and breathed tenderly on her crushed fingers.

The professor gave her a sidelong look—nothing more. But the professor's sister, yet on shore, had put up her long-handle double eyeglass to look at the scene. She dropped it with a faint rattle.

"I've never in my life heard anything so crude said to a lady," she murmured, passing before Renouard with a perfectly erect head. When, a moment afterward, softening suddenly, she turned to throw a

212

good-bye to that young man, she saw only his back in the distance moving toward the bungalow. She watched him go in—amazed—before she too left the soil of Malata.

Nobody disturbed Renouard in that room where he had shut himself in to breathe the evanescent perfume of her who for him was no more, till late in the afternoon when the half-caste was heard on the other side of the door.

He wanted the master to know that the trader *Janet* was just entering the cove.

Renouard's strong voice on his side of the door gave him most unexpected instructions. He was to pay off the boys with the cash in the office and arrange with the captain of the *Janet* to take every worker away from Malata, returning them to their respective homes. An order on the Dunster firm would be given to him in payment.

And again the silence of the bungalow remained unbroken till, next morning, the half-caste came to report that everything was done. The plantation boys were embarking now.

Through a crack in the door a hand thrust at him a piece of paper, and the door slammed to so sharply that Luiz stepped back. Then approaching cringingly the keyhole, in a propitiatory tone he asked:

"Do I go too, master?"

"Yes. You too. Everybody."

"Master stop here alone?"

Silence. And the half-caste's eyes grew wide with wonder. But he also, like those "ignorant savages," the plantation boys, was only too glad to leave an island haunted by the ghost of a white man. He backed away noiselessly from the mysterious silence in that closed room, and only in the very doorway of the bungalow allowed himself to give vent to his feelings by a deprecatory and pained—

"Tse! Tse! Tse!"

CHAPTER TWELVE

The Moorsoms did manage to catch the homeward mail boat all right, but had only twenty-four hours in town. Thus the sentimental Willie could not see very much of them. This did not prevent him afterward from relating at great length, with manly tears in his eyes, how poor Miss Moorsom—the fashionable and clever beauty—found her betrothed in Malata only to see him die in her arms. Most people were deeply touched by the sad story. It was the talk of a good many days.

But the all-knowing Editor, Renouard's only friend and crony, wanted to know more than the rest of the world. From professional incontinence, perhaps, he thirsted for a full cup of harrowing detail. And when he noticed Renouard's schooner lying in port day after day he sought the sailing master to learn the reason. The man told him that such were his instructions. He had been ordered to lie there a month before returning to Malata. And the month was nearly up. "I will ask you to give me a passage," said the Editor.

He landed in the morning at the bottom of the garden and found peace, stillness, sunshine reigning everywhere, the doors and windows of the bungalow standing wide open, no sight of a human being any-where, the plants growing rank and tall in the deserted fields. For hours the Editor and the schooner's crew, excited by the mystery, roamed over the island shouting Renouard's name; and at last set themselves in grim silence to explore systematically the uncleared bush and the deeper ravines in search of his corpse. What had happened? Had he been murdered by the boys? Or had he simply, capricious and secretive, abandoned his plantation taking the people with him. It was impossible to tell what had happened. At last, toward the decline of the day, the Editor and the sailing master discovered a track of sandals crossing a strip of sandy beach on the north shore of the bay. Following this track fearfully, they passed round the spur of the headlands, and there on a large stone found the sandals, Renouard's white jacket, and the Malay sarong of chequered pattern which the planter of Malata was well known to wear when going to bathe. These things made a little heap, and the sailor remarked, after gazing at it in silence—

"Birds have been hovering over this for many a day."

"He's gone bathing and got drowned," cried the Editor in dismay.

"I doubt it, sir. If he had been drowned anywhere within a mile from the shore the body would have been washed out on the reefs. And our boats have found nothing so far."

Nothing was ever found—and Renouard's disappearance remained in the main inexplicable. For to whom could it have occurred that a man would set out calmly to swim beyond the confines of life—with a steady stroke—his eyes fixed on a star!

Next evening, from the receding schooner, the Editor looked back for the last time at the deserted island. A black cloud hung listlessly over the high rock on the middle hill; and under the mysterious si-lence of that shadow Malata lay mournful, with an air of anguish in the wild sunset, as if remembering the heart that was broken there.

Dec., 1913.

An Outpost of Progress

THERE were two white men in charge of the trading station. Kayerts, the chief, was short and fat; Carlier, the assistant, was tall, with a large head and a very broad trunk perched upon a long pair of thin legs. The third man on the staff was a Sierra Leone nigger, who maintained that his name was Henry Price. However, for some reason or other, the natives down the river had given him the name of Makola, and it stuck to him through all his wanderings about the country. He spoke English and French with a warbling accent, wrote a beautiful hand, understood bookkeeping, and cherished in his innermost heart the worship of evil spirits. His wife was a negress from Loanda, very large and very noisy. Three children rolled about in sunshine before the door of his low, shed-like dwelling. Makola, taciturn and impenetrable, despised the two white men. He had charge of a small clay storehouse with a dried-grass roof, and pretended to keep a correct account of beads, cotton cloth, red kerchiefs, brass wire, and other trade goods it contained. Besides the storehouse and Makola's hut, there was only one large building in the cleared ground of the station. It was built neatly of reeds, with a verandah on all the four sides. There were three rooms in it. The one in the middle was the living-room, and had two rough tables and a few stools in it. The other two were the bedrooms for the white men. Each had a bedstead and a mosquito net for all furniture. The plank floor was littered with the belongings of the white men; open half-empty boxes, torn wearing apparel, old boots; all the things dirty, and all the things broken, that accumulate mysteriously round untidy men. There was also another dwelling-place some distance away from the buildings. In it, under a tall cross much out of the perpendicular, slept the man who had seen the beginning of all this; who had planned and had watched the construction of this outpost of progress. He had been, at home, an unsuccessful painter who, weary of pursuing fame on an empty stomach, had gone out there through high protections. He had been the first chief of that station. Makola had watched the energetic artist die of fever in the just finished house with his usual kind of "I told you so" indifference. Then, for a time, he dwelt alone with his family, his accounts books, and the Evil Spirit that rules the lands under the equator. He got on very well with his god. Perhaps he had propitiated him by a promise of more white men to play with, by and by. At any rate the director of the Great Trading Company, coming up in a steamer that resembled an enormous sardine box with a flat-roofed shed erected on it, found the station in good order, and Makola as usual quietly diligent. The director had the cross put up over the first agent's grave, and appointed Kayerts to the post. Carlier was told off as second in charge. The director was a man ruthless and efficient, who at times, but very imperceptibly, indulged in grim humour. He made a speech to Kayerts and Carlier, pointing out to them the promising aspect of their station. The nearest trading-post was about three hundred miles away. It was an exceptional opportunity for them to distinguish themselves and to earn percentages on the trade. This appointment was a favour done to beginners. Kayerts was moved almost to tears by his director's kindness. He would, he said, by doing his best, try to justify the flattering confidence, &c., &c. Kayerts had been in the Administration of the Telegraphs, and knew how to express himself correctly. Carlier, an ex-non-commissioned officer of cavalry in an army guaranteed from harm by several European Powers, was less impressed. If there were commissions to get, so much the better; and, trailing a sulky glance over the river, the forests, the impenetrable bush that seemed to cut off the station from the rest of the world, he muttered between his teeth, "We shall see, very soon."

Next day, some bales of cotton goods and a few cases of provisions having been thrown on shore, the sardine-box steamer went off, not to return for another six months. On the deck the Director touched his cap to the two agents, who stood on the bank waving their hats, and turning to an old servant of the Company on his passage to headquarters, said, "Look at those two imbeciles. They must be mad at home to send me such specimens. I told those fellows to plant a vegetable garden, build new storehouses and fences, and construct a landing-stage. I bet nothing will be done! They won't know how to begin. I always thought the station on this river useless, and they just fit the station!"

"They will form themselves there," said the old stager with a quiet smile.

"At any rate, I am rid of them for six months," retorted the Director.

The two men watched the steamer round the bend, then ascending arm in arm the slope of the bank, returned to the station. They had been in this vast and dark country only a very short time, and as yet always in the midst of other white men, under the eye and guidance of their superiors. And now, dull as they were to the subtle influences of surroundings, they felt themselves very much alone, when suddenly left unassisted to face the wilderness; a wilderness rendered more strange, more incomprehensible by the mysterious glimpses of the vigorous life it contained. They were two perfectly insignificant and incapable individuals, whose existence is only rendered possible through the high organization of civilized crowds. Few men realize that their life, the very essence of their character, their capabilities and their audacities, are only the expression of their belief in the safety of their ities, are only the expression of their belief in the safety of their surroundings. The courage, the composure, the confidence; the emotions and principles; every great and every insignificant thought belongs not to the individual but to the crowd: to the crowd that believes blindly in the irresistible force of its institutions and of its morals, in the power of its police and of its opinion. But the contact with pure unmitigated savagery, with primitive nature and primitive man, brings sudden and profound trouble into the heart. To the sentiment of being alone of one's kind, to the clear perception of the loneliness of one's thoughts, of one's sensations—to the negation of the habitual, which is safe, there is added the affirmation of the unusual, which is dangerous; a suggestion of things vague, uncontrollable, and repulsive, whose discomposing intrusion excites the imagination and tries the civilized nerves of the foolish and the wise alike.

Kayerts and Carlier walked arm in arm, drawing close to one another as children do in the dark; and they had the same, not altogether unpleasant, sense of danger which one half suspects to be imaginary. They chatted persistently in familiar tones. "Our station is prettily situated," said one. The other assented with enthusiasm, enlarging volubly on the beauties of the situation. Then they passed near the grave. "Poor devil!" said Kayerts. "He died of fever, didn't he?" muttered Carlier, stopping short. "Why," retorted Kayerts, with indignation, "I've been told that the fellow exposed himself recklessly to the sun. The climate here, everybody says, is not at all worse than at home, as long as you keep out of the sun. Do you hear that, Carlier? I am chief here, and my orders are that you should not expose yourself to the sun!" He assumed his superiority jocularly, but his meaning was serious. The idea that he would, perhaps, have to bury Carlier and remain alone, gave him an inward shiver. He felt suddenly that this Carlier was more precious to him here, in the centre of Africa, than a brother could be anywhere else. Carlier, entering into the spirit of the thing, made a military salute and answered in a brisk tone, "Your orders shall be attended to, chief!" Then he burst out laughing, slapped Kayerts on the back and shouted, "We shall let life run easily here! Just sit still and gather in the ivory those savages will bring. This country has its good points, after all!" They both laughed loudly while

Carlier thought: "That poor Kayerts; he is so fat and unhealthy. It would be awful if I had to bury him here. He is a man I respect." . . . Before they reached the verandah of their house they called one another "my dear fellow."

The first day they were very active, pottering about with hammers and nails and red calico, to put up curtains, make their house habitable and pretty; resolved to settle down comfortably to their new life. For them an impossible task. To grapple effectually with even purely material problems requires more serenity of mind and more lofty courage than people generally imagine. No two beings could have been more unfitted for such a struggle. Society, not from any tenderness, but because of its strange needs, had taken care of those two men, forbidding them all independent thought, all initiative, all departure from routine; and forbidding it under pain of death. They could only live on condition of being machines. And now, released from the fostering care of men with pens behind the ears, or of men with gold lace on the sleeves, they were like those lifelong prisoners who, liberated after many years, do not know what use to make of their freedom. They did not know what use to make of their faculties, being both, through want of practice, incapable of independent thought.

At the end of two months Kayerts often would say, "If it was not for my Melie, you wouldn't catch me here." Melie was his daughter. He had thrown up his post in the Administration of the Telegraphs, though he had been for seventeen years perfectly happy there, to earn a dowry for his girl. His wife was dead, and the child was being brought up by his sisters. He regretted the streets, the pavements, the cafés, his friends of many years; all the things he used to see, day after day; all the thoughts suggested by familiar things—the thoughts effortless, monotonous, and soothing of a Government clerk; he regretted all the gossip, the small enmities, the mild venom, and the little jokes of Government offices. "If I had had a decent brother-in-law," Carlier would remark, "a fellow with a heart, I would not be here." He had left the army and had made himself so obnoxious to his family by his laziness and impudence, that an exasperated brother-in-law had made superhuman efforts to procure him an appointment in the Company as a second-class agent. Having not a penny in the world he was compelled to accept this means of livelihood as soon as it became quite clear to him that there was nothing more to squeeze out of his relations. He, like Kayerts, regretted his old life. He regretted the clink of sabre and spurs on a fine afternoon, the barrack-room witticisms, the girls of garrison towns; but, besides, he had also a sense of grievance. He was evidently a much ill-used man. This made him moody, at times. But the two men got on well together in the fellowship of their stupidity and laziness. Together they did nothing, absolutely nothing, and enjoyed the sense of the idleness for which they were paid. And in time they came to feel something resembling affection for one another.

They lived like blind men in a large room, aware only of what came in contact with them (and of that only imperfectly), but unable to see the general aspect of things. The river, the forest, all the great land throbbing with life, were like a great emptiness. Even the brilliant sunshine disclosed nothing intelligible. Things appeared and disappeared before their eyes in an unconnected and aimless kind of way. The river seemed to come from nowhere and flow nowhither. It flowed through a void. Out of that void, at times, came canoes, and men with spears in their hands would suddenly crowd the yard of the station. They were naked, glossy black, ornamented with snowy shells and glistening brass wire, perfect of limb. They made an uncouth babbling noise when they spoke, moved in a stately manner, and sent quick, wild glances out of their startled, never-resting eyes. Those warriors would squat in long rows, four or more deep, before the verandah, while their chiefs bargained for hours with Makola over an elephant tusk. Kayerts sat on his chair and looked down on the proceedings, understanding nothing. He stared at them with his round blue eyes, called out to Carlier, "Here, look! look at that fellow there—and that other one, to the left. Did you ever see such a face? Oh, the funny brute!"

Carlier, smoking native tobacco in a short wooden pipe, would swagger up twirling his moustaches, and surveying the warriors with haughty indulgence, would say—

"Fine animals. Brought any bone? Yes? It's not any too soon. Look at the muscles of that fellow—third from the end. I wouldn't care to get a punch on the nose from him. Fine arms, but legs no good below the knee. Couldn't make cavalry men of them." And after glancing down complacently at his own shanks, he always concluded: "Pah! Don't they stink! You, Makola! Take that herd over to the fetish" (the storehouse was in every station called the fetish, perhaps because of the spirit of civilization it contained) "and give them up some of the rubbish you keep there. I'd rather see it full of bone than full of rags."

Kayerts approved.

"Yes, yes! Go and finish that palaver over there, Mr. Makola. I will come round when you are ready, to weigh the tusk. We must be careful." Then turning to his companion: "This is the tribe that lives down the river; they are rather aromatic. I remember, they had been once before here. D'ye hear that row? What a fellow has got to put up with in this dog of a country! My head is split."

Such profitable visits were rare. For days the two pioneers of trade and progress would look on their empty courtyard in the vibrating brilliance of vertical sunshine. Below the high bank, the silent river flowed on glittering and steady. On the sands in the middle of the stream, hippos and alligators sunned themselves side by side. And stretching away in all directions, surrounding the insignificant cleared spot of the trading post, immense forests, hiding fateful complications of fantastic life, lay in the eloquent silence of mute greatness. The two men understood nothing, cared for nothing but for the passage of days that separated them from the steamer's return. Their predecessor had left some torn books. They took up these wrecks of novels, and, as they had never read anything of the kind before, they were surprised and amused. Then during long days there were interminable and silly discussions about plots and personages. In the centre of Africa they made acquaintance of Richelieu and of d'Artagnan, of Hawk's Eye and of Father Goriot, and of many other people. All these imaginary personages became subjects for gossip as if they had been living friends. They discounted their virtues, suspected their motives, decried their successes; were scandalized at their duplicity or were doubtful about their courage. The accounts of crimes filled them with indignation, while tender or pathetic passages moved them deeply. Carlier cleared his throat and said in a soldierly voice, "What nonsense!" Kayerts, his round eyes suffused with tears, his fat cheeks quivering, rubbed his bald head, and declared, "This is a splendid book. I had no idea there were such clever fellows in the world." They also found some old copies of a home paper. That print discussed what it was pleased to call "Our Colonial Expansion" in high-flown language. It spoke much of the rights and duties of civilization, of the sacredness of the civilizing work, and extolled the merits of those who went about bringing light, and faith and commerce to the dark places of the earth. Carlier and Kayerts read, wondered, and began to think better of themselves. Carlier said one evening, waving his hand about, "In a hundred years, there will be perhaps a town here. Quays, and warehouses, and barracks, and—and—billiard-rooms. Civilization, my boy, and virtue—and all. And then, chaps will read that two good fellows, Kayerts and Carlier, were the first civilized men to live in this very spot!" Kayerts nodded, "Yes, it is a consolation to think of that." They seemed to forget their dead predecessor; but, early one day, Carlier went out and replanted the cross firmly. "It used to make me squint whenever I walked that way," he explained to Kayerts over the morning coffee. "It made me squint, leaning over so much. So I just planted it upright. And solid, I promise you! I suspended myself with both hands to the cross-piece. Not a move. Oh, I did that properly."

At times Gobila came to see them. Gobila was the chief of the neighbouring villages. He was a gray-headed savage, thin and black, with a white cloth round his loins and a mangy panther skin hanging over his back. He came up with long strides of his skeleton legs, swinging a staff as tall as himself, and, entering the common room of the station, would squat on his heels to the left of the door. There he sat, watching Kayerts, and now and then making a speech which the other did not understand. Kayerts, without interrupting his occupation, would from time to time say in a friendly manner: "How goes it, you old image?" and they would smile at one another. The two whites had a liking for that old and incomprehensible creature, and called him Father Gobila. Gobila's manner was paternal, and he seemed really to love all white men. They all appeared to him very young, indistinguishably alike (except for stature), and he knew that they were all brothers, and also immortal. The death of the artist, who was the first white man whom he knew intimately, did not disturb this belief, because he was firmly convinced that the white stranger had pretended to die and got himself buried for some mysterious purpose of his own, into which it was useless to inquire. Perhaps it was his way of going home to his own country? At any rate, these were his brothers, and he transferred his absurd affection to them. They returned it in a way. Carlier slapped him on the back, and recklessly struck off matches for his amusement. Kayerts was always ready to let him have a sniff at the ammonia bottle. In short, they behaved just like that other white creature that had hidden itself in a hole in the ground. Gobila considered them attentively. Perhaps they were the same being with the other—or one of them was. He couldn't decide—clear up that mystery; but he remained always very friendly. In consequence of that friendship the women of Gobila's village walked in single file through the reedy grass, bringing every morning to the station, fowls, and sweet potatoes, and palm wine, and sometimes a goat. The Company never provisions the stations fully, and the agents required those local supplies to live. They had them through the good-will of Gobila, and lived well. Now and then one of them had a bout of fever, and the other nursed him with gentle devotion. They did not think much of it. It left them weaker, and their appearance changed for the worse. Carlier was hollow-eyed and irritable. Kayerts showed a drawn, flabby face above the rotundity of his stomach, which gave him a weird aspect. But being constantly together, they did not notice the change that took place gradually in their appearance, and also in their dispositions.

Five months passed in that way.

Then, one morning, as Kayerts and Carlier, lounging in their chairs under the verandah, talked about the approaching visit of the steamer, a knot of armed men came out of the forest and advanced towards the station. They were strangers to that part of the country. They were tall, slight, draped classically from neck to heel in blue fringed cloths, and carried percussion muskets over their bare right shoulders. Makola showed signs of excitement, and ran out of the storehouse (where he spent all his days) to meet these visitors. They came into the courtyard and looked about them with steady, scornful glances. Their leader, a powerful and determined-looking negro with bloodshot eyes, stood in front of the verandah and made a long speech. He gesticulated much, and ceased very suddenly.

There was something in his intonation, in the sounds of the long sentences he used, that startled the two whites. It was like a reminiscence of something not exactly familiar, and yet resembling the speech of civilized men. It sounded like one of those impossible languages which sometimes we hear in our dreams.

"What lingo is that?" said the amazed Carlier. "In the first moment I fancied the fellow was going to speak French. Anyway, it is a different kind of gibberish to what we ever heard."

"Yes," replied Kayerts. "Hey, Makola, what does he say? Where do they come from? Who are they?"

But Makola, who seemed to be standing on hot bricks, answered hurriedly, "I don't know. They come from very far. Perhaps Mrs. Price will understand. They are perhaps bad men."

The leader, after waiting for a while, said something sharply to Makola, who shook his head. Then the man, after looking round, noticed Makola's hut and walked over there. The next moment Mrs. Makola was heard speaking with great volubility. The other strangers—they were six in all—strolled about with an air of ease, put their heads through the door of the storeroom, congregated round the grave, pointed understandingly at the cross, and generally made themselves at home.

"I don't like those chaps—and, I say, Kayerts, they must be from the coast; they've got firearms," observed the sagacious Carlier.

Kayerts also did not like those chaps. They both, for the first time, became aware that they lived in conditions where the unusual may be dangerous, and that there was no power on earth outside of themselves to stand between them and the unusual. They became uneasy, went in and loaded their revolvers. Kayerts said, "We must order Makola to tell them to go away before dark."

The strangers left in the afternoon, after eating a meal prepared for them by Mrs. Makola. The immense woman was excited, and talked much with the visitors. She rattled away shrilly, pointing here and there at the forests and at the river. Makola sat apart and watched. At times he got up and whispered to his wife. He accompanied the strangers across the ravine at the back of the station-ground, and returned slowly looking very thoughtful. When questioned by the white men he was very strange, seemed not to understand, seemed to have forgotten French—seemed to have forgotten how to speak altogether. Kayerts and Carlier agreed that the nigger had had too much palm wine.

There was some talk about keeping a watch in turn, but in the evening everything seemed so quiet and peaceful that they retired as usual. All night they were disturbed by a lot of drumming in the villages. A deep, rapid roll near by would be followed by another far off—then all ceased. Soon short appeals would rattle out here and there, then all mingle together, increase, become vigorous and sustained, would spread out over the forest, roll through the night, unbroken and ceaseless, near and far, as if the whole land had been one immense drum booming out steadily an appeal to heaven. And through the deep and tremendous noise sudden yells that resembled snatches of songs from a madhouse darted shrill and high in discordant jets of sound which seemed to rush far above the earth and drive all peace from under the stars.

Carlier and Kayerts slept badly. They both thought they had heard shots fired during the night—but they could not agree as to the direction. In the morning Makola was gone somewhere. He returned about noon with one of yesterday's strangers, and eluded all Kayerts' attempts to close with him: had become deaf apparently. Kayerts wondered. Carlier, who had been fishing off the bank, came back and remarked while he showed his catch, "The niggers seem to be in a deuce of a stir; I wonder what's up. I saw about fifteen canoes cross the river during the two hours I was there fishing." Kayerts, worried, said, "Isn't this Makola very queer to-day?" Carlier advised, "Keep all our men together in case of some trouble."

CHAPTER TWO

There were ten station men who had been left by the Director. Those fellows, having engaged themselves to the Company for six months (without having any idea of a month in particular and only a very faint notion of time in general), had been serving the cause of progress for upwards of two years. Belonging to a tribe from a very distant part of the land of darkness and sorrow, they did not run away, naturally supposing that as wandering strangers they would be killed by the inhabitants of the country; in which they were right. They lived in straw huts on the slope of a ravine overgrown with reedy grass, just behind the station buildings. They were not happy, regretting the festive incantations, the sorceries, the human sacrifices of their own land; where they also had parents, brothers, sisters, admired chiefs, respected magicians, loved friends, and other ties supposed generally to be human. Besides, the rice rations served out by the Company did not agree with them, being a food unknown to their land, and to which they could not get used. Consequently they were unhealthy and miserable. Had they been of any other tribe they would have made up their minds to die—for nothing is easier to certain savages than suicide —and so have escaped from the puzzling difficulties of existence. But belonging, as they did, to a warlike tribe with filed teeth, they had more grit, and went on stupidly living through disease and sorrow. They did very little work, and had lost their splendid physique. Carlier and Kayerts doctored them assiduously without being able to bring them back into condition again. They were mustered every morning and told off to different tasks—grass-cutting, fence-building, tree-felling, &c., &c., which no power on earth could induce them to execute efficiently. The two whites had practically very little control over them.

In the afternoon Makola came over to the big house and found Kayerts watching three heavy columns of smoke rising above the forests. "What is that?" asked Kayerts. "Some villages burn," answered Makola, who seemed to have regained his wits. Then he said abruptly: "We have got very little ivory; bad six months' trading. Do you like get a little more ivory?"

"Yes," said Kayerts, eagerly. He thought of percentages which were low.

"Those men who came yesterday are traders from Loanda who have got more ivory than they can carry home. Shall I buy? I know their camp."

"Certainly," said Kayerts. "What are those traders?"

"Bad fellows," said Makola, indifferently. "They fight with people, and catch women and children. They are bad men and got guns. There is a great disturbance in the country. Do you want ivory?"

"Yes," said Kayerts. Makola said nothing for a while. Then: "Those workmen of ours are no good at all," he muttered, looking round. "Station in very bad order, sir. Director will growl. Better get a fine lot of ivory, then he say nothing."

"I can't help it; the men won't work," said Kayerts. "When will you get that ivory?"

"Very soon," said Makola. "Perhaps to-night. You leave it to me, and keep indoors, sir. I think you had better give some palm wine to our men to make a dance this evening. Enjoy themselves. Work better to-morrow. There's plenty palm wine—gone a little sour."

Kayerts said "yes," and Makola, with his own hands carried big calabashes to the door of his hut. They stood there till the evening, and Mrs. Makola looked into every one. The men got them at sunset. When Kayerts and Carlier retired, a big bonfire was flaring before the men's huts. They could hear their shouts and drumming. Some men from Gobila's village had joined the station hands, and the entertainment was a great success.

In the middle of the night, Carlier waking suddenly, heard a man shout loudly; then a shot was fired. Only one. Carlier ran out and met Kayerts on the verandah. They were both startled. As they went across the yard to call Makola, they saw shadows moving in the night. One of them cried, "Don't shoot! It's me, Price." Then Makola appeared close to them. "Go back, go back, please," he urged, "you spoil all." "There are strange men about," said Carlier. "Never mind; I know," said Makola. Then he whispered, "All right. Bring ivory. Say nothing! I know my business." The two white men reluctantly went back to the house, but did not sleep. They heard footsteps, whispers, some groans. It seemed as if a lot of men came in, dumped heavy things on the ground, squabbled a long time, then went away. They lay on their hard beds and thought: "This Makola is invaluable." In the morning Carlier came out, very sleepy, and pulled at the cord of the big bell. The station hands mustered every morning to the sound of the bell. That morning nobody came. Kayerts turned out also, yawning. Across the yard they saw Makola come out of his hut, a tin basin of soapy water in his hand. Makola, a civilized nigger, was very neat in his person. He threw the soapsuds skilfully over a wretched little yellow cur he had, then turning his face to the agent's house, he shouted from the distance, "All the men gone last night!"

They heard him plainly, but in their surprise they both yelled out together: "What!" Then they stared at one another. "We are in a proper fix now," growled Carlier. "It's incredible!" muttered Kayerts. "I will go to the huts and see," said Carlier, striding off. Makola coming up found Kayerts standing alone.

"I can hardly believe it," said Kayerts, tearfully. "We took care of them as if they had been our children."

"They went with the coast people," said Makola after a moment of hesitation.

"What do I care with whom they went—the ungrateful brutes!" exclaimed the other. Then with sudden suspicion, and looking hard at Makola, he added: "What do you know about it?"

Makola moved his shoulders, looking down on the ground. "What do I know? I think only. Will you come and look at the ivory I've got there? It is a fine lot. You never saw such."

He moved towards the store. Kayerts followed him mechanically, thinking about the incredible desertion of the men. On the ground before the door of the fetish lay six splendid tusks.

"What did you give for it?" asked Kayerts, after surveying the lot with satisfaction.

"No regular trade," said Makola. "They brought the ivory and gave it to me. I told them to take what they most wanted in the station. It is a beautiful lot. No station can show such tusks. Those traders wanted carriers badly, and our men were no good here. No trade, no entry in books; all correct."

Kayerts nearly burst with indignation. "Why!" he shouted, "I believe you have sold our men for these tusks!" Makola stood impassive and silent. "I—I—will—I," stuttered Kayerts. "You fiend!" he yelled out.

"I did the best for you and the Company," said Makola, imperturbably. "Why you shout so much? Look at this tusk."

"I dismiss you! I will report you—I won't look at the tusk. I forbid you to touch them. I order you to throw them into the river. You—you!"

"You very red, Mr. Kayerts. If you are so irritable in the sun, you will get fever and die—like the first chief!" pronounced Makola impressively.

They stood still, contemplating one another with intense eyes, as if they had been looking with effort across immense distances. Kayerts shivered. Makola had meant no more than he said, but his words seemed to Kayerts full of ominous menace! He turned sharply and went away to the house. Makola retired into the bosom of his family; and the tusks, left lying before the store, looked very large and valuable in the sunshine.

Carlier came back on the verandah. "They're all gone, hey?" asked Kayerts from the far end of the common room in a muffled voice. "You did not find anybody?"

"Oh, yes," said Carlier, "I found one of Gobila's people lying dead before the huts—shot through the body. We heard that shot last night."

Kayerts came out quickly. He found his companion staring grimly over the yard at the tusks, away by the store. They both sat in silence for a while. Then Kayerts related his conversation with Makola. Carlier said nothing. At the midday meal they ate very little. They hardly exchanged a word that day. A great silence seemed to lie heavily over the station and press on their lips. Makola did not open the store; he spent the day playing with his children. He lay full-length on a mat outside his door, and the youngsters sat on his chest and clambered all over him. It was a touching picture. Mrs. Makola was busy cooking all day as usual. The white men made a somewhat better meal in the evening. Afterwards, Carlier smoking his pipe strolled over to the store; he stood for a long time over the tusks, touched one or two with his foot, even tried to lift the largest one by its small end. He came back to his chief, who had not stirred from the verandah, threw himself in the chair and said—

"I can see it! They were pounced upon while they slept heavily after drinking all that palm wine you've allowed Makola to give them. A put-up job! See? The worst is, some of Gobila's people were there, and got carried off too, no doubt. The least drunk woke up, and got shot for his sobriety. This is a funny country. What will you do now?"

"We can't touch it, of course," said Kayerts.

"Of course not," assented Carlier.

"Slavery is an awful thing," stammered out Kayerts in an unsteady voice.

"Frightful—the sufferings," grunted Carlier with conviction.

They believed their words. Everybody shows a respectful deference to certain sounds that he and his fellows can make. But about feelings people really know nothing. We talk with indignation or enthusiasm; we talk about oppression, cruelty, crime, devotion, self-sacrifice, virtue, and we know nothing real beyond the words. Nobody knows what suffering or sacrifice mean—except, perhaps the victims of the mysterious purpose of these illusions.

Next morning they saw Makola very busy setting up in the yard the big scales used for weighing ivory. By and by Carlier said: "What's that filthy scoundrel up to?" and lounged out into the yard. Kayerts followed. They stood watching. Makola took no notice. When the balance was swung true, he tried to lift a tusk into the scale. It was too heavy. He looked up helplessly without a word, and for a minute they stood round that balance as mute and still as three statues. Suddenly Carlier said: "Catch hold of the other end, Makola—you beast!" and together they swung the tusk up. Kayerts trembled in every limb. He muttered, "I say! O! I say!" and putting his hand in his pocket found there a dirty bit of paper and the stump of a pencil. He turned his back on the others, as if about to do something tricky, and noted stealthily the weights which Carlier shouted out to him with unnecessary loudness. When all was over Makola whispered to himself: "The sun's very strong here for the tusks." Carlier said to Kayerts in a careless tone: "I say, chief, I might just as well give him a lift with this lot into the store."

As they were going back to the house Kayerts observed with a sigh: "It had to be done." And Carlier said: "It's deplorable, but, the men being Company's men the ivory is Company's ivory. We must look after it." "I will report to the Director, of course," said Kayerts. "Of course; let him decide," approved Carlier.

At midday they made a hearty meal. Kayerts sighed from time to time. Whenever they mentioned Makola's name they always added to it an opprobrious epithet. It eased their conscience. Makola gave himself a half-holiday, and bathed his children in the river. No one from Gobila's villages came near the station that day. No one came the next day, and the next, nor for a whole week. Gobila's people might have been dead and buried for any sign of life they gave. But they were only mourning for those they had lost by the witchcraft of white men, who had brought wicked people into their country. The wicked people were gone, but fear remained. Fear always remains. A man may destroy everything within himself, love and hate and belief, and even doubt; but as long as he clings to life he cannot destroy fear: the fear, subtle, indestructible, and terrible, that pervades his being; that tinges his thoughts; that lurks in his heart; that watches on his lips the struggle of his last breath. In his fear, the mild old Gobila offered extra human sacrifices to all the Evil Spirits that had taken possession of his white friends. His heart was heavy. Some warriors spoke about burning and killing, but the cautious old savage dissuaded them. Who could foresee the woe those mysterious creatures, if irritated, might bring? They should be left alone. Perhaps in time they would disappear into the earth as the first one had disappeared. His people must keep away from them, and hope for the best.

Kayerts and Carlier did not disappear, but remained above on this earth, that, somehow, they fancied had become bigger and very empty. It was not the absolute and dumb solitude of the post that impressed them so much as an inarticulate feeling that something from within them was gone, something that worked for their safety, and had kept the wilderness from interfering with their hearts. The images of home; the memory of people like them, of men that thought and felt as they used to think and feel, receded into distances made indistinct by the glare of unclouded sunshine. And out of the great silence of the surrounding wilderness, its very hopelessness and savagery seemed to approach them nearer, to draw them gently, to look upon them, to envelop them with a solicitude irresistible, familiar, and disgusting.

Days lengthened into weeks, then into months. Gobila's people drummed and yelled to every new moon, as of yore, but kept away from the station. Makola and Carlier tried once in a canoe to open communications, but were received with a shower of arrows, and had to fly back to the station for dear life. That attempt set the country up and down the river into an uproar that could be very distinctly heard for days. The steamer was late. At first they spoke of delay jauntily, then anxiously, then gloomily. The matter was becoming serious. Stores were running short. Carlier cast his lines off the bank, but the river was low, and the fish kept out in the stream. They dared not stroll far away from the station to shoot. Moreover, there was no game in the impenetrable forest. Once Carlier shot a hippo in the river. They had no boat to secure it, and it sank. When it floated up it drifted away, and Gobila's people secured the carcase. It was the occasion for a national holiday, but Carlier had a fit of rage over it and talked about the necessity of exterminating all the niggers before the country could be made habitable. Kayerts mooned about silently; spent hours looking at the portrait of his Melie. It represented a little girl with long bleached tresses and a rather sour face. His legs were much swollen, and he could hardly walk. Carlier, undermined by fever, could not swagger any more, but kept tottering about, still with a devil-may-care air, as became a man who remembered his crack regiment. He had become hoarse, sarcastic, and inclined to say unpleasant things. He called it "being frank with you." They had long ago reckoned their percentages on trade, including in them that last deal of "this infamous Makola." They had also concluded not to say anything about it. Kayerts hesitated at first—was afraid of the Director.

"He has seen worse things done on the quiet," maintained Carlier, with a hoarse laugh. "Trust him! He won't thank you if you blab. He is no better than you or me. Who will talk if we hold our tongues? There is nobody here."

That was the root of the trouble! There was nobody there; and being left there alone with their weakness, they became daily more like a pair of accomplices than like a couple of devoted friends. They had heard nothing from home for eight months. Every evening they said, "To-morrow we shall see the steamer." But one of the Company's steamers had been wrecked, and the Director was busy with the other, relieving very distant and important stations on the main river. He thought that the useless station, and the useless men, could wait. Meantime Kayerts and Carlier lived on rice boiled without salt, and cursed the Company, all Africa, and the day they were born. One must have lived on such diet to discover what ghastly trouble the necessity of swallowing one's food may become. There was literally nothing else in the station but rice and coffee; they drank the coffee without sugar. The last fifteen lumps Kayerts had solemnly locked away in his box, together with a half-bottle of Cognâc, "in case of sickness," he explained. Carlier approved. "When one is sick," he said, "any little extra like that is cheering."

They waited. Rank grass began to sprout over the courtyard. The bell never rang now. Days passed, silent, exasperating, and slow. When the two men spoke, they snarled; and their silences were bitter, as if tinged by the bitterness of their thoughts.

One day after a lunch of boiled rice, Carlier put down his cup untasted, and said: "Hang it all! Let's have a decent cup of coffee for once. Bring out that sugar, Kayerts!"

"For the sick," muttered Kayerts, without looking up.

"For the sick," mocked Carlier. "Bosh! . . . Well! I am sick."

"You are no more sick than I am, and I go without," said Kayerts in a peaceful tone.

"Come! out with that sugar, you stingy old slave-dealer."

Kayerts looked up quickly. Carlier was smiling with marked insolence. And suddenly it seemed to Kayerts that he had never seen that man before. Who was he? He knew nothing about him. What was he capable of? There was a surprising flash of violent emotion within him, as if in the presence of something undreamt-of, dangerous, and final. But he managed to pronounce with composure—

"That joke is in very bad taste. Don't repeat it."

"Joke!" said Carlier, hitching himself forward on his seat. "I am hungry—I am sick—I don't joke! I hate hypocrites. You are a hypocrite. You are a slave-dealer. I am a slave-dealer. There's nothing but slave-dealers in this cursed country. I mean to have sugar in my coffee to-day, anyhow!"

"I forbid you to speak to me in that way," said Kayerts with a fair show of resolution.

"You!—What?" shouted Carlier, jumping up.

Kayerts stood up also. "I am your chief," he began, trying to master the shakiness of his voice.

"What?" yelled the other. "Who's chief? There's no chief here. There's nothing here: there's nothing but you and I. Fetch the sugar—you pot-bellied ass."

"Hold your tongue. Go out of this room," screamed Kayerts. "I dismiss you—you scoundrel!"

Carlier swung a stool. All at once he looked dangerously in earnest. "You flabby, good-for-nothing civilian—take that!" he howled.

Kayerts dropped under the table, and the stool struck the grass inner wall of the room. Then, as Carlier was trying to upset the table, Kayerts in desperation made a blind rush, head low, like a cornered pig would do, and over-turning his friend, bolted along the verandah, and into his room. He locked the door, snatched his revolver, and stood panting. In less than a minute Carlier was kicking at the door furiously, howling, "If you don't bring out that sugar, I will shoot you at sight, like a dog. Now then—one—two—three. You won't? I will show you who's the master."

Kayerts thought the door would fall in, and scrambled through the square hole that served for a window in his room. There was then the whole breadth of the house between them. But the other was apparently not strong enough to break in the door, and Kayerts heard him running round. Then he also began to run laboriously on his swollen legs. He ran as quickly as he could, grasping the revolver, and unable yet to understand what was happening to him. He saw in succession Makola's house, the store, the river, the ravine, and the low bushes; and he saw all those things again as he ran for the second time round the house. Then again they flashed past him. That morning he could not have walked a yard without a groan.

And now he ran. He ran fast enough to keep out of sight of the other man.

Then as, weak and desperate, he thought, "Before I finish the next round I shall die," he heard the other man stumble heavily, then stop. He stopped also. He had the back and Carlier the front of the house, as before. He heard him drop into a chair cursing, and suddenly his own legs gave way, and he slid down into a sitting posture with his back to the wall. His mouth was as dry as a cinder, and his face was wet with perspiration—and tears. What was it all about? He thought it must be a horrible illusion; he thought he was dreaming; he thought he was going mad! After a while he collected his senses. What did they quarrel about? That sugar! How absurd! He would give it to him—didn't want it himself. And he began scrambling to his feet with a sudden feeling of security. But before he had fairly stood upright, a common-sense reflection occurred to him and drove him back into despair. He thought: "If I give way now to that brute of a soldier, he will begin this horror again to-morrow—and the day after—every day—raise other pretensions, trample on me, torture me, make me his slave—and I will be lost! Lost! The steamer may not come for days—may never come." He shook so that he had to sit down on the floor again. He shivered forlornly. He felt he could not, would not move any more. He was completely distracted by the sudden perception that the position was without issue—that death and life had in a moment become equally difficult and terrible.

All at once he heard the other push his chair back; and he leaped to his feet with extreme facility. He listened and got confused. Must run again! Right or left? He heard footsteps. He darted to the left, grasping his revolver, and at the very same instant, as it seemed to him, they came into violent collision. Both shouted with surprise. A loud explosion took place between them; a roar of red fire, thick smoke; and Kayerts, deafened and blinded, rushed back thinking: "I am hit—it's all over." He expected the other to come round—to gloat over his agony. He caught hold of an upright of the roof—"All over!" Then he heard a crashing fall on the other side of the house, as if somebody had tumbled headlong over a chair—then silence. Nothing more happened. He did not die. Only his shoulder felt as if it had been badly wrenched, and he had lost his revolver. He was disarmed and helpless! He waited for his fate. The other man made no sound. It was a stratagem. He was stalking him now! Along what side? Perhaps he was taking aim this very minute.

After a few moments of an agony frightful and absurd, he decided to go and meet his doom. He was prepared for every surrender. He turned the corner, steadying himself with one hand on the wall; made a few paces, and nearly swooned. He had seen on the floor, protruding past the other corner, a pair of turned-up feet. A pair of white naked feet in red slippers. He felt deadly sick, and stood for a time in profound darkness. Then Makola appeared before him, saying quietly: "Come along, Mr. Kayerts. He is dead." He burst into tears of gratitude; a loud, sobbing fit of crying. After a time he found himself sitting in a chair and looking at Carlier, who lay stretched on his back. Makola was kneeling over the body.

"Is this your revolver?" asked Makola, getting up.

"Yes," said Kayerts; then he added very quickly, "He ran after me to shoot me—you saw!"

"Yes, I saw," said Makola. "There is only one revolver; where's his?"

"Don't know," whispered Kayerts in a voice that had become suddenly very faint.

"I will go and look for it," said the other, gently. He made the round along the verandah, while Kayerts sat still and looked at the corpse. Makola came back empty-handed, stood in deep thought, then stepped quietly into the dead man's room, and came out directly with a revolver, which he held up before Kayerts. Kayerts shut his eyes. Everything was going round. He found life more terrible and difficult than death. He had shot an unarmed man.

After meditating for a while, Makola said softly, pointing at the dead man who lay there with his right eye blown out—

"He died of fever." Kayerts looked at him with a stony stare. "Yes," repeated Makola, thoughtfully, stepping over the corpse, "I think he died of fever. Bury him to-morrow."

And he went away slowly to his expectant wife, leaving the two white men alone on the verandah.

Night came, and Kayerts sat unmoving on his chair. He sat quiet as if he had taken a dose of opium. The violence of the emotions he had passed through produced a feeling of exhausted serenity. He had plumbed in one short afternoon the depths of horror and despair, and now found repose in the conviction that life had no more secrets for him: neither had death! He sat by the corpse thinking; thinking very actively, thinking very new thoughts. He seemed to have broken loose from himself altogether. His old thoughts, convictions, likes and dislikes, things he respected and things he abhorred, appeared in their true light at last! Appeared contemptible and childish, false and ridiculous. He revelled in his new wisdom while he sat by the man he had killed. He argued with himself about all things under heaven with that kind of wrong-headed lucidity which may be observed in some lunatics. Incidentally he reflected that the fellow dead there had been a noxious beast anyway; that men died every day in thousands; perhaps in hundreds of thousands—who could tell?—and that in the number, that one death could not possibly make any difference; couldn't have any importance, at least to a thinking creature. He, Kayerts, was a thinking creature. He had been all his life, till that moment, a believer in a lot of nonsense like the rest of mankind—who are fools; but now he thought! He knew! He was at peace; he was familiar with the highest wisdom! Then he tried to imagine himself dead, and Carlier sitting in his chair watching him; and his attempt met with such unexpected success, that in a very few moments he became not at all sure who was dead and who was alive. This extraordinary achievement of his fancy startled him, however, and by a clever and timely effort of mind he saved himself just in time from becoming Carlier. His heart thumped, and he felt hot all over at the thought of that danger. Carlier! What a beastly thing! To compose his now disturbed nerves—and no wonder! —he tried to whistle a little. Then, suddenly, he fell asleep, or thought he had slept; but at any rate there was a fog, and somebody had whistled in the fog.

He stood up. The day had come, and a heavy mist had descended upon the land: the mist penetrating, enveloping, and silent; the morning mist of tropical lands; the mist that clings and kills; the mist white and deadly, immaculate and poisonous. He stood up, saw the body, and threw his arms above his head with a cry like that of a man who, waking from a trance, finds himself immured forever in a tomb. *"Help!* . . . *My God!"*

A shriek inhuman, vibrating and sudden, pierced like a sharp dart the white shroud of that land of sorrow. Three short, impatient screeches followed, and then, for a time, the fog-wreaths rolled on, undisturbed, through a formidable silence. Then many more shrieks, rapid and piercing, like the yells of some exasperated and ruthless creature, rent the air. Progress was calling to Kayerts from the river. Progress and civilization and all the virtues. Society was calling to its accomplished child to come, to be taken care of, to be instructed, to be judged, to be condemned; it called him to return to that rubbish heap from which he had wandered away, so that justice could be done.

Kayerts heard and understood. He stumbled out of the verandah, leaving the other man quite alone for the first time since they had been thrown there together. He groped his way through the fog, calling in his ignorance upon the invisible heaven to undo its work. Makola flitted by in the mist, shouting as he ran—

"Steamer! Steamer! They can't see. They whistle for the station. I go ring the bell. Go down to the landing, sir. I ring."

He disappeared. Kayerts stood still. He looked upwards; the fog rolled low over his head. He looked round like a man who has lost his way; and he saw a dark smudge, a cross-shaped stain, upon the shifting purity of the mist. As he began to stumble towards it, the station bell rang in a tumultuous peal its answer to the impatient clamour of the steamer.

The Managing Director of the Great Civilizing Company (since we know that civilization follows trade) landed first, and incontinently lost sight of the steamer. The fog down by the river was exceedingly dense; above, at the station, the bell rang unceasing and brazen.

The Director shouted loudly to the steamer:

"There is nobody down to meet us; there may be something wrong, though they are ringing. You had better come, too!"

And he began to toil up the steep bank. The captain and the engine-driver of the boat followed behind. As they scrambled up the fog thinned, and they could see their Director a good way ahead. Suddenly they saw him start forward, calling to them over his shoulder: —"Run! Run to the house! I've found one of them. Run, look for the other!"

He had found one of them! And even he, the man of varied and startling experience, was somewhat discomposed by the manner of this finding. He stood and fumbled in his pockets (for a knife) while he faced Kayerts, who was hanging by a leather strap from the cross. He had evidently climbed the grave, which was high and narrow, and after tying the end of the strap to the arm, had swung himself off. His toes were only a couple of inches above the ground; his arms hung stiffly down; he seemed to be standing rigidly at attention, but with one purple cheek playfully posed on the shoulder. And, irreverently, he was putting out a swollen tongue at his Managing Director.

Falk: A Reminiscence

SEVERAL of us, all more or less connected with the sea, were dining in a small river-hostelry not more than thirty miles from London, and less than twenty from that shallow and dangerous puddle to which our coasting men give the grandiose name of "German Ocean." And through the wide windows we had a view of the Thames; an enfilading view down the Lower Hope Reach. But the dinner was execrable, and all the feast was for the eyes.

That flavour of salt-water which for so many of us had been the very water of life permeated our talk. He who hath known the bitterness of the Ocean shall have its taste for ever in his mouth. But one or two of us, pampered by the life of the land, complained of hunger. It was impossible to swallow any of that stuff. And indeed there was a strange mustiness in everything. The wooden dining-room stuck out over the mud of the shore like a lacustrine dwelling; the planks of the floor seemed rotten; a decrepid old waiter tottered pathetically to and fro before an antediluvian and worm-eaten sideboard; the chipped plates might have been disinterred from some kitchen midden near an inhabited lake; and the chops recalled times more ancient still. They brought forcibly to one's mind the night of ages when the primeval man, evolving the first rudiments of cookery from his dim consciousness, scorched lumps of flesh at a fire of sticks in the company of other good fellows; then, gorged and happy, sat him back among the gnawed bones to tell his artless tales of experience—the tales of hunger and hunt—and of women, perhaps!

But luckily the wine happened to be as old as the waiter. So, comparatively empty, but upon the whole fairly happy, we sat back and told our artless tales. We talked of the sea and all its works. The sea never changes, and its works for all the talk of men are wrapped in mystery. But we agreed that the times were changed. And we talked of old ships, of sea-accidents, of break-downs, dismastings; and of a man who brought his ship safe to Liverpool all the way from the River Platte under a jury rudder. We talked of wrecks, of short rations and of heroism—or at least of what the newspapers would have called heroism at sea—a manifestation of virtues quite different from the heroism of primitive times. And now and then falling silent all together we gazed at the sights of the river.

A P. & O. boat passed bound down. "One gets jolly good dinners on board these ships," remarked one of our band. A man with sharp eyes read out the name on her bows: *Arcadia.* "What a beautiful model of a ship!" murmured some of us. She was followed by a small cargo-steamer, and the flag they hauled down aboard while we were looking showed her to be a Norwegian. She made an awful lot of smoke, and before it had quite blown away, a high-sided, short, wooden barque, in ballast and towed by a paddle-tug, appeared in front of the windows. All her hands were forward busy setting up the headgear; and aft a woman in a red hood, quite alone with the man at the wheel, paced the length of the poop back and forth, with the gray wool of some knitting work in her hands.

"German I should think," muttered one. "The skipper has his wife on board," remarked another; and the light of the crimson sunset all ablaze behind the London smoke, throwing a glow of Bengal light upon the barque's spars, faded away from the Hope Reach.

Then one of us, who had not spoken before, a man of more than fifty, that had commanded ships for a quarter of a century, looking after the barque now gliding far away, all black on the lustre of the river, said:

This reminds me of an absurd episode in my life, now many years ago, when I got first the command of an iron barque, loading then in a certain Eastern seaport. It was also the capital of an Eastern kingdom, lying up a river as might be London lies up this old Thames of ours. No more need be said of the place; for this sort of thing might have happened anywhere where there are ships, skippers, tug-boats, and orphan nieces of indescribable splendour. And the absurdity of the episode concerns only me, my enemy Falk, and my friend Hermann.

There seemed to be something like peculiar emphasis on the words "My friend Hermann," which caused one of us (for we had just been speaking of heroism at sea) to say idly and nonchalantly:

"And was this Hermann a hero?"

Not at all, said our grizzled friend. No hero at all. He was a Schiff-führer: Ship-conductor. That's how they call a Master Mariner in Germany. I prefer our way. The alliteration is good, and there is some-thing in the nomenclature that gives to us as a body the sense of corporate existence: Apprentice, Mate, Master, in the ancient and honourable craft of the sea. As to my friend Hermann, he might have been a consummate master of the honourable craft, but he was called officially Schiff-führer, and had the simple, heavy appearance of a well-to-do farmer, combined with the good-natured shrewdness of a small shopkeeper. With his shaven chin, round limbs, and heavy eyelids he did not look like a toiler, and even less like an adventurer of the sea. Still, he toiled upon the seas, in his own way, much as a shopkeeper works behind his counter. And his ship was the means by which he maintained his growing family.

She was a heavy, strong, blunt-bowed affair, awakening the ideas of primitive solidity, like the wooden plough of our forefathers. And there were, about her, other suggestions of a rustic and homely nature. The extraordinary timber projections which I have seen in no other vessel made her square stern resemble the tail end of a miller's waggon. But the four stern ports of her cabin, glazed with six little greenish panes each, and framed in wooden sashes painted brown, might have been the windows of a cottage in the country. The tiny white curtains and the greenery of flower-pots behind the glass completed the resemblance. On one or two occasions when passing under her stern I had detected from my boat a round arm in the act of tilting a watering-pot, and the bowed sleek head of a maiden whom I shall always call Hermann's niece, because as a matter of fact I've never heard her name, for all my intimacy with the family.

This, however, sprang up later on. Meantime in common with the rest of the shipping in that Eastern port, I was left in no doubt as to Hermann's notions of hygienic clothing. Evidently he believed in wearing good stout flannel next his skin. On most days little frocks and pinafores could be seen drying in the mizzen rigging of his ship, or a tiny row of socks fluttering on the signal halyards; but once a fortnight the family washing was exhibited in force. It covered the poop entirely. The afternoon breeze would incite to a weird and flabby activity all that crowded mass of clothing, with its vague suggestions of drowned, mutilated and flattened humanity. Trunks without heads waved at you arms without hands; legs without feet kicked fantastically with collapsible flourishes; and there were long white garments, that taking the wind fairly through their neck openings edged with lace, became for a moment violently distended as by the passage of obese and invisible bodies. On these days you could make out that ship at a great distance by the multi-coloured grotesque riot going on abaft her mizzen-mast.

She had her berth just ahead of me, and her name was *Diana*,— Diana not of Ephesus but of Bremen. This was proclaimed in white letters a foot long spaced widely across the stern (somewhat like the lettering of a shop-sign) under the cottage windows. This ridiculously unsuitable name struck one as an impertinence towards the memory of the most charming of goddesses; for, apart from the fact that the old craft was physically incapable of engaging in any sort of chase, there was a gang of four children belonging to her. They peeped over the rail at passing boats and occasionally dropped various objects into them. Thus, sometime before I knew Hermann to speak to, I received on my hat a horrid rag-doll belonging to Hermann's eldest daughter. However, these youngsters were upon the whole well behaved. They had fair heads, round eyes, round little knobby noses, and they resembled their father a good deal.

This *Diana* of Bremen was a most innocent old ship and seemed to know nothing of the wicked sea, as there are on shore households that know nothing of the corrupt world. And the sentiments she suggested were unexceptionable and mainly of a domestic order. She was a home. All these dear children had learned to walk on her roomy quarter-deck. In such thoughts there is something pretty, even touching. Their teeth, I should judge, they cut on the ends of her running gear. I have many times observed the baby Hermann (Nicholas) engaged in gnawing the whipping of the fore-royal brace. Nicholas' favourite place of residence was under the main fife-rail. Directly he was let loose he would crawl off there, and the first seaman who came along would bring him, carefully held aloft in tarry hands, back to the cabin door. I fancy there must have been a standing order to that effect. In the course of these transportations the baby, who was the only peppery person in the ship, tried to smite these stalwart young German sailors on the face.

Mrs. Hermann, an engaging, stout housewife, wore on board baggy blue dresses with white dots. When, as happened once or twice, I caught her at an elegant little wash-tub rubbing hard on white collars, baby's socks, and Hermann's summer neckties, she would blush in girlish confusion, and raising her wet hands greet me from afar with many friendly nods. Her sleeves would be rolled up to the elbows, and the gold hoop of her wedding ring glittered among the soap-suds. Her voice was pleasant, she had a serene brow, smooth bands of very fair hair, and a good-humoured expression of the eyes. She was motherly and moderately talkative. When this simple matron smiled, youthful dimples broke out on her fresh broad cheeks. Hermann's niece, on the other hand, an orphan and very silent, I never saw attempt a smile. This, however, was not gloom on her part but the restraint of youthful gravity.

They had carried her about with them for the last three years, to help with the children and be company for Mrs. Hermann, as Hermann mentioned once to me. It had been very necessary while they were all little, he had added in a vexed manner. It was her arm and her sleek head that I had glimpsed one morning, through the stern-windows of the cabin, hovering over the pots of fuchsias and mignonette; but the first time I beheld her full length I surrendered to her proportions. They fix her in my mind, as great beauty, great intelligence, quickness of wit or kindness of heart might have made some other woman memorable.

With her it was form and size. It was her physical personality that had this imposing charm. She might have been witty, intelligent, and kind to an exceptional degree. I don't know, and this is not to the point. All I know is that she was built on a magnificent scale. Built is the only word. She was constructed, she was erected, as it were, with regal lavishness. It staggered you to see this reckless expenditure of material upon a chit of a girl. She was youthful and also perfectly mature, as though she had been some fortunate immortal. She was heavy, too, perhaps, but that's nothing. It only added to that notion of permanence. She was barely nineteen. But such shoulders! Such round arms! Such a shadowing forth of mighty limbs when with three long strides she pounced across the deck upon the overturned Nicholas—it's perfectly indescribable! She seemed a good, quiet girl, vigilant as to Lena's needs, Gustav's tumbles, the state of Karl's dear little nose—conscientious, hardworking, and all that. But what magnificent hair she had! Abundant, long, thick, of a tawny colour. It had the sheen of precious metals. She wore it plaited tightly into one single tress hanging girlishly down her back; and its end reached down to her waist. The massiveness of it surprised you. On my word it reminded one of a club. Her face was big, comely, of an unruffled expression. She had a good complexion, and her blue eyes were so pale that she appeared to look at the world with the empty white candour of a statue. You could not call her good-looking. It was something much more impressive. The simplicity of her apparel, the opulence of her form, her imposing stature, and the extraordinary sense of vigorous life that seemed to emanate from her like a perfume exhaled by a flower, made her beautiful with a beauty of a rustic and olympian order. To watch her reaching up to the clothes-line with both arms raised high above her head, caused you to fall a musing in a strain of pagan piety. Excellent Mrs. Hermann's baggy cotton gowns had some sort of rudimentary frills at neck and bottom, but this girl's print frocks hadn't even a wrinkle; nothing but a few straight folds in the skirt falling to her feet, and these, when she stood still, had a severe and statuesque quality. She was inclined naturally to be still whether sitting or standing. However, I don't mean to say she was statuesque. She was too generously alive; but she could have stood for an allegoric statue of the Earth. I don't mean the worn-out earth of our possession, but a young Earth, a virginal planet undisturbed by the vision of a future teeming with the monstrous forms of life, clamorous with the cruel battles of hunger and thought.

The worthy Hermann himself was not very entertaining, though his English was fairly comprehensible. Mrs. Hermann, who always let off one speech at least at me in an hospitable, cordial tone (and in Platt-Deutsch, I suppose), I could not understand. As to their niece, however satisfactory to look upon (and she inspired you somehow with a hopeful view as to the prospects of mankind) she was a modest and silent presence, mostly engaged in sewing, only now and then, as I observed, falling over that work into a state of maidenly meditation. Her aunt sat opposite her, sewing also, with her feet propped on a wooden footstool. On the other side of the deck Hermann and I would get a couple of chairs out of the cabin and settle down to a smoking match, accompanied at long intervals by the pacific exchange of a few words. I came nearly every evening. Hermann I would find in his shirt-sleeves. As soon as he returned from the shore on board his ship he commenced operations by taking off his coat; then he put on his head an embroidered round cap with a tassel, and changed his boots for a pair of cloth slippers. Afterwards he smoked at the cabin door, looking at his children with an air of civic virtue, till they got caught one after another and put to bed in various staterooms. Lastly, we would drink some beer in the cabin, which was furnished with a wooden table on cross legs, and with black straight-backed chairs—more like a farm kitchen than a ship's cuddy. The sea and all nautical affairs seemed very far removed from the hospitality of this exemplary family.

And I liked this because I had a rather worrying time on board my own ship. I had been appointed ex-officio by the British Consul to take charge of her after a man who had died suddenly, leaving for the guidance of his successor some suspiciously unreceipted bills, a few dry-dock estimates hinting a bribery, and a quantity of vouchers for three years' extravagant expenditure; all these mixed up together in a dusty old violin-case lined with ruby velvet. I found besides a large account-book, which, when opened hopefully, turned out to my infinite consternation to be filled with verses—page after page of rhymed doggerel of a jovial and improper character, written in the neatest minute hand I ever did see. In the same fiddle-case a photograph of my predecessor, taken lately in Saigon, represented in front of a garden view and in company of a female in strange draperies, an elderly, squat, rugged man of stern aspect in a clumsy suit of black broadcloth, and with the hair brushed forward above the temples in a manner reminding one of a boar's tusks. Of a fiddle, however, the only trace on board was the case, its empty husk as it were; but of the two last freights the ship had indubitably earned of late, there were not even the husks left. It was impossible to say where all that money had gone to. It wasn't on board. It had not been remitted home; for a letter from the owners, preserved in a desk evidently by the merest accident, complained mildly enough that they had not been favoured by a scratch of the pen for the last eighteen months. There were next to no stores on board, not an inch of spare rope or a yard of canvas. The ship had been run bare, and I foresaw no end of difficulties before I could get her ready for sea.

As I was young then—not thirty yet—I took myself and my troubles very seriously. The old mate, who had acted as chief mourner at the captain's funeral, was not particularly pleased at my coming. But the fact is the fellow was not legally qualified for command, and the Consul was bound, if at all possible, to put a properly certificated man on board. As to the second mate, all I can say is his name was Tottersen, or something like that. His practice was to wear on his head, in that tropical climate, a mangy fur cap. He was, without exception, the stupidest man I had ever seen on board ship. And he looked it, too. He looked so confoundedly stupid that it was a matter of surprise for me when he answered to his name.

I drew no great comfort from their company, to say the least of it; while the prospect of making a long sea passage with those two fellows was depressing. And my other thoughts in solitude could not be of a gay complexion. The crew was sickly, the cargo was coming very slow; I foresaw I would have lots of trouble with the charterers, and doubted whether they would advance me enough money for the ship's expenses. Their attitude towards me was unfriendly. Altogether I was not getting on. I would discover at odd times (generally about midnight) that I was totally inexperienced, greatly ignorant of business, and hopelessly unfit for any sort of command; and when the steward had to be taken to the hospital ill with choleraic symptoms I felt bereaved of the only decent person at the after end of the ship. He was fully expected to recover but in the meantime had to be replaced by some sort of servant. And on the recommendation of a certain Schomberg, the proprietor of the smaller of the two hotels in the place, I engaged a Chinaman. Schomberg, a brawny, hairy Alsatian, and an awful gossip, assured me that it was all right. "First-class boy that. Came in the *suite* of his Excellency Tseng the Commissioner—you know. His Excellency Tseng lodged with me here for three weeks."

He mouthed the Chinese Excellency at me with great unction, though the specimen of the "*suite*" did not seem very promising. At the time, however, I did not know what an untrustworthy humbug Schomberg was. The "boy" might have been forty or a hundred and forty for all you could tell—one of those Chinamen of the death's-head type of face and completely inscrutable. Before the end of the third day he had revealed himself as a confirmed opium-smoker, a gambler, a most audacious thief, and a first-class sprinter. When he departed at the top of his speed with thirty-two golden sovereigns of my own hard-earned savings it was the last straw. I had reserved that money in case my difficulties came to the worst. Now it was gone I felt as poor and naked as a fakir. I clung to my ship, for all the bother she caused me, but what I could not bear were the long lonely evenings in her cuddy, where the atmosphere, made smelly by a leaky lamp, was agitated by the snoring of the mate. That fellow shut himself up in his stuffy cabin punctually at eight, and made gross and revolting noises like a water-logged trombone. It was odious not to be able to worry oneself in comfort on board one's own ship. Everything in this world, I reflected, even the command of a nice little barque, may be made a delusion and a snare for the unwary spirit of pride in man.

From such reflections I was glad to make my escape on board that Bremen *Diana*. There apparently no whisper of the world's iniquities had ever penetrated. And yet she lived upon the wide sea: and the sea tragic and comic, the sea with its horrors and its peculiar scandals, the sea peopled by men and ruled by iron necessity is indubitably a part of the world. But that patriarchal old tub, like some saintly retreat, echoed nothing of it. She was world proof. Her venerable innocence apparently put a restraint on the roaring lusts of the sea. And yet I have known the sea too long to believe in its respect for decency. An elemental force is ruthlessly frank. It may, of course, have been Hermann's skilful seamanship, but to me it looked as if the allied oceans had refrained from smashing these high bulwarks, unshipping the lumpy rudder, frightening the children, and generally opening this family's eyes out of sheer reticence. It looked like reticence. The ruthless disclosure was, in the end, left for a man to make; a man strong and elemental enough and driven to unveil some secrets of the sea by the power of a simple and elemental desire.

This, however, occurred much later, and meantime I took sanctuary in that serene old ship early every evening. The only person on board that seemed to be in trouble was little Lena, and in due course I perceived that the health of the rag-doll was more than delicate. This object led a sort of "in extremis" existence in a wooden box placed against the starboard mooring-bitts tended and nursed with the greatest sympathy and care by all the children, who greatly enjoyed pulling long faces and moving with hushed footsteps. Only the baby— Nicholas—looked on with a cold, ruffianly leer, as if he had belonged to another tribe altogether. Lena perpetually sorrowed over the box, and all of them were in deadly earnest. It was wonderful the way these children would work up their compassion for that bedraggled thing I wouldn't have touched with a pair of tongs. I suppose they were exercising and developing their racial sentimentalism by the means of that dummy. I was only surprised that Mrs. Hermann let

Lena cherish and hug that bundle of rags to that extent, it was so disreputably and completely unclean. But Mrs. Hermann would raise her fine womanly eyes from her needlework to look on with amused sympathy, and did not seem to see it, somehow, that this object of affection was a disgrace to the ship's purity. Purity, not cleanliness, is the word. It was pushed so far that I seemed to detect in this, too, a sentimental excess, as if dirt had been removed in very love. It is impossible to give you an idea of such a meticulous neatness. It was as if every morning that ship had been arduously explored with—with toothbrushes. Her very bowsprit three times a week had its toilette made with a cake of soap and a piece of soft flannel. Arrayed—I *must* say arrayed—arrayed artlessly in dazzling white paint as to wood and dark green as to ironwork the simple-minded distribution of these colours evoked the images of guileless peace, of arcadian felicity; and the childish comedy of disease and sorrow struck me sometimes as an abominably real blot upon that ideal state.

I enjoyed it greatly, and on my part I brought a little mild excitement into it. Our intimacy arose from the pursuit of that thief. It was in the evening, and Hermann, who, contrary to his habits, had stayed on shore late that day, was extricating himself backwards out of a little gharry on the river bank, opposite his ship, when the hunt passed. Realizing the situation as though he had eyes in his shoulder-blades, he joined us with a leap and took the lead. The Chinaman fled silent like a rapid shadow on the dust of an extremely oriental road. I followed. A long way in the rear my mate whooped like a savage. A young moon threw a bashful light on a plain like a monstrous waste ground: the architectural mass of a Buddhist temple far away projected itself in dead black on the sky. We lost the thief of course; but in my disappointment I had to admire Hermann's presence of mind. The velocity that stodgy man developed in the interests of a complete stranger earned my warm gratitude—there was something truly cordial in his exertions.

He seemed as vexed as myself at our failure, and would hardly listen to my thanks. He said it was "nothings," and invited me on the spot to come on board his ship and drink a glass of beer with him. We poked sceptically for a while amongst the bushes, peered w 'hout conviction into a ditch or two. There was not a sound: patches of slime glimmered feebly amongst the reeds. Slowly we trudged back, drooping under the thin sickle of the moon, and I heard him mutter to himself, "Himmel! Zwei und dreissig Pfund!" He was impressed by the figure of my loss. For a long time we had ceased to hear the mate's whoops and yells.

Then he said to me, "Everybody has his troubles," and as we went on remarked that he would never have known anything of mine hadn't he by an extraordinary chance been detained on shore by Captain Falk. He didn't like to stay late ashore—he added with a sigh. The something doleful in his tone I put to his sympathy with my misfortune, of course.

On board the *Diana* Mrs. Hermann's fine eyes expressed much interest and commiseration. We had found the two women sewing face to face under the open skylight in the strong glare of the lamp. Hermann walked in first, starting in the very doorway to pull off his coat, and encouraging me with loud, hospitable ejaculations: "Come in! This way! Come in, captain!" At once, coat in hand, he began to tell his wife all about it. Mrs. Hermann put the palms of her plump hands together; I smiled and bowed with a heavy heart: the niece got up from her sewing to bring Hermann's slippers and his embroidered calotte, which he assumed pontifically, talking (about me) all the time. Billows of white stuff lay between the chairs on the cabin floor; I caught the words "Zwei und dreissig Pfund" repeated several times, and presently came the beer, which seemed delicious to my throat, parched with running and the emotions of the chase.

I didn't get away till well past midnight, long after the women had retired. Hermann had been trading in the East for three years or more, carrying freights of rice and timber mostly. His ship was well known in all the ports from Vladivostok to Singapore. She was his own property. The profits had been moderate, but the trade answered well enough while the children were small yet. In another year or so he hoped he would be able to sell the old *Diana* to a firm in Japan for a fair price. He intended to return home, to Bremen, by mail-boat, second class, with Mrs. Hermann and the children. He told me all this stolidly, with slow puffs at his pipe. I was sorry when knocking the ashes out he began to rub his eyes. I would have sat with him till morning. What had I to hurry on board my own ship for? To face the broken rifled drawer in my stateroom. Ugh! The very thought made me feel unwell.

I became their daily guest, as you know. I think that Mrs. Hermann from the first looked upon me as a romantic person. I did not, of course, tear my hair *coram populo* over my loss, and she took it for lordly indifference. Afterwards, I daresay, I did tell them some of my adventures—such as they were—and they marvelled greatly at the extent of my experience. Hermann would translate what he thought the most striking passages. Getting upon his legs, and as if delivering a lecture on a phenomenon, he addressed himself, with gestures, to the two women, who would let their sewing sink slowly on their laps. Meantime I sat before a glass of Hermann's beer, trying to look modest. Mrs. Hermann would glance at me quickly, emit slight "Ach's!" The girl never made a sound. Never. But she, too, would sometimes raise her pale eyes to look at me in her unseeing, gentle way. Her glance was by no means stupid; it beamed out soft and diffuse as the moon beams upon a landscape—quite differently from the scrutinizing inspection of the stars. You were drowned in it, and imagined yourself to appear blurred. And yet this same glance when turned upon Christian Falk must have been as efficient as the searchlight of a battle-ship.

Falk was the other assiduous visitor on board, but from his behaviour he might have been coming to see the quarter-deck capstan. He certainly used to stare at it a good deal when keeping us company outside the cabin door, with one muscular arm thrown over the back of the chair, and his big shapely legs, in very tight white trousers, extended far out and ending in a pair of black shoes as roomy as punts. On arrival he would shake Hermann's hand with a mutter, bow to the women, and take up his careless and misanthropic attitude by our side. He departed abruptly, with a jump, going through the performance of grunts, handshakes, bow, as if in a panic. Sometimes, with a sort of discreet and convulsive effort, he approached the women and exchanged a few low words with them, half a dozen at most. On these occasions Hermann's usual stare became positively glassy and Mrs. Hermann's kind countenance would colour up. The girl herself never turned a hair.

Falk was a Dane or perhaps a Norwegian, I can't tell now. At all events he was a Scandinavian of some sort, and a bloated monopolist to boot. It is possible he was unacquainted with the word, but he had a clear perception of the thing itself. His tariff of charges for towing ships in and out was the most brutally inconsiderate document of the sort I had ever seen. He was the commander and owner of the only tug-boat on the river, a very trim white craft of 150 tons or more, as elegantly neat as a yacht, with a round wheelhouse rising like a glazed turret high above her sharp bows, and with one slender varnished pole mast forward. I daresay there are yet a few shipmasters afloat who remember Falk and his tug very well. He extracted his pound and a half of flesh from each of us merchant-skippers with an inflexible sort of indifference which made him detested and even feared. Schomberg used to remark: "I won't talk about the fellow. I don't think he has six drinks from year's end to year's end in my place. But my advice is, gentlemen, don't you have anything to do with him, if you can help it."

This advice, apart from unavoidable business relations, was easy to follow because Falk intruded upon no one. It seems absurd to compare a tug-boat skipper to a centaur: but he reminded me somehow of an engraving in a little book I had as a boy, which represented centaurs at a stream, and there was one especially, in the foreground, prancing bow and arrows in hand, with regular severe features and an immense curled wavy beard, flowing down his breast. Falk's face reminded me of that centaur. Besides, he was a composite creature. Not a man-horse, it is true, but a man-boat. He lived on board his tug, which was always dashing up and down the river from early morn till dewy eve. In the last rays of the setting sun, you could pick out far away down the reach his beard borne high up on the white structure, foaming up stream to anchor for the night. There was the white-clad man's body, and the rich brown patch of the hair, and nothing below the waist but the 'thwart-ship white lines of the bridge-screens, that led the eye to the sharp white lines of the bows cleaving the muddy water of the river.

Separated from his boat, to me at least he seemed incomplete. The tug herself without his head and torso on the bridge looked mutilated as it were. But he left her very seldom. All the time I remained in harbour I saw him only twice on shore. On the first occasion it was at my charterers, where he came in misanthropically to get paid for towing out a French barque the day before. The second time I could hardly believe my eyes, for I beheld him reclining under his beard in a cane-bottomed chair in the billiard-room of Schomberg's hotel.

It was very funny to see Schomberg ignoring him pointedly. The artificiality of it contrasted strongly with Falk's natural unconcern. The big Alsatian talked loudly with his other customers, going from one little table to the other, and passing Falk's place of repose with his eyes fixed straight ahead. Falk sat there with an untouched glass at his elbow. He must have known by sight and name every white man in the room, but he never addressed a word to anybody. He acknowledged my presence by a drop of his eyelids, and that was all. Sprawling there in the chair, he would, now and again, draw the palms of both his hands down his face, giving at the same time a slight, almost imperceptible, shudder.

It was a habit he had, and of course I was perfectly familiar with it, since you could not remain an hour in his company without being made to wonder at such a passionate and inexplicable gesture breaking some long period of stillness. He used to make it at all sorts of times; as likely as not after he had been listening to little Lena's chatter about the suffering doll, for instance. The Hermann children always besieged him about his legs closely, though, in a gentle way, he shrank from them a little. He seemed, however, to feel a great affection for the whole family. For Hermann himself especially. He sought his company. In this case, for instance, he must have been waiting for him, because as soon as he appeared Falk rose hastily, and they went out together. Then Schomberg expounded in my hearing to three or four people his theory that Falk was after Captain Hermann's niece, and asserted confidently that nothing would come of it. It was the same last year when Captain Hermann was loading here, he said.

Naturally, I did not believe Schomberg, but I own that for a time I observed closely what went on. All I discovered was some impatience on Hermann's part. At the sight of Falk, stepping over the gangway, the excellent man would begin to mumble and chew between his teeth something that sounded like German swear-words. However, as I've said, I'm not familiar with the language, and Hermann's soft, round-eyed countenance remained unchanged. Staring stolidly ahead he greeted him with, "Wie geht's," or in English, "How are you?" with a throaty enunciation. The girl would look up for an instant and move her lips slightly: Mrs. Hermann let her hands rest on her lap to talk volubly to him for a minute or so in her pleasant voice before she went on with her sewing again. Falk would throw himself into a chair, stretch his big legs, as like as not draw his hands down his face passionately. As to myself, he was not pointedly impertinent: it was rather as though he could not be bothered with such trifles as my existence; and the truth is that being a monopolist he was under no necessity to be amiable. He was sure to get his own extortionate terms out of me for towage whether he frowned or smiled. As a matter of fact, he did neither: but before many days went by he managed to astonish me not a little and to set Schomberg's tongue clacking more than ever.

It came about in this way. There was a shallow bar at the mouth of the river which ought to have been kept down, but the authorities of the State were piously busy gilding afresh the great Buddhist Pagoda just then, and had no money to spare for dredging operations. I don't know how it may be now, but at the time I speak of that sandbank was a great nuisance to the shipping. One of its consequences was that vessels of a certain draught of water, like Hermann's or mine, could not complete their loading in the river. After taking in as much as possible of their cargo, they had to go outside to fill up. The whole procedure was an unmitigated bore. When you thought you had as much on board as your ship could carry safely over the bar, you went and gave notice to your agents. They, in their turn, notified Falk that so-and-so was ready to go out. Then Falk (ostensibly when it fitted in with his other work, but, if the truth were known, simply when his arbitrary spirit moved him), after ascertaining carefully in the office that there was enough money to meet his bill, would come along unsympathetically, glaring at you with his yellow eyes from the bridge, and would drag you out dishevelled as to rigging, lumbered as to the decks, with unfeeling haste, as if to execution. And he would force you, too, to take the end of his own wire hawser, for the use of which there was of course an extra charge. To your shouted remonstrances against this extortion this towering trunk with one hand on the engine-room telegraph only shook its bearded head above the splash, the racket and the clouds of smoke, in which the tug, backing and filling in the smother of churning paddle-wheels behaved like a ferocious and impatient creature. He had her manned by the cheekiest gang of lascars I ever did see, whom he allowed to bawl at you insolently, and, once fast, he plucked you out of your berth as if he did not care what he smashed. Eighteen miles down the river you had to go behind him, and then three more along the coast to where a group of uninhabited rocky islets enclosed a sheltered anchorage. There you would have to lie at single anchor with your naked spars showing to seaward over these barren fragments of land scattered upon a very intensely blue sea. There was nothing to look at besides but a bare coast, the muddy edge of the brown plain with the sinuosities of the river you had left, traced in dull green, and the Great Pagoda up-rising lonely and massive with shining curves and pinnacles like the gorgeous and stony efflorescence of tropical rocks. You had nothing to do but to wait fretfully for the balance of your cargo, which was sent out of the river with the greatest irregularity. And it was open to you to console yourself with the thought that, after all, this stage of bother meant that your departure from these shores was indeed approaching at last.

We both had to go through that stage, Hermann and I, and there was a sort of tacit emulation between the ships as to which should be ready first. We kept on neck and neck almost to the finish, when I won the race by going personally to give notice in the forenoon; whereas Hermann, who was very slow in making up his mind to go ashore, did not get to the agents' office till late in the day. They told him there that my ship was first on turn for next morning, and I believe he told them he was in no hurry. It suited him better to go the day after.

That evening, on board the *Diana*, he sat staring with his plump knees well apart and puffing at the curved mouthpiece of his pipe. Presently he spoke with some impatience to his niece about putting the children to bed. Mrs. Hermann, who was talking to Falk, stopped short and looked at her husband uneasily, but the girl got up at once and drove the children before her into the cabin. In a little while Mrs. Hermann had to leave us to quell what, from the sounds inside, must have been a dangerous mutiny. At this Hermann grumbled to himself. For half an hour longer Falk left alone with us fidgeted on his chair, sighed lightly, then at last, after drawing his hands down his face, got up, and as if renouncing the hope of making himself understood (he hadn't opened his mouth once) he said in English:

"Well . . . Good night, Captain Hermann." He stopped for a moment before my chair and looked down fixedly, I may even say he glared, and he went so far as to make a deep noise in his throat. All this was so marked that for the first time in our limited intercourse of nods and grunts he excited in me something like interest. But next moment he disappointed me—for he strode away hastily without a nod even.

His manner was usually odd it is true, and I certainly did not pay much attention to it; but that sort of obscure intention, which seemed to lurk in his nonchalance like a wary old carp in a pond, had never before come so near the surface. He had distinctly aroused my expectations. I would have been unable to say what it was I expected, but at all events I did not expect the absurd developments he sprung upon me no later than the break of the very next day.

I remember only that there was, on that evening, enough point in his behaviour to make me, after he had fled, wonder audibly what he might mean. To this Hermann, crossing his legs with a swing and settling himself viciously away from me in his chair, said: "That fellow don't know himself what he means."

There might have been some insight in such a remark. I said nothing, and, still averted, Hermann added: "When I was here last year he was just the same." An eruption of tobacco smoke enveloped his head as if his temper had exploded like gunpowder.

I had half a mind to ask him point blank whether he, at least, didn't know why Falk, a notoriously unsociable man, had taken to visiting his ship with such assiduity. After all, I reflected suddenly, it was a most remarkable thing. I wonder now what Hermann would have said. As it turned out he didn't let me ask. Forgetting all about Falk apparently, he started a monologue on his plans for the future: the selling of the ship, the going home; and falling into a reflective and calculating mood he mumbled between regular jets of smoke about the expense. The necessity of disbursing passage-money for all his tribe seemed to disturb him in a manner that was the more striking because otherwise he gave no signs of a miserly disposition. And yet he fussed over the prospect of that voyage home in a mail-boat like a sedentary grocer who has made up his mind to see the world. He was racially thrifty I suppose, and for him there must have been a great novelty in finding himself obliged to pay for travelling—for sea travelling which was the normal state of life for the family—from the very cradle for most of them. I could see he grudged prospectively every single shilling which must be spent so absurdly. It was rather funny. He would become doleful over it, and then again, with a fretful sigh, he would suppose there was nothing for it now but to take three second-class tickets—and there were the four children to pay for besides. A lot of money that to spend at once. A big lot of money.

I sat with him listening (not for the first time) to these heart-searchings till I grew thoroughly sleepy, and then I left him and turned in on board my ship. At daylight I was awakened by a yelping of shrill voices, accompanied by a great commotion in the water, and the short, bullying blasts of a steam-whistle. Falk with his tug had come for me.

I began to dress. It was remarkable that the answering noise on board my ship together with the patter of feet above my head ceased suddenly. But I heard more remote guttural cries which seemed to express surprise and annoyance. Then the voice of my mate reached me howling expostulations to somebody at a distance. Other voices joined, apparently indignant; a chorus of something that sounded like abuse replied. Now and then the steam-whistle screeched.

Altogether that unnecessary uproar was distracting, but down there in my cabin I took it calmly. In another moment, I thought, I should be going down that wretched river, and in another week at the most I should be totally quit of the odious place and all the odious people in it.

Greatly cheered by the idea, I seized the hair-brushes and looking at myself in the glass began to use them. Suddenly a hush fell upon the noise outside, and I heard (the ports of my cabin were thrown open)—I heard a deep calm voice, not on board my ship, however, hailing resolutely in English, but with a strong foreign twang, "Go ahead!"

There may be tides in the affairs of men which taken at the flood . . . and so on. Personally I am still on the look-out for that important turn. I am, however, afraid that most of us are fated to flounder for ever in the dead water of a pool the shores of which are arid indeed. But I know that there are often in men's affairs unexpectedly—even irrationally—illuminating moments when an otherwise insignificant sound, perhaps only some perfectly commonplace gesture, suffices to reveal to us all the unreason, all the fatuous unreason, of our complacency. "Go ahead" are not particularly striking words even when pronounced with a foreign accent; yet they petrified me in the very act of smiling at myself in the glass. And then, refusing to believe my ears, but already boiling with indignation, I ran out of the cabin and up on deck.

It was incredibly true. It was perfectly true. I had no eyes for anything but the *Diana*. It was she that was being taken away. She was already out of her berth and shooting athwart the river. "The way this loonatic plucked that ship out is a caution," said the awed voice of my mate close to my ear. "Hey! Hallo! Falk! Hermann! What's this infernal trick?" I yelled in a fury.

Nobody heard me. Falk certainly could not hear me. His tug was turning at full speed away under the other bank. The wire hawser between her and the *Diana*, stretched as taut as a harpstring, vibrated alarmingly.

The high black craft careened over to the awful strain. A loud crack came out of her, followed by the tearing and splintering of wood. "There!" said the awed voice in my ear. "He's carried away their towing chock." And then, with enthusiasm, "Oh! Look! Look, sir! Look at them Dutchmen skipping out of the way on the forecastle. I hope to goodness he'll break a few of their shins before he's done with 'em."

I yelled my vain protests. The rays of the rising sun coursing level along the plain warmed my back, but I was hot enough with rage. I could not have believed that a simple towing operation could suggest so plainly the idea of abduction, of rape. Falk was simply running off with the *Diana*.

The white tug careered out into the middle of the river. The red floats of her paddle-wheels revolving with mad rapidity tore up the whole reach into foam. The *Diana* in mid-stream waltzed round with as much grace as an old barn, and flew after her ravisher. Through the ragged fog of smoke driving headlong upon the water I had a glimpse of Falk's square motionless shoulders under a white hat as big as a cart-wheel, of his red face, his yellow staring eyes, his great beard. Instead of keeping a look-out ahead, he was deliberately turning his back on the river to glare at his tow. The tall heavy craft, never so used before in her life, seemed to have lost her senses; she took a wild sheer against her helm, and for a moment came straight at us, menacing and clumsy, like a runaway mountain. She piled up a streaming, hissing, boiling wave halfway up her blunt stem, my crew let out one great howl,—and then we held our breaths. It was a near thing. But Falk had her! He had her in his clutch. I fancied I could hear the steel hawser ping as it surged across the *Diana's* forecastle, with the hands on board of her bolting away from it in all directions. It was a near thing. Hermann, with his hair rumpled, in a snuffy flannel shirt and a pair of mustard-coloured trousers, had rushed to help with the wheel. I saw his terrified round face; I saw his very teeth uncovered by a sort of ghastly fixed grin; and in a great leaping tumult of water between the two ships the *Diana* whisked past so close that I could have flung a hair-brush at his head, for, it seems, I had kept them in my hands all the time. Meanwhile Mrs. Hermann sat placidly on the skylight, with a woollen shawl on her shoulders. The excellent woman in response to my indignant gesticulations fluttered a handkerchief, nodding and smiling in the kindest way imaginable. The boys, only half-dressed, were jumping about the poop in great glee, displaying their gaudy braces; and Lena in a short scarlet petti-

coat, with peaked elbows and thin bare arms, nursed the rag-doll with
devotion. The whole family passed before my sight as if dragged across
a scene of unparalleled violence. The last I saw was Hermann's niece
with the baby Hermann in her arms standing apart from the others.
Magnificent in her close-fitting print frock, she displayed something so
commanding in the manifest perfection of her figure that the sun
seemed to be rising for her alone. The flood of light brought out the
opulence of her form and the vigour of her youth in a glorifying way.
She went by perfectly motionless and as if lost in meditation; only
the hem of her skirt stirred in the draught; the sun rays broke on
her sleek tawny hair; that bald-headed ruffian, Nicholas, was whacking
her on the shoulder. I saw his tiny fat arm rise and fall in a workman-
like manner. And then the four cottage windows of the *Diana* came
into view retreating swiftly down the river. The sashes were up, and
one of the white calico curtains fluttered straight out like a streamer
above the agitated water of the wake.

To be thus tricked out of one's turn was an unheard of occurrence.
In my agent's office, where I went to complain at once, they protested
with apologies they couldn't understand how the mistake arose: but
Schomberg, when I dropped in later to get some tiffin, though surprised to see me, was perfectly ready with an explanation. I found
him seated at the end of a long narrow table, facing his wife—a
scraggy little woman, with long ringlets and a blue tooth, who smiled
abroad stupidly and looked frightened when you spoke to her. Between them a waggling punkah fanned twenty vacant cane-bottomed
chairs and two rows of shiny plates. Three Chinamen in white jackets
loafed with napkins in their hands around that desolation. Schomberg's pet *table d'hôte* was not much of a success that day. He was
feeding himself furiously and seemed to overflow with bitterness.

He began by ordering in a brutal voice the chops to be brought
back for me, and turning in his chair: "Mistake, they told you? Not
a bit of it! Don't you believe it for a moment, captain! Falk isn't
a man to make mistakes unless on purpose." His firm conviction was
that Falk had been trying all along to curry favour on the cheap with
Hermann. "On the cheap—mind you! It doesn't cost him a cent to
put that insult upon you, and Captain Hermann gets in a day ahead
of your ship. Time's money! Eh? You are very friendly with Captain
Hermann I believe, but a man is bound to be pleased at any little
advantage he may get. Captain Hermann is a good business man, and
there's no such thing as a friend in business. Is there?" He leaned
forward and began to cast stealthy glances as usual. "But Falk is,
and always was, a miserable fellow. I would despise him."

I muttered, grumpily, that I had no particular respect for Falk.
"I would despise him," he insisted, with an appearance of anxiety

which would have amused me if I had not been fathoms deep in discontent. To a young man fairly conscientious and as well-meaning as only the young man can be, the current ill-usage of life comes with a peculiar cruelty. Youth that is fresh enough to believe in guilt, in innocence, and in itself, will always doubt whether it have not perchance deserved its fate. Sombre of mind and without appetite, I struggled with the chop while Mrs. Schomberg sat with her everlasting stupid grin and Schomberg's talk gathered way like a slide of rubbish.

"Let me tell you. It's all about that girl. I don't know what Captain Hermann expects, but if he asked me I could tell him something about Falk. He's a miserable fellow. That man is a perfect slave. That's what I call him. A slave. Last year I started this *table d'hôte*, and sent cards out—you know. You think he had one meal in the house? Give the thing a trial? Not once. He has got hold now of a Madras cook —a blamed fraud that I hunted out of my cookhouse with a rattan. He was not fit to cook for white men. No, not for the white men's dogs either; but see, any damned native that can boil a pot of rice is good enough for Mr. Falk. Rice and a little fish he buys for a few cents from the fishing-boats outside is what he lives on. You would hardly credit it—eh? A white man, too. . . ."

He wiped his lips, using the napkin with indignation, and looking at me. It flashed through my mind in the midst of my depression that if all the meat in the town was like these *table d'hôte* chops, Falk wasn't so much to blame. I was on the point of saying this, but Schomberg's stare was intimidating. "He's a vegetarian, perhaps," I murmured instead.

"He's a miser. A miserable miser," affirmed the hotel-keeper with great force. "The meat here is not so good as at home—of course. And dear, too. But look at me. I only charge a dollar for the tiffin, and one dollar and fifty cents for the dinner. Show me anything cheaper. Why am I doing it? There's little profit in this game. Falk wouldn't look at it. I do it for the sake of a lot of young white fellows here that hadn't a place where they could get a decent meal and eat it decently in good company. There's first-rate company always at my table."

The convinced way he surveyed the empty chairs made me feel as if I had intruded upon a tiffin of ghostly Presences.

"A white man should eat like a white man, dash it all," he burst out impetuously. "Ought to eat meat, must eat meat. I manage to get meat for my patrons all the year round. Don't I? I am not catering for a dam' lot of coolies: Have another chop, captain. . . . No? You, boy—take away!"

He threw himself back and waited grimly for the curry. The half-closed jalousies darkened the room pervaded by the smell of fresh whitewash; a swarm of flies buzzed and settled in turns, and poor Mrs. Schomberg's smile seemed to express the quintessence of all the imbecility that had ever spoken, had ever breathed, had ever been fed on infamous buffalo meat within these bare walls. Schomberg did not open his lips till he was ready to thrust therein a spoonful of greasy rice. He rolled his eyes ridiculously before he swallowed the hot stuff, and only then broke out afresh.

"It is the most degrading thing. They take the dish up to the wheelhouse for him with a cover on it, and he shuts both the doors before he begins to eat. Fact! Must be ashamed of himself. Ask the engineer. He can't do without an engineer—don't you see—and as no respectable man can be expected to put up with such a table, he allows them fifteen dollars a month extra mess money. I assure you it is so! You just ask Mr. Ferdinand da Costa. That's the engineer he has now. You may have seen him about my place, a delicate dark young man, with very fine eyes and a little moustache. He arrived here a year ago from Calcutta. Between you and me, I guess the moneylenders there must have been after him. He rushes here for a meal every chance he can get, for just please tell me what satisfaction is that for a well-educated young fellow to feed all alone in his cabin —like a wild beast? That's what Falk expects his engineers to put up with for fifteen dollars extra. And the rows on board every time a little smell of cooking gets about the deck! You wouldn't believe! The other day da Costa got the cook to fry a steak for him—a turtle steak it was, too, not beef at all—and the fat caught or something. Young da Costa himself was telling me of it here in this room. 'Mr. Schomberg'—says he—'if I had let a cylinder cover blow off through my negligence Captain Falk couldn't have been more savage. He frightened the cook so that he won't put anything on the fire for me now.' Poor da Costa had tears in his eyes. Only try to put yourself in his place, captain: a sensitive gentlemanly young fellow. Is he expected to eat his food raw? But that's your Falk all over. Ask any one you like. I suppose the fifteen dollars extra he has to give keep on rankling—in there."

And Schomberg tapped his manly breast. I sat half stunned by his irrelevant babble. Suddenly he gripped my forearm in an impressive and cautious manner, as if to lead me into a very cavern of confidence.

"It's nothing but enviousness," he said in a lowered tone, which had a stimulating effect upon my wearied hearing. "I don't suppose there is one person in this town that he isn't envious of. I tell you he's dangerous. Even I myself am not safe from him. I know for certain he tried to poison. . . ."

"Oh, come now," I cried, disgusted.

"But I know for certain. The people themselves came and told me of it. He went about saying everywhere I was a worse pest to this town than the cholera. He had been talking against me ever since I opened this hotel. And he poisoned Captain Hermann's mind, too. Last time the *Diana* was loading here Captain Hermann used to come in every day for a drink or a cigar. This time he hasn't been here twice in a week. How do you account for that?"

He squeezed my arm till he extorted from me some sort of mumble.

"Falk makes ten times the money I do. I've another hotel to fight against, and there is no other tug on the river. I am not in his way, am I? He wouldn't be fit to run an hotel if he tried. But that's just his nature. He can't bear to think I am making a living. I only hope it makes him properly wretched. He's like that in everything. He would like to keep a decent table well enough. But no—for the sake of a few cents. Can't do it. It's too much for him. That's what I call being a slave to it. But he's mean enough to kick up a row when his nose gets tickled a bit. See that? That just paints him. Miserly and envious. You can't account for it any other way. Can you? I have been studying him these three years."

He was anxious I should assent to his theory. And indeed on thinking it over it would have been plausible enough if there hadn't been always the essential falseness of irresponsibility in Schomberg's chatter. However, I was not disposed to investigate the psychology of Falk. I was engaged just then in eating despondently a piece of stale Dutch cheese, being too much crushed to care what I swallowed myself, let alone bothering my head about Falk's ideas of gastronomy. I could expect from their study no clue to his conduct in matters of business, which seemed to me totally unrestrained by morality or even by the commonest sort of decency. How insignificant and contemptible I must appear, for the fellow to dare treat me like this—I reflected suddenly, writhing in silent agony. And I consigned Falk and all his peculiarities to the devil with so much mental fervour as to forget Schomberg's existence, till he grabbed my arm urgently. "Well, you may think and think till every hair of your head falls off, captain; but you can't explain it in any other way."

For the sake of peace and quietness I admitted hurriedly that I couldn't; persuaded that now he would leave off. But the only result was to make his moist face shine with the pride of cunning. He removed his hand for a moment to scare a black mass of flies off the sugar-basin, and caught hold of my arm again.

"To be sure. And in the same way everybody is aware he would like to get married. Only he can't. Let me quote you an instance. Well, two years ago a Miss Vanlo, a very ladylike girl, came from home to keep house for her brother, Fred, who had an engineering shop for small repairs by the waterside. Suddenly Falk takes to going up to their bungalow after diner and sitting for hours on the verandah saying nothing. The poor girl couldn't tell for the life of her what to do with such a man, so she would keep on playing the piano and singing to him evening after evening till she was ready to drop. And it wasn't as if she had been a strong young woman either. She was thirty, and the climate had been playing the deuce with her. Then— don't you see—Fred had to sit up with them for propriety, and during whole weeks on end never got a chance to get to bed before midnight. That was not pleasant for a tired man—was it? And besides Fred had worries then because his shop didn't pay and he was dropping money fast. He just longed to get away from here and try his luck somewhere else, but for the sake of his sister he hung on and on till he ran himself into debt over his ears—I can tell you. I, myself, could show a handful of his chits for meals and drinks in my drawer. I could never find out tho' where Fred found all the money at last. Can't be but he must have got something out of that brother of his, a coal merchant in Port Said. Anyhow he paid everybody before he left, but the girl nearly broke her heart. Disappointment, of course, and at her age, don't you know. . . . Mrs. Schomberg here was very friendly with her, and she could tell you. Awful despair. Fainting fits. It was a scandal. A notorious scandal. To that extent that old Mr. Siegers—not your present charterer, but Mr. Siegers, the father, the old gentleman who retired from business on a fortune and got buried at sea going home, he had to interview Falk in his private office. He was a man who could speak like a Dutch Uncle, and, besides, Messrs. Siegers had been helping Falk with a good bit of money from the start. In fact, you may say they made him as far as that goes. It so happened that just at the time he turned up here, their firm was chartering a lot of sailing-ships every year, and it suited their business that there should be good towing facilities on the river. See? . . . Well—there's always an ear at the keyhole—isn't there? In fact," he lowered his tone confidentially, "in this case it was a good friend of mine; a man you can see here any evening; only they conversed rather low. Anyhow my friend's certain that Falk was trying to make all sorts of excuses, and old Mr. Siegers was coughing a lot. And yet Falk wanted all the time to be married, too. Why! It's notorious the man has been longing for years to make a home for himself. Only he can't face the expense. When it comes to putting his hand in his pocket—it chokes him off. That's the truth and no other. I've always said so, and everybody agrees with me by this time. What do you think of that—eh?"

He appealed confidently to my indignation, but having a mind to annoy him I remarked, "that it seemed to me very pitiful—if true."

He bounced in his chair as if I had run a pin into him. I don't know what he might have said, only at that moment we heard through the half-open door of the billiard-room the footsteps of two men entering from the verandah, a murmur of two voices; at the sharp tapping of a coin on a table Mrs. Schomberg half rose irresolutely. "Sit still," he hissed at her, and then, in an hospitable, jovial tone, contrasting amazingly with the angry glance that had made his wife sink in her chair, he cried very loud: "Tiffin still going on in here, gentlemen."

There was no answer, but the voices dropped suddenly. The head Chinaman went out. We heard the clink of ice in the glasses, pouring sounds, the shuffling feet, the scraping of chairs. Schomberg, after wondering in a low mutter who the devil could be there at this time of the day, got up napkin in hand to peep through the doorway cautiously. He retreated rapidly on tip-toe, and whispering behind his hand informed me that it was Falk, Falk himself who was in there, and what's more, he had Captain Hermann with him.

The return of the tug from the outer Roads was unexpected but possible, for Falk had taken away the *Diana* at half-past five, and it was now two o'clock. Schomberg wished me to observe that neither of these men would spend a dollar on a tiffin, which they must have wanted. But by the time I was ready to leave the dining-room Falk had gone. I heard the last of his big boots on the planks of the verandah. Hermann was sitting quite alone in the large, wooden room with the two lifeless billiard tables shrouded in striped covers, mopping his face diligently. He wore his best go ashore clothes, a stiff collar, black coat, large white waistcoat, gray trousers. A white cotton sunshade with a cane handle reposed between his legs, his side whiskers were neatly brushed, his chin had been freshly shaved; and he only distantly resembled the dishevelled and terrified man in a snuffy night shirt and ignoble old trousers I had seen in the morning hanging on to the wheel of the *Diana*.

He gave a start at my entrance, and addressed me at once in some confusion, but with genuine eagerness. He was anxious to make it clear he had nothing to do with what he called the "tam pizness" of the morning. It was most inconvenient. He had reckoned upon another day up in town to settle his bills and sign certain papers. There were also some few stores to come, and sundry pieces of "my iron-work," as he called it quaintly, landed for repairs, had been left behind. Now he would have to hire a native boat to take all this out to the ship. It would cost five or six dollars perhaps. He had had no warning from Falk. Nothing. . . . He hit the table with his dumpy fist. . . . Der verfluchte Kerl came in the morning like a "tam' ropper," making a great noise, and took him away. His mate was not prepared, his ship was moored fast—he protested it was shameful to come upon a man in that way. Shameful! Yet such was the power Falk had on the river that when I suggested in a chilling tone that he might have simply refused to have his ship moved, Hermann was quite startled at the idea. I never realized so well before that this is an age of steam. The exclusive possession of a marine boiler had given Falk the whip hand of us all. Hermann, recovering, put it to me appealingly that I knew very well how unsafe it was to contradict that fellow. At this I only smiled distantly.

"Der Kerl!" he cried. He was sorry he had not refused. He was indeed. The damage! The damage! What for all that damage! There was no occasion for damage. Did I know how much damage he had done? It gave me a certain satisfaction to tell him that I had heard his old waggon of a ship crack fore and aft as she went by. "You passed close enough to me," I added, significantly.

He threw both his hands up to heaven at the recollection. One of them grasped by the middle the white parasol, and he resembled curiously a caricature of a shopkeeping citizen in one of his own German comic papers. "Ach! That was dangerous," he cried. I was amused. But directly he added with an appearance of simplicity, "The side of your iron ship would have been crushed in like—like this matchbox."

"Would it?" I growled, much less amused now; but by the time I had decided that this remark was not meant for a dig at me he had worked himself into a high state of resentfulness against Falk. The inconvenience, the damage, the expense! Gottferdam! Devil take the fellow. Behind the bar Schomberg, with a cigar in his teeth, pretended to be writing with a pencil on a large sheet of paper; and as Hermann's excitement increased it made me comfortingly aware of my own calmness and superiority. But it occurred to me while I listened to his revilings, that after all the good man had come up in the tug. There perhaps—since he must come to town—he had no option. But evidently he had had a drink with Falk, either accepted or offered. How was that? So I checked him by saying loftily that I hoped he would make Falk pay for every penny of the damage.

"That's it! That's it! Go for him," called out Schomberg from the bar, flinging his pencil down and rubbing his hands.

We ignored his noise. But Hermann's excitement suddenly went off the boil as when you remove a saucepan from the fire. I urged on his consideration that he had done now with Falk and Falk's confounded tug. He, Hermann, would not, perhaps, turn up again in this part of the world for years to come, since he was going to sell the *Diana* at the end of this very trip ("Go home passenger in a mail-boat," he murmured mechanically). He was therefore safe from Falk's malice. All he had to do was to race off to his consignees and stop payment of the towage bill before Falk had the time to get in and lift the money.

Nothing could have been less in the spirit of my advice than the thoughtful way in which he set about to make his parasol stay propped against the edge of the table.

While I watched his concentrated efforts with astonishment he threw at me one or two perplexed, half-shy glances. Then he sat down. "That's all very well," he said, reflectively.

It cannot be doubted that the man had been thrown off his balance by being hauled out of the harbour against his wish. His stolidity had been profoundly stirred, else he would never have made up his mind to ask me unexpectedly whether I had not remarked that Falk had been casting eyes upon his niece. "No more than myself," I answered with literal truth. The girl was of the sort one necessarily casts eyes at in a sense. She made no noise, but she filled most satisfactorily a good bit of space.

"But you, captain, are not the same kind of man," observed Hermann.

I was not, I am happy to say, in a position to deny this. "What about the lady?" I could not help asking. At this he gazed for a time into my face, earnestly, and made as if to change the subject. I heard him beginning to mutter something unexpected, about his children growing old enough to require schooling. He would have to leave them ashore with their grandmother when he took up that new command he expected to get in Germany.

This constant harping on his domestic arrangements was funny. I suppose it must have been like the prospect of a complete alteration in his life. An epoch. He was going, too, to part with the *Diana!* He had served in her for years. He had inherited her. From an uncle, if I remember rightly. And the future loomed big before him, occupying his thought exclusively with all its aspects as on the eve of a venturesome enterprise. He sat there frowning and biting his lip, and suddenly he began to fume and fret.

I discovered to my momentary amusement that he seemed to imagine I could, should or ought, have caused Falk in some way to declare himself. Such a hope was incomprehensible, but funny. Then the contact with all this foolishness irritated me. I said crossly that I had seen no symptoms, but if there were any—since he, Hermann, was so sure—then it was still worse. What pleasure Falk found in humbugging people in just that way I couldn't say. It was, however, my solemn duty to warn him. It had lately, I said, come to my knowledge that there was a man (not a very long time ago either) who had been taken in just like this.

All this passed in undertones, and at this point Schomberg, ex-

asperated at our secrecy, went out of the room, slamming the door
with a crash that positively lifted us in our chairs. This, or else what
I had said, huffed my Hermann. He supposed, with a contemptuous
toss of his head towards the door which trembled yet, that I had got
hold of some of that man's silly tales. It looked, indeed, as though
his mind had been thoroughly poisoned against Schomberg. "His
tales were—they were," he repeated, seeking for the word—"trash."
They were trash, he reiterated and moreover I was young yet . . .

This horrid aspersion (I regret I am no longer exposed to that sort
of insult) made me huffy, too. I felt ready in my own mind to back
up every assertion of Schomberg's and on any subject. In a moment,
devil only knows why, Hermann and I were looking at each other
most inimically. He caught up his hat without more ado and I gave
myself the pleasure of calling after him:

"Take my advice and make Falk pay for breaking up your ship. You
aren't likely to get anything else out of him."

When I got on board my ship, the old mate, who was very full of
the events of the morning, remarked:

"I saw the tug coming back from the outer Roads just before two
p.m." (He never by any chance used the words morning or afternoon.
Always p.m. or a.m., log-book style.) "Smart work that. Man's always
in a state of hurry. He's a regular chucker-out, ain't he, sir? There's
a few pubs I know of in the East-end of London that would be all the
better for one of his sort around the bar." He chuckled at his joke.
"A regular chucker-out. Now he has fired out that Dutchman head
over heels, I suppose our turn's coming to-morrow morning."

We were all on deck at break of day (even the sick—poor devils—
had crawled out) ready to cast off in the twinkling of an eye. Nothing
came. Falk did not come. At last, when I began to think that probably something had gone wrong in his engine-room, we perceived
the tug going by, full pelt, down the river, as if we hadn't existed.
For a moment I entertained the wild notion that he was going to
turn round in the next reach. Afterwards, I watched his smoke appear
above the plain, now here, now there, according to the windings of
the river. It disappeared. Then without a word I went down to breakfast. I just simply went down to breakfast.

Not one of us uttered a sound till the mate, after imbibing—by
means of suction out of a saucer—his second cup of tea, exclaimed:
"Where the devil is the man gone to?"

"Courting!" I shouted, with such a fiendish laugh that the old chap
didn't venture to open his lips any more.

I started to the office perfectly calm. Calm with excessive rage.
Evidently they knew all about it already, and they treated me to a
show of consternation. The manager, a soft-footed, obese man, breath-

ing short, got up to meet me, while all round the room the young clerks, bending over their desks, cast glances in my direction. The fat man, without waiting for my complaint, wheezing heavily and in a tone as if he himself were incredulous, conveyed to me the news that Falk—Captain Falk—had declined—had absolutely declined—to tow my ship—to have anything to do with my ship—this day or any other day. Never!

I did my best to preserve a cool appearance, but, all the same, I must have shown how much taken aback I was. We were talking in the middle of the room. Suddenly, behind my back some ass blew his nose with a great noise and at the same time another quill-driver got up and went out on the landing hastily. It occurred to me I was cutting a foolish figure there. I demanded angrily to see the principal in his private room.

The skin of Mr. Siegers' head showed dead white between the iron gray streaks of hair lying plastered cross-wise from ear to ear over the top of his skull in the manner of a bandage. His narrow sunken face was of an uniform and permanent terra-cotta colour, like a piece of pottery. He was sickly, thin, and short, with wrists like a boy of ten. But from that debile body there issued a bullying voice, tremendously loud, harsh and resonant, as if produced by some powerful mechanical contrivance in the nature of a fog-horn. I do not know what he did with it in the private life of his home, but in the larger sphere of business it presented the advantage of overcoming arguments without the slightest mental effort, by the mere volume of sound. We had had several passages of arms. It took me all I knew to guard the interest of my owners—whom, *nota bene,* I had never seen—while Siegers (who had made their acquaintance some years before, during a business tour in Australia) pretended to the knowledge of their innermost minds, and, in the character of "our very good friends," threw them perpetually at my head.

He looked at me with a jaundiced eye (there was no love lost between us), and declared at once that it was strange, very strange. His pronunciation of English was so extravagant that I can't even attempt to reproduce it. For instance, he said "Fferie strantch." Combined with the bellowing intonation it made the language of one's childhood sound weirdly startling, and even if considered purely as a kind of unmeaning noise it filled you with astonishment at first. "They had," he continued, "been acquainted with Captain Falk for very many years, and never had any reason. . . ."

"That's why I come to you, of course," I interrupted. "I've the right to know the meaning of this infernal nonsense." In the half-light of the room, which was greenish, because of the tree-tops screening the window, I saw him writhe his meagre shoulders. It came into my head, as disconnected ideas will come at all sorts of times into one's head, that this, most likely, was the very room where, if the tale were true, Falk had been lectured by Mr. Siegers, the father. Mr. Siegers' (the son's) overwhelming voice, in brassy blasts, as though he had been trying to articulate words through a trumpet, was expressing his great regret at conduct characterized by a very marked want of discretion . . . As I lived I was being lectured, too! His deafening gibberish was difficult to follow, but it was *my* conduct— mine!—that . . . Damn! I wasn't going to stand this.

"What on earth are you driving at?" I asked in a passion. I put my hat on my head (he never offered a seat to anybody), and as he seemed for the moment struck dumb by my irreverence, I turned my back on him and marched out. His vocal arrangements blared after me a few threats of coming down on the ship for the demurrage of the lighters, and all the other expenses consequent upon the delays arising from my frivolity.

Once outside in the sunshine my head swam. It was no longer a question of mere delay. I perceived myself involved in hopeless and humiliating absurdities that were leading me to something very like a disaster. "Let us be calm," I muttered to myself, and ran into the shade of a leprous wall. From that short side-street I could see the broad main thoroughfare ruinous and gay, running away, away between stretches of decaying masonry, bamboo fences, ranges of arcades of brick and plaster, hovels of lath and mud, lofty temple gates of carved timber, huts of rotten mats—an immensely wide thoroughfare, loosely packed as far as the eye could reach with a barefooted and brown multitude paddling ankle deep in the dust. For a moment I felt myself about to go out of my mind with worry and desperation.

Some allowance must be made for the feelings of a young man new to responsibility. I thought of my crew. Half of them were ill, and I really began to think that some of them would end by dying on board if I couldn't get them out to sea soon. Obviously I should have to take my ship down the river, either working under canvas or dredging with the anchor down; operations which, in common with many modern sailors, I only knew theoretically. And I almost shrank from undertaking them shorthanded and without local knowledge of the river bed, which is so necessary for the confident handling of a ship. There were no pilots, no beacons, no buoys of any sort; but there was a very devil of a current for anybody to see, no end of shoal places, and at least two obviously awkward turns of the channel between me and the sea. But how dangerous these turns were I could not tell. I didn't even know what my ship was capable of! I had never handled her in my life. A misunderstanding between a man and his ship, in a difficult river with no room to make it up, is bound to end in trouble for the man. On the other hand, it must be owned I had not much reason to count upon a general run of good luck. And suppose I had the misfortune to pile up high and dry on some beastly shoal? That would have been the final undoing of that voyage. It was plain that if Falk refused to tow me out he would also refuse to pull me off. This meant—what? A day lost at the very best; but more likely a whole fortnight of frizzling on some pestilential mudflat, of desperate work, of discharging cargo; more than likely it meant borrowing money at an exorbitant rate of interest—from the Siegers' gang, too, at that. They were a power in the port. And that elderly seaman of mine, Gambril, had looked pretty ghastly when I went forward to dose him with quinine that morning. *He* would certainly die—not to speak of two or three others that seemed nearly as bad, and of the rest of them just ready to catch any tropical disease going. Horror, ruin and everlasting remorse. And no help. None. I had fallen amongst a lot of unfriendly lunatics!

At any rate, if I must take my ship down myself it was my duty to produce if possible some local knowledge. But that was not easy. The only person I could think of for that service was a certain Johnson, formerly captain of a country ship, but now spliced to a country wife and gone utterly to the bad. I had only heard of him in the vaguest way, as living concealed in the thick of two hundred thousand natives, and only emerging into the light of day for the purpose of hunting up some brandy. I had a notion that if I could lay my hands on him I would sober him on board my ship and use him for a pilot. Better than nothing. Once a sailor always a sailor—and he had known the river for years. But in our Consulate (where I arrived dripping after a sharp walk) they could tell me nothing. The excellent young men on the staff, though willing to help me, belonged to a sphere of the white colony for which that sort of Johnson does not exist. Their suggestion was that I should hunt the man up myself with the help of the Consulate's constable—an ex-sergeant-major of a regiment of Hussars.

This man, whose usual duty apparently consisted in sitting behind a little table in an outer room of Consular offices, when ordered to assist me in my search for Johnson displayed lots of energy and a marvellous amount of local knowledge of a sort. But he did not conceal an immense and sceptical contempt for the whole business. We explored together on that afternoon an infinity of infamous grog shops, gambling dens, opium dens. We walked up narrow lanes where our gharry—a tiny box of a thing on wheels, attached to a jibbing Burmah pony—could by no means have passed. The constable seemed to be on terms of scornful intimacy with Maltese, with Eurasians, with Chinamen, with Klings, and with the sweepers belonging to a temple, with whom he talked at the gate. We interviewed also through a grating in a mud wall closing a blind alley an immensely corpulent Italian, who, the ex-sergeant-major remarked to me perfunctorily, had "killed another man last year." Thereupon he addressed him as "Antonio" and "Old Buck," though that bloated carcase, apparently more than half filling the sort of cell wherein it sat, recalled rather a fat pig in a stye. Familiar and never unbending, the sergeant chucked—absolutely chucked—under the chin a horribly wrinkled and shrivelled old hag propped on a stick, who had volunteered some sort of information: and with the same stolid face he kept up an animated conversation with the groups of swathed brown women, who sat smoking cheroots on the door-steps of a long range of clay hovels. We got out of the gharry and clambered into dwellings airy like packing crates, or descended into places sinister like cellars. We got in, we drove on, we got out again for the sole purpose, as it seemed, of looking behind a heap of rubble. The sun declined; my companion was curt and sardonic in his answers, but it appears we were just missing Johnson all along. At last our conveyance stopped once more with a jerk, and the driver jumping down opened the door.

A black mudhole blocked the lane. A mound of garbage crowned with the dead body of a dog arrested us not. An empty Australian beef tin bounded cheerily before the toe of my boot. Suddenly we clambered through a gap in a prickly fence. . . .

It was a very clean native compound: and the big native woman, with bare brown legs as thick as bedposts, pursuing on all fours a silver dollar that came rolling out from somewhere, was Mrs. Johnson herself. "Your man's at home," said the ex-sergeant, and stepped aside in complete and marked indifference to anything that might follow. Johnson—at home—stood with his back to a native house built on posts and with its walls made of mats. In his left hand he held a banana. Out of the right he dealt another dollar into space. The woman captured this one on the wing, and there and then plumped down on the ground to look at us with greater comfort.

"My man" was sallow of face, grizzled, unshaven, muddy on elbows and back; where the seams of his serge coat yawned you could see his white nakedness. The vestiges of a paper collar encircled his neck. He looked at us with a grave, swaying surprise. "Where do you come from?" he asked. My heart sank. How could I have been stupid enough to waste energy and time for this?

But having already gone so far I approached a little nearer and declared the purpose of my visit. He would have to come at once with me, sleep on board my ship, and to-morrow, with the first of the ebb, he would give me his assistance in getting my ship down to the sea, without steam. A six-hundred-ton barque, drawing nine feet aft.

I proposed to give him eighteen dollars for his local knowledge; and all the time I was speaking he kept on considering attentively the various aspects of the banana, holding first one side up to his eye, then the other.

"You've forgotten to apologize," he said at last with extreme precision. "Not being a gentleman yourself, you don't know apparently when you intrude upon a gentleman. I am one. I wish you to understand that when I am in funds I don't work, and now . . ."

I would have pronounced him perfectly sober had he not paused in great concern to try and brush a hole off the knee of his trousers.

"I have money—and friends. Every gentleman has. Perhaps you would like to know my friend? His name is Falk. You could borrow some money. Try to remember. F-A-L-K. Falk." Abruptly his tone changed. "A noble heart," he said, muzzily.

"Has Falk been giving you some money?" I asked, appalled by the detailed finish of the dark plot.

"Lent me, my good man, not given me," he corrected, suavely. "Met me taking the air last evening, and being as usual anxious to oblige—— Hadn't you better go to the devil out of my compound?"

And upon this, without other warning, he let fly with the banana, which missed my head and took the constable just under the left eye. He rushed at the miserable Johnson, stammering with fury. They fell. . . . But why dwell on the wretchedness, the breathlessness, the degradation, the senselessness, the weariness, the ridicule and humiliation and—and—the perspiration, of these moments? I dragged the ex-hussar off. He was like a wild beast. It seems he had been greatly annoyed at losing his free afternoon on my account. The garden of his bungalow required his personal attention, and at the slight blow of the banana the brute in him had broken loose. We left Johnson on his back still black in the face, but beginning to kick feebly. Meantime, the big woman had remained sitting on the ground, apparently paralyzed with extreme terror.

For half an hour we jolted inside our rolling box, side by side, in profound silence. The ex-sergeant was busy staunching the blood of a long scratch on his cheek. "I hope you're satisfied," he said, suddenly. "That's what comes of all that tomfool business. If you hadn't quarrelled with that tugboat skipper over some girl or other, all this wouldn't have happened."

"You heard *that* story?" I said.

"Of course I heard. And I shouldn't wonder if the Consul-General himself doesn't come to hear of it. How am I to go before him tomorrow with that thing on my cheek—I want to know. It's *you* who ought to have got this!"

After that, till the gharry stopped and he jumped out without leave-

taking, he swore to himself steadily, horribly; muttering great, purposeful, trooper oaths, to which the worst a sailor can do is like the
prattle of a child. For my part I had just the strength to crawl into
Schomberg's coffee-room, where I wrote at a little table a note to the
mate instructing him to get everything ready for dropping down the
river next day. I couldn't face my ship. Well! she had a clever sort of
skipper and no mistake—poor thing! What a horrid mess! I took my
head between my hands. At times the obviousness of my innocence
would reduce me to despair. What had I done? If I had done something to bring about the situation I should at least have learned not
to do it again. But I felt guiltless to the point of imbecility. The
room was empty yet; only Schomberg prowled round me goggle-eyed
and with a sort of awed respectful curiosity. No doubt he had set the
story going himself; but he was a good-hearted chap, and I am really
persuaded he participated in all my troubles. He did what he could
for me. He ranged aside the heavy matchstand, set a chair straight,
pushed a spittoon slightly with his foot—as you show small attentions
to a friend under a great sorrow—sighed, and at last, unable to hold
his tongue:

"Well! I warned you, captain. That's what comes of running your
head against Mr. Falk. Man'll stick at nothing."

I sat without stirring, and after surveying me with a sort of commiseration in his eyes, he burst out in a hoarse whisper: "But for a
fine lump of a girl, she's a fine lump of a girl." He made a loud smack-
ing noise with his thick lips. "The finest lump of a girl that I ever
. . ." he was going on with great unction, but for some reason or
other broke off. I fancied myself throwing something at his head. "I
don't blame you, captain. Hang me if I do," he said with a patronizing
air.

"Thank you," I said, resignedly. It was no use fighting against this
false fate. I don't know even if I was sure myself where the truth of
the matter began. The conviction that it would end disastrously had
been driven into me by all the successive shocks my sense of security
had received. I began to ascribe an extraordinary potency to agents
in themselves powerless. It was as if Schomberg's baseless gossip had
the power to bring about the thing itself or the abstract enmity of Falk
could put my ship ashore.

I have already explained how fatal this last would have been. For
my further action, my youth, my inexperience, my very real concern
for the health of my crew must be my excuse. The action itself, when
it came, was purely impulsive. It was set in movement quite un-
diplomatically and simply by Falk's appearance in the doorway of the
coffee-room.

The room was full by then and buzzing with voices. I had been looked at with curiosity by every one, but how am I to describe the sensation produced by the appearance of Falk himself blocking the doorway? The tension of expectation could be measured by the profundity of the silence that fell upon the very click of the billiard balls. As to Schomberg, he looked extremely frightened; he hated mortally any sort of row (*fracas* he called it) in his establishment. *Fracas* was bad for business, he affirmed; but in truth, this specimen of portly, middle-aged manhood was of a timid disposition. I don't know what, considering my presence in the place, they all hoped would come of it. A sort of stag fight, perhaps. Or they may have supposed Falk had come in only to annihilate me completely. As a matter of fact, Falk had come in because Hermann had asked him to inquire after the precious white cotton parasol which, in the worry and excitement of the previous day, he had forgotten at the table where we had held our little discussion.

It was this that gave me my opportunity. I don't think I would have gone to seek Falk out. No. I don't think so. There are limits. But there was an opportunity and I seized it—I have already tried to explain why. Now I will merely state that, in my opinion, to get his sickly crew into the sea air and secure a quick despatch for his ship a skipper would be justified in going to any length, short of absolute crime. He should put his pride in his pocket; he may accept confidences; he must explain his innocence as if it were a sin; he may take advantage of misconceptions, of desires and weaknesses; he ought to conceal his horror and other emotions, and, if the fate of a human being, and that human being a magnificent young girl, is strangely involved—why, he should contemplate that fate (whatever it might seem to be) without turning a hair. And all these things I have done; the explaining, the listening, the pretending—even to the discretion —and nobody, not even Hermann's voice, I believe, need throw stones at me now. Schomberg at all events needn't, since from first to last, I am happy to say there was not the slightest "*fracas.*"

Overcoming a nervous contraction of the windpipe, I had managed to exclaim "Captain Falk!" His start of surprise was perfectly genuine, but afterwards he neither smiled nor scowled. He simply waited. Then when I had said, "I must have a talk with you," and had pointed to a chair at my table, he moved up to me, though he didn't sit down. Schomberg, however, with a long tumbler in his hand, was making towards us prudently, and I discovered then the only sign of weakness in Falk. He had for Schomberg a repulsion resembling that sort of physical fear some people experience at the sight of a toad. Perhaps to a man so essentially and silently concentrated upon himself (though he could talk well enough, as I was to find out presently) the other's irrepressible loquacity, embracing every human being

within range of the tongue, might have appeared unnatural, disgusting, and monstrous. He suddenly gave signs of restiveness—positively
like a horse about to rear, and, muttering hurriedly as if in great pain,
"No. I can't stand that fellow," seemed ready to bolt. This weakness
of his gave me the advantage at the very start. "Verandah," I suggested,
as if rendering him a service, and walked him out by the arm. We
stumbled over a few chairs; we had the feeling of open space before
us, and felt the fresh breath of the river—fresh, but tainted. The
Chinese theatres across the water made, in the sparsely twinkling
masse of gloom an Eastern town presents at night, blazing centres of
light, and of a distant and howling uproar. I felt him become suddenly tractable again like an animal, like a good-tempered horse when
the object that scares him is removed. Yes. I felt in the darkness there
how tractable he was, without my conviction of his inflexibility—
tenacity, rather, perhaps—being in the least weakened. His very arm
abandoning itself to my grasp was as hard as marble—like a limb of
iron. But I heard a tumultuous scuffling of boot-soles within. The
unspeakable idiots inside were crowding to the windows, climbing
over each other's backs behind the blinds, billiard cues and all. Somebody broke a window-pane, and with the sound of falling glass, so
suggestive of riot and devastation, Schomberg reeled out after us in a
state of funk which had prevented him from parting with his brandy
and soda. He must have trembled like an aspen leaf. The piece of ice
in the long tumbler he held in his hand tinkled with an effect of chat-
tering teeth. "I beg you, gentlemen," he expostulated, thickly. "Come!
Really, now, I must insist . . .

How proud I am of my presence of mind! "Hallo," I said instantly in a loud and naïve tone, "somebody's breaking your windows,
Schomberg. Would you please tell one of your boys to bring out here
a pack of cards and a couple of lights? And two drinks. Will you?"

To receive an order soothed him at once. It was business. "Certainly," he said in an immensely relieved tone. The night was rainy,
with wandering gusts of wind, and while we waited for the candles
Falk said, as if to justify his panic, "I don't interfere in anybody's
business. I don't give any occasion for talk. I am a respectable man.
But this fellow is always making out something wrong, and can never
rest till he gets somebody to believe him."

This was the first of my knowledge of Falk. This desire of respectability, of being like everybody else, was the only recognition he vouchsafed to the organization of mankind. For the rest he might have
been the member of a herd, not a society. Self-preservation was his
only concern. Not selfishness, but mere self-preservation. Selfishness
presupposes consciousness, choice, the presence of other men; but his
instinct acted as though he were the last of mankind nursing that

law like the only spark of a sacred fire. I don't mean to say that living naked in a cavern would have satisfied him. Obviously he was the creature of the conditions to which he was born. No doubt self-preservation meant also the preservation of these conditions. But essentially it meant something much more simple, natural, and powerful. How shall I express it? It meant the preservation of the five senses of his body—let us say—taking it in its narrowest as well as in its widest meaning. I think you will admit before long the justice of this judgment. However, as we stood there together on the dark verandah I had judged nothing as yet—and I had no desire to judge—which is an idle practice anyhow. The light was long in coming.

"Of course," I said in a tone of mutual understanding, "it isn't exactly a game of cards I want with you."

I saw him draw his hands down his face—the vague stir of the passionate and meaningless gesture; but he waited in silent patience. It was only when the lights had been brought out that he opened his lips. I understood his mumble to mean that "he didn't know any card-games."

"Like this, Schomberg and all the other fools will have to keep off," I said, tearing open the pack. "Have you heard that we are universally supposed to be quarrelling about a girl? You know who—of course. I am really ashamed to ask, but is it possible that you do me the honour to think me dangerous?"

As I said these words I felt how absurd it was and also I felt flattered—for, really, what else could it be? His answer, spoken in his usual dispassionate undertone, made it clear that it was so, but not precisely as flattering as I supposed. He thought me dangerous with Hermann, more than with the girl herself; but, as to quarrelling, I saw at once how inappropriate the word was. We had no quarrel. Natural forces are not quarrelsome. You can't quarrel with the wind that inconveniences and humiliates you by blowing off your hat in a street full of people. He had no quarrel with me. Neither would a boulder, falling on my head, have had. He fell upon me in accordance with the law by which he was moved—not of gravitation, like a detached stone, but of self-preservation. Of course this is giving it a rather wide interpretation. Strictly speaking, he had existed and could have existed without being married. Yet he told me that he had found it more and more difficult to live alone. Yes. He told me this in his low, careless voice, to such a pitch of confidence had we arrived at the end of half an hour.

It took me just about that time to convince him that I had never dreamed of marrying Hermann's niece. Could any necessity have been more extravagant? And the difficulty was the greater because he was so hard hit himself that he couldn't imagine anybody else being able to remain in a state of indifference. Any man with eyes in his head, he seemed to think, could not help coveting so much bodily magnificence. This profound belief was conveyed by the manner he listened, sitting sideways to the table and playing absently with a few cards I had dealt to him at random. And the more I saw into him the more I saw of him. The wind swayed the lights so that his sunburnt face, whiskered to the eyes, seemed to successively flicker crimson at me and to go out. I saw the extraordinary breadth of the high cheekbones, the perpendicular style of the features, the massive forehead, steep like a cliff, denuded at the top, largely uncovered at the temples. The fact is I had never before seen him without his hat; but now, as if my fervour had made him hot, he had taken it off and laid it gently on the floor. Something peculiar in the shape and setting of his yellow eyes gave them the provoking silent intensity which characterized his glance. But the face was thin, furrowed, worn; I discovered this through the bush of his hair, as you may detect the gnarled shape of a tree trunk in a dense undergrowth. These overgrown cheeks were sunken. It was an anchorite's bony head fitted with a Capuchin's beard and adjusted to a herculean body. I don't mean athletic. Hercules, I take it, was not an athlete. He was a strong man, susceptible to female charms, and not afraid of dirt. And thus with Falk, who was a strong man. He was extremely strong, just as the girl (since I must think of them together) was magnificently attractive by the masterful power of flesh and blood, expressed in shape, in size, in attitude—that is by a straight appeal to the senses. His mind meantime, preoccupied with respectability, quailed before Schomberg's tongue and seemed absolutely impervious to my protestations; and I went so far as to protest that I would just as soon think of marrying my mother's (dear old lady!) faithful female cook as Hermann's niece. Sooner, I protested, in my desperation, much sooner; but it did not appear that he saw anything outrageous in the proposition, and in his sceptical immobility he seemed to nurse the argument that at all events the cook was very, very far away. It must be said that, just before, I had gone wrong by appealing to the evidence of my manner whenever I called on board the *Diana*. I had never attempted to approach the girl, or to speak to her, or even to look at her in any marked way. Nothing could be clearer. But, as his own idea of—let us say—courting, seemed to consist precisely in sitting silently for hours in the vicinity of the beloved object, that line of argument inspired him with distrust. Staring down his extended legs he let out a grunt—as much as to say, "That's all very fine, but you can't throw dust in *my* eyes."

As last I was exasperated into saying, "Why don't you put the matter at rest by talking to Hermann?" and I added, sneeringly: "You don't expect me perhaps to speak for you?"

To this he said, very loud for him, "Would you?"

And for the first time he lifted his head to look at me with wonder and incredulity. He lifted his head so sharply that there could be no mistake. I had touched a spring. I saw the whole extent of my opportunity, and could hardly believe in it.

"Why! Speak to . . . Well, of course," I proceeded very slowly, watching him with great attention, for, on my word, I feared a joke. "Not, perhaps, to the young lady herself. I can't speak German, you know. But . . ."

He interrupted me with the earnest assurance that Hermann had the highest opinion of me; and at once I felt the need for the greatest possible diplomacy at this juncture. So I demurred just enough to draw him on. Falk sat up, but except for a very noticeable enlargement of the pupils, till the irises of his eyes were reduced to two narrow yellow rings, his face, I should judge, was incapable of expressing excitement. "Oh, yes! Hermann did have the greatest . . ."

"Take up your cards. Here's Schomberg peeping at us through the blind!" I said.

We went through the motions of what might have been a game of écarté. Presently the intolerable scandalmonger withdrew, probably to inform the people in the billiard-room that we two were gambling on the verandah like mad.

We were not gambling, but it was a game; a game in which I felt I held the winning cards. The stake, roughly speaking, was the success of the voyage—for me; and he, I apprehended, had nothing to lose. Our intimacy matured rapidly, and before many words had been exchanged I perceived that the excellent Hermann had been making use of me. That simple and astute Teuton had been, it seems, holding me up to Falk in the light of a rival. I was young enough to be shocked at so much duplicity. "Did he tell you that in so many words?" I asked with indignation.

Hermann had not. He had given hints only; and of course it had not taken very much to alarm Falk; but, instead of declaring himself, he had taken steps to remove the family from under my influence. He was perfectly straightforward about it—as straightforward as a tile falling on your head. There was no duplicity in that man; and when I congratulated him on the perfection of his arrangements—even to the bribing of the wretched Johnson against me—he had a genuine movement of protest. Never bribed. He knew the man wouldn't work as long as he had a few cents in his pocket to get drunk on, and, naturally (he said—"*naturally*") he let him have a dollar or two. He was himself a sailor, he said, and anticipated the view another sailor, like myself, was bound to take. On the other hand, he was sure that I should have to come to grief. He hadn't been knocking about for the last seven years up and down that river for nothing. It would have been no disgrace to me—but he asserted confidently I would have had my ship very awkwardly ashore at a spot two miles below the Great Pagoda . . .

And with all that he had no ill-will. That was evident. This was a crisis in which his only object had been to gain time—I fancy. And presently he mentioned that he had written for some jewellery, real good jewellery—had written to Hong-Kong for it. It would arrive in a day or two.

"Well, then," I said, cheerily, "everything is all right. All you've got to do is to present it to the lady together with your heart, and live happy ever after."

Upon the whole he seemed to accept that view as far as the girl was concerned, but the eyelids drooped. There was still something in the way. For one thing Hermann disliked him so much. As to me, on the contrary, it seemed as though he could not praise me enough. Mrs. Hermann, too. He didn't know why they disliked him so. It made everything most difficult.

I listened impassive, feeling more and more diplomatic. His speech was not transparently clear. He was one of those men who seem to live, feel, suffer in a sort of mental twilight. But as to being fascinated by the girl and possessed by the desire of home life with her—it was as clear as daylight. So much being at stake, he was afraid of putting it to the hazard of the declaration. Besides, there was something else. And with Hermann being so set against him . . .

"I see," I said, thoughtfully, while my heart beat fast with the excitement of my diplomacy. "I don't mind sounding Hermann. In fact, to show you how mistaken you were, I am ready to do all I can for you in that way."

A light sigh escaped him. He drew his hands down his face, and it emerged, bony, unchanged of expression, as if all the tissues had been ossified. All the passion was in those big brown hands. He was satisfied. Then there was that other matter. If there were anybody on earth it was I who could persuade Hermann to take a reasonable view! I had a knowledge of the world and lots of experience. Hermann admitted this himself. And then I was a sailor, too. Falk thought that a sailor would be able to understand certain things best. . . .

He talked as if the Hermanns had been living all their life in a rural hamlet, and I alone had been capable, with my practice in life, of a large and indulgent view of certain occurrences. That was what my diplomacy was leading me to. I began suddenly to dislike it.

"I say, Falk," I asked quite brusquely, "you haven't already a wife put away somewhere?"

The pain and disgust of his denial were very striking. Couldn't I understand that he was as respectable as any white man hereabouts; earning his living honestly? He was suffering from my suspicion, and the low undertone of his voice made his protestations sound very pathetic. For a moment he shamed me, but, my diplomacy notwithstanding, I seemed to develop a conscience, as if in very truth it were in my power to decide the success of this matrimonial enterprise. By pretending hard enough we come to believe anything—anything to our advantage. And I had been pretending very hard, because I meant yet to be towed safely down the river. But, through conscience or stupidity, I couldn't help alluding to the Vanlo affair. "You acted rather badly there. Didn't you?" was what I ventured actually to say—for the logic of our conduct is always at the mercy of obscure and unforeseen impulses.

His dilated pupils swerved from my face, glancing at the window with a sort of scared fury. We heard behind the blinds the continuous and sudden clicking of ivory, a jovial murmur of many voices, and Schomberg's deep manly laugh.

"That confounded old woman of a hotel-keeper then would never, never let it rest!" Falk exclaimed. Well, yes! It had happened two years ago. When it came to the point he owned he couldn't make up his mind to trust Fred Vanlo—no sailor, a bit of a fool, too. He could not trust him, but, to stop his row, he had lent him enough money to pay all his debts before he left. I was greatly surprised to hear this. Then Falk could not be such a miser after all. So much the better for the girl. For a time he sat silent; then he picked up a card and while looking at it he said:

"You need not think of anything bad. It was an accident. I've been unfortunate once."

"Then in heaven's name say nothing about it."

As soon as these words were out of my mouth I fancied I had said something immoral. He shook his head negatively. It had to be told. He considered it proper that the relations of the lady should know. No doubt—I thought to myself—had Miss Vanlo not been thirty and damaged by the climate he would have found it possible to entrust Fred Vanlo with this confidence. And then the figure of Hermann's niece appeared before my mind's eye, with the wealth of her opulent form, her rich youth, her lavish strength. With that powerful and immaculate vitality, her girlish form must have shouted aloud of life to that man, whereas poor Miss Vanlo could only sing sentimental songs to the strumming of a piano.

"And that Hermann hates me, I know it!" he cried in his undertone, with a sudden recrudescence of anxiety. "I must tell them. It is proper that they should know. You would say so yourself."

He then murmured an utterly mysterious allusion to the necessity for peculiar domestic arrangements. Though my curiosity was excited I did not want to hear any of his confidences. I feared he might give me a piece of information that would make my assumed *rôle* of match-maker odious—however unreal it was. I was aware that he could have the girl for the asking; and keeping down a desire to laugh in his face, I expressed a confident belief in my ability to argue away Hermann's dislike for him. "I am sure I can make it all right," I said. He looked very pleased.

And when we rose not a word had been said about towage! Not a word! The game was won and the honour was safe. Oh! blessed white cotton umbrella! We shook hands, and I was holding myself with difficulty from breaking into a dance of joy when he came back, striding all the length of the verandah, and said doubtfully:

"I say, captain, I have your word? You—you—won't turn round?"

Heavens! The fright he gave me. Behind his tone of doubt there was something desperate and menacing. The infatuated ass. But I was equal to the situation.

"My dear Falk," I said, beginning to lie with a glibness and effrontery that amazed me even at the time—"confidence for confidence." (He had made no confidences.) "I will tell you that I am already engaged to an extremely charming girl at home, and so you understand . . ."

He caught my hand and wrung it in a crushing grip.

"Pardon me. I feel it every day more difficult to live alone . . ."

"On rice and fish," I interrupted smartly, giggling with the sheer nervousness of escaped danger.

He dropped my hand as if it had become suddenly red hot. A moment of profound silence ensued, as though something extraordinary had happened.

"I promise you to obtain Hermann's consent," I faltered out at last, and it seemed to me that he could not help seeing through that humbugging promise. "If there's anything else to get over I shall endeavour to stand by you," I conceded further, feeling somehow defeated and overborne; "but you must do your best yourself."

"I have been unfortunate once," he muttered, unemotionally, and turning his back on me he went away, thumping slowly the plank floor as if his feet had been shod with iron.

Next morning, however, he was lively enough as man-boat, a combination of splashing and shouting; of the insolent commotion below with the steady overbearing glare of the silent head-piece above. He turned us out most unnecessarily at an ungodly hour, but it was nearly eleven in the morning before he brought me up a cable's length from Hermann's ship. And he did it very badly, too, in a hurry, and nearly contriving to miss altogether the patch of good holding ground, because, forsooth, he had caught sight of Hermann's niece on the poop. And so did I; and probably as soon as he had seen her himself. I saw the modest, sleek glory of the tawny head, and the full, gray shape of the girlish print frock she filled so perfectly, so satisfactorily, with the seduction of unfaltering curves—a very nymph of Diana the Huntress. And *Diana* the ship sat, high-walled and as solid as an institution, on the smooth level of the water, the most uninspiring and respectable craft upon the seas, useful and ugly, devoted to the support of domestic virtues like any grocer's shop on shore. At once Falk steamed away; for there was some work for him to do. He would return in the evening.

He ranged close by us, passing out dead slow, without a hail. The beat of the paddle-wheels reverberating amongst the stony islets, as if from the ruined walls of a vast arena, filled the anchorage confusedly with the clapping sounds as of a mighty and leisurely applause. Abreast of Hermann's ship Falk stopped the engines; and a profound silence reigned over the rocks, the shore and the sea, for the time it took him to raise his hat aloft before the nymph of the gray print frock. I had snatched up my binoculars, and I can answer for it she didn't stir a limb, standing by the rail shapely and erect, with one of her hands grasping a rope at the height of her head, while the way of the tug carried slowly past her the lingering and profound homage of the man. There was for me an enormous significance in the scene, the sense of having witnessed a solemn declaration. The die was cast. After such a manifestation he couldn't back out. And I reflected that it was nothing whatever to me now. With a rush of black smoke belching suddenly out of the funnel, and a mad swirl of paddle-wheels provoking a burst of weird and precipitated clapping, the tug shot out of the desolate arena. The rocky islets lay on the sea like the heaps of a cyclopean ruin on a plain; the centipedes and scorpions lurked under the stones; there was not a single blade of grass in sight anywhere, not a single lizard sunning himself on a boulder by the shore. When I looked again at Hermann's ship the girl had disappeared. I could not detect the smallest dot of a bird on the immense sky, and the flatness of the land continued the flatness of the sea to the naked line of the horizon.

This is the setting now inseparably connected with my knowledge of Falk's misfortune. My diplomacy had brought me there, and now I had only to wait the time for taking up the *rôle* of an ambassador. My diplomacy was a success; my ship was safe; old Gambril would probably live; a feeble sound of a tapping hammer came intermittently from the *Diana*. During the afternoon I looked at times at the old homely ship, the faithful nurse of Hermann's progeny, or yawned towards the distant temple of Buddha, like a lonely hillock on the plain, where shaven priests cherish the thoughts of that Annihilation which is the worthy reward of us all. Unfortunate! He had been unfortunate once. Well, that was not so bad as life goes. And what the devil could be the nature of that misfortune? I remembered that I had known a man before who had declared himself to have fallen, years ago, a victim to misfortune: but this misfortune, whose effects appeared permanent (he looked desperately hard up) when considered dispassionately, seemed indistinguishable from a breach of trust. Could it be something of that nature? Apart, however, from the utter improbability that he would offer to talk of it even to his future uncle-in-law I had a strange feeling that Falk's physique unfitted him for that sort of delinquency. As the person of Hermann's niece exhaled the profound physical charm of feminine form, so her adorer's big frame embodied to my senses the hard, straight masculinity that would conceivably kill but would not condescend to cheat. The thing was obvious. I might just as well have suspected the girl of a curvature of the spine. And I perceived that the sun was about to set.

The smoke of Falk's tug hove in sight, far away at the mouth of the river. It was time for me to assume the character of an ambassador, and the negotiation would not be difficult except in the matter of keeping my countenance. It was all too extravagantly nonsensical, and I conceived that it would be best to compose for myself a grave demeanour. I practiced this in my boat as I went along, but the bashfulness that came secretly upon me the moment I stepped on the deck of the *Diana* is inexplicable. As soon as we had exchanged greetings Hermann asked me eagerly if I knew whether Falk had found his white parasol.

"He's going to bring it to you himself directly," I said with great solemnity. "Meantime, I am charged with an important message for which he begs your favourable consideration. He is in love with your niece . . ."

"*Ach So!*" he hissed with an animosity that made my assumed gravity change into the most genuine concern. What meant this tone? And I hurried on.

"He wishes, with your consent of course, to ask her to marry him at once—before you leave here, that is. He would speak to his Consul."

Hermann sat down and smoked violently. Five minutes passed in that furious meditation, and then, taking the long pipe out of his mouth, he burst into a hot diatribe against Falk—against his cupidity, his stupidity (a fellow that can hardly be got to say "yes" or "no" to the simplest question)—against his outrageous treatment of the shipping in port (because he saw they were at his mercy)—and against his manner of walking, which to his (Hermann's) mind showed a conceit positively unbearable. The damage to the old *Diana* was not forgotten, of course, and there was nothing of any nature said or done by Falk (even to the last offer of refreshment in the hotel) that did not seem to have been a cause of offence. "Had the cheek" to drag him (Hermann) into that coffee-room; as though a drink from him could make up for forty-seven dollars and fifty cents of damage in the cost of wood alone—not counting two days' work for the carpenter. Of course he would not stand in the girl's way. He was going home to Germany. There were plenty of poor girls walking about in Germany.

"He's very much in love," was all I found to say.

"Yes," he cried. "And it is time, too, after making himself and me talked about ashore the last voyage I was here, and then now again; coming on board every evening unsettling the girl's mind, and saying nothing. What sort of conduct is that?"

The seven thousand dollars the fellow was always talking about did not, in his opinion, justify such behaviour. Moreover, nobody had seen them. He (Hermann) seriously doubted if Falk possessed seven thousand cents, and the tug, no doubt, was mortgaged up to the firm of Siegers. But let that pass. He wouldn't stand in the girl's way. Her head was so turned that she had become no good to them of late. Quite unable even to put the children to bed without her aunt. It was bad for the children; they got unruly; and yesterday he actually had to give Gustav a thrashing.

For that, too, Falk was made responsible apparently. And looking at my Hermann's heavy, puffy, good-natured face, I knew he would not exert himself till greatly exasperated, and, therefore, would thrash very hard, and being fat would resent the necessity. How Falk had managed to turn the girl's head was more difficult to understand. I supposed Hermann would know. And then hadn't there been Miss Vanlo? It could not be his silvery tongue, or the subtle seduction of his manner; he had no more of what is called "manner" than an animal—which, however, on the other hand, is never, and can never be called vulgar. Therefore it must have been his bodily appearance, exhibiting a virility of nature as exaggerated as his beard, and resembling a sort of constant ruthlessness. It was seen in the very manner he lolled in the chair. He meant no offence, but his intercourse was characterized by that sort of frank disregard of susceptibilities a tall man, living in a world of dwarfs, would naturally assume, without in the least wishing to be unkind. But amongst men of his own stature, or nearly, this frank use of his advantages, in such matters as the awful towage bills for instance, caused much impotent gnashing of teeth. When attentively considered it seemed appalling at times. He was a strange beast. But maybe women liked it. Seen in that light he was well worth taming, and I suppose every woman at the bottom of her heart considers herself as a tamer of strange beasts. But Hermann arose with precipitation to carry the news to his wife. I had barely the time, as he made for the cabin door, to grab him by the seat of his inexpressibles. I begged him to wait till Falk in person had spoken with him. There remained some small matter to talk over as I understood.

He sat down again at once, full of suspicion.

"What matter?" he said, surlily. "I have had enough of his nonsense. There's no matter at all, as he knows very well; the girl has nothing in the world. She came to us in one thin dress when my brother died, and I have a growing family."

"It can't be anything of that kind," I opined. "He's desperately enamoured of your niece. I don't know why he did not say so before. Upon my word, I believe it is because he was afraid to lose, perhaps, the felicity of sitting near her on your quarter-deck."

I intimated my conviction that Falk's love was so great as to be in a sense cowardly. The effects of a great passion are unaccountable. It has been known to make a man timid. But Hermann looked at me as if I had raved; and the twilight was dying out rapidly.

"You don't believe in passion, do you, Hermann?" I continued, cheerily. "The passion of fear will make a cornered rat courageous. Falk's in a corner. He will take her off your hands in one thin frock just as she came to you. And after ten years' service it isn't a bad bargain," I added.

Far from taking offence, he resumed his air of civic virtue. The sudden night came upon him while he stared placidly along the deck, bringing in contact with his thick lips, and taking away again after a jet of smoke, the curved mouthpiece fitted to the stem of his pipe. The night came upon him and buried in haste his whiskers, his globular eyes, his puffy pale face, his fat knees and the vast flat slippers on his fatherly feet. Only his short arms in respectable white shirt-sleeves remained very visible, propped up like the flippers of seal reposing on the strand.

"Falk wouldn't settle anything about repairs. Told me to find out first how much wood I should require and he would see," he remarked; and after he had spat peacefully in the dusk we heard over the water the beat of the tug's floats. There is, on a calm night, nothing more suggestive of fierce and headlong haste than the rapid sound made by the paddle-wheels of a boat threshing her way through a quiet sea; and the approach of Falk towards his fate seemed to be urged by an

impatient and passionate desire. The engines must have been driven
to the very utmost of their revolutions. We heard them slow down at
last, and, vaguely, the white hull of the tug appeared moving against
the black islets, whilst a slow and rhythmical clapping as of thousands
of hands rose on all sides. It ceased all at once, just before Falk
brought her up. A single brusque splash was followed by the long-
drawn rumbling of iron links running through the hawse pipe. Then
a solemn silence fell upon the roadstead.

"He will soon be here," I murmured, and after that we waited
for him without a word. Meantime, raising my eyes, I beheld the glitter
of a lofty sky above the *Diana's* mastheads. The multitude of stars
gathered into clusters, in rows, in lines, in masses, in groups, shone
all together, unanimously—and the few isolated ones, blazing by themselves in the midst of dark patches, seemed to be of a superior
kind and of an inextinguishable nature. But long striding footsteps
were heard hastening along the deck; the high bulwarks of the *Diana*
made a deeper darkness. We rose from our chairs quickly, and Falk,
appearing before us, all in white, stood still.

Nobody spoke at first, as though we had been covered with confusion. His arrival was fiery, but his white bulk, of indefinite shape
and without features, made him loom up like a man of snow.

"The captain here has been telling me . . ." Hermann began in a
homely and amicable voice; and Falk gave a low, nervous laugh. His
cool, negligent undertone had no inflexions, but the strength of a
powerful emotion made him ramble in his speech. He had always
desired a home. It was difficult to live alone, though he was not answer-
able. He was domestic; there had been difficulties; but since he had
seen Hermann's niece he found that it had become at last impossible
to live by himself. "I mean—impossible," he repeated with no sort of
emphasis and only with the slightest of pauses, but the word fell into
my mind with the force of a new idea.

"I have not said anything to her yet," Hermann observed, quietly.
And Falk dismissed this by a "That's all right. Certainly. Very proper."
There was a necessity for perfect frankness—in marrying, especially.
Hermann seemed attentive, but he seized the first opportunity to ask
us into the cabin. "And by-the-by, Falk," he said, innocently, as we
passed in, "the timber came to no less than forty-seven dollars and
fifty cents."

Falk, uncovering his head, lingered in the passage. "Some other
time," he said; and Hermann nudged me angrily—I don't know why.
The girl alone in the cabin sat sewing at some distance from the
table. Falk stopped short in the doorway. Without a word, without
a sign, without the the slightest inclination of his bony head, by the
silent intensity of his look alone, he seemed to lay his herculean frame

at her feet. Her hands sank slowly on her lap, and raising her clear eyes, she let her soft, beaming glance enfold him from head to foot like a slow and pale caress. He was very hot when he sat down; she, with bowed head, went on with her sewing; but her neck was very white under the light of the lamp; but Falk, hiding his face in the palms of his hands shuddered faintly. He drew them down, even to his beard, and his uncovered eyes astonished me by their tense and irrational expression—as though he had just swallowed a heavy gulp of alcohol. It passed away while he was binding us to secrecy. Not that he cared, but he did not like to be spoken about; and I looked at the girl's marvellous, at her wonderful, at her regal hair, plaited tight into that one astonishing and maidenly tress. Whenever she moved her well-shaped head it would stir stiffly to and fro on her back. The thin cotton sleeve fitted the irreproachable roundness of her arm like a skin; and her very dress, stretched on her bust, seemed to palpitate like a living tissue with the strength of vitality animating her body. How good her complexion was, the outline of her soft cheek and the small convoluted conch of her rosy ear! To pull her needle she kept the little finger apart from the others; it seemed a waste of power to see her sewing—eternally sewing—with that industrious and precise movement of her arm, going on eternally upon all the oceans, under all the skies, in innumerable harbours. And suddenly I heard Falk's voice declare that he could not marry a woman unless she knew of something in his life that had happened ten years ago. It was an accident. An unfortunate accident. It would affect the domestic arrangements of their home, but, once told, it need not be alluded to again for the rest of their lives. "I should want my wife to feel for me," he said. "It has made me unhappy." And how could he keep the knowledge of it to himself—he asked us—perhaps through years and years of companionship? What sort of companionship would that be? He had thought it over. A wife must know. Then why not at once? He counted on Hermann's kindness for presenting the affair in the best possible light. And Hermann's countenance, mystified before, became very sour. He stole an inquisitive glance at me. I shook my head blankly. Some people thought, Falk went on, that such an experience changed a man for the rest of his life. He couldn't say. It was hard, awful, and not to be forgotten, but he did not think himself a worse man than before. Only he talked in his sleep now, he believed. . . . At last I began to think he had accidentally killed someone; perhaps a friend—his own father maybe; when he went on to say that probably we were aware he never touched meat. Throughout he spoke English, of course on my account.

He swayed forward heavily.

The girl, with her hands raised before her pale eyes, was threading her needle. He glanced at her and his mighty trunk overshadowed the table, bringing nearer to us the breadth of his shoulders, the thickness of his neck, and that incongruous, anchorite head, burnt in the desert, hollowed and lean as if by excesses of vigils and fasting. His beard flowed imposingly downwards, out of sight, between the two brown hands gripping the edge of the table, and his persistent glance made sombre by the wide dilations of the pupils, fascinated.

"Imagine to yourselves," he said in his ordinary voice, "that I have eaten man."

I could only ejaculate a faint "Ah!" of complete enlightenment. But Hermann, dazed by the excessive shock, actually murmured, "Himmel! What for?"

"It was my terrible misfortune to do so," said Falk in a measured undertone. The girl, unconscious, sewed on. Mrs. Hermann was absent in one of the staterooms, sitting up with Lena, who was feverish; but Hermann suddenly put both his hands up with a jerk. The embroidered calotte fell, and, in the twinkling of an eye, he had rumpled his hair all ends up in a most extravagant manner. In this state he strove to speak; with every effort his eyes seemed to start further out of their sockets; his head looked like a mop. He choked, gasped, swallowed, and managed to shriek out the one word, "Beast!"

From that moment till Falk went out of the cabin the girl, with her hands folded on the work lying in her lap, never took her eyes off him. His own, in the blindness of his heart, darted all over the cabin, only seeking to avoid the sight of Hermann's raving. It was ridiculous, and was made almost terrible by the stillness of every other person present. It was contemptible, and was made appalling by the man's overmastering horror of this awful sincerity, coming to him suddenly, with the confession of such a fact. He walked with great strides; he gasped. He wanted to know from Falk how dared he to come and tell him this? Did he think himself a proper person to be sitting in this cabin where his wife and children lived? Tell his niece! Expected him to tell his niece! His own brother's daughter! Shameless! Did I ever hear tell of such impudence?—he appealed to me. "This man here ought to have gone and hidden himself out of sight instead of . . ."

"But it's a great misfortune for me. But it's a great misfortune for me," Falk would ejaculate from time to time.

However, Hermann kept on running frequently against the corners of the table. At last he lost a slipper, and crossing his arms on his breast, walked up with one stocking foot very close to Falk, in order to ask him whether he did think there was anywhere on earth a woman abandoned enough to mate with such a monster. "Did he? Did he? Did he?" I tried to restrain him. He tore himself out of my hands;

he found his slipper, and, endeavouring to put it on, stormed standing on one leg—and Falk, with a face unmoved and averted eyes, grasped all his mighty beard in one vast palm.

"Was it right then for me to die myself?" he asked thoughtfully. I laid my hand on his shoulder.

"Go away," I whispered imperiously, without any clear reason for this advice, except that I wished to put an end to Hermann's odious noise. "Go away."

He looked searchingly for a moment at Hermann before he made a move. I left the cabin, too, to see him out of the ship. But he hung about the quarter-deck.

"It is my misfortune," he said in a steady voice.

"You were stupid to blurt it out in such a manner. After all, we don't hear such confidences every day."

"What does the man mean?" he mused in deep undertones. "Somebody had to die—but why me?"

He remained still for a time in the dark—silent; almost invisible. All at once he pinned my elbows to my sides. I felt utterly powerless in his grip, and his voice, whispering in my ear, vibrated.

"It's worse than hunger. Captain, do you know what that means? And I could kill then—or be killed. I wish the crowbar had smashed my skull ten years ago. And I've got to live now. Without her. Do you understand? Perhaps many years. But how? What can be done? If I had allowed myself to look at her once I would have carried her off before that man in my hands—like this."

I felt myself snatched off the deck, then suddenly dropped—and I staggered backwards, feeling bewildered and bruised. What a man! All was still; he was gone. I heard Hermann's voice declaiming in the cabin, and went in.

I could not at first make out a single word, but Mrs. Hermann, who, attracted by the noise, had come in some time before, with an expression of surprise and mild disapproval depicted broadly on her face, was giving now all the signs of profound, helpless agitation. Her husband shot a string of guttural words at her, and instantly putting out one hand to the bulkhead as if to save herself from falling, she clutched the loose bosom of her dress with the other. He harangued the two women extraordinarily, with much of his shirt hanging out of his waistbelt, stamping his foot, turning from one to the other, sometimes flinging both his arms straight up above his rumpled hair and keeping them in that position while he uttered a passage of loud denunciation; at others folding them tight across his breast—and then he hissed with indignation, elevating his shoulders and protruding his head. The girl was crying.

She had not changed her attitude. From her steady eyes that, following Falk in his retreat, had remained fixed wistfully on the cabin door, the tears fell rapid, thick, on her hands, on the work in her lap, warm and gentle like a shower in spring. She wept without grimacing, without noise—very touching, very quiet, with something more of pity than of pain in her face, as one weeps in compassion rather than grief—and Hermann, before her, declaimed. I caught several times the words "Mensch," man; and also "Fressen," which last I looked up afterwards in my dictionary. It means "Devour." Hermann seemed to be requesting an answer of some sort from her; his whole body swayed. She remained mute and perfectly still; at last his agitation gained her; she put the palms of her hands together, her full lips parted, no sound came. His voice scolded shrilly, his arms went like a windmill—suddenly he shook his thick fist at her. She burst out into loud sobs. He seemed stupefied.

Mrs. Hermann rushed forward babbling rapidly.

The two women fell on each other's necks, and, with an arm round her niece's waist, she led her away. Her own eyes were simply streaming, her face was flooded. She shook her head back at me negatively, I wonder why to this day. The girl's head dropped heavily on her shoulder. They disappeared together.

Then Hermann sat down and stared at the cabin floor.

"We don't know all the circumstances," I ventured to break the silence. He retorted tartly that he didn't want to know of any. According to his ideas no circumstances could excuse a crime—and certainly not such a crime. This was the opinion generally received. The duty of a human being was to starve. Falk therefore was a beast, an animal; base, low, vile, despicable, shameless, and deceitful. He had been deceiving him since last year. He was, however, inclined to think that Falk must have gone mad quite recently; for no sane person, without necessity, uselessly, for no earthly reason, and regardless of another's self-respect and peace of mind, would own to having devoured human flesh. "Why tell?" he cried. "Who was asking him?" It showed Falk's brutality because after all he had selfishly caused him (Hermann) much pain. He would have preferred not to know that such an unclean creature had been in the habit of caressing his children. He hoped I would say nothing of all this ashore, though. He wouldn't like it to get about that he had been intimate with an eater of men—a common cannibal. As to the scene he had made (which I judged quite unnecessary) he was not going to inconvenience and restrain himself for a fellow that went about courting and upsetting girls' heads, while he knew all the time that no decent housewifely girl would think of marrying him. At least he (Hermann) could not conceive how any girl could. "Fancy Lena! . . . No, it was impossible. The thoughts that would come into their heads every time they sat down to a meal. Horrible! Horrible!"

"You are too squeamish, Hermann," I said.

He seemed to think it was eminently proper to be squeamish if the word meant disgust at Falk's conduct; and turning up his eyes sentimentally he drew my attention to the horrible fate of the victims —the victims of that Falk. I said that I knew nothing about them. He seemed surprised. Could not anybody imagine without knowing? He—for instance—felt he would like to avenge them. But what if— said I—there had not been any? They might have died as it were, naturally—of starvation. He shuddered. But to be eaten—after death! To be devoured! He gave another deep shudder, and asked suddenly, "Do you think it is true?"

His indignation and his personality together would have been enough to spoil the reality of the most authentic thing. When I looked at him I doubted the story—but the remembrance of Falk's words, looks, gestures, invested it not only with an air of reality but the absolute truth of primitive passion.

"It is true just as much as you are able to make it; and exactly in the way you like to make it. For my part, when I hear you clamouring about it, I don't believe it is true at all."

And I left him pondering. The men in my gig lying at the foot of *Diana's* side-ladder, told me that the captain of the tug had gone away in his boat some time ago.

I let my fellows pull an easy stroke; because of the heavy dew the clear sparkle of the stars seemed to fall on me cold and wetting. There was a sense of lurking gruesome horror somewhere in my mind, and it was mingled with clear and grotesque images. Schomberg's gastronomic tittle-tattle was responsible for these; and I half hoped I should never see Falk again. But the first thing my anchor-watchman told me was that the captain of the tug was on board. He had sent his boat away and was now waiting for me in the cuddy.

He was lying full length on the stern settee, his face buried in the cushions. I had expected to see it discomposed, contorted, despairing. It was nothing of the kind; it was just as I had seen it twenty times, steady and glaring from the bridge of the tug. It was immovably set and hungry, dominated like the whole man by the singleness of one instinct.

He wanted to live. He had always wanted to live. So we all do—but in us the instinct serves a complex conception, and in him this instinct existed alone. There is in such simple development a gigantic force, and like the pathos of a child's naïve and uncontrolled desire. He wanted that girl, and the utmost that can be said for him was that he wanted that particular girl alone. I think I saw then the obscure beginning, the seed germinating in the soil of an unconscious need, the first shoot of that tree bearing now for a mature mankind the flower and the fruit, the infinite gradation in shades and in flavour of our discriminating love. He was a child. He was as frank as a child, too. He was hungry for the girl, terribly hungry, as he had been terribly hungry for food.

Don't be shocked if I declare that in my belief it was the same need, the same pain, the same torture. We are in his case allowed to contemplate the foundation of all the emotions—that one joy which is to live, and the one sadness at the root of the innumerable torments. It was made plain by the way he talked. He had never suffered so. It was gnawing, it was fire; it was there, like this! And after pointing below his breastbone, he made a hard wringing motion with his hands. And I assure you that, seen as I saw it with my bodily eyes, it was anything but laughable. And again, as he was presently to tell me (alluding to an early incident of the disastrous voyage when some damaged meat had been flung overboard), he said that a time soon came when his heart ached (that was the expression he used), and he was ready to tear his hair out at the thought of all that rotten beef thrown away.

I heard all this; I witnessed his physical struggles, seeing the working of the rack and hearing the true voice of pain. I witnessed it all patiently, because the moment I came into the cuddy he had called upon me to stand by him—and this, it seems, I had diplomatically promised.

His agitation was impressive and alarming in the little cabin, like the floundering of a great whale driven into a shallow cove in a coast. He stood up; he flung himself down headlong; he tried to tear the cushion with his teeth; and again hugging it fiercely to his face he let himself fall on the couch. The whole ship seemed to feel the shock of his despair; and I contemplated with wonder the lofty forehead, the noble touch of time on the uncovered temples, the unchanged hungry character of the face—so strangely ascetic and so incapable of portraying emotion.

What should he do? He had lived by being near her.

He had sat—in the evening—I knew?—all his life! She sewed. Her head was bent—so. Her head—like this—and her arms. Ah! Had I seen? Like this.

He dropped on a stool, bowed his powerful neck whose nape was red, and with his hands stitched the air, ludicrous, sublimely imbecile and comprehensible.

And now he couldn't have her? No! That was too much. After thinking, too, that . . . What had he done? What was my advice? Take her by force? No? Mustn't he? Who was there to stop him?

For the first time I saw one of his features move; a fighting teeth-baring curl of the lip. . . . "Not Hermann, perhaps." He lost himself in thought as though he had fallen out of the world.

I may note that the idea of suicide apparently did not enter his head for a single moment. It occurred to me to ask:

"Where was it that this shipwreck of yours took place?"

"Down south," he said, vaguely, with a start.

"You are not down south now," I said. "Violence won't do. They would take her away from you in no time. And what was the name of the ship?"

"*Borgmester Dahl*," he said. "It was no shipwreck."

He seemed to be waking up by degrees from that trance, and waking up calmed.

"Not a shipwreck? What was it?"

"Break down," he answered, looking more like himself every moment. By this only I learned that it was a steamer. I had till then supposed they had been starving in boats or on a raft—or perhaps on a barren rock.

"She did not sink then?" I asked in surprise. He nodded. "We sighted the southern ice," he pronounced, dreamily.

"And you alone survived?"

He sat down. "Yes. It was a terrible misfortune for me. Everything went wrong. All the men went wrong. I survived."

Remembering the things one reads of it was difficult to realize the true meaning of his answers. I ought to have seen at once—but I did not; so difficult is it for our minds, remembering so much, instructed so much, informed of so much, to get in touch with the real actuality at our elbow. And with my head full of preconceived notions as to how a case of "Cannibalism and suffering at sea" should be managed I said—"You were then so lucky in the drawing of lots?"

"Drawing of lots?" he said. "What lots? Do you think I would have allowed my life to go for the drawing of lots?"

Not if he could help it, I perceived, no matter what other life went.

"It was a great misfortune. Terrible. Awful," he said. "Many heads went wrong, but the best men would live."

"The toughest, you mean," I said. He considered the word. Perhaps it was strange to him, though his English was so good.

"Yes," he asserted at last. "The best. It was everybody for himself at last and the ship open to all."

Thus from question to question I got the whole story. I fancy it was the only way I could that night have stood by him. Outwardly at least he was himself again; the first sign of it was the return of that incongruous trick he had of drawing both his hands down his face—and it had its meaning now, with that slight shudder of the frame and the passionate anguish of these hands uncovering a hungry immovable face, the wide pupils of the intent, silent, fascinating eyes.

It was an iron steamer of a most respectable origin. The burgomaster of Falk's native town had built her. She was the first steamer ever launched there. The burgomaster's daughter had christened her. Country people drove in carts from miles around to see her. He told me all this. He got the berth as, what we would call, chief mate. He seemed to think it had been a feather in his cap; and, in his own corner of the world, this lover of life was of good parentage.

The burgomaster had advanced ideas in the shipowning line. At that time not everyone would have known enough to think of despatching a cargo steamer to the Pacific. But he loaded her with pitch-pine deals and sent her off to hunt for her luck. Wellington was to be the first port, I fancy. It doesn't matter, because in latitude 44° south and somewhere halfway between Good Hope and New Zealand the tail-shaft broke and the propeller dropped off.

They were steaming then with a fresh gale on the quarter and all their canvas set, to help the engines. But by itself the sail power was not enough to keep way on her. When the propeller went the ship broached-to at once, and the masts got whipped overboard.

The disadvantage of being dismasted consisted in this, that they had nothing to hoist flags on to make themselves visible at a distance. In the course of the first few days several ships failed to sight them; and the gale was drifting them out of the usual track. The voyage had been, from the first, neither very successful nor very harmonious. There had been quarrels on board. The captain was a clever, melancholic man, who had no unusual grip on his crew. The ship had been amply provisioned for the passage, but, somehow or other, several barrels of meat were found spoiled on opening, and had been thrown overboard soon after leaving home, as a sanitary measure. Afterwards the crew of the *Borgmester Dahl* thought of that rotten carrion with tears of regret, covetousness and despair.

She drove south. To begin with, there had been an appearance of organization, but soon the bonds of discipline became relaxed. A sombre idleness succeeded. They looked with sullen eyes at the horizon. The gales increased, she lay in the trough and the seas made a clean breach over her. One frightful night, when they expected their hulk to turn over with them every moment, a heavy sea broke on board, deluged the store-rooms and spoiled the best part of the remaining provisions. It seems the hatch had not been properly secured. This instance of neglect is characteristic of utter discouragement. Falk tried to inspire some energy into his captain, but failed. From that time he retired more into himself, always trying to do his utmost in the situation. It grew worse. Gale succeeded gale, with black mountains of water hurling themselves on the *Borgmester Dahl*. Some of the men never left their bunks; many became quarrelsome. The chief-engineer, an old man, refused to speak at all to anybody. Others shut themselves up in their berths to cry. On calm days the inert steamer rolled on a leaden sea under a murky sky, or showed, in sunshine, the squalor of sea waifs, the dried white salt, the rust, the jagged broken places. Then the gales came again. They kept body and soul together on short rations. Once, an English ship, scudding in a storm, tried to stand by them, heaving-to pluckily under their lee. The seas swept her decks; the men in oilskins clinging to her rigging looked at them, and they made desperate signs over their shattered bulwarks. Suddenly her main-topsail went, yard and all, in a terrific squall; she had to bear up under bare poles and disappeared.

Other ships had spoken them before, but at first they had refused to be taken off, expecting the assistance of some steamer. There were very few steamers in those latitudes then; and when they desired to leave this dead and drifting carcase, no ship came in sight. They had drifted south out of men's knowledge. They failed to attract the attention of a lonely whaler: and very soon the edge of the polar ice-cap rose from the sea and closed the southern horizon like a wall. One morning they were alarmed by finding themselves floating amongst detached pieces of ice. But the fear of sinking passed away like their vigour, like their hopes; the shocks of the floes knocking against the ship's side could not rouse them from their apathy: and the *Borgmester Dahl* drifted out again, unharmed, into open water. They hardly noticed the change.

The funnel had gone overboard in one of the heavy rolls; two of their three boats had disappeared, washed away in bad weather, and the davits swung to and fro, unsecured, with chafed rope's ends waggling to the roll. Nothing was done on board, and Falk told me how he had often listened to the water washing about the dark engine-room where the engines, stilled for ever, were decaying slowly into a mass of rust, as the stilled heart decays within the lifeless body. At first, after the loss of the motive power, the tiller had been thoroughly secured by lashings. But in course of time these had rotted, chafed, rusted, parting one by one; and the rudder, freed, banged heavily to and fro night and day, sending dull shocks through the whole frame of the vessel. This was dangerous. Nobody cared enough to lift a little finger. He told me that even now sometimes waking up at night, he fancied he could hear the dull vibrating thuds. The pintles carried away, and it dropped off at last.

The final catastrophe came with the sending off of their one remaining boat. It was Falk who had managed to preserve her intact, and now it was agreed that some of the hands should sail away into the track of the shipping to procure assistance. She was provisioned with all the food they could spare for the six who were to go. They waited for a fine day. It was long in coming. At last one morning they lowered her into the water.

Directly, in that demoralized crowd, trouble broke out. Two men who had no business there had jumped into the boat under the pretence of unhooking the tackles, while some sort of squabble arose on the deck amongst these weak, tottering spectres of a ship's company. The captain, who had been for days living secluded and unapproachable in the chart-room, came to the rail. He ordered the two men to come up on board and threatened them with his revolver. They pretended to obey, but suddenly cutting the boat's painter, gave a shove against the ship's side and made ready to hoist the sail.

"Shoot, sir! Shoot them down!" cried Falk—"and I will jump overboard to regain the boat." But the captain, after taking aim with an irresolute arm, turned suddenly away.

A howl of rage arose. Falk dashed into his cabin for his own pistol. When he returned it was too late. Two more men had leaped into the water, but the fellows in the boat beat them off with the oars, hoisted the boat's lug and sailed away. They were never heard of again.

Consternation and despair possessed the remaining ship's company, till the apathy of utter hopelessness re-asserted its sway. That day a fireman committed suicide, running up on deck with his throat cut from ear to ear, to the horror of all hands. He was thrown overboard. The captain had locked himself in the chart-room, and Falk, knocking vainly for admittance, heard him reciting over and over again the names of his wife and children, not as if calling upon them or commending them to God, but in a mechanical voice like an exercise of memory. Next day the doors of the chart-room were swinging open to the roll of the ship, and the captain had disappeared. He must during the night have jumped into the sea. Falk locked both the doors and kept the keys.

The organized life of the ship had come to an end. The solidarity of the men had gone. They became indifferent to each other. It was Falk who took in hand the distribution of such food as remained. Sometimes whispers of hate were heard passing between the languid skeletons that drifted endlessly to and fro, north and south, east and west, upon that carcase of a ship.

And in this lies the grotesque horror of this sombre story. The last extremity of sailors, overtaking a small boat or a frail craft, seems easier to bear, because of the direct danger of the seas. The confined space, the close contact, the imminent menace of the waves, seem to draw men together, in spite of madness, suffering and despair. But

FALK

there was a ship—safe, convenient, roomy: a ship with beds, bedding, knives, forks, comfortable cabins, glass and china, and a complete cook's galley, pervaded, ruled and possessed by the pitiless spectre of starvation. The lamp oil had been drunk, the wicks cut up for food, the candles eaten. At night she floated dark in all her recesses and full of fears. One day Falk came upon a man gnawing a splinter of pine wood. Suddenly he threw the piece of wood away, tottered to the rail, and fell over. Falk, too late to prevent the act, saw him claw the ship's side desperately before he went down. Next day another man did the same thing, after uttering horrible imprecations. But this one somehow managed to get hold of the broken rudder chains and hung on there, silently. Falk set about trying to save him, and all the time the man, holding with both hands, looked at him anxiously with his sunken eyes. Then, just as Falk was ready to put his hand on him, the man let go his hold and sank like a stone. Falk reflected on these sights. His heart revolted against the horror of death, and he said to himself that he would struggle for every precious minute of his life.

One afternoon—as the survivors lay about on the after-deck—the carpenter, a tall man with a black beard, spoke of the last sacrifice. There was nothing eatable left on board. Nobody said a word to this; but that company separated quickly, these listless feeble spectres slunk off one by one to hide in fear of each other. Falk and the carpenter remained on deck together. Falk liked the big carpenter. He had been the best man of the lot, helpful and ready as long as there was anything to do, the longest hopeful, and had preserved to the last some vigour and decision of mind.

They did not speak to each other. Henceforth no voices were to be heard conversing sadly on board that ship. After a time the carpenter tottered away forward; but later in the day Falk going to drink at the fresh-water pump, had the inspiration to turn his head. The carpenter had stolen upon him from behind, and, summoning all his strength, was aiming with a crowbar a blow at the back of his skull.

Dodging just in time, Falk made his escape and ran into his cabin. While he was loading his revolver there, he heard the sound of heavy blows struck upon the bridge. The locks of the chart-room doors were slight, they flew open, and the carpenter, possessing himself of the captain's revolver, fired a shot of defiance.

Falk was about to go on deck and have it out at once, when he remarked that one of the ports of his cabin commanded the approaches of the fresh-water pump. Instead of going out he stayed within and secured the door. "The best man shall survive," he said to himself—and the other, he reasoned, must at some time or other come there to drink. These starving men would drink often to cheat the pangs of their hunger. But the carpenter, too, must have noticed the position of the port. They were the two best men in the ship, and the game was with them. All the rest of the day Falk saw no one and heard no sound. At night he strained his eyes. It was dark—he heard a rustling noise once, but he was certain that no one could have come near the pump. It was to the left of his deck port, and he could not have failed to see a man, for the night was clear and starry. He saw nothing; towards morning another faint noise made him suspicious. Deliberately and quietly he unlocked his door. He had not slept, and had not given way to the horror of the situation. He wanted to live.

But during the night the carpenter, without even trying to approach the pump, had managed to creep quietly along the starboard bulwark, and, unseen, had crouched down right under Falk's deck port. When daylight came he rose up suddenly, looked in, and putting his arm through the round, brass-framed opening, fired at Falk within a foot. He missed—and Falk, instead of attempting to seize the arm holding the weapon, opened his door unexpectedly, and with the muzzle of his revolver nearly touching the other's side, shot him dead.

The best man had survived. Both of them had at the beginning just strength enough to stand on their feet, and both had displayed pitiless resolution, endurance, cunning and courage—all the qualities of classic heroism. At once Falk threw overboard the captain's revolver. He was a born monopolist. Then after the report of the two shots, followed by a profound silence, there crept out into the cold, cruel dawn of Antarctic regions, from various hiding-places, over the deck of that dismantled corpse of a ship floating on a gray sea ruled by iron necessity and with a heart of ice—there crept into view one by one, cautious, slow, eager, glaring, and unclean, a band of hungry and livid skeletons. Falk faced them, the possessor of the only fire-arm on board; and the second best man—the carpenter—was lying dead between him and them.

"He was eaten, of course," I said.

Falk bent his head slowly, shuddered a little, drawing his hands over his face, and said, "I had never any quarrel with that man. But there were our lives between him and me."

Why continue the story of that ship, that story before which—with its fresh-water pump like a spring of death, its man with the weapon, the sea ruled by iron necessity, its spectral band swayed by terror and hope, its mute and unhearing heaven—the fable of the *Flying Dutchman* with its convention of crime and its sentimental retribution fades like a graceful wreath, like a wisp of white mist. What is there to say that everyone of us cannot guess for himself? I believe Falk began by going through the ship, revolver in hand, to annex all the matches. Those starving wretches had plenty of matches! He had no mind to have the ship set on fire under his feet, either from hate or from despair. He lived in the open, camping on the bridge, commanding all the after-deck and the only approach to the pump. He lived! Some of the others lived, too—concealed, anxious, coming out one by one from their hiding-places at the seductive sound of a shot. And he was not selfish. They shared all alike. But only three of them all remained alive when a whaler, returning from her cruising-ground, nearly ran over the water-logged hull of the *Borgmester Dahl*, which, it seems, in the end had in some way sprung a leak in both her holds, but being loaded with deals could not sink.

"They all died," Falk said. "These three, too, afterwards. But I would not die. All died, all! under this terrible misfortune. But was I, too, to throw away my life? Could I? Tell me, captain? I was alone there, quite alone, just like the others. Each man was alone. Was I to give up my revolver? Who to? Or was I to throw it into the sea? What would have been the good? Only the best man would survive. It was a great, terrible, and cruel misfortune."

He had survived! I saw him before me as though preserved for a witness to the mighty truth of an unerring and eternal principle. Great beads of perspiration stood on his forehead. And suddenly it struck the table with a heavy blow, as he fell forward throwing his hands out.

"And this is worse," he cried. "This is a worse pain! This is more terrible."

He made my heart thump with the profound conviction of his cry. And after he had left me to go on board his ship I called up before my mental eye the image of the girl weeping silently, abundantly, patiently, and as if irresistibly. I thought of her tawny hair. I thought how, if unplaited, it would have covered her all round as low as the hips, like the hair of a siren. And she had bewitched him. Fancy a man who would guard his own life with the inflexibility of a pitiless and immovable fate, being brought to lament that once a crowbar had missed his skull! The sirens sing and lure to death, but this one had been weeping silently as if for the pity of his life. She was the tender and voiceless siren of this appalling navigator. He evidently wanted to live his whole conception of life. Nothing else would do. And she, too, was a servant of that life that, in the midst of death, cries aloud to our senses. She was eminently fitted to interpret for him its feminine side. And in her own way, and with her own profusion of sensuous charms she also seemed to illustrate the eternal truth of an unerring principle. I don't know though what sort of principle Hermann illustrated when he turned up early on board my ship with a most perplexed air. It struck me, however, that he, too, would do his best to survive. He seemed greatly calmed on the subject of Falk, but still very full of it.

"What is it you said I was last night? You know—" he asked after some preliminary talk. "Too—too—I don't know. A very funny word."

"Squeamish?" I suggested.

"Yes. What does it mean?"

"That you exaggerate things—to yourself. Without inquiry, and so on."

He seemed to turn it over in his mind. We went on talking. This Falk was the plague of his life. Upsetting everybody like this! Mrs. Hermann was unwell this morning. His niece was crying still. There was nobody to look after the children. He struck his umbrella on the deck. The girl would be like that for months. Fancy carrying all the way home, second class, a perfectly useless girl who is crying all the time. It was bad for Lena, too, he observed; but on what grounds I could not guess. Perhaps of the bad example. That child was already sorrowing and crying enough over the rag-doll. Nicholas was really the least sentimental person of the family.

"Why does your niece weep?" I asked.

"From pity," cried Hermann.

It was impossible to make out women. Mrs. Hermann was the only one he pretended to understand. She was very, very upset and doubtful.

"Doubtful about what?" I asked.

He averted his eyes and did not answer this. It was impossible to make women out. For instance, his niece was weeping for Falk. Now he (Hermann) would like to wring his neck—but then . . . He supposed he had too tender a heart. "Frankly," he asked at last, "what do you think of what we heard last night, captain?"

"In all these tales," I observed, "there is always a good deal of exaggeration."

And not letting him recover from his surprise I assured him that I knew all the details. He begged me not to repeat them. His heart was too tender. They would make him feel unwell. Then, looking at his feet and speaking very slowly, he supposed that he need not see much of them after they were married. For, indeed, he could not bear the sight of Falk. On the other hand, it was ridiculous to take home a girl with her head turned. A girl that weeps all the time and is of no help to her aunt.

"Now you will be able to do with one cabin only on your passage home," I said.

"Yes, I had thought of that," he said brightly, almost. Yes! Himself, his wife, four children—one cabin might do. Whereas if his niece went . . .

"And what does Mrs. Hermann say to it?" I inquired.

Mrs. Hermann did not know whether a man of that sort could make a girl happy—she had been greatly deceived in Captain Falk. She had passed a very bad night.

Those good people did not seem to be able to retain an impression for a whole twelve hours. I assured him on my own personal knowledge that Falk possessed in himself all the qualities to make his niece's future prosperous. He said he was glad to hear this, and that he would tell his wife. Then the object of the visit came out. He wished me to help him to resume relations with Falk. His niece, he said, had expressed the hope I would do so in my kindness. He was evidently anxious that I should, for though he seemed to have forgotten nine-tenths of his last night's opinions and the whole of his indignation, yet he evidently feared to be sent to the right-about. "You told me he was very much in love," he concluded, slyly, and leered in a sort of bucolic way.

As soon as he had left my ship I called Falk on board by signal—the tug still lying at the anchorage. He took the news with calm gravity, as though he had all along trusted the stars to fight for him in their courses.

I saw them once more together, and only once—on the quarter-deck of the *Diana*. Hermann sat smoking with a shirt-sleeved elbow hooked over the back of his chair. Mrs. Hermann was sewing alone. As Falk stepped over the gangway, Hermann's niece, with a slight swish of the skirt and a friendly nod to me, glided past my chair.

Those two met in sunshine abreast of the mainmast. He held her hands and looked down at them, and she looked up at him with her candid and unseeing glance. It seemed to me they had come together as if attracted, drawn and guided to each other by a mysterious influence. They were a complete couple. In her gray frock, palpitating with life, generous of form, olympian and simple, she was indeed the siren to fascinate that dark navigator, this ruthless lover of the five senses. From afar I seemed to feel the masculine strength with which he grasped those hands she had extended to him with a womanly swiftness. Lena, a little pale, nursing her beloved lump of dirty rags, ran towards her big friend; and then in the drowsy silence of the good old ship Mrs. Hermann's voice rang out so changed that it made me spin round in my chair to see what was the matter.

"Lena, come here!" she screamed. And this good-natured matron gave me a wavering glance, dark and full of fearsome distrust. The child ran back, surprised, to her knee. But the two, standing before each other in sunlight with clasped hands, had heard nothing, had seen nothing and no one. Three feet away from them, in the shade, a seaman sat on a spar, very busy splicing a strop and dipping his fingers into a tar-pot, as if utterly unaware of their existence.

When I returned in command of another vessel some five years afterwards, Mr. and Mrs. Falk had left the place. I shouldn't wonder if Schomberg's tongue had succeeded at last in scaring Falk away for good; and, indubitably, there was some vague tale still going about the town of a certain Falk, owner of a tug, who had won his wife at cards from the captain of an English ship.

Prince Roman

E VENTS which happened seventy years ago are perhaps rather too far off to be dragged aptly into a mere conversation. Of course the year 1831 is for us an historical date, one of these fatal years when in the presence of the world's passive indignation and eloquent sympathies we had once more to murmur 'Vœ Victis' and count the cost in sorrow. Not that we were ever very good at calculating, either, in prosperity or in adversity. That's a lesson we could never learn, to the great exasperation of our enemies who have bestowed upon us the epithet of Incorrigible. . . ."

The speaker was of Polish nationality, that nationality not so much alive as surviving, which persists in thinking, breathing, speaking, hoping, and suffering in its grave, railed in by a million of bayonets and triple-sealed with the seals of three great empires.

The conversation was about aristocracy. How did this, nowadays discredited, subject come up? It is some years ago now and the precise recollection has faded. But I remember that it was not considered practically as an ingredient in the social mixture; and I verily believed that we arrived at that subject through some exchange of ideas about patriotism—a somewhat discredited sentiment, because the delicacy of our humanitarians regards it as a relic of barbarism. Yet neither the great Florentine painter who closed his eyes in death thinking of his city, nor St. Francis blessing with his last breath the town of Assisi, were barbarians. It requires a certain greatness of soul to interpret patriotism worthily—or else a sincerity of feeling denied to the vulgar refinement of modern thought which cannot understand the august simplicity of a sentiment proceeding from the very nature of things and men.

The aristocracy we were talking about was the very highest, the great families of Europe, not impoverished, not converted, not liberalized, the most distinctive and specialized class of all classes, for which even ambition itself does not exist among the usual incentives to activity and regulators of conduct.

The undisputed right of leadership having passed away from them, we judged that their great fortunes, their cosmopolitanism brought about by wide alliances, their elevated station, in which there is so little to gain and so much to lose, must make their position difficult in times of political commotion or national upheaval. No longer born to command—which is the very essence of aristocracy—it becomes difficult for them to do aught else but hold aloof from the great movements of popular passion.

We had reached that conclusion when the remark about far-off events was made and the date of 1831 mentioned. And the speaker continued:

"I don't mean to say that I knew Prince Roman at that remote time. I begin to feel pretty ancient, but I am not so ancient as that. In fact Prince Roman was married the very year my father was born. It was in 1828; the 19th Century was young yet and the Prince was even younger than the century, but I don't know exactly by how much. In any case his was an early marriage. It was an ideal alliance from every point of view. The girl was young and beautiful, an orphan heiress of a great name and of a great fortune. The Prince, then an officer in the Guards and distinguished amongst his fellows by something reserved and reflective in his character, had fallen headlong in love with her beauty, her charm, and the serious qualities of her mind and heart. He was a rather silent young man; but his glances, his bearing, his whole person expressed his absolute devotion to the woman of his choice, a devotion which she returned in her own frank and fascinating manner.

"The flame of this pure young passion promised to burn for ever; and for a season it lit up the dry, cynical atmosphere of the great world of St. Petersburg. The Emperor Nicholas himself, the grandfather of the present man, the one who died from the Crimean War, the last perhaps of the Autocrats with a mystical belief in the Divine character of his mission, showed some interest in this pair of married lovers. It is true that Nicholas kept a watchful eye on all the doings of the great Polish nobles. The young people leading a life appropriate to their station were obviously wrapped up in each other; and society, fascinated by the sincerity of a feeling moving serenely among the artificialities of its anxious and fastidious agitation, watched them with benevolent indulgence and an amused tenderness.

"The marriage was the social event of 1828, in the capital. Just forty years afterwards I was staying in the country house of my mother's brother in our southern provinces.

"It was the dead of winter. The great lawn in front was as pure and smooth as an alpine snowfield, a white and feathery level sparkling under the sun as if sprinkled with diamond-dust, declining gently to the lake—a long, sinuous piece of frozen water looking bluish and more solid than the earth. A cold brilliant sun glided low above an undulating horizon of great folds of snow in which the villages of Ukrainian peasants remained out of sight, like clusters of boats hidden in the hollows of a running sea. And everything was very still.

"I don't know now how I had managed to escape at eleven o'clock in the morning from the schoolroom. I was a boy of eight, the little girl, my cousin, a few months younger than myself, though hereditarily more quick-tempered, was less adventurous. So I had escaped alone; and presently I found myself in the great stone-paved hall, warmed by a monumental stove of white tiles, a much more pleasant locality than the schoolroom, which for some reason or other, perhaps hygienic, was always kept at a low temperature.

"We children were aware that there was a guest staying in the house. He had arrived the night before just as we were being driven off to bed. We broke back through the line of beaters to rush and flatten our noses against the dark window panes; but we were too late to see him alight. We had only watched in a ruddy glare the big travelling carriage on sleigh-runners harnessed with six horses, a black mass against the snow, going off to the stables, preceded by a horseman carrying a blazing ball of tow and resin in an iron basket at the end of a long stick swung from his saddle bow. Two stable boys had been sent out early in the afternoon along the snow-tracks to meet the expected guest at dusk and light his way with these road torches. At that time, you must remember, there was not a single mile of railways in our southern provinces. My little cousin and I had no knowledge of trains and engines, except from picture-books, as of things rather vague, extremely remote, and not particularly interesting unless to grown-ups who travelled abroad.

"Our notion of princes, perhaps a little more precise, was mainly literary and had a glamour reflected from the light of fairy tales, in which princes always appear young, charming, heroic, and fortunate. Yet, as well as any other children, we could draw a firm line between the real and the ideal. We knew that princes were historical personages. And there was some glamour in that fact, too. But what had driven me to roam cautiously over the house like an escaped prisoner was the hope of snatching an interview with a special friend of mine, the head forester, who generally came to make his report at that time of the day. I yearned for news of a certain wolf. You know, in a country where wolves are to be found, every winter almost brings forward an individual eminent by the audacity of his misdeeds, by his more perfect wolfishness—so to speak. I wanted to hear some new thrilling tale of that wolf—perhaps the dramatic story of his death. . . .

"But there was no one in the hall.

"Deceived in my hopes, I became suddenly very much depressed. Unable to slip back in triumph to my studies I elected to stroll spiritlessly into the billiard room where certainly I had no business. There was no one there either, and I felt very lost and desolate under its high ceiling, all alone with the massive English billiard table which seemed, in heavy, rectilinear silence, to disapprove of that small boy's intrusion.

"As I began to think of retreat I heard footsteps in the adjoining drawing room; and, before I could turn tail and flee, my uncle and his guest appeared in the doorway. To run away after having been seen would have been highly improper, so I stood my ground. My uncle looked surprised to see me; the guest by his side was a spare man, of average stature, buttoned up in a black frock coat and holding himself very erect with a stiffly soldier-like carriage. From the folds of a soft white cambric neck-cloth peeped the points of a collar close against each shaven cheek. A few wisps of thin gray hair were brushed smoothly across the top of his bald head. His face, which must have been beautiful in its day, had preserved in age the harmonious simplicity of its lines. What amazed me was its even, almost deathlike pallor. He seemed to me to be prodigiously old. A faint smile, a mere momentary alteration in the set of his thin lips acknowledged my blushing confusion; and I became greatly interested to see him reach into the inside breastpocket of his coat. He extracted therefrom a lead pencil and a block of detachable pages, which he handed to my uncle with an almost imperceptible bow.

"I was very much astonished, but my uncle received it as a matter of course. He wrote something at which the other glanced and nodded slightly. A thin wrinkled hand—the hand was older than the face— patted my cheek and then rested on my head lightly. An unringing voice, a voice as colourless as the face itself, issued from his sunken lips, while the eyes, dark and still, looked down at me kindly.

" 'And how old is this shy little boy?' "

"Before I could answer my uncle wrote down my age on the pad. I was deeply impressed. What was this ceremony? Was this personage too great to be spoken to? Again he glanced at the pad, and again gave a nod, and again that impersonal, mechanical voice was heard: 'He resembles his grandfather.'

"I remembered my paternal grandfather. He had died not long before. He, too, was prodigiously old. And to me it seemed perfectly natural that two such ancient and venerable persons should have known each other in the dim ages of creation before my birth. But my uncle obviously had not been aware of the fact. So obviously that the mechanical voice explained: 'Yes, yes. Comrades in '31. He was one of those who knew. Old times, my dear sir, old times. . . .'

"He made a gesture as if to put aside an importunate ghost. And now they were both looking down at me. I wondered whether anything was expected from me. To my round, questioning eyes my uncle remarked: 'He's completely deaf.' And the unrelated, inexpressive voice said: 'Give me your hand.'

"Acutely conscious of inky fingers I put it out timidly. I had never seen a deaf person before and was rather startled. He pressed it firmly and then gave me a final pat on the head.

"My uncle addressed me weightily: 'You have shaken hands with Prince Roman S——. It's something for you to remember when you grow up.'

"I was impressed by his tone. I had enough historical information to know vaguely that the Princes S—— counted amongst the sovereign Princes of Ruthenia till the union of all Rutheian lands to the kingdom of Poland, when they became great Polish magnates, sometime at the beginning of the 15th Century. But what concerned me most was the failure of the fairy-tale glamour. It was shocking to discover a prince who was deaf, bald, meagre, and so prodigiously old. It never occurred to me that this imposing and disappointing man had been young, rich, beautiful; I could not know that he had been happy in the felicity of an ideal marriage uniting two young hearts, two great names and two great fortunes; happy with a happiness which, as in fairy tales, seemed destined to last forever. . . .

"But it did not last forever. It was fated not to last very long even by the measure of the days allotted to men's passage on this earth where enduring happiness is only found in the conclusion of fairy tales. A daughter was born to them and shortly afterwards, the health of the young princess began to fail. For a time she bore up with smiling intrepidity, sustained by the feeling that now her existence was necessary for the happiness of two lives. But at last the husband, thoroughly alarmed by the rapid changes in her appearance, obtained an unlimited leave and took her away from the capital to his parents in the country.

"The old prince and princess were extremely frightened at the state of their beloved daughter-in-law. Preparations were at once made for a journey abroad. But it seemed as if it were already too late; and the invalid herself opposed the project with gentle obstinacy. Thin and pale in the great armchair, where the insidious and obscure nervous malady made her appear smaller and more frail every day without effacing the smile of her eyes or the charming grace of her wasted face, she clung to her native land and wished to breathe her native air. Nowhere else could she expect to get well so quickly, nowhere else would it be so easy for her to die.

"She died before her little girl was two years old. The grief of the husband was terrible and the more alarming to his parents because perfectly silent and dry-eyed. After the funeral, while the immense bare-headed crowd of peasants surrounding the private chapel on the grounds was dispersing, the Prince, waving away his friends and relations, remained alone to watch the masons of the estate closing the family vault. When the last stone was in position he uttered a groan, the first sound of pain which had escaped from him for days, and walking away with lowered head shut himself up again in his apartments.

"His father and mother feared for his reason. His outward tranquillity was appalling to them. They had nothing to trust to but that very youth which made his despair so self-absorbed and so intense. Old Prince John, fretful and anxious, repeated: 'Poor Roman should be roused somehow. He's so young.' But they could find nothing to rouse him with. And the old princess, wiping her eyes, wished in her heart he were young enough to come and cry at her knee.

"In time Prince Roman, making an effort, would join now and again the family circle. But it was as if his heart and his mind had been buried in the family vault with the wife he had lost. He took to wandering in the woods with a gun, watched over secretly by one of the keepers, who would report in the evening that 'His Serenity has never fired a shot all day.' Sometimes walking to the stables in the morning he would order in subdued tones a horse to be saddled, wait switching his boot till it was led up to him, then mount without a word and ride out of the gates at a walking pace. He would be gone all day. People saw him on the roads looking neither to the right nor to the left, white-faced, sitting rigidly in the saddle like a horseman of stone on a living mount.

"The peasants working in the fields, the great unhedged fields, looked after him from the distance; and sometimes some sympathetic old woman on the threshold of a low, thatched hut was moved to make the sign of the cross in the air behind his back; as though he were one of themselves, a simple village soul struck by a sore affliction.

"He rode looking straight ahead, seeing no one, as if the earth were empty and all mankind buried in that grave which had opened so suddenly in his path to swallow up his happiness. What were men to him with their sorrows, joys, labours and passions from which she who had been all the world to him had been cut off so early?

"They did not exist; and he would have felt as completely lonely and abandoned as a man in the toils of a cruel nightmare if it had not been for this countryside where he had been born and had spent his happy boyish years. He knew it well—every slight rise crowned with trees amongst the ploughed fields, every dell concealing a village. The dammed streams made a chain of lakes set in the green meadows. Far away to the north the great Lithuanian forest faced the sun, no higher than a hedge; and to the south, the way to the plains, the vast brown spaces of the earth touched the blue sky.

"And this familiar landscape associated with the days without thought and without sorrow, this land the charm of which he felt without even looking at it soothed his pain, like the presence of an old friend who sits silent and disregarded by one in some dark hour of life.

"One afternoon, it happened that the Prince after turning his horse's head for home remarked a low dense cloud of dark dust cutting off slantwise a part of the view. He reined in on a knoll and peered. There were slender gleams of steel here and there in that cloud, and it contained moving forms which revealed themselves at last as a long line of peasant carts full of soldiers, moving slowly in double file under the escort of mounted Cossacks.

"It was like an immense reptile creeping over the fields; its head dipped out of sight in a slight hollow and its tail went on writhing and growing shorter as though the monster were eating its way slowly into the very heart of the land.

"The Prince directed his way through a village lying a little off the track. The roadside inn with its stable, byre, and barn under one enormous thatched roof resembled a deformed, hunch-backed, ragged giant, sprawling amongst the small huts of the peasants. The inn-keeper, a portly, dignified Jew, clad in a black satin coat reaching down to his heels and girt with a red sash, stood at the door stroking his long silvery beard.

"He watched the Prince approach and bowed gravely from the waist, not expecting to be noticed even, since it was well known that their young lord had no eyes for anything or anybody in his grief. It was quite a shock for him when the Prince pulled up and asked:

" 'What's all this, Yankel?'

" 'That is, please your Serenity, that is a convoy of footsoldiers they are hurrying down to the south.'

"He glanced right and left cautiously, but as there was no one near but some children playing in the dust of the village street, he came up close to the stirrup.

" 'Doesn't your Serenity know? It has begun already down there. All the landowners great and small are out in arms and even the common people have risen. Only yesterday the saddler from Grodek (it was a tiny market-town near by) went through here with his two apprentices on his way to join. He left even his cart with me. I gave him a guide through our neighbourhood. You know, your Serenity, our people they travel at lot and they see all that's going on, and they know all the roads.'

"He tried to keep down his excitement, for the Jew Yankel, inn-keeper and tenant of all the mills on the estate, was a Polish patriot. And in a still lower voice:

" 'I was already a married man when the French and all the other nations passed this way with Napoleon. Tse! Tse! That was a great harvest for death, nu! Perhaps this time God will help.'

"The Prince nodded. 'Perhaps'—and falling into deep meditation he let his horse take him home.

"That night he wrote a letter, and early in the morning sent a mounted express to the post town. During the day he came out of his taciturnity, to the great joy of the family circle, and conversed with his father of recent events—the revolt in Warsaw, the flight of the Grand Duke Constantine, the first slight successes of the Polish army (at that time there was a Polish army); the risings in the provinces. Old Prince John, moved and uneasy, speaking from a purely aristocratic point of view, mistrusted the popular origins of the movement, regretted its democratic tendencies, and did not believe in the possibility of success. He was sad, inwardly agitated.

" 'I am judging all this calmly. There are secular principles of legitimity and order which have been violated in this reckless enterprise for the sake of most subversive illusions. Though of course the patriotic impulses of the heart . . .'

"Prince Roman had listened in a thoughtful attitude. He took advantage of the pause to tell his father quietly that he had sent that morning a letter to St. Petersburg resigning his commission in the Guards.

"The old prince remained silent. He thought that he ought to have been consulted. His son was also ordnance officer to the Emperor and he knew that the Tsar would never forget this appearance of defection in a Polish noble. In a discontented tone he pointed out to his son that as it was he had an unlimited leave. The right thing would have been to keep quiet. They had too much tact at Court to recall a man of his name. Or at worst some distant mission might have been asked for—to the Caucasus for instance—away from this unhappy struggle which was wrong in principle and therefore destined to fail.

" 'Presently you shall find yourself without any interest in life and with no occupation. And you shall need something to occupy you, my poor boy. You have acted rashly, I fear.'

"Prince Roman murmured.

" 'I thought it better.'

"His father faltered under his steady gaze.

" 'Well, well—perhaps! But as ordnance officer to the Emperor and in favour with all the Imperial family . . .'

" 'Those people had never been heard of when our house was already illustrious,' the young man let fall disdainfully.

"This was the sort of remark to which the old prince was sensible.

" 'Well—perhaps it is better,' he conceded at last.

"The father and son parted affectionately for the night. The next day Prince Roman seemed to have fallen back into the depths of his indifference. He rode out as usual. He remembered that the day before he had seen a reptile-like convoy of soldiery, bristling with bayonets, crawling over the face of that land which was his. The woman he loved had been his, too. Death had robbed him of her. Her loss had been to him a moral shock. It had opened his heart to a greater sorrow, his mind to a vaster thought, his eyes to all the past and to the existence of another love fraught with pain but as mysteriously imperative as that lost one to which he had entrusted his happiness.

"That evening he retired earlier than usual and rang for his personal servant.

" 'Go and see if there is light yet in the quarters of the Master-of-the-Horse. If he is still up ask him to come and speak to me.'

"While the servant was absent on this errand the Prince tore up hastily some papers, locked the drawers of his desk, and hung a medallion, containing the miniature of his wife, round his neck against his breast.

"The man the Prince was expecting belonged to that past which the death of his love had called to life. He was of a family of small nobles who for generations had been adherents, servants, and friends of the Princes S——. He remembered the times before the last partition and had taken part in the struggles of the last hour. He was a typical old Pole of that class, with a great capacity for emotion, for blind enthusiasm; with martial instincts and simple beliefs; and even with the old-time habit of larding his speech with Latin words. And his kindly shrewd eyes, his ruddy face, his lofty brow and his thick, gray, pendent moustache were also very typical of his kind.

" 'Listen, Master Francis,' the Prince said familiarly and without preliminaries. 'Listen, old friend. I am going to vanish from here quietly. I go where something louder than my grief and yet something with a voice very like it calls me. I confide in you alone. You will say what's necessary when the time comes.'

"The old man understood. His extended hands trembled exceedingly. But as soon as he found his voice he thanked God aloud for letting him live long enough to see the descendant of the illustrious family in its youngest generation give an example *coram Gentibus* of the love of his country and of valour in the field. He doubted not of his dear Prince attaining a place in council and in war worthy of his high birth; he saw already that *in fulgore* of family glory *affulget patride serenitas*. At the end of the speech he burst into tears and fell into the Prince's arms.

"The Prince quieted the old man and when he had him seated in an armchair and comparatively composed he said:

" 'Don't misunderstand me, Master Francis. You know how I loved my wife. A loss like that opens one's eyes to unsuspected truths. There is no question here of leadership and glory. I mean to go alone and to fight obscurely in the ranks. I am going to offer my country what is mine to offer, that is my life, as simply as the saddler from Grodek who went through yesterday with his apprentices.'

"The old man cried out at this. That could never be. He could not allow it. But he had to give way before the arguments and the express will of the Prince.

" 'Ha! If you say that it is a matter of feeling and conscience—so be it. But you cannot go utterly alone. Alas! that I am too old to be of any use. *Cripit verba dolor*, my dear Prince, at the thought that I am over seventy and of no more account in the world than a cripple on the church porch. It seems that to sit at home and pray to God for the nation and for you is all I am fit for. But there is my son, my youngest son, Peter. He will make a worthy companion for you. And as it happens he's staying with me here. There has not been for ages a Prince S—— hazarding his life without a companion of our name to ride by his side. You must have by you somebody who knows who you are if only to let your parents and your old servant hear what is happening to you. And when does your Princely Mightiness mean to start?'

" 'In an hour,' said the Prince; and the old man hurried off to warn his son.

"Prince Roman took up a candlestick and walked quietly along a dark corridor in the silent house. The head-nurse said afterwards that waking up suddenly she saw the Prince looking at his child, one hand shading the light from its eyes. He stood and gazed at her for some time, and then putting the candlestick on the floor bent over the cot and kissed lightly the little girl who did not wake. He went out noiselessly, taking the light away with him. She saw his face perfectly well, but she could read nothing of his purpose in it. It was pale but perfectly calm and after he turned away from the cot he never looked back at it once.

"The only other trusted person, besides the old man and his son Peter, was the Jew Yankel. When he asked the Prince where precisely he wanted to be guided the Prince answered: 'To the nearest party.' A grandson of the Jew, a lanky youth, conducted the two young men by little-known paths across woods and morasses, and led them in sight of the few fires of a small detachment camped in a hollow. Some invisible horses neighed, a voice in the dark cried: 'Who goes there?'

. . . and the young Jew departed hurriedly, explaining that he must make haste home to be in time for keeping the Sabbath.

"Thus humbly and in accord with the simplicity of the vision of duty he saw when death had removed the brilliant bandage of happiness from his eyes, did Prince Roman bring his offering to his country. His companion made himself known as the son of the Master-of-the-Horse to the Prince S—— and declared him to be a relation, a distant cousin from the same parts as himself and, as people presumed, of the same name. In truth no one inquired much. Two more young men clearly of the right sort had joined. Nothing more natural.

"Prince Roman did not remain long in the south. One day while scouting with several others, they were ambushed near the entrance of a village by some Russian infantry. The first discharge laid low a good many and the rest scattered in all directions. The Russians, too, did not stay, being afraid of a return in force. After some time, the peasants coming to view the scene extricated Prince Roman from under his dead horse. He was unhurt but his faithful companion had been one of the first to fall. The Prince helped the peasants to bury him and the other dead.

"Then alone, not certain where to find the body of partizans which was constantly moving about in all directions, he resolved to try and join the main Polish army facing the Russians on the borders of Lithuania. Disguised in peasant clothes, in case of meeting some marauding Cossacks, he wandered a couple of weeks before he came upon a village occupied by a regiment of Polish cavalry on outpost duty.

"On a bench, before a peasant hut of a better sort, sat an elderly officer whom he took for the colonel. The Prince approached respectfully, told his story shortly and stated his desire to enlist; and when asked his name by the officer, who had been looking him over carefully, he gave on the spur of the moment the name of his dead companion.

"The elderly officer thought to himself: Here's the son of some peasant proprietor of the liberated class. He liked his appearance.

" 'And can you read and write, my good fellow?' he asked.

" 'Yes, your honour, I can,' said the Prince.

" 'Good. Come along inside the hut; the regimental adjutant is there. He will enter your name and administer the oath to you.'

"The adjutant stared very hard at the newcomer but said nothing. When all the forms had been gone through and the recruit gone out, he turned to his superior officer.

" 'Do you know who that is?'

" 'Who? That Peter? A likely chap.'

" 'That's Prince Roman S——.'

" 'Nonsense.'

"But the adjutant was positive. He had seen the Prince several times, about two years before, in the Castle in Warsaw. He had even spoken to him once at a reception of officers held by the Grand Duke.

" 'He's changed. He seems much older, but I am certain of my man. I have a good memory for faces.'

"The officers looked at each other in silence.

" 'He's sure to be recognized sooner or later,' murmured the adjutant. The colonel shrugged his shoulders.

" 'It's no affair of ours—if he has a fancy to serve in the ranks. As to being recognized it's not so likely. All our officers and men come from the other end of Poland.'

"He meditated gravely for a while, then smiled. 'He told me he could read and write. There's nothing to prevent me making him a sergeant at the first opportunity. He's sure to shape all right.'

"Prince Roman as a non-commissioned officer surpassed the colonel's expectations. Before long Sergeant Peter became famous for his resourcefulness and courage. It was not the reckless courage of a desperate man; it was a self-possessed, as if conscientious, valour which nothing could dismay; a boundless but equable devotion, unaffected by time, by reverses, by the discouragement of endless retreats, by the bitterness of waning hopes and the horrors of pestilence added to the toils and perils of war. It was in this year that the cholera made its first appearance in Europe. It devastated the camps of both armies, affecting the firmest minds with the terror of a mysterious death stalking silently between the piled-up arms and around the bivouac fires.

"A sudden shriek would wake up the harassed soldiers and they would see in the glow of embers one of themselves writhe on the ground like a worm trodden on by an invisible foot. And before the dawn broke he would be stiff and cold. Parties so visited have been known to rise like one man, abandon the fire and run off into the night in mute panic. Or a comrade talking to you on the march would stammer suddenly in the middle of a sentence, roll affrighted eyes, and fall down with distorted face and blue lips, breaking the ranks with the convulsions of his agony. Men were struck in the saddle, on sentry duty in the firing line, carrying orders, serving the guns. I have been told that in a battalion forming under fire with perfect steadiness for the assault of a village, three cases occurred within five minutes at the head of the column; and the attack could not be delivered because the leading companies scattered all over the fields like chaff before the wind.

"Sergeant Peter, young as he was, had a great influence over his men. It was said that the number of desertions in the squadron in

which he served was less than in any other in the whole of that cavalry division. Such was supposed to be the compelling example of
one man's quiet intrepidity in facing every form of danger and terror.

"However that may be, he was liked and trusted generally. When
the end came and the remnants of that army corps, hard pressed
on all sides, were preparing to cross the Prussian frontier, Sergeant
Peter had enough influence to rally round him a score of troopers.
He managed to escape with them at night, from the hemmed-in army.
He led this band through 200 miles of country covered by numerous
Russian detachments and ravaged by the cholera. But this was not
to avoid captivity, to go into hiding and try to save themselves. No.
He led them into a fortress which was still occupied by the Poles, and
where the last stand of the vanquished revolution was to be made.

"This looks like mere fanaticism. But fanaticism is human. Man
has adored ferocious divinities. There is ferocity in every passion, even
in love itself. The religion of undying hope resembles the mad cult
of despair, of death, of annihilation. The difference lies in the moral
motive springing from the secret needs and the unexpressed aspiration
of the believers. It is only to vain men that all is vanity; and all is
deception only to those who have never been sincere with themselves.

"It was in the fortress that my grandfather found himself together
with Sergeant Peter. My grandfather was a neighbour of the S——
family in the country but he did not know Prince Roman, who however knew his name perfectly well. The Prince introduced himself
one night as they both sat on the ramparts, leaning against a gun
carriage.

"The service he wished to ask for was, in case of his being killed,
to have the intelligence conveyed to his parents.

"They talked in low tones, the other servants of the piece lying
about near them. My grandfather gave the required promise, and
then asked frankly—for he was greatly interested by the disclosure
so unexpectedly made:

" 'But tell me, Prince, why this request? Have you any evil forebodings as to yourself?'

" 'Not in the least; I was thinking of my people. They have no
idea where I am,' answered Prince Roman. 'I'll engage to do as
much for you, if you like. It's certain that half of us at least shall
be killed before the end, so there's an even chance of one of us
surviving the other.'

"My grandfather told him where, as he supposed, his wife and
children were then. From that moment till the end of the siege the
two were much together. On the day of the great assault my grandfather received a severe wound. The town was taken. Next day the

citadel itself, its hospital full of dead and dying, its magazines empty, its defenders having burnt their last cartridge, opened its gates.

"During all the campaign the Prince, exposing his person conscientiously on every occasion, had not received a scratch. No one had recognized him or at any rate had betrayed his identity. Till then, as long as he did his duty, it had mattered nothing who he was.

"Now, however, the position was changed. As ex-guardsman and as late ordnance officer to the Emperor, this rebel ran a serious risk of being given special attention in the shape of a firing squad at ten paces. For more than a month he remained lost in the miserable crowd of prisoners packed in the casemates of the citadel, with just enough food to keep body and soul together but otherwise allowed to die from wounds, privation, and disease at the rate of forty or so a day.

"The position of the fortress being central, new parties, captured in the open in the course of a thorough pacification, were being sent in frequently. Amongst such newcomers there happened to be a young man, a personal friend of the Prince from his school days. He recognized him, and in the extremity of his dismay cried aloud: 'My God! Roman, you here!'

"It is said that years of life embittered by remorse paid for this momentary lack of self-control. All this happened in the main quadrangle of the citadel. The warning gesture of the Prince came too late. An officer of the gendarmes on guard had heard the exclamation. The incident appeared to him worth inquiring into. The investigation which followed was not very arduous because the Prince, asked categorically for his real name, owned up at once.

"The intelligence of the Prince S—— being found amongst the prisoners was sent to St. Petersburg. His parents were already there living in sorrow, incertitude, and apprehension. The capital of the Empire was the safest place to reside in for a noble whose son had disappeared so mysteriously from home in a time of rebellion. The old people had not heard from him, or of him, for months. They took care not to contradict the rumours of suicide from despair circulating in the great world, which remembered the interesting love-match, the charming and frank happiness brought to an end by death. But they hoped secretly that their son survived, and that he had been able to cross the frontier with that part of the army which had surrendered to the Prussians.

"The news of his captivity was a crushing blow. Directly, nothing could be done for him. But the greatness of their name, of their position, their wide relations and connections in the highest spheres, enabled his parents to act indirectly and they moved heaven and earth, as the saying is, to save their son from the 'consequences of his madness,' as poor Prince John did not hesitate to express himself. Great personages were approached by society leaders, high dignitaries were interviewed, powerful officials were induced to take an interest in that affair. The help of every possible secret influence was enlisted. Some private secretaries got heavy bribes. The mistress of a certain senator obtained a large sum of money.

"But, as I have said, in such a glaring case no direct appeal could be made and no open steps taken. All that could be done was to incline by private representation the mind of the President of the Military Commission to the side of clemency. He ended by being impressed by the hints and suggestions, some of them from very high quarters, which he received from St. Petersburg. And, after all, the gratitude of such great nobles as the Prince S—— was something worth having from a worldly point of view. He was a good Russian but he was also a good-natured man. Moreover, the hate of Poles was not at that time a cardinal article of patriotic creed as it became some thirty years later. He felt well disposed at first sight towards that young man, bronzed, thin-faced, worn out by months of hard campaigning, the hardships of the siege and the rigours of captivity.

"The Commission was composed of three officers. It sat in the citadel in a bare vaulted room behind a long black table. Some clerks occupied the two ends, and besides the gendarmes who brought in the Prince there was no one else there.

"Within those four sinister walls shutting out from him all the sights and sounds of liberty, all hopes of the future, all consoling illusions—alone in the face of his enemies erected for judges, who can tell how much love of life there was in Prince Roman? How much remained in that sense of duty, revealed to him in sorrow? How much of his awakened love for his native country? That country which demands to be loved as no other country has ever been loved, with the mournful affection one bears to the unforgotten dead and with the unextinguishable fire of a hopeless passion which only a living, breathing, warm ideal can kindle in our breasts for our pride, for our weariness, for our exultation, for our undoing.

"There is something monstrous in the thought of such an exaction till it stands before us embodied in the shape of a fidelity without fear and without reproach. Nearing the supreme moment of his life the Prince could only have had the feeling that it was about to end. He answered the questions put to him clearly, concisely—with the most profound indifference. After all those tense months of action, to talk was a weariness to him. But he concealed it, lest his foes should suspect in his manner the apathy of discouragement or the numbness of a crushed spirit. The details of his conduct could have no importance one way or another; with his thoughts these men had nothing to do. He preserved a scrupulously courteous tone. He had refused the permission to sit down.

"What happened at this preliminary examination is only known from the presiding officer. Pursuing the only possible course in that glaringly bad case he tried from the first to bring to the Prince's mind the line of defence he wished him to take. He absolutely framed his questions so as to put the right answers in the culprit's mouth, going so far as to suggest the very words: how, distracted by excessive grief after his young wife's death, rendered irresponsible for his conduct by his despair, in a moment of blind recklessness, without realizing the highly reprehensible nature of the act, nor yet its danger and its dishonour, he went off to join the nearest rebels on a sudden impulse. And that now, penitently . . .

"But Prince Roman was silent. The military judges looked at him hopefully. In silence he reached for a pen and wrote on a sheet of paper he found under his hand: 'I joined the national rising from conviction.'

"He pushed the paper across the table. The president took it up, showed it in turn to his two colleagues sitting to the right and left, then looking fixedly at Prince Roman let it fall from his hand. And the silence remained unbroken till he spoke to the gendarmes ordering them to remove the prisoner.

"Such was the written testimony of Prince Roman in the supreme moment of his life. I have heard that the Princes of the S—— family, in all its branches, adopted the last two words: 'From conviction' for the device under the armorial bearings of their house. I don't know whether the report is true. My uncle could not tell me. He remarked only, that naturally, it was not to be seen on Prince Roman's own seal.

"He was condemned for life to Siberian mines. Emperor Nicholas, who always took personal cognizance of all sentences on Polish nobility, wrote with his own hand in the margin: 'The authorities are severely warned to take care that this convict walks in chains like any other criminal every step of the way.'

"It was a sentence of deferred death. Very few survived entombment in these mines for more than three years. Yet as he was reported as still alive at the end of that time he was allowed, on a petition of his parents and by way of exceptional grace, to serve as common soldier in the Caucasus. All communication with him was forbidden. He had no civil rights. For all practical purposes except that of suffering he was a dead man. The little child he had been so careful not to wake up when he kissed her in her cot, inherited all the fortune after Prince John's death. Her existence saved those immense estates from confiscation.

"It was twenty-five years before Prince Roman, stone deaf, his health broken, was permitted to return to Poland. His daughter married splendidly to a Polish Austrian *grand seigneur* and, moving in the cosmopolitan sphere of the highest European aristocracy, lived mostly abroad in Nice and Vienna. He, settling down on one of her estates, not the one with the palatial residence but another where there was a modest little house, saw very little of her.

"But Prince Roman did not shut himself up as if his work were done. There was hardly anything done in the private and public life of the neighbourhood, in which Prince Roman's advice and assistance were not called upon, and never in vain. It was well said that his days did not belong to himself but to his fellow citizens. And especially he was the particular friend of all returned exiles, helping them with purse and advice, arranging their affairs and finding them means of livelihood.

"I heard from my uncle many tales of his devoted activity, in which he was always guided by a simple wisdom, a high sense of honour, and the most scrupulous conception of private and public probity. He remains a living figure for me because of that meeting in a billiard room, when, in my anxiety to hear about a particularly wolfish wolf, I came in momentary contact with a man who was preëminently a man amongst all men capable of feeling deeply, of believing steadily, of loving ardently.

"I remember to this day the grasp of Prince Roman's bony, wrinkled hand closing on my small inky paw, and my uncle's half-serious, half-amused way of looking down at his trespassing nephew.

"They moved on and forgot that little boy. But I did not move; I gazed after them, not so much disappointed as disconcerted by this prince so utterly unlike a prince in a fairy tale. They moved very slowly across the room. Before reaching the other door the Prince stopped, and I heard him—I seem to hear him now—saying: 'I wish you would write to Vienna about filling up that post. He's a most deserving fellow—and your recommendation would be decisive.'

"My uncle's face turned to him expressed genuine wonder. It said as plainly as any speech could say: What better recommendation than a father's can be needed? The Prince was quick at reading expressions. Again he spoke with the toneless accent of a man who has not heard his own voice for years, for whom the soundless world is like an abode of silent shades.

"And to this day I remember the very words: 'I ask you because, you see, my daughter and my son-in-law don't believe me to be a good judge of men. They think that I let myself be guided too much by mere sentiment.'"

Amy Foster

KENNEDY is a country doctor, and lives in Colebrook, on the shores of Eastbay. The high ground rising abruptly behind the red roofs of the little town crowds the quaint High Street against the wall which defends it from the sea. Beyond the sea-wall there curves for miles in a vast and regular sweep the barren beach of shingle, with the village of Brenzett standing out darkly across the water, a spire in a clump of trees; and still further out the perpendicular column of a lighthouse, looking in the distance no bigger than a lead pencil, marks the vanishing-point of the land. The country at the back of Brenzett is low and flat; but the bay is fairly well sheltered from the seas, and occasionally a big ship, windbound or through stress of weather, makes use of the anchoring ground a mile and a half due north from you as you stand at the back door of the "Ship Inn" in Brenzett. A dilapidated windmill near by, lifting its shattered arms from a mound no loftier than a rubbish-heap, and a Martello tower squatting at the water's edge half a mile to the south of the Coast-guard cottages, are familiar to the skippers of small craft. These are the official seamarks for the patch of trustworthy bottom represented on the Admiralty charts by an irregular oval of dots enclosing several figures six, with a tiny anchor engraved among them, and the legend "mud and shells" over all.

The brow of the upland overtops the square tower of the Colebrook Church. The slope is green and looped by a white road. Ascending along this road, you open a valley broad and shallow, a wide green trough of pastures and hedges merging inland into a vista of purple tints and flowing lines closing the view.

In this valley down to Brenzett and Colebrook and up to Darnford, the market town fourteen miles away, lies the practice of my friend Kennedy. He had begun life as surgeon in the Navy, and afterwards had been the companion of a famous traveller, in the days when there were continents with unexplored interiors. His papers on the fauna and flora made him known to scientific societies. And now he had come to a country practice—from choice. The penetrating power of his mind, acting like a corrosive fluid, had destroyed his ambition, I fancy. His intelligence is of a scientific order, of an investigating habit, and of that unappeasable curiosity which believes that there is a particle of a general truth in every mystery.

A good many years ago now, on my return from abroad, he invited me to stay with him. I came readily enough, and as he could not neglect his patients to keep me company, he took me on his rounds —thirty miles or so of an afternoon, sometimes. I waited for him on the roads; the horse reached after the leafy twigs, and, sitting high in the dogcart, I could hear Kennedy's laugh through the half-open door of some cottage. He had a big, hearty laugh that would have fitted a man twice his size, a brisk manner, a bronzed face, and a pair of gray, profoundly attentive eyes. He had the talent of making people talk to him freely, and an inexhaustible patience in listening to their tales.

One day, as we trotted out of a large village into a shady bit of road I saw on our left hand a low, black cottage, with diamond panes in the windows, a creeper on the end wall, a roof of shingle, and some roses climbing on the rickety trellis-work of the tiny porch. Kennedy pulled up to a walk. A woman, in full sunlight, was throwing a dripping blanket over a line stretched between two old apple-trees. And as the bobtailed, long-necked chestnut, trying to get his head, jerked the left hand, covered by a thick dogskin glove, the doctor raised his voice over the hedge: "How's your child, Amy?"

I had the time to see her dull face, red, not with a mantling blush, but as if her flat cheeks had been vigorously slapped, and to take in the squat figure, the scanty, dusty brown hair drawn into a tight knot at the back of the head. She looked quite young. With a distinct catch in her breath, her voice sounded low and timid.

"He's well, thank you."

We trotted again. "A young patient of yours," I said; and the doctor, flicking the chestnut absently, muttered, "Her husband used to be."

"She seems a dull creature," I remarked, listlessly.

"Precisely," said Kennedy. "She is very passive. It's enough to look at the red hands hanging at the end of those short arms, at those slow, prominent brown eyes, to know the inertness of her mind—an inertness that one would think made it everlastingly safe from all the surprises of imagination. And yet which of us is safe? At any rate, such as you see her, she had enough imagination to fall in love. She's the daughter of one Isaac Foster, who from a small farmer has sunk into a shepherd; the beginning of his misfortunes dating from his runaway marriage with the cook of his widowed father—well-to-do, apoplectic grazier, who passionately struck his name off his will, and had been heard to utter threats against his life. But this old affair, scandalous enough to serve as a motive for a Greek tragedy, arose from the similarity of their characters. There are other tragedies, less scandalous and of a subtler poignancy, arising from irreconcilable differences and from that fear of the Incomprehensible that hangs over all our heads —over all our heads. . . ."

The tired chestnut dropped into a walk; and the rim of the sun, all red in a speckless sky, touched familiarly the smooth top of a ploughed rise near the road as I had seen it times innumerable touch the distant horizon of the sea. The uniform brownness of the harrowed field glowed with a rose tinge, as though the powdered clods had sweated out in minute pearls of blood the toil of uncounted plough-men. From the edge of a copse a waggon with two horses was rolling gently along the ridge. Raised above our heads upon the sky-line, it loomed up against the red sun, triumphantly big, enormous, like a chariot of giants drawn by two slow-stepping steeds of legendary pro-portions. And the clumsy figure of the man plodding at the head of the leading horse projected itself on the background of the Infinite with a heroic uncouthness. The end of his carter's whip quivered high up in the blue. Kennedy discoursed.

"She's the eldest of a large family. At the age of fifteen they put her out to service at the New Barns Farm. I attended Mrs. Smith, the tenant's wife, and saw that girl there for the first time. Mrs. Smith, a genteel person with a sharp nose, made her put on a black dress every afternoon. I don't know what induced me to notice her at all. There are faces that call your attention by a curious want of definiteness in their whole aspect, as, walking in a mist, you peer attentively at a vague shape which, after all, may be nothing more curious or strange than a signpost. The only peculiarity I perceived in her was a slight hesitation in her utterance, a sort of preliminary stammer which passes away with the first word. When sharply spoken to, she was apt to lose her head at once; but her heart was of the kindest. She had never been heard to express a dislike for a single human being, and she was tender to every living creature. She was devoted to Mrs. Smith, to Mr. Smith, to their dogs, cats, canaries; and as to Mrs. Smith's gray parrot, its peculiarities exercised upon her a positive fascination. Never-theless, when that outlandish bird, attacked by the cat, shrieked for help in human accents, she ran out into the yard stopping her ears, and did not prevent the crime. For Mrs. Smith this was another evi-dence of her stupidity; on the other hand, her want of charm, in view of Smith's well-known frivolousness, was a great recommendation. Her short-sighted eyes would swim with pity for a poor mouse in a trap, and she had been seen once by some boys on her knees in the wet grass helping a toad in difficulties. If it's true, as some German fellow has said, that without phosphorous there is no thought, it is still more true that there is no kindness of heart without a certain amount of imagination. She had some. She had even more than is necessary to understand suffering and to be moved by pity. She fell in love under circumstances that leave no room for doubt in the matter; for you need imagination to form a notion of beauty at all, and still more to discover your ideal in an unfamiliar shape.

"How this aptitude came to her, what it did feed upon, is an inscrutable mystery. She was born in the village, and had never been further away from it than Colebrook or perhaps Darnford. She lived for four years with the Smiths. New Barns is an isolated farmhouse a mile away from the road, and she was content to look day after day at the same fields, hollows, rises; at the trees and the hedgerows; at the faces of the four men about the farm, always the same—day after day, month after month, year after year. She never showed a desire for conversation, and, as it seemed to me, she did not know how to smile. Sometimes of a fine Sunday afternoon she would put on her best dress, a pair of stout boots, a large gray hat trimmed with a black feather (I've seen her in that finery), seize an absurdly slender parasol, climb over two stiles, tramp over three fields and along two hundred yards of road—never further. There stood Foster's cottage. She would help her mother to give their tea to the younger children, wash up the crockery, kiss the little ones, and go back to the farm. That was all. All the rest, all the change, all the relaxation. She never seemed to wish for anything more. And then she fell in love. She fell in love silently, obstinately—perhaps helplessly. It came slowly, but when it came it worked like a powerful spell; it was love as the Ancients understood it: an irresistible and fateful impulse—a possession! Yes, it was in her to become haunted and possessed by a face, by a presence, fatally, as though she had been a pagan worshipper of form under a joyous sky—and to be awakened at last from that mysterious forgetfulness of self, from that enchantment, from that transport, by a fear resembling the unaccountable terror of a brute. . . ."

With the sun hanging low on its western limit, the expanse of the grass-lands framed in the counter-scarps of the rising ground took on a gorgeous and sombre aspect. A sense of penetrating sadness, like that inspired by a grave strain of music, disengaged itself from the silence of the fields. The men we met walked past, slow, unsmiling, with downcast eyes, as if the melancholy of an over-burdened earth had weighted their feet, bowed their shoulders, borne down their glances.

"Yes," said the doctor to my remark, "one would think the earth is under a curse, since of all her children these that cling to her the closest are uncouth in body and as leaden of gait as if their very hearts were loaded with chains. But here on this same road you might have seen amongst these heavy men a being lithe, supple and long-limbed, straight like a pine, with something striving upwards in his appearance as though the heart within him had been buoyant. Perhaps it was only the force of the contrast, but when he was passing one of these villagers here, the soles of his feet did not seem to me to touch the dust of the road. He vaulted over the stiles, paced these slopes with a long elastic stride that made him noticeable at a great distance, and had lustrous black eyes. He was so different from the mankind around that, with his freedom of movement, his soft—a little startled, glance, his olive complexion and graceful bearing, his humanity suggested to me the nature of a woodland creature. He came from there."

The doctor pointed with his whip, and from the summit of the descent seen over the rolling tops of the trees in a park by the side of the road, appeared the level sea far below us, like the floor of an immense edifice inlaid with bands of dark ripple, with still trails of glitter, ending in a belt of glassy water at the foot of the sky. The light blurr of smoke, from an invisible steamer, faded on the great clearness of the horizon like the mist of a breath on a mirror; and, inshore, the white sails of a coaster, with the appearance of disentangling themselves slowly from under the branches, floated clear of the foliage of the trees.

"Shipwrecked in the bay?" I said.

"Yes; he was a castaway. A poor emigrant from Central Europe bound to America and washed ashore here in a storm. And for him, who knew nothing of the earth, England was an undiscovered country. It was some time before he learned its name; and for all I know he might have expected to find wild beasts or wild men here, when, crawling in the dark over the sea-wall, he rolled down the other side into a dyke, where it was another miracle he didn't get drowned. But he struggled instinctively like an animal under a net, and this blind struggle threw him out into a field. He must have been, indeed, of a tougher fibre than he looked to withstand without expiring such buffetings, the violence of his exertions, and so much fear. Later on, in his broken English that resembled curiously the speech of a young child, he told me himself that he put his trust in God, believing he was no longer in this world. And truly—he would add—how was he to know? He fought his way against the rain and the gale on all fours, and crawled at last among some sheep huddled close under the lee of a hedge. They ran off in all directions, bleating in the darkness, and he welcomed the first familiar sound he heard on these shores. It must have been two in the morning then. And this is all we know of the manner of his landing, though he did not arrive unattended by any means. Only his grisly company did not begin to come ashore till much later in the day. . . ."

The doctor gathered the reins, clicked his tongue; we trotted down the hill. Then turning, almost directly, a sharp corner into High Street, we rattled over the stones and were home.

Late in the evening Kennedy, breaking a spell of moodiness that had come over him, returned to the story. Smoking his pipe, he paced the long room from end to end. A reading-lamp concentrated all its light upon the papers on his desk; and, sitting by the open window, I saw, after the windless, scorching day, the frigid splendour of a hazy sea lying motionless under the moon. Not a whisper, not a splash, not a stir of the shingle, not a footstep, not a sigh came up from the earth below—never a sign of life but the scent of climbing jasmine: and Kennedy's voice, speaking behind me, passed through the wide casement, to vanish outside in a chill and sumptuous stillness.

". . . The relations of shipwrecks in the olden time tell us of much suffering. Often the castaways were only saved from drowning to die miserably from starvation on a barren coast; others suffered violent death or else slavery, passing through years of precarious existence with people to whom their strangeness was an object of suspicion, dislike or fear. We read about these things, and they are very pitiful. It is indeed hard upon a man to find himself a lost stranger, helpless, incomprehensible, and of a mysterious origin, in some obscure corner of the earth. Yet amongst all the adventurers shipwrecked in all the wild parts of the world, there is not one, it seems to me, that ever had to suffer a fate so simply tragic as the man I am speaking of, the most innocent of adventurers cast out by the sea in the bight of this bay, almost within sight from this very window.

"He did not know the name of his ship. Indeed in the course of time we discovered he did not even know that ships had names— 'like Christian people'; and when, one day, from the top of Talfourd Hill, he beheld the sea lying open to his view, his eyes roamed afar, lost in an air of wild surprise, as though he had never seen such a sight before. And probably he had not. As far as I could make out, he had been hustled together with many others on board an emigrant ship at the mouth of the Elbe, too bewildered to take note of his surroundings, too weary to see anything, too anxious to care. They were driven below into the 'tween-deck and battened down from the very start. It was a low timber dwelling—he would say—with wooden beams overhead, like the houses in his country, but you went into it down a ladder. It was very large, very cold, damp and sombre, with places in the manner of wooden boxes where people had to sleep one above another, and it kept on rocking all ways at once all the time. He crept into one of these boxes and lay down there in the clothes in which he had left his home many days before, keeping his bundle and his stick by his side. People groaned, children cried, water dripped, the lights went out, the walls of the place creaked, and everything was being shaken so that in one's little box one dared not lift one's head. He had lost touch with his only companion (a young man from the same valley, he said), and all the time a great noise of wind went on out-

side and heavy blows fell—boom! boom! An awful sickness overcame
him, even to the point of making him neglect his prayers. Besides,
one could not tell whether it was morning or evening. It seemed always to be night in that place.

"Before that he had been travelling a long, long time on the iron
track. He looked out of the window, which had a wonderfully clear
glass in it, and the trees, the houses, the fields, and the long roads
seemed to fly round and round about him till his head swam. He
gave me to understand that he had on his passage beheld uncounted
multitudes of people—whole nations—all dressed in such clothes as
the rich wear. Once he was made to get out of the carriage, and
slept through a night on a bench in a house of bricks with his bundle
under his head; and once for many hours he had to sit on a floor
of flat stones, dozing, with his knees up and with his bundle between
his feet. There was a roof over him, which seemed made of glass,
and was so high that the tallest mountain-pine he had ever seen would
have had room to grow under it. Steam-machines rolled in at one
end and out at the other. People swarmed more than you can see
on a feast-day round the miraculous Holy Image in the yard of the
Carmelite Convent down in the plains where, before he left his home,
he drove his mother in a wooden cart:—a pious old woman who
wanted to offer prayers and make a vow for his safety. He could
not give me an idea of how large and lofty and full of noise and
smoke and gloom, and clang of iron, the place was, but someone
had told him it was called Berlin. Then they rang a bell, and another
steam-machine came in, and again he was taken on and on through
a land that wearied his eyes by its flatness without a single bit of
a hill to be seen anywhere. One more night he spent shut up in a
building like a good stable with a litter of straw on the floor, guarding
his bundle amongst a lot of men, of whom not one could understand
a single word he said. In the morning they were all led down to the
stony shores of an extremely broad muddy river, flowing not between
hills but between houses that seemed immense. There was a steam-
machine that went on the water, and they all stood upon it packed
tight, only now there were with them many women and children
who made much noise. A cold rain fell, the wind blew in his face;
he was wet through, and his teeth chattered. He and the young
man from the same valley took each other by the hand.

"They thought they were being taken to America straight away, but
suddenly the steam-machine bumped against the side of a thing like
a great house on the water. The walls were smooth and black, and
there uprose, growing from the roof as it were, bare trees in the shape
of crosses, extremely high. That's how it appeared to him then, for
he had never seen a ship before. This was the ship that was going

to swim all the way to America. Voices shouted, everything swayed; there was a ladder dipping up and down. He went up on his hands and knees in mortal fear of falling into the water below, which made a great splashing. He got separated from his companion, and when he descended into the bottom of that ship his heart seemed to melt suddenly within him.

"It was then also, as he told me, that he lost contact for good and all with one of those three men who the summer before had been going about through all the little towns in the foothills of his country. They would arrive on market-days driving in a peasant's cart, and would set up an office in an inn or some other Jew's house. There were three of them, of whom one with a long beard looked venerable; and they had red cloth collars round their necks and gold lace on their sleeves like Government officials. They sat proudly behind a long table; and in the next room, so that the common people shouldn't hear, they kept a cunning telegraph machine, through which they could talk to the Emperor of America. The fathers hung about the door, but the young men of the mountains would crowd up to the table asking many questions, for there was work to be got all the year round at three dollars a day in America, and no military service to do.

"But the American Kaiser would not take everybody. Oh, no! He himself had a great difficulty in getting accepted, and the venerable man in uniform had to go out of the room several times to work the telegraph on his behalf. The American Kaiser engaged him at last at three dollars, he being young and strong. However, many able young men backed out, afraid of the great distance; besides, those only who had some money could be taken. There were some who sold their huts and their land because it cost a lot of money to get to America; but then, once there, you had three dollars a day, and if you were clever you could find places where true gold could be picked up on the ground. His father's house was getting over full. Two of his brothers were married and had children. He promised to send money home from America by post twice a year. His father sold an old cow, a pair of piebald mountain ponies of his own raising, and a cleared plot of fair pasture land on the sunny slope of a pine-clad pass to a Jew inn-keeper, in order to pay the people of the ship that took men to America to get rich in a short time.

"He must have been a real adventurer at heart, for how many of the greatest enterprises in the conquest of the earth had for their beginning just such a bargaining away of the paternal cow for the mirage or true gold far away! I have been telling you more or less in my own words what I learned fragmentarily in the course of two or three years, during which I seldom missed an opportunity of a friendly chat with him. He told me this story of his adventure with many flashes of white teeth and lively glances of black eyes, at first in a sort of anxious baby-talk, then, as he acquired the language, with great fluency, but always with that singing, soft, and at the same time vibrating intonation that instilled a strangely penetrating power into the sound of the most familiar English words, as if they had been the words of an unearthly language. And he always would come to an end, with many emphatic shakes of his head, upon that awful sensation of his heart melting within him directly he set foot on board that ship. Afterwards there seemed to come for him a period of blank ignorance, at any rate as to facts. No doubt he must have been abominably seasick and abominably unhappy—this soft and passionate adventurer, taken thus out of his knowledge, and feeling bitterly as he lay in his emigrant bunk his utter loneliness; for his was a highly sensitive·nature. The next thing we know of him for certain is that he had been hiding in Hammond's pig-pound by the side of the road to Norton, six miles, as the crow flies, from the sea. Of these experiences he was unwilling to speak: they seemed to have seared into his soul a sombre sort of wonder and indignation. Through the rumours of the country-side, which lasted for a good many days after his arrival, we know that the fishermen of West Colebrook had been disturbed and startled by heavy knocks against the walls of weatherboard cottages, and by a voice crying piercingly strange words in the night. Several of them turned out even, but, no doubt, he had fled in sudden alarm at their rough angry tones hailing each other in the darkness. A sort of frenzy must have helped him up the steep Norton hill. It was he, no doubt, who early the following morning had been seen lying (in a swoon, I should say) on the roadside grass by the Brenzett carrier, who actually got down to have a nearer look, but drew back, intimidated by the perfect immobility, and by something queer in the aspect of that tramp, sleeping so still under the showers. As the day advanced, some children came dashing into school at Norton in such a fright that the schoolmistress went out and spoke indignantly to a 'horrid-looking man' on the road. He edged away, hanging his head, for a few steps, and then suddenly ran off with extraordinary fleetness. The driver of Mr. Bradley's milk-cart made no secret of it that he had lashed with his whip at a hairy sort of gipsy fellow who, jumping up at a turn of the road by the Vents, made a snatch at the pony's bridle. And he caught him a good one, too, right over the face, he said, that made him drop down in the mud a jolly sight quicker than he had jumped up; but it was a good half a mile before he could stop the pony. Maybe that in his desperate endeavours to get help, and in his need to get in touch with someone, the poor devil had tried to stop the cart. Also three boys confessed afterwards to throwing stones at a funny tramp, knocking about all wet and muddy, and, it seemed, very drunk, in the narrow deep lane by the limekilns. All this was the talk of three villages for days; but we have Mrs. Finn's (the wife of Smith's waggoner) unimpeachable testimony that she saw him get over the low wall of Hammond's pig-pound and lurch straight at her, babbling aloud in a voice that was enough to make one die of fright. Having the baby with her in a perambulator, Mrs. Finn called out to him to go away, and as he persisted in coming nearer, she hit him courageously with her um-brella over the head, and, without once looking back, ran like the wind with the perambulator as far as the first house in the village. She stopped then, out of breath, and spoke to old Lewis, hammering there at a heap of stones; and the old chap, taking off his immense black wire goggles, got up on his shaky legs to look where she pointed. Together they followed with their eyes the figure of the man running over a field; they saw him fall down, pick himself up, and run on again, staggering and waving his long arms above his head, in the direction of the New Barns Farm. From that moment he is plainly in the toils of his obscure and touching destiny. There is no doubt after this of what happened to him. All is certain now: Mrs. Smith's intense terror; Amy Foster's stolid conviction held against the other's nervous attack, that the man 'meant no harm': Smith's exasperation (on his return from Darnford Market) at finding the dog barking himself into a fit, the back-door locked, his wife in hysterics; and all for an unfortunate dirty tramp, supposed to be even then lurking in his stackyard, Was he? He would teach him to frighten women.

"Smith is notoriously hot-tempered, but the sight of some nonde-script and miry creature sitting cross-legged amongst a lot of loose straw, and swinging itself to and fro like a bear in a cage, made him pause. Then this tramp stood up silently before him, one mass of mud and filth from head to foot. Smith, alone amongst his stacks with this apparition, in the stormy twilight ringing with the in-furiated barking of the dog, felt the dread of an inexplicable strange-ness. But when that being, parting with his black hands the long matted locks that hung before his face, as you part the two halves of a curtain, looked out at him with glistening, wild, black-and-white eyes, the weirdness of this silent encounter fairly staggered him. He has admitted since (for the story has been a legitimate subject of conversation about here for years) that he made more than one step backwards. Then a sudden burst of rapid, senseless speech persuaded him at once that he had to do with an escaped lunatic. In fact, that impression never wore off completely. Smith has not in his heart given up his secret conviction of the man's essential insanity to this very day.

"As the creature approached him, jabbering in a most discomposing manner, Smith (unaware that he was being addressed as 'gracious lord,' and adjured in God's name to afford food and shelter) kept on speaking firmly but gently to it, and retreating all the time into the other yard. At last, watching his chance, by a sudden charge he bundled him headlong into the wood-lodge, and instantly shot the bolt. Thereupon he wiped his brow, though the day was cold. He had done his duty to the community by shutting up a wandering and probably dangerous maniac. Smith isn't a hard man at all, but he had room in his brain only for that one idea of lunacy. He was not imaginative enough to ask himself whether the man might not be perishing with cold and hunger. Meantime, at first, the maniac made a great deal of noise in the lodge. Mrs. Smith was screaming upstairs, where she had locked herself in her bedroom; but Amy Foster sobbed piteously at the kitchen-door, wringing her hands and muttering, 'Don't! don't!' I daresay Smith had a rough time of it that evening with one noise and another, and this insane, disturbing voice crying obstinately through the door only added to his irritation. He couldn't possibly have connected this troublesome lunatic with the sinking of a ship in Eastbay, of which there had been a rumour in the Darnford market place. And I daresay the man inside had been very near to insanity on that night. Before his excitement collapsed and he became unconscious he was throwing himself violently about in the dark, rolling on some dirty sacks, and biting his fists with rage, cold, hunger, amazement, and despair.

"He was a mountaineer of the eastern range of the Carpathians, and the vessel sunk the night before in Eastbay was the Hamburg emigrant-ship *Herzogin Sophia-Dorothea*, of appalling memory.

"A few months later we could read in the papers the accounts of the bogus 'Emigration Agencies' among the Sclavonian peasantry in the more remote provinces of Austria. The object of these scoundrels was to get hold of the poor ignorant people's homesteads, and they were in league with the local usurers. They exported their victims through Hamburg mostly. As to the ship, I had watched her out of this very window, reaching close-hauled under short canvas into the bay on a dark, threatening afternoon. She came to an anchor, correctly by the chart, off the Brenzett Coastguard station. I remember before the night fell looking out again at the outlines of her spars and rigging that stood out dark and pointed on a background of ragged, slaty clouds like another and a slighter spire to the left of the Brenzett church-tower. In the evening the wind rose. At midnight I could hear in my bed the terrific gusts and the sounds of a driving deluge.

"About that time the Coastguardmen thought they saw the lights of a steamer over the anchoring-ground. In a moment they vanished; but it is clear that another vessel of some sort had tried for shelter in the bay on that awful, blind night, had rammed the German ship amidships (a breach—as one of the divers told me afterwards— 'that you could sail a Thames barge through'), and then had gone out either scathless or damaged, who shall say; but had gone out, unknown, unseen, and fatal, to perish mysteriously at sea. Of her nothing ever came to light, and yet the hue and cry that was raised all over the world would have found her out if she had been in existence anywhere on the face of the waters.

"A completeness without a clue, and a stealthy silence as of a neatly executed crime, characterize this murderous disaster, which, as you may remember, had its gruesome celebrity. The wind would have prevented the loudest outcries from reaching the shore; there had been evidently no time for signals of distress. It was death without any sort of fuss. The Hamburg ship, filling all at once, capsized as she sank, and at daylight there was not even the end of a spar to be seen above water. She was missed, of course, and at first the Coastguardmen surmised that she had either dragged her anchor or parted her cable some time during the night, and had been blown out to sea. Then, after the tide turned, the wreck must have shifted a little and released some of the bodies, because a child—a little fair-haired child in a red frock—came ashore abreast of the Martello tower. By the afternoon you could see along three miles of beach dark figures with bare legs dashing in and out of the tumbling foam, and rough-looking men, women with hard faces, children, mostly fair-haired, were being carried, stiff and dripping, on stretches, on wattles, on ladders, in a long procession past the door of the "Ship Inn," to be laid out in a row under the north wall of the Brenzett Church.

"Officially, the body of the little girl in the red frock is the first thing that came ashore from that ship. But I have patients amongst the seafaring population of West Colebrook, and, unofficially, I am informed that very early that morning two brothers, who went down to look after their cobble hauled up on the beach, found a good way from Brenzett, an ordinary ship's hencoop, lying high and dry on the shore, with eleven drowned ducks inside. Their families ate the birds, and the hencoop was split into firewood with a hatchet. It is possible that a man (supposing he happened to be on deck at the time of the accident) might have floated ashore on that hencoop. He might. I admit it is improbable, but there was the man—and for days, nay, for weeks—it didn't enter our heads that we had amongst us the only living soul that had escaped from that disaster. The man himself, even when he learned to speak intelligibly, could tell us very little. He remembered he had felt better (after the ship had anchored,

I suppose), and that the darkness, the wind, and the rain took his breath away. This looks as if he had been on deck some time during that night. But we musn't forget he had been taken out of his knowledge, that he had been sea-sick and battened down below for four days, that he had no general notion of a ship or of the sea, and therefore could have no definite idea of what was happening to him. The rain, the wind, the darkness he knew; he understood the bleating of the sheep, and he remembered the pain of his wretchedness and misery, his heartbroken astonishment that it was neither seen nor understood, his dismay at finding all the men angry and all the women fierce. He had approached them as a beggar, it is true, he said; but in his country, even if they gave nothing, they spoke gently to beggars. The children in his country were not taught to throw stones at those who asked for compassion. Smith's strategy overcame him completely. The wood-lodge presented the horrible aspect of a dungeon. What would be done to him next? . . . No wonder that Amy Foster appeared to his eyes with the aureole of an angel of light. The girl had not been able to sleep for thinking of the poor man, and in the morning, before the Smiths were up, she slipped out across the back yard. Holding the door of the wood-lodge ajar, she looked in and extended to him half a loaf of white bread—'such bread as the rich eat in my country,' he used to say.

"At this he got up slowly from amongst all sorts of rubbish, stiff, hungry, trembling, miserable, and doubtful. 'Can you eat this?' she asked in her soft and timid voice. He must have taken her for a 'gracious lady.' He devoured ferociously, and tears were falling on the crust. Suddenly he dropped the bread, seized her wrist, and imprinted a kiss on her hand. She was not frightened. Through his forlorn condition she had observed that he was good-looking. She shut the door and walked back slowly to the kitchen. Much later on, she told Mrs. Smith, who shuddered at the bare idea of being touched by that creature.

"Through this act of impulsive pity he was brought back again within the pale of human relations with his new surroundings. He never forgot it—never.

"That very same morning old Mr. Swaffer (Smith's nearest neighbour) came over to give his advice, and ended by carrying him off. He stood, unsteady on his legs, meek, and caked over in half-dried mud, while the two men talked around him in an incomprehensible tongue. Mrs. Smith had refused to come downstairs till the madman was off the premises; Amy Foster, far from within the dark kitchen, watched through the open back-door; and he obeyed the signs that were made to him to the best of his ability. But Smith was full of mistrust. 'Mind, sir! It may be all his cunning,' he cried repeatedly in a tone of warning. When Mr. Swaffer started the mare, the deplorable being sitting humbly by his side, through weakness, nearly fell out over the back of the high two-wheeled cart. Swaffer took him straight home. And it is then that I come upon the scene.

"I was called in by the simple process of the old man beckoning to me with his forefinger over the gate of his house as I happened to be driving past. I got down, of course.

" 'I've got something here,' he mumbled, leading the way to an outhouse at a little distance from his other farm-buildings.

"It was there that I saw him first, in a long, low room taken upon the space of that sort of coach-house. It was bare and whitewashed, with a small square aperture glazed with one cracked, dusty pane at its further end. He was lying on his back upon a straw pallet; they had given him a couple of horse-blankets, and he seemed to have spent the remainder of his strength in the exertion of cleaning himself. He was almost speechless; his quick breathing under the blankets pulled up to his chin, his glittering, restless black eyes reminded me of a wild bird caught in a snare. While I was examining him, old Swaffer stood silently by the door, passing the tips of his fingers along his shaven upper lip. I gave some directions, promised to send a bottle of medicine, and naturally made some inquiries.

" 'Smith caught him in the stackyard at New Barns,' said the old chap in his deliberate, unmoved manner, and as if the other had been indeed a sort of wild animal. 'That's how I came by him. Quite a curiosity, isn't he? Now tell me, doctor—you've been all over the world—don't you think that's a bit of a Hindoo we've got hold of here?'

"I was greatly surprised. His long black hair scattered over the straw bolster contrasted with the olive pallor of his face. It occurred to me he might be a Basque. It didn't necessarily follow that he should understand Spanish; but I tried him with the few words I know, and also with some French. The whispered sounds I caught by bending my ear to his lips puzzled me utterly. That afternoon the young ladies from the Rectory (one of them read Goethe with a dictionary, and the other had struggled with Dante for years), coming to see Miss Swaffer, tried their German and Italian on him from the doorway. They retreated, just the least bit scared by the flood of passionate speech which, turning on his pallet, he let out at them. They admitted that the sound was pleasant, soft, musical—but, in conjunction with his looks perhaps, it was startling—so excitable, so utterly unlike anything one had ever heard. The village boys climbed up the bank to have a peep through the little square aperture. Everybody was wondering what Mr. Swaffer would do with him.

"He simply kept him.

"Swaffer would be called eccentric were he not so much respected. They will tell you that Mr. Swaffer sits up as late as ten o'clock at night to read books, and they will tell you also that he can write a cheque for two hundred pounds without thinking twice about it. He himself would tell you that the Swaffers had owned land between this and Darnford for these three hundred years. He must be eighty-five to-day, but he does not look a bit older than when I first came here. He is a great breeder of sheep, and deals extensively in cattle. He attends market days for miles around in every sort of weather, and drives sitting bowed low over the reins, his lank gray hair curling over the collar of his warm coat, and with a green plaid rug round his legs. The calmness of advanced age gives a solemnity to his manner. He is clean-shaved; his lips are thin and sensitive; something rigid and monachal in the set of his features lends a certain elevation to the character of his face. He has been known to drive miles in the rain to see a new kind of rose in somebody's garden, or a monstrous cabbage grown by a cottager. He loves to hear tell of or to be shown something what he calls 'outlandish.' Perhaps it was just that outlandishness of the man which influenced old Swaffer. Perhaps it was only an inexplicable caprice. All I know is that at the end of three weeks I caught sight of Smith's lunatic digging in Swaffer's kitchen garden. They had found out he could use a spade. He dug barefooted.

"His black hair flowed over his shoulders. I suppose it was Swaffer who had given him the striped old cotton shirt; but he wore still the national brown cloth trousers (in which he had been washed ashore) fitting to the legs almost like tights; was belted with a broad leather belt studded with little brass discs; and had never yet ventured into the village. The land he looked upon seemed to him kept neatly, like the grounds round a landowner's house; the size of the cart-horses struck him with astonishment; the roads resembled garden walks, and the aspect of the people, especially on Sundays, spoke of opulence. He wondered what made them so hardhearted and their children so bold. He got his food at the back-door, carried it in both hands, carefully, to his outhouse, and, sitting alone on his pallet, would make the sign of the cross before he began. Beside the same pallet, kneeling in the early darkness of the short days, he recited aloud the Lord's Prayer before he slept. Whenever he saw old Swaffer he would bow with veneration from the waist, and stand erect while the old man, with his fingers over his upper lip, surveyed him silently. He bowed also to Miss Swaffer, who kept house frugally for her father—a broad-shouldered, big-boned woman of forty-five, with the pocket of her dress full of keys, and a gray, steady eye. She was Church—as people said (while her father was one of the trustees of the Baptist Chapel)—

and wore a little steel cross at her waist. She dressed severely in black, in memory of one of the innumerable Bradleys of the neighbourhood, to whom she had been engaged some twenty-five years ago—a young farmer who broke his neck out hunting on the eve of the wedding-day. She had the unmoved countenance of the deaf, spoke very seldom, and her lips, thin like her father's, astonished one sometimes by a mysteriously ironic curl.

"These were the people to whom he owed allegiance, and an overwhelming loneliness seemed to fall from the leaden sky of that winter without sunshine. All the faces were sad. He could talk to no one, and had no hope of ever understanding anybody. It was as if these had been the faces of people from the other world—dead people— he used to tell me years afterwards. Upon my word, I wonder he did not go mad. He didn't know where he was. Somewhere very far from his mountains—somewhere over the water. Was this America, he wondered?

"If it hadn't been for the steel cross at Miss Swaffer's belt he would not, he confessed, have known whether he was in a Christian country at all. He used to cast stealthy glances at it, and feel comforted. There was nothing here the same as in his country! The earth and the water were different; there were no images of the Redeemer by the roadside. The very grass was different, and the trees. All the trees but the three old Norway pines on the bit of lawn before Swaffer's house, and these reminded him of his country. He had been detected once, after dusk, with his forehead against the trunk of one of them, sobbing, and talking to himself. They had been like brothers to him at that time, he affirmed. Everything else was strange. Conceive you the kind of an existence over-shadowed, oppressed, by the everyday material appearances, as if by the visions of a nightmare. At night, when he could not sleep, he kept on thinking of the girl who gave him the first piece of bread he had eaten in this foreign land. She had been neither fierce nor angry, nor frightened. Her face he remembered as the only comprehensible face amongst all these faces that were as closed, as mysterious, and as mute as the faces of the dead who are possessed of a knowledge beyond the comprehension of the living. I wonder whether the memory of her compassion prevented him from cutting his throat. But there! I suppose I am an old sentimentalist, and forget the instinctive love of life which it takes all the strength of an uncommon despair to overcome.

"He did the work which was given him with an intelligence which surprised old Swaffer. By-and-by it was discovered that he could help at the ploughing, could milk the cows, feed the bullocks in the cattle-yard, and was of some use with the sheep. He began to pick up words, too, very fast; and suddenly, one fine morning in spring, he rescued from an untimely death a grandchild of old Swaffer.

"Swaffer's younger daughter is married to Willcox, a solicitor and the Town Clerk of Colebrook. Regularly twice a year they come to stay with the old man for a few days. Their only child, a little girl not three years old at the time, ran out of the house alone in her little white pinafore, and, toddling across the grass of a terraced garden, pitched herself over a low wall head first into the horsepond in the yard below.

"Our man was out with the waggoner and the plough in the field nearest to the house, and as he was leading the team round to begin a fresh furrow, he saw, through the gap of a gate, what for anybody else would have been a mere flutter of something white. But he had straight-glancing, quick, far-reaching eyes, that only seemed to flinch and lose their amazing power before the immensity of the sea. He was barefooted and looking as outlandish as the heart of Swaffer could desire. Leaving the horses on the turn, to the inexpressible disgust of the waggoner he bounded off, going over the ploughed ground in long leaps, and suddenly appeared before the mother, thrust the child into her arms, and strode away.

"The pond was not very deep; but still, if he had not had such good eyes, the child would have perished—miserably suffocated in the foot or so of sticky mud at the bottom. Old Swaffer walked out slowly into the field, waited till the plough came over to his side, had a good look at him, and without saying a word went back to the house. But from that time they laid out his meals on the kitchen table; and at first, Miss Swaffer, all in black and with an inscrutable face, would come and stand in the doorway of the living-room to see him make a big sign of the cross before he fell to. I believe that from that day, too, Swaffer began to pay him regular wages.

"I can't follow step by step his development. He cut his hair short, was seen in the village and along the road going to and fro to his work like any other man. Children ceased to shout after him. He became aware of social differences, but remained for a long time surprised at the bare poverty of the churches among so much wealth. He couldn't understand either why they were kept shut up on weekdays. There was nothing to steal in them. Was it to keep people from praying too often? The rectory took much notice of him about that time, and I believe the young ladies attempted to prepare the ground for his conversion. They could not, however, break him of his habit of crossing himself, but he went so far as to take off the string with a couple of brass medals the size of a sixpence, a tiny metal cross, and a square sort of scapulary which he wore round his neck. He hung them on the wall by the side of his bed, and he was still to be heard every evening reciting the Lord's Prayer, in incomprehensible words and in a slow, fervent tone, as he had heard his old father do at the head of all the kneeling family, big and little, on every evening of his life. And though he wore corduroys at work, and a slop-made pepper-and-salt suit on Sundays, strangers would turn round to look after him on the road. His foreignness had a peculiar and indelible stamp. At last people became used to seeing him. But they never became used to him. His rapid, skimming walk; his swarthy complexion; his hat cocked on the left ear; his habit, on warm evenings, of wearing his coat over one shoulder, like a hussar's dolman; his manner of leaping over the stiles, not as a feat of agility, but in the ordinary course of progression—all these peculiarities were, as one may say, so many causes of scorn and offence to the inhabitants of the village. They wouldn't in their dinner hour lie flat on their backs on the grass to stare at the sky. Neither did they go about the fields screaming dismal tunes. Many times have I heard his high-pitched voice from behind the ridge of some sloping sheep-walk, a voice light and soaring, like a lark's, but with a melancholy human note, over our fields that hear only the song of birds. And I would be startled myself. Ah! He was different; innocent of heart, and full of good will, which nobody wanted, this castaway, that, like a man transplanted into another planet, was separated by an immense space from his past and by an immense ignorance from his future. His quick, fervent utterance positively shocked everybody. 'An excitable devil,' they called him. One evening, in the tap-room of the Coach and Horses, (having drunk some whisky), he upset them all by singing a love-song of his country. They hooted him down, and he was pained; but Preble, the lame wheelwright, and Vincent, the fat blacksmith, and the other notables, too, wanted to drink their evening beer in peace. On another occasion he tried to show them how to dance. The dust rose in clouds from the sanded floor; he leaped straight up amongst the deal tables, struck his heels together, squatted on one heel in front of old Preble, shooting out the other leg, uttered wild and exulting cries, jumped up to whirl on one foot, snapping his fingers above his head—and a strange carter who was having a drink in there began to swear, and cleared out with his half-pint in his hand into the bar. But when suddenly he sprang upon a table and continued to dance among the glasses, the landlord interfered. He didn't want any 'acrobat tricks in the tap-room.' They laid their hands on him. Having had a glass or two, Mr. Swaffer's foreigner tried to expostulate: was ejected forcibly: got a black eye.

"I believe he felt the hostility of his human surroundings. But he was tough—tough in spirit, too, as well as in body. Only the memory of the sea frightened him, with that vague terror that is left by a bad dream. His home was far away; and he did not want now to go to America. I had often explained to him that there is no place on earth where true gold can be found lying ready and to be got for the trouble of the picking up. How, then, he asked, could he ever return home with empty hands when there had been sold a cow, two ponies, and a bit of land to pay for his going? His eyes would fill with tears, and, averting them from the immense shimmer of the sea, he would throw himself face down on the grass. But sometimes, cocking his hat with a little conquering air, he would defy my wisdom. He had found his bit of true gold. That was Amy Foster's heart; which was 'a golden heart, and soft to people's misery,' he would say in the accents of overwhelming conviction.

"He was called Yanko. He had explained that this meant Little John; but as he would also repeat very often that he was a mountaineer (some word sounding in the dialect of his country like Goorall) he got it for his surname. And this is the only trace of him that the succeeding ages may find in the marriage register of the parish. There it stands—Yanko Goorall—in the rector's handwriting. The crooked cross made by the castaway, a cross whose tracing no doubt seemed to him the most solemn part of the whole ceremony, is all that remains now to perpetuate the memory of his name.

"His courtship had lasted some time—ever since he got his precarious footing in the community. It began by his buying for Amy Foster a green satin ribbon in Darnford. This was what you did in his country. You bought a ribbon at a Jew's stall on a fair-day. I don't suppose the girl knew what to do with it, but he seemed to think that his honourable intentions could not be mistaken.

"It was only when he declared his purpose to get married that I fully understood how, for a hundred futile and inappreciable reasons, how—shall I say odious?—he was to all the countryside. Every old woman in the village was up in arms. Smith, coming upon him near the farm, promised to break his head for him if he found him about again. But he twisted his little black moustache with such a bellicose air and rolled such big, black fierce eyes at Smith that this promise came to nothing. Smith, however, told the girl that she must be mad to take up with a man who was surely wrong in his head. All the same, when she heard him in the gloaming whistle from beyond the orchard a couple of bars of a weird and mournful tune, she would drop whatever she had in her hand—she would leave Mrs. Smith in the middle of a sentence—and she would run out to his call. Mrs. Smith called her a shameless hussy. She answered nothing. She said nothing at all to anybody, and went on her way as if she had been deaf. She and I alone in all the land, I fancy, could see his very real beauty. He was very good-looking, and most graceful in his bearing, with that something wild as of a woodland creature in his aspect. Her mother moaned over her dismally whenever the girl came to see her on her day out. The father was surly, but pretended not to know; and Mrs. Finn once told her plainly that 'this man, my dear, will do you some harm some day yet.' And so it went on. They could be seen on the roads, she tramping stolidly in her finery—gray dress, black feather, stout boots, prominent white cotton gloves that caught your eye a hundred yards away; and he, his coat slung picturesquely over one shoulder, pacing by her side, gallant of bearing and casting tender glances upon the girl with the golden heart. I wonder whether he saw how plain she was. Perhaps among types so different from what he had ever seen, he had not the power to judge; or perhaps he was seduced by the divine quality of her pity.

"Yanko was in great trouble meantime. In his country you get an old man for an ambassador in marriage affairs. He did not know how to proceed. However, one day in the midst of sheep in a field (he was now Swaffer's under-shepherd with Foster) he took off his hat to the father and declared himself humbly. 'I daresay she's fool enough to marry you,' was all Foster said. 'And then,' he used to relate, 'he puts his hat on his head, looks black at me as if he wanted to cut my throat, whistles the dog, and off he goes, leaving me to do the work.' The Fosters, of course, didn't like to lose the wages the girl earned: Amy used to give all her money to her mother. But there was in Foster a very genuine aversion to that match. He contended that the fellow was very good with sheep, but was not fit for any girl to marry. For one thing, he used to go along the hedges muttering to himself like a dam' fool; and then, these foreigners behave very queerly to women sometimes. And perhaps he would want to carry her off somewhere—or run off himself. It was not safe. He preached it to his daughter that the fellow might ill-use her in some way. She made no answer. It was, they said in the villge, as if the man had done something to her. People discussed the matter. It was quite an excitement, and the two went on 'walking out' together in the face of opposition. Then something unexpected happened.

"I don't know whether old Swaffer ever understood how much he was regarded in the light of a father by his foreign retainer. Anyway the relation was curiously feudal. So when Yanko asked formally for an interview—'and the Miss, too' (he called the severe, deaf Miss Swaffer simply *Miss*)—it was to obtain their permission to marry. Swaffer heard him unmoved, dismissed him by a nod, and then shouted the intelligence into Miss Swaffer's best ear. She showed no surprise, and only remarked grimly, in a veiled blank voice, 'He certainly won't get any other girl to marry him.'

"It is Miss Swaffer who has all the credit of the munificence: but in a very few days it came out that Mr. Swaffer had presented Yanko with a cottage (the cottage you've seen this morning) and something like an acre of ground—had made it over to him in absolute property. Willcox expedited the deed, and I remember him telling me he had a great pleasure in making it ready. It recited: 'In consideration of saving the life of my beloved grandchild, Bertha Willcox.'

"Of course, after that no power on earth could prevent them from getting married.

"Her infatuation endured. People saw her going out to meet him in the evening. She stared with unblinking, fascinated eyes up the road where he was expected to appear, walking freely, with a swing from the hip, and humming one of the love-tunes of his country. When the boy was born, he got elevated at the 'Coach and Horses,' essayed again a song and a dance, and was again ejected. People expressed their commiseration for a woman married to that Jack-in-the-box. He didn't care. There was a man now (he told me boastfully) to whom he could sing and talk in the language of his country, and show how to dance by-and-by.

"But I don't know. To me he appeared to have grown less springy of step, heavier in body, less keen of eye. Imagination, no doubt; but it seems to me now as if the net of fate had been drawn closer round him already.

"One day I met him on the footpath over the Talfourd Hill. He told me that 'women were funny.' I had heard already of domestic differences. People were saying that Amy Foster was beginning to find out what sort of man she had married. He looked upon the sea with indifferent, unseeing eyes. His wife had snatched the child out of his arms one day as he sat on the doorstep crooning to it a song such as the mothers sing to babies in his mountains. She seemed to think he was doing it some harm. Women are funny. And she had objected to him praying aloud in the evening. Why? He expected the boy to repeat the prayer aloud after him by-and-by, as he used to do after his old father when he was a child—in his own country. And I discovered he longed for their boy to grow up so that he could have a man to talk with in that language that to our ears sounded so disturbing, so passionate, and so bizarre. Why his wife should dislike the idea he couldn't tell. But that would pass, he said. And tilting his head knowingly, he tapped his breastbone to indicate that she had a good heart: not hard, not fierce, open to compassion, charitable to the poor!

"I walked away thoughtfully; I wondered whether his difference, his strangeness, were not penetrating with repulsion that dull nature they had begun by irresistibly attracting. I wondered. . . ."

The Doctor came to the window and looked out at the frigid

splendour of the sea, immense in the haze, as if enclosing all the earth with all the hearts lost among the passions of love and fear.

"Physiologically, now," he said, turning away abruptly, "it was possible. It was possible."

He remained silent. Then went on—

"At all events, the next time I saw him he was ill—lung trouble. He was tough, but I daresay he was not acclimatized as well as I had supposed. It was a bad winter; and, of course, these mountaineers do get fits of home sickness; and a state of depression would make him vulnerable. He was lying half dressed on a couch downstairs.

"A table covered with a dark oilcloth took up all the middle of the little room. There was a wicker cradle on the floor, a kettle spouting steam on the hob, and some child's linen lay drying on the fender. The room was warm, but the door opens right into the garden, as you noticed perhaps.

"He was very feverish, and kept on muttering to himself. She sat on a chair and looked at him fixedly across the table with her brown, blurred eyes. 'Why don't you have him upstairs?' I asked. With a start and a confused stammer she said, 'Oh! ah! I couldn't sit with him upstairs, sir.'

"I gave her certain directions; and going outside, I said again that he ought to be in bed upstairs. She wrung her hands. 'I couldn't. I couldn't. He keeps on saying something—I don't know what.' With the memory of all the talk against the man that had been dinned into her ears, I looked at her narrowly. I looked into her short-sighted eyes, at her dumb eyes that once in her life had seen an enticing shape, but seemed, staring at me, to see nothing at all now. But I saw she was uneasy.

" 'What's the matter with him?' she asked in a sort of vacant trepidation. 'He doesn't look very ill. I never did see anybody look like this before. . . .

" 'Do you think,' I asked indignantly, 'he is shamming?'

" 'I can't help it, sir,' she said, stolidly. And suddenly she clapped her hands and looked right and left. 'And there's the baby. I am so frightened. He wanted me just now to give him the baby. I can't understand what he says to it.'

" 'Can't you ask a neighbour to come in to-night?' I asked.

" 'Please, sir, nobody seems to care to come,' she muttered, dully resigned all at once.

"I impressed upon her the necessity of the greatest care, and then had to go. There was a good deal of sickness that winter. 'Oh, I hope he won't talk!' she exclaimed softly just as I was going away.

"I don't know how it is I did not see—but I didn't. And yet, turning

in my trap, I saw her lingering before the door, very still, as if meditating a flight up the miry road.

"Towards the night his fever increased.

"He tossed, moaned, and now and then muttered a complaint. And
she sat with the table between her and the couch, watching every
movement and every sound, with the terror, the unreasonable terror,
of that man she could not understand creeping over her. She had
drawn the wicker cradle close to her feet. There was nothing in her
now but the maternal instinct and that unaccountable fear.

"Suddenly coming to himself, parched, he demanded a drink of
water. She did not move. She had not understood, though he may
have thought he was speaking in English. He waited, looking at her,
burning with fever, amazed at her silence and immobility, and then
he shouted impatiently, 'Water! Give me water!'

"She jumped to her feet, snatched up the child, and stood still.
He spoke to her, and his passionate remonstrances only increased
her fear of that strange man. I believe he spoke to her for a long
time, entreating, wondering, pleading, ordering, I suppose. She says
she bore it as long as she could. And then a gust of rage came over
him.

"He sat up and called out terribly one word—some word. Then
he got up as though he hadn't been ill at all, she says. And as in
fevered dismay, indignation, and wonder he tried to get to her round
the table, she simply opened the door and ran out with the child
in her arms. She heard him call twice after her down the road in a
terrible voice—and fled. . . . Ah! but you should have seen stirring
behind the dull, blurred glance of those eyes the spectre of the fear
which had haunted her on that night three miles and a half to the door
of Foster's cottage! I did the next day.

"And it was I who found him lying face down and his body in a
puddle, just outside the little wicker-gate.

"I had been called out that night to an urgent case in the village,
and on my way home at daybreak passed by the cottage. The door
stood open. My man helped me to carry him in. We laid him on
the couch. The lamp smoked, the fire was out, the chill of the stormy
night oozed from the cheerless yellow paper on the wall. 'Amy!' I called
aloud, and my voice seemed to lose itself in the emptiness of this
tiny house as if I had cried in a desert. He opened his eyes. 'Gone!'
he said, distinctly. 'I had only asked for water—only for a little
water. . . .'

"He was muddy. I covered him up and stood waiting in silence,
catching a painfully gasped word now and then. They were no longer
in his own language. The fever had left him, taking with it the heat
of life. And with his panting breast and lustrous eyes he reminded

me again of a wild creature under the net, of a bird caught in a snare. She had left him. She had left him—sick—helpless—thirsty. The spear of the hunter had entered his very soul. 'Why?' he cried, in the penetrating and indignant voice of a man calling to a responsible Maker. A gust of wind and a swish of rain answered.

"And as I turned away to shut the door he pronounced the word 'Merciful!' and expired.

"Eventually I certified heart-failure as the immediate cause of death. His heart must have indeed failed him, or else he might have stood this night of storm and exposure, too. I closed his eyes and drove away. Not very far from the cottage I met Foster walking sturdily between the dripping hedges with his collie at his heels.

" 'Do you know where your daughter is?' I asked.

" 'Don't I!' he cried. 'I am going to talk to him a bit. Frightening a poor woman like this.'

" 'He won't frighten her any more,' I said. 'He is dead.'

"He struck with his stick at the mud.

" 'And there's the child.'

"Then, after thinking deeply for a while—

" 'I don't know that it isn't for the best.'

"That's what he said. And she says nothing at all now. Not a word of him. Never. Is his image as utterly gone from her mind as his lithe and striding figure, his carolling voice are gone from our fields? He is no longer before her eyes to excite her imagination into a passion of love or fear; and his memory seems to have vanished from her dull brain as a shadow passes away upon a white screen. She lives in the cottage and works for Miss Swaffer. She is Amy Foster for everybody, and the child is 'Amy Foster's boy.' She calls him Johnny—which means Little John.

"It is impossible to say whether this name recalls anything to her. Does she ever think of the past? I have seen her hanging over the boy's cot in a very passion of maternal tenderness. The little fellow was lying on his back, a little frightened at me, but very still, with his big black eyes, with his fluttered air of a bird in a snare. And looking at him I seemed to see again the other one—the father, cast out mysteriously by the sea to perish in the supreme disaster of loneliness and despair."

The Secret Agent

MR. VERLOC, going out in the morning, left his shop nominally in charge of his brother-in-law. It could be done, because there was very little business at any time, and practically none at all before the evening. Mr. Verloc cared but little about his ostensible business. And, moreover, his wife was in charge of his brother-in-law.

The shop was small, and so was the house. It was one of those grimy brick houses which existed in large quantities before the era of reconstruction dawned upon London. The shop was a square box of a place, with the front glazed in small panes. In the daytime the door remained closed; in the evening it stood discreetly but suspiciously ajar.

The window contained photographs of more or less undressed dancing girls; nondescript packages in wrappers like patent medicines; closed yellow paper envelopes, very flimsy, and marked two-and-six in heavy black figures; a few numbers of ancient French comic publications hung across a string as if to dry; a dingy blue china bowl, a casket of black wood, bottles of marking ink, and rubber stamps; a few books, with titles hinting at impropriety; a few apparently old copies of obscure newspapers, badly printed, with titles like *The Torch*, *The Gong*—rousing titles. And the two gas-jets inside the panes were always turned low, either for economy's sake or for the sake of the customers.

These customers were either very young men, who hung about the window for a time before slipping in suddenly; or men of a more mature age, but looking generally as if they were not in funds. Some of that last kind had the collars of their overcoats turned right up to their moustaches, and traces of mud on the bottom of their nether garments, which had the appearance of being much worn and not very valuable. And the legs inside them did not, as a general rule, seem of much account either. With their hands plunged deep in the side pockets of their coats, they dodged in sideways, one shoulder first, as if afraid to start the bell going.

The bell, hung on the door by means of a curved ribbon of steel, was difficult to circumvent. It was hopelessly cracked; but of an evening, at the slightest provocation, it clattered behind the customer with impudent virulence.

It clattered; and at that signal, through the dusty glass door behind the painted deal counter, Mr. Verloc would issue hastily from the parlour at the back. His eyes were naturally heavy; he had an air of having wallowed, fully dressed, all day on an unmade bed. Another man would have felt such an appearance a distinct disadvantage. In a commercial transaction of the retail order much depends on the seller's engaging and amiable aspect. But Mr. Verloc knew his business, and remained undisturbed by any sort of æsthetic doubt about his appearance. With a firm, steady-eyed impudence, which seemed to hold back the threat of some abominable menace, he would proceed to sell over the counter some object looking obviously and scandalously not worth the money which passed in the transaction: a small cardboard box with apparently nothing inside, for instance, or one of those carefully closed yellow flimsy envelopes, or a soiled volume in paper covers with a promising title. Now and then it happened that one of the faded, yellow dancing girls would get sold to an amateur, as though she had been alive and young.

Sometimes it was Mrs. Verloc who would appear at the call of the cracked bell. Winnie Verloc was a young woman with a full bust, in a tight bodice, and with broad hips. Her hair was very tidy. Steady-eyed like her husband, she preserved an air of unfathomable indifference behind the rampart of the counter. Then the customer of comparatively tender years would get suddenly disconcerted at having to deal with a woman, and with rage in his heart would proffer a request for a bottle of marking ink, retail value sixpence (price in Verloc's shop one-and-sixpence), which, once outside, he would drop stealthily into the gutter.

The evening visitors—the men with collars turned up and soft hats rammed down—nodded familiarly to Mrs. Verloc, and with a muttered greeting, lifted up the flap at the end of the counter in order to pass into the back parlour, which gave access to a passage and to a steep flight of stairs. The door of the shop was the only means of entrance to the house in which Mr. Verloc carried on his business of a seller of shady wares, exercised his vocation of a protector of society, and cultivated his domestic virtues. These last were pronounced. He was thoroughly domesticated. Neither his spiritual, nor his mental, nor his physical needs were of the kind to take him much abroad. He found at home the ease of his body and the peace of his conscience,

together with Mrs. Verloc's wifely attentions and Mrs. Verloc's
mother's deferential regard.

Winnie's mother was a stout, wheezy woman, with a large brown
face. She wore a black wig under a white cap. Her swollen legs
rendered her inactive. She considered herself to be of French descent,
which might have been true; and after a good many years of married
life with a licenced victualler of the more common sort, she provided
for the years of widowhood by letting furnished apartments for gentlemen near Vauxhall Bridge Road in a square once of some splendour
and still included in the district of Belgravia. This topographical fact
was of some advantage in advertising her rooms; but the patrons of
the worthy widow were not exactly of the fashionable kind. Such
as they were, her daughter Winnie, helped to look after them. Traces
of the French descent which the widow boasted of were apparent in
Winnie, too. They were apparent in the extremely neat and artistic
arrangement of her glossy dark hair. Winnie had also other charms:
her youth; her full, rounded form; her clear complexion; the provocation of her unfathomable reserve, which never went so far as to prevent
conversation, carried on on the lodger's part with animation, and on
hers with an equable amiability. It must be that Mr. Verloc was
susceptible to these fascinations. Mr. Verloc was an intermittent
patron. He came and went without any very apparent reason. He
generally arrived in London (like the influenza) from the Continent,
only he arrived unheralded by the Press; and his visitations set in
with great severity. He breakfasted in bed, and remained wallowing
there with an air of quiet enjoyment till noon every day—and sometimes even to a later hour. But when he went out he seemed to
experience a great difficulty in finding his way back to his temporary
home in the Belgravian square. He left it late, and returned to it
early—as early as three or four in the morning; and on waking up
at ten addressed Winnie, bringing in the breakfast tray, with jocular,
exhausted civility, in the hoarse, failing tones of a man who had been
talking vehemently for many hours together. His prominent, heavy-
lidded eyes rolled sideways amorously and languidly, the bedclothes
were pulled up to his chin, and his dark smooth moustache covered
his thick lips capable of much honeyed banter.

In Winnie's mother's opinion Mr. Verloc was a very nice gentleman.
From her life's experience gathered in various "business houses" the
good woman had taken into her retirement an ideal of gentlemanli-
ness as exhibited by the patrons of private-saloon bars. Mr. Verloc
approached that ideal; he attained it, in fact.

"Of course, we'll take over your furniture, mother," Winnie had
remarked.

The lodging-house was to be given up. It seems it would not answer to carry it on. It would have been too much trouble for Mr. Verloc. It would not have been convenient for his other business. What his business was he did not say; but after his engagement to Winnie he took the trouble to get up before noon, and descending the basement stairs, make himself pleasant to Winnie's mother in the breakfast-room downstairs where she had her motionless being. He stroked the cat, poked the fire, had his lunch served to him there. He left its slightly stuffy cosiness with evident reluctance, but, all the same, remained out till the night was far advanced. He never offered to take Winnie to theatres, as such a nice gentleman ought to have done. His evenings were occupied. His work was in a way political, he told Winnie once. She would have, he warned her, to be very nice to his political friends. And with her straight, unfathomable glance she answered that she would be so, of course.

How much more he told her as to his occupation it was impossible for Winnie's mother to discover. The married couple took her over with the furniture. The mean aspect of the shop surprised her. The change from the Belgravian square to the narrow street in Soho affected her legs adversely. They became of an enormous size. On the other hand, she experienced a complete relief from material cares. Her son-in-law's heavy good nature inspired her with a sense of absolute safety. Her daughter's future was obviously assured, and even as to her son Stevie she need have no anxiety. She had not been able to conceal from herself that he was a terrible encumbrance, that poor Stevie. But in view of Winnie's fondness for her delicate brother, and of Mr. Verloc's kind and generous disposition, she felt that the poor boy was pretty safe in this rough world. And in her heart of hearts she was not perhaps displeased that the Verlocs had no children. As that circumstance seemed perfectly indifferent to Mr. Verloc, and as Winnie found an object of quasi-maternal affection in her brother, perhaps this was just as well for poor Stevie.

For he was difficult to dispose of, that boy. He was delicate and, in a frail way, good-looking, too, except for the vacant droop of his lower lip. Under our excellent system of compulsory education he had learned to read and write, notwithstanding the unfavourable aspect of the lower lip. But as errand-boy he did not turn out a great success. He forgot his messages; he was easily diverted from the straight path of duty by the attractions of stray cats and dogs, which he followed down narrow alleys into unsavoury courts; by the comedies of the streets, which he contemplated open-mouthed, to the detriment of his employer's interests; or by the dramas of fallen horses, whose pathos and violence induced him sometimes to shriek piercingly in a crowd, which disliked to be disturbed by sounds of distress in its quiet enjoyment of the national spectacle. When led away by a grave and protecting policeman, it would often become apparent that poor Stevie had forgotten his address—at least for a time. A brusque question caused him to stutter to the point of suffocation. When startled by anything perplexing he used to squint horribly. However, he never had any fits (which was encouraging); and before the natural outbursts of impatience on the part of his father he could always, in his childhood's days, run for protection behind the short skirts of his sister Winnie. On the other hand, he might have been suspected of hiding a fund of reckless naughtiness. When he had reached the age of fourteen a friend of his late father, an agent for a foreign preserved milk firm, having given him an opening as office-boy, he was discovered one foggy afternoon, in the chief's absence, busy letting off fireworks on the staircase. He touched off in quick succession a set of fierce rockets, angry catherine wheels, loudly exploding squibs—and the matter might have turned out very serious. An awful panic spread through the whole building. Wild-eyed, choking clerks stampeded through the passages full of smoke, silk hats and elderly business men could be seen rolling independently down the stairs. Stevie did not seem to derive any personal gratification from what he had done. His motives for this stroke of originality were difficult to discover. It was only later on that Winnie obtained from him a misty and confused confession. It seems that two other office-boys in the building had worked upon his feelings by tales of injustice and oppression till they had wrought his compassion to the pitch of that frenzy. But his father's friend, of course, dismissed him summarily as likely to ruin his business. After that altruistic exploit Stevie was put to help wash the dishes in the basement kitchen, and to black the boots of the gentlemen patronizing the Belgravian mansion. There was obviously no future in such work. The gentlemen tipped him a shilling now and then. Mr. Verloc showed himself the most generous of lodgers. But altogether all that did not amount to much either in the way of gain or prospects; so that when Winnie announced her engagement to Mr. Verloc her mother could not help wondering, with a sigh and a glance towards the scullery, what would become of poor Stephen now.

It appeared that Mr. Verloc was ready to take him over together with his wife's mother and with the furniture, which was the whole visible fortune of the family. Mr. Verloc gathered everything as it came to his broad, good-natured breast. The furniture was disposed to the best advantage all over the house, but Mrs. Verloc's mother was confined to two back rooms on the first floor. The luckless Stevie slept in one of them. By this time a growth of thin fluffy hair had come to blur, like golden mist, the sharp line of his small lower jaw. He helped his sister with blind love and docility in her household duties. Mr. Verloc thought that some occupation would be good for him. His spare time he occupied by drawing circles with compass and pencil on a piece of paper. He applied himself to that pastime with great industry, with his elbows spread out and bowed low over the kitchen table. Through the open door of the parlour at the back of the shop Winnie, his sister, glanced at him from time to time with maternal vigilance.

CHAPTER TWO

Such was the house, the household, and the business Mr. Verloc left behind him on his way westward at the hour of half-past ten in the morning. It was unusually early for him; his whole person exhaled the charm of almost dewy freshness; he wore his blue cloth overcoat unbuttoned; his boots were shiny; his cheeks, freshly shaven, had a sort of gloss; and even his heavy-lidded eyes, refreshed by a night of peaceful slumber, sent out glances of comparative alertness. Through the park railings these glances beheld men and women riding in the Row, couples cantering past harmoniously, others advancing sedately at a walk, loitering groups of three or four, solitary horsemen looking unsociable, and solitary women followed at a long distance by a groom with a cockade to his hat and a leather belt over his tight-fitting coat. Carriages went bowling by, mostly two-horse broughams, with here and there a victoria with the skin of some wild beast inside and a woman's face and hat emerging above the folded hood. And a peculiarly London sun—against which nothing could be said except that it looked bloodshot—glorified all this by its stare. It hung at a moderate elevation above Hyde Park Corner with an air of punctual and benign vigilance. The very pavement under Mr. Verloc's feet had an old-gold tinge in that diffused light, in which neither wall, nor tree, nor beast, nor man cast a shadow. Mr. Verloc was going westward through a town without shadows in an atmosphere of powdered old gold. There were red, coppery gleams on the roofs of houses, on the corners of walls, on the panels of carriages, on the very coats of the horses, and on the broad back of Mr. Verloc's overcoat, where they produced a dull effect of rustiness. But Mr. Verloc was not in the least conscious of having got rusty. He surveyed through the park railings the evidence of the town's opulence and luxury with an approving eye. All these people had to be protected. Protection is the first necessity of opulence and luxury. They had to be protected; and their horses, carriages, houses, servants had to be protected; and the source of their wealth had to be protected in the heart of the city and the heart of the country; the whole social order favourable to their hygienic idleness had to be protected against the shallow enviousness of unhygienic labour. It had to—and Mr. Verloc would have rubbed his hands with satisfaction had he not been constitutionally averse from every superfluous exertion. His idleness was not hygienic, but it suited him very well. He was in a manner devoted to it with a sort of inert fanaticism, or perhaps rather with a fanatical inertness. Born of industrious parents for a life of toil, he had embraced indolence from an impulse as profound, as inexplicable, and as imperious as the impulse which directs a man's preference for one particular woman in a given thousand. He was too lazy even for a mere demagogue, for a workman orator, for a leader of labour. It was too much trouble. He required a more perfect form of ease; of it might have been that he was the victim of a philosophical unbelief in the effectiveness of every human effort. Such a form of indolence requires, implies, a certain amount of intelligence. Mr. Verloc was not devoid of intelligence—and at the notion of a menaced social order he would perhaps have winked to himself if there had not been an effort to make in that sign of scepticism. His big, prominent eyes were not well adapted to winking. They were rather of the sort that closes solemnly in slumber with majestic effect.

Undemonstrative and burly in a fat-pig style, Mr. Verloc, without either rubbing his hands with satisfaction or winking sceptically at his thoughts, proceeded on his way. He trod the pavement heavily with his shiny boots, and his general get-up was that of a well-to-do mechanic in business for himself. He might have been anything from a picture-frame maker to a locksmith; an employer of labour in a small way. But there was also about him an indescribable air which no mechanic could have acquired in the practice of his handicraft however dishonestly exercised: the air common to men who live on the vices, the follies, or the baser fears of mankind; the air of moral nihilism common to keepers of gambling hells and disorderly houses; to private detectives and inquiry agents; to drink sellers and, I should say, to the sellers of invigorating electric belts and to the inventors of patent medicines. But of that last I am not sure, not having carried my investigations so far into the depths. For all I know, the expression of these last may be perfectly diabolic. I shouldn't be surprised. What I want to affirm is that Mr. Verloc's expression was by no means diabolic.

Before reaching Knightsbridge, Mr. Verloc took a turn to the left out of the busy main thoroughfare, uproarious with the traffic of swaying omnibuses and trotting vans, into the almost silent, swift flow of hansoms. Under his hat, worn with a slight backward tilt, his hair had been carefully brushed into respectful sleekness; for his business was with an Embassy. And Mr. Verloc, steady like a rock—a soft kind of rock—marched now along a street which could with every propriety be described as private. In its breadth, emptiness, and extent it had the majesty of inorganic nature, of matter that never dies. The only reminder of mortality was a doctor's brougham arrested in august solitude close to the curbstone. The polished knockers of the doors gleamed as far as the eye could reach, the clean windows shone with a dark opaque lustre. And all was still. But a milk cart rattled noisily across the distant perspective; a butcher boy, driving with the noble recklessness of a charioteer at Olympic Games, dashed round the corner sitting high above a pair of red wheels. A guilty-looking cat issuing from under the stones ran for a while in front of Mr. Verloc, then dived into another basement; and a thick police constable, looking a stranger to every emotion, as if he, too, were part of inorganic nature, surging apparently out of a lamp-post, took not the slightest notice of Mr. Verloc. With a turn to the left Mr. Verloc pursued his way along a narrow street by the side of a yellow wall which, for some inscrutable reason, had No. 1 Chesham Square written on it in black letters. Chesham Square was at least sixty yards away, and Mr. Verloc, cosmopolitan enough not to be deceived by London's topographical mysteries, held on steadily, without a sign of surprise or indignation. At last, with business-like persistency, he reached the Square, and made diagonally for the number 10. This belonged to an imposing carriage gate in a high, clean wall between two houses, of which one rationally enough bore the number 9 and the other was numbered 37; but the fact that this last belonged to Porthill Street, a street well known in the neighbourhood, was proclaimed by an inscription placed above the ground-floor windows by whatever highly efficient authority is charged with the duty of keeping track of London's strayed houses. Why powers are not asked of Parliament (a short act would do) for compelling those edifices to return where they belong is one of the mysteries of municipal administration. Mr. Verloc did not trouble his head about it, his mission in life being the protection of the social mechanism, not its perfectionment or even its criticism.

It was so early that the porter of the Embassy issued hurriedly out of his lodge still struggling with the left sleeve of his livery coat. His waistcoat was red, and he wore knee-breeches, but his aspect was flustered. Mr. Verloc, aware of the rush on his flank, drove it off by simply holding out an envelope stamped with the arms of the Embassy, and passed on. He produced the same talisman also to the footman who opened the door, and stood back to let him enter the hall.

A clear fire burned in a tall fireplace, and an elderly man standing with his back to it, in evening dress and with a chain round his neck, glanced up from the newspaper he was holding spread out in both hands before his calm and severe face. He didn't move; but another lackey, in brown trousers and clawhammer coat edged with thin yellow cord, approaching Mr. Verloc listened to the murmur of his name, and turning round on his heel in silence, began to walk, without looking back once. Mr. Verloc, thus led along a ground-floor passage to the left of the great carpeted staircase, was suddenly motioned to enter a quite small room furnished with a heavy writing-table and a few chairs. The servant shut the door, and Mr. Verloc remained alone. He did not take a seat. With his hat and stick held in one hand he glanced about, passing his other podgy hand over his uncovered sleek head.

Another door opened noiselessly, and Mr. Verloc immobilizing his glance in that direction saw at first only black clothes, the bald top of a head, and a drooping dark grey whisker on each side of a pair of wrinkled hands. The person who had entered was holding a batch of papers before his eyes and walked up to the table with a rather mincing step, turning the papers over the while. Privy Councillor Wurmt, Chancelier d'Ambassade, was rather shortsighted. This meritorious official, laying the papers on the table, disclosed a face of pasty complexion and of melancholy ugliness surrounded by a lot of fine, long dark grey hairs, barred heavily by thick and bushy eyebrows. He put on a black-framed pince-nez upon a blunt and shapeless nose, and seemed struck by Mr. Verloc's appearance. Under the enormous eyebrows his weak eyes blinked pathetically through the glasses.

He made no sign of greeting; neither did Mr. Verloc who certainly knew his place; but a subtle change about the general outlines of his shoulders and back suggested a slight bending of Mr. Verloc's spine under the vast surface of his overcoat. The effect was of unobtrusive deference.

"I have here some of your reports," said the bureaucrat in an unexpectedly soft and weary voice, and pressing the tip of his forefinger on the papers with force. He paused; and Mr. Verloc, who had recognized his own handwriting very well, waited in an almost breathless silence. "We are not very satisfied with the attitude of the police here," the other continued, with every appearance of mental fatigue.

The shoulders of Mr. Verloc, without actually moving, suggested a shrug. And for the first time since he left his home that morning his lips opened.

"Every country has its police," he said, philosophically. But as the official of the Embassy went on blinking at him steadily he felt constrained to add: "Allow me to observe that I have no means of action upon the police here."

"What is desired," said the man of papers, "is the occurrence of something definite which should stimulate their vigilance. That is within your province—is it not so?"

Mr. Verloc made no answer except by a sigh, which escaped him involuntarily, for instantly he tried to give his face a cheerful expression. The official blinked doubtfully, as if affected by the dim light of the room. He repeated vaguely:

"The vigilance of the police—and the severity of the magistrates. The general leniency of the judicial procedure here, and the utter absence of all repressive measures, are a scandal to Europe. What is wished for just now is the accentuation of the unrest—of the fermentation which undoubtedly exists——"

"Undoubtedly, undoubtedly," broke in Mr. Verloc in a deep, deferential bass of an oratorical quality, so utterly different from the tone in which he had spoken before that his interlocutor remained profoundly surprised. "It exists to a dangerous degree. My reports for the last twelve months make it sufficiently clear."

"Your reports for the last twelve months," State Councillor Wurmt began in his gentle and dispassionate tone, "have been read by me. I failed to discover why you wrote them at all."

A sad silence reigned for a time. Mr. Verloc seemed to have swallowed his tongue, and the other gazed at the papers on the table fixedly. At last he gave them a slight push.

"The state of affairs you expose there is assumed to exist as the first condition of your employment. What is required at present is not writing, but the bringing to light of a distinct, significant fact—I would almost say of an alarming fact."

"I need not say that all my endeavours shall be directed to that end," Mr. Verloc said, with convinced modulations in his conversational husky tone. But the sense of being blinked at watchfully behind the blind glitter of these eyeglasses on the other side of the table disconcerted him. He stopped short with a gesture of absolute devotion. The useful hard-working, if obscure member of the Embassy had an air of being impressed by some newly-born thought.

"You are very corpulent," he said.

This observation, really of a psychological nature, and advanced with the modest hesitation of an officeman more familiar with ink and paper than with the requirements of active life, stung Mr. Verloc in the manner of a rude personal remark. He stepped back a pace.

"Eh? What were you pleased to say?" he exclaimed, with husky resentment.

The Chancelier d'Ambassade, entrusted with the conduct of this interview, seemed to find it too much for him.

"I think," he said, "that you had better see Mr. Vladimir. Yes, decidedly I think you ought to see Mr. Vladimir. Be good enough to wait here," he added, and went out with mincing steps.

At once Mr. Verloc passed his hand over his hair. A slight perspiration had broken out on his forehead. He let the air escape from his pursed-up lips like a man blowing at a spoonful of hot soup. But when the servant in brown appeared at the door silently, Mr. Verloc had not moved an inch from the place he had occupied throughout the interview. He had remained motionless, as if feeling himself surrounded by pitfalls.

He walked along a passage lighted by a lonely gas-jet, then up a flight of winding stairs, and through a glazed and cheerful corridor on the first floor. The footman threw open a door, and stood aside. The feet of Mr. Verloc felt a thick carpet. The room was large, with three windows; and a young man with a shaven, big face, sitting in a roomy armchair before a vast mahogany writing-table, said in French to the Chancelier d'Ambassade, who was going out with the papers in his hand:

"You are quite right, mon cher. He's fat—the animal."

Mr. Vladimir, First Secretary, had a drawing-room reputation as an agreeable and entertaining man. He was something of a favourite in society. His wit consisted in discovering droll connections between incongruous ideas; and when talking in that strain he sat well forward on his seat, with his left hand raised, as if exhibiting his funny demonstrations between the thumb and forefinger, while his round and clean-shaven face wore an expression of merry perplexity.

But there was no trace of merriment or perplexity in the way he looked at Mr. Verloc. Lying far back in the deep armchair, with squarely spread elbows, and throwing one leg over a thick knee, he had with his smooth and rosy countenance the air of a preternaturally thriving baby that will not stand nonsense from anybody.

"You understand French, I suppose?" he said.

Mr. Verloc stated huskily that he did. His whole vast bulk had a forward inclination. He stood on the carpet in the middle of the room, clutching his hat and stick in one hand; the other hung lifelessly by his side. He muttered unobtrusively somewhere deep down in his throat something about having done his military service in the French artillery. At once, with contemptuous perversity, Mr. Vladimir changed the language, and began to speak idiomatic English without the slightest trace of a foreign accent.

"Ah! Yes. Of course. Let's see. How much did you get for obtaining the design of the improved breech-block of their new field-gun?"

"Five years' rigorous confinement in a fortress," Mr. Verloc answered, unexpectedly, but without any sign of feeling.

"You got off easily," was Mr. Vladimir's comment. "And, anyhow, it served you right for letting yourself get caught. What made you go in for that sort of thing—eh?"

Mr. Verloc's husky conversational voice was heard speaking of youth, of a fatal infatuation for an unworthy——

"Aha! Cherchez la femme," Mr. Vladimir deigned to interrupt, unbending, but without affability; there was, on the contrary, a touch of grimness in his condescension. "How long have you been employed by the Embassy here?" he asked.

"Ever since the time of the late Baron Stott-Wartenheim," Mr. Verloc answered in subdued tones, and protruding his lips sadly, in sign of sorrow for the deceased diplomat. The First Secretary observed this play of physiognomy steadily.

"Ah! ever since. . . . Well! What have you got to say for yourself?" he asked, sharply.

Mr. Verloc answered with some surprise that he was not aware of having anything special to say. He had been summoned by a letter—— And he plunged his hand busily into the side pocket of his overcoat, but before the mocking, cynical watchfulness of Mr. Vladimir, concluded to leave it there.

"Bah!" said the latter. "What do you mean by getting out of condition like this? You haven't got even the physique of your profession. You—a member of a starving proletariat—never! You—a desperate socialist or anarchist—which is it?"

"Anarchist," stated Mr. Verloc in a deadened tone.

"Bosh!" went on Mr. Vladimir, without raising his voice. "You startled old Wurmt himself. You wouldn't deceive an idiot. They all are that by-the-by, but you seem to me simply impossible. So you began your connection with us by stealing the French gun designs. And you got yourself caught. That must have been very disagreeable to our Government. You don't seem to be very smart."

Mr. Verloc tried to exculpate himself huskily.

"As I've had occasion to observe before, a fatal infatuation for an unworthy——"

Mr. Vladimir raised a large, white, plump hand.

"Ah, yes. The unlucky attachment—of your youth. She got hold of the money, and then sold you to the police—eh?"

The doleful change in Mr. Verloc's physiognomy, the momentary drooping of his whole person, confessed that such was the regrettable case. Mr. Vladimir's hand clasped the ankle reposing on his knee. The sock was a dark blue silk.

"You see, that was not very clever of you. Perhaps you are too susceptible."

Mr. Verloc intimated in a throaty, veiled murmur that he was no longer young.

"Oh! That's a failing which age does not cure," Mr. Vladimir remarked, with sinister familiarity. "But no! You are too fat for that. You could not have come to look like this if you had been at all susceptible. I'll tell you what I think is the matter: you are a lazy fellow. How long have you been drawing pay from this Embassy?"

"Eleven years," was the answer, after a moment of sulky hesitation. "I've been charged with several missions to London while His Excellency Baron Stott-Wartenheim was still Ambassador in Paris. Then by his Excellency's instructions I settled down in London. I am English."

"You are! Are you? Eh?"

"A natural-born British subject," Mr. Verloc said, stolidly. "But my father was French, and so——"

"Never mind explaining," interrupted the other. "I dare say you could have been legally a Marshal of France and a Member of Parliament in England—and then, indeed, you would have been of some use to our Embassy."

This flight of fancy provoked something like a faint smile on Mr. Verloc's face. Mr. Vladimir retained an imperturbable gravity.

"But, as I've said, you are a lazy fellow; you don't use your opportunities. In the time of Baron Stott-Wartenheim we had a lot of soft-headed people running this Embassy. They caused fellows of your sort to form a false conception of the nature of a secret service fund. It is my business to correct this misapprehension by telling you what the secret service is not. It is not a philanthropic institution. I've had you called here on purpose to tell you this."

Mr. Valdimir observed the forced expression of bewilderment on Verloc's face, and smiled sarcastically.

"I see that you understand me perfectly. I daresay you are intelligent enough for your work. What we want now is activity—activity."

On repeating this last word Mr. Vladimir laid a long white forefinger on the edge of the desk. Every trace of huskiness disappeared from Verloc's voice. The nape of his gross neck became crimson above the velvet collar of his overcoat. His lips quivered before they came widely open.

"If you'll only be good enough to look up my record," he boomed out in his great, clear, oratorical bass, "you'll see I gave a warning only three months ago on the occasion of the Grand Duke Romuald's visit to Paris, which was telegraphed from here to the French police, and——"

"Tut, tut!" broke out Mr. Vladimir, with a frowning grimace. "The French police had no use for your warning. Don't roar like this. What the devil do you mean?"

With a note of proud humility Mr. Verloc apologized for forgetting himself. His voice, famous for years at open-air meetings and at workmen's assemblies in large halls, had contributed, he said, to his reputation of a good and trustworthy comrade. It was, therefore, a part of his usefulness. It had inspired confidence in his principles. "I was always put up to speak by the leaders at a critical moment," Mr. Verloc declared, with obvious satisfaction. There was no uproar above which he could not make himself heard, he added; and suddenly he made a demonstration.

"Allow me," he said. With lowered forehead, without looking up, swiftly and ponderously, he crossed the room to one of the French windows. As if giving way to an uncontrollable impulse, he opened it a little. Mr. Vladimir, jumping up amazed from the depths of the armchair, looked over his shoulder; and below, across the courtyard of the Embassy, well beyond the open gate, could be seen the broad back of a policeman watching idly the gorgeous perambulator of a wealthy baby being wheeled in state across the Square.

"Constable!" said Mr. Verloc, with no more effort than if he were whispering; and Mr. Vladimir burst into a laugh on seeing the policeman spin round as if prodded by a sharp instrument. Mr. Verloc shut the window quietly, and returned to the middle of the room.

"With a voice like that," he said, putting on the husky conversational pedal, "I was naturally trusted. And I knew what to say, too."

"Mr. Vladimir, arranging his cravat, observed him in the glass over the mantelpiece.

"I daresay you have the social revolutionary jargon by heart well enough," he said, contemptuously. "Vox et. . . . You haven't ever studied Latin—have you?"

"No," growled Mr. Verloc. "You did not expect me to know it. I belong to the million. Who knows Latin? Only a few hundred imbeciles who aren't fit to take care of themselves."

For some thirty seconds longer Mr. Vladimir studied in the mirror the fleshy profile, the gross bulk, of the man behind him. And at the same time he had the advantage of seeing his own face, clean-shaved and round, rosy about the gills, and with the thin, sensitive lips formed exactly for the utterance of those delicate witticisms which had made him such a favourite in the very highest society. Then he turned, and advanced into the room with such determination that the very ends of his quaintly old-fashioned bow necktie seemed to bristle with unspeakable menaces. The movement was so swift and fierce that Mr. Verloc, casting an oblique glance, quailed inwardly.

"Aha! You dare be impudent," Mr. Vladimir began, with an amazingly guttural intonation not only utterly un-English, but absolutely un-European, and startling even to Mr. Verloc's experience of cosmopolitan slums. "You dare! Well, I am going to speak plain English to you. Voice won't do. We have no use for your voice. We don't want a voice. We want facts—startling facts—damn you!" he added, with a sort of ferocious discretion, right into Mr. Verloc's face.

"Don't you try to come over me with your Hyperborean manners," Mr. Verloc defended himself, huskily, looking at the carpet. At this his interlocutor, smiling mockingly above the bristling bow of his necktie, switched the conversation into French.

"You give yourself for an 'agent provocateur.' The proper business of an 'agent provocateur' is to provoke. As far as I can judge from your record kept here, you have done nothing to earn your money for the last three years."

"Nothing!" exclaimed Verloc, stirring not a limb, and not raising his eyes, but with the note of sincere feeling in his tone. "I have several times prevented what might have been—"

"There is a proverb in this country which says prevention is better than cure," interrupted Mr. Vladimir, throwing himself into the armchair. "It is stupid in a general way. There is no end to prevention. But it is characteristic. They dislike finality in this country. Don't you be too English. And in this particular instance, don't be absurd. The evil is already here. We don't want prevention—we want cure."

He paused, turned to the desk, and turning over some papers lying there, spoke in a changed, business-like tone, without looking at Mr. Verloc.

"You know, of course, of the International Conference assembled in Milan?"

Mr. Verloc intimated hoarsely that he was in the habit of reading the daily papers. To a further question his answer was that, of course, he understood what he read. At this Mr. Vladimir, smiling faintly at the documents he was still scanning one after another, murmured "As long as it is not written in Latin, I suppose."

"Or Chinese," added Mr. Verloc, stolidly.

"H'm. Some of your revolutionary friends' effusions are written in a *charabia* every bit as incomprehensible as Chinese—" Mr. Vladimir let fall disdainfully a grey sheet of printed matter. "What are all these leaflets headed F. P., with a hammer, pen, and torch crossed? What does it mean, this F. P.?" Mr. Verloc approached the imposing writing-table.

"The Future of the Proletariat. It's a society," he explained, standing ponderously by the side of the armchair, "not anarchist in principle, but open to all shades of revolutionary opinion."

"Are you in it?"

"One of the Vice-Presidents," Mr. Verloc breathed out heavily; and the First Secretary of the Embassy raised his head to look at him.

"Then you ought to be ashamed of yourself," he said, incisively. "Isn't your society capable of anything else but printing this prophetic bosh in blunt type on this filthy paper—eh? Why don't you do something? Look here. I've this matter in hand now, and I tell you plainly that you will have to earn your money. The good old Stott-Wartenheim times are over. No work, no pay."

Mr. Verloc felt a queer sensation of faintness in his stout legs. He stepped back one pace, and blew his nose loudly.

He was, in truth, startled and alarmed. The rusty London sunshine struggling clear of the London mist shed a lukewarm brightness into the First Secretary's private room: and in the silence Mr. Verloc heard against a window-pane the faint buzzing of a fly—his first fly of the year—heralding better than any number of swallows the approach of spring. The useless fussing of that tiny, energetic organism affected unpleasantly this big man threatened in his indolence.

In the pause Mr. Vladimir formulated in his mind a series of disparaging remarks concerning Mr. Verloc's face and figure. The fellow was unexpectedly vulgar, heavy, and impudently unintelligent. He looked uncommonly like a master plumber come to present his bill. The First Secretary of the Embassy, from his occasional excursions into the field of American humour, had formed a special notion of that class of mechanic as the embodiment of fraudulent laziness and incompetency.

This was then the famous and trusty secret agent, so secret that he was never designated otherwise but by the symbol $\triangle$ in the late Baron Stott-Wartenheim's official, semi-official, and confidential correspondence; the celebrated agent $\triangle$, whose warnings had the power to change the schemes and the dates of royal, imperial, or grand-ducal journeys, and sometimes cause them to be put off altogether! This fellow! And Mr. Vladimir indulged mentally in an enormous and derisive fit of merriment, partly at his own astonishment, which he judged naïve, but mostly at the expense of the universally regretted Baron Stott-Wartenheim. His late Excellency, whom the august favour of his Imperial master had imposed as Ambassador upon several reluctant Ministers of Foreign Affairs, had enjoyed in his lifetime a fame for an owlish, pessimistic gullibility. His Excellency had the social revolution on the brain. He imagined himself to be a diplomatist set apart by a special dispensation to watch the end of diplomacy, and pretty nearly the end of the world, in a horrid, democratic upheaval. His prophetic and doleful despatches had been for years the joke of Foreign Offices. He was said to have exclaimed on his deathbed (visited by his Imperial friend and master): "Unhappy Europe! Thou shalt perish by the moral insanity of thy children!" He was fated to be the victim of the first humbugging rascal that came along, thought Mr. Vladimir, smiling vaguely at Mr. Verloc.

"You ought to venerate the memory of Baron Stott-Wartenheim," he exclaimed, suddenly.

352

The lowered physiognomy of Mr. Verloc expressed a sombre and weary annoyance.

"Permit me to observe to you," he said, "that I came here because I was summoned by a peremptory letter. I have been here only twice before in the last eleven years, and certainly never at eleven in the morning. It isn't very wise to call me up like this. There is just a chance of being seen. And that would be no joke for me."

Mr. Vladimir shrugged his shoulders.

"It would destroy my usefulness," continued the other hotly.

"That's your affair," murmured Mr. Vladimir, with soft brutality. "When you cease to be useful you shall cease to be employed. Yes. Right off. Cut short. You shall——" Mr. Vladimir, frowning, paused, at a loss for a sufficiently idiomatic expression, and instantly brightened up, with a grin of beautifully white teeth. "You shall be chucked," he brought out ferociously.

Once more Mr. Verloc had to react with all the force of his will against that sensation of faintness running down one's legs which once upon a time had inspired some poor devil with the felicitous expression: "My heart went down into my boots." Mr. Verloc, aware of the sensation, raised his head bravely.

Mr. Vladimir bore the look of heavy inquiry with perfect serenity.

"What we want is to administer a tonic to the Conference in Milan," he said, airily. "Its deliberations upon international action for the suppression of political crime don't seem to get anywhere. England lags. This country is absurd with its sentimental regard for individual liberty. It's intolerable to think that all your friends have got only to come over to—"

"In that way I have them all under my eye," Mr. Verloc interrupted, huskily.

"It would be much more to the point to have them all under lock and key. England must be brought into line. The imbecile bourgeoisie of this country make themselves the accomplices of the very people whose aim is to drive them out of their houses to starve in ditches. And they have the political power still, if they only had the sense to use it for their preservation. I suppose you agree that the middle classes are stupid?"

Mr. Verloc agreed hoarsely.

"They are."

"They have no imagination. They are blinded by an idiotic vanity. What they want just now is a jolly good scare. This is the psychological moment to set your friends to work. I have had you called here to develop to you my idea."

And Mr. Vladimir developed his idea from on high, with scorn and condescension, displaying at the same time an amount of ignorance as to the real aims, thoughts, and methods of the revolutionary world which filled the silent Mr. Verloc with inward consternation. He confounded causes with effects more than was excusable; the most distinguished propagandists with impulsive bomb throwers; assumed organization where in the nature of things it could not exist; spoke of the social revolutionary party one moment as of a perfectly disciplined army, where the word of chiefs was supreme, and at another as if it had been the loosest association of desperate brigands that ever camped in a mountain gorge. Once Mr. Verloc had opened his mouth for a protest, but the raising of a shapely, large white hand arrested him. Very soon he became too appalled to even try to protest. He listened in a stillness of dread which resembled the immobility of profound attention.

"A series of outrages," Mr. Vladimir continued, calmly, "executed here in this country; not only *planned* here—that would not do—they would not mind. Your friends could set half the Continent on fire without influencing the public opinion here in favour of a universal repressive legislation. They will not look outside their backyard here."

Mr. Verloc cleared his throat, but his heart failed him, and he said nothing.

"These outrages need not be especially sanguinary," Mr. Vladimir went on, as if delivering a scientific lecture, "but they must be sufficiently startling—effective. Let them be directed against buildings, for instance. What is the fetish of the hour that all the bourgeoisie recognise—eh, Mr. Verloc?"

Mr. Verloc opened his hands and shrugged his shoulders slightly.

"You are too lazy to think," was Mr. Vladimir's comment upon that gesture. "Pay attention to what I say. The fetish of to-day is neither royalty nor religion. Therefore the palace and the church should be left alone. You understand what I mean, Mr. Verloc?"

The dismay and the scorn of Mr. Verloc found vent in an attempt at levity.

"Perfectly. But what of the Embassies? A series of attacks on the various Embassies," he began; but he could not withstand the cold, watchful stare of the First Secretary.

"You can be facetious, I see," the latter observed, carelessly. "That's all right. It may enliven your oratory at socialistic congresses. But this room is no place for it. It would be infinitely safer for you to follow carefully what I am saying. As you are being called upon to furnish facts instead of cock-and-bull stories, you had better try to make your profit off what I am taking the trouble to explain to you. The sacrosanct fetish of to-day is science. Why don't you get some of your friends to go for that wooden-faced panjandrum—eh? Is it not part of these institutions which must be swept away before the F. P. comes along?"

Mr. Verloc said nothing. He was afraid to open his lips lest a groan should escape him.

"This is what you should try for. An attempt upon a crowned head or on a president is sensational enough in a way, but not so much as it used to be. It has entered into the general conception of the existence of all chiefs of state. It's almost conventional—especially since so many presidents have been assassinated. Now let us take an outrage upon—say a church. Horrible enough at first sight, no doubt, and yet not so effective as a person of an ordinary mind might think. No matter how revolutionary and anarchist in inception, there would be fools enough to give such an outrage the character of a religious manifestation. And that would detract from the especial alarming significance we wish to give to the act. A murderous attempt on a restaurant or a theatre would suffer in the same way from the suggestion of non-political passion; the exasperation of a hungry man, an act of social revenge. All this is used up; it is no longer instructive as an object lesson in revolutionary anarchism. Every newspaper has ready-made phrases to explain such manifestations away. I am about to give you the philosophy of bomb throwing from my point of view; from the point of view you pretend to have been serving for the last eleven years. I will try not to talk above your head. The sensibilities of the class you are attacking are soon blunted. Property seems to them an indestructible thing. You can't count upon their emotions either of pity or fear for very long. A bomb outrage to have any influence on public opinion now must go beyond the intention of vengeance or terrorism. It must be purely destructive. It must be that, and only that, beyond the faintest suspicion of any other object. You anarchists should make it clear that you are perfectly determined to make a clean sweep of the whole social creation. But how to get that appallingly absurd notion into the heads of the middle classes so that there should be no mistake? That's the question. By directing your blows at something outside the ordinary passions of humanity is the answer. Of course, there is art. A bomb in the National Gallery would make some noise. But it would not be serious enough. Art has never been their fetish. It's like breaking a few back windows in a man's house; whereas, if you want to make him really sit up, you must try at least to raise the roof. There would be some screaming of course, but from whom? Artists—art critics and such like—people of no account. Nobody minds what they say. But there is learning—science. Any imbecile that has got an income believes in that. He does not know why, but he believes it matters somehow. It is the sacrosanct fetish. All the damned professors are radicals at heart. Let them know that their great panjandrum has got to go, too, to make room for the Future of the Proletariat. A howl from all these intellectual idiots is bound to help forward the labours of the Milan Conference. They will be writing to the papers. Their indignation would be above suspicion, no material interests being openly at stake, and it will alarm every selfishness of the class which should be impressed. They believe that in some mysterious way science is at the source of their material prosperity. They do. And the absurd ferocity of such a demonstration will affect them more profoundly than the mangling of a whole street—or theatre—full of their own kind. To that last they can always say: 'Oh! it's mere class hate.' But what is one to say to an act of destructive ferocity so absurd as to be incomprehensible, inexplicable, almost unthinkable; in fact, mad? Madness alone is truly terrifying, inasmuch as you cannot placate it either by threats, persuasion, or bribes. Moreover, I am a civilized man. I would never dream of directing you to organize a mere butchery, even if I expected the best results from it. But I wouldn't expect from a butchery the result I want. Murder is always with us. It is almost an institution. The demonstration must be against learning—science. But not every science will do. The attack must have all the shocking senselessness of gratuitous blasphemy. Since bombs are your means of expression, it would be really telling if one could throw a bomb into pure mathematics. But that is impossible. I have been trying to educate you; I have expounded to you the higher philosophy of your usefulness, and suggested to you some serviceable arguments. The practical application of my teaching interests *you* mostly. But from the moment I have undertaken to interview you I have also given some attention to the practical aspect of the question. What do you think of having a go at astronomy?"

For sometime already Mr. Verloc's immobility by the side of the armchair resembled a state of collapsed coma—a sort of passive insensibility interrupted by slight convulsive starts, such as may be observed in the domestic dog having a nightmare on the hearthrug. And it was in an uneasy, doglike growl that he repeated the word:

"Astronomy."

He had not recovered thoroughly as yet from the state of bewilderment brought about by the effort to follow Mr. Vladimir's rapid, incisive utterance. It had overcome his power of assimilation. It had made him angry. This anger was complicated by incredulity. And suddenly it dawned upon him that all this was an elaborate joke. Mr. Vladimir exhibited his white teeth in a smile, with dimples on his round, full face posed with a complacent inclination above the bristling bow of his necktie. The favourite of intelligent society women had assumed his drawing-room attitude accompanying the delivery of delicate witticisms. Sitting well forward, his white hand upraised, he seemed to hold delicately between his thumb and forefinger the subtlety of his suggestion.

"There could be nothing better. Such an outrage combines the greatest possible regard for humanity with the most alarming display of ferocious imbecility. I defy the ingenuity of journalists to persuade their public that any given member of the proletariat can have a personal grievance against astronomy. Starvation itself could hardly be dragged in there—eh? And there are other advantages. The whole civilized world has heard of Greenwich. The very boot-blacks in the basement of Charing Cross Station know something of it. See?"

The features of Mr. Vladimir, so well known in the best society by their humorous urbanity, beamed with cynical self-satisfaction, which would have astonished the intelligent women his wit entertained so exquisitely. "Yes," he continued, with a contemptuous smile, "the blowing up of the first meridian is bound to raise a howl of execration."

"A difficult business," Mr. Verloc mumbled, feeling that this was the only safe thing to say.

"What is the matter? Haven't you the whole gang under your hand? The very pick of the basket? That old terrorist Yundt is here. I see him walking about Piccadilly in his green havelock almost every day. And Michaelis, the ticket-of-leave apostle—you don't mean to say you don't know where he is? Because if you don't, I can tell you," Mr. Vladimir went on menacingly. "If you imagine that you are the only one on the secret fund list, you are mistaken."

This perfectly gratuitous suggestion caused Mr. Verloc to shuffle his feet slightly.

"And the whole Lausanne lot—eh? Haven't they been flocking over here at the first hint of the Milan Conference? This is an absurd country."

"It will cost money," Mr. Verloc said, by a sort of instinct.

"That cock won't fight," Mr. Vladimir retorted, with an amazingly genuine English accent. "You'll get your screw every month, and no more till something happens. And if nothing happens very soon you won't get even that. What's your ostensible occupation? What are you supposed to live by?"

"I keep a shop," answered Mr. Verloc.

"A shop! What sort of shop?"

"Stationery, newspapers. My wife——"

"Your what?" interrupted Mr. Vladimir in his guttural Central Asian tones.

"My wife." Mr. Verloc raised his husky voice slightly. "I am married."

"That be damned for a yarn," exclaimed the other in unfeigned astonishment. "Married! And you a professed anarchist, too! What is this confounded nonsense? But I suppose it's merely a manner of speaking. Anarchists don't marry. It's well known. They can't. It would be apostasy."

"My wife isn't one," Mr. Verloc mumbled, sulkily. "Moreover, it's no concern of yours."

"Oh, yes, it is," snapped Mr. Vladimir. "I am beginning to be convinced that you are not at all the man for the work you've been employed on. Why you must have discredited yourself completely in your own world by your marriage. Couldn't you have managed without? This is your virtuous attachment—eh? What with one sort of attachment and another you are doing away with your usefulness."

Mr. Verloc, puffing out his cheeks, let the air escape violently, and that was all. He had armed himself with patience. It was not to be tried much longer. The First Secretary became suddenly very curt, detached, final.

"You may go now," he said. "A dynamite outrage must be provoked. I give you a month. The sittings of the Conference are suspended. Before it reassembles again something must have happened here, or your connection with us ceases."

He changed the note once more with an unprincipled versatility.

"Think over my philosophy, Mr.—Mr.—Verloc," he said, with a sort of chaffing condescension, waving his hand towards the door. "Go for the first meridian. You don't know the middle classes as well as I do. Their sensibilities are jaded. The first meridian. Nothing better, and nothing easier, I should think."

He got up, and with his thin sensitive lips twitching humorously, watched in the glass over the mantelpiece Mr. Verloc backing out of the room heavily, hat and stick in hand. The door closed.

The footman in trousers, appearing suddenly in the corridor, led Mr. Verloc another way out and through a small door in the corner of the courtyard. The porter standing at the gate ignored his exit completely; and Mr. Verloc retraced the path of his morning's pilgrimage as if a dream—an angry dream. This detachment from the material world was so complete that, though the mortal envelope of Mr. Verloc had not hastened unduly along the streets, that part of him to which it would be unwarrantably rude to refuse immortality, found itself at the shop door all at once, as borne from west to east on the wings of a great wind. He walked straight behind the counter, and sat down on a wooden chair that stood there. No one appeared to disturb his solitude. Stevie, put into a green baize apron, was now sweeping and dusting upstairs, intent and conscientious, as though he were playing at it; and Mrs. Verloc, warned in the kitchen by the clatter of the cracked bell, had merely come to the glazed door of the parlour, and putting the curtain aside a little, had peered into the dim shop. Seeing her husband sitting there shadowy and bulky, with his hat tilted far back on his head, she had at once returned to her stove. An hour or more later she took the green baize apron off her brother Stevie, and instructed him to wash his hands and face in the peremptory tone she had used in that connection for fifteen years or so—ever since she had, in fact, ceased to attend to the boy's hands and face herself. She spared presently a glance away from her dishing-up for the inspection of that face and those hands which Stevie, approaching the kitchen table, offered for her approval with an air of self-assurance hiding a perpetual residue of anxiety. Formerly the anger of the father was the supremely effective sanction of these rites, but Mr. Verloc's placidity in domestic life would have made all mention of anger incredible—even to poor Stevie's nervousness. The theory was that Mr. Verloc would have been inexpressibly pained and shocked by any deficiency of cleanliness at meal times. Winnie after the death of her father found considerable consolation in the feeling that she need no longer tremble for poor Stevie. She could not bear to see the boy hurt. It maddened her. As a little girl she had often faced with blazing eyes the irascible licenced victualler in defence of her brother. Nothing now in Mrs. Verloc's appearance could lead one to suppose that she was capable of a passionate demonstration.

She finished her dishing-up. The table was laid in the parlour. Going to the foot of the stairs she screamed out "Mother!" Then opening the glazed door leading to the shop, she said quietly, "Adolf!" Mr. Verloc had not changed his position; he had not apparently stirred a limb for an hour and a half. He got up heavily, and came to his dinner in his overcoat and with his hat on, without uttering a word. His silence in itself had nothing startlingly unusual in this household, hidden in the shades of the sordid street seldom touched by the sun, behind the dim shop with its wares of disreputable rubbish. Only that day Mr. Verloc's taciturnity was so obviously thoughtful that the two women were impressed by it. They sat silent themselves, keeping a watchful eye on poor Stevie, lest he should break out into one of his fits of loquacity. He faced Mr. Verloc across the table, and remained very good and quiet, staring vacantly. The endeavour to keep him from making himself objectionable in any way to the master of the house put no inconsiderable anxiety into these two women's lives. "That boy," as they alluded to him softly between themselves, had been a source of that sort of anxiety almost from the very day of his birth. The late licenced victualler's humiliation at having such a very peculiar boy for a son manifested itself by a propensity to brutal treatment; for he was a person of fine sensibilities, and his sufferings as a man and a father were perfectly genuine. Afterwards Stevie had to be kept from making himself a nuisance to the single gentlemen lodgers, who are themselves a queer lot, and are easily aggrieved. And there was always the anxiety of his mere existence to face. Visions of a workhouse infirmary for her child had haunted the old woman in the basement breakfast-room of the decayed Belgravian house. "If you had not found such a good husband, my dear," she used to say to her daughter, "I don't know what would have become of that poor boy."

Mr. Verloc extended as much recognition to Stevie as a man not particularly fond of animals may give to his wife's beloved cat; and this recognition, benevolent and perfunctory, was essentially of the same quality. Both women admitted to themselves that not much more could be reasonably expected. It was enough to earn for Mr. Verloc the old woman's reverential gratitude. In the early days, made sceptical by the trials of friendless life, she used sometimes to ask anxiously: "You don't think, my dear, that Mr. Verloc is getting tired of seeing Stevie about?" To this Winnie replied habitually by a slight toss of her head. Once, however, she retorted, with a rather grim pertness: "He'll have to get tired of me first." A long silence ensued. The mother, with her feet propped up on a stool, seemed to be trying to get to the bottom of that answer, whose feminine profundity had struck her all of a heap. She had never really understood why Winnie had married Mr. Verloc. It was very sensible of her, and evidently had turned out for the best, but her girl might have naturally hoped to find somebody of a more suitable age. There had been a steady young fellow, only son of a butcher in the next street, helping his father in business, with whom Winnie had been walking out with obvious gusto. He was dependent on his father, it is true; but the business was good, and his prospects excellent. He took her girl to the theatre on several evenings. Then just as she began to dread to hear of their engagement (for what could she have done with that big house alone, with Stevie on her hands?), that romance came to an abrupt end, and Winnie went about looking very dull. But Mr. Verloc, turning up providentially to occupy the first-floor front bed-room, there had been no more question of the young butcher. It was clearly providential.

CHAPTER THREE

". . . All idealization makes life poorer. To beautify it is to take away its character of complexity—it is to destroy it. Leave that to the moralists, my boy. History is made by men, but they do not make it in their heads. The ideas that are born in their consciousness play an insignificant part in the march of events. History is dominated and determined by the tool and the production—by the force of economic conditions. Capitalism has made socialism, and the laws made by capitalism for the protection of property are responsible for anarchism. No one can tell what form the social organization may take in the future. Then why indulge in prophetic phantasies? At best they can only interpret the mind of the prophet, and can have no objective value. Leave that pastime to the moralists, my boy."

Michaelis, the ticket-of-leave apostle, was speaking in an even voice, a voice that wheezed as if deadened and oppressed by the layer of fat on his chest. He had come out of a highly hygienic prison round like a tub, with an enormous stomach and distended cheeks of a pale, semi-transparent complexion, as though for fifteen years the servants of an outraged society had made a point of stuffing him with fattening foods in a damp and lightless cellar. And ever since he had never managed to get his weight down as much as an ounce.

It was said that for three seasons running a very wealthy old lady had sent him for a cure to Marienbad—where he was about to share the public curiosity once with a crowned head—but the police on that occasion ordered him to leave within twelve hours. His martyrdom was continued by forbidding him all access to the healing waters. But he was resigned now.

With his elbow presenting no appearance of a joint, but more like a bend in a dummy's limb, thrown over the back of a chair, he leaned forward slightly over his short and enormous thighs to spit into the grate.

"Yes! I had the time to think things out a little," he added without emphasis. "Society has given me plenty of time for meditation."

On the other side of the fireplace, in the horse-hair armchair where Mrs. Verloc's mother was generally privileged to sit, Karl Yundt giggled grimly, with a faint black grimace of a toothless mouth. The terrorist, as he called himself, was old and bald, with a narrow, snow-white wisp of a goatee hanging limply from his chin. An extraordinary expression of underhand malevolence survived in his extinguished eyes. When he rose painfully the thrusting forward of a skinny groping hand deformed by gouty swellings suggested the effort of a moribund murderer summoning all his remaining strength for a last stab. He leaned on a thick stick, which trembled under his other hand.

"I have always dreamed," he mouthed, fiercely, "of a band of men absolute in their resolve to discard all scruples in the choice of means, strong enough to give themselves frankly the name of destroyers, and free from the taint of that resigned pessimism which rots the world. No pity for anything on earth, including themselves, and death enlisted for good and all in the service of humanity—that's what I would have liked to see."

His little bald head quivered, imparting a comical vibration to the wisp of white goatee. His enunciation would have been almost totally unintelligible to a stranger. His worn-out passion, resembling in its impotent fierceness the excitement of a senile sensualist, was badly served by a dried throat and toothless gums which seemed to catch the tip of his tongue. Mr. Verloc, established in the corner of the sofa at the other end of the room, emitted two hearty grunts of assent.

The old terrorist turned slowly his head on his skinny neck from side to side.

"And I could never get as many as three such men together. So much for your rotten pessimism," he snarled at Michaelis, who uncrossed his thick legs similar to bolsters, and slid his feet abruptly under his chair in sign of exasperation.

He a pessimist! Preposterous! He cried out that the charge was outrageous. He was so far from pessimism that he saw already the end of all private property coming along logically, unavoidably, by the mere development of its inherent viciousness. The possessors of property had not only to face the awakened proletariat, but they had also to fight amongst themselves. Yes. Struggle, warfare, was the condition of private ownership. It was fatal. Ah! he did not depend upon emotional excitement to keep up his belief, no declamations, no anger, no visions of blood-red flags waving, or metaphorical lurid suns of vengeance rising above the horizon of a doomed society. Not he! Cold reason, he boasted, was the basis of his optimism. Yes, optimism——

His laborious wheezing stopped, then, after a gasp or two, he added:

"Don't you think that, if I had not been the optimist I am, I could have found in fifteen years some means to cut my throat? And, in the last instance, there were always the walls of my cell to dash my head against."

The shortness of breath took all fire, all animation out of his voice; his great, pale cheeks hung like filled pouches, motionless, without a quiver; but in his blue eyes, narrowed as if peering, there was the same look of confident shrewdness, a little crazy in its fixity, they must have had while the indomitable optimist sat thinking at night in his cell. Before him, Karl Yundt remained standing, one wing of his faded greenish havelock thrown back cavalierly over his shoulder. Seated in front of the fireplace, Comrade Ossipon, ex-medical student, the principal writer of the F. P. leaflets, stretched out his robust legs, keeping the soles of his boots turned up to the glow in the grate. A bush of crinkly yellow hair topped his red, freckled face, with a flattened nose and prominent mouth cast in the rough mould of the negro type. His almond-shaped eyes leered languidly over the high cheek-bones. He wore a grey flannel shirt, the loose ends of a black silk tie hung down the buttoned breast of his serge coat; and his head resting on the back of his chair, his throat largely exposed, he raised to his lips a cigarette in a long wooden tube, puffing jets of smoke straight up at the ceiling.

Michaelis pursued his idea—*the* idea of his solitary reclusion—the thought vouchsafed to his captivity and growing like a faith revealed in visions. He talked to himself, indifferent to the sympathy or hostility of his hearers, indifferent indeed to their presence, from the habit he had acquired of thinking aloud hopefully in the solitude of the four whitewashed walls of his cell, in the sepulchral silence of the great blind pile of bricks near a river, sinister and ugly like a colossal mortuary for the socially drowned.

He was no good in discussion, not because any amount of argument could shake his faith, but because the mere fact of hearing another voice disconcerted him painfully, confusing his thoughts at once— these thoughts that for so many years, in a mental solitude more barren than a waterless desert, no living voice had ever combatted, commented, or approved.

No one interrupted him now, and he made again the confession of his faith, mastering him irresistible and complete like an act of grace: the secret of fate discovered in the material side of life; the economic condition of the world responsible for the past and shaping the future; the source of all history, of all ideas, guiding the mental development of mankind and the very impulses of their passion——

A harsh laugh from Comrade Ossipon cut the tirade dead short in a sudden faltering of the tongue and a bewildered unsteadiness of the apostle's mildly exalted eyes. He closed them slowly for a moment, as if to collect his routed thoughts. A silence fell; but what with the two gas-jets over the table and the glowing grate the little parlour behind Mr. Verloc's shop had become frightfully hot. Mr. Verloc, getting off the sofa with ponderous reluctance, opened the door leading into the kitchen to get more air, and thus disclosed the innocent Stevie, seated very good and quiet at a deal table, drawing circles, circles, circles; innumerable circles, concentric, eccentric; a coruscating whirl of circles that by their tangled multitude of repeated curves, uniformity of form, and confusion of intersecting lines suggested a rendering of cosmic chaos, the symbolism of a mad art attempting the inconceivable. The artist never turned his head; and in all his soul's application to the task his back quivered, his thin neck, sunk into a deep hollow at the base of the skull, seemed ready to snap.

Mr. Verloc, after a grunt of disapproving surprise, returned to the sofa. Alexander Ossipon got up, tall in his threadbare blue serge suit under the low ceiling, shook off the stiffness of long immobility, and strolled away into the kitchen (down two steps) to look over Stevie's shoulder. He came back, pronouncing oracularly: "Very good. Very characteristic, perfectly typical."

"What's very good?" grunted, inquiringly, Mr. Verloc, settled again in the corner of the sofa. The other explained his meaning negligently, with a shade of condescension and a toss of his head towards the kitchen:

"Typical of this form of degeneracy—these drawings, I mean."

"You would call that lad a degenerate, would you?" mumbled Mr. Verloc.

Comrade Alexander Ossipon—nicknamed the Doctor, ex-medical student without a degree; afterwards wandering lecturer to working-men's associations upon the socialistic aspects of hygiene; author of a popular quasi-medical study (in the form of a cheap pamphlet seized promptly by the police) entitled "The Corroding Vices of the Middle Classes"; special delegate of the more or less mysterious Red Committee, together with Karl Yundt and Michaelis for the work of literary propaganda—turned upon the obscure familiar of at least two Embassies that glance of insufferable, hopelessly dense sufficiency which nothing but the frequentation of science can give to the dulness of common mortals.

"That's what he may be called scientifically. Very good type, too, altogether, of that sort of degenerate. It's enough to glance at the lobes of his ears. If you read Lombroso——"

Mr. Verloc, moody and spread largely on the sofa, continued to look down the row of his waistcoat buttons; but his cheeks became tinged by a faint blush. Of late even the merest derivative of the word science (a term in itself inoffensive and of indefinite meaning) had the curious power of evoking a definitely offensive mental vision of Mr. Vladimir, in his body as he lived, with an almost supernatural clearness. And this phenomenon, deserving justly to be classed amongst the marvels of science, induced in Mr. Verloc an emotional state of dread and exasperation tending to express itself in violent swearing. But he said nothing. It was Karl Yundt who was heard, implacable to his last breath.

"Lombroso is an ass."

Comrade Ossipon met the shock of this blasphemy by an awful, vacant stare. And the other, his extinguished eyes without gleams blackening the deep shadows under the great, bony forehead, mumbled, catching the tip of his tongue between his lips at every second word as though he were chewing it angrily:

"Did you ever see such an idiot? For him the criminal is the prisoner. Simple, is it not? What about those who shut him up there—forced him in there? Exactly. Forced him in there. And what is crime? Does he know that, this imbecile who has made his way in this world of gorged fools by looking at the ears and teeth of a lot of poor, luckless devils? Teeth and ears mark the criminal? Do they? And what about the law that marks him still better—the pretty branding instrument invented by the overfed to protect themselves against the hungry? Red-hot applications on their vile skins—hey? Can't you smell and hear from here the thick hide of the people burn and sizzle? That's how criminals are made for your Lombrosos to write their silly stuff about."

The knob of his stick and his legs shook together with passion, whilst the trunk, draped in the wings of the havelock, preserved his historic attitude of defiance. He seemed to sniff the tainted air of social cruelty, to strain his ear for its atrocious sounds. There was an extraordinary force of suggestion in this posturing. The all but moribund veteran of dynamite wars had been a great actor in his time—actor on platforms, in secret assemblies, in private interviews. The famous terrorist had never in his life raised personally as much as his little finger against the social edifice. He was no man of action; he was not even an orator of torrential eloquence, sweeping the masses along in the rushing noise and foam of a great enthusiasm. With a more subtle intention, he took the part of an insolent and venomous evoker of sinister impulses which lurk in the blind envy and exasperated vanity of ignorance, in the suffering and misery of poverty, in all the hopeful and noble illusions of righteous anger, pity, and revolt. The shadow of his evil gift clung to him yet like the smell of a deadly drug in an old vial of poison, emptied now, useless, ready to be thrown away upon the rubbish-heap of things that had served their time.

Michaelis, the ticket-of-leave apostle, smiled vaguely with his glued lips; his pasty moon face drooped under the weight of melancholy assent. He had been a prisoner himself. His own skin had sizzled under the red-hot brand, he murmured softly. But Comrade Ossipon, nicknamed the Doctor, had got over the shock by that time.

"You don't understand," he began, disdainfully, but stopped short, intimidated by the dead blackness of the cavernous eyes in the face turned slowly towards him with a blind stare, as if guided only by the sound. He gave the discussion up, with a slight shrug of the shoulders.

Stevie, accustomed to move about disregarded, had got up from the kitchen table, carrying off his drawing to bed with him. He had reached the parlour door in time to receive in full the shock of Karl Yundt's eloquent imagery. The sheet of paper covered with circles dropped out of his fingers, and he remained staring at the old terrorist, as if rooted suddenly to the spot by his morbid horror and dread of physical pain. Stevie knew very well that hot iron applied to one's skin hurt very much. His scared eyes blazed with indignation: it would hurt terribly. His mouth dropped open.

Michaelis by staring unwinkingly at the fire had regained that sentiment of isolation necessary for the continuity of his thought. His
optimism had begun to flow from his lips. He saw Capitalism doomed
in its cradle, born with the poison of the principle of competition in
its system. The great capitalists devouring the little capitalists, concen-
trating the power and the tools of production in great masses, perfecting industrial processes, and in the madness of self-aggrandizement
only preparing, organizing, enriching, making ready the lawful inheritance of the suffering proletariat. Michaelis pronounced the great
word "Patience"—and his clear blue glance, raised to the low ceiling
of Mr. Verloc's parlour, had a character of seraphic trustfulness. In
the doorway Stevie, calmed, seemed sunk in hebetude.

Comrade Ossipon's face twitched with exasperation.

"Then it's no use doing anything—no use whatever."

"I don't say that," protested Michaelis, gently. His vision of truth
had grown so intense that the sound of a strange voice failed to rout
it this time. He continued to look down at the red coals. Preparation
for the future was necessary, and he was willing to admit that the
great change would perhaps come in the upheaval of a revolution. But
he argued that revolutionary propaganda was a delicate work of high
conscience. It was the education of the masters of the world. It should
be as careful as the education given to kings. He would have it advance
its tenets cautiously, even timidly, in our ignorance of the effect that
may be produced by any given economic change upon the happiness,
the morals, the intellect, the history of mankind. For history is made
with tools, not with ideas; and everything is changed by economic
conditions—art, philosophy, love, virtue—truth itself!

The coals in the grate settled down with a slight crash; and Michaelis, the hermit of visions in the desert of a penitentiary, got up impetuously. Round like a distended balloon, he opened his short, thick arms,
as if in a pathetically hopeless attempt to embrace and hug to his
breast a self-regenerated universe. He gasped with ardour.

"The future is as certain as the past—slavery, feudalism, individual-
ism, collectivism. This is the statement of a law, not an empty
prophecy."

The disdainful pout of Comrade Ossipon's thick lips accentuated
the negro type of his face.

"Nonsense," he said, calmly enough. "There is no law and no certainty. The teaching propaganda be hanged. What the people knows
does not matter, were its knowledge ever so accurate. The only thing
that matters to us is the emotional state of the masses. Without emotion there is no action."

He paused, then added with modest firmness:

"I am speaking now to you scientifically—scientifically—— Eh? What did you say, Verloc?"

"Nothing," growled from the sofa Mr. Verloc, who, provoked by the abhorrent sound, had merely muttered a "Damn."

The venomous spluttering of the old terrorist without teeth was heard.

"Do you know how I would call the nature of the present economic conditions? I would call it cannibalistic. That's what it is! They are nourishing their greed on the quivering flesh and the warm blood of the people—nothing else."

Stevie swallowed the terrifying statement with an audible gulp, and at once, as though it had been swift poison, sank limply in a sitting posture on the steps of the kitchen door.

Michaelis gave no signs of having heard anything. His lips seemed glued together for good; not a quiver passed over his heavy cheeks. With troubled eyes he looked for his round, hard hat, and put it on his round head. His round and obese body seemed to float low between the chairs under the sharp elbow of Karl Yundt. The old terrorist, raising an uncertain and clawlike hand, gave a swaggering tilt to a black felt sombrero shading the hollows and ridges of his wasted face. He got in motion slowly, striking the floor with his stick at every step. It was rather an affair to get him out of the house because, now and then, he would stop, as if to think, and did not offer to move again till impelled forward by Michaelis. The gentle apostle grasped his arm with brotherly care; and behind them, his hands in his pockets, the robust Ossipon yawned vaguely. A blue cap with a patent leather peak set well at the back of his yellow bush of hair gave him the aspect of a Norwegian sailor bored with the world after a thundering spree. Mr. Verloc saw his guests off the premises, attending them bareheaded, his heavy overcoat hanging open, his eyes on the ground.

He closed the door behind their backs with restrained violence, turned the key, shot the bolt. He was not satisfied with his friends. In the light of Mr. Vladimir's philosophy of bomb throwing they appeared hopelessly futile. The part of Mr. Verloc in revolutionary politics having been to observe, he could not all at once, either in his own home or in larger assemblies, take the initiative of action. He had to be cautious. Moved by the just indignation of a man well over forty, menaced in what is dearest to him—his repose and his security—he asked himself scornfully what else could have been expected from such a lot, this Karl Yundt, this Michaelis—this Ossipon.

Pausing in his intention to turn off the gas burning in the middle of the shop, Mr. Verloc descended into the abyss of moral reflections. With the insight of a kindred temperament he pronounced his verdict. A lazy lot—this Karl Yundt, nursed by a blear-eyed old woman, a woman he had years ago enticed away from a friend, and afterwards had tried more than once to shake off into the gutter. Jolly lucky for Yundt that she had persisted in coming up time after time, or else there would have been no one now to help him out of the 'bus by the Green Park railings, where that spectre took its constitutional crawl every fine morning. When that indomitable snarling old witch died the swaggering spectre would have to vanish, too—there would be an end to fiery Karl Yundt. And Mr. Verloc's morality was offended also by the optimism of Michaelis, annexed by his wealthy old lady, who had taken lately to sending him to a cottage she had in the country. The ex-prisoner could moon about the shady lanes for days together in a delicious and humanitarian idleness. As to Ossipon, that beggar was sure to want for nothing as long as there were silly girls with savings-bank books in the world. And Mr. Verloc, temperamentally identical with his associates, drew fine distinctions in his mind on the strength of insignificant differences. He drew them with a certain complacency, because the instinct of conventional respectability was strong within him, being only overcome by his dislike of all kinds of recognized labour—a temperamental defect which he shared with a large proportion of revolutionary reformers of a given social state. For obviously one does not revolt against the advantages and opportunities of that state, but against the price which must be paid for the same in the coin of accepted morality, self-restraint, and toil. The majority of revolutionists are the enemies of discipline and fatigue mostly. There are natures, too, to whose sense of justice the price exacted looms up monstrously enormous, odious, oppressive, worrying, humiliating, extortionate, intolerable. Those are the fanatics. The remaining portion of social rebels is accounted for by vanity, the mother of all noble and vile illusions, the companion of poets, reformers, charlatans, prophets, and incendiaries.

Lost for a whole minute in the abyss of meditation, Mr. Verloc did not reach the depth of these abstract considerations. Perhaps he was not able. In any case he had not the time. He was pulled up painfully by the sudden recollection of Mr. Vladimir, another of his associates, whom in virtue of subtle moral affinities he was capable of judging correctly. He considered him as dangerous. A shade of envy crept into his thoughts. Loafing was all very well for these fellows, who knew not Mr. Vladimir, and had women to fall back upon; whereas he had a woman to provide for——

At this point, by a simple association of ideas, Mr. Verloc was brought face to face with the necessity of going to bed some time or other that evening. Then why not go now—at once? He sighed. The necessity was not so normally pleasurable as it ought to have been for a man of his age and temperament. He dreaded the demon of sleeplessness, which he felt had marked him for its own. He raised his arm, and turned off the flaring gas-jet above his head.

A bright band of light fell through the parlour door into the part of the shop behind the counter. It enabled Mr. Verloc to ascertain at a glance the number of silver coins in the till. These were but few; and for the first time since he opened his shop he took a commercial survey of its value. This survey was unfavourable. He had gone into trade for no commercial reasons. He had been guided in the selection of this peculiar line of business by an instinctive leaning towards shady transactions, where money is picked up easily. Moreover, it did not take him out of his own sphere—the sphere which is watched by the police. On the contrary, it gave him a publicly confessed standing in that sphere, and as Mr. Verloc had unconfessed relations which made him familiar with yet careless of the police, there was a distinct advantage in such a situation. But as a means of livelihood it was by itself insufficient.

He took the cash-box out of the drawer, and turning to leave the shop, became aware that Stevie was still downstairs.

What on earth is he doing there? Mr. Verloc asked himself. What's the meaning of these antics? He looked dubiously at his brother-in-law, but he did not ask him for information. Mr. Verloc's intercourse with Stevie was limited to the casual mutter of a morning, after breakfast, "My boots," and even that was more a communication at large of a need than a direct order or request. Mr. Verloc perceived with some surprise that he did not know really what to say to Stevie. He stood still in the middle of the parlour, and looked into the kitchen in silence. Nor yet did he know what would happen if he did say anything. And this appeared very queer to Mr. Verloc in view of the fact, borne upon him suddenly, that he had to provide for this fellow, too. He had never given a moment's thought till then to that aspect of Stevie's existence.

Positively he did not know how to speak to the lad. He watched him gesticulating and murmuring in the kitchen. Stevie prowled round the table like an excited animal in a cage. A tentative "Hadn't you better go to bed now?" produced no effect whatever; and Mr. Verloc, abandoning the stony contemplation of his brother-in-law's behaviour, crossed the parlour wearily, cash-box in hand. The cause of the general lassitude he felt while climbing the stairs being purely mental, he became alarmed by its inexplicable character. He hoped he was not sickening for anything. He stopped on the dark landing to examine his sensations. But a slight and continuous sound of snoring pervading the obscurity interfered with their clearness. The sound came from his mother-in-law's room. Another one to provide for, he thought—and on this thought walked into the bedroom.

Mrs. Verloc had fallen asleep with the lamp (no gas was laid up-stairs) turned up full on the table by the side of the bed. The light thrown down by the shade fell dazzlingly on the white pillow sunk by the weight of her head reposing with closed eyes and dark hair done up in several plaits for the night. She woke up with the sound of her name in her ears, and saw her husband standing over her.

"Winnie! Winnie!"

At first, she did not stir, lying very quiet and looking at the cash-box in Mr. Verloc's hand. But when she understood that her brother was "capering all over the place downstairs" she swung out in one sudden movement on to the edge of the bed. Her bare feet, as if poked through the bottom of an unadorned, sleeved calico sack buttoned tightly at neck and wrists, felt over the rug for the slippers while she looked upward into her husband's face.

"I don't know how to manage him," Mr. Verloc explained, peevishly. "Won't do to leave him downstairs alone with the lights."

She said nothing, glided across the room swiftly, and the door closed upon her white form.

Mr. Verloc deposited the cash-box on the night table, and began the operation of undressing by flinging his overcoat on to a distant chair. His coat and waistcoat followed. He walked about the room in his stockinged feet, and his burly figure, with the hands worrying nervously at his throat, passed and repassed across the long strip of looking-glass in the door of his wife's wardrobe. Then after slipping his braces off his shoulders he pulled up violently the venetian blind, and leaned his forehead against the cold window-pane—a fragile film of glass stretched between him and the enormity of cold, black, wet, muddy, inhospitable accumulation of bricks, slates, and stones, things in themselves unlovely and unfriendly to man.

Mr. Verloc felt the latent unfriendliness of all out of doors with a force approaching to positive bodily anguish. There is no occupation that fails a man more completely than that of a secret agent of police. It's like your horse suddenly falling dead under you in the midst of an uninhabited and thirsty plain. The comparison occurred to Mr. Verloc because he had sat astride various army horses in his time, and had now the sensation of an incipient fall. The prospect was as black as the window-pane against which he was leaning his forehead. And suddenly the face of Mr. Vladimir, clean-shaved and witty, appeared enhaloed in the glow of its rosy complexion like a sort of pink seal impressed on the fatal darkness.

This luminous and mutilated vision was so ghastly physically that Mr. Verloc started away from the window, letting down the venetian blind with a great rattle. Discomposed and speechless with the appre-hension of more such visions, he beheld his wife re-enter the room and get into bed in a calm, businesslike manner which made him feel hopelessly lonely in the world. Mrs. Verloc expressed her surprise at seeing him up yet.

"I don't feel very well," he muttered, passing his hands over his moist brow.

"Giddiness?"

"Yes. Not at all well."

Mrs. Verloc, with all the placidity of an experienced wife, expressed a confident opinion as to the cause, and suggested the usual remedies; but her husband, rooted in the middle of the room, shook his lowered head sadly.

"You'll catch cold standing there," she observed.

Mr. Verloc made an effort, finished undressing, and got into bed. Down below in the quiet, narrow street measured footsteps approached the house, then died away, unhurried and firm, as if the passer-by had started to pace out all eternity, from gas-lamp to gas-lamp in a night without end; and the drowsy ticking of the old clock on the landing became distinctly audible in the bedroom.

Mrs. Verloc, on her back, and staring at the ceiling, made a remark.

"Takings very small to-day."

Mr. Verloc, in the same position, cleared his throat as if for an important statement, but merely inquired:

"Did you turn off the gas downstairs?"

"Yes; I did," answered Mrs. Verloc, conscientiously. "That poor boy is in a very excited state to-night," she murmured, after a pause which lasted for three ticks of the clock.

Mr. Verloc cared nothing for Stevie's excitement, but he felt horribly wakeful, and dreaded facing the darkness and silence that would follow the extinguishing of the lamp. This dread led him to make the remark that Stevie had disregarded his suggestion to go to bed. Mrs. Verloc, falling into the trap, started to demonstrate at length to her husband that this was not "impudence" of any sort, but simply "excitement." There was no young man of his age in London more willing and docile than Stephen, she affirmed; none more affectionate and ready to please, and even useful, as long as people did not upset his poor head. Mrs. Verloc, turning towards her recumbent husband, raised herself on her elbow, and hung over him in her anxiety that he should believe Stevie to be a useful member of the family. That ardour of protecting compassion exalted morbidly in her childhood by the misery of another child tinged her sallow cheeks with a faint dusky blush, made her big eyes gleam under the dark lids. Mrs. Verloc then looked younger; she looked as young as Winnie used to look, and much more animated than the Winnie of the Belgravian mansion days had ever allowed herself to appear to gentlemen lodgers. Mr.

Verloc's anxieties had prevented him attaching any sense to what his wife was saying. It was as if her voice was talking on the other side of a very thick wall. It was her aspect that recalled him to himself.

He appreciated this woman, and the sentiment of this appreciation, stirred by a display of something resembling emotion, only added another pang to his mental anguish. When her voice ceased he moved uneasily, and said:

"I haven't been feeling well for the last few days."

He might have meant this as an opening to a complete confidence; but Mrs. Verloc laid her head on the pillow again, and staring upward, went on:

"That boy hears too much of what is talked about here. If I had known they were coming to-night I would have seen to it that he went to bed at the same time I did. He was out of his mind with something he overheard about eating people's flesh and drinking blood. What's the good of talking like that?"

There was a note of indignant scorn in her voice. Mr. Verloc was fully responsive now.

"Ask Karl Yundt," he growled, savagely.

Mrs. Verloc, with great decision, pronounced Karl Yundt "a disgusting old man." She declared openly her affection for Michaelis. Of the robust Ossipon, in whose presence she always felt uneasy behind an attitude of stony reserve, she said nothing whatever. And continuing to talk of that brother, who had been for so many years an object of care and fears:

"He isn't fit to hear what's said here. He believes it's all true. He knows no better. He gets into his passions over it."

Mr. Verloc made no comment.

"He glared at me, as if he didn't know who I was, when I went downstairs. His heart was going like a hammer. He can't help being excitable. I woke mother up, and asked her to sit with him till he went to sleep. It isn't his fault. He's no trouble when he's left alone."

Mr. Verloc made no comment.

"I wish he had never been to school," Mrs. Verloc began again, brusquely. "He's always taking away those newspapers from the window to read. He gets a red face poring over them. We don't get rid of a dozen numbers in a month. They only take up room in the front window. And Mr. Ossipon brings every week a pile of these F. P. tracts to sell at a halfpenny each. I wouldn't give a halfpenny for the whole lot. It's silly reading—that's what it is. There's no sale for it. The other day Stevie got hold of one, and there was a story in it of a German soldier officer tearing half-off the ear of a recruit, and nothing was done to him for it. The brute! I couldn't do anything with Stevie that afternoon. The story was enough, too, to make one's blood boil.

But what's the use of printing things like that? We aren't German slaves here, thank God. It's not our business—is it?"

Mr. Verloc made no reply.

"I had to take the carving knife from the boy," Mrs. Verloc continued, a little sleepily now. "He was shouting and stamping and sobbing. He can't stand the notion of any cruelty. He would have struck that officer like a pig if he had seen him then. It's true, too! Some people don't deserve much mercy." Mrs. Verloc's voice ceased, and the expression of her motionless eyes became more and more contemplative and veiled during the long pause. "Comfortable, dear?" she asked in a faint, far-away voice. "Shall I put out the light now?"

The dreary conviction that there was no sleep for him held Mr. Verloc mute and hopelessly inert in his fear of darkness. He made a great effort.

"Yes. Put it out," he said at last in a hollow tone.

CHAPTER FOUR

Most of the thirty or so little tables covered by red cloths with a white design stood ranged at right angles to the deep brown wainscoting of the underground hall. Bronze chandeliers with many globes depended from the low, slightly vaulted ceiling, and the fresco paintings ran flat and dull all round the walls without windows, representing scenes of the chase and of outdoor revelry in mediæval costumes. Varlets in green jerkins brandished hunting knives and raised on high tankards of foaming beer.

"Unless I am very much mistaken, you are the man who would know the inside of this confounded affair," said the robust Ossipon, leaning over, his elbows far out on the table and his feet tucked back completely under his chair. His eyes stared with wild eagerness.

An upright semi-grand piano near the door, flanked by two palms in pots, executed suddenly all by itself a valse tune with aggressive virtuosity. The din it raised was deafening. When it ceased, as abruptly as it had started, the bespectacled, dingy little man who faced Ossipon behind a heavy glass mug full of beer emitted calmly what had the sound of a general proposition.

"In principle what one of us may or may not know as to any given fact can't be a matter for inquiry to the others."

"Certainly not," Comrade Ossipon agreed in a quiet undertone. "In principle."

With his big florid face held between his hands he continued to stare hard, while the dingy little man in spectacles coolly took a drink of beer and stood the glass mug back on the table. His flat, large ears departed widely from the sides of his skull, which looked frail enough for Ossipon to crush between thunb and forefinger; the dome of the forehead seemed to rest on the rim of the spectacles; the flat cheeks, of a greasy, unhealthy complexion, were merely smudged by the miserable poverty of a thin dark whisker. The lamentable inferiority of the whole physique was made ludicrous by the supremely self-confident bearing of the individual. His speech was curt, and he had a particularly impressive manner of keeping silent.

Ossipon spoke again from between his hands in a mutter.

"Have you been out much to-day?"

"No. I stayed in bed all the morning," answered the other. "Why?"

"Oh! Nothing," said Ossipon, gazing earnestly and quivering inwardly with the desire to find out something, but obviously intimidated by the little man's overwhelming air of unconcern. When talking with this comrade—which happened but rarely—the big Ossipon suffered from a sense of moral and even physical insignificance. However, he ventured another question. "Did you walk down here?"

"No; omnibus," the little man answered, readily enough. He lived far away in Islington, in a small house down a shabby street, littered with straw and dirty paper, where out of school hours a troop of assorted children ran and squabbled with a shrill, joyless, rowdy clamour. His single back room, remarkable for having an extremely large cupboard, he rented furnished from two elderly spinsters, dressmakers in a humble way with a clientele of servant girls mostly. He had a heavy padlock put on the cupboard, but otherwise he was a model lodger, giving no trouble, and requiring practically no attendance. His oddities were that he insisted on being present when his room was being swept, and that when he went out he locked his door, and took the key away with him.

Ossipon had a vision of these round black-rimmed spectacles progressing along the streets on the top of an omnibus, their self-confident glitter falling here and there on the walls of houses or lowered upon the heads of the unconscious stream of people on the pavements. The ghost of a sickly smile altered the set of Ossipon's thick lips at the thought of the walls nodding, of people running for life at the sight of those spectacles. If they had only known! What a panic! He murmured interrogatively: "Been sitting long here?"

"An hour or more," answered the other, negligently, and took a pull at the dark beer. All his movements—the way he grasped the mug, the act of drinking, the way he set the heavy glass down and folded his arms—had a firmness, an assured precision which made the big and muscular Ossipon, leaning forward with staring eyes and protruding lips, look the picture of eager indecision.

"An hour," he said. "Then it may be you haven't heard yet the news I've heard just now—in the street. Have you?"

The little man shook his head negatively the least bit. But as he gave no indication of curiosity Ossipon ventured to add that he had heard it just outside the place. A newspaper boy had yelled the thing under his very nose, and not being prepared for anything of that sort, he was very much startled and upset. He had to come in there with a dry mouth. "I never thought of finding you here," he added, murmuring steadily, with his elbows planted on the table.

"I come here sometimes," said the other, preserving his provoking coolness of demeanour.

"It's wonderful that you of all people should have heard nothing of it," the big Ossipon continued. His eyelids snapped nervously upon the shining eyes. "You of all people," he repeated, tentatively. This obvious restraint argued an incredible and inexplicable timidity of the big fellow before the calm little man, who again lifted the glass mug, drank, and put it down with brusque and assured movements. And that was all.

Ossipon, after waiting for something, word or sign, that did not come, made an effort to assume a sort of indifference.

"Do you," he said, deadening his voice still more, "give your stuff to anybody who's up to asking you for it?"

My absolute rule is never to refuse anybody—as long as I have a pinch by me," answered the little man with decision.

"That's a principle?" commented Ossipon.

"It's a principle."

"And you think it's sound?"

The large round spectacles, which gave a look of staring self-confidence to the sallow face, confronted Ossipon like sleepless, unwinking orbs flashing a cold fire.

"Perfectly. Always. Under every circumstance. What could stop me? Why should I not? Why should I think twice about it?"

Ossipon gasped, as it were, discreetly.

"Do you mean to say you would hand it over to a 'tec' if one came to ask you for your wares?"

The other smiled faintly.

"Let them come and try it on, and you will see," he said. "They know me, but I know also every one of them. They won't come near me—not they."

His thin, livid lips snapped together firmly. Ossipon began to argue.

"But they could send someone—rig a plant on you. Don't you see? Get the stuff from you in that way, and then arrest you with the proof in their hands."

"Proof of what? Dealing in explosives without a licence perhaps."

This was meant for a contemptuous jeer, though the expression of the thin, sickly face remained unchanged, and the utterance was negligent. "I don't think there's one of them anxious to make that arrest. I don't think they could get one of them to apply for a warrant. I mean one of the best. Not one."

"Why?" Ossipon asked.

"Because they know very well I take care never to part with the last handful of my wares. I've it always by me." He touched the breast of his coat lightly. "In a thick glass flask," he added.

"So I have been told," said Ossipon, with a shade of wonder in his voice. "But I didn't know if—"

"They know," interrupted the little man, crisply, leaning against the straight chair back, which rose higher than his fragile head. "I shall never be arrested. The game isn't good enough for any policeman of them all. To deal with a man like me you require sheer, naked, inglorious heroism."

Again his lips closed with a self-confident snap. Ossipon repressed a movement of impatience.

"Or recklessness—or simply ignorance," he retorted. "They've only to get somebody for the job who does not know you carry enough stuff in your pocket to blow yourself and everything within sixty yards of you to pieces."

"I never affirmed I could not be eliminated," rejoined the other. "But that wouldn't be an arrest. Moreover, it's not so easy as it looks."

"Bah!" Ossipon contradicted. "Don't be too sure of that. What's to prevent half-a-dozen of them jumping upon you from behind in the street? With your arms pinned to your sides you could do nothing —could you?"

"Yes; I could. I am seldom out in the streets after dark," said the little man, impassively, "and never very late. I walk always with my left hand closed round the india-rubber ball which I have in my trouser pocket. The pressing of this ball actuates a detonator inside the flask I carry in my pocket. It's the principle of the pneumatic instantaneous shutter for a camera lens. The tube leads up——"

With a swift, disclosing gesture he gave Ossipon a glimpse of an india-rubber tube, resembling a slender brown worm, issuing from the armhole of his waistcoat and plunging into the inner breast pocket of his jacket. His clothes, of a nondescript brown mixture, were threadbare and marked with stains, dusty in the folds, with ragged buttonholes. "The detonator is partly mechanical, partly chemical," he explained, with casual condescension.

"It is instantaneous, of course?" murmured Ossipon, with a slight shudder.

"Far from it," confessed the other, with a reluctance which seemed to twist his mouth dolorously. "A full twenty seconds must elapse from the moment I press the ball till the explosion takes place."

"Phew!" whistled Ossipon, completely appalled. "Twenty seconds! Horrors! You mean to say that you could face that? I should go crazy——"

"Wouldn't matter if you did. Of course, it's the weak point of this special system, which is only for my own use. The worst is that the manner of exploding is always the weak point with us. I am trying to invent a detonator that would adjust itself to all conditions of action, and even to unexpected changes of conditions. A variable and yet perfectly precise mechanism. A really intelligent detonator."

"Twenty seconds," muttered Ossipon again. "Ough! And then——"

With a slight turn of the head the glitter of the spectacles seemed to gauge the size of the beer saloon in the basement of the renowned Silenus Restaurant.

"Nobody in this room could hope to escape," was the verdict of that survey. "Nor yet this couple going up the stairs now."

The piano at the foot of the staircase clanged through a mazurka with brazen impetuosity, as though a vulgar and impudent ghost were showing off. The keys sank and rose mysteriously. Then all became still. For a moment Ossipon imagined the overlighted place changed into a dreadful black hole belching horrible fumes choked with ghastly rubbish of smashed brickwork and mutilated corpses. He had such a distinct perception of ruin and death that he shuddered again. The other observed, with an air of calm sufficiency:

"In the last instance it is character alone that makes for one's safety. There are very few people in the world whose character is as well established as mine."

"I wonder how you managed it," growled Ossipon.

"Force of personality," said the other, without raising his voice; and coming from the mouth of that obviously miserable organism the assertion caused the robust Ossipon to bite his lower lip. "Force of personality," he repeated, with ostentatious calm.

"I have the means to make myself deadly, but that by itself, you understand, is absolutely nothing in the way of protection. What is effective is the belief those people have in my will to use the means. That's their impression. It is absolute. Therefore I am deadly."

"There are individuals of character amongst that lot, too," muttered Ossipon ominously.

"Possibly. But it is a matter of degree obviously, since, for instance, I am not impressed by them. Therefore they are inferior. They cannot be otherwise. Their character is built upon conventional morality. It leans on the social order. Mine stands free from everything artificial. They are bound in all sorts of conventions. They depend on life, which, in this connection, is a historical fact surrounded by all sorts of restraints and considerations, a complex, organized fact open to attack at every point; whereas I depend on death, which knows no restraint and cannot be attacked. My superiority is evident."

"This is a transcendental way of putting it," said Ossipon, watching the cold glitter of the round spectacles. "I've heard Karl Yundt say much the same thing not very long ago."

"Karl Yundt," mumbled the other, contemptuously, "the delegate of the International Red Committee, has been a posturing shadow all his life. There are three of you delegates aren't there? I won't define the other two, as you are one of them. But what you say means nothing. You are the worthy delegates for revolutionary propaganda, but the trouble is not only that you are as unable to think independently as any respectable grocer or journalist of them all, but that you have no character whatever."

Ossipon could not restrain a start of indignation.

"But what do you want from us?" he exclaimed in a deadened voice. "What is it you are after yourself?"

"A perfect detonator," was the peremptory answer. "What are you making that face for? You see, you can't even bear the mention of something conclusive."

"I am not making a face," growled the annoyed Ossipon bearishly.

"You revolutionists," the other continued, with leisurely self-confidence, "are the slaves of the social convention, which is afraid of you; slaves of it as much as the very police that stands up in the defence of that convention. Clearly you are, since you want to revolutionize it. It governs your thought, of course, and your action, too, and thus neither your thought nor your action can ever be conclusive." He paused, tranquil, with that air of close, endless silence, then almost immediately went on: "You are not a bit better than the forces arrayed against you—than the police, for instance. The other day I came suddenly upon Chief Inspector Heat at the corner of Tottenham Court Road. He looked at me very steadily. But I did not look at him. Why should I give him more than a glance? He was thinking of many things—of his superiors, of his reputation, of the law courts, of his salary, of newspapers—of a hundred things. But I was thinking of my perfect detonator only. He meant nothing to me. He was as insignificant as—I can't call to mind anything insignificant enough to compare him with—except Karl Yundt perhaps. Like to like. The terrorist and the policeman both come from the same basket. Revolution, legality—counter moves in the same game; forms of idleness at bottom identical. He plays his little game—so do you propagandists. But I don't play; I work fourteen hours a day, and go hungry sometimes. My experiments cost money now and again, and then I must do without food for a day or two. You're looking at my beer. Yes. I have had two glasses already, and shall have another presently. This is a little holiday, and I celebrate it alone. Why not? I've the grit to work alone, quite alone, absolutely alone. I've worked alone for years."

Ossipon's face had turned dusky red.

"At the perfect detonator—eh?" he sneered, very low.

"Yes," retorted the other. "It is a good definition. You couldn't find anything half so precise to define the nature of your activity with all your committees and delegations. It is I who am the true propagandist."

"We won't discuss that point," said Ossipon, with an air of rising above personal considerations. "I am afraid I'll have to spoil your holiday for you, though. There's a man blown up in Greenwich Park this morning."

"How do you know?"

"They have been yelling the news in the streets since two o'clock. I bought the paper, and just ran in here. Then I saw you sitting at this table. I've got it in my pocket now."

He pulled the newspaper out. It was a good-sized, rosy sheet, as if flushed by the warmth of its own convictions, which were optimistic. He scanned the pages rapidly.

"Ah! Here it is. Bomb in Greenwich Park. There isn't much so far. Half-past eleven. Foggy morning. Effects of explosion felt as far as Romney Road and Park Place. Enormous hole in the ground under a tree filled with smashed roots and broken branches. All round fragments of a man's body blown to pieces. That's all. The rest's mere newspaper gup. No doubt a wicked attempt to blow up the Observatory, they say. H'm. That's hardly credible."

He looked at the paper for a while longer in silence then passed it to the other, who after gazing abstractedly at the print laid it down without comment.

It was Ossipon who spoke first—still resentful.

"The fragments of only *one* man, you note. Ergo: blew *himself* up. That spoils your day off for you—don't it? Were you expecting that sort of move? I hadn't the slightest idea—not the ghost of a notion of anything of the sort being planned to come off here—in this country. Under the present circumstances it's nothing short of criminal."

The little man lifted his thin black eyebrows with dispassionate scorn.

"Criminal! What is that? What *is* crime? What can be the meaning of such an assertion?"

"How am I to express myself? One must use the current words," said Ossipon, impatiently. "The meaning of this assertion is that this business may affect our position very adversely in this country. Isn't that crime enough for you? I am convinced you have been giving away some of your stuff lately."

Ossipon stared hard. The other, without flinching, lowered and raised his head slowly.

"You have!" burst out the editor of the F. P. leaflets in an intense whisper. "No! And are you really handing it over at large like this, for the asking, to the first fool that comes along?"

"Just so! The condemned social order has not been built up on paper and ink, and I don't fancy that a combination of paper and ink will ever put an end to it, whatever you may think. Yes, I would give the stuff with both hands to every man, woman, or fool that likes to come along. I know what you are thinking about. But I am not taking my cue from the Red Committee. I would see you all hounded out of here, or arrested—or beheaded for that matter—without turning a hair. What happens to us as individuals is not of the least consequence."

He spoke carelessly, without heat, almost without feeling, and Ossipon, secretly much affected, tried to copy this detachment.

"If the police here knew their business they would shoot you full of holes with revolvers, or else try to sandbag you from behind in broad daylight."

The little man seemed already to have considered that point of view in his dispassionate, self-confident manner.

"Yes," he assented with the utmost readiness. "But for that they would have to face their own institutions. Do you see? That requires uncommon grit. Grit of a special kind."

Ossipon blinked.

"I fancy that's exactly what would happen to you if you were to set up your laboratory in the States. They don't stand on ceremony with their institutions there."

"I am not likely to go and see. Otherwise your remark is just," admitted the other. "They have more character over there, and their character is essentially anarchistic. Fertile ground for us, the States— very good ground. The great Republic has the root of the destructive matter in her. The collective temperament is lawless. Excellent. They may shoot us down, but——"

"You are too transcendental for me," growled Ossipon, with moody concern.

"Logical," protested the other. "There are several kinds of logic. This is the enlightened kind. America is all right. It is this country that is dangerous, with her idealistic conception of legality. The social spirit of this people is wrapped up in scrupulous prejudices, and that is fatal to our work. You talk of England being our only refuge! So much the worse. Capua! What do we want with refuges? Here you talk, print, plot, and do nothing. I daresay it's very convenient for such Karl Yundts."

He shrugged his shoulders slightly, then added with the same leisurely assurance: "To break up the superstition and worship of legality should be our aim. Nothing would please me more than to see Inspector Heat and his likes take to shooting us down in broad daylight with the approval of the public. Half our battle would be won then; the disintegration of the old morality would have set in in its very temple. That is what you ought to aim at. But you revolutionists will never understand that. You plan the future, you lose yourselves in reveries of economical systems derived from what is; whereas what's wanted is a clean sweep and a clear start for a new conception of life. That sort of future will take care of itself if you will only make room for it. Therefore I would shovel my stuff in heaps at the corners of the streets if I had enough for that; and as I haven't, I do my best by perfecting a really dependable detonator."

Ossipon, who had been mentally swimming in deep waters, seized upon the last word as if it were a saving plank.

"Yes. Your detonators. I shouldn't wonder if it weren't one of your detonators that made a clean sweep of the man in the park."

A shade of vexation darkened the determined, sallow face confronting Ossipon.

"My difficulty consists precisely in experimenting practically with the various kinds. They must be tried, after all. Besides——"

Ossipon interrupted.

"Who could that fellow be? I assure you that we in London had no knowledge—— Couldn't you describe the person you gave the stuff to?"

The other turned his spectacles upon Ossipon like a pair of searchlights.

"Describe him," he repeated, slowly. "I don't think there can be the slightest objection now. I will describe him to you in one word—Verloc."

Ossipon, whom curiosity had lifted a few inches off his seat, dropped back, as if hit in the face.

"Verloc! Impossible."

The self-possessed little man nodded slightly once.

"Yes. He's the person. You can't say that in this case I was giving my stuff to the first fool that came along. He was a prominent member of the group as far as I understand."

"Yes," said Ossipon. "Prominent. No, not exactly. He was the centre for general intelligence, and usually received comrades coming over here. More useful than important. Man of no ideas. Years ago he used to speak at meetings—in France, I believe. Not very well, though. He was trusted by such men as Latorre, Moser, and all that old lot. The only talent he showed really was his ability to elude the attentions of the police somehow. Here, for instance, he did not seem to be looked after very closely. He was regularly married, you know. I suppose it's with her money that he started that shop. Seemed to make it pay, too."

Ossipon paused abruptly, muttered to himself "I wonder what that woman will do now?" and fell into thought.

The other waited with ostentatious indifference. His parentage was obscure, and he was generally known only by his nickname of Professor. His title to that designation consisted in his having been once assistant demonstrator in chemistry at some technical institute. He quarrelled with the authorities upon a question of unfair treatment. Afterwards he obtained a post in the laboratory of a manufactory of dyes. There, too, he had been treated with revolting injustice. His struggles, his privations, his hard work to raise himself in the social scale, had filled him with such an exalted conviction of his merits that it was extremely difficult for the world to treat him with justice—the standard of that notion depending so much upon the patience of the individual. The Professor had genius, but lacked the great social virtue of resignation.

"Intellectually a nonentity," Ossipon pronounced aloud, abandoning suddenly the inward contemplation of Mrs. Verloc's bereaved person and business. "Quite an ordinary personality. You are wrong in not keeping more in touch with the comrades, Professor," he added in a reproving tone. "Did he say anything to you—give you some idea of his intentions? I hadn't seen him for a month. It seems impossible that he should be gone."

"He told me it was going to be a demonstration against a building," said the Professor. "I had to know that much to prepare the missile. I pointed out to him that I had hardly a sufficient quantity for a completely destructive result, but he pressed me very earnestly to do my best. As he wanted something that could be carried openly in the hand, I proposed to make use of an old one-gallon copal varnish can I happened to have by me. He was pleased at the idea. It gave me some trouble, because I had to cut out the bottom first and solder it on again afterwards. When prepared for use, the can enclosed a wide-mouthed, well-corked jar of thick glass packed around with some wet clay and containing sixteen ounces of $X2$ green powder. The detonator was connected with the screw top of the can. It was ingenious—a combination of time and shock. I explained the system to him. It was a thin tube of tin enclosing a——"

Ossipon's attention had wandered.

"What do you think has happened?" he interrupted.

"Can't tell. Screwed the top on tight, which would make the connection, and then forgot the time. It was set for twenty minutes. On the other hand, the time contact being made, a sharp shock would bring about the explosion at once. He either ran the time too close, or simply let the thing fall. The contact was made all right—that's clear to me at any rate. The system's worked perfectly. And yet you would think that a common fool in a hurry would be much more likely to forget to make the contact altogether. I was worrying myself about that sort of failure mostly. But there are more kinds of fools than one can guard against. You can't expect a detonator to be absolutely foolproof."

He beckoned to a waiter. Ossipon sat rigid, with the abstracted gaze of mental travail. After the man had gone away with the money he roused himself, with an air of profound dissatisfaction.

"It's extremely unpleasant for me," he mused. "Karl has been in bed with bronchitis for a week. There's an even chance that he will never get up again. Michaelis is luxuriating in the country somewhere. A fashionable publisher has offered him five hundred pounds for a book. It will be a ghastly failure. He has lost the habit of consecutive thinking in prison, you know."

The Professor on his feet, now buttoning his coat, looked about him with perfect indifference.

"What are you going to do?" asked Ossipon, wearily. He dreaded the blame of the Central Red Committee, a body which had no permanent place of abode, and of whose membership he was not exactly informed. If this affair eventuated in the stoppage of the modest subsidy allotted to the publication of the F. P. pamphlets, then indeed he would have to regret Verloc's inexplicable folly.

"Solidarity with the extremest form of action is one thing, and silly recklessness is another," he said, with a sort of moody brutality. "I don't know what came to Verloc. There's some mystery there. However, he's gone. You may take it as you like, but under the circumstances the only policy for the militant revolutionary group is to disclaim all connection with this damned freak of yours. How to make the disclaimer convincing enough is what bothers me."

The little man on his feet, buttoned up and ready to go, was no taller than the seated Ossipon. He levelled his spectacles at the latter's face point-blank.

"You might ask the police for a testimonial of good conduct. They know where every one of you slept last night. Perhaps if you asked them they would consent to publish some sort of official statement."

"No doubt they are aware well enough that we had nothing to do with this," mumbled Ossipon, bitterly. "What they will say is another thing." He remained thoughtful, disregarding the short, owlish, shabby figure standing by his side. "I must lay hands on Michaelis at once, and get him to speak from his heart at one of our gatherings. The public has a sort of sentimental regard for that fellow. His name is known. And I am in touch with a few reporters on the big dailies. What he would say would be utter bosh, but he has a turn of talk that makes it go down all the same."

"Like treacle," interjected the Professor, rather low, keeping an impassive expression.

The perplexed Ossipon went on communing with himself half audibly, after the manner of a man reflecting in perfect solitude.

"Confounded ass! To leave such an imbecile business on my hands. And I dón't even know if——"

He sat with compressed lips. The idea of going for news straight to the shop lacked charm. His notion was that Verloc's shop might have been turned already into a police trap. They will be bound to make some arrests, he thought, with something resembling virtuous indignation, for the even tenor of his revolutionary life was menaced by no fault of his. And yet unless he went there he ran the risk of remaining in ignorance of what perhaps it would be very material for him to know. Then he reflected that, if the man in the park had been so very much blown to pieces as the evening papers said, he could not have been identified. And if so, the police could have no special reason for watching Verloc's shop more closely than any other place known to be frequented by marked anarchists—no more reason, in fact, than for watching the doors of the Silenus. There would be a lot of watching all round, no matter where he went. Still——

"I wonder what I had better do now?" he muttered, taking counsel with himself.

A rasping voice at his elbow said, with sedate scorn:

"Fasten yourself upon the woman for all she's worth."

After uttering these words the Professor walked away from the table. Ossipon, whom that piece of insight had taken unawares, gave one ineffectual start, and remained still, with a helpless gaze, as though nailed fast to the seat of his chair. The lonely piano, without as much as a music stool to help it, struck a few cords courageously, and beginning a selection of national airs, played him out at last to the tune of "The Bluebells of Scotland." The painfully detached notes grew faint behind his back while he went slowly upstairs, across the hall, and into the street.

In front of the great doorway a dismal row of newspaper sellers standing clear of the pavement dealt out their wares from the gutter. It was a raw, gloomy day of the early spring; and the grimy sky, the mud of the streets, the rags of the dirty men harmonized excellently with the eruption of the damp, rubbishy sheets of paper soiled with printers' ink. The posters, maculated with filth, garnished like tapestry the sweep of the curbstone. The trade in afternoon papers was brisk, yet, in comparison with the swift, constant march of foot traffic, the effect was of indifference, of a disregarded distribution. Ossipon looked hurriedly both ways before stepping out into the cross-currents, but the Professor was already out of sight.

CHAPTER FIVE

The Professor had turned into a street to the left, and walked along, with his head carried rigidly erect, in a crowd whose every individual almost overtopped his stunted stature. It was vain to pretend to himself that he was not disappointed. But that was mere feeling; the stoicism of his thought could not be disturbed by this or any other failure. Next time, or the time after next, a telling stroke would be delivered—something really startling—a blow fit to open the first crack in the imposing front of the great edifice of legal conceptions sheltering the atrocious injustice of society. Of humble origin, and with an appearance really so mean as to stand in the way of his considerable natural abilities, his imagination had been fired early by the tales of men rising from the depths of poverty to positions of authority and affluence. The extreme, almost ascetic purity of his thought, combined with an astounding ignorance of worldly conditions, had set before him a goal of power and prestige to be attained without the medium of arts, graces, tact, wealth—by sheer weight of merit alone. On that view he considered himself entitled to undisputed success. His father, a delicate dark enthusiast with a sloping forehead, had been an itinerant and rousing preacher of some obscure but rigid Christian sect— a man supremely confident in the privileges of his righteousness. In the son, individualist by temperament, once the science of colleges had replaced thoroughly the faith of conventicles, this moral attitude translated itself into a frenzied puritanism of ambition. He nursed it as something secularly holy. To see it thwarted opened his eyes to the true nature of the world, whose morality was artificial, corrupt, and blasphemous. The way of even the most justifiable revolutions is prepared by personal impulses disguised into creeds. The Professor's indignation found in itself a final cause that absolved him from the sin of turning to destruction as the agent of his ambition. To destroy public faith in legality was the imperfect formula of his pedantic fanaticism; but the subconscious conviction that the framework of an established social order cannot be effectually shattered except by some form of collective or individual violence was precise and correct. He was a moral agent—that was settled in his mind. By exercising his agency with ruthless defiance he procured for himself the appearances of power and personal prestige. That was undeniable to his vengeful bitterness. It pacified its unrest; and in their own way the most ardent of revolutionaries are perhaps doing no more but seeking for peace in common with the rest of mankind—the peace of soothed vanity, of satisfied appetites, or perhaps of appeased conscience.

Lost in the crowd, miserable and undersized, he meditated confidently on his power, keeping his hand in the left pocket of his trousers, grasping lightly the india-rubber ball, the supreme guarantee of his sinister freedom; but after a while he became disagreeably affected by the sight of the roadway thronged with vehicles and of the pavement crowded with men and women. He was in a long, straight street, peopled by a mere fraction of an immense multitude; but all round him, on and on, even to the limits of the horizon hidden by the enormous piles of bricks, he felt the mass of mankind mighty in its numbers. They swarmed numerous like locusts, industrious like ants, thoughtless like a natural force, pushing on blind and orderly and absorbed, impervious to sentiment, to logic, to terror, too, perhaps.

That was the form of doubt he feared most. Impervious to fear! Often while walking abroad, when he happened also to come out of himself, he had such moments of dreadful and sane mistrust of mankind. What if nothing could move them? Such moments come to all men whose ambition aims at a direct grasp upon humanity—to artists, politicians, thinkers, reformers, or saints. A despicable emotional state this, against which solitude fortifies a superior character; and with severe exultation the Professor thought of the refuge of his room, with its padlocked cupboard, lost in a wilderness of poor houses, the hermitage of the perfect anarchist. In order to reach sooner the point where he could take his omnibus, he turned brusquely out of the populous street into a narrow and dusky alley paved with flagstones. On one side the low brick houses had in their dusty windows the sightless, moribund look of incurable decay—empty shells awaiting demolition. From the other side life had not departed wholly as yet. Facing the only gas-lamp yawned the cavern of a second-hand furniture dealer, where, deep in the gloom of a sort of narrow avenue winding through a bizarre forest of wardrobes, with an undergrowth tangle of table legs, a tall pier-glass glimmered like a pool of water in a wood. An unhappy, homeless couch, accompanied by two unrelated chairs, stood in the open. The only human being making use of the alley besides the Professor, coming stalwart and erect from the opposite direction, checked his swinging pace suddenly.

"Hallo!" he said, and stood a little on one side watchfully.

The Professor had already stopped, with a ready half turn which brought his shoulders very near the other wall. His right hand fell lightly on the back of the outcast couch, the left remained purpose-fully plunged deep in the trousers pocket, and the roundness of the heavy rimmed spectacles imparted an owlish character to his moody, unperturbed face.

It was like a meeting in a side corridor of a mansion full of life. The stalwart man was buttoned up in a dark overcoat, and carried an umbrella. His hat, tilted back, uncovered a good deal of forehead, which appeared very white in the dusk. In the dark patches of the orbits the eyeballs glimmered piercingly. Long, drooping moustaches, the colour of ripe corn, framed with their points the square block of his shaved chin.

"I am not looking for you," he said, curtly.

The Professor did not stir an inch. The blended noises of the enormous town sank down to an inarticulate low murmur. Chief Inspector Heat of the Special Crime Department changed his tone.

"Not in a hurry to get home?" he asked, with mocking simplicity.

The unwholesome-looking little moral agent of destruction exulted silently in the possession of personal prestige, keeping in check this man armed with the defensive mandate of a menaced society. More fortunate than Caligula, who wished that the Roman Senate had only one head for the better satisfaction of his cruel lust, he beheld in that one man all the forces he had set at defiance: the force of law, property, oppression, and injustice. He beheld all his enemies and fear-lessly confronted them all in a supreme satisfaction of his vanity. They stood perplexed before him as if before a dreadful portent. He gloated inwardly over the chance of this meeting affirming his superiority over all the multitude of mankind.

It was in reality a chance meeting. Chief Inspector Heat had had a disagreeably busy day since his department received the first telegram from Greenwich a little before eleven in the morning. First of all, the fact of the outrage being attempted less than a week after he had assured a high official that no outbreak of anarchist activity was to be apprehended was sufficiently annoying. If he ever thought himself safe in making a statement, it was then. He had made that statement with infinite satisfaction to himself, because it was clear that the high official desired greatly to hear that very thing. He had affirmed that nothing of the sort could even be thought of without the department being aware of it within twenty-four hours; and he had spoken thus in his consciousness of being the great expert of his department. He had gone even so far as to utter words which true wisdom would have kept back. But Chief Inspector Heat was not very wise—at least not truly so. True wisdom, which is not certain of anything in this world of contradictions, would have prevented him from attaining his present position. It would have alarmed his superiors, and done away with his chances of promotion. His promotion had been very rapid.

"There isn't one of them, sir, that we couldn't lay our hands on at any time of night and day. We know what each of them is doing hour by hour," he had declared. And the high official had deigned to smile. This was so obviously the right thing to say for an officer of Chief Inspector Heat's reputation that it was perfectly delightful. The high official believed the declaration, which chimed in with his idea of the fitness of things. His wisdom was of an official kind, or else he might have reflected upon a matter not of theory but of experience that in the close-woven stuff of relations between conspirator and police there occur unexpected solutions of continuity, sudden holes in space and time. A given anarchist may be watched inch by inch and minute by minute, but a moment always comes when somehow all sight and touch of him are lost for a few hours, during which something (generally an explosion) more or less deplorable does happen. But the high official, carried away by his sense of the fitness of things, had smiled, and now the recollection of that smile was very annoying to Chief Inspector Heat, principal expert in anarchist procedure.

This was not the only circumstance whose recollection depressed the usual serenity of the eminent specialist. There was another dating back only to that very morning. The thought that when called urgently to his Assistant Commissioner's private room he had been unable to conceal his astonishment was distinctly vexing. His instinct of a successful man had taught him long ago that, as a general rule, a reputation is built on manner as much as on achievement. And he felt that his manner when confronted with the telegram had not been impressive. He had opened his eyes widely, and had exclaimed "Impossible!" exposing himself thereby to the unanswerable retort of a finger-tip laid forcibly on the telegram which the Assistant Commissioner, after reading it aloud, had flung on the desk. To be crushed, as it were, under the tip of a forefinger was an unpleasant experience. Very damaging, too! Furthermore, Chief Inspector Heat was conscious of not having mended matters by allowing himself to express a conviction.

"One thing I can tell you at once: none of our lot had anything to do with this."

He was strong in his integrity of a good detective, but he saw now that an impenetrably attentive reserve towards this incident would have served his reputation better. On the other hand, he admitted to himself that it was difficult to preserve one's reputation if rank outsiders were going to take a hand in the business. Outsiders are the bane of the police as of other professions. The tone of the Assistant

Commissioner's remarks had been sour enough to set one's teeth on edge.

And since breakfast Chief Inspector Heat had not managed to get anything to eat.

Starting immediately to begin his investigation on the spot, he had swallowed a good deal of raw, unwholesome fog in the park. Then he had walked over to the hospital; and when the investigation in Greenwich was concluded at last he had lost his inclination for food. Not accustomed, as the doctors are, to examine closely the mangled remains of human beings, he had been shocked by the sight disclosed to his view when a waterproof sheet had been lifted off a table in a certain apartment of the hospital.

Another waterproof sheet was spread over that table in the manner of a tablecloth, with the corners turned up over a sort of mound—a heap of rags, scorched and bloodstained, half concealing what might have been an accumulation of raw material for a cannibal feast. It required considerable firmness of mind not to recoil before that sight. Chief Inspector Heat, an efficient officer of his department, stood his ground, but for a whole minute he did not advance. A local constable in uniform cast a sidelong glance, and said with stolid simplicity:

"He's all there. Every bit of him. It was a job."

He had been the first man on the spot after the explosion. He mentioned the fact again. He had seen something like a heavy flash of lightning in the fog. At that time he was standing at the door of the King William Street Lodge talking to the keeper. The concussion made him tingle all over. He ran between the trees towards the Observatory. "As fast as my legs would carry me," he repeated twice.

Chief Inspector Heat, bending forward over the table in a gingerly and horrified manner, let him run on. The hospital porter and another man turned down the corners of the cloth, and stepped aside. The Chief Inspector's eyes searched the gruesome detail of that heap of mixed things, which seemed to have been collected in shambles and rag shops.

"You used a shovel," he remarked, observing a sprinkling of small gravel, tiny brown bits of bark, and particles of splintered wood as fine as needles.

"Had to in one place," said the stolid constable. "I sent a keeper to fetch a spade. When he heard me scraping the ground with it he leaned his forehead against a tree, and was as sick as a dog."

The Chief Inspector, stooping guardedly over the table fought down the unpleasant sensation in his throat. The shattering violence of destruction which had made of that body a heap of nameless fragments affected his feelings with a sense of ruthless cruelty, though his reason told him the effect must have been as swift as a flash of lightning. The man, whoever he was, had died instantaneously; and yet it seemed impossible to believe that a human body could have reached that state of disintegration without passing through the pangs of inconceivable agony. No physiologist, and still less of a meta-physician, Chief Inspector Heat rose by the force of sympathy, which is a form of fear, above the vulgar conception of time. Instantaneous! He remembered all he had ever read in popular publications of long and terrifying dreams dreamed in the instant of waking; of the whole past life lived with frightful intensity by a drowning man as his doomed head bobs up, streaming, for the last time. The inexplicable mysteries of conscious existence beset Chief Inspector Heat till he evolved a horrible notion that ages of atrocious pain and mental tor-ture could be contained between two successive winks of an eye. And meantime the Chief Inspector went on peering at the table with a calm face and the slightly anxious attention of an indigent customer bending over what may be called the by-products of a butcher's shop with a view to an inexpensive Sunday dinner. All the time his trained faculties of an excellent investigator, who scorns no chance of infor-mation, followed the self-satisfied, disjointed loquacity of the con-stable.

"A fair-haired fellow," the last observed in a placid tone, and paused. "The old woman who spoke to the sergeant noticed a fair-haired fellow coming out of Maze Hill Station." He paused. "And he was a fair-haired fellow. She noticed two men coming out of the station after the uptrain had gone on," he continued, slowly. "She couldn't tell if they were together. She took no particular notice of the big one, but the other was a fair, slight chap, carrying a tin varnish can in one hand." The constable ceased.

"Know the woman?" muttered the Chief Inspector, with his eyes fixed on the table, and a vague notion in his mind of an inquest to be held presently upon a person likely to remain for ever unknown.

"Yes. She's housekeeper to a retired publican, and attends the chapel in Park Place sometimes," the constable uttered weightily, and paused, with another oblique glance at the table. Then suddenly: "Well, here he is—all of him I could see. Fair. Slight—slight enough. Look at that foot there. I picked up the legs first, one after another. He was that scattered you didn't know where to begin."

The constable paused; the least flicker of an innocent, self-laudatory smile invested his round face with an infantile expression.

"Stumbled," he announced, positively. "I stumbled once myself, and pitched on my head, too, while running up. Them roots do stick out all about the place. Stumbled against the root of a tree and fell, and that thing he was carrying must have gone off right under his chest, I expect."

The echo of the words "Person unknown" repeating itself in his inner consciousness bothered the Chief Inspector considerably. He would have liked to trace this affair back to its mysterious origin for his own information. He was professionally curious. Before the public he would have liked to vindicate the efficiency of his department by establishing the identity of that man. He was a loyal servant. That, however, appeared impossible. The first term of the problem was un-readable—lacked all suggestion but that of atrocious cruelty.

Overcoming his physical repugnance, Chief Inspector Heat stretched out his hand without conviction for the salving of his con-science, and took up the least soiled of the rags. It was a narrow strip of velvet with a larger triangular piece of dark blue cloth hanging from it. He held it up to his eyes; and the police constable spoke.

"Velvet collar. Funny the old woman should have noticed the velvet collar. Dark blue overcoat with a velvet collar, she has told us. He was the chap she saw, and no mistake. And here he is all complete, velvet collar and all. I don't think I missed a single piece as big as a postage stamp."

At this point the trained faculties of the Chief Inspector ceased to hear the voice of the constable. He moved to one of the windows for better light. His face, averted from the room, expressed a startled, in-tense interest while he examined closely the triangular piece of broad-cloth. By a sudden jerk he detached it, and only after stuffing it into his pocket turned round to the room, and flung the velvet collar back on the table.

"Cover up," he directed the attendants, curtly, without another look and, saluted by the constable, carried off his spoil hastily.

A convenient train whirled him up to town, alone and pondering deeply, in a third-class compartment. That singed piece of cloth was incredibly valuable, and he could not defend himself from astonish-ment at the casual manner it had come into his possession. It was as if Fate had thrust that clue into his hands. And after the manner of the average man, whose ambition is to command events, he began to mis-trust such a gratuitous and accidental success—just because it seemed forced upon him. The practical value of success depends not a little on the way you look at it. But Fate looks at nothing. It has no dis-cretion. He no longer considered it eminently desirable all round to establish publicly the identity of the man who had blown himself up that morning with such horrible completeness. But he was not certain of the view his department would take. A department is to those it employs a complex personality with ideas and even fads of its own. It depends on the loyal devotion of its servants, and the devoted

loyalty of trusted servants is associated with a certain amount of affectionate contempt, which keeps it sweet, as it were. By a benevolent
provision of Nature no man is a hero to his valet, or else the heroes
would have to brush their own clothes. Likewise no department appears perfectly wise to the intimacy of its workers. A department does
not know so much as some of its servants. Being a dispassionate
organism, it can never be perfectly informed. It would not be good
for its efficiency to know too much. Chief Inspector Heat got out
of the train in a state of thoughtfulness entirely untainted with dis-
loyalty, but not quite free of that jealous mistrust which so often
springs on the ground of perfect devotion, whether to women or to
institutions.

It was in this mental disposition, physically very empty but still
nauseated by what he had seen, that he had come upon the Professor.
Under these conditions which make for irascibility in a sound, normal
man, this meeting was specially unwelcome to Chief Inspector Heat.
He had not been thinking of the Professor; he had not been thinking
of any individual anarchist at all. The complexion of that case had
somehow forced upon him the general idea of the absurdity of things
human, which in the abstract is sufficiently annoying to an unphilo-
sophical temperament, and in concrete instances becomes exasperating
beyond endurance. At the beginning of his career Chief Inspector
Heat had been concerned with the more energetic forms of thieving.
He had gained his spurs in that sphere, and naturally enough had
kept for it, after his promotion to another department, a feeling not
very far removed from affection. Thieving was not a sheer absurdity.
It was a form of human industry, perverse indeed, but still an industry exercised in an industrious world; it was work undertaken for the
same reason as the work in potteries, in coal mines, in fields, in tool-
grinding shops. It was labour, whose practical difference from the
other forms of labour consisted in the nature of its risk, which did
not lie in ankylosis, or lead poisoning, or fire-damp, or gritty dust,
but in what may be briefly defined in its own special phraseology as
"Seven years hard." Chief Inspector Heat was, of course, not insensible to the gravity of moral differences. But neither were the thieves
he had been looking after. They submitted to the severe sanctions of
a morality familiar to Chief Inspector Heat with a certain resignation. They were his fellow-citizens gone wrong because of imperfect
education, Chief Inspector Heat believed; but allowing for that difference, he could understand the mind of a burglar, because, as a matter
of fact, the mind and the instincts of a burglar are of the same kind
as the mind and the instincts of a police officer. Both recognize the
same conventions, and have a working knowledge of each other's
methods and of the routine of their respective trades. They under-

stand each other, which is advantageous to both, and establishes a sort of amenity in their relations. Products of the same machine, one classed as useful and the other as noxious, they take the machine for granted in different ways, but with a seriousness essentially the same. The mind of Chief Inspector Heat was inaccessible to ideas of revolt. But his thieves were not rebels. His bodily vigour, his cool, inflexible manner, his courage, and his fairness, had secured for him much respect and some adulation in the sphere of his early successes. He had felt himself revered and admired. And Chief Inspector Heat, arrested within six paces of the anarchist nicknamed the Professor, gave a thought of regret to the world of thieves—sane, without morbid ideals, working by routine, respectful of constituted authorities, free from all taint of hate and despair.

After paying this tribute to what is normal in the constitution of society (for the idea of thieving appeared to his instinct as normal as the idea of property), Chief Inspector Heat felt very angry with himself for having stopped, for having spoken, for having taken that way at all on the ground of it being a short cut from the station to the headquarters. And he spoke again in his big, authoritative voice, which, being moderated, had a threatening character.

"You are not wanted, I tell you," he repeated.

The anarchist did not stir. An inward laugh of derision uncovered not only his teeth but his gums as well, shook him all over, without the slightest sound. Chief Inspector Heat was led to add, against his better judgment:

"Not yet. When I want you I shall know where to find you."

Those were perfectly proper words, within the tradition and suitable to his character of a police officer addressing one of his special flock. But the reception they got departed from tradition and propriety. It was outrageous. The stunted, weakly figure before him spoke at last.

"I've no doubt the papers would give you an obituary notice then. You know best what that would be worth to you. I should think you can imagine easily the sort of stuff that would be printed. But you may be exposed to the unpleasantness of being buried together with me, though I suppose your friends would make an effort to sort us out as much as possible."

With all his healthy contempt for the spirit dictating such speeches, the atrocious allusiveness of the words had its effect on Chief Inspector Heat. He had too much insight, and too much exact information as well, to dismiss them as rot. The dusk of this narrow lane took on a sinister tint from the dark, frail little figure, its back to the wall, and speaking with a weak, self-confident voice. To the vigorous, tenacious vitality of the Chief Inspector, the physical wretchedness of that being, so obviously not fit to live, was ominous; for it seemed to him that if he had the misfortune to be such a miserable object he would not have cared how soon he died. Life had such a strong hold upon him that a fresh wave of nausea broke out in slight perspiration upon his brow. The murmur of town life, the subdued rumble of wheels in the two invisible streets to the right and left, came through the curve of the sordid lane to his ears with a precious familiarity and an appealing sweetness. He was human. But Chief Inspector Heat was also a man, and he could not let such words pass.

"All this is good to frighten children with," he said. "I'll have you yet."

It was very well said, without scorn, wtih an almost austere quietness.

"Doubtless," was the answer; "but there's no time like the present, believe me. For a man of real convictions this is a fine opportunity of self-sacrifice. You may not find another so favourable, so humane. There isn't even a cat near us, and these condemned old houses would make a good heap of bricks where you stand. You'll never get me at so little cost of life and property, which you are paid to protect."

"You don't know who you're speaking to," said Chief Inspector Heat, firmly. "If I were to lay my hands on you now I would be no better than yourself."

"Ah! The game!"

"You may be sure our side will win in the end. It may yet be necessary to make people believe that some of you ought to be shot at sight like mad dogs. Then that will be the game. But I'll be damned if I know what yours is. I don't believe you know yourselves. You'll never get anything by it."

"Meantime, it's you who get something from it—so far. And you get it easily, too. I won't speak of your salary, but haven't you made your name simply by not understanding what we are after?"

"What are you after, then?" asked Chief Inspector Heat, with scornful haste, like a man in a hurry who perceives he is wasting his time.

The perfect anarchist answered by a smile which did not part his thin, colourless lips; and the celebrated Chief Inspector felt a sense of superiority which induced him to raise a warning finger.

"Give it up—whatever it is," he said in an admonishing tone, but not so kindly as if he were condescending to give good advice to a cracksman of repute. "Give it up. You'll find we are too many for you."

The fixed smile on the Professor's lips wavered, as if the mocking spirit within had lost its assurance. Chief Inspector Heat went on:

"Don't you believe me—eh? Well, you've only got to look about you. We are. And anyway, you're not doing it well. You're always making a mess of it. Why, if the thieves didn't know their work better they would starve."

The hint of an invincible multitude behind that man's back roused a sombre indignation in the breast of the Professor. He smiled no longer his enigmatic and mocking smile. The resisting power of numbers, the unattackable stolidity of a great multitude, was the haunting fear of his sinister loneliness. His lips trembled for some time before he managed to say in a strangled voice:

"I am doing my work better than you're doing yours."

"That'll do now," interrupted Chief Inspector Heat, hurriedly; and the Professor laughed right out this time. While still laughing he moved on; but he did not laugh long. It was a sad-faced, miserable little man who emerged from the narrow passage into the bustle of the broad thoroughfare. He walked with the nerveless gait of a tramp going on, still going on, indifferent to rain or sun in a sinister detachment from the aspects of sky and earth. Chief Inspector Heat, on the other hand, after watching him for a while, stepped out with the purposeful briskness of a man disregarding indeed the inclemencies of the weather, but conscious of having an authorized mission on this earth and the moral support of his kind. All the inhabitants of the immense town, the population of the whole country, and even the teeming millions struggling upon the planet, were with him—down to the very thieves and mendicants. Yes, the thieves themselves were sure to be with him in his present work. The consciousness of universal support in his general activity heartened him to grapple with the particular problem.

The problem immediately before the Chief Inspector was that of managing the Assistant Commissioner of his department, his immediate superior. This is the perennial problem of trusty and loyal servants; anarchism gave it its particular complexion, but nothing more. Truth to say, Chief Inspector Heat thought but little of anarchism. He did not attach undue importance to it, and could never bring himself to consider it seriously. It had more the character of disorderly conduct; disorderly without the human excuse of drunkenness, which at any rate implies good feeling and an amiable leaning towards festivity. As criminals, anarchists were distinctly no class—no class at all. And recalling the Professor, Chief Inspector Heat, without checking his swinging pace, muttered through his teeth:

"Lunatic."

Catching thieves was another matter altogether. It had that quality of seriousness belonging to every form of open sport where the best man wins under perfectly comprehensible rules. There were no rules for dealing with anarchists. And that was distasteful to the Chief Inspector. It was all foolishness, but that foolishness excited the public mind, affected persons in high places, and touched upon international relations. A hard, merciless contempt settled rigidly on the Chief Inspector's face as he walked on. His mind ran over all the anarchists of his flock. Not one of them had half the spunk of this or that burglar he had known. Not half—not one tenth.

At headquarters the Chief Inspector was admitted at once to the Assistant Commissioner's private room. He found him, pen in hand, bent over a great table bestrewn with papers, as if worshipping an enormous double inkstand of bronze and crystal. Speaking tubes resembling snakes were tied by the heads to the back of the Assistant Commissioner's wooden armchair, and their gaping mouths seemed ready to bite his elbows. And in this attitude he raised only his eyes, whose lids were darker than his face and very much creased. The reports had come in: every anarchist had been exactly accounted for.

After saying this he lowered his eyes, signed rapidly two single sheets of paper, and only then laid down his pen, and sat well back, directing an inquiring gaze at his renowned subordinate. The Chief Inspector stood it well, deferential but inscrutable.

"I daresay you were right," said the Assistant Commissioner, "in telling me at first that the London anarchists had nothing to do with this. I quite appreciate the excellent watch kept on them by your men. On the other hand, this, for the public, does not amount to more than a confession of ignorance."

The Assistant Commissioner's delivery was leisurely, as it were cautious. His thought seemed to rest poised on a word before passing to another, as though words had been the stepping-stones for his intellect picking its way across the waters of error. "Unless you have brought something useful from Greenwich," he added.

The Chief Inspector began at once the account of his investigation in a clear, matter-of-fact manner. His superior, turning his chair a little and crossing his thin legs, leaned sideways on his elbow, with one hand shading his eyes. His listening attitude had a sort of angular and sorrowful grace. Gleams as of highly burnished silver played on the sides of his ebony black head when he inclined it slowly at the end.

Chief Inspector Heat waited with the appearance of turning over in his mind all he had just said, but, as a matter of fact, considering the advisability of saying something more. The Assistant Commissioner cut his hesitation short.

"You believe there were two men?" he asked, without uncovering his eyes.

The Chief Inspector thought it more than probable. In his opinion, the two men had parted from each other within a hundred yards from the Observatory walls. He explained also how the other man could have got out of the park speedily without being observed. The fog, though not very dense, was in his favour. He seemed to have escorted the other to the spot, and then to have left him there to do the job single-handed. Taking the time those two were seen coming out of Maze Hill Station by the old woman, and the time when the explosion was heard, the Chief Inspector thought that the other man might have been actually at the Greenwich Park Station, ready to catch the next train up, at the moment his comrade was destroying himself so thoroughly.

"Very thoroughly—eh?" murmured the Assistant Commissioner from under the shadow of his hand.

The Chief Inspector in a few vigorous words described the aspect of the remains. "The coroner's jury will have a treat," he added, grimly.

The Assistant Commissioner uncovered his eyes.

"We shall have nothing to tell them," he remarked, languidly.

He looked up, and for a time watched the markedly noncommittal attitude of his Chief Inspector. His nature was one that is not easily accessible to illusions. He knew that a department is at the mercy of its subordinate officers, who have their own conceptions of loyalty. His career had begun in a tropical colony. He had liked his work there. It was police work. He had been very successful in tracking and breaking up certain nefarious secret societies amongst the natives. Then he took his long leave, and got married rather impulsively. It was a good match from a worldly point of view, but his wife formed an unfavourable opinion of the colonial climate on hearsay evidence. On the other hand, she had influential connections. It was an excellent match. But he did not like the work he had to do now. He felt himself dependent on too many subordinates and too many masters. The near presence of that strange emotional phenomenon called public opinion weighed upon his spirits, and alarmed him by its irrational nature. No doubt that from ignorance he exaggerated to himself its power for good and evil—especially for evil; and the rough east winds of the English spring (which agreed with his wife) augmented his general mistrust of men's motives and of the efficiency of their organization. The futility of office work especially appalled him on those days so trying to his sensitive liver.

He got up, unfolding himself to his full height, and with a heaviness of step remarkable in so slender a man, moved across the room to the window. The panes streamed with rain, and the short street he looked down into lay wet and empty, as if swept clear suddenly by a great flood. It was a very trying day, choked in raw fog to begin with, and now drowned in cold rain. The flickering, blurred flames of gas-lamps seemed to be dissolving in a watery atmosphere. And the lofty pretensions of a mankind oppressed by the miserable indignities of the weather appeared as a colossal and hopeless vanity deserving of scorn, wonder, and compassion.

"Horrible, horrible!" thought the Assistant Commissioner to himself, with his face near the window-pane. "We have been having this sort of thing now for ten days; no, a fortnight—a fortnight." He ceased to think completely for a time. That utter stillness of his brain lasted about three seconds. Then he said, perfunctorily: "You have set inquiries on foot for tracing that other man up and down the line?"

He had no doubt that everything needful had been done. Chief Inspector Heat knew, of course, thoroughly the business of manhunting. And these were the routine steps, too, that would be taken as a matter of course by the merest beginner. A few inquiries amongst the ticket collectors and the porters of the two small railway stations would give additional details as to the appearance of the two men; the inspection of the collected tickets would show at once where they came from that morning. It was elementary, and could not have been neglected. Accordingly, the Chief Inspector answered that all this had been done directly the old woman had come forward with her deposition. And he mentioned the name of a station. "That's where they came from, sir," he went on. "The porter who took the tickets at Maze Hill remembers two chaps answering to the description passing the barrier. They seemed to him two respectable working-men of a superior sort—sign painters or house decorators. The big man got out of a third-class compartment backward, with a bright tin can in his hand. On the platform he gave it to carry to the fair young fellow who followed him. All this agrees exactly with what the old woman told the police sergeant in Greenwich."

The Assistant Commissioner, still with his face turned to the window, expressed his doubt as to these two men having had anything to do with the outrage. All this theory rested upon the utterances of an old charwoman who had been nearly knocked down by a man in a hurry. Not a very substantial authority indeed, unless of the ground of sudden inspiration, which was hardly tenable.

"Frankly now, could she have been really inspired?" he queried, with grave irony, keeping his back to the room, as if entranced by the contemplation of the town's colossal forms half lost in the night. He did not even look round when he heard the mutter of the word "Providential" from the principal subordinate of his department, whose name, printed sometimes in the papers, was familiar to the great public as that of one of its zealous and hard-working protectors. Chief Inspector Heat raised his voice a little.

"Strips and bits of bright tin were quite visible to me," he said. "That's a pretty good corroboration."

398

"And these men came from that little country station," the Assistant Commissioner mused aloud, wondering. He was told that such was the name on two tickets out of three given up out of that train at Maze Hill. The third person who got out was a hawker from Gravesend well known to the porters. The Chief Inspector imparted that information in a tone of finality with some ill humour, as loyal servants will do in the consciousness of their fidelity and with the sense of the value of their loyal exertions. And still the Assistant Commissioner did not turn away from the darkness outside, as vast as a sea.

"Two foreign anarchists coming from that place," he said, apparently to the window-pane. "It's rather unaccountable."

"Yes, sir. But it would be still more unaccountable if that Michaelis weren't staying in a cottage in the neighbourhood."

At the sound of that name, falling unexpectedly into this annoying affair, the Assistant Commissioner dismissed brusquely the vague rememberance of his daily whist party at his club. It was the most comforting habit of his life, in a mainly successful display of his skill without the assistance of any subordinate. He entered his club to play from five to seven, before going home to dinner, forgetting for those two hours whatever was distasteful in his life, as though the game were a beneficent drug for allaying the pangs of moral discontent. His partners were the gloomily humorous editor of a celebrated magazine; a silent, elderly barrister with malicious little eyes; and a highly martial, simple-minded old Colonel with nervous brown hands. They were his club acquaintances merely. He never met them elsewhere except at the card table. But they all seemed to approach the game in the spirit of co-sufferers, as if it were indeed a drug against the secret ills of existence; and every day as the sun declined over the countless roofs of the town, a mellow, pleasurable impatience, resembling the impulse of a sure and profound friendship, lightened his professional labours. And now this pleasurable sensation went out of him with something resembling a physical shock, and was replaced by a special kind of interest in his work of social protection—an improper sort of interest, which may be defined best as a sudden and alert mistrust of the weapon in his hand.

CHAPTER SIX

The lady patroness of Michaelis, the ticket-of-leave apostle of humanitarian hopes, was one of the most influential and distinguished connections of the Assistant Commissioner's wife, whom she called Annie, and treated still rather as a not very wise and utterly inexperienced young girl. But she had consented to accept him on a friendly footing, which was by no means the case with all of his wife's influential connections. Married young and splendidly at some remote epoch of the past, she had had for a time a close view of great affairs and even of some great men. She herself was a great lady. Old now in the number of her years, she had that sort of exceptional temperament which defies time with scornful disregard, as if it were a rather vulgar convention submitted to by the mass of inferior mankind. Many other conventions easier to set aside, alas! failed to obtain her recognition, also on temperamental grounds—either because they bored her, or else because they stood in the way of her scorns and sympathies. Admiration was a sentiment unknown to her (it was one of the secret griefs of her most noble husband against her)—first, as always more or less tainted with mediocrity, and next as being in a way an admission of inferiority. And both were frankly inconceivable to her nature. To be fearlessly outspoken in her opinions came easily to her, since she judged solely from the standpoint of her social position. She was equally untrammelled in her actions; and as her tactfulness proceeded from genuine humanity, her bodily vigour remained remarkable and her superiority was serene and cordial, three generations had admired her infinitely, and the last she was likely to see had pronounced her a wonderful woman. Meantime, intelligent, with a sort of lofty simplicity, and curious at heart, but not like many women merely of social gossip, she amused her age by attracting within her ken through the power of her great, almost historical, social prestige everything that rose above the dead level of mankind, lawfully or unlawfully, by position, wit, audacity, fortune or misfortune. Royal Highnesses, artists, men of science, young statesmen, and charlatans of all ages and conditions, who, unsubstantial and light, bobbing up like corks, show best the direction of the surface currents, had been welcomed in that house, listened to, penetrated, understood, appraised, for her own edification. In her own words, she liked to watch what the world was coming to. And as she had a practical mind her judgment of men and things, though based on special prejudices, was seldom totally wrong, and almost never wrong-headed. Her drawing-room was probably the only place in the wide world where an Assistant Commissioner of Police could meet a convict liberated on a ticket-of-leave on other than professional and official ground. Who had brought Michaelis there one afternoon the Assistant Commissioner did not remember very well. He had a notion it must have been a certain Member of Parliament of illustrious parentage and unconventional sympathies, which were the standing joke of the comic papers. The notabilities and even the simple notorieties of the day brought each other freely to that temple of an old woman's not ignoble curiosity. You never could guess whom you were likely to come upon being received in semi-privacy within the faded blue silk and gilt frame screen, making a cosy nook for a couch and a few arm-chairs in the great drawing-room, with its hum of voices and the groups of people seated or standing in the light of six tall windows.

Michaelis had been the object of a revulsion of popular sentiment, the same sentiment which years ago had applauded the ferocity of the life sentence passed upon him for complicity in a rather mad attempt to rescue some prisoners from a police van. The plan of the conspirators had been to shoot down the horses and overpower the escort. Unfortunately, one of the police constables got shot, too. He left a wife and three small children, and the death of that man aroused through the length and breadth of a realm for whose defence, welfare, and glory men die every day as matter of duty, an outburst of furious indignation, of a raging, implacable pity for the victim. Three ring-leaders got hanged. Michaelis, young and slim, locksmith by trade, and great frequenter of evening schools, did not even know that anybody had been killed, his part with a few others being to force open the door at the back of the special conveyance. When arrested he had a bunch of skeleton keys in one pocket, a heavy chisel in another, and a short crowbar in his hand: neither more nor less than a burglar. But no burglar would have received such a heavy sentence. The death of the constable had made him miserable at heart, but the failure of the plot also. He did not conceal either of these sentiments from his empanelled countrymen, and that sort of com-punction appeared shockingly imperfect to the crammed court. The judge on passing sentence commented feelingly upon the depravity and callousness of the young prisoner.

That made the groundless fame of his condemnation; the fame of his release was made for him on no better grounds by people who wished to exploit the sentimental aspect of his imprisonment either for purposes of their own or for no intelligible purpose. He let them do so in the innocence of his heart and the simplicity of his mind. Nothing that happened to him individually had any importance. He was like those saintly men whose personality is lost in the contem-plation of their faith. His ideas were not in the nature of convictions. They were inaccessible to reasoning. They formed in all their contra-dictions and obscurities an invincible and humanitarian creed, which he confessed rather than preached, with an obstinate gentleness, a smile of pacific assurance on his lips, and his candid blue eyes cast down because the sight of faces troubled his inspiration developed in solitude. In that characteristic attitude, pathetic in his grotesque and incurable obesity which he had to drag like a galley slave's bullet to the end of his days, the Assistant Commissioner of Police beheld the ticket-of-leave apostle filling a privileged armchair within the screen. He sat there by the head of the old lady's couch, mild-voiced and quiet, with no more self-consciousness than a very small child, and with something of a child's charm—the appealing charm of trustfulness. Confident of the future, whose secret ways had been revealed to him within the four walls of a well-known penitentiary, he had no reason to look with suspicion upon anybody. If he could not give the great and curious lady a very definite idea as to what the world was coming to, he had managed without effort to impress her by his unembittered faith, by the sterling quality of his optimism.

A certain simplicity of thought is common to serene souls at both ends of the social scale. The great lady was simple in her own way. His views and beliefs had nothing in them to shock or startle her, since she judged them from the standpoint of her lofty position. Indeed, her sympathies were easily accessible to a man of that sort. She was not an exploiting capitalist herself; she was, as it were, above the play of economic conditions. And she had a great capacity of pity for the more obvious forms of common human miseries, precisely because she was such a complete stranger to them that she had to translate her conception into terms of mental suffering before she could grasp the notion of their cruelty. The Assistant Commissioner remembered very well the conversation between these two. He had listened in silence. It was something as exciting in a way, and even touching in its foredoomed futility, as the efforts at moral intercourse between the inhabitants of remote planets. But this grotesque incarnation of humanitarian passion appealed, somehow, to one's imagination. At last Michaelis rose, and taking the great lady's extended hand, shook it, retained it for a moment in his great cushioned palm with unembarrassed friendliness, and turned upon the semi-private nook of the drawing-room his back, vast and square, and as if distended under the short tweed jacket. Glancing about in serene benevolence, he waddled along to the distant door between the knots of other visitors. The murmur of conversations paused on his passage. He smiled innocently at a tall, brilliant girl, whose eyes met his accidentally, and went out unconscious of the glances following him across the room. Michaelis' first appearance in the world was a success—a success of esteem unmarred by a single murmur of derision. The interrupted conversations were resumed in their proper tone, grave or light. Only a well-set-up, long-limbed, active-looking man of forty talking with two ladies near a window remarked aloud, with an unexpected depth of feeling: "Eighteen stone, I should say, and not five foot six. Poor fellow! It's terrible—terrible."

The lady of the house, gazing absently at the Assistant Commissioner, left alone with her on the private side of the screen, seemed to be rearranging her mental impressions behind the thoughtful immobility of her handsome old face. Men with grey moustaches and full, healthy, vaguely smiling countenances approached, circling round the screen; two mature women with a matronly air of gracious resolution; a clean-shaved individual with sunken cheeks, and dangling a gold-mounted eyeglass on a broad black ribbon with an old-world, dandified effect. A silence deferential, but full of reserves, reigned for a moment, and then the great lady exclaimed, not with resentment, but with a sort of protesting indignation:

"And that officially is supposed to be a revolutionist! What nonsense." She looked hard at the Assistant Commissioner, who murmured, apologetically:

"Not a dangerous one perhaps."

"Not dangerous—I should think not indeed. He is a mere believer. It's the temperament of a saint," declared the great lady in a firm tone. "And they kept him shut up for twenty years. One shudders at the stupidity of it. And now they have let him out everybody belonging to him is gone away somewhere or dead. His parents are dead; the girl he was to marry has died while he was in prison; he has lost the skill necessary for his manual occupation. He told me all this himself with the sweetest patience; but then, he said, he had had plenty of time to think out things for himself. A pretty compensation! If that's the stuff revolutionists are made of some of us may well go on our knees to them," she continued in a slightly bantering voice, while the banal society smiles hardened on the worldly faces turned towards her with conventional deference. "The poor creature is obviously no longer in a position to take care of himself. Somebody will have to look after him a little."

"He should be recommended to follow a treatment of some sort," the soldierly voice of the active-looking man was heard advising earnestly from a distance. He was in the pink of condition for his age, and even the texture of his long frock coat had a character of elastic soundness, as if it were a living tissue. "The man is virtually a cripple," he added with unmistakable feeling.

Other voices, as if glad of the opening, murmured hasty compassion. "Quite startling," "Monstrous," "Most painful to see." The lank man, with the eyeglass on a broad ribbon, pronounced mincingly the word "Grotesque," whose justness was appreciated by those standing near him. They smiled at each other.

The Assistant Commissioner had expressed no opinion either then or later, his position making it impossible for him to ventilate any independent view of a ticket-of-leave convict. But, in truth, he shared the view of his wife's friend and patron that Michaelis was a humanitarian sentimentalist, a little mad, but upon the whole incapable of hurting a fly intentionally. So when that name cropped up suddenly in this vexing bomb affair he realized all the danger of it for the ticket-of-leave apostle, and his mind reverted at once to the old lady's well-established infatuation. Her arbitrary kindness would not brook patiently any interference with Michaelis' freedom. It was a deep, calm, convinced infatuation. She had not only felt him to be inoffensive, but she had said so, which last by a confusion of her absolutist mind became a sort of incontrovertible demonstration. It was as if the monstrosity of the man, with his candid infant's eyes and a fat angelic smile, had fascinated her. She had come to believe almost his theory of the future, since it was not repugnant to her prejudices. She disliked the new element of plutocracy in the social compound, and industrialism as a method of human development appeared to her singularly repulsive in its mechanical and unfeeling character. The humanitarian hopes of the mild Michaelis tended not towards utter destruction, but merely towards the complete economic ruin of the system. And she did not really see where was the moral harm of it. It would do away with all the multitude of the "parvenus," whom she disliked and mistrusted, not because they had arrived anywhere (she denied that), but because of their profound unintelligence of the world, which was the primary cause of the crudity of their perceptions and the aridity of their hearts. With the annihilation of all capital they would vanish, too; but universal ruin (providing it was universal, as it was revealed to Michaelis) would leave the social values untouched. The disappearance of the last piece of money could not affect people of position. She could not conceive how it could affect her position, for instance. She had developed these discoveries to the Assistant Commissioner with all the serene fearlessness of an old woman who had escaped the blight of indifference. He had made for himself the rule to receive everything of that sort in a silence which he took care from policy and inclination not to make offensive. He had an affection for the aged disciple of Michaelis, a complex sentiment depending a little on her prestige, on her personality, but most of all on the instinct of flattered gratitude. He felt himself really liked in her house. She was kindness personified. And she was practically wise, too, after the manner of experienced women. She made his married life much easier than it would have been without her generously full recognition of his rights as Annie's husband. Her influence upon his wife, a woman devoured by all sorts of small selfishnesses, small envies, small jealousies, was excellent. Unfortunately, both her kindness and her wisdom were of unreasonable complexion, distinctly feminine, and difficult to deal with. She remained a perfect woman all along her full tale of years, and not as some of them do become— a sort of slippery, pestilential old man in petticoats. And it was as of a woman that he thought of her—the specially choice incarnation of the feminine, wherein is recruited the tender, ingenuous, and fierce bodyguard for all sorts of men who talk under the influence of an emotion, true or fraudulent; for preachers, seers, prophets, or reformers.

Appreciating the distinguished and good friend of his wife, and himself, in that way, the Assistant Commissioner became alarmed at the convict Michaelis' possible fate. Once arrested on suspicion of being in some way, however remote, a party to this outrage, the man could hardly escape being sent back to finish his sentence at least. And that would kill him; he would never come out alive. The Assistant Commissioner made a reflection extremely unbecoming his official position without being really creditable to his humanity.

"If the fellow is laid hold of again," he thought, "she will never forgive me."

The frankness of such a secretly outspoken thought could not go without some derisive self-criticism. No man engaged in a work he does not like can preserve many saving illusions about himself. The distaste, the absence of glamour, extend from the occupation to the personality. It is only when our appointed activities seem by a lucky accident to obey the particular earnestness of our temperament that we can taste the comfort of complete self-deception. The Assistant Commissioner did not like his work at home. The police work he had been engaged on in a distant part of the globe had the saving character of an irregular sort of warfare or at least the risk and excitement of open-air sport. His real abilities, which were mainly of an administrative order, were combined with an adventurous disposition. Chained to a desk in the thick of four millions of men, he considered himself the victim of an ironic fate—the same, no doubt, which had brought about his marriage with a woman exceptionally sensitive in the matter of colonial climate, besides other limitations testifying to the delicacy of her nature—and her tastes. Though he judged his alarm sardonically he did not dismiss the improper thought from his mind. The instinct of self-preservation was strong within him. On the contrary, he repeated it mentally with profane emphasis and a fuller precision: "Damn it! If that infernal Heat has his way the fellow'll die in prison smothered in his fat, and she'll never forgive me."

His black, narrow figure, with the white band of the collar under the silvery gleams on the close-cropped hair at the back of the head, remained motionless. The silence had lasted such a long time that Chief Inspector Heat ventured to clear his throat. This noise produced its effect. The zealous and intelligent officer was asked by his superior, whose back remained turned to him immovably:

"You connect Michaelis with this affair?"

Chief Inspector Heat was very positive, but cautious.

"Well, sir," he said, "we have enough to go upon. A man like that has no business to be at large, anyhow."

"You will want some conclusive evidence," came the observation in a murmur.

Chief Inspector Heat raised his eyebrows at the black, narrow back, which remained obstinately presented to his intelligence and his zeal.

"There will be no difficulty in getting up sufficient evidence against *him*," he said, with virtuous complacency. "You may trust me for that, sir," he added, quite unnecessarily, out of the fullness of his heart; for it seemed to him an excellent thing to have that man in hand to be thrown down to the public should it think fit to roar with any special indignation in this case. It was impossible to say yet whether it would roar or not. That in the last instance depended, of course, on the newspaper press. But in any case, Chief Inspector Heat, purveyor of prisons by trade, and a man of legal instincts, did logically believe that incarceration was the proper fate for every declared enemy of the law. In the strength of that conviction he committed a fault of tact. He allowed himself a little conceited laugh, and repeated:

"Trust me for that, sir."

This was too much for the forced calmness under which the Assistant Commissioner had for upwards of eighteen months concealed his irritation with the system and the subordinates of his office. A square peg forced into a round hole, he had felt like a daily outrage that long-established smooth roundness into which a man of less sharply angular shape would have fitted himself, with voluptuous acquiescence, after a shrug or two. What he resented most was just the necessity of taking so much on trust. At the little laugh of Chief Inspector Heat's he spun swiftly on his heels, as if whirled away from the window-pane by an electric shock. He caught on the latter's face not only the complacency proper to the occasion lurking under the moustache, but the vestiges of experimental watchfulness in the round eyes, which had been, no doubt, fastened on his back, and now met his glance for a second before the intent character of their stare had the time to change to a merely startled appearance.

The Assistant Commissioner of Police had really some qualifications for his post. Suddenly his suspicion was awakened. It is but fair to say that his suspicion of the police methods (unless the police happened to be a semi-military body organized by himself) was not difficult to arouse. If it ever slumbered from sheer weariness, it was but lightly; and his appreciation of Chief Inspector Heat's zeal and ability, moderate in itself, excluded all notion of moral confidence. "He's up to something," he exclaimed, mentally, and at once became angry. Crossing over to his desk with headlong strides, he sat down violently. "Here I am stuck in a litter of paper," he reflected, with unreasonable resentment, "supposed to hold all the threads in my hands, and yet I can but hold what is put in my hand, and nothing else. And they can fasten the other ends of the threads where they please."

He raised his head, and turned towards his subordinate a long, meagre face with the accentuated features of an energetic Don Quixote.

"Now what is it you've got up your sleeve?"

The other stared. He stared without winking in a perfect immobility of his round eyes, as he was used to staring at the various members of the criminal class when, after being duly cautioned, they made their statements in the tones of injured innocence, or false simplicity, or sullen resignation. But behind that professional and stony fixity there was some surprise, too, for in such a tone, combining nicely the note of contempt and impatience, Chief Inspector Heat, the right-hand man of the department, was not used to be addressed. He began in a procrastinating manner, like a man taken unawares by a new and unexpected experience.

"What I've got against that man Michaelis you mean, sir?"

The Assistant Commissioner watched the bullet head; the points of that Norse rover's moustache, falling below the line of the heavy jaw; the whole full and pale physiognomy, whose determined character was marred by too much flesh; at the cunning wrinkles radiating from the outer corners of the eyes—and in that purposeful contemplation of the valuable and trusted officer he drew a conviction so sudden that it moved him like an inspiration.

"I have reason to think that when you came into this room," he said in measured tones, "it was not Michaelis who was in your mind; not principally—perhaps not at all."

"You have reason to think, sir?" muttered Chief Inspector Heat, with every appearance of astonishment, which up to a certain point was genuine enough. He had discovered in this affair a delicate and perplexing side, forcing upon the discoverer a certain amount of insincerity—that sort of insincerity which, under the names of skill, prudence, discretion, turns up at one point or another in most human affairs. He felt at the moment like a tight-rope artist might feel if suddenly, in the middle of the performance, the manager of the Music Hall were to rush out of the proper managerial seclusion and begin to shake the rope. Indignation, the sense of moral insecurity engendered by such a treacherous proceeding joined to the immediate apprehension of a broken neck, would, in the colloquial phrase, put him in a state. And there would be also some scandalized concern for his art, too, since a man must identify himself with something more tangible than his own personality, and establish his pride somewhere, either in his social position, or in the quality of the work he is obliged to do, or simply in the superiority of the idleness he may be fortunate enough to enjoy.

"Yes," said the Assistant Commissioner; "I have. I do not mean to say that you have not thought of Michaelis at all. But you are giving the fact you've mentioned a prominence which strikes me as not quite candid, Inspector Heat. If that is really the track of discovery, why haven't you followed it up at once, either personally or by sending one of your men to that village?"

"Do you think, sir, I have failed in my duty there?" the Chief Inspector asked, in a tone which he sought to make simply reflective. Forced unexpectedly to concentrate his faculties upon the task of preserving his balance, he had seized upon that point, and exposed himself to a rebuke; for, the Assistant Commissioner, frowning slightly, observed that this was a very improper remark to make.

"But since you've made it," he continued, coldly, "I'll tell you that this is not my meaning."

He paused, with a straight glance of his sunken eyes which was a full equivalent of the unspoken termination "and you know it." The head of the so-called Special Crimes Department, debarred by his position from going out of doors personally in quest of secrets locked up in guilty breasts, had a propensity to exercise his considerable gifts for the detection of incriminating truth upon his own subordinates. That peculiar instinct could hardly be called a weakness. It was natural. He was a born detective. It had unconsciously governed his choice of a career, and if it ever failed him in life it was perhaps in the one exceptional circumstance of his marriage—which was also natural. It fed, since it could not roam abroad, upon the human material which was brought to it in its official seclusion. We can never cease to be ourselves.

His elbow on the desk, his thin legs crossed and nursing his cheek in the palm of his meagre hand, the Assistant Commissioner in charge of the Special Crimes branch was getting hold of the case with growing interest. His Chief Inspector, if not an absolutely worthy foeman of his penetration, was at any rate the most worthy of all within his reach. A mistrust of established reputations was strictly in character with the Assistant Commissioner's ability as detector. His memory evoked a certain old fat and wealthy native chief in the distant colony whom it was a tradition for the successive Colonial Governors to trust and make much of as a firm friend and supporter of the order and legality established by white men; whereas, when examined sceptically, he was found out to be principally his own good friend, and nobody else's. Not precisely a traitor, but still a man of many dangerous reservations in his fidelity, caused by a due regard for his own advantage, comfort, and safety. A fellow of some innocence in his naïve duplicity, but none the less dangerous. He took some finding out. He was physically a big man, too, and (allowing for the difference of colour, of course) Chief Inspector Heat's appearance recalled him to the memory of his superior. It was not the eyes nor yet the lips exactly. It was bizarre. But does not Alfred Wallace relate in his famous book on the Malay Archipelago how, amongst the Aru Islanders, he discovered in an old and naked savage with a sooty skin a peculiar resemblance to a dear·friend at home?

For the first time since he took up his appointment the Assistant Commissioner felt as if he were going to do some real work for his salary. And that was a pleasurable sensation. "I'll turn him inside out like an old glove," thought the Assistant Commissioner, with his eyes resting pensively upon Chief Inspector Heat.

"No, that was not my thought," he began again. "There is no doubt about you knowing your business—no doubt at all; and that's precisely why I——" He stopped short, and changing his tone: "What could you bring up against Michaelis of a definite nature? I mean apart from the fact that the two men under suspicion—you're certain there were two of them—came last from a railway station within three miles of the village where Michaelis is living now."

"This by itself is enough for us to go upon, sir, with that sort of man," said the Chief Inspector, with returning composure. The slight, approving movement of the Assistant Commissioner's head went far to pacify the resentful astonishment of the renowned officer. For Chief Inspector Heat was a kind man, an excellent husband, a devoted father; and the public and departmental confidence he enjoyed acting favourably upon an amiable nature, disposed him to feel friendly towards the successive Assistant Commissioners he had seen pass through that very room. There had been three in his time. The first one, a soldierly, abrupt, red-faced person, with white eyebrows and an explosive temper, could be managed with a silken thread. He left on reaching the age limit. The second, a perfect gentleman, knowing his own and everybody else's place to a nicety, on resigning to take up a higher appointment out of England got decorated for (really) Inspector Heat's services. To work with him had been a pride and a pleasure. The third, a bit of a dark horse from the first, was at the end of eighteen months something of a dark horse still to the department. Upon the whole Chief Inspector Heat believed him to be in the main harmless—odd-looking, but harmless. He was speaking now, and the Chief Inspector listened with outward deference (which means nothing, being a matter of duty) and inwardly with benevolent toleration.

"Michaelis reported himself before leaving London for the country?"

"Yes, sir. He did."

"And what may he be doing there?" continued the Assistant Commissioner, who was perfectly informed on that point. Fitted with painful tightness into an old wooden armchair, before a worm-eaten oak table in an upstairs room of a four-roomed cottage with a roof of moss-grown tiles, Michaelis was writing night and day in a shaky, slanting hand that "Autobiography of a Prisoner" which was to be like a book of Revelation in the history of mankind. The conditions of confined space, seclusion, and solitude in a small four-roomed cottage were favourable to his inspiration. It was like being in prison, except that one was never disturbed for the odious purpose of taking exercise according to the tyrannical regulations of his old home in the penitentiary. He could not tell whether the sun still shone on the earth or not. The perspiration of the literary labour dropped from his brow. A delightful enthusiasm urged him on. It was the liberation of his inner life, the letting out of his soul into the wide world. And the zeal of his guileless vanity (first awakened by the offer of five hundred pounds from a publisher) seemed something predestined and holy.

"It would be, of course, most desirable to be informed exactly," insisted the Assistant Commissioner, uncandidly.

Chief Inspector Heat, conscious of renewed irritation at this display of scrupulousness, said that the county police had been notified from the first of Michaelis' arrival, and that a full report could be obtained in a few hours. A wire to the superintendent——

Thus he spoke, rather slowly, while his mind seemed already to be weighing the consequences. A slight knitting of the brow was the outward sign of this. But he was interrupted by a question.

"You've sent that wire already?"

"No, sir," he answered, as if surprised.

The Assistant Commissioner uncrossed his legs suddenly. The briskness of that movement contrasted with the casual way in which he threw out a suggestion.

"Would you think that Michaelis had anything to do with the preparation of that bomb, for instance?"

The Chief Inspector assumed a reflective manner.

"I wouldn't say so. There's no necessity to say anything at present. He associates with men who are classed as dangerous. He was made a delegate of the Red Committee less than a year after his release on licence. A sort of compliment, I suppose."

And the Chief Inspector laughed a little angrily, a little scornfully. With a man of that sort scrupulousness was a misplaced and even an illegal sentiment. The celebrity bestowed upon Michaelis on his release two years ago by some emotional journalists in want of special copy had rankled ever since in his breast. It was perfectly legal to arrest that man on the barest suspicion. It was legal and expedient on the face

of it. His two former chiefs would have seen the point at once; whereas
this one, without saying either yes or no, sat there, as if lost in a
dream. Moreover, besides being legal and expedient, the arrest of
Michaelis solved a little personal difficulty which worried Chief Inspector Heat somewhat. This difficulty had its bearing upon his reputation, upon his comfort, and even upon the efficient performance of
his duties. For, if Michaelis no doubt knew something about this outrage, the Chief Inspector was fairly certain that he did not know too
much. This was just as well. He knew much less—the Chief Inspector
was positive—than certain other individuals he had in his mind, but
whose arrest seemed to him inexpedient, besides being a more complicated matter, on account of the rules of the game. The rules of the
game did not protect so much Michaelis, who was an ex-convict. It
would be stupid not to take advantage of legal facilities, and the
journalists who had written him up with emotional gush would be
ready to write him down with emotional indignation.

This prospect, viewed with confidence, had the attraction of a personal triumph for Chief Inspector Heat. And deep down in his blameless bosom of an average married citizen, almost unconscious but
potent nevertheless, the dislike of being compelled by events to meddle
with the desperate ferocity of the Professor had its say. This dislike
had been strengthened by the chance meeting in the lane. The encounter did not leave behind with Chief Inspector Heat that satisfactory sense of superiority the members of the police force get from
the unofficial but intimate side of their intercourse with the criminal
classes, by which the vanity of power is soothed, and the vulgar love
of domination over our fellow-creatures is flattered as worthily as it
deserves.

The perfect anarchist was not recognized as a fellow-creature by
Chief Inspector Heat. He was impossible—a mad dog to be left alone.
Not that the Chief Inspector was afraid of him; on the contrary, he
meant to have him some day. But not yet: he meant to get hold of
him in his own time, properly and effectively, according to the rules of
the game. The present was not the right time for attempting that feat,
not the right time for many reasons, personal and of public service.
This being the strong feeling of Inspector Heat, it appeared to him
just and proper that this affair should be shunted off its obscure and
inconvenient track, leading goodness knows where, into a quiet (and
lawful) siding called Michaelis. And he repeated, as if reconsidering
the suggestion conscientiously:

"The bomb. No, I would not say that exactly. We may never find
that out. But it's clear that he is connected with this in some way,
which we can find out without much trouble."

His countenance had that look of grave, overbearing indifference once well known and much dreaded by the better sort of thieves. Chief Inspector Heat, though what is called a man, was not a smiling animal. But his inward state was that of satisfaction at the passively receptive attitude of the Assistant Commissioner, who murmured gently:

"And you really think that the investigation should be made in that direction?"

"I do, sir."

"Quite convinced?"

"I am, sir. That's the true line for us to take."

The Assistant Commissioner withdrew the support of his hand from his reclining head with a suddenness that, considering his languid attitude, seemed to menace his whole person with collapse. But, on the contrary, he sat up, extremely alert, behind the great writing-table on which his hand had fallen with the sound of a sharp blow.

"What I want to know is what put it out of your head till now."

"Put it out of my head," repeated the Chief Inspector very slowly.

"Yes. Till you were called into this room—you know."

The Chief Inspector felt as if the air between his clothing and his skin had become unpleasantly hot. It was the sensation of an unprecedented and incredible experience.

"Of course," he said, exaggerating the deliberation of his utterance to the utmost limits of possibility, "if there is a reason, of which I know nothing, for not interfering with the convict Michaelis, perhaps it's just as well I didn't start the county police after him."

This took such a long time to say that the unflagging attention of the Assistant Commissioner seemed a wonderful feat of endurance. His retort came without delay.

"No reason whatever that I know of. Come, Chief Inspector, this finessing with me is highly improper on your part—highly improper. And it's also unfair, you know. You shouldn't leave me to puzzle things out for myself like this. Really, I am surprised."

He paused, then added smoothly: "I need scarcely tell you that this conversation is altogether unofficial."

These words were far from pacifying the Chief Inspector. The indignation of a betrayed tight-rope performer was strong within him. In his pride of a trusted servant he was affected by the assurance that the rope was not shaken for the purpose of breaking his neck, as by an exhibition of impudence. As if anybody were afraid! Assistant Commissioners come and go, but a valuable Chief Inspector is not an ephemeral office phenomenon. He was not afraid of getting a broken neck. To have his performance spoiled was more than enough to account for the glow of honest indignation. And as thought is no respecter of persons, the thought of Chief Inspector Heat took a threatening and prophetic shape. "You, my boy," he said to himself, keeping his round and habitually roving eyes fastened upon the Assistant Commissioner's face—"you, my boy, you don't know your place, and your place won't know you very long either, I bet."

As if in provoking answer to that thought, something like the ghost of an amiable smile passed on the lips of the Assistant Commissioner. His manner was easy and businesslike while he persisted in administering another shake to the tightrope.

"Let us come now to what you have discovered on the spot, Chief Inspector," he said.

"A fool and his job are soon parted," went on the train of prophetic thought in Chief Inspector Heat's head. But it was immediately followed by the reflection that a higher official, even when "fired out" (this was the precise image), has still the time as he flies through the door to launch a nasty kick at the shinbones of a subordinate. Without softening very much the basilisk nature of his stare, he said, impassively:

"We are coming to that part of my investigation, sir."

"That's right. Well, what have you brought away from it?"

The Chief Inspector, who had made up his mind to jump off the rope, came to the ground with gloomy frankness.

"I've brought away an address," he said, pulling out of his pocket without haste a singed rag of dark blue cloth. "This belongs to the overcoat the fellow who got himself blown to pieces was wearing. Of course, the overcoat may not have been his, and may even have been stolen. But that's not at all probable if you look at this."

The Chief Inspector, stepping up to the table, smoothed out carefully the rag of blue cloth. He had picked it up from the repulsive heap in the mortuary, because a tailor's name is found sometimes under the collar. It is not often of much use, but still—— He only half expected to find anything useful, but certainly he did not expect to find—not under the collar at all, but stitched carefully on the under side of the lapel—a square piece of calico with an address written on it in marking ink.

The Chief Inspector removed his smoothing hand.

"I carried it off with me without anybody taking notice," he said. "I thought it best. It can always be produced if required."

The Assistant Commissioner, rising a little in his chair, pulled the cloth over to his side of the table. He sat looking at it in silence. Only the number 32 and the name of Brett Street were written in marking ink on a piece of calico slightly larger than an ordinary cigarette paper. He was genuinely surprised.

"Can't understand why he should have gone about labelled like this," he said, looking up at Chief Inspector Heat. "It's a most extraordinary thing."

"I met once in the smoking-room of a hotel an old gentleman who went about with his name and address sewn on in all his coats in case of an accident or sudden illness," said the Chief Inspector. "He professed to be eighty-four years old, but he didn't look his age. He told me he was also afraid of losing his memory suddenly, like those people he had been reading of in the papers."

A question from the Assistant Commissioner, who wanted to know what was No. 32 Brett Street, interrupted that reminiscence abruptly. The Chief Inspector, driven down to the ground by unfair artifices, had elected to walk the path of unreserved openness. If he believed firmly that to know too much was not good for the department, the judicious holding back of knowledge was as far as his loyalty dared to go for the good of the service. If the Assistant Commissioner wanted to mismanage this affair nothing, of course, could prevent him. But, on his own part, he now saw no reason for a display of alacrity. So he answered concisely:

"It's a shop, sir."

The Assistant Commissioner, with his eyes lowered on the rag of blue cloth, waited for more information. As that did not come he proceeded to obtain it by a series of questions propounded with gentle patience. Thus he acquired an idea of the nature of Mr. Verloc's commerce, of his personal appearance, and heard at last his name. In a pause the Assistant Commissioner raised his eyes, and discovered some animation on the Chief Inspector's face. They looked at each other in silence.

"Of course," said the latter, "the department has no record of that man."

"Did any of my predecessors have any knowledge of what you have told me now?" asked the Assistant Commissioner, putting his elbows on the table and raising his joined hands before his face, as if about to offer prayer, only that his eyes had not a pious expression.

"No, sir; certainly not. What would have been the object? That sort of man could never be produced publicly to any good purpose. It was sufficient for me to know who he was, and to make use of him in a way that could be used publicly."

"And do you think that sort of private knowledge consistent with the official position you occupy?"

"Perfectly, sir. I think it's quite proper. I will take the liberty to tell you, sir, that it makes me what I am—and I am looked upon as a man who knows his work. It's a private affair of my own. A personal friend of mine in the French police gave me the hint that the fellow was an Embassy spy. Private friendship, private information, private use of it—that's how I look upon it."

The Assistant Commissioner, after remarking to himself that the mental state of the renowned Chief Inspector seemed to affect the outline of his lower jaw, as if the lively sense of his high professional distinction had been located in that part of his anatomy, dismissed the point for the moment with a calm "I see." Then leaning his cheek on his joined hands:

"Well, then—speaking privately if you like—how long have you been in private touch with this Embassy spy?"

To this inquiry the private answer of the Chief Inspector, so private that it was never shaped into audible words, was:

"Long before you were even thought of for your place here."

The so-to-speak public utterance was much more precise.

"I saw him for the first time in my life a little more than seven years ago, when two Imperial Highnesses and the Imperial Chancellor were on a visit here. I was put in charge of all the arrangements for looking after them. Baron Stott-Wartenheim was Ambassador then. He was a very nervous old gentleman. One evening, three days before the Guildhall Banquet, he sent word that he wanted to see me for a moment. I was downstairs, and the carriages were at the door to take the Imperial Highnesses and the Chancellor to the opera. I went up at once. I found the Baron walking up and down his bedroom in a pitiable state of distress, squeezing his hands together. He assured me he had the fullest confidence in our police and in my abilities, but he had there a man just come over from Paris whose information could be trusted implicitly. He wanted me to hear what that man had to say. He took me at once into a dressing-room next door, where I saw a big fellow in a heavy overcoat sitting all alone on a chair, and holding his hat and stick in one hand. The Baron said to him in French, 'Speak, my friend.' The light in that room was not very good. I talked with him for some five minutes perhaps. He certainly gave me a piece of very startling news. Then the Baron took me aside nervously to praise him up to me, and when I turned round again I discovered that the fellow had vanished like a ghost. Got up and sneaked out down some back stairs, I suppose. There was no time to run after him, as I had to hurry off after the Ambassador down the great staircase, and see the party started safe for the opera. However, I acted upon the information that very night. Whether it was perfectly correct or not, it did look serious enough. Very likely it saved us from an ugly trouble on the day of the Imperial visit to the City.

"Some time later, a month or so after my promotion to Chief Inspector, my attention was attracted to a big burly man, I thought I had seen somewhere before, coming out in a hurry from a jeweller's shop in the Strand. I went after him, as it was on my way towards Charing Cross, and there seeing one of our detectives across the road, I beckoned him over, and pointed out the fellow to him, with instructions to watch his movements for a couple of days, and then report to me. No later than next afternoon my man turned up to tell me that the fellow had married his landlady's daughter at a registrar's office that very day at 11.30 A.M., and had gone off with her to Margate for a week. Our man had seen the luggage being put on the cab. There were some old Paris labels on one of the bags. Somehow I couldn't get the fellow out of my head, and the very next time I had to go to Paris on service I spoke about him to that friend of mine in the Paris police. My friend said: 'From what you tell me I think you must mean a rather well-known hanger-on and emissary of the Revolutionary Red Committee. He says he is an Englishman by birth. We have an idea that he has been for a good few years now a secret agent of one of the foreign Embassies in London.' This woke up my memory completely. He was the vanishing fellow I saw sitting on a chair in Baron Stott-Wartenheim's bathroom. I told my friend that he was quite right. The fellow was a secret agent to my certain knowledge. Afterwards my friend took the trouble to ferret out the complete record of that man for me. I thought I had better know all there was to know; but I don't suppose you want to hear his history now, sir?"

The Assistant Commissioner shook his supported head. "The history of your relations with that useful personage is the only thing that matters just now," he said, closing slowly his weary, deep-set eyes, and then opening them swiftly with a greatly refreshed glance.

"There's nothing official about them," said the Chief Inspector, bitterly. "I went into his shop one evening, told him who I was, and reminded him of our first meeting. He didn't as much as twitch an eyebrow. He said that he was married and settled now, and that all he wanted was not to be interfered in his little business. I took it upon myself to promise him that, as long as he didn't go in for anything obviously outrageous, he would be left alone by the police. That was worth something to him, because a word from us to the Custom-House people would have been enough to get some of these packages he gets from Paris and Brussels opened in Dover, with confiscation to follow for certain, and perhaps a prosecution as well at the end of it."

"That's a very precarious trade," murmured the Assistant Commissioner. "Why did he go in for that?"

The Chief Inspector raised scornful eyebrows dispassionately.

"Most likely got a connection—friends on the Continent—amongst people who deal in such wares. They would be just the sort he would consort with. He's a lazy dog, too—like the rest of them."

"What do you get from him in exchange for your protection?"

The Chief Inspector was not inclined to enlarge on the value of Mr. Verloc's services.

"He would not be much good to anybody but myself. One has got to know a good deal beforehand to make use of a man like that. I can understand the sort of hint he can give. And when I want a hint he can generally furnish it to me."

The Chief Inspector lost himself suddenly in a discreet reflective mood; and the Assistant Commissioner repressed a smile at the fleeting thought that the reputation of Chief Inspector Heat might possibly have been made in a great part by the Secret Agent Verloc.

"In a more general way of being of use, all our men of the Special Crimes section on duty at Charing Cross and Victoria have orders to take careful notice of anybody they may see with him. He meets the new arrivals frequently, and afterwards keeps track of them. He seems to have been told off for that sort of duty. When I want an address in a hurry, I can always get it from him. Of course, I know how to manage our relations. I haven't seen him to speak to three times in the last two years. I drop him a line, unsigned, and he answers me in the same way at my private address."

From time to time the Assistant Commissioner gave an almost imperceptible nod. The Chief Inspector added that he did not suppose Mr. Verloc to be deep in the confidence of the prominent members of the Revolutionary International Council, but that he was generally trusted there could be no doubt. "Whenever I've had reason to think there was something in the wind," he concluded, "I've always found he could tell me something worth knowing."

The Assistant Commissioner made a significant remark.

"He failed you this time."

"Neither had I wind of anything in any other way," retorted Chief Inspector Heat. "I asked him nothing so he could tell me nothing. He isn't one of our men. It isn't as if he were in our pay."

"No," muttered the Assistant Commissioner. "He's a spy in the pay of a foreign government. We could never confess to him."

"I must do my work in my own way," declared the Chief Inspector. "When it comes to that I would deal with the devil himself, and take the consequences. There are things not fit for everybody to know."

"Your idea of secrecy seems to consist in keeping the chief of your department in the dark. That's stretching it perhaps a little too far, isn't it? He lives over his shop?"

"Who—Verloc? Oh, yes. He lives over his shop. The wife's mother, I fancy, lives with them."

"Is the house watched?"

"Oh, dear, no. It wouldn't do. Certain people who come there are watched. My opinion is that he knows nothing of this affair."

"How do you account for this?" The Assistant Commissioner nodded at the cloth rag lying before him on the table.

"I don't account for it at all, sir. It's simply unaccountable. It can't be explained by what I know." The Chief Inspector made those admissions with the frankness of a man whose reputation is established as if on a rock. "At any rate not at this present moment. I think that the man who had most to do with it will turn out to be Michaelis."

"You do?"

"Yes, sir; because I can answer for all the others."

"What about that other man supposed to have escaped from the park?"

"I should think he's far away by this time," opined the Chief Inspector.

The Assistant Commissioner looked hard at him, and rose suddenly, as though having made up his mind to some course of action. As a matter of fact, he had that very moment succumbed to a fascinating temptation. The Chief Inspector heard himself dismissed with instructions to meet his superior early next morning for further consultation upon the case. He listened with an impenetrable face, and walked out of the room with measured steps.

Whatever might have been the plans of the Assistant Commissioner they had nothing to do with that desk work, which was the bane of his existence because of its confined nature and apparent lack of reality. It could not have had, or else the general air of alacrity that came upon the Assistant Commissioner would have been inexplicable. As soon as he was left alone he looked for his hat impulsively, and put it on his head. Having done that, he sat down again to reconsider the whole matter. But as his mind was already made up, this did not take long. And before Chief Inspector Heat had gone very far on the way home, he also left the building.

CHAPTER SEVEN

The Assistant Commissioner walked along a short and narrow street like a wet, muddy ditch, then crossing a very broad thoroughfare entered a public edifice, and sought speech with a young private secretary (unpaid) of a great personage.

This fair, smooth-faced young man, whose symmetrically arranged hair gave him the air of a large and neat schoolboy, met the Assistant Commissioner's request with a doubtful look, and spoke with bated breath.

"Would he see you? I don't know about that. He has walked over from the House an hour ago to talk with the permanent Under-

418

Secretary, and now he's ready to walk back again. He might have
sent for him; but he does it for the sake of a little exercise, I suppose.
It's all the exercise he can find time for while this session lasts. I don't
complain; I rather enjoy these little strolls. He leans on my arm, and
doesn't open his lips. But, I say, he's very tired, and—well—not in the
sweetest of tempers just now."

"It's in connection with that Greenwich affair."

"Oh! I say! He's very bitter against you people. But I will go and
see, if you insist."

"Do. That's a good fellow," said the Assistant Commissioner.

The unpaid secretary admired this pluck. Composing for himself
an innocent face, he opened a door, and went in with the assurance
of a nice and privileged child. And presently he reappeared, with a
nod to the Assistant Commissioner who, passing through the same
door left open for him, found himself with the great personage in a
large room.

Vast in bulk and stature, with a long white face, which, broadened
at the base by a big double chin, appeared egg-shaped in the fringe
of thin greyish whisker, the great personage seemed an expanding man.
Unfortunate from a tailoring point of view, the cross-folds in the
middle of a buttoned black coat added to the impression, as if the
fastenings of the garment were tried to the utmost. From the head,
set upward on a thick neck, the eyes, with puffy lower lids, stared with
a haughty droop on each side of a hooked, aggressive nose, nobly
salient in the vast pale circumference of the face. A shiny silk hat
and a pair of worn gloves lying ready on the end of a long table
looked expanded, too, enormous.

He stood on the hearthrug in big, roomy boots, and uttered no
word of greeting.

"I would like to know if this is the beginning of another dynamite
campaign," he asked at once in a deep, very smooth voice. "Don't
go into details. I have no time for that."

The Assistant Commissioner's figure before this big and rustic
Presence had the frail slenderness of a reed addressing an oak. And
indeed the unbroken record of that man's descent surpassed in the
number of centuries the age of the oldest oak in the country.

"No. As far as one can be positive about anything I can assure you
that it is not."

"Yes. But your idea of assurances over there," said the great man,
with a contemptuous wave of his hand towards a window giving on
the broad thoroughfare, "seems to consist mainly in making the Secretary of State look a fool. I have been told positively in this very room
less than a month ago that nothing of the sort was even possible."

The Assistant Commissioner glanced in the direction of the window calmly.

"You will allow me to remark, Sir Ethelred, that so far I have had no opportunity to give you assurances of any kind."

The haughty droop of the eyes was focussed now upon the Assistant Commissioner.

"True," confessed the deep, smooth voice. "I sent for Heat. You are still rather a novice in your new berth. And how are you getting on over there?"

"I believe I am learning something every day."

"Of course, of course. I hope you will get on."

"Thank you, Sir Ethelred. I've learned something to-day, and even within the last hour or so. There is much in this affair of a kind that does not meet the eye in a usual anarchist outrage, even if one looked into it as deep as can be. That's why I am here."

The great man put his arms akimbo, the backs of his big hands resting on his hips.

"Very well. Go on. Only no details, pray. Spare me the details."

"You shall not be troubled with them, Sir Ethelred," the Assistant Commissioner began, with a calm and untroubled assurance. While he was speaking the hands on the face of the clock behind the great man's back—a heavy, glistening affair of massive scrolls in the same dark marble as the mantelpiece, and with a ghostly, evanescent tick—had moved through the space of seven minutes. He spoke with a studious fidelity to a parenthetical manner, into which every little fact—that is, every detail—fitted with delightful ease. Not a murmur nor even a movement hinted at interruption. The great Personage might have been the statue of one of his own princely ancestors stripped of a crusader's war harness, and put into an ill-fitting frock coat. The Assistant Commissioner felt as though he were at liberty to talk for an hour. But he kept his head, and at the end of the time mentioned above he broke off with a sudden conclusion, which, reproducing the opening statement, pleasantly surprised Sir Ethelred by its apparent swiftness and force.

"The kind of thing which meets us under the surface of this affair, otherwise without gravity, is unusual—in this precise form at least—and requires special treatment."

The tone of Sir Ethelred was deepened, full of conviction.

"I should think so—involving the Ambassador of a foreign power!"

"Oh! The Ambassador!" protested the other, erect and slender, allowing himself a mere half smile. "It would be stupid of me to advance anything of the kind. And it is absolutely unnecessary, because if I am right in my surmises, whether ambassador or hall porter it's a mere detail."

Sir Ethelred opened a wide mouth, like a cavern, into which the hooked nose seemed anxious to peer; there came from it a subdued rolling sound, as from a distant organ with the scornful indignation stop.

"No! These people are too impossible. What do they mean by importing their methods of Crim-Tartary here? A Turk would have more decency."

"You forget, Sir Ethelred, that strictly speaking we know nothing positively—as yet."

"No! But how would you define it? Shortly?"

"Barefaced audacity amounting to childishness of a peculiar sort."

"We can't put up with the innocence of nasty little children," said the great and expanded Personage, expanding a little more, as it were. The haughty, drooping glance struck crushingly the carpet at the Assistant Commissioner's feet. "They'll have to get a hard rap on the knuckles over this affair. We must be in a position to—— What is your general idea, stated shortly? No need to go into details."

"No, Sir Ethelred. In principle, I should lay it down that the existence of secret agents should not be tolerated, as tending to augment the positive dangers of the evil against which they are used. That the spy will fabricate his information is a mere commonplace. But in the sphere of political and revolutionary action, relying partly on violence, the professional spy has every facility to fabricate the very facts themselves, and will spread the double evil of emulation in one direction, and of panic, hasty legislation, unreflecting hate, on the other. However, this is an imperfect world——"

The deep-voiced Presence on the hearthrug, motionless, with big elbows stuck out, said hastily:

"Be lucid, please."

"Yes, Sir Ethelred—— An imperfect world. Therefore directly the character of this affair suggested itself to me, I thought it should be dealt with with special secrecy, and ventured to come over here."

"That's right," approved the great Personage, glancing down complacently over his double chin. "I am glad there's somebody over at your shop who thinks that the Secretary of State may be trusted now and then."

The Assistant Commissioner had an amused smile.

"I was really thinking that it might be better at this stage for Heat to be replaced by——"

"What! Heat? An ass—eh?" exclaimed the great man, with distinct animosity.

"Not at all. Pray, Sir Ethelred, don't put that unjust interpretation on my remarks."

"Then what? Too clever by half?"

"Neither—at least not as a rule. All the grounds of my surmises I have from him. The only thing I've discovered by myself is that he has been making use of that man privately. Who could blame him? He's an old police hand. He told me virtually that he must have tools to work with. It occurred to me that this tool should be surrendered to the Special Crimes division as a whole, instead of remaining the private property of Chief Inspector Heat. I extend my conception of our departmental duties to the suppression of the secret agent. But Chief Inspector Heat is an old departmental hand. He would accuse me of perverting its morality and attacking its efficiency. He would define it bitterly as protection extended to the criminal class of revolutionists. It would mean just that to him."

"Yes. But what do you mean?"

"I mean to say, first, that there's but poor comfort in being able to declare that any given act of violence—damaging property or destroying life—is not the work of anarchism at all, but of something else altogether—some species of authorized scoundrelism. This, I fancy, is much more frequent than we suppose. Next, it's obvious that the existence of these people in the pay of foreign governments destroys in a measure the efficiency of our supervision. A spy of that sort can afford to be more reckless than the most reckless of conspirators. His occupation is free from all restraint. He's without as much faith as is necessary for complete negation, and without that much law as is implied in lawlessness. Thirdly, the existence of these spies amongst the revolutionary groups, which we are reproached for harbouring here, does away with all certitude. You have received a reassuring statement from Chief Inspector Heat some time ago. It was by no means groundless—and yet this episode happens. I call it an episode, because this affair, I make bold to say, is episodic; it is no part of any general scheme, however wild. The very peculiarities which surprise and perplex Chief Inspector Heat establish its character in my eyes. I am keeping clear of details, Sir Ethelred."

The Personage on the hearthrug had been listening with profound attention.

"Just so. Be as concise as you can."

The Assistant Commissioner intimated by an earnest, deferential gesture that he was anxious to be concise.

"There is a peculiar stupidity and feebleness in the conduct of this affair which gives me excellent hopes of getting behind it and finding there something else than an individual freak of fanaticism. For it is a planned thing, undoubtedly. The actual perpetrator seems to have been led by the hand to the spot, and then abandoned hurriedly to his own devices. The inference is that he was imported from abroad for the purpose of committing this outrage. At the same time one is forced to the conclusion that he did not know enough English to ask his way, unless one were to accept the fantastic theory that he was a deaf mute. I wonder now—— But this is idle. He has destroyed himself by an accident, obviously. Not an extraordinary accident. But an extraordinary little fact remains: the address on his clothing discovered by the merest accident, too. It is an incredible little fact, so incredible that the explanation which will account for it is bound to touch the bottom of this affair. Instead of instructing Heat to go on with this case, my intention is to seek this explanation personally—by myself, I mean—where it may be picked up. That is in a certain shop in Brett Street, and on the lips of a certain secret agent once upon a time the confidential and trusted spy of the late Baron Stott-Wartenheim, Ambassador of a Great Power to the Court of St. James."

The Assistant Commissioner paused, then added: "Those fellows are a perfect pest." In order to raise his drooping glance to the speaker's face, the Personage on the hearthrug had gradually tilted his head farther back, which gave him an aspect of extraordinary haughtiness.

"Why not leave it to Heat?"

"Because he is an old departmental hand. They have their own morality. My line of inquiry would appear to him an awful perversion of duty. For him the plain duty is to fasten the guilt upon as many prominent anarchists as he can on some slight indications he had picked up in the course of his investigation on the spot; whereas I, he would say, am bent upon vindicating their innocence. I am trying to be as lucid as I can in presenting this obscure matter to you without details."

"He would, would he?" muttered the proud head of Sir Ethelred from its lofty elevation.

"I am afraid so—with an indignation and disgust of which you or I can have no idea. He's an excellent servant. We must not put an undue strain on his loyalty. That's always a mistake. Besides, I want a free hand—a freer hand than it would be perhaps advisable to give Chief Inspector Heat. I haven't the slightest wish to spare this man Verloc. He will, I imagine, be extremely startled to find his connection with this affair, whatever it may be, brought home to him so quickly. Frightening him will not be very difficult. But our true objective lies behind him somewhere. I want your authority to give him such assurances of personal safety as I may think proper."

"Certainly," said the Personage on the hearthrug. "Find out as much as you can; find it out in your own way."

"I must set about it without loss of time, this very evening," said the Assistant Commissioner.

Sir Ethelred shifted one hand under his coat tails, and tilting back his head, looked at him steadily.

"We'll have a late sitting to-night," he said. "Come to the House with your discoveries if we are not gone home. I'll warn Toodles to look out for you. He'll take you into my room."

The numerous family and the wide connections of the youthful-looking Private Secretary cherished for him the hope of an austere and exalted destiny. Meantime, the social sphere he adorned in his hours of idleness chose to pet him under the above nickname. And Sir Ethelred, hearing it on the lips of his wife and girls every day (mostly at breakfast-time), had conferred upon it the dignity of un-smiling adoption.

The Assistant Commissioner was surprised and gratified extremely.

"I shall certainly bring my discoveries to the House on the chance of you having the time to——"

"I won't have the time," interrupted the great Personage. "But I will see you. I haven't the time now—— And you are going yourself?"

"Yes, Sir Ethelred. I think it the best way."

The Personage had tilted his head so far back that, in order to keep the Assistant Commissioner under his observation, he had to nearly close his eyes.

"H'm. Ha! And how do you propose—— Will you assume a disguise?"

"Hardly a disguise! I'll change my clothes, of course."

"Of course," repeated the great man, with a sort of absent-minded loftiness. He turned his big head slowly, and over his shoulder gave a haughty, oblique stare to the ponderous marble timepiece with the sly, feeble tick. The gilt hands had taken the opportunity to steal through no less than five and twenty minutes behind his back.

The Assistant Commissioner, who could not see them, grew a little nervous in the interval. But the great man presented to him a calm and undismayed face.

"Very well," he said, and paused, as if in deliberate contempt of the official clock. "But what first put you in motion in this direction?"

"I have been always of opinion," began the Assistant Commissioner.

"Ah. Yes! Opinion. That's of course. But the immediate motive?"

"What shall I say, Sir Ethelred? A new man's antagonism to old methods. A desire to know something at first hand. Some impatience. It's my old work, but the harness is different. It has been chafing me a little in one or two tender places."

"I hope you'll get on over there," said the great man, kindly, extending his hand, soft to the touch, but broad and powerful like the hand of a glorified farmer. The Assistant Commissioner shook it, and withdrew.

In the outer room Toodles, who had been waiting perched on the edge of a table, advanced to meet him, subduing his natural buoyancy.

"Well? Satisfactory?" he asked, with airy importance.

"Perfectly. You've earned my undying gratitude," answered the Assistant Commissioner, whose long face looked wooden in contrast with the peculiar character of the other's gravity, which seemed perpetually ready to break into ripples and chuckles.

"That's all right. But, seriously, you can't imagine how irritated he is by the attacks on his Bill for the Nationalization of Fisheries. They call it the beginning of social revolution. Of course, it is a revolutionary measure. But these fellows have no decency. The personal attacks——"

"I read the papers," remarked the Assistant Commissioner.

"Odious? Eh? And you have no notion what a mass of work he has got to get through every day. He does it all himself. Seems unable to trust any one with these Fisheries."

"And yet he's given a whole half hour to the consideration of my very small sprat," interjected the Assistant Commissioner.

"Small! Is it? I'm glad to hear that. But it's a pity you didn't keep away, then. This fight takes it out of him frightfully. The man's getting exhausted. I feel it by the way he leans on my arm as we walk over. And, I say, is he safe in the streets? Mullins has been marching his men up here this afternoon. There's a constable stuck by every lamp-post, and every second person we meet between this and Palace Yard is an obvious 'tec.' It will get on his nerves presently. I say, these foreign scoundrels aren't likely to throw something at him—are they? It would be a national calamity. The country can't spare him."

"Not to mention yourself. He leans on your arm," suggested the Assistant Commissioner, soberly. "You would both go."

"It would be an easy way for a young man to go down into history! Not so many British Ministers have been assassinated as to make it a minor incident. But seriously now——"

"I am afraid that if you want to go down into history you'll have to do something for it. Seriously, there's no danger whatever for both of you but from overwork."

The sympathetic Toodles welcomed this opening for a chuckle.

"The Fisheries won't kill me. I am used to late hours," he declared, with ingenuous levity. But, feeling an instant compunction, he began to assume an air of statesmanlike moodiness, as one draws on a glove. "His massive intellect will stand any amount of work. It's his nerves that I am afraid of. The reactionary gang, with that abusive brute Cheeseman at their head, insult him every night."

"If he will insist on beginning a revolution!" murmured the Assistant Commissioner.

"The time has come, and he is the only man great enough for the work," protested the revolutionary Toodles, flaring up under the calm, speculative gaze of the Assistant Commissioner. Somewhere in a corridor a distant bell tinkled urgently, and with devoted vigilance the young man pricked up his ears at the sound. "He's ready to go now," he exclaimed in a whisper, snatched up his hat, and vanished from the room.

The Assistant Commissioner went out by another door in a less elastic manner. Again he crossed the wide thoroughfare, walked along a narrow street, and re-entered hastily his own departmental buildings. He kept up this accelerated pace to the door of his private room. Before he had closed it fairly his eyes sought his desk. He stood still for a moment, then walked up, looked all round on the floor, sat down in his chair, rang a bell, and waited.

"Chief Inspector Heat gone yet?"

"Yes, sir. Went away half-an-hour ago."

He nodded. "That will do." And sitting still, with his hat pushed off his forehead, he thought that it was just like Heat's confounded cheek to carry off quietly the only piece of material evidence. But he thought this without animosity. Old and valued servants will take liberties. The piece of overcoat with the address sewn on was certainly not a thing to leave about. Dismissing from his mind this manifestation of Chief Inspector Heat's mistrust, he wrote and despatched a note to his wife, charging her to make his apologies to Michaelis' great lady, with whom they were engaged to dine that evening.

The short jacket and the low, round hat he assumed in a sort of curtained alcove containing a washstand, a row of wooden pegs and a shelf, brought out wonderfully the length of his grave, brown face. He stepped back into the full light of the room, looking like the vision of a cool, reflective Don Quixote, with the sunken eyes of a dark enthusiast and a very deliberate manner. He left the scene of his daily labours quickly like an unobtrusive shadow. His descent into the street was like the descent into a slimy aquarium from which the water had been run off. A murky, gloomy dampness enveloped him. The walls of the houses were wet, the mud of the roadway glistened with an effect of phosphorescence, and when he emerged into the Strand out of a narrow street by the side of Charing Cross Station the genius of the locality assimilated him. He might have been but one more of the queer foreign fish that can be seen of an evening about there flitting round the dark corners.

He came to a stand on the very edge of the pavement, and waited. His exercised eyes had made out in the confused movements of lights and shadows thronging the roadway the crawling approach of a hansom. He gave no sign; but when the low step gliding along the curbstone came to his feet he dodged in skilfully in front of the big turning wheel, and spoke up through the little trap door almost before the man gazing supinely ahead from his perch was aware of having been boarded by a fare.

It was not a long drive. It ended by signal abruptly, nowhere in particular, between two lamp-posts before a large drapery establishment—a long range of shops already lapped up in sheets of corrugated iron for the night. Tendering a coin through the trap door the fare slipped out and away, leaving an effect of uncanny, eccentric ghostliness upon the driver's mind. But the size of the coin was satisfactory to his touch, and his education not being literary, he remained untroubled by the fear of finding it presently turned to a dead leaf in his pocket. Raised above the world of fares by the nature of his calling, he contemplated their action with a limited interest. The sharp pulling of his horse right round expressed his philosophy.

Meantime, the Assistant Commissioner was already giving his order to a waiter in a little Italian restaurant round the corner—one of those traps for the hungry, long and narrow, baited with a perspective of mirrors and white napery; without air, but with an atmosphere of their own—an atmosphere of fraudulent cookery mocking an abject mankind in the most pressing of its miserable necessities. In this immoral atmosphere the Assistant Commissioner, reflecting upon his enterprise, seemed to lose some more of his identity. He had a sense of loneliness, of evil freedom. It was rather pleasant. When, after paying for his short meal, he stood up and waited for his change, he saw himself in the sheet of glass, and was struck by his foreign appearance. He contemplated his own image with a melancholy and inquisitive gaze, then by sudden inspiration raised the collar of his jacket. This arrangement appeared to him commendable, and he completed it by giving an upward twist to the ends of his black moustache. He was satisfied by the subtle modification of his personal aspect caused by these small changes. "That'll do very well," he thought. "I'll get a little wet, a little splashed——"

He became aware of the waiter at his elbow and of a small pile of silver coins on the edge of the table before him. The waiter kept one eye on it, while his other eye followed the long back of a tall, not very young girl, who passed up to a distant table, looking perfectly sightless and altogether unapproachable. She seemed to be an habitual customer.

On going out the Assistant Commissioner made to himself the observation that the patrons of the place had lost in the frequentation of fraudulent cookery all their national and private characteristics. And this was strange, since the Italian restaurant is such a peculiarly British institution. But these people were as denationalized as the dishes set before them with every circumstance of unstamped respectability. Neither was their personality stamped in any way, professionally, socially, or racially. They seemed created for the Italian restaurant, unless the Italian restaurant had been perchance created for them. But that last hypothesis was unthinkable, since one could not place them anywhere outside those special establishments. One never met these enigmatical persons elsewhere. It was impossible to form a precise idea what occupations they followed by day and where they went to bed at night. And he himself had become unplaced. It would have been impossible for anybody to guess his occupation. As to going to bed, there was a doubt even in his own mind. Not indeed in regard to his domicile itself, but very much so in respect of the time when he would be able to return there. A pleasurable feeling of independence possessed him when he heard the glass doors swing to behind his back with a sort of imperfect baffled thud. He advanced at once into an immensity of greasy slime and damp plaster interspersed with lamps, and enveloped, oppressed, penetrated, choked, and suffocated by the blackness of a wet London night, which is composed of soot and drops of water.

Brett Street was not very far away. It branched off, narrow, from the side of an open triangular space surrounded by dark and mysterious houses, temples of petty commerce emptied of traders for the night. Only a fruiterer's stall at the corner made a violent blaze of light and colour. Beyond all was black, and the few people passing in that direction vanished at one stride beyond the glowing heaps of oranges and lemons. No footsteps echoed. They would never be heard of again. The adventurous head of the Special Crimes Department watched these disappearances from a distance with an interested eye. He felt light-hearted, as though he had been ambushed all alone in a jungle many thousands of miles away from departmental desks and official inkstands. This joyousness and dispersion of thought before a task of some importance seems to prove that this world of ours is not such a very serious affair after all. For the Assistant Commissioner was not constitutionally inclined to levity.

The policeman on the beat projected his sombre and moving form against the luminous glory of oranges and lemons, and entered Brett Street without haste. The Assistant Commissioner, as though he were a member of the criminal classes, lingered out of sight, awaiting his return. But this constable seemed to be lost for ever to the force. He never returned: must have gone out at the other end of Brett Street.

The Assistant Commissioner, reaching this conclusion, entered the street in his turn, and came upon a large van arrested in front of the dimly lit window-panes of a carters' eating-house. The man was refreshing himself inside, and the horses, their big heads lowered to the ground, fed out of nose-bags steadily. Farther on, on the opposite side of the street, another suspect patch of dim light issued from Mr. Verloc's shop front, hung with papers, heaving with vague piles of cardboard boxes and the shapes of books. The Assistant Commissioner stood observing it across the roadway. There could be no mistake. By the side of the front window, encumbered by the shadows of nondescript things, the door, standing ajar, let escape on the pavement a narrow, clear streak of gaslight within.

Behind the Assistant Commissioner the van and horses, merged into one mass, seemed something alive—a square-backed black monster blocking half the street, with sudden iron-shod stampings, fierce jingles, and heavy, blowing sighs. The harshly festive, ill-omened glare of a large and prosperous public-house faced the other end of Brett Street across a wide road. This barrier of blazing lights, opposing the shadows gathered about the humble abode of Mr. Verloc's domestic happiness, seemed to drive the obscurity of the street back upon itself, make it more sullen, brooding, and sinister.

CHAPTER EIGHT

Having infused by persistent importunities some sort of heat into the chilly interest of several licenced victuallers (the acquaintances once upon a time of her late unlucky husband), Mrs. Verloc's mother had at last secured her admission to certain almshouses founded by a wealthy innkeeper for the destitute widows of the trade.

This end, conceived in the astuteness of her uneasy heart, the old woman had pursued with secrecy and determination. That was the time when her daughter Winnie could not help passing a remark to Mr. Verloc that "mother has been spending half-crowns and five shillings almost every day this last week in cab fares." But the remark was not made grudgingly. Winnie respected her mother's infirmities. She was only a little surprised at this sudden mania for locomotion. Mr. Verloc, who was sufficiently magnificent in his way, had grunted the remark impatiently aside as interfering with his meditations. These were frequent, deep, and prolonged; they bore upon a matter more important than five shillings. Distinctly more important, and beyond all comparison more difficult to consider in all its aspects with philosophical serenity.

Her object attained in astute secrecy, the heroic old woman had made a clean breast of it to Mrs. Verloc. Her soul was triumphant and her heart tremulous. Inwardly she quaked, because she dreaded and admired the calm, self-contained character of her daughter Winnie, whose displeasure was made redoubtable by a diversity of dieadful silences. But she did not allow her inward apprehensions to rob her of the advantage of venerable placidity conferred upon her outward person by her triple chin, the floating ampleness of her ancient form, and the impotent condition of her legs.

The shock of the information was so unexpected that Mrs. Verloc, against her usual practice when addressed, interrupted the domestic occupation she was engaged upon. It was the dusting of the furniture in the parlour behind the shop. She turned her head towards her mother.

"Whatever did you want to do that for?" she exclaimed, in scandalized astonishment.

The shock must have been severe to make her depart from that distant and uninquiring acceptance of facts which was her force and her safeguard in life.

"Weren't you made comfortable enough here?"

She had lapsed into these inquiries, but next moment she saved the consistency of her conduct by resuming her dusting, while the old woman sat scared and dumb under her dingy white cap and lustreless dark wig.

Winnie finished the chair, and ran the duster along the mahogany at the back of the horsehair sofa on which Mr. Verloc loved to take his ease in hat and overcoat. She was intent on her work, but presently she permitted herself another question.

"How in the world did you manage it, mother?"

As not affecting the inwardness of things, which it was Mrs. Verloc's principle to ignore, this curiosity was excusable. It bore merely on the methods. The old woman welcomed it eagerly as bringing forward something that could be talked about with much sincerity.

She favoured her daughter by an exhaustive answer full of names and enriched by side comments upon the ravages of time as observed in the alteration of human countenances. The names were principally the names of licenced victuallers—"poor daddy's friends, my dear." She enlarged with special appreciation on the kindness and condescension of a large brewer, a Baronet and an M.P., the Chairman of the Governors of the Charity. She expressed herself thus warmly because she had been allowed to interview by appointment his Private Secretary—"a very polite gentleman, all in black, with a gentle, sad voice, but so very, very thin and quiet. He was like a shadow, my dear."

Winnie, prolonging her dusting operations till the tale was told to the end, walked out of the parlour into the kitchen (down two steps) in her usual manner, without the slightest comment.

Shedding a few tears in sign of rejoicing at her daughter's mansuetude in this terrible affair, Mrs. Verloc's mother gave play to her astuteness in the direction of her furniture, because it was her own;

and sometimes she wished it hadn't been. Heroism is all very well, but there are circumstances when the disposal of a few tables and chairs, brass bedsteads, and so on, may be big with remote and disastrous consequences. She required a few pieces herself, the Foundation which, after many importunities, had gathered her to its charitable breast, giving nothing but bare planks and cheaply papered bricks to the objects of its solicitude. The delicacy guiding her choice to the least valuable and most dilapidated articles passed unacknowledged, because Winnie's philosophy consisted in not taking notice of the inside facts; she assumed that mother took what suited her best. As to Mr. Verloc, his intense meditation, like a sort of Chinese wall, isolated him completely from the phenomena of this world of vain effort and illusory appearances.

Her selection made, the disposal of the rest became a perplexing question in a particular way. She was leaving it in Brett Street, of course. But she had two children. Winnie was provided for by her sensible union with that excellent husband, Mr. Verloc. Stevie was destitute—and a little peculiar. His position had to be considered before the claims of legal justice and even the promptings of partiality. The possession of the furniture would not be in any sense a provision. He ought to have it—the poor boy. But to give it to him would be like tampering with his position of complete dependence. It was a sort of claim which she feared to weaken. Moreover, the susceptibilities of Mr. Verloc would perhaps not brook being beholden to his brother-in-law for the chairs he sat on. In a long experience of gentlemen lodgers, Mrs. Verloc's mother had acquired a dismal but resigned notion of the fantastic side of human nature. What if Mr. Verloc suddenly took it into his head to tell Stevie to take his blessed sticks somewhere out of that? A division, on the other hand, however carefully made, might give some cause of offence to Winnie. No. Stevie must remain destitute and dependent. And at the moment of leaving Brett Street she had said to her daughter: "No use waiting till I am dead, is there? Everything I leave here is altogether your own now, my dear."

Winnie, with her hat on, silent behind her mother's back, went on arranging the collar of the old woman's cloak. She got her handbag, an umbrella, with an impassive face. The time had come for the expenditure of the sum of three-and-sixpence on what might well be supposed the last cab drive of Mrs. Verloc's mother's life. They went out at the shop door.

The conveyance awaiting them would have illustrated the proverb that "truth can be more cruel than caricature," if such a proverb existed. Crawling behind an infirm horse, a metropolitan hackney carriage drew up on wobbly wheels and with a maimed driver on the box. This last peculiarity caused some embarrassment. Catching sight of a hooked iron contrivance protruding from the left sleeve of the man's coat, Mrs. Verloc's mother lost suddenly the heroic courage of these days. She really couldn't trust herself. "What do you think, Winnie?" She hung back. The passionate expostulations of the big-faced cabman seemed to be squeezed out of a blocked throat. Leaning over from his box, he whispered with mysterious indignation. What was the matter now? Was it possible to treat a man so? His enormous and unwashed countenance flamed red in the muddy stretch of the street. Was it likely they would have given him a licence, he inquired desperately, if——

The police constable of the locality quieted him by a friendly glance; then addressing himself to the two women without marked consideration, said:

"He's been driving a cab for twenty years. I never knew him to have an accident."

"Accident!" shouted the driver in a scornful whisper.

The policeman's testimony settled it. The modest assemblage of seven people, mostly under age, dispersed. Winnie followed her mother into the cab. Stevie climbed on the box. His vacant mouth and distressed eyes depicted the state of his mind in regard to the transactions which were taking place. In the narrow streets the progress of the journey was made sensible to those within by the near fronts of the houses gliding past slowly and shakily, with a great rattle and jingling of glass, as if about to collapse behind the cab; and the infirm horse, with the harness hung over his sharp backbone flapping very loose about his thighs, appeared to be dancing mincingly on his toes with infinite patience. Later on, in the wider space of Whitehall, all visual evidences of motion became imperceptible. The rattle and jingle of glass went on indefinitely in front of the long Treasury building— and time itself seemed to stand still.

At last Winnie observed: "This isn't a very good horse."

Her eyes gleamed in the shadow of the cab straight ahead, immovable. On the box, Stevie shut his vacant mouth first, in order to ejaculate earnestly: "Don't."

The driver, holding high the reins twisted around the hook, took no notice. Perhaps he had not heard. Stevie's breast heaved.

"Don't whip."

The man turned slowly his bloated and sodden face of many colours bristling with white hairs. His little red eyes glistened with moisture. His big lips had a violet tint. They remained closed. With the dirty back of his whip-hand he rubbed the stubble sprouting on his enormous chin.

"You mustn't," stammered out Stevie, violently, "it hurts."

"Mustn't whip?" queried the other in a thoughtful whisper, and immediately whipped. He did this, not because his soul was cruel and his heart evil, but because he had to earn his fare. And for a time the walls of St. Stephen's, with its towers and pinnacles, contemplated in immobility and silence a cab that jingled. It rolled, too, however. But on the bridge there was a commotion. Stevie suddenly proceeded to get down from the box. There were shouts on the pavement, people ran forward, the driver pulled up, whispering curses of indignation and astonishment. Winnie lowered the window, and put her head out, white as a ghost. In the depths of the cab, her mother was exclaiming, in tones of anguish: "Is that boy hurt? Is that boy hurt?"

Stevie was not hurt, he had not even fallen, but excitement as usual had robbed him of the power of connected speech. He could do no more than stammer at the window: "Too heavy. Too heavy." Winnie put out her hand on to his shoulder.

"Stevie! Get up on the box directly, and don't try to get down again."

"No. No. Walk. Must walk."

In trying to state the nature of that necessity he stammered himself into utter incoherence. No physical impossibility stood in the way of his whim. Stevie could have managed easily to keep pace with the infirm, dancing horse without getting out of breath. But his sister withheld her consent decisively. "The idea! Who ever heard of such a thing! Run after a cab!" Her mother, frightened and helpless in the depths of the conveyance, entreated:

"Oh, don't let him, Winnie. He'll get lost. Don't let him."

"Certainly not. What next! Mr. Verloc will be sorry to hear of this nonsense, Stevie—I can tell you. He won't be happy at all."

The idea of Mr. Verloc's grief and unhappiness acting as usual powerfully upon Stevie's fundamentally docile disposition, he abandoned all resistance, and climbed up again on the box, with a face of despair.

The cabby turned at him his enormous and inflamed countenance truculently. "Don't you go for trying this silly game again, young fellow."

After delivering himself thus in a stern whisper, strained almost to extinction, he drove on, ruminating solemnly. To his mind the incident remained somewhat obscure. But his intellect, though it had lost its pristine vivacity in the benumbing years of sedentary exposure to the weather, lacked not independence or sanity. Gravely he dismissed the hypothesis of Stevie being a drunken young nipper.

Inside the cab the spell of silence, in which the two women had endured shoulder to shoulder the jolting, rattling, and jingling of the journey, had been broken by Stevie's outbreak. Winnie raised her voice.

"You've done what you wanted, mother. You'll have only yourself to thank for it if you aren't happy afterwards. And I don't think you'll be. That I don't. Weren't you comfortable enough in the house? Whatever people'll think of us—you throwing yourself like this on a Charity?"

"My dear," screamed the old woman earnestly above the noise, "you've been the best of daughters to me. As to Mr. Verloc—there——"

Words failing her on the subject of Mr. Verloc's excellence, she turned her old tearful eyes to the roof of the cab. Then she averted her head on the pretence of looking out of the window, as if to judge of their progress. It was insignificant, and went on close to the curbstone. Night, the early dirty night, the sinister, noisy, hopeless, and rowdy night of South London, had overtaken her on her last cab drive. In the gaslight of the low-fronted shops her big cheeks glowed with an orange hue under a black and mauve bonnet.

Mrs. Verloc's mother's complexion had become yellow by the effect of age and from a natural predisposition to biliousness, favoured by the trials of a difficult and worried existence, first as wife, then as widow. It was a complexion that under the influence of a blush would take on an orange tint. And this woman, modest indeed but hardened in the fires of adversity, of an age, moreover, when blushes are not expected, had positively blushed before her daughter. In the privacy of a four-wheeler, on her way to a charity cottage (one of a row) which by the exiguity of its dimensions and the simplicity of its accommodation, might well have been devised in kindness as a place of training for the still more straitened circumstances of the grave, she was forced to hide from her own child a blush of remorse and shame.

Whatever people will think? She knew very well what they did think, the people Winnie had in her mind—the old friends of her husband, and others too, whose interest she had solicited with such flattering success. She had not known before what a good beggar she could be. But she guessed very well what inference was drawn from her application. On account of that shrinking delicacy, which exists side by side with aggressive brutality in masculine nature, the inquiries into her circumstances had not been pushed very far. She had checked them by a visible compression of the lips and some display of an emotion determined to be eloquently silent. And the men would become suddenly incurious, after the manner of their kind. She congratulated herself more than once on having nothing to do with women, who being naturally more callous and avid of details, would have been anxious to be exactly informed by what sort of unkind conduct her daughter and son-in-law had driven her to that sad extremity. It was only before the Secretary of the great brewer M. P. and Chairman of the Charity, who, acting for his principal, felt bound to be conscientiously inquisitive as to the real circumstances of the applicant, that she had burst into tears outright and aloud, as a cornered woman will weep. The thin and polite gentleman, after contemplating her with an air of being "struck all of a heap," abandoned his position under the cover of soothing remarks. She must not distress herself. The deed of the Charity did not absolutely specify "childless widows." In fact, it did not by any means disqualify her. But the discretion of the Committee must be an informed discretion. One could understand very well her unwillingness to be a burden, etc., etc. Thereupon, to his profound disappointment, Mrs. Verloc's mother wept some more with an augmented vehemence.

The tears of that large female in a dark, dusty wig, and ancient silk dress festooned with dingy white cotton lace, were the tears of genuine distress. She had wept because she was heroic and unscrupulous and full of love for both her children. Girls frequently get sacrificed to the welfare of the boys. In this case she was sacrificing Winnie. By the suppression of truth she was slandering her. Of course, Winnie was independent, and need not care for the opinion of people that she would never see and who would never see her; whereas poor Stevie had nothing in the world he could call his own except his mother's heroism and unscrupulousness.

The first sense of security following on Winnie's marriage wore off in time (for nothing lasts), and Mrs. Verloc's mother, in the seclusion of the back bedroom, had recalled the teaching of that experience which the world impresses upon a widowed woman. But she had recalled it without vain bitterness; her store of resignation amounted almost to dignity. She reflected stoically that everything decays, wears out, in this world; that the way of kindness should be made easy to the well disposed; that her daughter Winnie was a most devoted sister, and a very self-confident wife indeed. As regards Winnie's sisterly devotion, her stoicism flinched. She excepted that sentiment from the rule of decay affecting all things human and some things divine. She could not help it; not to do so would have frightened her too much. But in considering the conditions of her daughter's married state, she rejected firmly all flattering illusions. She took the cold and reasonable view that the less strain put on Mr. Verloc's kindness the longer its effects were likely to last. That excellent man loved his wife, of course, but he would, no doubt, prefer to keep as few of her relations as was consistent with the proper display of that sentiment. It would be better if its whole effect were concentrated on poor

Stevie. And the heroic old woman resolved on going away from her children as an act of devotion and as a move of deep policy.

The "virtue" of this policy consisted in this (Mrs. Verloc's mother was subtle in her way), that Stevie's moral claim would be strengthened. The poor boy—a good, useful boy, if a little peculiar—had not a sufficient standing. He had been taken over with his mother, somewhat in the same way as the furniture of the Belgravian mansion had been taken over, as if on the ground of belonging to her exclusively. What will happen, she asked herself (for Mrs. Verloc's mother was in a measure imaginative), when I die? And when she asked herself that question it was with dread. It was also terrible to think that she would not then have the means of knowing what happened to the poor boy. But by making him over to his sister, by going thus away, she gave him the advantage of a directly dependent position. This was the more subtle sanction of Mrs. Verloc's mother's heroism and unscrupulousness. Her act of abandonment was really an arrangement for settling her son permanently in life. Other people made material sacrifices for such an object, she in that way. It was the only way. Moreover, she would be able to see how it worked. Ill or well she would avoid the horrible incertitude on her death-bed. But it was hard, hard, cruelly hard.

The cab rattled, jingled, jolted; in fact, the last was quite extraordinary. By its disproportionate violence and magnitude it obliterated every sensation of onward movement; and the effect was of being shaken in a stationary apparatus like a mediæval device for the punishment of crime, or some very new-fangled invention for the cure of a sluggish liver. It was extremely distressing; and the raising of Mrs. Verloc's mother's voice sounded like a wail of pain.

"I know, my dear, you'll come to see me as often as you can spare the time. Won't you?"

"Of course," answered Winnie, shortly, staring straight before her.

And the cab jolted in front of a steamy, greasy shop in a blaze of gas and in the smell of fried fish.

The old woman raised a wail again.

"And, my dear, I must see that poor boy every Sunday. He won't mind spending the day with his old mother——"

Winnie screamed out stolidly:

"Mind! I should think not. That poor boy will miss you something cruel. I wish you had thought a little of that, mother."

Not think of it! The heroic woman swallowed a playful and inconvenient object like a billiard ball, which had tried to jump out of her throat. Winnie sat mute for a while, pouting at the front of the cab, then snapped out, which was an unusual tone with her:

"I expect I'll have a job with him at first, he'll be that restless——"

"Whatever you do, don't let him worry your husband, my dear."

Thus they discussed on familiar lines the bearings of a new situation. And the cab jolted. Mrs. Verloc's mother expressed some misgivings. Could Stevie be trusted to come all that way alone? Winnie maintained that he was much less "absent-minded" now. They agreed as to that. It could not be denied. Much less—hardly at all. They shouted at each other in the jingle with comparative cheerfulness. But suddenly the maternal anxiety broke out afresh. There were two omnibuses to take, and a short walk between. It was too difficult! The old woman gave way to grief and consternation.

Winnie stared forward.

"Don't you upset yourself like this, mother. You must see him, of course."

"No, my dear. I'll try not to."

She mopped her streaming eyes.

"But you can't spare the time to come with him, and if he should forget himself and lose his way and somebody spoke to him sharply, his name and address may slip his memory, and he'll remain lost for days and days——"

The vision of a workhouse infirmary for poor Stevie—if only during inquires—wrung her heart. For she was a proud woman. Winnie's stare had grown hard, intent, inventive.

"I can't bring him to you myself every week," she cried. "But don't you worry, mother. I'll see to it that he don't get lost for long."

They felt a peculiar bump; a vision of brick pillars lingered before the rattling windows of the cab; a sudden cessation of atrocious jolting and uproarious jingling dazed the two women. What had happened? They sat motionless and scared in the profound stillness, till the door came open, and a rough, strained whispering was heard:

" 'Ere you are!"

A range of gabled little houses, each with one dim yellow window, on the ground floor, surrounded the dark open space of a grass plot planted with shrubs and railed off from the patchwork of lights and shadows in the wide road, resounding with the dull rumble of traffic. Before the door of one of these tiny houses—one without a light in the little downstairs window—the cab had come to a standstill. Mrs. Verloc's mother got out first, backwards, with a key in her hand. Winnie lingered on the flagstone path to pay the cabman. Stevie, after helping to carry inside a lot of small parcels, came out and stood under the light of a gas-lamp belonging to the Charity. The cabman looked at the pieces of silver, which, appearing very minute in his big, grimy palm, symbolized the insignificant results which reward the ambitious courage and toil of a mankind whose day is short on this earth of evil.

He had been paid decently—four one-shilling pieces—and he con-

templated them in perfect stillness, as if they had been the surprising
terms of a melancholy problem. The slow transfer of that treasure to
an inner pocket demanded much laborious groping in the depths of
decayed clothing. His form was squat and without flexibility. Stevie,
slender, his shoulders a little up, and his hands thrust deep in the side
pockets of his warm overcoat, stood at the edge of the path, pouting.

The cabman, pausing in his deliberate movements, seemed struck
by some misty recollection.

"Oh! 'Ere you are, young fellow," he whispered. "You'll know him
again—won't you?"

Stevie was staring at the horse, whose hind quarters appeared unduly elevated by the effect of emaciation. The little stiff tail seemed
to have been fitted in for a heartless joke; and at the other end the
thin, flat neck, like a plank covered with old horse-hide, drooped to
the ground under the weight of an enormous bony head. The ears
hung at different angles, negligently; and the macabre figure of that
mute dweller on the earth steamed straight up from ribs and backbone
in the muggy stillness of the air.

The cabman struck lightly Stevie's breast with the iron hook protruding from a ragged, greasy sleeve.

"Look 'ere, young feller. 'Ow'd *you* like to sit behind this 'oss up
to two o'clock in the morning p'raps?"

Stevie looked vacantly into the fierce little eyes with red-edged lids.

"He ain't lame," pursued the other, whispering with energy. "He
ain't got no sore places on 'im. 'Ere he is. 'Ow would *you* like——"

His strained, extinct voice invested his utterance with a character
of vehement secrecy. Stevie's vacant gaze was changing slowly into
dread.

"You may well look! Till three and four o'clock in the morning.
Cold and 'ungry. Looking for fares. Drunks."

His jovial purple cheeks bristled with white hairs; and like Virgil's
Silenus, who, his face smeared with the juice of berries, discoursed of
Olympian Gods to the innocent shepherds of Sicily, he talked to
Stevie of domestic matters and the affairs of men whose sufferings
are great and immortality by no means assured.

"I am a night cabby, I am," he whispered, with a sort of boastful
exasperation. "I've got to take out what they will blooming well give
me at the yard. I've got my missus and four kids at 'ome."

The monstrous nature of that declaration of paternity seemed to
strike the world dumb. A silence reigned, during which the flanks of
the old horse, the steed of apocalyptic misery, smoked upwards in the
light of the charitable gas-lamp.

The cabman grunted, then added in his mysterious whisper:

"This ain't an easy world."

Stevie's face had been twitching for some time and at last his feelings burst out in their usual concise form.

"Bad! Bad!"

His gaze remained fixed on the ribs of the horse, self-conscious and sombre, as though he were afraid to look about him at the badness of the world. And his slenderness, his rosy lips and pale, clear complexion, gave him the aspect of a delicate boy, notwithstanding the fluffy growth of golden hair on his cheeks. He pouted in a scared way like a child. The cabman, short and broad, eyed him with his fierce little eyes that seemed to smart in a clear and corroding liquid.

"'Ard on 'osses, but dam' sight 'arder on poor chaps like me," he wheezed just audibly.

"Poor! Poor!" stammered out Stevie, pushing his hands deeper into his pockets with convulsive sympathy. He could say nothing; for the tenderness to all pain and all misery, the desire to make the horse happy and the cabman happy, had reached the point of a bizarre longing to take them to bed with him. And that, he knew, was impossible. For Stevie was not mad. It was, as it were, a symbolic longing; and at the same time it was very distinct, because springing from experience, the mother of wisdom. Thus when as a child he cowered in a dark corner scared, wretched, sore, and miserable with the black, black misery of the soul, his sister Winnie used to come along, and carry him off to bed with her, as into a heaven of consoling peace. Stevie, though apt to forget mere facts, such as his name and address for instance, had a faithful memory of sensations. To be taken into a bed of compassion was the supreme remedy, with the only one disadvantage of being difficult of application on a large scale. And looking at the cabman, Stevie perceived this clearly, because he was reasonable.

The cabman went on with his leisurely preparations as if Stevie had not existed. He made as if to hoist himself on the box, but at the last moment, from some obscure motive, perhaps merely from disgust with carriage exercise, desisted. He approached instead the motionless partner of his labours, and stooping to seize the bridle, lifted up the big, weary head to the height of his shoulder with one effort of his right arm, like a feat of strength.

"Come on," he whispered, secretly.

Limping, he led the cab away. There was an air of austerity in this departure, the scrunched gravel of the drive crying out under the slowly turning wheels, the horse's lean thighs moving with ascetic deliberation away from the light into the obscurity of the open space bordered dimly by the pointed roofs and the feebly shining windows of the little almshouses. The plaint of the gravel travelled slowly all round the drive. Between the lamps of the charitable gateway the slow cortège reappeared, lighted up for a moment, the short, thick man limping busily, with the horse's head held aloft in his fist, the lank animal walking in stiff and forlorn dignity, the dark, low box on wheels rolling behind comically with an air of waddling. They turned to the left. There was a pub down the street, within fifty yards of the gate.

Stevie left alone beside the private lamp-post of the Charity, his hands thrust deep into his pockets, glared with vacant sulkiness. At the bottom of his pockets his incapable, weak hands were clinched hard into a pair of angry fists. In the face of anything which affected directly or indirectly his morbid dread of pain, Stevie ended by turning vicious. A magnanimous indignation swelled his frail chest to bursting, and caused his candid eyes to squint. Supremely wise in knowing his own powerlessness, Stevie was not wise enough to restrain his passions. The tenderness of his universal charity had two phases as indissolubly joined and connected as the reverse and obverse sides of a medal. The anguish of immoderate compassion was succeeded by the pain of an innocent but pitiless rage. Those two states expressing themselves outwardly by the same signs of futile bodily agitation, his sister Winnie soothed his excitement without ever fathoming its two-fold character. Mrs. Verloc wasted no portion of this transient life in seeking for fundamental information. This is a sort of economy having all the appearances and some of the advantages of prudence. Obviously it may be good for one not to know too much. And such a view accords very well with constitutional indolence.

On that evening on which it may be said that Mrs. Verloc's mother having parted for good from her children had also departed this life, Winnie Verloc did not investigate her brother's psychology. The poor boy was excited, of course. After once more assuring the old woman on the threshold that she would know how to guard against the risk of Stevie losing himself for very long on his pilgrimages of filial piety, she took her brother's arm to walk away. Stevie did not even mutter to himself, but with the special sense of sisterly devotion developed in her earliest infancy, she felt that the boy was very much excited indeed. Holding tight to his arm, under the appearance of leaning on it, she thought of some words suitable to the occasion.

"Now, Stevie, you must look well after me at the crossings, and get first into the bus, like a good brother."

This appeal to manly protection was received by Stevie with his usual docility. It flattered him. He raised his head and threw out his chest.

"Don't be nervous, Winnie. Mustn't be nervous! 'Bus all right," he answered in a brusque, slurring stammer partaking of the timorousness of a child and the resolution of a man. He advanced fearlessly with the woman on his arm, but his lower lip dropped.

Nevertheless, on the pavement of the squalid and wide thoroughfare, whose poverty in all the amenities of life stood foolishly exposed by a mad profusion of gas-lights, their resemblance to each other was so pronounced as to strike the casual passers-by.

Before the doors of the public-house at the corner, where the profusion of gas-light reached the height of positive wickedness, a four-wheeled cab standing by the curbstone, with no one on the box, seemed cast out into the gutter on account of irremediable decay. Mrs. Verloc recognized the conveyance. Its aspect was so profoundly lamentable, with such a perfection of grotesque misery and weirdness of macabre detail, as if it were the Cab of Death itself, that Mrs. Verloc, with that ready compassion of a woman for a horse (when she is not sitting behind him), exclaimed vaguely:

"Poor brute!"

Hanging back suddenly, Stevie inflicted an arresting jerk upon his sister.

"Poor! Poor!" he ejaculated, appreciatively. "Cabman poor, too. He told me himself."

The contemplation of the infirm and lonely steed overcame him. Jostled, but obstinate, he would remain there, trying to express the view newly opened to his sympathies of the human and equine misery in close association. But it was very difficult. "Poor brute, poor people!" was all he could repeat. It did not seem forcible enough, and he came to a stop with an angry splutter: "Shame!" Stevie was no master of phrases, and perhaps for that very reason his thoughts lacked clearness and precision. But he felt with greater completeness and some profundity. That little word contained all his sense of indignation and horror at one sort of wretchedness having to feed upon the anguish of the other—at the poor cabman beating the poor horse in the name, as it were, of his poor kids at home. And Stevie knew what it was to be beaten. He knew it from experience. It was a bad world. Bad! Bad!

Mrs. Verloc, his only sister, guardian, and protector, could not pretend to such depths of insight. Moreover, she had not experienced the magic of the cabman's eloquence. She was in the dark as to the inwardness of the word "Shame." And she said placidly:

"Come along, Stevie. You can't help that."

The docile Stevie went along; but now he went along without pride, shamblingly, and muttering half words, and even words that would have been whole if they had not been made up of halves that did not belong to each other. It was as though he had been trying to fit all the words he could remember to his sentiments in order to get some sort of corresponding idea. And, as a matter of fact, he got it at last. He hung back to utter it at once.

"Bad world for poor people."

Directly he had expressed that thought he became aware that it was familiar to him already in all its consequences. This circumstance strengthened his conviction immensely, but also augmented his indignation. Somebody, he felt, ought to be punished for it—punished with great severity. Being no sceptic, but a moral creature, he was in a manner at the mercy of his righteous passions.

"Beastly!" he added, concisely.

It was clear to Mrs. Verloc that he was greatly excited.

"Nobody can help that," she said. "Do come along. Is that the way you're taking care of me?"

Stevie mended his pace obediently. He prided himself on being a good brother. His morality, which was very complete, demanded that from him. Yet he was pained at the information imparted by his sister Winnie—who was good. Nobody could help that! He came along gloomily, but presently he brightened up. Like the rest of mankind, perplexed by the mystery of the universe, he had his moments of consoling trust in the organized powers of the earth.

"Police," he suggested, confidently.

"The police aren't for that," observed Mrs. Verloc, cursorily, hurrying on her way.

Stevie's face lengthened considerably. He was thinking. The more intense his thinking, the slacker was the droop of his lower jaw. And it was with an aspect of hopeless vacancy that he gave up his intellectual enterprise.

"Not for that?" he mumbled, resigned but surprised. "Not for that?" He had formed for himself an ideal conception of the metropolitan police as a sort of benevolent institution for the suppression of evil. The notion of benevolence especially was very closely associated with his sense of the power of the men in blue. He had liked all police constables tenderly, with a guileless trustfulness. And he was pained. He was irritated, too, by a suspicion of duplicity in the members of the force. For Stevie was frank and as open as the day himself. What did they mean by pretending then? Unlike his sister, who put her trust in face values, he wished to go to the bottom of the matter. He carried on his inquiry by means of an angry challenge.

"What are they for then, Winn? What are they for? Tell me."

Winnie disliked controversy. But fearing most a fit of black depression consequent on Stevie missing his mother very much at first, she did not altogether decline the discussion. Guiltless of all irony, she answered yet in a form which was not perhaps unnatural in the wife of Mr. Verloc, Delegate of the Central Red Committee, personal friend of certain anarchists, and a votary of social revolution.

"Don't you know what the police are for, Stevie? They are there so that them as have nothing shouldn't take anything away from them who have."

She avoided using the verb "to steal," because it always made her brother uncomfortable. For Stevie was delicately honest. Certain simple principles had been instilled into him so anxiously (on account of his "queerness") that the mere names of certain transgressions filled him with horror. He had been always easily impressed by speeches. He was impressed and startled now, and his intelligence was very alert.

"What?" he asked at once, anxiously. "Not even if they were hungry? Mustn't they?"

The two had paused in their walk.

"Not if they were ever so," said Mrs. Verloc, with the equanimity of a person untroubled by the problem of the distribution of wealth, and exploring the perspective of the roadway for an omnibus of the right colour. "Certainly not. But what's the use of talking about all that? You aren't ever hungry."

She cast a swift glance at the boy, like a young man, by her side. She saw him amiable, attractive, affectionate, and only a little, a very little peculiar. And she could not see him otherwise, for he was connected with what there was of the salt of passion in her tasteless life—the passion of indignation, of courage, of pity, and even of self-sacrifice. She did not add: "And you aren't likely ever to be as long as I live." But she might very well have done so, since she had taken effectual steps to that end. Mr. Verloc was a very good husband. It was her honest impression that nobody could help liking the boy. She cried out suddenly:

"Quick, Stevie. Stop that green 'bus."

And Stevie, tremulous and important with his sister Winnie on his arm, flung up the other high above his head at the approaching 'bus, with complete success.

An hour afterwards Mr. Verloc raised his eyes from a newspaper he was reading, or at any rate looking at, behind the counter, and in the expiring clatter of the door-bell beheld Winnie, his wife, enter and cross the shop on her way upstairs, followed by Stevie, his brother-in-law. The sight of his wife was agreeable to Mr. Verloc. It was his idiosyncrasy. The figure of his brother-in-law remained imperceptible to him because of the morose thoughtfulness that lately had fallen like a veil between Mr. Verloc and the appearances of the world of senses. He looked after his wife fixedly, without a word, as though she had been a phantom. His voice for home use was husky and placid, but now it was heard not at all. It was not heard at supper, to which he was called by his wife in the usual brief manner: "Adolf." He sat down to consume it without conviction, wearing his hat pushed far back on his head. It was not devotion to an outdoor life, but the frequentation of foreign cafés which was responsible for that habit, investing with a character of unceremonious impermanency Mr. Verloc's steady fidelity to his own fireside. Twice at the clatter of the cracked bell he arose without a word, disappeared into the shop, and came back silently. During these absences Mrs. Verloc, becoming acutely aware of the vacant place at her right hand, missed her mother very much, and stared stonily; while Stevie, from the same reason, kept on shuffling his feet, as though the floor under the table were uncomfortably hot. When Mr. Verloc returned to sit in his place, like the very embodiment of silence, the character of Mrs. Verloc's stare underwent a subtle change, and Stevie ceased to fidget with his feet, because of his great and awed regard for his sister's husband. He directed at him glances of respectful compassion. Mr. Verloc was sorry. His sister Winnie had impressed upon him (in the omnibus) that Mr. Verloc would be found at home in a state of sorrow, and must not be worried. His father's anger, the irritability of gentlemen lodgers, and Mr. Verloc's predisposition to immoderate grief, had been the main sanctions of Stevie's self-restraint. Of these sentiments, all easily provoked, but not always easy to understand, the last had the greatest moral efficiency—because Mr. Verloc was *good*. His mother and his sister had established that ethical fact on an unshakable foundation. They had established, erected, consecrated it behind Mr. Verloc's back, for reasons that had nothing to do with abstract morality. And Mr. Verloc was not aware of it. It is but bare justice to him to say that he had no notion of appearing good to Stevie. Yet so it was. He was even the only man so qualified in Stevie's knowledge, because the gentlemen lodgers had been too transient and too remote to have anything very distinct about them but perhaps their boots; and as regards the disciplinary measures of his father, the desolation of his mother and sister shrank from setting up a theory of goodness before the victim. It would have been too cruel. And it was even possible that Stevie would not have believed them. As far as Mr. Verloc was concerned, nothing could stand in the way of Stevie's belief. Mr. Verloc was obviously yet mysteriously *good*. And the grief of a good man is august.

Stevie gave glances of reverential compassion to his brother-in-law. Mr. Verloc was sorry. The brother of Winnie had never before felt himself in such close communion with the mystery of that man's goodness. It was an understandable sorrow. And Stevie himself was sorry. He was very sorry. The same sort of sorrow. And his attention being drawn to this unpleasant state, Stevie shuffled his feet. His feelings were habitually manifested by the agitation of his limbs.

"Keep your feet quiet, dear," said Mrs. Verloc, with authority and tenderness; then turning towards her husband in an indifferent voice, the masterly achievement of instinctive tact: "Are you going out to-night?" she asked.

The mere suggestion seemed repugnant to Mr. Verloc. He shook his head moodily, and then sat still with downcast eyes, looking at the piece of cheese on his plate for a whole minute. At the end of that time he got up, and went out—went right out in the clatter of shop-door bell. He acted thus inconsistently, not from any desire to make himself unpleasant, but because of an unconquerable restless-ness. It was no earthly good going out. He could not find anywhere in London what he wanted. But he went out. He led a cortège of dismal thoughts along dark streets, through lighted streets, in and out of two flash bars, as if in a half-hearted attempt to make a night of it, and finally back again to his menaced home, where he sat down fatigued behind the counter, and they crowded urgently round him, like a pack of hungry black hounds. After locking up the house and putting out the gas he took them upstairs with him—a dreadful escort for a man going to bed. His wife had preceded him some time before, and with her ample form defined vaguely under the counterpane, her head on the pillow, and a hand under the cheek, offered to his distraction the view of early drowsiness arguing the possession of an equable soul. Her big eyes stared wide open, inert and dark against the snowy whiteness of the linen. She did not move.

She had an equable soul. She felt profoundly that things do not stand much looking into. She made her force and her wisdom of that instinct. But the taciturnity of Mr. Verloc had been lying heavily upon her for a good many days. It was, as a matter of fact, affecting her nerves. Recumbent and motionless, she said placidly:

"You'll catch cold walking about in your socks like this."

This speech, becoming the solicitude of the wife and the prudence of the woman, took Mr. Verloc unawares. He had left his boots down-stairs, but he had forgotten to put on his slippers, and he had been turning about the bedroom on noiseless pads like a bear in a cage. At the sound of his wife's voice he stopped and stared at her with a somnambulistic, expressionless gaze so long that Mrs. Verloc moved her limbs slightly under the bedclothes. But she did not move her black head sunk in the white pillow, one hand under her cheek and the big, dark, unwinking eyes.

Under her husband's expressionless stare, and remembering her mother's empty room across the landing, she felt an acute pang of loneliness. She had never been parted from her mother before. They had stood by each other. She felt that they had, and she said to herself that now mother was gone—gone for good. Mrs. Verloc had no il-lusions. Stevie remained, however. And she said:

"Mother's done what she wanted to do. There's no sense in it that I can see. I'm sure she couldn't have thought you had enough of her. It's perfectly wicked, leaving us like that."

Mr. Verloc was not a well-read person; his range of allusive phrases was limited, but there was a peculiar aptness in circumstances which made him think of rats leaving a doomed ship. He very nearly said so. He had grown suspicious and embittered. Could it be that the old woman had such an excellent nose? But the unreasonableness of such suspicion was patent, and Mr. Verloc held his tongue. Not altogether, however. He muttered, heavily:

"Perhaps it's just as well."

He began to undress. Mrs. Verloc kept very still, perfectly still, with her eyes fixed in a dreamy, quiet stare. And her heart for the fraction of a second seemed to stand still, too. That night she was "not quite herself," as the saying is, and it was borne upon her with some force that a simple sentence may hold several diverse meanings—mostly disagreeable. *How* was it just as well? And why? But she did not allow herself to fall into the idleness of barren speculation. She was rather confirmed in her belief that things did not stand being looked into. Practical and subtle in her way, she brought Stevie to the front without loss of time, because in her the singleness of purpose had the unerring nature and the force of an instinct.

"What I am going to do to cheer up that boy for the first few days I'm sure I don't know. He'll be worrying himself from morning till night before he gets used to mother being away. And he's such a good boy. I couldn't do without him."

Mr. Verloc went on divesting himself of his clothing with the unnoticing inward concentration of a man undressing in the solitude of a vast and hopeless desert. For thus inhospitably did this fair earth, our common inheritance, present itself to the mental vision of Mr. Verloc. All was so still without and within that the lonely ticking of the clock on the landing stole into the room as if for the sake of company.

Mr. Verloc, getting into bed on his own side, remained prone and mute behind Mrs. Verloc's back. His thick arms rested abandoned on the outside of the counterpane like dropped weapons, like discarded tools. At that moment he was within a hair's breadth of making a clean breast of it all to his wife. The moment seemed propitious. Looking out of the corners of his eyes, he saw her ample shoulders draped in white, the back of her head, with the hair done for the night in three plaits tied up with black tapes at the ends. And he forbore. Mr. Verloc loved his wife as a wife should be loved—that is, maritally, with the regard one has for one's chief possession. This head arranged for the night, those ample shoulders, had an aspect of familiar sacredness—

the sacredness of domestic peace. She moved not, massive and shapeless like a recumbent statue in the rough; he remembered her wide-open eyes looking into the empty room. She was mysterious, with the mysteriousness of living beings. The far-famed secret agent △ of the late Baron Stott-Wartenheim's alarmist despatches was not the man to break into such mysteries. He was easily intimidated. And he was also indolent, with the indolence which is so often the secret of good nature. He forbore touching that mystery out of love, timidity, and indolence. There would be always time enough. For several minutes he bore his sufferings silently in the drowsy silence of the room. And then he disturbed it by a resolute declaration.

"I am going on the Continent to-morrow."

His wife might have fallen asleep already. He could not tell. As a matter of fact, Mrs. Verloc had heard him. Her eyes remained very wide open, and she lay very still, confirmed in her instinctive conviction that things don't bear looking into very much. And yet it was nothing very unusual for Mr. Verloc to take such a trip. He renewed his stock from Paris and Brussels. Often he went over to make his purchases personally. A little select connection of amateurs was forming around the shop in Brett Street, a secret connection eminently proper for any business undertaken by Mr. Verloc, who, by a mystic accord of temperament and necessity, had been set apart to be a secret agent all his life.

He waited for a while, then added: "I'll be away a week or perhaps a fortnight. Get Mrs. Neale to come for the day."

Mrs. Neale was the charwoman of Brett Street. Victim of her marriage with a debauched joiner, she was oppressed by the needs of many infant children. Red-armed, and aproned in coarse sacking up to the arm-pits, she exhaled the anguish of the poor in a breath of soap-suds and rum, in the uproar of scrubbing, in the clatter of tin pails.

Mrs. Verloc, full of deep purpose, spoke in the tone of the shallowest indifference.

"There is no need to have the woman here all day. I shall do very well with Stevie."

She let the lonely clock on the landing count off fifteen ticks into the abyss of eternity, and asked:

"Shall I put the light out?"

Mr. Verloc snapped at his wife huskily.

"Put it out."

Mr. Verloc, returning from the Continent at the end of ten days, brought back a mind evidently unrefreshed by the wonders of foreign travel and a countenance unlighted by the joys of home-coming. He entered in the clatter of the shop-bell with an air of sombre and vexed exhaustion. His bag in hand, his head lowered, he strode straight behind the counter, and let himself fall into the chair, as though he had tramped all the way from Dover. It was early morning. Stevie, dusting various objects displayed in the front windows, turned to gape at him with reverence and awe.

"Here!" said Mr. Verloc, giving a slight kick to the gladstone bag on the floor; and Stevie flung himself upon it, seized it, bore it off with triumphant devotion. He was so prompt that Mr. Verloc was distinctly surprised.

Already at the clatter of the shop-bell Mrs. Neale, black-leading the parlour grate, had looked through the door, and rising from her knees had gone, aproned, and grimy with everlasting toil, to tell Mrs. Verloc in the kitchen that "there was the master come back."

Winnie came no farther than the inner shop door.

"You'll want some breakfast," she said from a distance.

Mr. Verloc moved his hands slightly, as if overcome by an impossible suggestion. But once enticed into the parlour he did not reject the food set before him. He ate as if in a public place, his hat pushed off his forehead, the skirts of his heavy overcoat hanging in a triangle on each side of the chair. And across the length of the table covered with brown oilcloth Winnie, his wife, talked evenly at him the wifely talk, as artfully adapted, no doubt, to the circumstances of this return as the talk of Penelope to the return of the wandering Odysseus. Mrs. Verloc, however, had done no weaving during her husband's absence. But she had had all the upstairs rooms cleaned thoroughly, had sold some wares, had seen Mr. Michaelis several times. He had told her the last time that he was going away to live in a cottage in the country, somewhere on the London, Chatham, and Dover line. Karl Yundt had come, too, once, led under the arm by that "wicked old housekeeper of his." He was "a disgusting old man." Of Comrade Ossipon, whom she had received curtly, entrenched behind the counter with a stony face and a faraway gaze, she said nothing, her mental reference to the robust anarchist being marked by a short pause, with the faintest possible blush. And bringing in her brother Stevie as soon as she could into the current of domestic events, she mentioned that the boy had moped a good deal.

"It's all along of mother leaving us like this."

Mr. Verloc neither said "Damn!" nor yet "Stevie be hanged!" And Mrs. Verloc, not let into the secret of his thoughts, failed to appreciate the generosity of this restraint.

"It isn't that he doesn't work as well as ever," she continued. "He's been making himself very useful. You'd think he couldn't do enough for us."

Mr. Verloc directed a casual and somnolent glance at Stevie, who sat on his right, delicate, pale-faced, his rosy mouth open vacantly. It was not a critical glance. It had no intention. And if Mr. Verloc thought for a moment that his wife's brother looked uncommonly useless, it was only a dull and fleeting thought, devoid of that force and durability which enables sometimes a thought to move the world. Leaning back, Mr. Verloc uncovered his head. Before his extended arm could put down the hat Stevie pounced upon it, and bore it off reverently into the kitchen. And again Mr. Verloc was surprised.

"You could do anything with that boy, Adolf," Mrs. Verloc said, with her best air of inflexible calmness. "He would go through fire for you. He——"

She paused attentive, her ear turned towards the door of the kitchen.

There Mrs. Neale was scrubbing the floor. At Stevie's appearance she groaned lamentably, having observed that he could be induced easily to bestow for the benefit of her infant children the shilling his sister Winnie presented him with from time to time. On all fours amongst the puddles, wet and begrimed, like a sort of amphibious and domestic animal living in ashbins and dirty water, she uttered the usual exordium: "It's all very well for you, kept doing nothing like a gentleman." And she followed it with the everlasting plaint of the poor, pathetically mendacious, miserably authenticated by the horrible breath of cheap rum and soap-suds. She scrubbed hard, snuffling all the time, and talking volubly. And she was sincere. And on each side of her thin red nose her bleared, misty eyes swam in tears, because she felt really the want of some sort of stimulant in the morning.

In the parlour Mrs. Verloc observed, with knowledge:

"There's Mrs. Neale at it again with her harrowing tales about her little children. They can't be all so little as she makes them out. Some of them must be big enough by now to try to do something for themselves. It only makes Stevie angry."

These words were confirmed by a thud as of a fist striking the kitchen table. In the normal evolution of his sympathy Stevie had become angry on discovering that he had no shilling in his pocket. In his inability to relieve at once Mrs. Neale's "little 'uns'" privations, he felt that somebody should be made to suffer for it. Mrs. Verloc rose, and went into the kitchen to "stop that nonsense." And she did it firmly but gently. She was well aware that directly Mrs. Neale received her money she went round the corner to drink ardent spirits in a mean and musty public-house—the unavoidable station on the *via dolorosa* of her life. Mrs. Verloc's comment upon this practice had an unexpected profundity, as coming from a person disinclined to look under the surface of things. "Of course, what is she to do to keep up? If I were like Mrs. Neale I expect I wouldn't act any different."

In the afternoon of the same day, as Mr. Verloc, coming with a start out of the last of a long series of dozes before the parlour fire, declared his intention of going out for a walk, Winnie said from the shop:

"I wish you would take that boy out with you, Adolf."

For the third time that day Mr. Verloc was surprised. He stared stupidly at his wife. She continued in her steady manner. The boy, whenever he was not doing anything, moped in the house. It made her uneasy; it made her nervous, she confessed. And that from the calm Winnie sounded like exaggeration. But, in truth, Stevie moped in the striking fashion of an unhappy domestic animal. He would go up on the dark landing, to sit on the floor at the foot of the tall clock, with his knees drawn up and his head in his hands. To come upon his pallid face, with its big eyes gleaming in the dusk, was discomposing; to think of him up there was uncomfortable.

Mr. Verloc got used to the startling novelty of the idea. He was fond of his wife as a man should be—that is, generously. But a weighty objection presented itself to his mind, and he formulated it.

"He'll lose sight of me perhaps, and get lost in the street," he said.

Mrs. Verloc shook her head competently.

"He won't. You don't know him. That boy just worships you. But if you should miss him——"

Mrs. Verloc paused for a moment, but only for a moment.

"You just go on, and have your walk out. Don't worry. He'll be all right. He's sure to turn up safe here before very long."

This optimism procured for Mr. Verloc his fourth surprise of the day.

"Is he?" he grunted, doubtfully. But perhaps his brother-in-law was not such an idiot as he looked. His wife would know best. He turned away his heavy eyes, saying huskily: "Well, let him come along, then," and relapsed into the clutches of black care, that perhaps prefers to sit behind a horseman, but knows also how to tread close on the heels of people not sufficiently well off to keep horses—like Mr. Verloc, for instance.

Winnie, at the shop door, did not see this fatal attendant upon Mr. Verloc's walks. She watched the two figures down the squalid street, one tall and burly, the other slight and short, with a thin neck, and the peaked shoulders raised slightly under the large semi-transparent ears. The material of their overcoats was the same, their hats were black and round in shape. Inspired by the similarity of wearing apparel, Mrs. Verloc gave rein to her fancy.

"Might be father and son," she said to herself. She thought also that Mr. Verloc was as much of a father as poor Stevie ever had in his life. She was aware also that it was her work. And with peaceful pride she congratulated herself on a certain resolution she had taken a few years before. It had cost her some effort, and even a few tears.

She congratulated herself still more on observing in the course of days that Mr. Verloc seemed to be taking kindly to Stevie's companionship. Now, when ready to go out for his walk, Mr. Verloc called aloud to the boy, in the spirit, no doubt, in which a man invites the attendance of the household dog, though, of course, in a different manner. In the house Mr. Verloc could be detected staring curiously at Stevie a good deal. His own demeanour had changed. Taciturn still, he was not so listless. Mrs. Verloc thought that he was rather jumpy at times. It might have been regarded as an improvement. As to Stevie, he moped no longer at the foot of the clock, but muttered to himself in corners instead in a threatening tone. When asked "What is it you're saying, Stevie?" he merely opened his mouth, and squinted at his sister. At odd times he clenched his fists without apparent cause, and when discovered in solitude would be scowling at the wall, with the sheet of paper and the pencil given him for drawing circles lying blank and idle on the kitchen table. This was a change, but it was no improvement. Mrs. Verloc, including all these vagaries under the general definition of excitement, began to fear that Stevie was hearing more than was good for him of her husband's conversations with his friends. During his "walks" Mr. Verloc, of course, met and conversed with various persons. It could hardly be otherwise. His walks were an integral part of his outdoor activities, which his wife had never looked deeply into. Mrs. Verloc felt that the position was delicate, but she faced it with the same impenetrable calmness which impressed and even astonished the customers of the shop and made the other visitors keep their distance a little wonderingly. No! She feared that there were things not good for Stevie to hear of, she told her husband. It only excited the poor boy, because he could not help them being so. Nobody could.

It was in the shop. Mr. Verloc made no comment. He made no retort, and yet the retort was obvious. But he refrained from pointing out to his wife that the idea of making Stevie the companion of his walks was her own, and nobody else's. At that moment, to an impartial observer, Mr. Verloc would have appeared more than human in his magnanimity. He took down a small cardboard box from a shelf, peeped in to see that the contents were all right, and put it down gently on the counter. Not till that was done did he break the silence, to the effect that most likely Stevie would profit greatly by being sent out of town for a while; only he supposed his wife could not get on without him.

"Could not get on without him!" repeated Mrs. Verloc, slowly. "I couldn't get on without him if it were for his good! The idea! Of course, I can get on without him. But there's nowhere for him to go."

Mr. Verloc got out some brown paper and a ball of string; and meanwhile he muttered that Michaelis was living in a little cottage in the country. Michaelis wouldn't mind giving Stevie a room to sleep in. There were no visitors and no talk there. Michaelis was writing a book.

Mrs. Verloc declared her affection for Michaelis; mentioned her abhorrence of Karl Yundt, "nasty old man"; and of Ossipon she said nothing. As to Stevie, he could be no other than very pleased. Mr. Michaelis was always so nice and kind to him. He seemed to like the boy. Well, the boy was a good boy.

"You, too, seem to have grown quite fond of him of late," she added, after a pause, with her inflexible assurance.

Mr. Verloc, tying up the cardboard box into a parcel for the post, broke the string by an injudicious jerk, and muttered several swear words confidentially to himself. Then raising his tone to the usual husky mutter, he announced his willingness to take Stevie into the country himself, and leave him all safe with Michaelis.

He carried out this scheme on the very next day. Stevie offered no objection. He seemed rather eager, in a bewildered sort of way. He turned his candid gaze inquisitively to Mr. Verloc's heavy countenance at frequent intervals, especially when his sister was not looking at him. His expression was proud, apprehensive, and concentrated, like that of a small child entrusted for the first time with a box of matches and the permission to strike a light. But Mrs. Verloc, gratified by her brother's docility, recommended him not to dirty his clothes unduly in the country. At this Stevie gave his sister, guardian, and protector a look, which for the first time in his life seemed to lack the quality of perfect childlike trustfulness. It was haughtily gloomy. Mrs. Verloc smiled.

"Goodness me! You needn't be offended. You know you do get yourself very untidy when you get a chance, Stevie."

Mr. Verloc was already gone some way down the street.

Thus in consequence of her mother's heroic proceedings, and of her brother's absence on this villeggiatura, Mrs. Verloc found herself oftener than usual all alone not only in the shop, but in the house.

For Mr. Verloc had to take his walks. She was alone longer than usual on the day of the attempted bomb outrage in Greenwich Park, because Mr. Verloc went out very early that morning and did not come back till nearly dusk. She did not mind being alone. She had no desire to go out. The weather was too bad, and the shop was cosier than the streets. Sitting behind the counter with some sewing, she did not raise her eyes from her work when Mr. Verloc entered in the aggressive clatter of the bell. She had recognized his step on the pavement outside.

She did not raise her eyes, but as Mr. Verloc, silent, and with his hat rammed down upon his forehead, made straight for the parlour door, she said, serenely:

"What a wretched day. You've been perhaps to see Stevie?"

"No! I haven't," said Mr. Verloc, softly, and slammed the glazed parlour door behind him with unexpected energy.

For some time Mrs. Verloc remained quiescent, with her work dropped in her lap, before she put it away under the counter and got up to light the gas. This done, she went into the parlour on her way to the kitchen. Mr. Verloc would want his tea presently. Confident of the power of her charms, Winnie did not expect from her husband in the daily intercourse of their married life a ceremonious amenity of address and courtliness of manner; vain and antiquated forms at best, probably never very exactly observed, discarded nowadays even in the highest spheres, and always foreign to the standards of her class. She did not look for courtesies from him. But he was a good husband, and she had a loyal respect for his rights.

Mrs. Verloc would have gone through the parlour and on to her domestic duties in the kitchen with the perfect serenity of a woman sure of the power of her charms. But a slight, very slight, and rapid rattling sound grew upon her hearing. Bizarre and incomprehensible, it arrested Mrs. Verloc's attention. Then as its character became plain to the ear she stopped short, amazed and concerned. Striking a match on the box she held in her hand, she turned on and lighted, above the parlour table, one of the two gas-burners, which, being defective, first whistled as if astonished, and then went on purring comfortably like a cat.

Mr. Verloc, against his usual practice, had thrown off his overcoat. It was lying on the sofa. His hat, which he must also have thrown off, rested overturned under the edge of the sofa. He had dragged a chair in front of the fireplace, and his feet planted inside the fender, his head held between his hands, he was hanging low over the glowing grate. His teeth rattled with an ungovernable violence, causing his whole enormous back to tremble at the same rate. Mrs. Verloc was startled.

"You've been getting wet," she said.

"Not very," Mr. Verloc managed to falter out, in a profound shudder. By a great effort he suppressed the rattling of his teeth.

"I'll have you laid up on my hands," she said, with genuine uneasiness.

"I don't think so," remarked Mr. Verloc, snuffling huskily.

He had certainly contrived somehow to catch an abominable cold between seven in the morning and five in the afternoon. Mrs. Verloc looked at his bowed back.

"Where have you been to-day?" she asked.

"Nowhere," answered Mr. Verloc in a low, choked nasal tone. His attitude suggested aggrieved sulks or a severe headache. The insufficiency and uncandidness of his answer became painfully apparent in the dead silence of the room. He snuffled apologetically, and added: "I've been to the bank."

Mrs. Verloc became attentive.

"You have!" she said, dispassionately. "What for?"

Mr. Verloc mumbled, with his nose over the grate, and with marked unwillingness:

"Draw the money out!"

"What do you mean? All of it?"

"Yes. All of it."

Mrs. Verloc spread out with care the scanty tablecloth, got two knives and two forks out of the table drawer, and suddenly stopped in her methodical proceedings.

"What did you do that for?"

"May want it soon," snuffled vaguely Mr. Verloc, who was coming to the end of his calculated indiscretions.

"I don't know what you mean," remarked his wife in a tone perfectly casual, but standing stock still between the table and the cupboard.

"You know you can trust me," Mr. Verloc remarked to the grate, with hoarse feeling.

Mrs. Verloc turned slowly towards the cupboard, saying with deliberation:

"Oh, yes. I can trust you."

And she went on with her methodical proceedings. She laid two plates, got the bread, the butter, going to and fro quietly between the table and the cupboard in the peace and silence of her home. On the point of taking out the jam, she reflected practically: "He will be feeling hungry, having been away all day," and she returned to the cupboard once more to get the cold beef. She set it under the purring gas-jet, and with a passing glance at her motionless husband hugging the fire, she went (down two steps) into the kitchen. It was only when coming back, carving knife and fork in hand, that she spoke again.

"If I hadn't trusted you I wouldn't have married you."

Bowed under the overmantel, Mr. Verloc, holding his head in both hands, seemed to have gone to sleep. Winnie made the tea, and called out in an undertone:

"Adolf."

Mr. Verloc got up at once, and staggered a little before he sat down at the table. His wife, examining the sharp edge of the carving knife, placed it on the dish, and called his attention to the cold beef. He remained insensible to the suggestion, with his chin on his breast.

"You should feed your cold," Mrs. Verloc said, dogmatically.

He looked up, and shook his head. His eyes were bloodshot and his face red. His fingers had ruffled his hair into a dissipated untidiness. Altogether he had a disreputable aspect, expressive of the discomfort, the irritation, and the gloom following a heavy debauch. But Mr. Verloc was not a debauched man. In his conduct he was respectable. His appearance might have been the effect of a feverish cold. He drank three cups of tea, but abstained from food entirely. He recoiled from it with sombre aversion when urged by Mrs. Verloc, who said at last:

"Aren't your feet wet? You had better put on your slippers. You aren't going out any more this evening."

Mr. Verloc intimated by morose grunts and signs that his feet were not wet, and that anyhow he did not care. The proposal as to slippers was disregarded as beneath his notice. But the question of going out in the evening received an unexpected development. It was not of going out in the evening that Mr. Verloc was thinking. His thoughts embraced a vaster scheme. From moody and incomplete phrases it became apparent that Mr. Verloc had been considering the expediency of emigrating. It was not very clear whether he had in his mind France or California.

The utter unexpectedness, improbability, and inconceivableness of such an event robbed this vague declaration of all its effect. Mrs. Verloc, as placidly as if her husband had been threatening her with the end of the world, said:

"The idea!"

Mr. Verloc declared himself sick and tired of everything, and be-sides—— She interrupted him.

"You've a bad cold."

It was indeed obvious that Mr. Verloc was not in his usual state, physically and even mentally. A sombre irresolution held him silent for a while. Then he murmured a few ominous generalities on the theme of necessity.

"Will have to," repeated Winnie, sitting calmly back, with folded arms, opposite her husband. "I should like to know who's to make you. You ain't a slave. No one need be a slave in this country—and don't you make yourself one." She paused, and with invincible and steady candour: "The business isn't so bad," she went on. "You've a comfortable home."

She glanced all round the parlour, from the corner cupboard to the good fire in the grate. Ensconced cosily behind the shop of doubtful wares, with the mysteriously dim window, and its door suspiciously ajar in the obscure and narrow street, it was in all essentials of domestic propriety and domestic comfort a respectable home. Her devoted affection missed out of it her brother Stevie, now enjoying a damp villeggiatura in the Kentish lanes under the care of Mr. Michaelis. She missed him poignantly, with all the force of her protecting passion. This was the boy's home, too—the roof, the cupboard, the stoked grate. On this thought Mrs. Verloc rose, and walking to the other end of the table, said in the fulness of her heart:

"And you are not tired of me."

Mr. Verloc made no sound. Winnie leaned on his shoulder from behind, and pressed her lips to his forehead. Thus she lingered. Not a whisper reached them from the outside world. The sound of footsteps on the pavement died out in the discreet dimness of the shop. Only the gas-jet above the table went on purring equably in the brooding silence of the parlour.

During the contact of that unexpected and lingering kiss Mr. Verloc, gripping with both hands the edges of his chair, preserved a hieratic immobility. When the pressure was removed he let go the chair, rose, and went to stand before the fireplace. He turned no longer his back to the room. With his features swollen and an air of being drugged, he followed his wife's movements with his eyes.

Mrs. Verloc went about serenely, clearing up the table. Her tranquil voice commented on the idea thrown out in a reasonable and domestic tone. It wouldn't stand examination. She condemned it from every point of view. But her only real concern was Stevie's welfare. He appeared to her thought in that connection as sufficiently "peculiar" not to be taken rashly abroad. And that was all. But talking round that vital point, she approached absolute vehemence in her delivery. Meanwhile, with brusque movements, she arrayed herself in an apron for the washing up of cups. And as if excited by the sound of her uncontradicted voice, she went so far as to say in a tone almost tart:

"If you go abroad you'll have to go without me."

"You know I wouldn't," said Mr. Verloc, huskily, and the unresonant voice of his private life trembled with an enigmatical emotion.

Already Mrs. Verloc was regretting her words. They had sounded more unkind than she meant them to be. They had also the unwisdom of unnecessary things. In fact, she had not meant them at all. It was a sort of phrase that is suggested by the demon of perverse inspiration. But she knew a way to make it as if it had not been.

She turned her head over her shoulder and gave that man planted heavily in front of the fireplace a glance, half arch, half cruel, out of her large eyes—a glance of which the Winnie of the Belgravian mansion days would have been incapable, because of her respectability and her ignorance. But the man was her husband now, and she was no longer ignorant. She kept it on him for a whole second, with her grave face motionless like a mask, while she said playfully:

"You couldn't. You would miss me too much."

Mr. Verloc started forward.

"Exactly," he said in a louder tone, throwing his arms out and making a step towards her. Something wild and doubtful in his expression made it appear uncertain whether he meant to strangle or to embrace his wife. But Mrs. Verloc's attention was called away from that manifestation by the clatter of the shop-bell.

"Shop, Adolf. You go."

He stopped, his arms came down slowly.

"You go," repeated Mrs. Verloc. "I've got my apron on."

Mr. Verloc obeyed woodenly, stony-eyed, and like an automaton whose face had been painted red. And this resemblance to a mechanical figure went so far that he had an automaton's absurd air of being aware of the machinery inside of him.

He closed the parlour door, and Mrs. Verloc, moving briskly, carried the tray into the kitchen. She washed the cups and some other things before she stopped in her work to listen. No sound reached her. The customer was a long time in the shop. It was a customer, because if he had not been Mr. Verloc would have taken him inside. Undoing the strings of her apron with a jerk, she threw it on a chair, and walked back to the parlour slowly.

At that precise moment Mr. Verloc entered from the shop.

He had gone in red. He came out a strange papery white. His face, losing its drugged, feverish stupor, had in that short time acquired a bewildered and harassed expression. He walked straight to the sofa, and stood looking down at his overcoat lying there, as though he were afraid to touch it.

"What's the matter?" asked Mrs. Verloc in a subdued voice. Through the door left ajar she could see that the customer was not gone yet.

"I find I'll have to go out this evening," said Mr. Verloc. He did not attempt to pick up his outer garment.

Without a word Winnie made for the shop and, shutting the door after her, walked in behind the counter. She did not look overtly at the customer till she had established herself comfortably on the chair. But by that time she had noted that he was tall and thin, and wore his moustaches twisted up. In fact, he gave the sharp points a twist just then. His long, bony face rose out of a turned-up collar. He was a little splashed, a little wet. A dark man, with the ridge of the cheekbone well defined under the slightly hollow temple. A complete stranger. Not a customer, either.

Mrs. Verloc looked at him placidly.

"You came over from the Continent?" she said after a time.

The long, thin stranger, without exactly looking at Mrs. Verloc, answered only by a faint and peculiar smile.

Mrs. Verloc's steady, incurious gaze rested on him.

"You understand English, don't you?"

"Oh, yes. I understand English."

There was nothing foreign in his accent, except that he seemed in his slow enunciation to be taking pains with it. And Mrs. Verloc, in her varied experience, had come to the conclusion that some foreigners could speak better English than the natives. She said, looking at the door of the parlour fixedly:

"You don't think perhaps of staying in England for good?"

The stranger gave her again a silent smile. He had a kindly mouth and probing eyes. And he shook his head a little sadly, it seemed.

"My husband will see you through all right. Meantime, for a few days you couldn't do better than take lodgings with Mr. Guigliani. Continental Hotel it's called. Private. It's quiet. My husband will take you there."

"A good idea," said the thin, dark man, whose glance had hardened suddenly.

"You knew Mr. Verloc before—didn't you? Perhaps in France?"

"I have heard of him," admitted the visitor in his slow, painstaking tone, which yet had a certain curtness of intention.

There was a pause. Then he spoke again, in a far less elaborate manner.

"Your husband has not gone out to wait for me in the street by chance?"

"In the street!" repeated Mrs. Verloc, surprised. "He couldn't. There's no other door to the house."

For a moment she sat impassive, then left her seat to go and peep through the glazed door. Suddenly she opened it, and disappeared into the parlour.

Mr. Verloc had done no more than put on his overcoat. But why he should remain afterwards leaning over the table propped up on his two arms as though he were feeling giddy or sick, she could not understand. "Adolf," she called out half aloud; and when he had raised himself:

"Do you know that man?" she asked, rapidly.

"I've heard of him," whispered uneasily Mr. Verloc, darting a wild glance at the door.

Mrs. Verloc's fine, incurious eyes lighted up with a flash of abhorrence.

"One of Karl Yundt's friends—beastly old man."

"No! No!" protested Mr. Verloc, busy fishing for his hat. But when he got it from under the sofa he held it as if he did not know the use of a hat.

"Well—he's waiting for you," said Mrs. Verloc at last. "I say, Adolf, he ain't one of them Embassy people you have been bothered with of late?"

"Bothered with Embassy people," repeated Mr. Verloc, with a heavy start of surprise and fear. "Who's been talking to you of the Embassy people?"

"Yourself."

"I! I! Talked of the Embassy to you!"

Mr. Verloc seemed scared and bewildered beyond measure. His wife explained:

"You've been talking a little in your sleep of late, Adolf."

"What—what did I say? What do you know?"

"Nothing much. It seemed mostly nonsense. Enough to let me guess that something worried you."

Mr. Verloc rammed his hat on his head. A crimson flood of anger ran over his face.

"Nonsense—eh? The Embassy people! I would cut their hearts out one after another. But let them look out. I've got a tongue in my head."

He fumed, pacing up and down between the table and the sofa, his open overcoat catching against the angles. The red flood of anger ebbed out, and left his face all white, with quivering nostrils. Mrs. Verloc, for the purposes of practical existence, put down these appearances to the cold.

"Well," she said, "get rid of the man whoever he is, as soon as you can, and come back home to me. You want looking after for a day or two."

Mr. Verloc calmed down, and, with resolution imprinted on his pale face, had already opened the door, when his wife called him back in a whisper:

"Adolf! Adolf!" He came back, startled. "What about that money you drew out?" she asked. "You've got it in your pocket? Hadn't you better——"

Mr. Verloc gazed stupidly into the palm of his wife's extended hand for some time before he slapped his brow.

"Money! Yes! Yes! I didn't know what you meant."

He drew out of his breast pocket a new pigskin pocket-book. Mrs. Verloc received it without another word, and stood still till the bell, clattering after Mr. Verloc and Mr. Verloc's visitor, had quieted down. Only then she peeped in at the amount, drawing the notes out for the purpose. After this inspection she looked round thoughtfully, with an air of mistrust in the silence and solitude of the house. This abode of her married life appeared to her as lonely and unsafe as though it had been situated in the midst of a forest. No receptacle she could think of amongst the solid, heavy furniture seemed other but flimsy and particularly tempting to her conception of a house-breaker. It was an ideal conception, endowed with sublime faculties and a miraculous insight. The till was not to be thought of. It was the first spot a thief would make for. Mrs. Verloc, unfastening hastily a couple of hooks, slipped the pocket-book under the bodice of her dress. Having thus disposed of her husband's capital, she was rather glad to hear the clatter of the door-bell, announcing an arrival. Assuming the fixed, unabashed stare and the stony expression reserved for the casual customer, she walked in behind the counter.

A man standing in the middle of the shop was inspecting it with a swift, cool, all-round glance. His eyes ran over the walls, took in the ceiling, noted the floor—all in a moment. The points of a long fair moustache fell below the line of the jaw. He smiled the smile of an old if distant acquaintance, and Mrs. Verloc remembered having seen him before. Not a customer. She softened her "customer stare" to mere indifference, and faced him across the counter.

He approached, on his side, confidentially, but not too markedly so.

"Husband at home, Mrs. Verloc?" he asked in an easy, full tone.

"No. He's gone out."

"I am sorry for that. I've called to get from him a little private information."

This was the exact truth. Chief Inspector Heat had been all the way home and had even gone so far as to think of getting into his slippers, since practically he was, he told himself, chucked out of that case. He indulged in some scornful and in a few angry thoughts, and found the occupation so unsatisfactory that he resolved to seek relief out of doors. Nothing prevented him paying a friendly call on Mr. Verloc, casually as it were. It was in the character of a private citizen that walking out privately he made use of his customary conveyances. Their general direction was towards Mr. Verloc's home. Chief Inspector Heat respected his own private character so consistently that he took especial pains to avoid all the police constables on point and patrol duty in the vicinity of Brett Street. This precaution was much more necessary for a man of his standing than for an obscure Assistant Commissioner. Private Citizen Heat entered the street, manœuvring in a way which in a member of the criminal classes would have been stigmatized as slinking. The piece of cloth picked up in Greenwich was in his pocket. Not that he had the slightest intention of producing it in his private capacity. On the contrary, he wanted to know just what Mr. Verloc would be disposed to say voluntarily. He hoped Mr. Verloc's talk would be of a nature to incriminate Michaelis. It was a conscientiously professional hope in the main, but not without its moral value. For Chief Inspector Heat was a servant of justice. Finding Mr. Verloc from home, he felt disappointed.

"I would wait for him a little if I were sure he wouldn't be long," he said.

Mrs. Verloc volunteered no assurance of any kind.

"The information I need is quite private," he repeated. "You understand what I mean? I wonder if you could give me a notion where he's gone to?"

Mrs. Verloc shook her head.

"Can't say."

She turned away to range some boxes on the shelves behind the counter. Chief Inspector Heat looked at her thoughtfully for a time.

"I suppose you know who I am?" he said.

Mrs. Verloc glanced over her shoulder. Chief Inspector Heat was amazed at her coolness.

"Come! You know I am in the police," he said, sharply.

"I don't trouble my head much about it," Mrs. Verloc remarked, returning to the ranging of her boxes.

"My name is Heat. Chief Inspector Heat of the Special Crimes section."

Mrs. Verloc adjusted nicely in its place a small cardboard box, and turning round, faced him again, heavy-eyed, with idle hands hanging down. A silence reigned for a time.

"So your husband went out a quarter of an hour ago! And he didn't say when he would be back?"

"He didn't go out alone," Mrs. Verloc let fall negligently.

"A friend?"

Mrs. Verloc touched the back of her hair. It was in perfect order.

"A stranger who called."

"I see. What sort of man was that stranger? Would you mind telling me?"

Mrs. Verloc did not mind. And when Chief Inspector Heat heard of a man dark, thin, with a long face and turned-up moustaches, he gave signs of perturbation, and exclaimed:

"Dash me if I didn't think so! He hasn't lost any time."

He was intensely disgusted in the secrecy of his heart at the un-official conduct of his immediate chief. But he was not quixotic. He lost all desire to await Mr. Verloc's return. What they had gone out for he did not know, but he imagined it possible that they would return together. The case is not followed properly, it's being tampered with, he thought, bitterly.

"I am afraid I haven't time to wait for your husband," he said.

Mrs. Verloc received this declaration listlessly. Her detachment had impressed Chief Inspector Heat all along. At this precise moment it whetted his curiosity. Chief Inspector Heat hung in the wind, swayed by his passions like the most private of citizens.

"I think," he said, looking at her steadily, "that you could give me a pretty good notion of what's going on if you liked."

Forcing her fine, inert eyes to return his gaze, Mrs. Verloc murmured:

"Going on! What *is* going on?"

"Why, the affair I came to talk about a little with your husband."

That day Mrs. Verloc had glanced at a morning paper as usual. But she had not stirred out of doors. The newsboys never invaded Brett Street. It was not a street for their business. And the echo of their cries drifting along the populous thoroughfares, expired between the dirty brick walls without reaching the threshold of the shop. Her husband had not brought an evening paper home. At any rate she had not seen it. Mrs. Verloc knew nothing whatever of any affair. And she said so, with a genuine note of wonder in her quiet voice.

Chief Inspector Heat did not believe for a moment in so much ignorance. Curtly, without amiability, he stated the bare fact.

Mrs. Verloc turned away her eyes.

"I call it silly," she pronounced, slowly. She paused. "We ain't downtrodden slaves here."

The Chief Inspector waited watchfully. Nothing more came.

"And your husband didn't mention anything to you when he came home?"

Mrs. Verloc simply turned her face from right to left in sign of negation. A languid, baffling silence reigned in the shop. Chief Inspector Heat felt provoked beyond endurance.

"There was another small matter," he began in a detached tone, "which I wanted to speak to your husband about. There came into our hands a—a—what we believe is—a stolen overcoat."

Mrs. Verloc, with her mind specially aware of thieves that evening, touching lightly the bosom of her dress.

"We have lost no overcoat," she said, calmly.

"That's funny," continued Private Citizen Heat. "I see you keep a lot of marking ink here——"

He took up a small bottle, and looked at it against the gas-jet in the middle of the shop.

"Purple—isn't it?" he remarked, setting it down again. "As I said, it's strange. Because the overcoat has got a label sewn on the inside with your address written in marking ink."

Mrs. Verloc leaned over the counter with a low exclamation.

"That's my brother's, then."

"Where's your brother? Can I see him?" asked the Chief Inspector, briskly. Mrs. Verloc leaned a little more over the counter.

"No. He isn't here. I wrote that label myself."

"Where's your brother now?"

"He's been away living with—a friend—in the country."

"The overcoat comes from the country. And what's the name of the friend?"

"Michaelis," confessed Mrs. Verloc in an awed whisper.

The Chief Inspector let out a whistle. His eyes snapped.

"Just so. Capital. And your brother now, what's he like—a sturdy, darkish chap—eh?"

"Oh, no," exclaimed Mrs. Verloc, fervently. "That must be the thief. Stevie's slight and fair."

"Good," said the Chief Inspector in an approving tone. And while Mrs. Verloc, wavering between alarm and wonder, stared at him, he sought for information. Why have the address sewn like this inside the coat? And he heard that the mangled remains he had inspected that morning with extreme repugnance were those of a youth, nervous, absent-minded, peculiar, and also that the woman who was speaking to him had had the charge of that boy since he was a baby.

"Easily excitable?" he suggested.

"Oh, yes. He is. But how did he come to lose his coat——"

Chief Inspector Heat suddenly pulled out a pink newspaper he had bought less than half-an-hour ago. He was interested in horses. Forced by his calling into an attitude of doubt and suspicion towards his fellow-citizens, Chief Inspector Heat relieved the instinct of credulity implanted in the human breast by putting unbounded faith in the sporting prophets of that particular evening publication. Dropping the extra special on to the counter, he plunged his hand again into his pocket, and pulling out the piece of cloth fate had presented him with out of a heap of things that seemed to have been collected in shambles and rag shops, he offered it to Mrs. Verloc for inspection.

"I suppose you recognize this?"

She took it mechanically in both her hands. Her eyes seemed to grow bigger as she looked.

"Yes," she whispered, then raised her head, and staggered backward a little.

"Whatever for is it torn out like this?"

The Chief Inspector snatched across the counter the cloth out of her hands, and she sat heavily on the chair. He thought: identification's perfect. And in that moment he had a glimpse into the whole amazing truth. Verloc was the "other man."

"Mrs. Verloc," he said, "it strikes me that you know more of this bomb affair than even you yourself are aware of."

Mrs. Verloc sat still, amazed, lost in boundless astonishment. What was the connection? And she became so rigid all over that she was not able to turn her head at the clatter of the bell, which caused the private investigator Heat to spin round on his heel. Mr. Verloc had shut the door, and for a moment the two men looked at each other.

Mr. Verloc, without looking at his wife, walked up to the Chief Inspector, who was relieved to see him return alone.

"You here!" muttered Mr. Verloc, heavily. "Who are you after?"

"No one," said Chief Inspector Heat in a low tone. "Look here, I would like a word or two with you."

Mr. Verloc, still pale, had brought an air of resolution with him. Still he didn't look at his wife. He said:

"Come in here, then." And he led the way into the parlour.

The door was hardly shut when Mrs. Verloc, jumping up from the chair, ran to it as if to fling it open, but instead of doing so fell on her knees, with her ear to the keyhole. The two men must have stopped directly they were through, because she heard plainly the Chief Inspector's voice, though she could not see his finger pressed against her husband's breast emphatically.

"You are the other man, Verloc. Two men were seen entering the park."

And the voice of Mr. Verloc said:

"Well, take me now. What's to prevent you? You have the right."

"Oh, no! I know too well whom you have been giving yourself away to. He'll have to manage this little affair all by himself. But don't you make a mistake, it's I who found you out."

Then she heard only muttering. Inspector Heat must have been showing to Mr. Verloc the piece of Stevie's overcoat, because Stevie's sister, guardian, and protector heard her husband a little louder.

"I never noticed that she had hit upon that dodge."

Again for a time Mrs. Verloc heard nothing but murmurs, whose mysteriousness was less nightmarish to her brain than the horrible suggestions of shaped words. Then Chief Inspector Heat, on the other side of the door, raised his voice:

"You must have been mad."

And Mr. Verloc's voice answered, with a sort of gloomy fury:

"I have been mad for a month or more, but I am not mad now. It's all over. It shall all come out of my head, and hang the consequences."

There was a silence, and then Private Citizen Heat murmured: "What's coming out?"

"Everything," exclaimed the voice of Mr. Verloc, and then sank very low.

After a while it rose again.

"You have known me for several years now, and you've found me useful, too. You know I was a straight man. Yes, straight."

This appeal to old acquaintance must have been extremely distasteful to the Chief Inspector.

His voice took on a warning note.

"Don't you trust so much to what you have been promised. If I were you I would clear out. I don't think we will run after you."

Mr. Verloc was heard to laugh a little.

"Oh, yes; you hope the others will get rid of me for you—don't you? No, no; you don't shake me off now. I have been a straight man to those people too long, and now everything must come out."

"Let it come out, then," the different voice of Chief Inspector Heat assented. "But tell me now how did you get away?"

"I was making for Chesterfield Walk," Mrs. Verloc heard her husband's voice, "when I heard the bang. I started running then. Fog. I saw no one till I was past the end of George Street. Don't think I met any one till then."

"So easy as that!" marvelled the voice of Chief Inspector Heat. "The bang startled you, eh?"

"Yes; it came too soon," confessed the gloomy, husky voice of Mr. Verloc.

Mrs. Verloc pressed her ear to the keyhole; her lips were blue, her hands cold as ice, and her pale face, in which the two eyes seemed like two black holes, felt to her as if it were enveloped in flames.

On the other side of the door the voices sank very low. She caught words now and then, sometimes in her husband's voice, sometimes in the smooth tones of the Chief Inspector. She heard this last say:

"We believe he stumbled against the root of a tree."

There was a husky, voluble murmur, which lasted for some time, and then the Chief Inspector, as if answering some inquiry, spoke emphatically:

"Of course. Blown to small bits: limbs, gravel, clothing, bones, splinters—all mixed up together. I tell you they had to fetch a shovel to gather him up with."

Mrs. Verloc sprang up suddenly from her crouching position, and stopping her ears, reeled to and fro between the counter and the shelves on the wall towards the chair. Her crazed eyes noted the sporting sheet left by the Chief Inspector, and as she knocked herself against the counter she snatched it up, fell into the chair, tore the optimistic, rosy sheet right across in trying to open it, then flung it on the floor. On the other side of the door, Chief Inspector Heat was saying to Mr. Verloc, the secret agent:

"So your defence will be practically a full confession?"

"It will. I am going to tell the whole story."

"You won't be believed as much as you fancy you will."

And the Chief Inspector remained thoughtful. The turn this affair was taking meant the disclosure of many things—the laying waste of fields of knowledge, which, cultivated by a capable man, had a distinct value for the individual and for the society. It was sorry, sorry meddling. It would leave Michaelis unscathed; it would drag to light the Professor's home industry; disorganize the whole system of supervision; make no end of a row in the papers, which, from that point of view, appeared to him by a sudden illumination as invariably written by fools for the reading of imbeciles. Mentally he agreed with the words Mr. Verloc let fall at last in answer to his last remark.

"Perhaps not. But it will upset many things. I have been a straight man, and I shall keep straight in this——"

"If they let you," said the Chief Inspector, cynically. "You will be preached to, no doubt, before they put you into the dock. And in the end you may yet get let in for a sentence that will surprise you. I wouldn't trust too much the gentleman who's been talking to you."

Mr. Verloc listened, frowning.

"My advice to you is to clear out while you may. I have no instructions. There are some of them," continued Chief Inspector Heat, laying a peculiar stress on the word "them," "who think you are already out of the world."

"Indeed!" Mr. Verloc was moved to say. Though since his return from Greenwich he had spent most of his time sitting in the tap-room of an obscure little public-house, he could hardly have hoped for such favourable news.

"That's the impression about you." The Chief Inspector nodded at him. "Vanish. Clear out."

"Where to?" snarled Mr. Verloc. He raised his head, and gazing at the closed door of the parlour, muttered feelingly: "I only wish you would take me away to-night. I would go quietly."

"I daresay," assented sardonically the Chief Inspector, following the direction of his glance.

The brow of Mr. Verloc broke into slight moisture. He lowered his husky voice confidentially before the unmoved Chief Inspector.

"The lad was half-witted, irresponsible. Any court would have seen that at once. Only fit for the asylum. And that was the worst that would've happened to him if——"

The Chief Inspector, his hand on the door handle, whispered into Mr. Verloc's face:

"He may've been half-witted, but you must have been crazy. What drove you off your head like this?"

Mr. Verloc, thinking of Mr. Vladimir, did not hesitate in the choice of words.

"A Hyperborean swine," he hissed, forcibly. "A what you might call a—a gentleman."

The Chief Inspector, steady-eyed, nodded briefly his comprehension, and opened the door. Mrs. Verloc, behind the counter, might have heard but did not see his departure, pursued by the aggressive clatter of the bell. She sat at her post of duty behind the counter. She sat rigidly erect in the chair with two dirty pink pieces of paper lying spread at her feet. The palms of her hands were pressed convulsively to her face, with the tips of the fingers contracted against the forehead, as though the skin had been a mask which she was ready to tear off violently. The perfect immobility of her pose expressed the agitation of rage and despair, all the potential violence of tragic passions, better than any shallow display of shrieks, with the beating of a distracted head against the walls, could have done. Chief Inspector Heat, crossing the shop at his busy, swinging pace, gave her only a cursory glance. And when the cracked bell ceased to tremble on its curved ribbon of steel nothing stirred near Mrs. Verloc, as if her attitude had the locking power of a spell. Even the butterfly-shaped gas flames posed on the ends of the suspended T-bracket burned without a quiver. In that shop of shady wares fitted with deal shelves painted a dull brown, which seemed to devour the sheen of the light, the gold circlet of the wedding ring on Mrs. Verloc's left hand glittered exceedingly with the untarnished glory of a piece from some splendid treasure of jewels, dropped in a dust-bin.

The Assistant Commissioner, driven rapidly in a hansom from the neighbourhood of Soho in the direction of Westminster, got out at the very centre of the Empire on which the sun never sets. Some stalwart constables, who did not seem particularly impressed by the duty of watching the august spot, saluted him. Penetrating through a portal by no means lofty into the precincts of the House which is *the* House, *par excellence*, in the minds of many millions of men, he was met at last by the volatile and revolutionary Toodles.

That neat and nice young man concealed his astonishment at the early appearance of the Assistant Commissioner, whom he had been told to look out for some time about midnight. His turning up so early he concluded to be the sign that things, whatever they were, had gone wrong. With an extremely ready sympathy, which in nice young-sters goes often with a joyous temperament, he felt sorry for the Great Presence he called "The Chief," and also for the Assistant Commissioner, whose face appeared to him more ominously wooden than ever before, and quite wonderfully long. "What a queer, foreign-looking chap he is," he thought to himself, smiling from a distance with friendly buoyancy. And directly they came together he began to talk with the kind intention of burying the awkwardness of failure under a heap of words. It looked as if the great assault threatened for that night were going to fizzle out. An inferior henchman of "that brute Cheeseman" was up boring mercilessly a very thin House with some shamelessly cooked statistics. He, Toodles, hoped he would bore them into a count out every minute. But then he might be only mark-ing time to let that guzzling Cheeseman dine at his leisure. Anyway, the Chief could not be persuaded to go home.

"He will see you at once, I think. He's sitting all alone in his room thinking of all the fishes of the sea," concluded Toodles, airily. "Come along."

Notwithstanding the kindness of his disposition, the young private secretary (unpaid) was accessible to the common failings of humanity. He did not wish to harrow the feelings of the Assistant Commissioner, who looked to him uncommonly like a man who has made a mess of his job. But his curiosity was too strong to be restrained by mere com-passion. He could not help, as they went along, throwing over his shoulder lightly:

"And your sprat?"

"Got him," answered the Assistant Commissioner with a concision which did not mean to be repellent in the least.

"Good. You've no idea how these great men dislike to be disappointed in small things."

After this profound observation the experienced Toodles seemed to reflect. At any rate he said nothing for quite two seconds. Then:

"I'm glad. But—I say—is it really such a very small thing as you make it out?"

"Do you know what may be done with a sprat?" the Assistant Commissioner asked in his turn.

"He's sometimes put into a sardine box," chuckled Toodles, whose erudition on the subject of the fishing industry was fresh and, in comparison with his ignorance of all other industrial matters, immense. "There are sardine canneries on the Spanish coast which——"

The Assistant Commissioner interrupted the apprentice statesman.

"Yes. Yes. But a sprat is also thrown away sometimes in order to catch a whale."

"A whale. Phew!" exclaimed Toodles, with bated breath. "You're after a whale, then?"

"Not exactly. What I am after is more like a dog-fish. You don't know perhaps what a dog-fish is like."

"Yes; I do. We're buried in special books up to our necks—whole shelves full of them—with plates. . . . It's a noxious, rascally-looking, altogether detestable beast, with a sort of smooth face and moustaches."

"Described to a T," commended the Assistant Commissioner. "Only mine is clean-shaven altogether. You've seen him. It's a witty fish."

"I have seen him!" said Toodles, incredulously. "I can't conceive where I could have seen him."

"At the Explorers', I should say," dropped the Assistant Commissioner, calmly. At the name of that extremely exclusive club Toodles looked scared, and stopped short.

"Nonsense," he protested, but in an awestruck tone. "What do you mean? A member?"

"Honorary," muttered the Assistant Commissioner through his teeth.

"Heavens!"

Toodles looked so thunderstruck that the Assistant Commissioner smiled faintly.

"That's between ourselves strictly," he said.

"That's the beastliest thing I've ever heard in my life," declared Toodles, feebly, as if astonishment had robbed him of all his buoyant strength in a second.

The Assistant Commissioner gave him an unsmiling glance. Till they came to the door of the great man's room, Toodles preserved a scandalized and solemn silence, as though he were offended with the Assistant Commissioner for exposing such an unsavoury and disturbing fact. It revolutionized his idea of the Explorers' Club's extreme selectness, of its social purity. Toodles was revolutionary only in politics; his social beliefs and personal feelings he wished to preserve unchanged through all the years allotted to him on this earth which, upon the whole, he believed to be a nice place to live on.

He stood aside.

"Go in without knocking," he said.

Shades of green silk fitted low over all the lights imparted to the room something of a forest's deep gloom. The haughty eyes were physically the great man's weak point. This point was wrapped up in secrecy. When an opportunity offered, he rested them conscientiously. The Assistant Commissioner entering saw at first only a big pale hand supporting a big head, and concealing the upper part of a big pale face. An open despatch-box stood on the writing-table near a few oblong sheets of paper and a scattered handful of quill pens. There was absolutely nothing else on the large flat surface except a little bronze statuette draped in a toga, mysteriously watchful in its shadowy immobility. The Assistant Commissioner, invited to take a chair, sat down. In the dim light, the salient points of his personality, the long face, the black hair, his lankness, made him look more foreign than ever.

The great man manifested no surprise, no eagerness, no sentiment whatever. The attitude in which he rested his menaced eyes was profoundly meditative. He did not alter it the least bit. But his tone was not dreamy.

"Well! What is it that you've found out already? You came upon something unexpected on the first step."

"Not exactly unexpected, Sir Ethelred. What I mainly came upon was a psychological state."

The Great Presence made a slight movement.

"You must be lucid, please."

"Yes, Sir Ethelred. You know no doubt that most criminals at some time or other feel an irresistible need of confessing—of making a clean breast of it to somebody—to anybody. And they do it often to the police. In that Verloc whom Heat wished so much to screen I've found a man in that particular psychological state. The man, figuratively speaking, flung himself on my breast. It was enough on my part to whisper to him who I was and to add 'I know that you are at the bottom of this affair.' It must have seemed miraculous to him that we should know already, but he took it all in the stride. The wonderfulness of it never checked him for a moment. There remained for me only to put to him the two questions: Who put you up to it?

and Who was the man who did it? He answered the first with remarkable emphasis. As to the second question, I gather that the fellow with the bomb was his brother-in-law—quite a lad—a weak-minded creature. . . . It is rather a curious affair—too long perhaps to state fully just now."

"What then have you learned?" asked the great man.

"First, I've learned that the ex-convict Michaelis had nothing to do with it, though indeed the lad had been living with him temporarily in the country up to eight o'clock this morning. It is more than likely that Michaelis knows nothing of it to this moment."

"You are positive as to that?" asked the great man.

"Quite certain, Sir Ethelred. This fellow Verloc went there this morning, and took away the lad on the pretence of going out for a walk in the lanes. As it was not the first time that he did this, Michaelis could not have the slightest suspicion of anything unusual. For the rest, Sir Ethelred, the indignation of this man Verloc had left nothing in doubt—nothing whatever. He had been driven out of his mind almost by an extraordinary performance, which for you or me it would be difficult to take as seriously meant, but which produced a great impression obviously on him."

The Assistant Commissioner then imparted briefly to the great man, who sat still, resting his eyes under the screen of his hand, Mr. Verloc's appreciation of Mr. Vladimir's proceedings and character. The Assistant Commissioner did not seem to refuse it a certain amount of competency. But the Great Personage remarked:

"All this seems very fantastic."

"Doesn't it? One would think a ferocious joke. But our man took it seriously, it appears. He felt himself threatened. Formerly, you know, he was in direct communication with old Stott-Wartenheim himself, and had come to regard his services as indispensable. It was an extremely rude awakening. I imagine that he lost his head. He became angry and frightened. Upon my word, my impression is that he thought these Embassy people quite capable not only of throwing him out, but of giving him away, too, in some manner or other——"

"How long were you with him?" interrupted the Presence from behind his big hand.

"Some forty minutes, Sir Ethelred, in a house of bad repute called the Continental Hotel, closeted in a room which by-the-by I took for the night. I found him under the influence of that reaction which follows the effort of crime. The man cannot be defined as a hardened criminal. It is obvious that he did not plan the death of that wretched lad—his brother-in-law. That was a shock to him—I could see that. Perhaps he is a man of strong sensibilities. Perhaps he was even fond of the lad—who knows? He might have hoped that the fellow would get clear away; in which case it would have been almost impossible to bring this thing home to any one. At any rate, he risked consciously nothing more than arrest for him."

The Assistant Commisioner paused in his speculations to reflect for a moment.

"Though how, in that last case, he could hope to have his own share in the business concealed is more than I can tell," he continued, in his ignorance of poor Stevie's devotion to Mr. Verloc (who was good), and of his truly peculiar dumbness, which in the old affair of fireworks on the stairs had for many years resisted entreaties, coaxing, anger, and other means of investigation used by his beloved sister. For Stevie was loyal. . . . "No, I can't imagine. It's possible that he never thought of that at all. It sounds an extravagant way of putting it, Sir Ethelred, but his state of dismay suggested to me an impulsive man who, after committing suicide with the notion that it would end all his troubles, had discovered that it did nothing of the kind."

The Assistant Commissioner gave this definition in an apologetic voice. But in truth there is a sort of lucidity proper to extravagant language, and the great man was not offended. A slight jerky movement of the big body half lost in the gloom of the green silk shades, of the big head leaning on the big hand, accompanied an intermittent stifled but powerful sound. The great man had laughed.

"What have you done with him?"

The Assistant Commissioner answered very readily:

"As he seemed very anxious to get back to his wife in the shop I let him go, Sir Ethelred."

"You did? But the fellow will disappear."

"Pardon me. I don't think so. Where could he go to? Moreover, you must remember that he has got to think of the danger from his comrades, too. He's there at his post. How could he explain leaving it? But even if there were no obstacles to his freedom of action he would do nothing. At present he hasn't enough moral energy to take a resolution of any sort. Permit me also to point out that if I had detained him we would have been committed to a course of action on which I wished to know your precise intentions first."

The Great Personage rose heavily, an imposing, shadowy form in the greenish gloom of the room.

"I'll see the Attorney-General to-night, and will send for you to-morrow morning. Is there anything more you'd wish to tell me now?"

The Assistant Commissioner had stood up also, slender and flexible.

"I think not, Sir Ethelred, unless I were to enter into details which——"

"No. No details, please."

The great shadowy form seemed to shrink away as if in physical dread of details; then came forward, expanded, enormous, and weighty, offering a large hand. "And you say that this man has got a wife?"

"Yes, Sir Ethelred," said the Assistant Commissioner, pressing deferentially the extended hand. "A genuine wife and a genuinely, respectably, marital relation. He told me that after his interview at the Embassy he would have thrown everything up, would have tried to sell his shop, and leave the country, only he felt certain that his wife would not even hear of going abroad. Nothing could be more characteristic of the respectable bond than that," went on, with a touch of grimness, the Assistant Commissioner, whose own wife, too, had refused to hear of going abroad. "Yes, a genuine wife. And the victim was a genuine brother-in-law. From a certain point of view we are here in the presence of a domestic drama."

The Assistant Commissioner laughed a little; but the great man's thoughts seemed to have wandered far away, perhaps to the questions of his country's domestic policy, the battle-ground of his crusading valour against the paynim Cheeseman. The Assistant Commissioner withdrew quietly, unnoticed, as if already forgotten.

He had his own crusading instincts. This affair, which, in one way or another, disgusted Chief Inspector Heat, seemed to him a providentially given starting-point for a crusade. He had it much at heart to begin. He walked slowly home, meditating that enterprise on the way, and thinking over Mr. Verloc's psychology in a composite mood of repugnance and satisfaction. He walked all the way home. Finding the drawing-room dark, he went upstairs, and spent some time between the bedroom and the dressing-room changing his clothes, going to and fro with the air of a thoughtful somnambulist. But he shook it off before going out again to join his wife at the house of the great lady patroness of Michaelis.

He knew he would be welcomed there. On entering the smaller of the two drawing-rooms he saw his wife in a small group near the piano. A youngish composer in process of becoming famous was discoursing from a music stool to two thick men whose backs looked old, and three slender women whose backs looked young. Behind the screen the great lady had only two persons with her: a man and a woman, who sat side by side on armchairs at the foot of her couch. She extended her hand to the Assistant Commissioner.

"I never hoped to see you here to-night. Annie told me——"

"Yes. I had no idea myself that my work would be over so soon."

The Assistant Commissioner added in a low tone: "I am glad to tell you that Michaelis is altogether clear of this——"

The patroness of the ex-convict received this assurance indignantly.

"Why? Were your people stupid enough to connect him with——"

"Not stupid," interrupted the Assistant Commissioner, contradicting deferentially. "Clever enough—quite clever enough for that."

A silence fell. The man at the foot of the couch had stopped speaking to the lady, and looked on with a faint smile.

"I don't know whether you ever met before," said the great lady.

Mr. Vladimir and the Assistant Commissioner, introduced, acknowledged each other's existence with punctilious and guarded courtesy.

"He's been frightening me," declared suddenly the lady who sat by the side of Mr. Vladimir, with an inclination of the head towards that gentleman. The Assistant Commissioner knew the lady.

"You do not look frightened," he pronounced, after surveying her conscientiously with his tired and equable gaze. He was thinking meantime to himself that in this house one met everybody sooner or later. Mr. Vladimir's rosy countenance was wreathed in smiles, because he was witty, but his eyes remained serious, like the eyes of a convinced man.

"Well, he tried to at least," amended the lady.

"Force of habit perhaps," said the Assistant Commissioner, moved by an irresistible inspiration.

"He has been threatening society with all sorts of horrors," continued the lady, whose enunciation was caressing and slow, "apropos of this explosion in Greenwich Park. It appears we all ought to quake in our shoes at what's coming if those people are not suppressed all over the world. I had no idea this was such a grave affair."

Mr. Vladimir, affecting not to listen, leaned towards the couch, talking amiably in subdued tones, but he heard the Assistant Commissioner say:

"I've no doubt that Mr. Vladimir has a very precise notion of the true importance of this affair."

Mr. Vladimir asked himself what that confounded and intrusive policeman was driving at. Descended from generations victimized by the instruments of an arbitrary power, he was racially, nationally, and individually afraid of the police. It was an inherited weakness, altogether independent of his judgment, of his reason, of his experience. He was born to it. But that sentiment, which resembled the irrational horror some people have of cats, did not stand in the way of his immense contempt for the English police. He finished the sentence addressed to the great lady, and turned slightly in his chair.

"You mean that we have a great experience of these people. Yes; indeed, we suffer greatly from their activity, while you"—Mr. Vladimir hesitated for a moment, in smiling perplexity—"while you suffer their presence gladly in your midst," he finished, displaying a dimple in each clean-shaven cheek. Then he added more gravely: "I may even say—because you do."

When Mr. Vladimir ceased speaking the Assistant Commissioner lowered his glance, and the conversation dropped. Almost immediately afterwards Mr. Vladimir took leave. Directly his back was turned on the couch the Assistant Commissioner rose, too.

"I thought you were going to stay and take Annie home," said the lady patroness of Michaelis.

"I find that I've yet a little work to do to-night."

"In connection——?"

"Well, yes—in a way."

"Tell me, what is it really—this horror?"

"It's difficult to say what it is, but it may yet be a *cause célèbre*," said the Assistant Commissioner.

He left the drawing-room hurriedly, and found Mr. Vladimir still in the hall, wrapping up his throat carefully in a large silk handkerchief. Behind him a footman waited, holding his overcoat. Another stood ready to open the door. The Assistant Commissioner was duly helped into his coat, and let out at once. After descending the front steps he stopped, as if to consider the way he should take. On seeing this through the door held open, Mr. Vladimir lingered in the hall to get out a cigar and asked for a light. It was furnished to him by an elderly man out of livery with an air of calm solicitude. But the match went out; the footman then closed the door, and Mr. Vladimir lighted his large Havana with leisurely care. When at last he got out of the house, he saw with disgust the "confounded policeman" still standing on the pavement.

"Can he be waiting for me?" thought Mr. Vladimir, looking up and down for some signs of a hansom. He saw none. A couple of carriages waited by the curbstone, their lamps blazing steadily, the horses standing perfectly still, as if carved in stone, the coachmen sitting motionless under the big fur capes, without as much as a quiver stirring the white thongs of their big whips. Mr. Vladimir walked on, and the "confounded policeman" fell into step at his elbow. He said nothing. At the end of the fourth stride Mr. Vladimir felt infuriated and uneasy. This could not last.

"Rotten weather," he growled, savagely.

"Mild," said the Assistant Commissioner without passion. He remained silent for a little while. "We've got hold of a man called Verloc," he announced, casually.

Mr. Vladimir did not stumble, did not stagger back, did not change his stride. But he could not prevent himself from exclaiming: "What?" The Assistant Commissioner did not repeat his statement. "You know him," he went on in the same tone.

Mr. Vladimir stopped, and became guttural.

"What makes you say that?"

"I don't. It's Verloc who says that."

"A lying dog of some sort," said Mr. Vladimir in somewhat Oriental phraseology. But in his heart he was almost awed by the miraculous cleverness of the English police. The change of his opinion on the subject was so violent that it made him for a moment feel slightly sick. He threw away his cigar, and moved on.

"What pleased me most in this affair," the Assistant went on, talking slowly, "is that it makes such an excellent starting-point for a piece of work which I've felt must be taken in hand—that is, the clearing out of this country of all the foreign political spies, police, and that sort of—of—dogs. In my opinion they are a ghastly nuisance; also an element of danger. But we can't very well seek them out individually. The only way is to make their employment unpleasant to their employers. The thing's becoming indecent. And dangerous, too, for us, here."

Mr. Vladimir stopped again for a moment.

"What do you mean?"

"The prosecution of this Verloc will demonstrate to the public both the danger and the indecency."

"Nobody will believe what a man of that sort says," said Mr. Vladimir, contemptuously.

"The wealth and precision of detail will carry conviction to the great mass of the public," advanced the Assistant Commissioner gently.

"So that is seriously what you mean to do?"

"We've got the man; we have no choice."

"You will be only feeding up the lying spirit of these revolutionary scoundrels," Mr. Vladimir protested. "What do you want to make a scandal for?—from morality—of what?"

Mr. Vladimir's anxiety was obvious. The Assistant Commissioner, having ascertained in this way that there must be some truth in the summary statements of Mr. Verloc, said indifferently:

"There's a practical side, too. We have really enough to do to look after the genuine article. You can't say we are not effective. But we don't intend to let ourselves be bothered by shams under any pretext whatever."

Mr. Vladimir's tone became lofty.

"For my part, I can't share your view. It is selfish. My sentiments for my own country cannot be doubted; but I've always felt that we ought to be good Europeans besides—I mean governments and men."

"Yes," said the Assistant Commissioner simply. "Only you look at Europe from its other end. But," he went on in a good-natured tone, "the foreign governments cannot complain of the inefficiency of our police. Look at this outrage; a case specially difficult to trace inasmuch as it was a sham. In less than twelve hours we have established the identity of a man literally blown to shreds, have found the organizer of the attempt, and have had a glimpse of the inciter behind him. And we could have gone further; only we stopped at the limits of our territory."

"So this instructive crime was planned abroad," Mr. Vladimir said, quickly. "You admit it was planned abroad?"

"Theoretically. Theoretically only, on foreign territory; abroad only by a fiction," said the Assistant Commissioner, alluding to the character of Embassies which are supposed to be part and parcel of the country to which they belong. "But that's a detail. I talked to you of this business because it's your government that grumbles most at our police. You see that we are not so bad. I wanted particularly to tell you of our success."

"I'm sure I'm very grateful," muttered Mr. Vladimir through his teeth.

"We can put our finger on every anarchist here," went on the Assistant Commissioner, as though he were quoting Chief Inspector Heat. "All that's wanted now is to do away with the agent provocateur to make everything safe."

Mr. Vladimir held up his hand to a passing hansom.

"You're not going in here?" remarked the Assistant Commissioner, looking at a building of noble proportions and hospitable aspect, with the light of a great hall falling through its glass doors on a broad flight of steps.

But Mr. Vladimir, sitting, stony-eyed, inside the hansom, drove off without a word.

The Assistant Commissioner himself did not turn into the noble building. It was the Explorers' Club. The thought passed through his mind that Mr. Vladimir, honorary member, would not be seen very often there in the future. He looked at his watch. It was only half-past ten. He had had a very full evening.

CHAPTER ELEVEN

After Chief Inspector Heat had left him Mr. Verloc moved about the parlour. From time to time he eyed his wife through the open door. "She knows all about it now," he thought to himself with commiseration for her sorrow and with some satisfaction as regarded himself. Mr. Verloc's soul, if lacking greatness perhaps, was capable of tender sentiments. The prospect of having to break the news to her had put him into a fever. Chief Inspector Heat had relieved him of the task. That was good as far as it went. It remained for him now to face her grief.

Mr. Verloc had never expected to have to face it on account of death, whose catastrophic character cannot be argued away by sophisticated reasoning or persuasive eloquence. Mr. Verloc never meant Stevie to perish with such abrupt violence. He did not mean him to perish at all. Stevie dead was a much greater nuisance than ever he had been when alive. Mr. Verloc had augured a favourable issue to his enterprise, basing himself not on Stevie's intelligence, which sometimes plays queer tricks with a man, but on the blind docility and on the blind devotion of the boy. Though not much of a psychologist, Mr. Verloc had gauged the depth of Stevie's fanaticism. He dared cherish the hope of Stevie walking away from the walls of the Observatory as he had been instructed to do, taking the way shown to him several times previously, and rejoining his brother-in-law, the wise and good Mr. Verloc, outside the precincts of the park. Fifteen minutes ought to have been enough for the veriest fool to deposit the engine and walk away. And the Professor had guaranteed more than fifteen minutes. But Stevie had stumbled within five minutes of being left to himself. And Mr. Verloc was shaken morally to pieces. He had foreseen everything but that. He had foreseen Stevie distracted and lost—sought for—found in some police station or provincial workhouse in the end. He had foreseen Stevie arrested, and was not afraid, because Mr. Verloc had a great opinion of Stevie's loyalty, which had been carefully indoctrinated with the necessity of silence in the course of many walks. Like a peripatetic philosopher, Mr. Verloc, strolling along the streets of London, had modified Stevie's view of the police by conversations full of subtle reasonings. Never had a sage a more attentive and admiring disciple. The submission and worship were so apparent that Mr. Verloc had come to feel something like a liking for the boy. In any case, he had not foreseen the swift bringing home of his connection. That his wife should hit upon the precaution of sewing the boy's address inside his overcoat was the last thing Mr. Verloc would have thought of. One can't think of everything. That was what she meant when she said that he need not worry if he lost Stevie during their walks. She had assured him that the boy would turn up all right. Well, he had turned up with a vengeance!

"Well, well," muttered Mr. Verloc in his wonder. What did she mean by it? Spare him the trouble of keeping an anxious eye on Stevie? Most likely she had meant well. Only she ought to have told him of the precaution she had taken.

Mr. Verloc walked behind the counter of the shop. His intention was not to overwhelm his wife with bitter reproaches. Mr. Verloc felt no bitterness. The unexpected march of events had converted him to the doctrine of fatalism. Nothing could be helped now. He said:

"I didn't mean any harm to come to the boy."

Mrs. Verloc shuddered at the sound of her husband's voice. She did not uncover her face. The trusted secret agent of the late Baron Stott-Wartenheim looked at her for a time with a heavy, persistent, undiscerning glance. The torn evening paper was lying at her feet. It could not have told her much. Mr. Verloc felt the need of talking to his wife.

"It's that damned Heat—eh?" he said. "He upset you. He's a brute, blurting it out like this to a woman. I made myself ill thinking how to break it to you. I sat for hours in the little parlour of the Cheshire Cheese thinking over the best way. You understand I never meant any harm to come to that boy."

Mr. Verloc, the Secret Agent, was speaking the truth. It was his marital affection that had received the greatest shock from the premature explosion. He added:

"I didn't feel particularly gay sitting there and thinking of you."

He observed another slight shudder of his wife, which affected his sensibility. As she persisted in hiding her face in her hands, he thought he had better leave her alone for a while. On this delicate impulse Mr. Verloc withdrew into the parlour again, where the gas-jet purred like a contented cat. Mrs. Verloc's wifely forethought had left the cold beef on the table with carving knife and fork and half a loaf of bread for Mr. Verloc's supper. He noticed all these things now for the first time, and cutting himself a piece of bread and meat, began to eat.

His appetite did not proceed from callousness. Mr. Verloc had not eaten any breakfast that day. He had left his home fasting. Not being an energetic man, he found his resolution in nervous excitement, which seemed to hold him mainly by the throat. He could not have swallowed anything solid. Michaelis' cottage was as destitute of provisions as the cell of a prisoner. The ticket-of-leave apostle lived on a little milk and crusts of stale bread. Moreover, when Mr. Verloc arrived he had already gone upstairs after his frugal meal. Absorbed in the toil and delight of literary composition, he had not even answered Mr. Verloc's shout up the little staircase.

"I am taking this young fellow home for a day or two."

And, in truth, Mr. Verloc did not wait for an answer, but had marched out of the cottage at once, followed by the obedient Stevie.

Now that all action was over and his fate taken out of his hands with unexpected swiftness, Mr. Verloc felt terribly empty physically. He carved the meat, cut the bread, and devoured his supper standing by the table, and now and then casting a glance towards his wife. Her prolonged immobility disturbed the comfort of his refection. He walked again into the shop, and came up very close to her. This sorrow with a veiled face made Mr. Verloc uneasy. He expected, of course, his wife to be very much upset, but he wanted her to pull herself together. He needed all her assistance and all her loyalty in these new conjunctures his fatalism had already accepted.

"Can't be helped," he said in a tone of gloomy sympathy. "Come, Winnie, we've got to think of to-morrow. You'll want all your wits about you after I am taken away."

He paused. Mrs. Verloc's breast heaved convulsively. This was not reassuring to Mr. Verloc, in whose view the newly created situation required from the two people most concerned in it calmness, decision, and other qualities incompatible with the mental disorder of passionate sorrow. Mr. Verloc was a humane man; he had come home prepared to allow every latitude to his wife's affection for her brother. Only he did not understand either the nature or the whole extent of that sentiment. And in this he was excusable, since it was impossible for him to understand it without ceasing to be himself. He was startled and disappointed, and his speech conveyed it by a certain roughness of tone.

"You might look at a fellow," he observed after waiting a while.

As if forced through the hands covering Mrs. Verloc's face the answer came, deadened, almost pitiful.

"I don't want to look at you as long as I live."

"Eh? What!" Mr. Verloc was merely startled by the superficial and literal meaning of this declaration. It was obviously unreasonable, the mere cry of exaggerated grief. He threw over it the mantle of his marital indulgence. The mind of Mr. Verloc lacked profundity. Under the mistaken impression that the value of individuals consists in what they are in themselves, he could not possibly comprehend the value of Stevie in the eyes of Mrs. Verloc. She was taking it confoundedly hard, he thought to himself. It was all the fault of that damned Heat. What did he want to upset the woman for? But she mustn't be allowed, for her own good, to carry on so till she got quite beside herself.

"Look here! You can't sit like this in the shop," he said with affected severity, in which there was some real annoyance; for urgent practical matters must be talked over if they had to sit up all night. "Somebody might come in at any minute," he added, and waited again. No effect was produced, and the idea of the finality of death occurred to Mr. Verloc during the pause. He changed his tone. "Come. This won't bring him back," he said, gently, feeling ready to take her in his arms and press her to his breast, where impatience and compassion dwelt side by side. But except for a short shudder Mrs. Verloc remained apparently unaffected by the force of that terrible truism. It was Mr. Verloc himself who was moved. He was moved in his simplicity to urge moderation by asserting the claims of his own personality.

"Do be reasonable, Winnie. What would it have been if you had lost me?"

He had vaguely expected to hear her cry out. But she did not budge. She leaned back a little, quieted down to a complete, unreadable stillness. Mr. Verloc's heart began to beat faster with exasperation and something resembling alarm. He laid his hand on her shoulder, saying:

"Don't be a fool, Winnie."

She gave no sign. It was impossible to talk to any purpose with a woman whose face one cannot see. Mr. Verloc caught hold of his wife's wrists. But her hands seemed glued fast. She swayed forward bodily to his tug, and nearly went off the chair. Startled to feel her so helplessly limp, he was trying to put her back on the chair when she stiffened suddenly all over, tore herself out of his hands, ran out of the shop, across the parlour, and into the kitchen. This was very swift. He had just a glimpse of her face and that much of her eyes that he knew she had not looked at him.

It all had the appearance of a struggle for the possession of a chair, because Mr. Verloc instantly took his wife's place in it. Mr. Verloc did not cover his face with his hands, but a sombre thoughtfulness veiled his features. A term of imprisonment could not be avoided. He did not wish now to avoid it. A prison was a place as safe from certain unlawful vengeances as the grave, with this advantage, that in a prison there is room for hope. What he saw before him was a term of imprisonment, an early release, and then life abroad somewhere, such as he had contemplated already, in case of failure. Well, it was a failure, if not exactly the sort of failure he had feared. It had been so near success that he could have positively terrified Mr. Vladimir out of his ferocious scoffing with this proof of occult efficiency. So at least it seemed now to Mr. Verloc. His prestige with the Embassy would have been immense if—if his wife had not had the unlucky notion of sewing on the address inside Stevie's overcoat. Mr. Verloc, who was no fool, had soon perceived the extraordinary character of the influence he had over Stevie, though he did not understand exactly its origin—the doctrine of his supreme wisdom and goodness inculcated by two anxious women. In all the eventualities he had foreseen Mr. Verloc had calculated with correct insight on Stevie's instinctive loyalty and blind discretion. The eventuality he had not foreseen had appalled him as a humane man and a fond husband. From every other point of view it was rather advantageous. Nothing can equal the everlasting discretion of death. Mr. Verloc, sitting perplexed and frightened in the small parlour of the Cheshire Cheese, could not help acknowledging that to himself, because his sensibility did not stand in the way of his judgment. Stevie's violent disintegration, however disturbing to think about, only assured the success; for, of course, the knocking down of a wall was not the aim of Mr. Vladimir's menaces, but the production of a moral effect. With much trouble and distress on Mr. Verloc's part the effect might be said to have been produced. When, however, most unexpectedly, it came home to roost in Brett Street, Mr. Verloc, who had been struggling like a man in a nightmare for the preservation of his position, accepted the blow in the spirit of a convinced fatalist. The position was gone through no one's fault really. A small, tiny fact had done it. It was like slipping on a bit of orange peel in the dark and breaking your leg.

Mr. Verloc drew a weary breath. He nourished no resentment against his wife. He thought: She will have to look after the shop while they keep me locked up. And thinking also how cruelly she would miss Stevie at first, he felt greatly concerned about her health and spirits. How would she stand her solitude—absolutely alone in that house? It would not do for her to break down while he was locked up. What would become of the shop then? The shop was an asset. Though Mr. Verloc's fatalism accepted his undoing as a secret agent, he had no mind to be utterly ruined, mostly, it must be owned, from regard for his wife.

Silent, and out of his line of sight in the kitchen, she frightened him. If only she had her mother with her. But that silly old woman—— An angry dismay possessed Mr. Verloc. He must talk with his wife. He could tell her certainly that a man does get desperate under certain circumstances. But he did not go incontinently to impart to her that information. First of all, it was clear to him that this evening was no time for business. He got up to close the street door and put the gas out in the shop.

Having thus assured a solitude around his hearthstone Mr. Verloc walked into the parlour, and glanced down into the kitchen. Mrs. Verloc was sitting in the place where poor Stevie usually established himself of an evening with paper and pencil for the pastime of drawing those coruscations of innumerable circles suggesting chaos and eternity. Her arms were folded on the table, and her head was lying on her arms. Mr. Verloc contemplated her back and the arrangement of her hair for a time, then walked away from the kitchen door. Mrs. Verloc's philosophical, almost disdainful incuriosity, the foundation of their accord in domestic life, made it extremely difficult to get into contact with her now this tragic necessity had arisen. Mr. Verloc felt this difficulty acutely. He turned around the table in the parlour with his usual air of a large animal in a cage.

Curiosity being one of the forms of self-revelation, a systematically incurious person remains always partly mysterious. Every time he passed near the door Mr. Verloc glanced at his wife uneasily. It was not that he was afraid of her. Mr. Verloc imagined himself loved by that woman. But she had not accustomed him to make confidences. And the confidence he had to make was of a profound psychological order. How with his want of practice could he tell her what he himself felt but vaguely: that there are conspiracies of fatal destiny, that a notion grows in a mind sometimes till it acquires an outward existence, an independent power of its own, and even a suggestive voice? He could not inform her that a man may be haunted by a fat, witty, clean-shaved face till the wildest expedient to get rid of it appears a child of wisdom.

On this mental reference to a First Secretary of a great Embassy, Mr. Verloc stopped in the doorway, and looking down into the kitchen with an angry face and clenched fists, addressed his wife.

"You don't know what a brute I had to deal with."

He started off to make another perambulation of the table; then when he had come to the door again he stopped, glaring in from the height of two steps.

"A silly, jeering, dangerous brute, with no more sense than—— After all these years! A man like me! And I have been playing my head at that game. You didn't know. Quite right, too. What was the good of telling you that I stood the risk of having a knife stuck into me any time these seven years we've been married? I am not a chap to worry a woman that's fond of me. You had no business to know."

Mr. Verloc took another turn round the parlour, fuming.

"A venomous beast," he began again from the doorway. "Drive me out into a ditch to starve for a joke. I could see he thought it was a damned good joke. A man like me! Look here! Some of the highest in the world got to thank me for walking on their two legs to this day. That's the man you've got married to, my girl!"

He perceived that his wife had sat up. Mrs. Verloc's arms remained lying stretched on the table. Mr. Verloc watched her back as if he could read there the effect of his words.

"There isn't a murdering plot for the last eleven years that I hadn't my finger in at the risk of my life. There's scores of these revolutionists I've sent off, with their bombs in their blamed pockets, to get themselves caught on the frontier. The old Baron knew what I was worth to his country. And here suddenly a swine comes along—an ignorant, overbearing swine."

Mr. Verloc, stepping slowly down two steps, entered the kitchen, took a tumbler off the dresser, and holding it in his hand, approached the sink, without looking at his wife.

"It wasn't the old Baron who would have had the wicked folly of getting me to call on him at eleven in the morning. There are two or three in this town that, if they had seen me going in, would have made no bones about knocking me on the head sooner or later. It was a silly, murderous trick to expose for nothing a man—like me."

Mr. Verloc, turning on the tap above the sink, poured three glasses of water, one after another, down his throat to quench the fires of his indignation. Mr. Vladimir's conduct was like a hot brand which set his internal economy in a blaze. He could not get over the dis-loyalty of it. This man, who would not work at the usual hard tasks which society sets to its humbler members, had exercised his secret industry with an indefatigable devotion. There was in Mr. Verloc a fund of loyalty. He had been loyal to his employers, to the cause of social stability—and to his affections, too—as became apparent when, after standing the tumbler in the sink, he turned about, saying:

"If I hadn't thought of you I would have taken the bullying brute by the throat and rammed his head into the fireplace. I'd have been more than a match for that pink-faced, smooth-shaved——"

Mr. Verloc neglected to finish the sentence, as if there could be no doubt of the terminal word. For the first time in his life he was taking that incurious woman into his confidence. The singularity of the event, the force and importance of the personal feelings aroused in the course of this confession, drove Stevie's fate clean out of Mr. Verloc's mind. The boy's stuttering existence of fears and indig-nations, together with the violence of his end, had passed out of Mr. Verloc's mental sight for a time. For that reason, when he looked up he was startled by the inappropriate character of his wife's stare. It was not a wild stare, and it was not inattentive, but its attention was peculiar and not satisfactory, inasmuch that it seemed concen-trated upon some point beyond Mr. Verloc's person. The impression was so strong that Mr. Verloc glanced over his shoulder. There was nothing behind him: there was just the whitewashed wall. The excel-lent husband of Winnie Verloc saw no writing on the wall. He turned to his wife again, repeating, with some emphasis:

"I would have taken him by the throat. As true as I stand here, if I hadn't thought of you then I would have half choked the life out of the brute before I let him get up. And don't you think he would have been anxious to call the police—either. He wouldn't have dared. You understand why—don't you?"

He blinked at his wife knowingly.

"No," said Mrs. Verloc in an unresonant voice, and without looking at him at all. "What are you talking about?"

A great discouragement, the result of fatigue, came upon Mr. Verloc. He had had a very full day, and his nerves had been tried to the utmost. After a month of maddening worry, ending in an unexpected catastrophe, the storm-tossed spirit of Mr. Verloc longed for repose. His career as a secret agent had come to an end in a way no one could have foreseen; only, now, perhaps he could manage to get a night's sleep at last. But looking at his wife, he doubted it. She was taking it very hard—not at all like herself, he thought. He made an effort to speak.

"You'll have to pull yourself together, my girl," he said, sympathetically. "What's done can't be undone."

Mrs. Verloc gave a slight start, though not a muscle of her white face moved in the least. Mr. Verloc, who was not looking at her, continued ponderously:

"You go to bed now. What you want is a good cry."

This opinion had nothing to recommend it but the general consent of mankind. It is universally understood that, as if it were nothing more substantial than vapour floating in the sky, every emotion of a woman is bound to end in a shower. And it is very probable that had Stevie died in his bed under her despairing gaze, in her protecting arms, Mrs. Verloc's grief would have found relief in a flood of bitter and pure tears. Mrs. Verloc, in common with other human beings, was provided with a fund of unconscious resignation sufficient to meet the normal manifestation of human destiny. Without "troubling her head about it," she was aware that it "did not stand looking into very much." But the lamentable circumstances of Stevie's end, which to Mr. Verloc's mind had only an episodic character, as part of a greater disaster, dried her tears at their very source. It was the effect of a white-hot iron drawn across her eyes; at the same time her heart, hardened and chilled into a lump of ice, kept her body in an inward shudder, set her features into a frozen, contemplative immobility addressed to a whitewashed wall with no writing on it. The exigencies of Mrs. Verloc's temperament, which, when stripped of its philosophical reserve, was maternal and violent, forced her to roll a series of thoughts in her motionless head. These thoughts were rather imagined than expressed. Mrs. Verloc was a woman of singularly few words, either for public or private use. With the rage and dismay of a betrayed woman, she reviewed the tenor of her life in visions concerned mostly with Stevie's difficult existence from its earliest days. It was a life of single purpose and of a noble unity of inspiration, like those rare lives that have left their mark on the thoughts and feelings of mankind. But the visions of Mrs. Verloc lacked nobility and magnificence.

She saw herself putting the boy to bed by the light of a single candle on the deserted top floor of a "business house," dark under the roof and scintillating exceedingly with lights and cut glass at the level of the street like a fairy palace. That meretricious splendour was the only one to be met in Mrs. Verloc's visions. She remembered brushing the boy's hair and tying his pinafores—herself in a pinafore still; the consolations administered to a small and badly scared creature by another creature nearly as small but not quite so badly scared; she had the vision of the blows intercepted (often with her own head), of a door held desperately shut against a man's rage (not for very long); of a poker flung once (not very far), which stilled that particular storm into the dumb and awful silence which follows a thunderclap. And all these scenes of violence came and went accompanied by the unrefined noise of deep vociferations proceeding from a man wounded in his paternal pride, declaring himself obviously accursed since one of his kids was a "slobbering idjut and the other a wicked she-devil." It was of her that this had been said many years ago.

Mrs. Verloc heard the words again in a ghostly fashion, and then the dreary shadow of the Belgravian mansion descended upon her shoulders. It was a crushing memory, an exhausting vision of countless breakfast trays carried up and down innumerable stairs, of endless haggling over pence, of the endless drudgery of sweeping, dusting, cleaning, from basement to attics; while the impotent mother, staggering on swollen legs, cooked in a grimy kitchen, and poor Stevie, the unconscious presiding genius of all their toil, blacked the gentlemen's boots in the scullery. But this vision had a breath of a hot London summer in it, and for a central figure a young man wearing his Sunday best, with a straw hat on his dark head and a wooden pipe in his mouth. Affectionate and jolly, he was a fascinating companion for a voyage down the sparkling stream of life; only his boat was very small. There was room in it for a girl-partner at the oar, but no accommodation for passengers. He was allowed to drift away from the threshold of the Belgravian mansion while Winnie averted her tearful eyes. He was not a lodger. The lodger was Mr. Verloc, indolent and keeping late hours, sleepily jocular of a morning from under his bedclothes, but with gleams of infatuation in his heavy-lidded eyes, and always with some money in his pockets. There was no sparkle of any kind on the lazy stream of his life. It flowed through secret places. But his barque seemed a roomy craft, and his taciturn magnanimity accepted as a matter of course the presence of passengers.

Mrs. Verloc pursued the visions of seven years' security for Stevie loyally paid for on her part; of security growing into confidence, into a domestic feeling, stagnant and deep like a placid pool, whose guarded surface hardly shuddered on the occasional passage of Comrade

Ossipon, the robust anarchist with shamelessly inviting eyes, whose glance had a corrupt clearness sufficient to enlighten any woman not absolutely imbecile.

A few seconds only had elapsed since the last word had been uttered aloud in the kitchen, and Mrs. Verloc was staring already at the vision of an episode not more than a fortnight old. With eyes whose pupils were extremely dilated she stared at the vision of her husband and poor Stevie walking up Brett Street side by side away from the shop. It was the last scene of an existence created by Mrs. Verloc's genius; an existence foreign to all grace and charm, without beauty and almost without decency, but admirable in the continuity of feeling and tenacity of purpose. And this last vision had such plastic relief, such nearness of form, such a fidelity of suggestive detail, that it wrung from Mrs. Verloc an anguished and faint murmur, reproducing the supreme illusion of her life, an appalled murmur that died out on her blanched lips.

"Might have been father and son."

Mr. Verloc stopped, and raised a careworn face. "Eh? What did you say?" he asked. Receiving no reply, he resumed his sinister tramping. Then with a menacing flourish of a thick, fleshy fist, he burst out:

"Yes. The Embassy people. A pretty lot, ain't they! Before a week's out I'll make some of them wish themselves twenty feet under ground. Eh? What?"

He glanced sideways, with his head down. Mrs. Verloc gazed at the whitewashed wall. A blank wall—perfectly blank. A blankness to run at and dash your head against. Mrs. Verloc remained immovably seated. She kept still as the population of half the globe would keep still in astonishment and despair, were the sun suddenly put out in the summer sky by the perfidy of a trusted providence.

"The Embassy," Mr. Verloc began again, after a preliminary grimace which bared his teeth wolfishly. "I wish I could get loose in there with a cudgel for half-an-hour. I would keep on hitting till there wasn't a single unbroken bone left amongst the whole lot. But never mind, I'll teach them yet what it means trying to throw out a man like me to rot in the streets. I've a tongue in my head. All the world shall know what I've done for them. I am not afraid. I don't care. Everything'll come out. Every damned thing. Let them look out!"

In these terms did Mr. Verloc declare his thirst for revenge. It was a very appropriate revenge. It was in harmony with the promptings of Mr. Verloc's genius. It had also the advantage of being within the range of his powers and of adjusting itself easily to the practice of his life, which had consisted precisely in betraying the secret and unlawful proceedings of his fellow-men. Anarchists or diplomats were all one to him. Mr. Verloc was temperamentally no respecter of persons. His scorn was equally distributed over the whole field of his operations. But as a member of a revolutionary proletariat—which he undoubtedly was—he nourished a rather inimical sentiment against social distinction.

"Nothing on earth can stop me now," he added, and paused, looking fixedly at his wife, who was looking fixedly at a blank wall.

The silence in the kitchen was prolonged, and Mr. Verloc felt disappointed. He had expected his wife to say something. But Mrs. Verloc's lips, composed in their usual form, preserved a statuesque immobility like the rest of her face. And Mr. Verloc was disappointed. Yet the occasion did not, he recognized, demand speech from her. She was a woman of very few words. For reasons involved in the very foundation of his psychology, Mr. Verloc was inclined to put his trust in any woman who had given herself to him. Therefore he trusted his wife. Their accord was perfect, but it was not precise. It was a tacit accord, congenial to Mrs. Verloc's incuriosity and to Mr. Verloc's habits of mind, which were indolent and secret. They refrained from going to the bottom of facts and motives.

This reserve, expressing, in a way, their profound confidence in each other, introduced at the same time a certain element of vagueness into their intimacy. No system of conjugal relations is perfect. Mr. Verloc presumed that his wife had understood him but he would have been glad to hear her say what she thought at the moment. It would have been a comfort.

There were several reasons why this comfort was denied him. There was a physical obstacle: Mrs. Verloc had not sufficient command over her voice. She did not see any alternative between screaming and silence, and instinctively she chose the silence. Winnie Verloc was temperamentally a silent person. And there was the paralyzing atrocity of the thought which occupied her. Her cheeks were blanched, her lips ashy, her immobility amazing. And she thought without looking at Mr. Verloc: "This man took the boy away to murder him. He took the boy away from his home to murder him. He took the boy away from me to murder him!"

Mrs. Verloc's whole being was racked by that inconclusive and maddening thought. It was in her veins, in her bones, in the roots of her hair. Mentally she assumed the biblical attitude of mourning—the covered face, the rent garments; the sound of wailing and lamentation filled her head. But her teeth were violently clenched, and her tearless eyes were hot with rage, because she was not a submissive creature. The protection she had extended over her brother had been in its origin of a fierce and indignant complexion. She had to love him with a militant love. She had battled for him—even against herself. His loss had the bitterness of defeat, with the anguish of a baffled passion. It was not an ordinary stroke of death. Moreover, it was not death that took Stevie from her. It was Mr. Verloc who took him away. She had seen him. She had watched him, without raising a hand, take the boy away. And she had let him go, like—like a fool—a blind fool. Then after he had murdered the boy he came home to her. Just came home like any other man would come home to his wife. . . .

Through her set teeth Mrs. Verloc muttered at the wall:

"And I thought he had caught a cold."

Mr. Verloc heard these words and appropriated them.

"It was nothing," he said, moodily. "I was upset. I was upset on your account."

Mrs. Verloc, turning her head slowly, transferred her stare from the wall to her husband's person. Mr. Verloc, with the tips of his fingers between his lips, was looking on the ground.

"Can't be helped," he mumbled, letting his hand fall. "You must pull yourself together. You'll want all your wits about you. It is you who brought the police about our ears. Never mind, I won't say anything more about it," continued Mr. Verloc, magnanimously. "You couldn't know."

"I couldn't," breathed out Mrs. Verloc. It was as if a corpse had spoken. Mr. Verloc took up the thread of his discourse.

"I don't blame you. I'll make them sit up. Once under lock and key it will be safe enough for me to talk—you understand. You must reckon on me being two years away from you," he continued, in a tone of sincere concern. "It will be easier for you than for me. You'll have something to do, while I—— Look here, Winnie, what you must do is to keep this business going for two years. You know enough for that. You've a good head on you. I'll send you word when it's time to go about trying to sell. You'll have to be extra careful. The comrades will be keeping an eye on you all the time. You'll have to be as artful as you know how, and as close as the grave. No one must know what you are going to do. I have no mind to get a knock on the head or a stab in the back directly I am let out."

Thus spoke Mr. Verloc, applying his mind with ingenuity and forethought to the problems of the future. His voice was sombre, because he had a correct sentiment of the situation. Everything which he did not wish to happen had come to pass. The future had become precarious. His judgment, perhaps, had been momentarily obscured by his dread of Mr. Vladimir's truculent folly. A man somewhat over forty may be excusably thrown into considerable disorder by the prospect of losing his employment, especially if the man is a secret agent of political police, dwelling secure in the consciousness of his high value and in the esteem of high personages. He was excusable.

Now the thing had ended in a crash. Mr. Verloc was cool; but he was not cheerful. A secret agent who throws his secrecy to the winds from desire of vengeance, and flaunts his achievements before the public eye, becomes the mark for desperate and bloodthirsty indignations. Without unduly exaggerating the danger, Mr. Verloc tried to bring it clearly before his wife's mind. He repeated that he had no intention of letting the revolutionists do away with him.

He looked straight into his wife's eyes. The enlarged pupils of the woman received his stare into their unfathomable depths.

"I am too fond of you for that," he said, with a little nervous laugh.

A faint flush coloured Mrs. Verloc's ghastly and motionless face. Having done with the visions of the past, she had not only heard, but had also understood the words uttered by her husband. By their extreme disaccord with her mental condition these words produced on her a slightly suffocating effect. Mrs. Verloc's mental condition had the merit of simplicity; but it was not sound. It was governed too much by a fixed idea. Every nook and cranny of her brain was filled with the thought that this man, with whom she had lived without distaste for seven years, had taken the "poor boy" away from her in order to kill him—the man to whom she had grown accustomed in body and mind; the man whom she had trusted, took the boy away to kill him! In its form, in its substance, in its effect, which was universal, altering even the aspect of inanimate things, it was a thought to sit still and marvel at for ever and ever. Mrs. Verloc sat still. And across that thought (not across the kitchen) the form of Mr. Verloc went to and fro, familiarly in hat and overcoat, stamping with his boots upon her brain. He was probably talking, too; but Mrs. Verloc's thought for the most part covered the voice.

Now and then, however, the voice would make itself heard. Several connected words emerged at times. Their purport was generally hopeful. On each of these occasions Mrs. Verloc's dilated pupils, losing their far-off fixity, followed her husband's movements with the effect of black care and impenetrable attention. Well informed upon all matters, relating to his secret calling, Mr. Verloc augured well for the success of his plans and combinations. He really believed that it would be upon the whole easy for him to escape the knife of infuriated revolutionists. He had exaggerated the strength of their fury and the length of their arm (for professional purposes) too often to have many illusions one way or the other. For to exaggerate with judgment one must begin by measuring with nicety. He knew also how much virtue and how much infamy is forgotten in two years—

two long years. His first really confidential discourse to his wife was optimistic from conviction. He also thought it good policy to display all the assurance he could muster. It would put heart into the poor woman. On his liberation, which, harmonizing with the whole tenor of his life, would be secret, of course, they would vanish together without loss of time. As to covering up the tracks, he begged his wife to trust him for that. He knew how it was to be done so that the devil himself——

He waved his hand. He seemed to boast. He wished only to put heart into her. It was a benevolent intention, but Mr. Verloc had the misfortune not to be in accord with his audience.

The self-confident tone grew upon Mrs. Verloc's ear which let most of the words go by; for what were words to her now? What could words do to her for good or evil in the face of her fixed idea? Her black glance followed that man who was asserting his impunity—the man who had taken poor Stevie from home to kill him somewhere. Mrs. Verloc could not remember exactly where, but her heart began to beat very perceptibly.

Mr. Verloc, in a soft and conjugal tone, was now expressing his firm belief that there were yet a good few years of quiet life before them both. He did not go into the question of means. A quiet life it must be and, as it were, nestling in the shade, concealed among men whose flesh is grass; modest, like the life of violets. The words used by Mr. Verloc were:

"Lie low for a bit." And far from England, of course. It was not clear whether Mr. Verloc had in his mind Spain or South America; but at any rate somewhere abroad.

This last word, falling into Mrs. Verloc's ear, produced a definite impression. This man was talking of going abroad. The impression was completely disconnected; and such is the force of mental habit that Mrs. Verloc at once and automatically asked herself: "And what of Stevie?"

It was a sort of forgetfulness; but instantly she became aware that there was no longer any occasion for anxiety on that score. There would never be any occasion any more. The poor boy had been taken out and killed. The poor boy was dead.

This shaking piece of forgetfulness stimulated Mrs. Verloc's intelligence. She began to perceive certain consequences which would have surprised Mr. Verloc. There was no need for her now to stay there, in that kitchen, in that house, with that man—since the boy was gone for ever. No need whatever. And on that Mrs. Verloc rose as if raised by a spring. But neither could she see what there was to keep her in the world at all. And this inability arrested her. Mr. Verloc watched her with marital solicitude.

"You're looking more like yourself," he said, uneasily. Something peculiar in the blackness of his wife's eyes disturbed his optimism. At that precise moment Mrs. Verloc began to look upon herself as released from all earthly ties. She had her freedom. Her contract with existence, as represented by that man standing over there, was at an end. She was a free woman. Had this view become in some way perceptible to Mr. Verloc he would have been extremely shocked. In his affairs of the heart Mr. Verloc had been always carelessly generous, yet always with no other idea than that of being loved for himself. Upon this matter, his ethical notions being in agreement with his vanity, he was completely incorrigible. That this should be so in the case of his virtuous and legal connection he was perfectly certain. He had grown older, fatter, heavier, in the belief that he lacked no fascination for being loved for his own sake. When he saw Mrs. Verloc starting to walk out of the kitchen without a word he was disappointed.

"Where are you going to?" he called out rather sharply. "Upstairs?"

Mrs. Verloc in the doorway turned at the voice. An instinct of prudence born of fear, the excessive fear of being approached and touched by that man, induced her to nod at him slightly (from the height of two steps), with a stir of the lips which the conjugal optimism of Mr. Verloc took for a wan and uncertain smile.

"That's right," he encouraged her gruffly. "Rest and quiet's what you want. Go on. It won't be long before I am with you."

Mrs. Verloc, the free woman who had had really no idea where she was going to, obeyed the suggestion with rigid steadiness.

Mr. Verloc watched her. She disappeared up the stairs. He was disappointed. There was that within him which would have been more satisfied if she had been moved to throw herself upon his breast. But he was generous and indulgent. Winnie was always undemonstrative and silent. Neither was Mr. Verloc himself prodigal of endearments and words as a rule. But this was not an ordinary evening. It was an occasion when a man wants to be fortified by open proofs of sympathy and affection. Mr. Verloc sighed, and put out the gas in the kitchen. Mr. Verloc's sympathy with his wife was genuine and intense. It almost brought tears into his eyes as he stood in the parlour reflecting on the loneliness hanging over her head. In this mood Mr. Verloc missed Stevie very much out of a difficult world. He thought mournfully of his end. If only that lad had not stupidly destroyed himself!

The sensation of unappeasable hunger, not unknown after the strain of a hazardous enterprise to adventurers of tougher fibre than Mr. Verloc, overcame him again. The piece of roast beef, laid out in the likeness of funereal baked meats for Stevie's obsequies, offered itself largely to his notice. And Mr. Verloc again partook. He partook ravenously, without restraint and decency, cutting thick slices with the sharp carving knife, and swallowing them without bread. In the course of that refection it occurred to Mr. Verloc that he was not hearing his wife move about the bedroom as he should have done. The thought of finding her perhaps sitting on the bed in the dark not only cut Mr. Verloc's appetite, but also took from him the inclination to follow her upstairs just yet. Laying down the carving knife, Mr. Verloc listened with careworn attention.

He was comforted by hearing her move at last. She walked suddenly across the room and threw the window up. After a period of stillness up there, during which he figured her to himself with her head out, he heard the sash being lowered slowly. Then she made a few steps, and sat down. Every resonance of his house was familiar to Mr. Verloc, who was thoroughly domesticated. When next he heard his wife's footsteps overhead he knew, as well as if he had seen her doing it, that she had been putting on her walking shoes. Mr. Verloc wriggled his shoulders slightly at this ominous symptom, and moving away from the table, stood with his back to the fireplace, his head on one side, and gnawing perplexedly at the tips of his fingers. He kept track of her movements by the sound. She walked here and there violently, with abrupt stoppages, now before the chest of drawers, then in front of the wardrobe. An immense load of weariness, the harvest of a day of shocks and surprises, weighed Mr. Verloc's energies to the ground.

He did not raise his eyes till he heard his wife descending the stairs. It was as he had guessed, she was dressed for going out.

Mrs. Verloc was a free woman. She had thrown open the window of the bedroom either with the intention of screaming Murder! Help! or of throwing herself out. For she did not exactly know what use to make of her freedom. Her personality seemed to have been torn into two pieces, whose mental operations did not adjust themselves very well to each other. The street, silent and deserted from end to end, repelled her by taking sides with that man who was so certain of his impunity. She was afraid to shout lest no one should come. Obviously no one would come. Her instinct of self-preservation recoiled from the depth of the fall into that sort of slimy, deep trench. Mrs. Verloc closed the window, and dressed herself to go out into the street by another way. She was a free woman. She had dressed herself thoroughly, down to the tying of a black veil over her face. As she appeared before him in the light of the parlour, Mr. Verloc observed that she had even her little handbag hanging from her left wrist . . . Flying off to her mother, of course.

The thought that women were wearisome creatures after all presented itself to his fatigued brain. But he was too generous to harbour it for more than an instant. This man, hurt cruelly in his vanity, remained magnanimous in his conduct, allowing himself no satisfaction of a bitter smile or of a contemptuous gesture. With true greatness of soul, he only glanced at the wooden clock on the wall, and said in a perfectly calm but forcible manner:

"Five and twenty minutes past eight, Winnie. There's no sense in going over there so late. You will never manage to get back to-night."

Before his extended hand Mrs. Verloc had stopped short. He added, heavily: "Your mother will be gone to bed before you get there. This is the sort of news that can wait."

Nothing was further from Mrs. Verloc's thoughts than going to her mother. She recoiled at the mere idea, and feeling a chair behind her, she obeyed the suggestion of the touch, and sat down. Her intention had been simply to get outside the door for ever. And if this feeling was correct, its mental form took an unrefined shape corresponding to her origin and station. "I would rather walk the streets all the days of my life," she thought. But this creature, whose moral nature had been subjected to a shock of which, in the physical order, the most violent earthquake of history could only be a faint and languid rendering, was at the mercy of mere trifles, of casual contacts. She sat down. With her hat and veil she had the air of a visitor, of having looked in on Mr. Verloc for a moment. Her instant docility encouraged him, whilst her aspect of only temporary and silent acquiescence provoked him a little.

"Let me tell you, Winnie," he said with authority, "that your place is here this evening. Hang it all! you brought the damned police high and low about my ears. I don't blame you—but it's your doing all the same. You'd better take this confounded hat off. I can't let you go out, old girl," he added in a softened voice.

Mrs. Verloc's mind got hold of that declaration with morbid tenacity. The man who had taken Stevie out from under her very eyes to murder him in a locality whose name was at the moment not present to her memory would not allow her to go out. Of course he wouldn't. Now he had murdered Stevie he would never let her go. He would want to keep her for nothing. And on this characteristic reasoning, having all the force of insane logic, Mrs. Verloc's disconnected wits went to work practically. She could slip by him, open the door, run out. But he would dash out after her, seize her round the body, drag her back into the shop. She could scratch, kick, and bite—and stab, too; but for stabbing she wanted a knife. Mrs. Verloc sat still under her black veil, in her own house, like a masked and mysterious visitor of impenetrable intentions.

Mr. Verloc's magnanimity was not more than human. She had exasperated him at last.

"Can't you say something? You have your own dodges for vexing a man. Oh, yes! I know your deaf-and-dumb trick. I've seen you at it before to-day. But just now it won't do. And to begin with, take this damned thing off. One can't tell whether one is talking to a dummy or to a live woman."

He advanced, and stretching out his hand, dragged the veil off, unmasking a still unreadable face, against which his nervous exasperation was shattered like a glass bubble flung against a rock. "That's better," he said, to cover his momentary uneasiness, and retreated back to his old station by the mantelpiece. It never entered his head that his wife could give him up. He felt a little ashamed of himself, for he was fond and generous. What could he do? Everything had been said already. He protested vehemently.

"By heavens! You know that I hunted high and low. I ran the risk of giving myself away to find somebody for that accursed job. And I tell you again I couldn't find any one crazy enough or hungry enough. What do you take me for—a murderer, or what? The boy is gone. Do you think I wanted him to blow himself up? He's gone. His troubles are over. Ours are just going to begin, I tell you, precisely because he did blow himself up. I don't blame you. But just try to understand that it was a pure accident; as much an accident as if he had been run over by a 'bus while crossing the street."

His generosity was not infinite, because he was a human being— and not a monster, as Mrs. Verloc believed him to be. He paused, and a snarl lifting his moustaches above a gleam of white teeth gave him the expression of a reflective beast, not very dangerous—a slow beast with a sleek head, gloomier than a seal, and with a husky voice.

"And when it comes to that, it's as much your doing as mine. That's so. You may glare as much as you like. I know what you can do in that way. Strike me dead if I ever would have thought of the lad for that purpose. It was you who kept on shoving him in my way when I was half distracted with the worry of keeping the lot of us out of trouble. What the devil made you? One would think you were doing it on purpose. And I am damned if I know that you didn't. There's no saying how much of what's going on you have got hold of on the sly with your infernal don't-care-a-damn way of looking nowhere in particular, and saying nothing at all. . . ."

His husky, domestic voice ceased for a while. Mrs. Verloc made no reply. Before that silence he felt ashamed of what he had said. But as often happens to peaceful men in domestic tiffs, being ashamed he pushed another point.

"You have a devilish way of holding your tongue sometimes,"

he began again, without raising his voice. "Enough to make some men go mad. It's lucky for you that I am not so easily put out as some of them would be by your deaf-and-dumb sulks. I am fond of you. But don't you go too far. This isn't the time for it. We ought to be thinking of what we've got to do. And I can't let you go out to-night, galloping off to your mother with some crazy tale or other about me. I won't have it. Don't you make any mistake about it; if you will have it that I killed the boy, then you've killed him as much as I."

In sincerity of feeling and openness of statement, these words went far beyond anything that had ever been said in this home, kept up on the wages of a secret industry eked out by the sale of more or less secret wares: the poor expedients devised by a mediocre mankind for preserving an imperfect society from the dangers of moral and physical corruption, both secret, too, of their kind. They were spoken because Mr. Verloc had felt himself really outraged; but the reticent decencies of this home life, nestling in a shady street behind a shop where the sun never shone, remained apparently undisturbed. Mrs. Verloc heard him out with perfect propriety, and then rose from her chair in her hat and jacket like a visitor at the end of a call. She advanced towards her husband, one arm extended as if for a silent leave-taking. Her net veil dangling down by one end on the left side of her face gave an air of disorderly formality to her restrained movements. But when she arrived as far as the hearthrug, Mr. Verloc was no longer standing there. He had moved off in the direction of the sofa, without raising his eyes to watch the effect of his tirade. He was tired, resigned in a truly marital spirit. But he felt hurt in the tender spot of his secret weakness. If she would go on sulking in that dreadful overcharged silence—why then she must. She was a master in that domestic art. Mr. Verloc flung himself heavily upon the sofa, disregarding as usual the fate of his hat, which, as if accustomed to take care of itself, made for a safe shelter under the table.

He was tired. The last particle of his nervous force had been expended in the wonders and agonies of this day full of surprising failures coming at the end of a harassing month of scheming and insomnia. He was tired. A man isn't made of stone. Hang everything! Mr. Verloc reposed characteristically, clad in his outdoor garments. One side of his open overcoat was lying partly on the ground. Mr. Verloc wallowed on his back. But he longed for a more perfect rest— for sleep—for a few hours of delicious forgetfulness. That would come later. Provisionally he rested. And he thought: "I wish she would give over this damned nonsense. It's exasperating."

There must have been something imperfect in Mrs. Verloc's sentiment of regained freedom. Instead of taking the way of the door she leaned back, with her shoulders against the tablet of the mantelpiece, as a wayfarer rests against a fence. A tinge of wildness in her aspect was derived from the black veil hanging like a rag against her cheek, and from the fixity of her black gaze where the light of the room was absorbed and lost without the trace of a single gleam. This woman, capable of a bargain the mere suspicion of which would have been infinitely shocking to Mr. Verloc's idea of love, remained irresolute, as if scrupulously aware of something wanting on her part for the formal closing of the transaction.

On the sofa Mr. Verloc wriggled his shoulders into perfect comfort, and from the fulness of his heart emitted a wish which was certainly as pious as anything likely to come from such a source.

"I wish to goodness," he growled, huskily, "I had never seen Greenwich Park or anything belonging to it."

The veiled sound filled the small room with its moderate volume, well adapted to the modest nature of the wish. The waves of air of the proper length, propagated in accordance with correct mathematical formulas, flowed around all the inanimate things in the room, lapped against Mrs. Verloc's head as if it had been a head of stone. And incredible as it may appear, the eyes of Mrs. Verloc seemed to grow still larger. The audible wish of Mr. Verloc's overflowing heart flowed into an empty place in his wife's memory. Greenwich Park. A park! That's where the boy was killed. A park—smashed branches, torn leaves, gravel, bits of brotherly flesh and bone, all spouting up together in the manner of a firework. She remembered now what she had heard, and she remembered it pictorially. They had to gather him up with the shovel. Trembling all over with irrepressible shudders, she saw before her the very implement with its ghastly load scraped up from the ground. Mrs. Verloc closed her eyes desperately, throwing upon that vision the night of her eyelids, where after a rainlike fall of mangled limbs the decapitated head of Stevie lingered suspended alone, and fading out slowly like the last star of a pyrotechnic display. Mrs. Verloc opened her eyes.

Her face was no longer stony. Anybody could have noted the subtle change on her features, in the stare of her eyes, giving her a new and startling expression; an expression seldom observed by competent persons under the conditions of leisure and security demanded for thorough analysis, but whose meaning could not be mistaken at a glance. Mrs. Verloc's doubts as to the end of the bargain no longer existed; her wits, no longer disconnected, were working under the control of her will. But Mr. Verloc observed nothing. He was reposing in that pathetic condition of optimism induced by excess of fatigue. He did not want any more trouble—with his wife, too—of all people in the world. He had been unanswerable in his vindication. He was loved for himself. The present phase of her silence he interpreted favourably. This was the time to make it up with her. The silence had lasted long enough. He broke it by calling to her in an undertone: "Winnie."

"Yes," answered obediently Mrs. Verloc, the free woman. She commanded her wits now, her vocal organs; she felt herself to be in an almost preternaturally perfect control of every fibre of her body. It was all her own, because the bargain was at an end. She was clearsighted. She had become cunning. She chose to answer him so readily for a purpose. She did not wish that man to change his position on the sofa which was very suitable to the circumstances. She succeeded. The man did not stir. But after answering him she remained leaning negligently against the mantelpiece in the attitude of a resting wayfarer. She was unhurried. Her brow was smooth. The head and shoulders of Mr. Verloc were hidden from her by the high side of the sofa. She kept her eyes fixed on his feet.

She remained thus mysteriously still and suddenly collected till Mr. Verloc was heard with an accent of marital authority, and moving slightly to make room for her to sit on the edge of the sofa.

"Come here," he said in a peculiar tone, which might have been the tone of brutality, but was intimately known to Mrs. Verloc as the note of wooing.

She started forward at once, as if she were still a loyal woman bound to that man by an unbroken contract. Her right hand skimmed slightly the end of the table, and when she had passed on towards the sofa the carving knife had vanished without the slightest sound from the side of the dish. Mr. Verloc heard the creaky plank in the floor, and was content. He waited. Mrs. Verloc was coming. As if the homeless soul of Stevie had flown for shelter straight to the breast of his sister, guardian, and protector, the resemblance of her face with that of her brother grew at every step, even to the droop of the lower lip, even to the slight divergence of the eyes. But Mr. Verloc did not see that. He was lying on his back and staring upwards. He saw partly on the ceiling and partly on the wall the moving shadow of an arm with a clenched hand holding a carving knife. It flickered up and down. Its movements were leisurely. They were leisurely enough for Mr. Verloc to recognize the limb and the weapon.

They were leisurely enough for him to take in the full meaning of the portent, and to taste the flavour of death rising in his gorge. His wife had gone raving mad—murdering mad. They were leisurely enough for the first paralyzing effect of this discovery to pass away before a resolute determination to come out victorious from the ghastly struggle with that armed lunatic. They were leisurely enough for Mr. Verloc to elaborate a plan of defence involving a dash behind the table, and the felling of the woman to the ground with a heavy wooden chair. But they were not leisurely enough to allow Mr. Verloc the time to move either hand or foot. The knife was already planted in his breast. It met no resistance on its way. Hazard has such accuracies. Into that plunging blow, delivered over the side of the couch, Mrs. Verloc had put all the inheritance of her immemorial and obscure descent, the simple ferocity of the age of caverns, and the unbalanced nervous fury of the age of bar-rooms. Mr. Verloc, the Secret Agent, turned slightly on his side with the force of a blow, expired without stirring a limb, in the muttered sound of the word "Don't" by way of protest.

Mrs. Verloc had let go the knife, and her extraordinary resemblance to her late brother had faded, had become very ordinary now. She drew a deep breath, the first easy breath since Chief Inspector Heat had exhibited to her the labelled piece of Stevie's overcoat. She leaned forward on her folded arms over the side of the sofa. She adopted that easy attitude not in order to watch or gloat over the body of Mr. Verloc, but because of the undulatory and swinging movements of the parlour, which for some time behaved as though it were at sea in a tempest. She was giddy but calm. She had become a free woman with a perfection of freedom which left her nothing to desire and absolutely nothing to do, since Stevie's urgent claim on her devotion no longer existed. Mrs. Verloc, who thought in images, was not troubled now by visions, because she did not think at all. And she did not move. She was a woman enjoying her complete irresponsibility and endless leisure, almost in the manner of a corpse. She did not move, she did not think. Neither did the mortal envelope of the late Mr. Verloc reposing on the sofa. Except for the fact that Mrs. Verloc breathed these two would have been perfectly in accord: that accord of prudent reserve without superfluous words, and sparing of signs, which had been the foundation of their respectable home life. For it had been respectable, covering by a decent reticence the problems that may arise in the practice of a secret profession and the commerce of shady wares. To the last its decorum had remained undisturbed by unseemly shrieks and other misplaced sincerities of conduct. And after the striking of the blow, this respectability was continued in immobility and silence.

Nothing moved in the parlour till Mrs. Verloc raised her head slowly and looked at the clock with inquiring mistrust. She had become aware of a ticking sound in the room. It grew upon her ear, while she remembered clearly that the clock on the wall was silent, had no audible tick. What did it mean by beginning to tick so loudly all of a sudden? Its face indicated ten minutes to nine. Mrs. Verloc cared nothing for time, and the ticking went on. She concluded it could not be the clock, and her sullen gaze moved along the walls, wavered, and became vague, while she strained her hearing to locate the sound. Tic, tic, tic.

After listening for some time Mrs. Verloc lowered her gaze deliberately on her husband's body. Its attitude of repose was so homelike and familiar that she could do so without feeling embarrassed by any pronounced novelty in the phenomena of her home life. Mr. Verloc was taking his habitual ease. He looked comfortable.

By the position of the body the face of Mr. Verloc was not visible to Mrs. Verloc, his widow. Her fine, sleepy eyes, travelling downward on the track of the sound, became contemplative on meeting a flat object of bone which protruded a little beyond the edge of the sofa. It was the handle of the domestic carving knife with nothing strange about it but its position at right angles to Mr. Verloc's waistcoat and the fact that something dripped from it. Dark drops fell on the floorcloth one after another, with a sound of ticking growing fast and furious like the pulse of an insane clock. At its highest speed this ticking changed into a continuous sound of trickling. Mrs. Verloc watched that transformation with shadows of anxiety coming and going on her face. It was a trickle, dark, swift, thin. . . . Blood!

At this unforeseen circumstance Mrs. Verloc abandoned her pose of idleness and irresponsibility.

With a sudden snatch at her skirts and a faint shriek she ran to the door, as if the trickle had been the first sign of a destroying flood. Finding the table in her way she gave it a push with both hands as though it had been alive, with such force that it went for some distance on its four legs, making a loud, scraping racket, whilst the big dish with the joint crashed heavily on the floor.

Then all became still. Mrs. Verloc on reaching the door had stopped. A round hat disclosed in the middle of the floor by the moving of the table rocked slightly on its crown in the wind of her flight.

CHAPTER TWELVE

Winnie Verloc, the widow of Mr. Verloc, the sister of the late faithful Stevie (blown to fragments in a state of innocence and in the conviction of being engaged in a humanitarian enterprise), did not run beyond the door of the parlour. She had indeed run away so far from a mere trickle of blood, but that was a movement of instinctive repulsion. And there she had paused, with staring eyes and lowered head. As though she had run through long years in her flight across the small parlour, Mrs. Verloc by the door was quite a different person from the woman who had been leaning over the sofa, a little swimmy in her head, but otherwise free to enjoy the profound calm of idleness and irresponsibility. Mrs. Verloc was no longer giddy. Her head was steady. On the other hand, she was no longer calm. She was afraid.

If she avoided looking in the direction of her reposing husband it was not because she was afraid of him. Mr. Verloc was not frightful to behold. He looked comfortable. Moreover, he was dead. Mrs. Verloc entertained no vain delusions on the subject of the dead. Nothing brings them back, neither love nor hate. They can do nothing to you. They are as nothing. Her mental state was tinged by a sort of austere contempt for that man who had let himself be killed so easily. He had been the master of a house, the husband of a woman, and the murderer of her Stevie. And now he was of no account in every respect. He was of less practical account than the clothing on his body, than his overcoat, than his boots—than that hat lying on the floor. He was nothing. He was not worth looking at. He was even no longer the murderer of poor Stevie. The only murderer that would be found in the room when people came to look for Mr. Verloc would be—herself!

Her hands shook so that she failed twice in the task of refastening her veil. Mrs. Verloc was no longer a person of leisure and irresponsibility. She was afraid. The stabbing of Mr. Verloc had been only a blow. It had relieved the pent-up agony of shrieks strangled in her throat, of tears dried up in her hot eyes, of the maddening and indignant rage at the atrocious part played by that man, who was less than nothing now, in robbing her of the boy. It had been an obscurely prompted blow. The blood trickling on the floor off the handle of the knife had turned it into an extremely plain case of murder. Mrs. Verloc, who always refrained from looking deep into things, was compelled to look into the very bottom of this thing. She saw there no haunting face, no reproachful shade, no vision of remorse, no sort of ideal conception. She saw there an object. That object was the gallows. Mrs. Verloc was afraid of the gallows.

She was terrified of them ideally. Having never set eyes on that last argument of men's justice except in illustrative wood-cuts to a certain type of tales, she first saw them erect against a black and stormy background, festooned with chains and human bones, circled about by birds that peck at dead men's eyes. This was frightful enough, but Mrs. Verloc, though not a well-informed woman, had a sufficient knowledge of the institutions of her country to know that gallows are no longer erected romantically on the banks of dismal rivers or on wind-swept headlands, but in the yards of jails. There within four high walls, as if into a pit, at dawn of day, the murderer was brought out to be executed, with a horrible quietness and, as the reports in the newspapers always said, "in the presence of the authorities." With her eyes staring on the floor, her nostrils quivering with anguish and shame, she imagined herself all alone amongst a lot of strange gentlemen in silk hats who were calmly proceeding about the business of hanging her by the neck. That—never! Never! And how was it done? The impossibility of imagining the details of such quiet execution added something maddening to her abstract terror. The newspapers never gave any details except one, but that one with some affectation was always there at the end of a meagre report. Mrs. Verloc remembered its nature. It came with a cruel burning pain into her head, as if the words "The drop given was fourteen feet" had been scratched on her brain with a hot needle. "The drop given was fourteen feet."

These words affected her physically, too. Her throat became convulsed in waves to resist strangulation; and the apprehension of the jerk was so vivid that she seized her head in both hands as if to save it from being torn off her shoulders. "The drop given was fourteen feet." No! that must never be. She could not stand *that*. The thought of it even was not bearable. She could not stand thinking of it. Therefore Mrs. Verloc formed the resolution to go at once and throw herself into the river off one of the bridges.

This time she managed to refasten her veil. With her face as if masked, all black from head to foot except for some flowers in her hat, she looked up mechanically at the clock. She thought it must have stopped. She could not believe that only two minutes had passed since she had looked at it last. Of course not. It had been stopped all the time. As a matter of fact, only three minutes had elapsed from the moment she had drawn the first deep, easy breath after the blow, to this moment when Mrs. Verloc formed the resolution to drown herself in the Thames. But Mrs. Verloc could not believe that. She seemed to have heard or read that clocks and watches always stopped at the moment of murder for the undoing of the murderer. She did not care. "To the bridge—and over I go." . . . But her movements were slow.

She dragged herself painfully across the shop, and had to hold on to the handle of the door before she found the necessary fortitude to open it. The street frightened her, since it led either to the gallows or to the river. She floundered over the doorstep head forward, arms thrown out, like a person falling over the parapet of a bridge. This entrance into the open air had a foretaste of drowning; a slimy dampness enveloped her, entered her nostrils, clung to her hair. It was not actually raining, but each gas-lamp had a rusty little halo of mist. The van and horses were gone, and in the black street the curtained window of the carters' eating-house made a square patch of soiled blood-red light glowing faintly very near the level of the pavement. Mrs. Verloc, dragging herself slowly towards it, thought that she was a very friendless woman. It was true. It was so true that in a sudden longing to see some friendly face, she could think of no one else but of Mrs. Neale, the charwoman. She had no acquaintances of her own. Nobody would miss her in a social way. It must not be imagined that the Widow Verloc had forgotten her mother. This was not so. Winnie had been a good daughter because she had been a devoted sister. Her mother had always leaned on her for support. No consolation or advice could be expected there. Now that Stevie was dead the bond seemed to be broken. She could not face the old woman with the horrible tale. Moreover, it was too far. The river was her present destination. Mrs. Verloc tried to forget her mother.

Each step cost her an effort of will which seemed the last possible. Mrs. Verloc had dragged herself past the red glow of the eating-house window. "To the bridge—and over I go," she repeated to herself with fierce obstinacy. She put out her hand just in time to steady herself against a lamp-post. "I'll never get there before morning," she thought. The fear of death paralyzed her efforts to escape the gallows. It seemed to her she had been staggering in that street for hours. "I'll never get there," she thought. "They'll find me knocking about the streets. It's too far." She held on, panting under her black veil.

"The drop given was fourteen feet."

She pushed the lamp-post away from her violently, and found herself walking. But another wave of faintness overtook her like a great sea, washing away her heart clean out of her breast. "I will never get there," she muttered, suddenly arrested, swaying lightly where she stood. "Never."

And perceiving the utter impossibility of walking as far as the nearest bridge, Mrs. Verloc thought of a flight abroad.

It came to her suddenly. Murderers escaped. They escaped abroad. Spain or California. Mere names. The vast world created for the glory of man was only a vast blank to Mrs. Verloc. She did not know which way to turn. Murderers had friends, relations, helpers—they had knowledge. She had nothing. She was the most lonely of murderers that ever struck a mortal blow. She was alone in London: and the whole town of marvels and mud, with its maze of streets and its mass of lights, was sunk in a hopeless night, rested at the bottom of a black abyss from which no unaided woman could hope to scramble out.

She swayed forward, and made a fresh start blindly, with an awful dread of falling down; but at the end of a few steps, unexpectedly, she found a sensation of support, of security. Raising her head, she saw a man's face peering closely at her veil. Comrade Ossipon was not afraid of strange women, and no feeling of false delicacy could prevent him from striking an acquaintance with a woman apparently very much intoxicated. Comrade Ossipon was interested in women. He held up this one between his two large palms, peering at her in a businesslike way till he heard her say faintly, "Mr. Ossipon!" and then he very nearly let her drop to the ground.

"Mrs. Verloc!" he exclaimed. "You here!"

It seemed impossible to him that she should have been drinking. But one never knows. He did not go into that question, but attentive not to discourage kind fate surrendering to him the widow of Comrade Verloc, he tried to draw her to his breast. To his astonishment she came quite easily, and even rested on his arm for a moment before she attempted to disengage herself. Comrade Ossipon would not be brusque with kind fate. He withdrew his arm in a natural way.

"You recognized me," she faltered out, standing before him, fairly steady on her legs.

"Of course I did," said Ossipon with perfect readiness. "I was afraid you were going to fall. I've thought of you too often lately not to recognize you anywhere, at any time. I've always thought of you—ever since I first set eyes on you."

Mrs. Verloc seemed not to hear. "You were coming to the shop?" she said nervously.

"Yes; at once," answered Ossipon. "Directly I read the paper."

In fact, Comrade Ossipon had been skulking for a good two hours in the neighbourhood of Brett Street, unable to make up his mind for a bold move. The robust anarchist was not exactly a bold conqueror. He remembered that Mrs. Verloc had never responded to his glances by the slightest sign of encouragement. Besides, he thought the shop might be watched by the police, and Comrade Ossipon did not wish the police to form an exaggerated notion of his revolutionary sympathies. Even now he did not know precisely what to do. In comparison with his usual amatory speculations this was a big and serious undertaking. He ignored how much there was in it and how far he would have to go in order to get hold of what there was to get—supposing there was a chance at all. These perplexities checking his elation imparted to his tone a soberness well in keeping with the circumstances.

"May I ask you where you were going?" he inquired in a subdued voice.

"Don't ask me!" cried Mrs. Verloc with a shuddering, repressed violence. All her strong vitality recoiled from the idea of death. "Never mind where I was going. . . ."

Ossipon concluded that she was very much excited but perfectly sober. She remained silent by his side for a moment, then all at once she did something which he did not expect. She slipped her hand under his arm. He was startled by the act itself certainly, and quite as much, too, by the palpably resolute character of this movement.

But this being a delicate affair, Comrade Ossipon behaved with delicacy. He contented himself by pressing the hand slightly against his robust ribs. At the same time he felt himself being impelled forward, and yielded to the impulse. At the end of Brett Street he became aware of being directed to the left. He submitted.

The fruiterer at the corner had put out the blazing glory of his oranges and lemons, and Brett Place was all darkness, interspersed with the misty halos of the few lamps defining its triangular shape, with a cluster of three lights on one stand in the middle. The dark forms of the man and woman glided slowly arm in arm along the walls with a loverlike and homeless aspect in the miserable night.

"What would you say if I were to tell you that I was going to find you?" Mrs. Verloc asked, gripping his arm with force.

"I would say that you couldn't find any one more ready to help you in your trouble," answered Ossipon, with a notion of making tremendous headway. In fact, the progress of this delicate affair was almost taking his breath away.

"In my trouble!" Mrs. Verloc repeated, slowly.

"Yes."

"And do you know what my trouble is?" she whispered with strange intensity.

"Ten minutes after seeing the evening paper," explained Ossipon with ardour, "I met a fellow whom you may have seen once or twice at the shop perhaps, and I had a talk with him which left no doubt whatever in my mind. Then I started for here, wondering whether you—— I've been fond of you beyond words ever since I set eyes on your face," he cried, as if unable to command his feelings.

Comrade Ossipon assumed correctly that no woman was capable of wholly disbelieving such a statement. But he did not know that Mrs. Verloc accepted it with all the fierceness the instinct of self-preservation imparts to the grip of a drowning person. To the widow of Mr. Verloc the robust anarchist was like a radiant messenger of life.

They walked slowly, in step. "I thought so," Mrs. Verloc murmured, faintly.

"You've read it in my eyes," suggested Ossipon with great assurance.

"Yes," she breathed out into his inclined ear.

"A love like mine could not be concealed from a woman like you," he went on, trying to detach his mind from material considerations such as the business value of the shop, and the amount of money Mr. Verloc might have left in the bank. He applied himself to the sentimental side of the affair. In his heart of hearts he was a little shocked at his success. Verloc had been a good fellow, and certainly a very decent husband as far as one could see. However, Comrade Ossipon was not going to quarrel with his luck for the sake of a dead man. Resolutely he suppressed his sympathy for the ghost of Comrade Verloc, and went on:

"I could not conceal it. I was too full of you. I daresay you could not help seeing it in my eyes. But I could not guess it. You were always so distant. . . ."

"What else did you expect?" burst out Mrs. Verloc. "I was a respectable woman——"

She paused, then added, as if speaking to herself, in sinister resentment: "Till he made me what I am."

Ossipon let that pass, and took up his running.

"He never did seem to me to be quite worthy of you," he began, throwing loyalty to the winds. "You were worthy of a better fate."

Mrs. Verloc interrupted bitterly:

"Better fate! He cheated me out of seven years of life."

"You seemed to live so happily with him." Ossipon tried to exculpate the lukewarmness of his past conduct. "It's that what's made me timid. You seemed to love him. I was surprised—and jealous," he added.

"Love him!" Mrs. Verloc cried out in a whisper full of scorn and rage. "Love him! I was a good wife to him. I am a respectable woman. You thought I loved him! You did! Look here, Tom——"

The sound of this name thrilled Comrade Ossipon with pride. For his name was Alexander, and he was called Tom by arrangement with the most familiar of his intimates. It was a name of friendship—of moments of expansion. He had no idea that she had ever heard it used by anybody. It was apparent that she had not only caught it, but had treasured it in her memory—perhaps in her heart.

"Look here, Tom! I was a young girl. I was done up. I was tired. I had two people depending on what I could do, and it did seem as if I couldn't do any more. Two people—mother and the boy. He was much more mine than mother's. I sat up nights and nights with him on my lap, all alone upstairs, when I wasn't more than eight years old myself. And then—— He was mine, I tell you. . . . You can't understand that. No man can understand it. What was I to do? There was a young fellow——"

The memory of the early romance with the young butcher survived, tenacious, like the image of a glimpsed ideal in that heart quailing before the fear of the gallows and full of revolt against death.

"That was the man I loved then," went on the widow of Mr. Verloc. "I suppose he could see it in my eyes, too. Five and twenty shillings a week, and his father threatened to kick him out of the business if he made such a fool of himself as to marry a girl with a crippled mother and a crazy idiot of a boy on her hands. But he would hang about me, till one evening I found the courage to slam the door in his face. I had to do it. I loved him dearly. Five and twenty shillings a week! There was that other man—a good lodger. What is a girl to do? Could I've gone on the streets? He seemed kind. He wanted me, anyhow. What was I to do with mother and that poor boy? Eh? I said yes. He seemed good-natured, he was freehanded, he had money, he never said anything. Seven years—seven years a good wife to him, the kind, the good, the generous, the—— And he loved me. Oh, yes. He loved me till I sometimes wished myself—— Seven years. Seven years a wife to him. And do you know what he was, that dear friend of yours? Do you know what he was? . . . He was a devil!"

The superhuman vehemence of that whispered statement completely stunned Comrade Ossipon. Winnie Verloc turning about held him by both arms, facing him under the falling mist in the darkness and solitude of Brett Place, in which all sounds of life seemed lost as if in a triangular well of asphalt and bricks, of blind houses and unfeeling stones.

"No; I didn't know," he declared, with a sort of flabby stupidity, whose comical aspect was lost upon a woman haunted by the fear of the gallows, "but I do now. I—I understand," he floundered on, his mind speculating as to what sort of atrocities Verloc could have practiced under the sleepy, placid appearances of his married estate. It was positively awful. "I understand," he repeated, and then by a sudden inspiration uttered an "Unhappy woman!" of lofty commiseration instead of the more familiar "Poor darling!" of his usual practice. This was no usual case. He felt conscious of something abnormal going on, while he never lost sight of the greatness of the stake. "Unhappy, brave woman!"

He was glad to have discovered that variation; but he could discover nothing else. "Ah, but he is dead now," was the best he could do. And he put a remarkable amount of animosity into his guarded exclamation. Mrs. Verloc caught at his arm with a sort of frenzy. "You guessed then he was dead," she murmured, as if beside herself. "You! You guessed what I had to do. Had to!"

There were suggestions of triumph, relief, gratitude in the indefinable tone of these words. It engrossed the whole attention of Ossipon to the detriment of mere literal sense. He wondered what was up with her, why she had worked herself into this state of wild excitement. He even began to wonder whether the hidden causes of that Greenwich Park affair did not lie deep in the unhappy circumstances of the Verlocs' married life. He went so far as to suspect Mr. Verloc of having selected that extraordinary manner of committing suicide. By Jove! that would account for the utter inanity and wrong-headedness of the thing. No anarchist manifestation was required by the circumstances. Quite the contrary; and Verloc was as well aware of that as any other revolutionist of his standing. What an immense joke if Verloc had simply made fools of the whole of Europe, of the revolutionary world, of the police, of the press, and of the cocksure Professor as well. Indeed, thought Ossipon, in astonishment, it seemed almost certain that he did! Poor begger! It struck him as very possible that of that household of two it wasn't precisely the man who was the devil.

Alexander Ossipon, nicknamed the Doctor, was naturally inclined to think indulgently of his men friends. He eyed Mrs. Verloc hanging on his arm. Of his women friends he thought in a specially practical way. Why Mrs. Verloc should exclaim at his knowledge of Mr. Verloc's death, which was no guess at all, did not disturb him beyond measure. Women often talked like lunatics. But he was curious to know how she had been informed. The papers could tell her nothing beyond the mere fact: the man blown to pieces in Greenwich Park not having been identified. It was inconceivable on any theory that Verloc should have given her an inkling of his intention—whatever it was. This problem interested Comrade Ossipon immensely. He stopped short. They had gone then along the three sides of Brett Place, and were near the end of Brett Street again.

"How did you first come to hear of it?" he asked in a tone he tried to render appropriate to the character of the revelations which had been made to him by the woman at his side.

She shook violently for a while before she answered in a listless voice:

"From the police. A chief inspector came. Chief Inspector Heat he said he was. He showed me——"

Mrs. Verloc choked. "Oh, Tom, they had to gather him up with a shovel."

Her breast heaved with dry sobs. In a moment Ossipon found his tongue.

"The police! Do you mean to say the police came already? That Chief Inspector Heat himself actually came to tell you?"

"Yes," she confirmed in the same listless tone. "He came. Just like this. He came. I didn't know. He showed me a piece of overcoat, and —— Just like that. 'Do you know this?' he says."

"Heat! Heat! And what did he do?"

Mrs. Verloc's head dropped. "Nothing. He did nothing. He went away. The police were on that man's side," she murmured, tragically. "Another one came, too."

"Another—another inspector, do you mean?" asked Ossipon, in great excitement, and very much in the tone of a scared child.

"I don't know. He came. He looked like a foreigner. He may have been one of them Embassy people."

Comrade Ossipon nearly collapsed under this new shock.

"Embassy! Are you aware what you are saying? What Embassy? What on earth do you mean by Embassy?"

"It's that place in Chesham Square. The people he cursed so. I don't know. What does it matter!"

"And that fellow, what did he do or say to you?"

"I don't remember. . . . Nothing. . . . I don't care. Don't ask me," she pleaded in a weary voice.

"All right. I won't," assented Ossipon, tenderly. And he meant it, too, not because he was touched by the pathos of the pleading voice, but because he felt himself losing his footing in the depths of this tenebrous affair. Police! Embassy! Phew! For fear of adventuring his intelligence into ways where its natural lights might fail to guide it safely he dismissed resolutely all suppositions, surmises, and theories out of his mind. He had the woman there, absolutely flinging herself at him, and that was the principal consideration. But after what he had heard nothing could astonish him any more. And when Mrs. Verloc, as if startled suddenly out of a dream of safety, began to urge upon him wildly the necessity of an immediate flight on the Continent, he did not exclaim in the least. He simply said with unaffected regret that there was no train till the morning, and stood looking thoughtfully at her face, veiled in black net, in the light of a gas-lamp veiled in a gauze of mist.

Near him, her black form merged in the night, like a figure half chiselled out of a block of black stone. It was impossible to say what she knew, how deep she was involved with policemen and Embassies. But if she wanted to get away, it was not for him to object. He was anxious to be off himself. He felt that the business, the shop so strangely familiar to chief inspectors and members of foreign Embassies, was not the place for him. That must be dropped. But there was the rest. These savings. The money!

"You must hide me till the morning somewhere," she said in a dismayed voice.

"Fact is, my dear, I can't take you where I live. I share the room with a friend."

He was somewhat dismayed himself. In the morning the blessed 'tecs will be out in all the stations, no doubt. And if they once got hold of her, for one reason or another she would be lost to him indeed.

"But you must. Don't you care for me at all—at all? What are you thinking of?"

She said this violently, but she let her clasped hands fall in discouragement. There was a silence, while the mist fell, and darkness reigned undisturbed over Brett Place. Not a soul, not even the vagabond, lawless, and amorous soul of a cat, came near the man and the woman facing each other.

"It would be possible perhaps to find a safe lodging somewhere," Ossipon spoke at last. "But the truth is, my dear, I have not enough money to go and try with—only a few pence. We revolutionists are not rich."

He had fifteen shillings in his pocket. He added:

"And there's the journey before us, too—first thing in the morning at that."

She did not move, made no sound, and Comrade Ossipon's heart sank a little. Apparently she had no suggestion to offer. Suddenly she clutched at her breast, as if she had felt a sharp pain there.

"But I have," she gasped. "I have the money. I have enough money. Tom! Let us go from here."

"How much have you got?" he inquired, without stirring to her tug; for he was a cautious man.

"I have the money, I tell you. All the money."

"What do you mean by it? All the money there was in the bank, or what?" he asked, incredulously, but ready not to be surprised at anything in the way of luck.

"Yes, yes!" she said, nervously. "All there was. I've it all."

"How on earth did you manage to get hold of it already?" he marvelled.

"He gave it to me," she murmured, suddenly subdued and trembling. Comrade Ossipon put down his rising surprise with a firm hand.

"Why, then—we are saved," he uttered, slowly.

She leaned forward, and sank against his breast. He welcomed her there. She had all the money. Her hat was in the way of very marked effusion; her veil, too. He was adequate in his manifestations, but no more. She received them without resistance and without abandonment, passively, as if only half-sensible. She freed herself from his lax embrace without difficulty.

"You will save me, Tom," she broke out, recoiling, but still keeping her hold on him by the two lapels of his damp coat. "Save me. Hide me. Don't let them have me. You must kill me first. I couldn't do it myself—I couldn't, I couldn't—not even for what I am afraid of."

She was confoundedly bizarre, he thought. She was beginning to inspire him with an indefinite uneasiness. He said surlily, for he was busy with important thoughts:

"What the devil *are* you afraid of?"

"Haven't you guessed what I was driven to do!" cried the woman. Distracted by the vividness of her dreadful apprehensions, her head ringing with forceful words, that kept the horror of her position before her mind, she had imagined her incoherence to be clearness itself. She had no conception of how little she had audibly said in the disjointed phrases completed only in her thought. She had felt the relief of a full confession, and she gave a special meaning to every sentence spoken by Comrade Ossipon, whose knowledge did not in the least resemble her own. "Haven't you guessed what I was driven to do!" Her voice fell. "You needn't be long in guessing then what I am afraid of," she continued, in a bitter and sombre murmur. "I won't have it! I won't! I won't! I won't! You must promise to kill me first!" She shook the lapels of his coat. "It must never be!"

He assured her curtly that no promises on his part were necessary, but he took good care not to contradict her in set terms, because he had had much to do with excited women, and he was inclined in general to let his experience guide his conduct in preference to applying his sagacity to each special case. His sagacity in this case was busy in other directions. Women's words fell into water, but the shortcomings of timetables remained. The insular nature of Great Britain obtruded itself upon his notice in an odious form. "Might just as well be put under lock and key every night," he thought irritably, as nonplussed as though he had a wall to scale with the woman on his back. Suddenly he slapped his forehead. He had by dint of cudgelling his brains just thought of the Southampton—St. Malo service. The boat left about midnight. There was a train at 10:30. He became cheery and ready to act.

"From Waterloo. Plenty of time. We are all right after all . . . What's the matter now? This isn't the way," he protested.

Mrs. Verloc, having hooked her arm into his, was trying to drag him into Brett Street again.

"I've forgotten to shut the shop door as I went out," she whispered, terribly agitated.

The shop and all that was in it had ceased to interest Comrade Ossipon. He knew how to limit his desires. He was on the point of saying "What of that? Let it be," but he refrained. He disliked argument about trifles. He even mended his pace considerably on the thought that she might have left the money in the drawer. But his willingness lagged behind her feverish impatience.

The shop seemed to be quite dark at first. The door stood ajar. Mrs. Verloc, leaning against the front, gasped out:

"Nobody has been in. Look! The light—the light in the parlour."

Ossipon, stretching his head forward, saw a faint gleam in the darkness of the shop.

"There is," he said.

"I forgot it." Mrs. Verloc's voice came from behind her veil faintly. And as he stood waiting for her to enter first, she said louder: "Go in and put it out—or I'll go mad."

He made no immediate objection to this proposal, so strangely motived. "Where's all that money?" he asked.

"On me! Go, Tom. Quick! Put it out. . . . Go in!" she cried, seizing him by both shoulders from behind.

Not prepared for a display of physical force, Comrade Ossipon stumbled far into the shop before her push. He was astonished at the strength of the woman and scandalized by her proceedings. But he did not retrace his steps in order to remonstrate with her severely in the street. He was beginning to be disagreeably impressed by her fantastic behaviour. Moreover, this or never was the time to humour the woman. Comrade Ossipon avoided easily the end of the counter, and approached calmly the glazed door of the parlour. The curtain over the panes being drawn back a little he, by a very natural impulse, looked in, just as he made ready to turn the handle. He looked in without a thought, without intention, without curiosity of any sort. He looked in because he could not help looking in. He looked in, and discovered Mr. Verloc reposing quietly on the sofa.

A yell coming from the innermost depths of his chest died out unheard and transformed into a sort of greasy, sickly taste on his lips. At the same time the mental personality of Comrade Ossipon executed a frantic leap backwards. But his body, left thus without intellectual guidance, held on to the door handle with the unthinking force of an instinct. The robust anarchist did not even totter. And he stared, his face close to the glass, his eyes protruding out of his head. He would have given anything to get away, but his returning reason informed him that it would not do to let go the door handle. What was it—madness, a nightmare, or a trap into which he had been decoyed with fiendish artfulness? Why—what for? He did not know. Without any sense of guilt in his breast, in the full peace of his conscience as far as these people were concerned, the idea that he would be murdered for mysterious reasons by the couple Verloc passed not so much across his mind as across the pit of his stomach, and went out, leaving behind a trail of sickly faintness—an indisposition. Comrade Ossipon did not feel very well in a very special way for a moment—a long moment. And he stared. Mr. Verloc lay very still meanwhile, simulating sleep for reasons of his own, while that savage woman of his was guarding the door—invisible and silent in the dark and deserted street. Was all this some sort of terrifying arrangement invented by the police for his especial benefit? His modesty shrank from that explanation.

But the true sense of the scene he was beholding came to Ossipon through the contemplation of the hat. It seemed an extraordinary thing, an ominous object, a sign. Black, and rim upward, it lay on the floor before the couch as if prepared to receive the contributions of pence from people who would come presently to behold Mr. Verloc in the fulness of his domestic ease reposing on a sofa. From the hat the eyes of the robust anarchist wandered to the displaced table, gazed at the broken dish for a time, received a kind of optical shock from observing a white gleam under the imperfectly closed eyelids of the man on the couch. Mr. Verloc did not seem so much asleep now as lying down with a bent head and looking insistently at his left breast. And when Comrade Ossipon had made out the handle of the knife he turned away from the glazed door, and retched violently.

The crash of the street door flung to made his very soul leap in a panic. This house with its harmless tenant could still be made a trap of—a trap of a terrible kind. Comrade Ossipon had no settled conception now of what was happening to him. Catching his thigh against the end of the counter, he spun round, staggered with a cry of pain, felt in the distracting clatter of the bell his arms pinned to his side by a convulsive hug, while the cold lips of a woman moved creepily on his very ear to form the words:

"Policeman! He has seen me!"

He ceased to struggle; she never let him go. Her hands had locked themselves with an inseparable twist of fingers on his robust back. While the footsteps approached, they breathed quickly, breast to breast, with hard, laboured breaths, as if theirs had been the attitude of a deadly struggle, while, in fact, it was the attitude of deadly fear. And the time was long.

The constable on the beat had in truth seen something of Mrs. Verloc; only coming from the lighted thoroughfare at the other end of Brett Street, she had been no more to him than a flutter in the darkness. And he was not even quite sure that there had been a flutter. He had no reason to hurry up. On coming abreast of the shop he observed that it had been closed early. There was nothing very unusual in that. The men on duty had special instructions about that shop: what went on about there was not to be meddled with unless absolutely disorderly, but any observations made were to be reported. There were no observations to make; but from a sense of duty and for the peace of his conscience, owing also to that doubtful flutter of the darkness, the constable crossed the road, and tried the door. The spring latch, whose key was reposing for ever off duty in the late Mr. Verloc's waistcoat pocket, held as well as usual. While the conscientious officer was shaking the handle, Ossipon felt the cold lips of the woman stirring again creepily against his very ear:

"If he comes in kill me—kill me, Tom."

The constable moved away, flashing as he passed the light of his dark lantern, merely for form's sake, at the shop window. For a moment longer the man and the woman inside stood motionless, panting, breast to breast; then her fingers came unlocked, her arms fell by her side slowly. Ossipon leaned against the counter. The robust anarchist wanted support badly. This was awful. He was almost too disgusted for speech. Yet he managed to utter a plaintive thought, showing at least that he realized his position.

"Only a couple of minutes later and you'd have made me blunder against the fellow poking about here with his damned dark lantern."

The widow of Mr. Verloc, motionless in the middle of the shop, said insistently:

"Go in and put that light out, Tom. It will drive me crazy."

She saw vaguely his vehement gesture of refusal. Nothing in the world would have induced Ossipon to go into the parlour. He was not superstitious, but there was too much blood on the floor; a beastly pool of it all round the hat. He judged he had been already too near that corpse for his peace of mind—for the safety of his neck, perhaps!

"At the meter then! There. Look. In that corner."

The robust form of Comrade Ossipon, striding brusque and shadowy across the shop, squatted in a corner obediently; but this obedience was without grace. He fumbled nervously—and suddenly in the sound of a muttered curse the light behind the glazed door flicked out to a gasping, hysterical sigh of a woman. Night, the inevitable reward of men's faithful labours on this earth, night had fallen on Mr. Verloc, the tried revolutionist—"one of the old lot"—the humble guardian of society; the invaluable Secret Agent $\triangle$ of Baron Stott-Wartenheim's despatches; a servant of law and order, faithful, trusted, accurate, admirable, with perhaps one single amiable weakness: the idealistic belief in being loved for himself.

Ossipon groped his way back through the stuffy atmosphere, as black as ink now, to the counter. The voice of Mrs. Verloc, standing in the middle of the shop, vibrated after him in that blackness with a desperate protest.

"I will not be hanged, Tom. I will not——"

She broke off. Ossipon from the counter issued a warning: "Don't shout like this," then seemed to reflect profoundly. "You did this thing quite by yourself?" he inquired in a hollow voice, but with an appearance of masterful calmness which filled Mrs. Verloc's heart with grateful confidence in his protecting strength.

"Yes," she whispered, invisible.

"I wouldn't have believed it possible," he muttered. "Nobody would." She heard him move about and the snapping of a lock in the parlour door. Comrade Ossipon had turned the key on Mr. Verloc's repose; and this he did not from reverence for its eternal nature or any other obscurely sentimental consideration, but for the precise reason that he was not at all sure that there was not someone else hiding somewhere in the house. He did not believe the woman, or rather he was incapable by now of judging what could be true, possible, or even probable on this astounding universe. He was terrified out of all capacity for belief or disbelief in regard to this extraordinary affair, which began with police inspectors and Embassies and would end goodness knows where—on the scaffold for someone. He was terrified at the thought that he could not prove the use he made of his time ever since seven o'clock, for he had been skulking about Brett Street. He was terrified at this savage woman who had brought him in there, and would probably saddle him with complicity, at least if he were not careful. He was terrified at the rapidity with which he had been involved in such danger—decoyed into it. It was some twenty minutes since he had met her—not more.

The voice of Mrs. Verloc rose subdued, pleading piteously: "Don't let them hang me, Tom! Take me out of the country. I'll work for you. I'll slave for you. I'll love you. I've no one in the world. . . . Who would look at me if you don't!" She ceased for a moment; then in the depths of the loneliness made round her by an insignificant thread of blood trickling off the handle of a knife, she found a dreadful inspiration to her—who had been the respectable girl of the Belgravian mansion, the loyal, respectable wife of Mr. Verloc. "I won't ask you to marry me," she breathed out in shamefaced accents.

She moved a step forward in the darkness. He was terrified at her. He would not have been surprised if she had suddenly produced another knife destined for his breast. He certainly would have made no resistance. He had really not enough fortitude in him just then to tell her to keep back. But he inquired in a cavernous, strange tone: "Was he asleep?"

"No," she cried, and went on rapidly: "He wasn't. Not he. He had been telling me that nothing could touch him. After taking the boy away from under my very eyes to kill him—the loving, innocent, harmless lad. My own, I tell you. He was lying on the couch quite easy—after killing the boy—my boy. I would have gone on the streets to get out of his sight. And he says to me like this: 'Come here,' after telling me I had helped to kill the boy. You hear, Tom? He says like this: 'Come here,' after taking my very heart out of me along with the boy to smash in the dirt."

She ceased, then dreamily repeated twice: "Blood and dirt. Blood and dirt." A great light broke upon Comrade Ossipon. It was that half-witted lad then who had perished in the park. And the fooling of everybody all round appeared more complete than ever—colossal. He exclaimed scientifically, in the extremity of his astonishment: "The degenerate—by heavens!"

" 'Come here.' " The voice of Mrs. Verloc rose again. "What did he think I was made of? Tell me, Tom. 'Come here!' Me! Like this! I had been looking at the knife, and I thought I would come then if he wanted me so much. Oh, yes! I came—for the last time. . . . With the knife."

He was excessively terrified at her—the sister of the degenerate—a degenerate herself of a murdering type . . . or else of the lying type. Comrade Ossipon might have been said to be terrified scientifically in addition to all other kinds of fear. It was an immeasurable and composite funk, which from its very excess gave him in the dark a false appearance of calm and thoughtful deliberation. For he moved and spoke with difficulty, being as if half frozen in his will and mind—and no one could see his ghastly face. He felt half dead.

He leaped a foot high. Unexpectedly Mrs. Verloc had desecrated the unbroken, reserved decency of her home by a shrill and terrible shriek.

"Help, Tom! Save me. I won't be hanged!"

He rushed forward, groping for her mouth with a silencing hand, and the shriek died out. But in his rush he had knocked her over. He felt her now clinging round his legs, and his terror reached its culminating point, became a sort of intoxication, entertained delusions, acquired the characteristics of delirium tremens. He positively saw snakes now. He saw the woman twined round him like a snake, not to be shaken off. She was not deadly. She was death itself—the companion of life.

Mrs. Verloc, as if relieved by the outburst, was very far from behaving noisily now. She was pitiful.

"Tom, you can't throw me off now," she murmured from the floor. "Not unless you crush my head under your heel. I won't leave you."

"Get up," said Ossipon.

His face was so pale as to be quite visible in the profound black darkness of the shop; while Mrs. Verloc, veiled, had no face, almost no discernible form. The trembling of something small and white, a flower in her hat, marked her place, her movements.

It rose in the blackness. She had got up from the floor, and Ossipon regretted not having run out at once into the street. But he perceived easily that it would not do. It would not do. She would run after him. She would pursue him shrieking till she sent every policeman within hearing in chase. And then goodness only knew what she would say of him. He was so frightened that for a moment the insane notion of strangling her in the dark passed through his mind. And he became more frightened than ever! She had him! He saw himself living in abject terror in some obscure hamlet in Spain or Italy; till some fine morning they found him dead, too, with a knife in his breast—like Mr. Verloc. He sighed deeply. He dared not move. And Mrs. Verloc waited in silence the good pleasure of her saviour, deriving comfort from his reflective silence.

Suddenly he spoke up in an almost natural voice. His reflections had come to an end.

"Let's get out, or we will lose the train."

"Where are we going to, Tom?" she asked, timidly. Mrs. Verloc was no longer a free woman.

"Let's get to Paris first, the best way we can. . . . Go out first, and see if the way's clear."

She obeyed. Her voice came subdued through the cautiously opened door.

"It's all right."

Ossipon came out. Notwithstanding his endeavours to be gentle, the cracked bell clattered behind the closed door in the empty shop, as if trying in vain to warn the reposing Mr. Verloc of the final departure of his wife—accompanied by his friend.

In the hansom they presently picked up, the robust anarchist became explanatory. He was still awfully pale, with eyes that seemed to have sunk a whole half-inch into his tense face. But he seemed to have thought of everything with extraordinary method.

"When we arrive," he discoursed in a queer, monotonous tone, "you must go into the station ahead of me, as if we did not know each other. I will take the tickets, and slip yours into your hand as I pass you. Then you will go into the first-class ladies' waiting-room, and sit there till ten minutes before the train starts. Then you come out. I shall be outside. You go in first on the platform, as if you did not know me. There may be eyes watching there that know what's what. Alone you are only a woman going off by train. I am known. With me, you may be guessed at as Mrs. Verloc running away. Do you understand, my dear?" he added, with an effort.

"Yes," said Mrs. Verloc, sitting there against him in the hansom all rigid with the dread of the gallows and the fear of death. "Yes, Tom." And she added to herself, like an awful refrain: "The drop given was fourteen feet."

Ossipon, not looking at her, and with a face like a fresh plaster cast of himself after a wasting illness, said: "By-the-by, I ought to have the money for the tickets now."

Mrs. Verloc, undoing some hooks of her bodice, while she went on staring ahead beyond the splashboard, handed over to him the new pigskin pocket-book. He received it without a word, and seemed to plunge it deep somewhere into his very breast. Then he slapped his coat on the outside.

All this was done without the exchange of a single glance; they were like two people looking out for the first sight of a desired goal.

It was not till the hansom swung round a corner and towards the bridge that Ossipon opened his lips again.

"Do you know how much money there is in that thing?" he asked, as if addressing slowly some hobgoblin sitting between the ears of the horse.

"No," said Mrs. Verloc. "He gave it to me. I didn't count. I thought nothing of it at the time. Afterwards——"

She moved her right hand a little. It was so expressive, that little movement of that right hand which had struck the deadly blow into a man's heart less than an hour before, that Ossipon could not repress a shudder. He exaggerated it then purposely, and muttered:

"I am cold. I got chilled through."

Mrs. Verloc looked straight ahead at the perspective of her escape. Now and then, like a sable streamer blown across a road, the words "The drop given was fourteen feet" got in the way of her tense stare. Through her black veil the whites of her big eyes gleamed lustrously like the eyes of a masked woman.

Ossipon's rigidity had something businesslike, a queer official expression. He was heard again all of a sudden, as though he had released a catch in order to speak.

"Look here! Do you know whether your—whether he kept his account at the bank in his own name or in some other name?"

Mrs. Verloc turned upon him her masked face and the big white gleam of her eyes.

"Other name?" she said, thoughtfully.

"Be exact in what you say," Ossipon lectured in the swift motion of the hansom. "It's extremely important. I will explain to you. The bank has the numbers of these notes. If they were paid to him in his own name, then when his—his death becomes known, the notes may serve to track us since we have no other money. You have no other money on you?"

She shook her head negatively.

"None whatever?" he insisted.

"A few coppers."

"It would be dangerous in that case. The money would have then to be dealt specially with. Very specially. We'd have perhaps to lose more than half the amount in order to get these notes changed in a certain safe place I know of in Paris. In the other case—I mean if he had his account and got paid out under some other name—say Smith, for instance—the money is perfectly safe to use. You understand? The bank has no means of knowing that Mr. Verloc and, say, Smith are one and the same person. Do you see how important it is that you should make no mistake in answering me? Can you answer that query at all? Perhaps not. Eh?"

She said composedly:

"I remember now! He didn't bank in his own name. He told me once that it was on deposit in the name of Prozor."

"You are sure?"

"Certain."

"You don't think the bank had any knowledge of his real name? Or anybody in the bank or——"

She shrugged her shoulders.

"How can I know? Is it likely, Tom?"

"No. I suppose it's not likely. It would have been more comfortable to know. . . . Here we are. Get out first, and walk straight in. Move smartly."

He remained behind, and paid the cabman out of his own loose silver. The programme traced by his minute foresight was carried out. When Mrs. Verloc, with her ticket for St. Malo in her hand, entered the ladies' waiting-room, Comrade Ossipon walked into the bar, and in seven minutes absorbed three goes of hot brandy and water.

"Trying to drive out a cold," he explained to the barmaid, with a friendly nod and a grimacing smile. Then he came out, bringing out from that festive interlude the face of a man who had drunk at the very Fountain of Sorrow. He raised his eyes to the clock. It was time. He waited.

Punctual, Mrs. Verloc came out, with her veil down, and all black—black as commonplace death itself, crowned with a few cheap and pale flowers. She passed close to a little group of men who were laughing, but whose laughter could have been struck dead by a single word. Her walk was indolent, but her back was straight, and Comrade Ossipon looked after it in terror before making a start himself.

The train was drawn up, with hardly anybody about its row of open doors. Owing to the time of the year and to the abominable weather there were but few passengers. Mrs. Verloc walked slowly along the line of empty compartments till Ossipon touched her elbow from behind.

"In here."

She got in, and he remained on the platform looking about. She bent forward, and in a whisper:

"What is it, Tom? Is there any danger?"

"Wait a moment. There's the guard."

She saw him accost the man in uniform. They talked for a while. She heard the guard say "Very well, sir," and saw him touch his cap. Then Ossipon came back, saying: "I told him not to let anybody get into our compartment."

She was leaning forward on her seat. "You think of everything. . . ."

You'll get me off, Tom?" she asked in a gust of anguish, lifting her veil brusquely to look at her saviour.

She had uncovered a face like adamant. And out of this face the eyes looked on, big, dry, enlarged, lightless, burnt out like two black holes in the white, shining globes.

"There is no danger," he said, gazing into them with an earnestness almost rapt, which to Mrs. Verloc, flying from the gallows, seemed to be full of force and tenderness. This devotion deeply moved her—and the adamantine face lost the stern rigidity of its terror. Comrade Alexander Ossipon, anarchist, nicknamed the Doctor, author of a medical (and improper) pamphlet, late lecturer on the social aspects of hygiene to working men's clubs, was free from the trammels of conventional morality—but he submitted to the rule of science. He was scientific, and he gazed scientifically at that woman, the sister of a degenerate, a degenerate herself—of a murdering type. He gazed at her, and invoked Lombroso, as an Italian peasant recommends himself to his favourite saint. He gazed scientifically. He gazed at her cheeks, at her nose, at her eyes, at her ears. . . . Bad! . . . Fatal! Mrs. Verloc's pale lips parting, slightly relaxed under his passionately attentive gaze, he gazed also at her teeth. . . . Not a doubt remained . . . a murdering type. . . . If Comrade Ossipon did not recommend his terrified soul to Lombroso, it was only because on scientific grounds he could not believe that he carried about him such a thing as a soul. But he had in him the scientific spirit, which moved him to testify on the platform of a railway station in nervous, jerky phrases.

"He was an extraordinary lad, that brother of yours. Most interesting to study. A perfect type in a way. Perfect!"

He spoke scientifically in his secret fear. And Mrs. Verloc, hearing these words of commendation vouchsafed to her beloved dead, swayed forward with a flicker of light in her sombre eyes, like a ray of sunshine heralding a tempest of rain.

"He was that indeed," she whispered, softly, with quivering lips. "You took a lot of notice of him, Tom. I loved you for it."

"It's almost incredible the resemblance there was between you two," pursued Ossipon, giving a voice to his abiding dread, and trying to conceal his nervous, sickening impatience for the train to start. "Yes, he resembled you."

These words were not especially touching or sympathetic. But the fact of that resemblance insisted upon was enough in itself to act upon her emotions powerfully. With a little faint cry, and throwing her arms out, Mrs. Verloc burst into tears at last.

Ossipon entered the carriage, hastily closed the door and looked out to see the time by the station clock. Eight minutes more. For the first three of these Mrs. Verloc wept violently and helplessly without pause or interruption. Then she recovered somewhat, and sobbed gently in an abundant fall of tears. She tried to talk to her saviour, to the man who was the messenger of life.

"Oh, Tom! How could I fear to die after he was taken away from me so cruelly? How could I! How could I be such a coward!"

She lamented aloud her love of life, that life without grace or charm, and almost without decency, but of an exalted faithfulness of purpose, even unto murder. And, as often happens in the lament of poor humanity rich in suffering but indigent in words, the truth—the very cry of truth—was found in a worn and artificial shape picked up somewhere among the phrases of sham sentiment.

"How could I be so afraid of death! Tom, I tried. But I am afraid. I tried to do away with myself. And I couldn't. Am I hard? I suppose the cup of horrors was not full enough for such as me. Then when you came. . . ."

She paused. Then in a gust of confidence and gratitude, "I will live all my days for you, Tom!" she sobbed out.

"Go over into the other corner of the carriage, away from the platform," said Ossipon, solicitously. She let her saviour settle her comfortably, and he watched the coming on of another crisis of weeping, still more violent than the first. He watched the symptoms with a sort of medical air, as if counting seconds. He heard the guard's whistle at last. An involuntary contraction of the upper lip bared his teeth with all the aspect of savage resolution as he felt the train beginning to move. Mrs. Verloc heard and felt nothing, and Ossipon, her saviour, stood still. He felt the train roll quicker, rumbling heavily to the sound of the woman's loud sobs, and then crossing the carriage in two long strides he opened the door deliberately, and leaped out.

He had leaped out at the very end of the platform; and such was his determination in sticking to his desperate plan that he managed by a sort of miracle, performed almost in the air, to slam to the door of the carriage. Only then did he find himself rolling head over heels like a shot rabbit. He was bruised, shaken, pale as death, and out of breath when he got up. But he was calm, and perfectly able to meet the excited crowd of railway men who had gathered round him in a moment. He explained, in gentle and convincing tones, that his wife had started at a moment's notice for Brittany to her dying mother; that, of course, she was greatly upset, and he considerably concerned at her state; that he was trying to cheer her up, and had absolutely failed to notice at first that the train was moving out. To the general exclamation "Why didn't you go to Southampton, then, sir?" he objected the inexperience of a young sister-in-law left alone in the house with three small children, and her alarm at his absence, the telegraph offices being closed. He had acted on impulse. "But I don't think I'll ever try that again," he concluded; smiled all round; distributed some small change, and marched without a limp out of the station.

Outside, Comrade Ossipon, flush of safe banknotes as never before in his life, refused the offer of a cab.

"I can walk," he said, with a little friendly laugh to the civil driver.

He could walk. He walked. He crossed the bridge. Later on the towers of the Abbey saw in their massive immobility the yellow bush of his hair passing under the lamps. The lights of Victoria saw him, too, and Sloane Square, and the railings of the park. And Comrade Ossipon once more found himself on a bridge. The river, a sinister marvel of still shadows and flowing gleams mingling below in a black silence, arrested his attention. He stood looking over the parapet for a long time. The clock tower boomed a brazen blast above his drooping head. He looked up at the dial. . . . Half-past twelve of a wild night in the Channel.

And again Comrade Ossipon walked. His robust form was seen that night in distant parts of the enormous town slumbering monstrously on a carpet of mud under a veil of raw mist. It was seen crossing the streets without life and sound, or diminishing in the interminable straight perspectives of shadowy houses bordering empty roadways lined by strings of gas-lamps. He walked through Squares, Places, Ovals, Commons, through monotonous streets with unknown names where the dust of humanity settles inert and hopeless out of the stream of life. He walked. And suddenly turning into a strip of a front garden with a mangy grass plot, he let himself into a small grimy house with a latchkey he took out of his pocket.

He threw himself down on his bed all dressed, and lay still for a whole quarter of an hour. Then he sat up suddenly, drawing up his knees, and clasping his legs. The first dawn found him open-eyed, in that same posture. This man who could walk so long, so far, so aimlessly, without showing a sign of fatigue, could also remain sitting still for hours without stirring a limb or an eyelid. But when the late sun sent its rays into the room he unclasped his hands, and fell back on the pillow. His eyes stared at the ceiling. And suddenly they closed. Comrade Ossipon slept in the sunlight.

CHAPTER THIRTEEN

The enormous iron padlock on the doors of the wall cupboard was the only object in the room on which the eye could rest without becoming afflicted by the miserable unloveliness of forms and the poverty of material. Unsaleable in the ordinary course of business on account of its noble proportions, it had been ceded to the Professor for a few pence by a marine dealer in the east of London. The room was large, clean, respectable, and poor with that poverty suggesting the starvation of every human need except mere bread. There was nothing on the walls but the paper, an expanse of arsenical green, soiled with indelible smudges here and there, and with stains resembling faded maps of uninhabited continents.

At a deal table near a window sat Comrade Ossipon, holding his head between his fists. The Professor, dressed in his only suit of shoddy tweeds, but flapping to and fro on the bare boards a pair of incredibly dilapidated slippers, had thrust his hands deep into the overstrained pockets of his jacket. He was relating to his robust guest a visit he had lately been paying to the Apostle Michaelis. The Perfect Anarchist had even been unbending a little.

"The fellow didn't know anything of Verloc's death. Of course! He never looks at the newspapers. They make him too sad, he says. But never mind. I walked into his cottage. Not a soul anywhere. I had to shout half-a-dozen times before he answered me. I thought he was fast asleep yet, in bed. But not at all. He had been writing his book for fours hours already. He sat in that tiny cage in a litter of manuscript. There was a half-eaten raw carrot on the table near him. His breakfast. He lives on a diet of raw carrots and a little milk now."

"How does he look on it?" asked Comrade Ossipon, listlessly.

"Angelic. . . . I picked up a handful of his pages from the floor. The poverty of reasoning is astonishing. He has no logic. He can't think consecutively. But that's nothing. He has divided his biography into three parts, entitled—'Faith, Hope, Charity.' He is elaborating now the idea of a world planned out like an immense and nice hospital, with gardens and flowers, in which the strong are to devote themselves to the nursing of the weak."

The Professor paused.

"Conceive you this folly, Ossipon? The weak! The source of all evil on this earth!" he continued with his grim assurance. "I told him that I dreamt of a world like shambles, where the weak would be taken in hand for utter extermination.

"Do you understand, Ossipon? The source of all evil! They are our sinister masters—the weak, the flabby, the silly, the cowardly, the faint of heart, and the slavish of mind. They have power. They are the multitude. Theirs is the kingdom of the earth. Exterminate, exterminate! That is the only way of progress. It is! Follow me, Ossipon? First the great multitude of the weak must go, then the only relatively strong. You see? First the blind, then the deaf and the dumb, then the halt and the lame—and so on. Every taint, every vice, every prejudice, every convention must meet its doom."

"And what remains?" asked Ossipon in a stifled voice.

"I remain—if I am strong enough," asserted the sallow little Professor, whose large ears, thin like membranes, and standing far out from the sides of his frail skull, took on suddenly a deep red tint.

"Haven't I suffered enough from this oppression of the weak?" he continued, forcibly. Then tapping the breast-pocket of his jacket: "And yet I *am* the force," he went on. "But the time! The time! Give me time! Ah! that multitude, too stupid to feel either pity or fear. Sometimes I think they have everything on their side. Everything—even death—my own weapon."

"Come and drink some beer with me at the Silenus," said the robust Ossipon after an interval of silence pervaded by the rapid flap, flap of the slippers on the feet of the Perfect Anarchist. The latter accepted. He was jovial that day in his own peculiar way. He slapped Ossipon's shoulder.

"Beer! So be it! Let us drink and be merry, for we are strong, and to-morrow we die."

He busied himself with putting on his boots, and talked meanwhile in his curt, resolute tones.

"What's the matter with you, Ossipon? You look glum and seek even my company. I hear that you are seen constantly in places where men utter foolish things over glasses of liquor. Why? Have you abandoned your collection of women? They are the weak who feed the strong—eh?"

He stamped one foot, and picked up his other laced boot, heavy, thick-soled, unblacked, mended many times. He smiled to himself grimly.

"Tell me, Ossipon, terrible man, has ever one of your victims killed herself for you—or are your triumphs so far incomplete—for blood alone puts a seal on greatness? Blood. Death. Look at history."

"You be damned," said Ossipon, without turning his head.

"Why? Let that be the hope of the weak, whose theology has invented hell for the strong. Ossipon, my feeling for you is amicable contempt. You couldn't kill a fly."

But rolling to the feast on the top of the omnibus the Professor lost his high spirits. The contemplation of the multitudes thronging the pavements extinguished his assurance under a load of doubt and uneasiness which he could shake off after a period of seclusion in the room with the large cupboard closed by an enormous padlock.

"And so," said over his shoulder Comrade Ossipon, who sat on the seat behind,—"and so Michaelis dreams of a world like a beautiful and cheery hospital."

"Just so. An immense charity for the healing of the weak," assented the Professor, sardonically.

"That's silly," admitted Ossipon. "You can't heal weakness. But after all Michaelis may not be so far wrong. In two hundred years doctors will rule the world. Science reigns already. It reigns in the shade maybe—but it reigns. And all science must culminate at last in the science of healing—not the weak, but the strong. Mankind wants to live—to live."

"Mankind," asserted the Professor with a self-confident glitter of his iron-rimmed spectacles, "does not know what it wants."

"But you do," growled Ossipon. "Just now you've been crying for time—time. Well, the doctors will serve you out your time—if you are good. You profess yourself to be one of the strong—because you carry in your pocket enough stuff to send yourself and, say, twenty other people into eternity. But eternity is a damned hole. It's time that you need. You—if you met a man who could give you for certain ten years of time, you would call him your master."

"My device is: No God! No master," said the Professor, sententiously, as he rose to get off the 'bus.

Ossipon followed. "Wait till you are lying flat on your back at the end of your time," he retorted, jumping off the footboard after the other. "Your scurvy, shabby, mangy little bit of time," he continued across the street, and hopping on to the curbstone.

"Ossipon, I think that you are a humbug," the Professor said, opening masterfully the doors of the renowned Silenus. And when they had established themselves at a little table he developed further this gracious thought. "You are not even a doctor. But you are funny. Your notion of a humanity universally putting out the tongue and taking the pill from pole to pole at the bidding of a few solemn jokers is worthy of the prophet. Prophecy! What's the good of thinking of what will be!" He raised his glass. "To the destruction of what is," he said, calmly.

He drank and relapsed into his peculiarly close manner of silence. The thought of a mankind as numerous as the sands of the seashore, as indestructible, as difficult to handle, oppressed him. The sound of exploding bombs was lost in their immensity of passive grains without an echo. For instance, this Verloc affair. Who thought of it now?

Ossipon, as if suddenly compelled by some mysterious force, pulled a much-folded newspaper out of his pocket. The Professor raised his head at the rustle.

"What's that paper? Anything in it?" he asked.

Ossipon started like a scared somnambulist.

"Nothing. Nothing whatever. The thing's ten days old. I forgot it in my pocket, I suppose."

But he did not throw the old thing away. Before returning it to his pocket he stole a glance at the last lines of a paragraph. They ran thus: "*An impenetrable mystery seems destined to hang for ever over this act of madness or despair.*"

Such were the end words of an item of news headed:

"Suicide of Lady Passenger from a cross-Channel Boat." Comrade Ossipon was familiar with the beauties of its journalistic style. "*An impenetrable mystery seems destined to hang for ever. . . .*" He knew every word by heart. "*An impenetrable mystery. . . .*" And the robust anarchist, hanging his head on his breast, fell into a long reverie.

He was menaced by this thing in the very sources of his existence. He could not issue forth to meet his various conquests, those that he courted on benches in Kensington Gardens, and those he met near area railings, without the dread of beginning to talk to them of an impenetrable mystery destined. . . . He was becoming scientifically afraid of insanity lying in wait for him amongst these lines. "*To hang for ever over.*" It was an obsession, a torture. He had lately failed to keep several of these appointments, whose note used to be an unbounded trustfulness in the language of sentiment and manly tenderness. The confiding disposition of various classes of women satisfied the needs of his self-love, and put some material means into his hand. He needed it to live. It was there. But if he could no longer make use of it, he ran the risk of starving his ideals and his body . . . "*This act of madness or despair.*"

"An impenetrable mystery" was sure "to hang for ever" as far as all mankind was concerned. But what of that if he alone of all men could never get rid of the cursed knowledge? And Comrade Ossipon's knowledge was as precise as the newspaper man could make it—up to the very threshold of the "*mystery destined to hang for ever. . . .*"

Comrade Ossipon was well informed. He knew what the gangway man of the steamer had seen: "A lady in a black dress and a black veil, wandering at midnight alongside, on the quay. 'Are you going by the boat, ma'am?' he had asked her encouragingly. 'This way.' She seemed not to know what to do. He helped her on board. She seemed weak."

And Ossipon knew also what the stewardess had seen: A lady in black with a white face standing in the middle of the empty ladies' cabin. The stewardess induced her to lie down there. The lady seemed quite unwilling to speak, and as if she were in some awful trouble. The next the stewardess knew she was gone from the ladies' cabin. The stewardess then went on deck to look for her, and Comrade Ossipon was informed that the good woman found the unhappy lady lying down in one of the hooded seats. Her eyes were open, but she would not answer anything that was said to her. She seemed very ill.

The stewardess fetched the chief steward, and those two people stood by the side of the hooded seat consulting over their extraordinary and tragic passenger. They talked in audible whispers (for she seemed past hearing) of St. Malo and the Consul there, of communicating with her people in England. Then they went away to arrange for her removal down below, for indeed by what they could see of her face she seemed to them to be dying. But Comrade Ossipon knew that behind that white mask there was struggling against terror and despair a vigour of vitality, a love of life that could resist the furious anguish which drives to murder and the fear, the blind, mad fear of the gallows. He knew. But the stewardess and the chief steward knew nothing, except that when they came back for her in less than five minutes the lady in black was no longer in the hooded seat. She was nowhere. She was gone. It was then five o'clock in the morning, and it was no accident either. An hour afterwards one of the steamer's hands found a wedding ring left lying on the seat. It had stuck to the wood in a bit of wet, and its glitter caught the man's eye. There was a date, 24th June, 1879, engraved inside. *"An impenetrable mystery is destined to hang for ever. . . ."*

And Comrade Ossipon raised his bowed head, beloved of various humble women of these isles, Apollo-like in the sunniness of its bush of hair.

The Professor had grown restless meantime. He rose.

"Stay," said Ossipon, hurriedly. "Here, what do you know of madness and despair?"

The Professor passed the tip of his tongue on his dry, thin lips, and said doctorally:

"There are no such things. All passion is lost now. The world is mediocre, limp, without force. And madness and despair are a force. And force is a crime in the eyes of the fools, the weak and the silly who rule the roost. You are mediocre. Verloc, whose affair the police has managed to smother so nicely, was mediocre. And the police murdered him. He was mediocre. Everybody is mediocre. Madness and despair! Give me that for a lever, and I'll move the world. Ossipon, you have my cordial scorn. You are incapable of conceiving even what the fat-fed citizen would call a crime. You have no force." He paused, smiling sardonically under the fierce glitter of his thick glasses.

"And let me tell you that this little legacy they say you've come into has not improved your intelligence. You sit at your beer like a dummy. Good-bye."

"Will you have it?" said Ossipon, looking up with an idiotic grin. "Have what?"

"The legacy. All of it."

The incorruptible Professor only smiled. His clothes were all but falling off him, his boots, shapeless with repairs, heavy like lead, let water in at every step. He said:

"I will send you by-and-by a small bill for certain chemicals which I shall order to-morrow. I need them badly. Understood—eh?"

Ossipon lowered his head slowly. He was alone. "*An impenetrable mystery. . . .*" It seemed to him that suspended in the air before him he saw his own brain pulsating to the rhythm of an impenetrable mystery. It was diseased clearly. . . . "*This act of madness or despair.*"

The mechanical piano near the door played through a valse cheekily, then fell silent all at once, as if gone grumpy.

Comrade Ossipon, nicknamed the Doctor, went out of the Silenus beer-hall. At the door he hesitated, blinking at a not too splendid sunlight—and the paper with the report of the suicide of a lady was in his pocket. His heart was beating against it. The suicide of a lady—*this act of madness or despair.*

He walked along the street without looking where he put his feet; and he walked in a direction which would not bring him to the place of appointment with another lady (an elderly nursery governess putting her trust in an Apollo-like ambrosial head). He was walking away from it. He could face no woman. It was ruin. He could neither think, work, sleep, nor eat. But he was beginning to drink with pleasure, with anticipation, with hope. It was ruin. His revolutionary career, sustained by the sentiment and trustfulness of many women, was menaced by an impenetrable mystery—the mystery of a human brain pulsating wrongfully to the rhythm of journalistic phrases. " . . . *Will hang for ever over this act. . . .*" It was inclining towards the gutter ". . . *of madness or despair. . . .*"

"I am seriously ill," he muttered to himself with scientific insight. Already his robust form, with an Embassy's secret-service money (inherited from Mr. Verloc) in his pockets, was marching in the gutter as if in training for the task of an inevitable future. Already he bowed his broad shoulders, his head of ambrosial locks, as if ready to receive the leather yoke of the sandwich board. As on that night, more than a week ago, Comrade Ossipon walked without looking where he put his feet, feeling no fatigue, feeling nothing, seeing nothing, hearing not a sound. "*An impenetrable mystery. . . .*" He walked disregarded. . . . "*This act of madness or despair.*"

And the incorruptible Professor walked, too, averting his eyes from the odious multitude of mankind. He had no future. He disdained it. He was a force. His thoughts caressed the images of ruin and destruction. He walked frail, insignificant, shabby, miserable—and terrible in the simplicity of his idea calling madness and despair to the regeneration of the world. Nobody looked at him. He passed on unsuspected and deadly, like a pest in the street full of men.

FINE WORKS OF FICTION AVAILABLE IN QUALITY PAPERBACK EDITIONS FROM CARROLL & GRAF

☐ Asch, Sholem/THE APOSTLE $10.95
☐ Asch, Sholem/MARY $10.95
☐ Asch, Sholem/THE NAZARENE $10.95
☐ Asch, Sholem/THREE CITIES $10.50
☐ Ashley, Mike (ed.)/THE MAMMOTH BOOK OF SHORT HORROR NOVELS $8.95
☐ Asimov, Isaac/THE MAMMOTH BOOK OF CLASSIC SCIENCE FICTION (1930s) $8.95
☐ Asimov, Isaac et al/THE MAMMOTH BOOK OF GOLDEN AGE SCIENCE FICTION (1940) $8.95
☐ Babel, Isaac/YOU MUST KNOW EVERYTHING $8.95
☐ Balzac, Honore de/BEATRIX $8.95
☐ Balzac, Honoré de/CESAR BIROTTEAU $8.95
☐ Balzac, Honoré de/THE LILY OF THE VALLEY $9.95
☐ Bellaman, Henry/KINGS ROW $8.95
☐ Bernanos, George/DIARY OF A COUNTRY PRIEST $7.95
☐ Brand, Christianna/GREEN FOR DANGER $8.95
☐ Céline, Louis-Ferdinand/CASTLE TO CASTLE $8.95
☐ Chekov, Anton/LATE BLOOMING FLOWERS $8.95
☐ Conrad, Joseph/SEA STORIES $8.95
☐ Conrad, Joseph & Ford Madox Ford/ THE INHERITORS $7.95
☐ Conrad, Joseph & Ford Madox Ford/ROMANCE $8.95
☐ Coward, Noel/A WITHERED NOSEGAY $8.95
☐ de Montherlant, Henry/THE GIRLS $11.95
☐ Dos Passos, John/THREE SOLDIERS $9.95
☐ Feuchtwanger, Lion/JEW SUSS $8.95
☐ Feuchtwanger, Lion/THE OPPERMANNS $8.95
☐ Fisher, R.L./THE PRINCE OF WHALES $5.95
☐ Fitzgerald, Penelope/OFFSHORE $7.95
☐ Fitzgerald, Penelope/INNOCENCE $7.95
☐ Flaubert, Gustave/NOVEMBER $7.95
☐ Fonseca, Rubem/HIGH ART $7.95
☐ Fuchs, Daniel/SUMMER IN WILLIAMSBURG $8.95

☐	Gold, Michael/JEWS WITHOUT MONEY	$7.95
☐	Greenberg & Waugh (eds.)/THE NEW ADVENTURES OF SHERLOCK HOLMES	$8.95
☐	Greene, Graham & Hugh/THE SPY'S BEDSIDE BOOK	$7.95
☐	Greenfeld, Josh/THE RETURN OF MR. HOLLYWOOD	$8.95
☐	Hamsun, Knut/MYSTERIES	$8.95
☐	Hardinge, George (ed.)/THE MAMMOTH BOOK OF MODERN CRIME STORIES	$8.95
☐	Hawkes, John/VIRGINIE: HER TWO LIVES	$7.95
☐	Higgins, George/TWO COMPLETE NOVELS	$9.95
☐	Hugo, Victor/NINETY-THREE	$8.95
☐	Huxley, Aldous/ANTIC HAY	$10.95
☐	Huxley, Aldous/EYELESS IN GAZA	$9.95
☐	Ibañez, Vincente Blasco/THE FOUR HORSEMEN OF THE APOCALYPSE	$8.95
☐	Jackson, Charles/THE LOST WEEKEND	$7.95
☐	James, Henry/GREAT SHORT NOVELS	$12.95
☐	Jones, Richard Glyn/THE MAMMOTH BOOK OF MURDER	$8.95
☐	Lewis, Norman/DAY OF THE FOX	$8.95
☐	Lowry, Malcolm/HEAR US O LORD FROM HEAVEN THY DWELLING PLACE	$9.95
☐	Lowry, Malcolm/ULTRAMARINE	$7.95
☐	Macaulay, Rose/CREWE TRAIN	$8.95
☐	Macaulay, Rose/KEEPING UP APPEARANCES	$8.95
☐	Macaulay, Rose/DANGEROUS AGES	$8.95
☐	Macaulay, Rose/THE TOWERS OF TREBIZOND	$8.95
☐	Mailer, Norman/BARBARY SHORE	$9.95
☐	Mauriac, François/THE DESERT OF LOVE	$6.95
☐	Mauriac, François/FLESH AND BLOOD	$8.95
☐	Mauriac, François/WOMAN OF THE PHARISEES	$8.95
☐	Mauriac, François/VIPER'S TANGLE	$8.95
☐	McElroy, Joseph/THE LETTER LEFT TO ME	$7.95
☐	McElroy, Joseph/LOOKOUT CARTRIDGE	$9.95
☐	McElroy, Joseph/PLUS	$8.95
☐	McElroy, Joseph/A SMUGGLER'S BIBLE	$9.50
☐	Moorcock, Michael/THE BROTHEL IN ROSENTRASSE	$6.95
☐	Munro, H.H./THE NOVELS AND PLAYS OF SAKI	$8.95

☐ Neider, Charles (ed.)/GREAT SHORT
    STORIES $11.95
☐ Neider, Charles (ed.)/SHORT NOVELS OF THE
    MASTERS $12.95
☐ O'Faolain, Julia/THE OBEDIENT WIFE $7.95
☐ O'Faolain, Julia/NO COUNTRY FOR YOUNG
    MEN $8.95
☐ O'Faolain, Julia/WOMEN IN THE WALL $8.95
☐ Olinto, Antonio/THE WATER HOUSE $9.95
☐ Plievier, Theodore/STALINGRAD $8.95
☐ Pronzini & Greenberg (eds.)/THE MAMMOTH
    BOOK OF PRIVATE EYE NOVELS $8.95
☐ Rechy, John/BODIES AND SOULS $8.95
☐ Rechy, John/MARILYN'S DAUGHTER $8.95
☐ Rhys, Jean/QUARTET $6.95
☐ Sand, George/MARIANNE $7.95
☐ Scott, Evelyn/THE WAVE $9.95
☐ Sigal, Clancy/GOING AWAY $9.95
☐ Singer, I.J./THE BROTHERS ASHKENAZI $9.95
☐ Taylor, Peter/IN THE MIRO DISTRICT $7.95
☐ Tolstoy, Leo/TALES OF COURAGE AND
    CONFLICT $11.95
☐ van Thal, Herbert/THE MAMMOTH BOOK OF
    GREAT DETECTIVE STORIES $8.95
☐ Wassermann, Jacob/CASPAR HAUSER $9.95
☐ Wassermann, Jabob/THE MAURIZIUS CASE $9.95
☐ Werfel, Franz/THE FORTY DAYS OF MUSA
    DAGH $9.95
☐ Winwood, John/THE MAMMOTH BOOK OF
    SPY THRILLERS $8.95

FINE WORKS OF NON-FICTION AVAILABLE IN QUALITY PAPERBACK EDITIONS FROM CARROLL & GRAF

☐ Anderson, Nancy/WORK WITH PASSION $8.95
☐ Arlett, Robert/THE PIZZA GOURMET $10.95
☐ Asprey, Robert/THE PANTHER'S FEAST $9.95
☐ Athill, Diana/INSTEAD OF A LETTER $7.95
☐ Bedford, Sybille/ALDOUS HUXLEY $14.95
☐ Berton, Pierre/KLONDIKE FEVER $10.95
☐ Blake, Robert/DISRAELI $14.50
☐ Blanch, Lesley/PIERRE LOTI $10.95
☐ Blanch, Lesley/THE SABRES OF PARADISE $9.95
☐ Blanch, Lesley/THE WILDER SHORES OF
LOVE $8.95
☐ Bowers, John/IN THE LAND OF NYX $7.95
☐ Buchan, John/PILGRIM'S WAY $10.95
☐ Carr, John Dickson/THE LIFE OF SIR ARTHUR
CONAN DOYLE $8.95
☐ Carr, Virginia Spencer/THE LONELY HUNTER:
A BIOGRAPHY OF CARSON McCULLERS $12.95
☐ Cherry-Garrard/THE WORST JOURNEY IN THE
WORLD $13.95
☐ Conot, Robert/JUSTICE AT NUREMBURG $11.95
☐ Cooper, Duff/OLD MEN FORGET $10.95
☐ Cooper, Lady Diana/AUTOBIOGRAPHY $13.95
☐ De Jonge, Alex/THE LIFE AND TIMES OF
GRIGORII RASPUTIN $10.95
☐ Edwards, Anne/SONYA: THE LIFE OF
COUNTESS TOLSTOY $8.95
☐ Elkington, John/THE GENE FACTORY $8.95
☐ Farson, Negley/THE WAY OF A
TRANSGRESSOR $9.95
☐ Garbus, Martin/TRAITORS AND HEROES $10.95
☐ Gill, Brendan/HERE AT THE NEW YORKER $12.95
☐ Goldin, Stephen & Sky, Kathleen/THE BUSINESS
OF BEING A WRITER $8.95
☐ Golenbock, Peter/HOW TO WIN AT ROTISSERIE
BASEBALL $8.95
☐ Green, Julian/DIARIES 1928–1957 $9.95

☐	Richelson, Hildy & Stan/INCOME WITHOUT TAXES	$9.95
☐	Roy, Jules/THE BATTLE OF DIENBIENPHU	$8.95
☐	Russell, Franklin/THE HUNTING ANIMAL	$7.95
☐	Salisbury, Harrison/A JOURNEY FOR OUR TIMES	$10.95
☐	Scott, Evelyn/ESCAPADE	$9.95
☐	Sloan, Allan/THREE PLUS ONE EQUALS BILLIONS	$8.95
☐	Stanway, Andrew/THE ART OF SENSUAL LOVING	$15.95
☐	Stein, Leon/THE TRIANGLE FIRE	$7.95
☐	Trench, Charles/THE ROAD TO KHARTOUM	$10.95
☐	Werth, Alexander/RUSSIA AT WAR: 1941–1945	$15.95
☐	White, Jon Manchip/CORTES	$10.95
☐	Wilmot, Chester/STRUGGLE FOR EUROPE	$14.95
☐	Wilson, Colin/THE MAMMOTH BOOK OF TRUE CRIME	$8.95
☐	Zuckmayer, Carl/A PART OF MYSELF	$9.95

Available from fine bookstores everywhere or use this coupon for ordering.

Carroll & Graf Publishers, Inc., 260 Fifth Avenue, N.Y., N.Y. 10001

Please send me the books I have checked above. I am enclosing $_____ (please add $1.00 per title to cover postage and handling.) Send check or money order—no cash or C.O.D.'s please. N.Y. residents please add 8¼% sales tax.

Mr/Mrs/Ms _____

Address _____

City _____ State/Zip _____
Please allow four to six weeks for delivery.